OXFORD WORLD'S CLASSICS

IVANHOE

A ROMANCE

°

SIR WALTER SCOTT

CHANCELLOR PRESS

Ivanhoe was first published in 1819, and in Oxford
World's Classics in 1903.

This edition first published in Great Britain in 1987 by

Chancellor Press
59 Grosvenor Street
London W1

under licence from

Oxford University Press
Walton Street
Oxford

'Oxford' is the trademark of Oxford University Press

ISBN 1 85152 043 0

Printed in Shenzhen, China

INTRODUCTION

THE Author of the Waverley Novels had hitherto
proceeded in an unabated course of popularity, and
might, in his peculiar district of literature, have
been termed *l'enfant gâté* of success. It was plain,
however, that frequent publication must finally
wear out the public favour, unless some mode could
be devised to give an appearance of novelty to
subsequent productions. Scottish manners, Scottish
dialect, and Scottish characters of note, being those
with which the Author was most intimately and
familiarly acquainted, were the groundwork upon
which he had hitherto relied for giving effect to his
narrative. It was, however, obvious that this kind
of interest must in the end occasion a degree of
sameness and repetition, if exclusively resorted to,
and that the reader was likely at length to adopt
the language of Edwin, in Parnell's *Tale:*—

> 'Reverse the spell,' he cries,
> 'And let it fairly now suffice,
> The gambol has been shown.'

Nothing can be more dangerous for the fame of
a professor of the fine arts than to permit (if he can
possibly prevent it) the character of a mannerist to
be attached to him, or that he should be supposed
capable of success only in a particular and limited
style. The public are, in general, very ready to
adopt the opinion that he who has pleased them in
one peculiar mode of composition is, by means of
that very talent, rendered incapable of venturing

upon other subjects. The effect of this disinclination, on the part of the public, towards the artificers of their pleasures, when they attempt to enlarge their means of amusing, may be seen in the censures usually passed by vulgar criticism upon actors or artists who venture to change the character of their efforts, that, in so doing, they may enlarge the scale of their art.

There is some justice in this opinion, as there always is in such as attain general currency. It may often happen on the stage, that an actor, by possessing in a pre-eminent degree the external qualities necessary to give effect to comedy, may be deprived of the right to aspire to tragic excellence ; and in painting or literary composition, an artist or poet may be master exclusively of modes of thought and powers of expression which confine him to a single course of subjects. But much more frequently the same capacity which carries a man to popularity in one department will obtain for him success in another, and that must be more particularly the case in literary composition than either in acting or painting, because the adventurer in that department is not impeded in his exertions by any peculiarity of features, or conformation of person, proper for particular parts, or, by any peculiar mechanical habits of using the pencil, limited to a particular class of subjects.

Whether this reasoning be correct or otherwise, the present Author felt that, in confining himself to subjects purely Scottish, he was not only likely to weary out the indulgence of his readers, but also greatly to limit his own power of affording them pleasure. In a highly polished country, where so much genius is monthly employed in catering for public amusement, a fresh topic, such as he had himself had the happiness to light upon, is the untasted spring of the desert :

Men bless their stars and call it luxury.

But when men and horses, cattle, camels, and dromedaries have poached the spring into mud, it becomes loathsome to those who at first drank of it with rapture; and he who had the merit of discovering it, if he would preserve his reputation with the tribe, must display his talent by a fresh discovery of untasted fountains.

If the author, who finds himself limited to a particular class of subjects, endeavours to sustain his reputation by striving to add a novelty of attraction to themes of the same character which have been formerly successful under his management, there are manifest reasons why, after a certain point, he is likely to fail. If the mine be not wrought out, the strength and capacity of the miner become necessarily exhausted. If he closely imitates the narratives which he has before rendered successful, he is doomed to 'wonder that they please no more.' If he struggles to take a different view of the same class of subjects, he speedily discovers that what is obvious, graceful, and natural has been exhausted; and, in order to obtain the indispensable charm of novelty, he is forced upon caricature, and, to avoid being trite, must become extravagant.

It is not, perhaps, necessary to enumerate so many reasons why the Author of the Scottish Novels, as they were then exclusively termed, should be desirous to make an experiment on a subject purely English. It was his purpose, at the same time, to have rendered the experiment as complete as possible, by bringing the intended work before the public as the effort of a new candidate for their favour, in order that no degree of prejudice, whether favourable or the reverse, might attach to it, as a new production of the Author of *Waverley*; but this intention was afterwards departed from, for reasons to be hereafter mentioned.

The period of the narrative adopted was the reign of Richard I., not only as abounding with characters

whose very names were sure to attract general
attention, but as affording a striking contrast betwixt the Saxons, by whom the soil was cultivated,
and the Normans, who still reigned in it as conquerors, reluctant to mix with the vanquished, or
acknowledge themselves of the same stock. The
idea of this contrast was taken from the ingenious
and unfortunate Logan's tragedy of *Runnamede*, in
which, about the same period of history, the Author
had seen the Saxon and Norman barons opposed to
each other on different sides of the stage. He does
not recollect that there was any attempt to contrast
the two races in their habits and sentiments ; and
indeed it was obvious that history was violated by
introducing the Saxons still existing as a high-
minded and martial race of nobles.

They did, however, survive as a people, and some
of the ancient Saxon families possessed wealth and
power, although they were exceptions to the humble
condition of the race in general. It seemed to the
Author that the existence of the two races in the
same country, the vanquished distinguished by their
plain, homely, blunt manners, and the free spirit
infused by their ancient institutions and laws ; the
victors, by the high spirit of military fame, personal
adventure, and whatever could distinguish them as
the flower of chivalry, might, intermixed with other
characters belonging to the same time and country,
interest the reader by the contrast, if the Author
should not fail on his part.

Scotland, however, had been of late used so exclusively as the scene of what is called historical
romance, that the preliminary letter of Mr. Laurence
Templeton became in some measure necessary. To
this, as to an Introduction, the reader is referred,
as expressing the Author's purpose and opinions in
undertaking this species of composition, under the
necessary reservation, that he is far from thinking
he has attained the point at which he aimed.

It is scarcely necessary to add, that there was no idea or wish to pass off the supposed Mr. Templeton as a real person. But a kind of continuation of the *Tales of my Landlord* had been recently attempted by a stranger, and it was supposed this Dedicatory Epistle might pass for some imitation of the same kind, and thus, putting inquirers upon a false scent, induce them to believe they had before them the work of some new candidate for their favour.

After a considerable part of the work had been finished and printed, the publishers, who pretended to discern in it a germ of popularity, remonstrated strenuously against its appearing as an absolutely anonymous production, and contended that it should have the advantage of being announced as by the Author of *Waverley.* The Author did not make any obstinate opposition, for he began to be of opinion with Dr. Wheeler, in Miss Edgeworth's excellent tale of *Manœuvring*, that 'trick upon trick' might be too much for the patience of an indulgent public, and might be reasonably considered as trifling with their favour.

The book, therefore, appeared as an avowed continuation of the Waverley Novels; and it would be ungrateful not to acknowledge that it met with the same favourable reception as its predecessors.

Such annotations as may be useful to assist the reader in comprehending the characters of the Jew, the Templar, the captain of the mercenaries, or Free Companians, as they were called, and others proper to the period, are added, but with a sparing hand, since sufficient information on these subjects is to be found in general history.

An incident in the tale, which had the good fortune to find favour in the eyes of many readers, is more directly borrowed from the stores of old romance. I mean the meeting of the King with Friar Tuck at the cell of that buxom hermit. The general tone of the story belongs to all ranks and all countries, which emulate each other in describing the rambles of a disguised sovereign, who, going in search of information or amusement into the lower ranks of life, meets with adventures diverting to the reader or hearer, from the contrast betwixt the monarch's outward appearance and his real character. The Eastern tale-teller has for his theme the disguised expeditions of Haroun Alraschid with his faithful attendants, Mesrour and Giafar, through the midnight streets of Bagdad; and Scottish tradition dwells upon the similar exploits of James V., distinguished during such excursions by the travelling name of the Goodman of Ballengeich, as the Commander of the Faithful, when he desired to be incognito, was known by that of Il Bondocani. The French minstrels are not silent on so popular a theme. There must have been a Norman original of the Scottish metrical romance of *Rauf Colziar*, in which Charlemagne is introduced as the unknown guest of a charcoal-man.[1] It seems to have been the original of other poems of the kind.

In merry England there is no end of popular ballads on this theme. The poem of *John the Reeve*, or Steward, mentioned by Bishop Percy, in the *Reliques of English Poetry*,[2] is said to have turned on such an incident; and we have, besides, the *King and the Tanner of Tamworth*, the *King and the Miller of Mansfield*, and others on the same topic. But the peculiar tale of this nature to which the Author of *Ivanhoe* has to acknowledge an obligation is more ancient by two centuries than any of these last mentioned.

It was first communicated to the public in that curious record of ancient literature which has been

[1] This very curious poem, long a *desideratum* in Scottish literature, and given up as irrecoverably lost, was lately brought to light by the researches of Dr. Irvine of the Advocates' Library, and has been reprinted by Mr. David Laing, Edinburgh. [2] Vol. ii. p. 167.

accumulated by the combined exertions of Sir
Egerton Brydges and Mr. Hazlewood, in the
periodical work entitled the *British Bibliographer*.
From thence it has been transferred by the Reverend
Charles Henry Hartshorne, M.A., editor of a very
curious volume, entitled *Ancient Metrical Tales,
printed chiefly from Original Sources*, 1829. Mr.
Hartshorne gives no other authority for the present
fragment, except the article in the *Bibliographer*,
where it is entitled the *Kyng and the Hermite*. A
short abstract of its contents will show its similarity
to the meeting of King Richard and Friar Tuck.

King Edward (we are not told which among the
monarchs of that name, but, from his temper and
habits, we may suppose Edward IV.) sets forth with
his court to a gallant hunting-match in Sherwood
Forest, in which, as is not unusual for princes in
romance, he falls in with a deer of extraordinary
size and swiftness, and pursues it closely, till he
has outstripped his whole retinue, tired out hounds
and horse, and finds himself alone under the gloom
of an extensive forest, upon which night is descending. Under the apprehensions natural to a situation
so uncomfortable, the king recollects that he has
heard how poor men, when apprehensive of a bad
night's lodging, pray to St. Julian, who, in the
Romish calendar, stands quarter-master-general to
all forlorn travellers that render him due homage.
Edward puts up his orisons accordingly, and by the
guidance, doubtless, of the good saint, reaches a
small path, conducting him to a chapel in the forest,
having a hermit's cell in its close vicinity. The
king hears the reverend man, with a companion of
his solitude, telling his beads within, and meekly
requests of him quarters for the night. 'I have no
accommodation for such a lord as ye be,' said the
hermit. 'I live here in the wilderness upon roots
and rinds, and may not receive into my dwelling
even the poorest wretch that lives, unless it were to

save his life.' The king inquires the way to the
next town, and, understanding it is by a road which
he cannot find without difficulty, even if he had
daylight to befriend him, he declares that, with or
without the hermit's consent, he is determined to
be his guest that night. He is admitted accordingly,
not without a hint from the recluse that, were he
himself out of his priestly weeds, he would care
little for his threats of using violence, and that he
gives way to him not out of intimidation, but simply
to avoid scandal.

The king is admitted into the cell; two bundles
of straw are shaken down for his accommodation,
and he comforts himself that he is now under shelter,
and that

> A night will soon be gone.

Other wants, however, arise. The guest becomes
clamorous for supper, observing,

> 'For certainly, as I you say,
> I ne had never so sorry a day,
> That I ne had a merry night.'

But this indication of his taste for good cheer,
joined to the annunciation of his being a follower
of the court, who had lost himself at the great
hunting-match, cannot induce the niggard hermit
to produce better fare than bread and cheese, for
which his guest showed little appetite, and 'thin
drink,' which was even less acceptable. At length
the king presses his host on a point to which he
had more than once alluded, without obtaining a
satisfactory reply:

> Then said the king, 'By Godys grace,
> Thou wert in a merry place,
>   To shoot should thou lere;
> When the foresters go to rest,
> Sometyme thou might have of the best,
>   All of the wild deer;
> I wold hold it for no scathe,
> Though thou hadst bow and arrows baith,
>   Althoff thou best a frere.'

The hermit, in return, expresses his apprehension that his guest means to drag him into some confession of offence against the forest laws, which, being betrayed to the king, might cost him his life. Edward answers by fresh assurances of secrecy, and again urges on him the necessity of procuring some venison. The hermit replies, by once more insisting on the duties incumbent upon him as a churchman, and continues to affirm himself free from all such breaches of order :

> 'Many day I have here been,
> And flesh-meat I eat never,
> But milk of the kye ;
> Warm thee well, and go to sleep,
> And I will lap thee with my cope,
> Softly to lye.'

It would seem that the manuscript is here imperfect, for we do not find the reasons which finally induce the curtal friar to amend the king's cheer. But, acknowledging his guest to be such a 'good fellow' as has seldom graced his board, the holy man at length produces the best his cell affords. Two candles are placed on a table, white bread and baked pasties are displayed by the light, besides choice of venison, both salt and fresh, from which they select collops. 'I might have eaten my bread dry,' said the king, 'had I not pressed thee on the score of archery, but now have I dined like a prince —if we had but drink enow.'

This too is afforded by the hospitable anchorite, who despatches an assistant to fetch a pot of four gallons from a secret corner near his bed, and the whole three set in to serious drinking. This amusement is superintended by the friar, according to the recurrence of certain fustian words, to be repeated by every compotator in turn before he drank—a species of high jinks, as it were, by which 'they regulated their potations, as toasts were given in latter times. The one toper says 'Fusty bandias,'

to which the other is obliged to reply, 'Strike
pantnere,' and the friar passes many jests on the
king's want of memory, who sometimes forgets the
words of action. The night is spent in this jolly
pastime. Before his departure in the morning, the
king invites his reverend host to court, promises, at
least, to requite his hospitality, and expresses himself much pleased with his entertainment. The
jolly hermit at length agrees to venture thither,
and to inquire for Jack Fletcher, which is the name
assumed by the king. After the hermit has shown
Edward some feats of archery, the joyous pair
separate. The king rides home, and rejoins his
retinue. As the romance is imperfect, we are not
acquainted how the discovery takes place; but it is
probably much in the same manner as in other
narratives turning on the same subject, where the
host, apprehensive of death for having trespassed on
the respect due to his sovereign, while incognito, is
agreeably surprised by receiving honours and reward.

In Mr. Hartshorn's collection, there is a romance
on the same foundation, called *King Edward and the
Shepherd*,[1] which, considered as illustrating manners,
is still more curious than *The King and the Hermit*;
but it is foreign to the present purpose. The reader
has here the original legend from which the incident
in the romance is derived; and the identifying the
irregular eremite with the Friar Tuck of Robin
Hood's story was an obvious expedient.

The name of Ivanhoe was suggested by an old
rhyme. All novelists have had occasion at some
time or other to wish with Falstaff that they knew
where a commodity of good names was to be had.

---

[1] Like the hermit, the shepherd makes havock amongst
the king's game; but by means of a sling, not of a bow;
like the hermit, too, he has his peculiar phrases of compo-
tation, the sign and countersign being Passelodion and
Berafriend. One can scarce conceive what humour our
ancestors found in this species of gibberish; but

I warrant it proved an excuse for the glass.

On such an occasion the Author chanced to call to memory a rhyme recording three names of the manors forfeited by the ancestor of the celebrated Hampden, for striking the Black Prince a blow with his racket, when they quarrelled at tennis :

> Tring, Wing, and Ivanhoe,
> For striking of a blow,
> Hampden did forego,
> And glad he could escape so.

The word suited the Author's purpose in two material respects—for, first, it had an ancient English sound ; and secondly, it conveyed no indication whatever of the nature of the story. He presumes to hold this last quality to be of no small importance. What is called a taking title serves the direct interest of the bookseller or publisher, who by this means sometimes sells an edition while it is yet passing the press. But if the Author permits an over degree of attention to be drawn to his work ere it has appeared, he places himself in the embarrassing condition of having excited a degree of expectation which, if he proves unable to satisfy, is an error fatal to his literary reputation. Besides, when we meet such a title as the Gunpowder Plot, or any other connected with general history, each reader, before he has seen the book, has formed to himself some particular idea of the sort of manner in which the story is to be conducted, and the nature of the amusement which he is to derive from it. In this he is probably disappointed, and in that case may be naturally disposed to visit upon the Author or the work the unpleasant feelings thus excited. In such a case the literary adventurer is censured, not for having missed the mark at which he himself aimed, but for not having shot off his shaft in a direction he never thought of.

On the footing of unreserved communication which the Author has established with the reader, he may here add the trifling circumstance, that a roll of

Norman warriors, occurring in the Auchinleck MS., gave him the formidable name of Front-de-Bœuf.

Ivanhoe was highly successful upon its appearance, and may be said to have procured for its Author the freedom of the rules, since he has ever since been permitted to exercise his powers of fictitious composition in England as well as Scotland.

The character of the fair Jewess found so much favour in the eyes of some fair readers, that the writer was censured because, when arranging the fates of the characters of the drama, he had not assigned the hand of Wilfred to Rebecca, rather than the less interesting Rowena. But, not to mention that the prejudices of the age rendered such an union almost impossible, the Author may, in passing, observe, that he thinks a character of a highly virtuous and lofty stamp is degraded rather than exalted by an attempt to reward virtue with temporal prosperity. Such is not the recompense which Providence has deemed worthy of suffering merit, and it is a dangerous and fatal doctrine to teach young persons, the most common readers of romance, that rectitude of conduct and of principle are either naturally allied with or adequately rewarded by the gratification of our passions, or attainment of our wishes. In a word, if a virtuous and self-denied character is dismissed with temporal wealth, greatness, rank, or the indulgence of such a rashly-formed or ill-assorted passion as that of Rebecca for Ivanhoe, the reader will be apt to say, 'Verily virtue has had its reward.' But a glance on the great picture of life will show that the duties of self-denial, and the sacrifice of passion to principle, are seldom thus remunerated ; and that the internal consciousness of their high-minded discharge of duty produces on their own reflections a more adequate recompense, in the form of that peace which the world cannot give or take away.

ABBOTSFORD, *1st September*, 1830.

IVANHOE

CHAPTER I

Thus communed these ; while to their lowly dome
The full-fed swine return'd with evening home,
Compell'd, reluctant, to the several sties,
With din obstreperous and ungrateful cries.
POPE's *Odyssey.*

In that pleasant district of merry England which is
watered by the river Don, there extended in ancient
times a large forest, covering the greater part of
the beautiful hills and valleys which lie between
Sheffield and the pleasant town of Doncaster. The
remains of this extensive wood are still to be seen
at the noble seats of Wentworth, of Wharncliffe
Park, and around Rotherham. Here haunted of
yore the fabulous Dragon of Wantley ; here were
fought many of the most desperate battles during
the Civil Wars of the Roses ; and here also flourished
in ancient times those bands of gallant outlaws
whose deeds have been rendered so popular in
English song.

Such being our chief scene, the date of our story
refers to a period towards the end of the reign of
Richard I., when his return from his long captivity
had become an event rather wished than hoped for
by his despairing subjects, who were in the meantime subjected to every species of subordinate

oppression. The nobles, whose power had become exorbitant during the reign of Stephen, and whom the prudence of Henry the Second had scarce reduced into some degree of subjection to the crown, had now resumed their ancient license in its utmost extent; despising the feeble interference of the English Council of State, fortifying their castles, increasing the number of their dependants, reducing all around them to a state of vassalage, and striving by every means in their power to place themselves each at the head of such forces as might enable him to make a figure in the national convulsions which appeared to be impending.

The situation of the inferior gentry, or franklins, as they were called, who, by the law and spirit of the English constitution, were entitled to hold themselves independent of feudal tyranny, became now unusually precarious. If, as was most generally the case, they placed themselves under the protection of any of the petty kings in their vicinity, accepted of feudal offices in his household, or bound themselves, by mutual treaties of alliance and protection, to support him in his enterprises, they might indeed purchase temporary repose; but it must be with the sacrifice of that independence which was so dear to every English bosom, and at the certain hazard of being involved as a party in whatever rash expedition the ambition of their protector might lead him to undertake. On the other hand, such and so multiplied were the means of vexation and oppression possessed by the great barons, that they never wanted the pretext, and seldom the will, to harass and pursue, even to the very edge of destruction, any of their less powerful neighbours who attempted to separate themselves from their authority, and to trust for their protection, during the dangers of the times, to their own inoffensive conduct and to the laws of the land.

A circumstance which greatly tended to enhance

the tyranny of the nobility and the sufferings of the inferior classes arose from the consequences of the Conquest by Duke William of Normandy. Four generations had not sufficed to blend the hostile blood of the Normans and Anglo-Saxons, or to unite, by common language and mutual interests, two hostile races, one of which still felt the elation of triumph, while the other groaned under all the consequences of defeat. The power had been completely placed in the hands of the Norman nobility by the event of the battle of Hastings, and it had been used, as our histories assure us, with no moderate hand. The whole race of Saxon princes and nobles had been extirpated or disinherited, with few or no exceptions; nor were the numbers great who possessed land in the country of their fathers, even as proprietors of the second or of yet inferior classes. The royal policy had long been to weaken, by every means, legal or illegal, the strength of a part of the population which was justly considered as nourishing the most inveterate antipathy to their victor. All the monarchs of the Norman race had shown the most marked predilection for their Norman subjects; the laws of the chase, and many others, equally unknown to the milder and more free spirit of the Saxon constitution, had been fixed upon the necks of the subjugated inhabitants, to add weight, as it were, to the feudal chains with which they were loaded. At court, and in the castles of the great nobles, where the pomp and state of a court was emulated, Norman-French was the only language employed; in courts of law, the pleadings and judgments were delivered in the same tongue. In short, French was the language of honour, of chivalry, and even of justice, while the far more manly and expressive Anglo-Saxon was abandoned to the use of rustics and hinds, who knew no other. Still, however, the necessary intercourse between the lords of the soil, and those oppressed inferior beings by whom that soil was cultivated, occasioned the gradual formation of a dialect, compounded betwixt the French and the Anglo-Saxon, in which they could render themselves mutually intelligible to each other; and from this necessity arose by degrees the structure of our present English language, in which the speech of the victors and the vanquished have been so happily blended together; and which has since been so richly improved by importations from the classical languages, and from those spoken by the southern nations of Europe.

This state of things I have thought it necessary to premise for the information of the general reader, who might be apt to forget that, although no great historical events, such as war or insurrection, mark the existence of the Anglo-Saxons as a separate people subsequent to the reign of William the Second, yet the great national distinctions betwixt them and their conquerors, the recollection of what they had formerly been, and to what they were now reduced, continued, down to the reign of Edward the Third, to keep open the wounds which the Conquest had inflicted, and to maintain a line of separation betwixt the descendants of the victor Normans and the vanquished Saxons.

The sun was setting upon one of the rich grassy glades of that forest which we have mentioned in the beginning of the chapter. Hundreds of broad-headed, short-stemmed, wide-branched oaks, which had witnessed perhaps the stately march of the Roman soldiery, flung their gnarled arms over a thick carpet of the most delicious green sward; in some places they were intermingled with beeches, hollies, and copsewood of various descriptions, so closely as totally to intercept the level beams of the sinking sun; in others they receded from each other, forming those long sweeping vistas in the intricacy of which the eye delights to lose itself, while imagination considers them as the paths to yet wilder scenes of silvan solitude. Here the red rays of the sun shot a broken and discoloured light, that partially hung upon the shattered boughs and mossy trunks of the trees, and there they illuminated in brilliant patches the portions of turf to which they made their way. A considerable open space, in the midst of this glade, seemed formerly to have been dedicated to the rites of Druidical superstition ; for, on the summit of a hillock, so regular as to seem artificial, there still remained part of a circle of rough, unhewn stones, of large dimensions. Seven stood upright ; the rest had been dislodged from their places, probably by the zeal of some convert to Christianity, and lay, some prostrate near their former site, and others on the side of the hill. One large stone only had found its way to the bottom, and, in stopping the course of a small brook which glided smoothly round the foot of the eminence, gave, by its opposition, a feeble voice of murmur to the placid and elsewhere silent streamlet.

The human figures which completed this landscape were in number two, partaking, in their dress and appearance, of that wild and rustic character which belonged to the woodlands of the West Riding of Yorkshire at that early period. The eldest of these men had a stern, savage, and wild aspect. His garment was of the simplest form imaginable, being a close jacket with sleeves, composed of the tanned skin of some animal, on which the hair had been originally left, but which had been worn off in so many places that it would have been difficult to distinguish, from the patches that remained, to what creature the fur had belonged. This primeval vestment reached from the throat to the knees, and served at once all the usual purposes of body-clothing ; there was no wider

opening at the collar than was necessary to admit
the passage of the head, from which it may be inferred
that it was put on by slipping it over the head
and shoulders, in the manner of a modern shirt, or
ancient hauberk. Sandals, bound with thongs made
of boar's hide, protected the feet, and a roll of thin
leather was twined artificially round the legs, and,
ascending above the calf, left the knees bare, like
those of a Scottish Highlander. To make the
jacket sit yet more close to the body, it was gathered
at the middle by a broad leathern belt, secured by a
brass buckle; to one side of which was attached a
sort of scrip, and to the other a ram's horn, accoutred
with a mouthpiece, for the purpose of blowing. In
the same belt was stuck one of those long, broad,
sharp-pointed, and two-edged knives, with a buck's-
horn handle, which were fabricated in the neighbourhood, and bore even at this early period the
name of a Sheffield whittle. The man had no
covering upon his head, which was only defended
by his own thick hair, matted and twisted together,
and scorched by the influence of the sun into a
rusty dark-red colour, forming a contrast with the
overgrown beard upon his cheeks, which was rather
of a yellow or amber hue. One part of his dress
only remains, but it is too remarkable to be suppressed; it was a brass ring, resembling a dog's
collar, but without any opening, and soldered fast
round his neck, so loose as to form no impediment
to his breathing, yet so tight as to be incapable of
being removed, excepting by the use of the file. On
this singular gorget was engraved, in Saxon characters, an inscription of the following purport:—
'Gurth, the son of Beowulph, is the born thrall of
Cedric of Rotherwood.'

Beside the swineherd, for such was Gurth's occupation, was seated, upon one of the fallen Druidical
monuments, a person about ten years younger in
appearance, and whose dress, though resembling his

companion's in form, was of better materials, and of
a more fantastic description. His jacket had been
stained of a bright purple hue, upon which there had
been some attempt to paint grotesque ornaments in
different colours. To the jacket he added a short
cloak, which scarcely reached half-way down his
thigh; it was of crimson cloth, though a good deal
soiled, lined with bright yellow; and as he could
transfer it from one shoulder to the other, or at his
pleasure draw it all around him, its width, contrasted
with its want of longitude, formed a fantastic piece
of drapery. He had thin silver bracelets upon his
arms, and on his neck a collar of the same metal,
bearing the inscription, 'Wamba, the son of Witless, is the thrall of Cedric of Rotherwood.' This
personage had the same sort of sandals with his
companion, but instead of the roll of leather thong,
his legs were cased in a sort of gaiters, of which one
was red and the other yellow. He was provided
also with a cap, having around it more than one
bell, about the size of those attached to hawks,
which jingled as he turned his head to one side or
other; and as he seldom remained a minute in the
same posture, the sound might be considered as
incessant. Around the edge of this cap was a stiff
bandeau of leather, cut at the top into open work,
resembling a coronet, while a prolonged bag arose
from within it, and fell down on one shoulder like
an old-fashioned nightcap, or a jelly-bag, or the
head-gear of a modern hussar. It was to this part
of the cap that the bells were attached; which circumstance, as well as the shape of his head-dress,
and his own half-crazed, half-cunning expression of
countenance, sufficiently pointed him out as belonging to the race of domestic clowns or jesters, maintained in the houses of the wealthy, to help away
the tedium of those lingering hours which they
were obliged to spend within doors. He bore, like
his companion, a scrip attached to his belt, but had

neither horn nor knife, being probably considered
as belonging to a class whom it is esteemed dangerous
to entrust with edge-tools. In place of these, he
was equipped with a sword of lath, resembling that
with which harlequin operates his wonders upon the
modern stage.

The outward appearance of these two men formed
scarce a stronger contrast than their look and demeanour. That of the serf, or bondsman, was sad
and sullen ; his aspect was bent on the ground with
an air of deep dejection, which might be almost
construed into apathy, had not the fire which
occasionally sparkled in his red eye manifested that
there slumbered, under the appearance of sullen
despondency, a sense of oppression, and a disposition
to resistance. The looks of Wamba, on the other
hand, indicated, as usual with his class, a sort of
vacant curiosity, and fidgety impatience of any
posture of repose, together with the utmost self-
satisfaction respecting his own situation and the
appearance which he made. The dialogue which
they maintained between them was carried on in
Anglo-Saxon, which, as we said before, was universally spoken by the inferior classes, excepting
the Norman soldiers and the immediate personal
dependants of the great feudal nobles. But to give
their conversation in the original would convey but
little information to the modern reader, for whose
benefit we beg to offer the following translation :—

'The curse of St. Withold upon these infernal
porkers !' said the swineherd, after blowing his horn
obstreperously, to collect together the scattered
herd of swine, which, answering his call with notes
equally melodious, made, however, no haste to
remove themselves from the luxurious banquet of
beech-mast and acorns on which they had fattened,
or to forsake the marshy banks of the rivulet, where
several of them, half-plunged in mud, lay stretched
at their ease, altogether regardless of the voice of

their keeper. 'The curse of St. Withold upon them and upon me !' said Gurth ; ' if the two-legged wolf snap not up some of them ere nightfall, I am no true man. Here, Fangs ! Fangs !' he ejaculated at the top of his voice to a ragged, wolfish-looking dog, a sort of lurcher, half mastiff, half greyhound, which ran limping about as if with the purpose of seconding his master in collecting the refractory grunters ; but which, in fact, from misapprehension of the swineherd's signals, ignorance of his own duty, or malice prepense, only drove them hither and thither, and increased the evil which he seemed to design to remedy. ' A devil draw the teeth of him,' said Gurth, ' and the mother of mischief confound the ranger of the forest, that cuts the foreclaws off our dogs, and makes them unfit for their trade ! Wamba, up and help me an thou beest a man ; take a turn round the back o' the hill to gain the wind on them ; and when thou'st got the weather-gage, thou mayst drive them before thee as gently as so many innocent lambs.'

' Truly,' said Wamba, without stirring from the spot, ' I have consulted my legs upon this matter, and they are altogether of opinion that to carry my gay garments through these sloughs would be an act of unfriendship to my sovereign person and royal wardrobe ; wherefore, Gurth, I advise thee to call off Fangs, and leave the herd to their destiny, which, whether they meet with bands of travelling soldiers, or of outlaws, or of wandering pilgrims, can be little else than to be converted into Normans before morning, to thy no small ease and comfort.'

' The swine turned Normans to my comfort !' quoth Gurth ; ' expound that to me, Wamba, for my brain is too dull and my mind too vexed to read riddles.'

' Why, how call you those grunting brutes running about on their four legs ?' demanded Wamba.

'Swine, fool—swine,' said the herd; 'every fool knows that.'

'And swine is good Saxon,' said the Jester; 'but how call you the sow when she is flayed, and drawn, and quartered, and hung up by the heels, like a traitor?'

'Pork,' answered the swineherd.

'I am very glad every fool knows that too,' said Wamba, 'and pork, I think, is good Norman-French; and so when the brute lives, and is in the charge of a Saxon slave, she goes by her Saxon name; but becomes a Norman, and is called pork, when she is carried to the castle hall to feast among the nobles. What dost thou think of this, friend Gurth, ha?'

'It is but too true doctrine, friend Wamba, however it got into thy fool's pate.'

'Nay, I can tell you more,' said Wamba in the same tone: 'there is old Alderman Ox continues to hold his Saxon epithet while he is under the charge of serfs and bondsmen such as thou, but becomes Beef, a fiery French gallant, when he arrives before the worshipful jaws that are destined to consume him. Mynherr Calf, too, becomes Monsieur de Veau in the like manner: he is Saxon when he requires tendance, and takes a Norman name when he becomes matter of enjoyment.'

'By St. Dunstan,' answered Gurth, 'thou speakest but sad truths; little is left to us but the air we breathe, and that appears to have been reserved with much hesitation, solely for the purpose of enabling us to endure the tasks they lay upon our shoulders. The finest and the fattest is for their board; the loveliest is for their couch; the best and bravest supply their foreign masters with soldiers, and whiten distant lands with their bones, leaving few here who have either will or the power to protect the unfortunate Saxon. God's blessing on our Master Cedric, he hath done the work of a man in

standing in the gap; but Reginald Front-de-Bœuf
is coming down to this country in person, and we
shall soon see how little Cedric's trouble will avail
him.   Here, here,' he exclaimed again, raising his
voice, 'So ho! so ho! well done, Fangs! thou hast
them all before thee now, and bring'st them on
bravely, lad.'

'Gurth,' said the Jester, 'I know thou thinkest
me a fool, or thou wouldst not be so rash in putting
thy head into my mouth.   One word to Reginald
Front-de-Bœuf or Philip de Malvoisin, that thou
hast spoken treason against the Norman—and thou
art but a castaway swineherd; thou wouldst waver
on one of these trees as a terror to all evil speakers
against dignities.'

'Dog, thou wouldst not betray me,' said Gurth,
'after having led me on to speak so much at disadvantage?'

'Betray thee!' answered the Jester; 'no, that
were the trick of a wise man; a fool cannot half so
well help himself.   But soft, whom have we here?'
he said, listening to the trampling of several horses
which became then audible.

'Never mind whom,' answered Gurth, who had
now got his herd before him, and, with the aid of
Fangs, was driving them down one of the long dim
vistas which we have endeavoured to describe.

'Nay, but I must see the riders,' answered
Wamba; 'perhaps they are come from Fairyland
with a message from King Oberon.'

'A murrain take thee!' rejoined the swineherd;
'wilt thou talk of such things, while a terrible storm
of thunder and lightning is raging within a few
miles of us?   Hark, how the thunder rumbles! and
for summer rain, I never saw such broad downright flat drops fall out of the clouds; the oaks,
too, notwithstanding the calm weather, sob and
creak with their great boughs as if announcing a
tempest.   Thou canst play the rational if thou wilt;

credit me for once, and let us home ere the storm
begins to rage, for the night will be fearful.'

Wamba seemed to feel the force of this appeal,
and accompanied his companion, who began his
journey after catching up a long quarter-staff which
lay upon the grass beside him. This second Eumæus
strode hastily down the forest glade, driving before
him, with the assistance of Fangs, the whole herd
of his inharmonious charge.

CHAPTER II

A monk there was, a fayre for the maistrie,
An outrider that loved venerie;
A manly man, to be an abbot able,
Full many a daintie horse had he in stable.
And whan he rode, men might his bridle hear
Gingeling in a whistling wind as clear,
And eke as loud, as doth the chapell bell,
There as this lord was keeper of the cell.

CHAUCER.

NOTWITHSTANDING the occasional exhortation and chiding of his companion, the noise of the horsemen's feet continuing to approach, Wamba could not be prevented from lingering occasionally on the road, upon every pretence which occurred; now catching from the hazel a cluster of half-ripe nuts, and now turning his head to leer after a cottage maiden who crossed their path. The horsemen, therefore, soon overtook them on the road.

Their numbers amounted to ten men, of whom the two who rode foremost seemed to be persons of considerable importance, and the others their attendants. It was not difficult to ascertain the condition and character of one of these personages. He was obviously an ecclesiastic of high rank; his dress was that of a Cistercian monk, but composed of materials much finer than those which the rule of that order admitted. His mantle and hood were of the best Flanders cloth, and fell in ample, and not ungraceful, folds around a handsome though some-

13

what corpulent person. His countenance bore as
little the marks of self-denial as his habit indicated
contempt of worldly splendour. His features might
have been called good, had there not lurked under
the penthouse of his eye that sly epicurean twinkle
which indicates the cautious voluptuary. In other
respects, his profession and situation had taught
him a ready command over his countenance, which
he could contract at pleasure into solemnity, although
its natural expression was that of good-humoured
social indulgence. In defiance of conventual rules
and the edicts of popes and councils, the sleeves of
this dignitary were lined and turned up with rich
furs, his mantle secured at the throat with a golden
clasp, and the whole dress proper to his order as
much refined upon and ornamented as that of a
Quaker beauty of the present day, who, while she
retains the garb and costume of her sect, continues
to give to its simplicity, by the choice of materials
and the mode of disposing them, a certain air of
coquettish attraction savouring but too much of the
vanities of the world.

This worthy churchman rode upon a well-fed,
ambling mule, whose furniture was highly decorated,
and whose bridle, according to the fashion of the
day, was ornamented with silver bells. In his seat
he had nothing of the awkwardness of the convent,
but displayed the easy and habitual grace of a well-
trained horseman. Indeed, it seemed that so humble
a conveyance as a mule, in however good case, and
however well broken to a pleasant and accommo-
dating amble, was only used by the gallant monk
for travelling on the road. A lay brother, one of
those who followed in the train, had, for his use on
other occasions, one of the most handsome Spanish
jennets ever bred in Andalusia, which merchants
used at that time to import, with great trouble and
risk, for the use of persons of wealth and distinction.
The saddle and housings of this superb palfrey were

covered by a long foot-cloth, which reached nearly to the ground, and on which were richly embroidered mitres, crosses, and other ecclesiastical emblems. Another lay brother led a sumpter mule, loaded probably with his superior's baggage; and two monks of his own order, of inferior station, rode together in the rear, laughing and conversing with each other, without taking much notice of the other members of the cavalcade.

The companion of the church dignitary was a man past forty, thin, strong, tall, and muscular; an athletic figure, which long fatigue and constant exercise seemed to have left none of the softer part of the human form, having reduced the whole to brawn, bones, and sinews, which had sustained a thousand toils, and were ready to dare a thousand more. His head was covered with a scarlet cap, faced with fur, of that kind which the French call *mortier*, from its resemblance to the shape of an inverted mortar. His countenance was therefore fully displayed, and its expression was calculated to impress a degree of awe, if not of fear, upon strangers. High features, naturally strong and powerfully expressive, had been burnt almost into Negro blackness by constant exposure to the tropical sun, and might, in their ordinary state, be said to slumber after the storm of passion had passed away; but the projection of the veins of the forehead, the readiness with which the upper lip and its thick black moustaches quivered upon the slightest emotion, plainly intimated that the tempest might be again and easily awakened. His keen, piercing, dark eyes told in every glance a history of difficulties subdued and dangers dared, and seemed to challenge opposition to his wishes, for the pleasure of sweeping it from his road by a determined exertion of courage and of will; a deep scar on his brow gave additional sternness to his countenance and a sinister expression to one of his eyes, which had been slightly injured on the same occasion, and of which the vision, though perfect, was in a slight and partial degree distorted.

The upper dress of this personage resembled that of his companion in shape, being a long monastic mantle; but the colour, being scarlet, showed that he did not belong to any of the four regular orders of monks. On the right shoulder of the mantle there was cut, in white cloth, a cross of a peculiar form. This upper robe concealed what at first view seemed rather inconsistent with its form, a shirt, namely, of linked mail, with sleeves and gloves of the same, curiously plaited and interwoven, as flexible to the body as those which are now wrought in the stocking-loom out of less obdurate materials. The fore-part of his thighs, where the folds of his mantle permitted them to be seen, were also covered with linked mail; the knees and feet were defended by splints, or thin plates of steel, ingeniously jointed upon each other; and mail hose, reaching from the ankle to the knee, effectually protected the legs, and completed the rider's defensive armour. In his girdle he wore a long and double-edged dagger, which was the only offensive weapon about his person.

He rode, not a mule, like his companion, but a strong hackney for the road, to save his gallant war-horse, which a squire led behind, fully accoutred for battle, with a chamfron or plaited head-piece upon his head, having a short spike projecting from the front. On one side of the saddle hung a short battle-axe, richly inlaid with Damascene carving; on the other the rider's plumed head-piece and hood of mail, with a long two-handed sword, used by the chivalry of the period. A second squire held aloft his master's lance, from the extremity of which fluttered a small banderole, or streamer, bearing a cross of the same form with that embroidered upon his cloak. He also carried his small triangular shield, broad enough at the top to protect the breast, and from thence diminishing to a point. It was covered with a scarlet cloth, which prevented the device from being seen.

These two squires were followed by two attendants, whose dark visages, white turbans, and the Oriental form of their garments, showed them to be natives of some distant Eastern country. The whole appearance of this warrior and his retinue was wild and outlandish; the dress of his squires was gorgeous, and his Eastern attendants wore silver collars round their throats, and bracelets of the same metal upon their swarthy legs and arms, of which the latter were naked from the elbow, and the former from mid-leg to ankle. Silk and embroidery distinguished their dresses, and marked the wealth and importance of their master; forming, at the same time, a striking contrast with the martial simplicity of his own attire. They were armed with crooked sabres, having the hilt and baldric inlaid with gold, and matched with Turkish daggers of yet more costly workmanship. Each of them bore at his saddle-bow a bundle of darts or javelins, about four feet in length, having sharp steel heads, a weapon much in use among the Saracens, and of which the memory is yet preserved in the martial exercise called *el jerrid*, still practised in the Eastern countries.

The steeds of these attendants were in appearance as foreign as their riders. They were of Saracen origin, and consequently of Arabian descent; and their fine slender limbs, small fetlocks, thin manes, and easy springy motion, formed a marked contrast with the large-jointed heavy horses, of which the race was cultivated in Flanders and in Normandy for mounting the men-at-arms of the period in all the panoply of plate and mail, and which, placed by the side of those Eastern coursers, might have passed for a personification of substance and of shadow

The singular appearance of this cavalcade not only attracted the curiosity of Wamba, but excited even that of his less volatile companion. The monk he instantly knew to be the Prior of Jorvaulx Abbey, well known for many miles around as a lover of the chase, of the banquet, and, if fame did him not wrong, of other worldly pleasures still more inconsistent with his monastic vows.

Yet so loose were the ideas of the times respecting the conduct of the clergy, whether secular or regular, that the Prior Aymer maintained a fair character in the neighbourhood of his abbey. His free and jovial temper, and the readiness with which he granted absolution from all ordinary delinquencies, rendered him a favourite among the nobility and principal gentry, to several of whom he was allied by birth, being of a distinguished Norman family. The ladies, in particular, were not disposed to scan too nicely the morals of a man who was a professed admirer of their sex, and who possessed many means of dispelling the *ennui* which was too apt to intrude upon the halls and bowers of an ancient feudal castle. The Prior mingled in the sports of the field with more than due eagerness, and was allowed to possess the best-trained hawks and the fleetest greyhounds in the North Riding—circumstances which strongly recommended him to the youthful gentry. With the old he had another part to play, which, when needful, he could sustain with great decorum. His knowledge of books, however superficial, was sufficient to impress upon their ignorance respect for his supposed learning ; and the gravity of his deportment and language, with the high tone which he exerted in setting forth the authority of the church and of the priesthood, impressed them no less with an opinion of his sanctity. Even the common people, the severest critics of the conduct of their betters, had commiseration with the follies of Prior Aymer. He was generous ; and charity,

as it is well known, covereth a multitude of sins,
in another sense than that in which it is said to do
so in Scripture. The revenues of the monastery,
of which a large part was at his disposal, while they
gave him the means of supplying his own very considerable expenses, afforded also those largesses
which he bestowed among the peasantry, and with
which he frequently relieved the distresses of the
oppressed. If Prior Aymer rode hard in the chase,
or remained long at the banquet, if Prior Aymer
was seen at the early peep of dawn to enter the
postern of the abbey, as he glided home from some
rendezvous which had occupied the hours of darkness, men only shrugged up their shoulders, and
reconciled themselves to his irregularities by recollecting that the same were practised by many of his
brethren who had no redeeming qualities whatsoever
to atone for them. Prior Aymer, therefore, and
his character, were well known to our Saxon serfs,
who made their rude obeisance, and received his
' *Benedicite, mes filz,*' in return.

But the singular appearance of his companion and
his attendants arrested their attention and excited
their wonder, and they could scarcely attend to the
Prior of Jorvaulx' question, when he demanded if
they knew of any place of harbourage in the vicinity;
so much were they surprised at the half-monastic,
half-military appearance of the swarthy stranger,
and at the uncouth dress and arms of his Eastern
attendants. It is probable, too, that the language
in which the benediction was conferred, and the
information asked, sounded ungracious, though not
probably unintelligible, in the ears of the Saxon
peasants.

' I asked you, my children,' said the Prior, raising
his voice, and using the *lingua Franca*, or mixed
language, in which the Norman and Saxon races
conversed with each other, ' if there be in this
neighbourhood any good man who, for the love of

God and devotion to Mother Church, will give two of her humblest servants, with their train, a night's hospitality and refreshment?'

This he spoke with a tone of conscious importance, which formed a strong contrast to the modest terms which he thought it proper to employ.

'Two of the humblest servants of Mother Church!' repeated Wamba to himself, but, fool as he was, taking care not to make his observation audible; 'I should like to see her seneschals, her chief butlers, and her other principal domestics!'

After this internal commentary on the Prior's speech, he raised his eyes and replied to the question which had been put.

'If the reverend fathers,' he said, 'loved good cheer and soft lodging, few miles of riding would carry them to the Priory of Brinxworth, where their quality could not but secure them the most honourable reception ; or if they preferred spending a penitential evening, they might turn down yonder wild glade, which would bring them to the hermitage of Copmanhurst, where a pious anchoret would make them sharers for the night of the shelter of his roof and the benefit of his prayers.'

The Prior shook his head at both proposals.

'Mine honest friend,' said he, 'if the jangling of thy bells had not dizzied thine understanding, thou mightst know *Clericus clericum non decimat* ; that is to say, we churchmen do not exhaust each other's hospitality, but rather require that of the laity, giving them thus an opportunity to serve God in honouring and relieving His appointed servants.'

'It is true,' replied Wamba, 'that I, being but an ass, am, nevertheless, honoured to bear the bells as well as your reverence's mule ; notwithstanding, I did conceive that the charity of Mother Church and her servants might be said, with other charity, to begin at home.'

'A truce to thine insolence, fellow,' said the

armed rider, breaking in on his prattle with a high
and stern voice, 'and tell us, if thou canst, the
road to——   How call'd you your franklin, Prior
Aymer?'

'Cedric,' answered the Prior—'Cedric the Saxon.
Tell me, good fellow, are we near his dwelling, and
can you show us the road?'

'The road will be uneasy to find,' answered Gurth,
who broke silence for the first time, 'and the family
of Cedric retire early to rest.'

'Tush, tell not me, fellow!' said the military
rider; ''tis easy for them to arise and supply the
wants of travellers such as we are, who will not
stoop to beg the hospitality which we have a right
to command.'

'I know not,' said Gurth, sullenly, 'if I should
show the way to my master's house to those who
demand as a right the shelter which most are fain
to ask as a favour.'

'Do you dispute with me, slave!' said the soldier;
and, setting spurs to his horse, he caused him make
a demi-volte across the path, raising at the same
time the riding rod which he held in his hand, with
a purpose of chastising what he considered as the
insolence of the peasant.

Gurth darted at him a savage and revengeful
scowl, and with a fierce yet hesitating motion laid
his hand on the haft of his knife; but the interference of Prior Aymer, who pushed his mule betwixt his companion and the swineherd, prevented
the meditated violence.

'Nay, by St. Mary, brother Brian, you must not
think you are now in Palestine, predominating over
heathen Turks and infidel Saracens; we islanders
love not blows, save those of Holy Church, who
chasteneth whom she loveth. Tell me, good fellow,'
said he to Wamba, and seconded his speech by a
small piece of silver coin, 'the way to Cedric the
Saxon's; you cannot be ignorant of it, and it is

your duty to direct the wanderer even when his character is less sanctified than ours.'

'In truth, venerable father,' answered the Jester, 'the Saracen head of your right reverend companion has frightened out of mine the way home: I am not sure I shall get there to-night myself.'

'Tush,' said the Abbot, 'thou canst tell us if thou wilt. This reverend brother has been all his life engaged in fighting among the Saracens for the recovery of the Holy Sepulchre; he is of the order of Knights Templars, whom you may have heard of: he is half a monk, half a soldier.'

'If he is but half a monk,' said the Jester, 'he should not be wholly unreasonable with those whom he meets upon the road, even if they should be in no hurry to answer questions that no way concern them.'

'I forgive thy wit,' replied the Abbot, 'on condition thou wilt show me the way to Cedric's mansion.'

'Well, then,' answered Wamba, 'your reverences must hold on this path till you come to a sunken cross, of which scarce a cubit's length remains above ground; then take the path to the left, for there are four which meet at Sunken Cross, and I trust your reverences will obtain shelter before the storm comes on.'

The Abbot thanked his sage adviser; and the cavalcade, setting spurs to their horses, rode on as men do who wish to reach their inn before the bursting of a night-storm.

As their horses' hoofs died away, Gurth said to his companion, 'If they follow thy wise direction, the reverend fathers will hardly reach Rotherwood this night.'

'No,' said the Jester, grinning, 'but they may reach Sheffield if they have good luck, and that is as fit a place for them. I am not so bad a woodsman as to show the dog where the deer lies, if I have no mind he should chase him.'

'Thou art right,' said Gurth; 'it were ill that Aymer saw the Lady Rowena; and it were worse, it may be, for Cedric to quarrel, as is most likely he would, with this military monk. But, like good servants, let us hear and see, and say nothing.'

We return to the riders, who had soon left the bondsmen far behind them, and who maintained the following conversation in the Norman-French language, usually employed by the superior classes, with the exception of the few who were still inclined to boast their Saxon descent:—

'What mean these fellows by their capricious insolence?' said the Templar to the Cistercian, 'and why did you prevent me from chastising it?'

'Marry, brother Brian,' replied the Prior, 'touching the one of them, it were hard for me to render a reason for a fool speaking according to his folly; and the other churl is of that savage, fierce, intractable race some of whom, as I have often told you, are still to be found among the descendants of the conquered Saxons, and whose supreme pleasure it is to testify, by all means in their power, their aversion to their conquerors.'

'I would soon have beat him into courtesy,' observed Brian; 'I am accustomed to deal with such spirits. Our Turkish captives are as fierce and intractable as Odin himself could have been; yet two months in my household, under the management of my master of the slaves, has made them humble, submissive, serviceable, and observant of your will. Marry, sir, you must beware of the poison and the dagger; for they use either with free will when you give them the slightest opportunity.'

'Ay, but,' answered Prior Aymer, 'every land has its own manners and fashions; and, besides that beating this fellow could procure us no information respecting the road to Cedric's house, it would have been sure to have established a quarrel betwixt you and him had we found our way thither. Remember

what I told you: this wealthy franklin is proud,
fierce, jealous, and irritable, a withstander of the
nobility, and even of his neighbours, Reginald Front-
de-Bœuf and Philip Malvoisin, who are no babes to
strive with.   He stands up so sternly for the privileges of his race, and is so proud of his uninterrupted
descent from Hereward, a renowned champion of
the Heptarchy, that he is universally called Cedric
the Saxon; and makes a boast of his belonging to
a people from whom many others endeavour to hide
their descent, lest they should encounter a share
of the *væ victis*, or severities imposed upon the
vanquished.'

'Prior Aymer,' said the Templar, 'you are a man
of gallantry, learned in the study of beauty, and as
expert as a troubadour in all matters concerning
the *arrêts* of love; but I shall expect much beauty
in this celebrated Rowena, to counterbalance the
self-denial and forbearance which I must exert if
I am to court the favour of such a seditious churl
as you have described her father Cedric.'

'Cedric is not her father,' replied the Prior, 'and
is but of remote relation: she is descended from
higher blood than even he pretends to, and is but
distantly connected with him by birth.   Her guardian,
however, he is, self-constituted as I believe; but
his ward is as dear to him as if she were his own
child.   Of her beauty you shall soon be judge; and
if the purity of her complexion, and the majestic
yet soft expression of a mild blue eye, do not
chase from your memory the black-tressed girls
of Palestine, ay, or the houris of old Mahound's
paradise, I am an infidel and no true son of the
church.'

'Should your boasted beauty,' said the Templar,
'be weighed in the balance and found wanting, you
know our wager?'

'My good collar,' answered the Prior, 'against
ten butts of Chian wine: they are mine as securely

as if they were already in the convent vaults, under
the key of old Dennis, the cellarer.'

'And I am myself to be judge,' said the Templar,
'and I am only to be convicted on my own admission
that I have seen no maiden so beautiful since Pentecost was a twelvemonth. Ran it not so? Prior, your
collar is in danger; I will wear it over my gorget
in the lists of Ashby-de-la-Zouche.'

'Win it fairly,' said the Prior, 'and wear it as
ye will; I will trust your giving true response, on
your word as a knight and as a churchman. Yet,
brother, take my advice, and file your tongue to a
little more courtesy than your habits of predominating over infidel captives and Eastern bondsmen
have accustomed you. Cedric the Saxon, if offended
—and he is noway slack in taking offence—is a man
who, without respect to your knighthood, my high
office, or the sanctity of either, would clear his house
of us, and send us to lodge with the larks, though
the hour were midnight. And be careful how you
look on Rowena, whom he cherishes with the most
jealous care; an he take the least alarm in that
quarter we are but lost men. It is said he banished
his only son from his family for lifting his eyes in
the way of affection towards this beauty, who may
be worshipped, it seems, at a distance, but is not
to be approached with other thoughts than such as
we bring to the shrine of the Blessed Virgin.'

'Well, you have said enough,' answered the
Templar; 'I will for a night put on the needful
restraint, and deport me as meekly as a maiden;
but as for the fear of his expelling us by violence,
myself and squires, with Hamet and Abdalla, will
warrant you against that disgrace. Doubt not that
we shall be strong enough to make good our
quarters.'

'We must not let it come so far,' answered the
Prior. 'But here is the clown's sunken cross, and
the night is so dark that we can hardly see which

of the roads we are to follow. He bid us turn, I
think, to the left.'

'To the right,' said Brian, 'to the best of my
remembrance.'

'To the left—certainly the left; I remember his
pointing with his wooden sword.'

'Ay, but he held his sword in his left hand, and
so pointed across his body with it,' said the Templar.

Each maintained his opinion with sufficient
obstinacy, as is usual in all such cases; the attendants were appealed to, but they had not been near
enough to hear Wamba's directions. At length
Brian remarked, what had at first escaped him in
the twilight—'Here is some one either asleep or
lying dead at the foot of this cross. Hugo, stir him
with the butt-end of thy lance.'

This was no sooner done than the figure arose,
exclaiming in good French, 'Whosoever thou art,
it is discourteous in you to disturb my thoughts.'

'We did but wish to ask you,' said the Prior,
'the road to Rotherwood, the abode of Cedric the
Saxon.'

'I myself am bound thither,' replied the stranger;
'and if I had a horse I would be your guide, for the
way is somewhat intricate, though perfectly well
known to me.'

'Thou shalt have both thanks and reward, my
friend,' said the Prior, 'if thou wilt bring us to
Cedric's in safety.'

And he caused one of his attendants to mount his
own led horse, and give that upon which he had
hitherto ridden to the stranger who was to serve for
a guide.

Their conductor pursued an opposite road from
that which Wamba had recommended for the purpose
of misleading them. The path soon led deeper into
the woodland, and crossed more than one brook,
the approach to which was rendered perilous by the
marshes through which it flowed; but the stranger

seemed to know, as if by instinct, the soundest ground and the safest points of passage; and, by dint of caution and attention, brought the party safely into a wider avenue than any they had yet seen; and, pointing to a large, low, irregular building at the upper extremity, he said to the Prior, 'Yonder is Rotherwood, the dwelling of Cedric the Saxon.'

This was a joyful intimation to Aymer, whose nerves were none of the strongest, and who had suffered such agitation and alarm in the course of passing through the dangerous bogs, that he had not yet had the curiosity to ask his guide a single question. Finding himself now at his ease and near shelter, his curiosity began to awake, and he demanded of the guide who and what he was.

'A palmer, just returned from the Holy Land,' was the answer.

'You had better have tarried there to fight for the recovery of the Holy Sepulchre,' said the Templar.

'True, Reverend Sir Knight,' answered the Palmer, to whom the appearance of the Templar seemed perfectly familiar; 'but when those who are under oath to recover the holy city are found travelling at such a distance from the scene of their duties, can you wonder that a peaceful peasant like me should decline the task which they have abandoned?'

The Templar would have made an angry reply, but was interrupted by the Prior, who again expressed his astonishment that their guide, after such long absence, should be so perfectly acquainted with the passes of the forest.

'I was born a native of these parts,' answered their guide, and as he made the reply they stood before the mansion of Cedric—a low, irregular building, containing several court-yards or inclosures, extending over a considerable space of ground,

and which, though its size argued the inhabitant to
be a person of wealth, differed entirely from the
tall, turreted, and castellated buildings in which
the Norman nobility resided, and which had become the universal style of architecture throughout
England.

Rotherwood was not, however, without defences ;
no habitation, in that disturbed period, could have
been so without the risk of being plundered and
burnt before the next morning. A deep fosse, or
ditch, was drawn round the whole building, and
filled with water from a neighbouring stream. A
double stockade, or palisade, composed of pointed
beams, which the adjacent forest supplied, defended
the outer and inner bank of the trench. There
was an entrance from the west through the outer
stockade, which communicated by a drawbridge
with a similar opening in the interior defences.
Some precautions had been taken to place those
entrances under the protection of projecting angles,
by which they might be flanked in case of need by
archers or slingers.

Before this entrance the Templar wound his horn
loudly ; for the rain, which had long threatened,
began now to descend with great violence.

CHAPTER III

Then (sad relief!) from the bleak coast that hears
The German Ocean roar, deep-blooming, strong,
And yellow-hair'd, the blue-eyed Saxon came.

THOMSON'S *Liberty.*

IN a hall, the height of which was greatly dispro-
portioned to its extreme length and width, a long
oaken table formed of planks rough-hewn from the
forest, and which had scarcely received any polish,
stood ready prepared for the evening meal of Cedric
the Saxon. The roof, composed of beams and
rafters, had nothing to divide the apartment from
the sky excepting the planking and thatch; there
was a huge fireplace at either end of the hall, but,
as the chimneys were constructed in a very clumsy
manner, at least as much of the smoke found its
way into the apartment as escaped by the proper
vent. The constant vapour which this occasioned
had polished the rafters and beams of the low-
browed hall, by encrusting them with a black var-
nish of soot. On the sides of the apartment hung
implements of war and of the chase, and there were
at each corner folding doors, which gave access to
other parts of the extensive building.

The other appointments of the mansion partook
of the rude simplicity of the Saxon period, which
Cedric piqued himself upon maintaining. The floor
was composed of earth mixed with lime, trodden
into a hard substance, such as is often employed in
flooring our modern barns. For about one quarter

of the length of the apartment the floor was raised
by a step, and this space, which was called the dais,
was occupied only by the principal members of the
family and visitors of distinction. For this purpose,
a table richly covered with scarlet cloth was placed
transversely across the platform, from the middle
of which ran the longer and lower board, at which
the domestics and inferior persons fed, down towards
the bottom of the hall. The whole resembled the
form of the letter T, or some of those ancient dinner-
tables which, arranged on the same principles, may
be still seen in the antique Colleges of Oxford or
Cambridge. Massive chairs and settles of carved
oak were placed upon the dais, and over these seats
and the more elevated table was fastened a canopy
of cloth, which served in some degree to protect the
dignitaries who occupied that distinguished station
from the weather, and especially from the rain,
which in some places found its way through the
ill-constructed roof.

The walls of this upper end of the hall, as far as
the dais extended, were covered with hangings or
curtains, and upon the floor there was a carpet,
both of which were adorned with some attempts at
tapestry or embroidery, executed with brilliant, or
rather gaudy, colouring. Over the lower range of
table, the roof, as we have noticed, had no covering ;
the rough plastered walls were left bare, and the
rude earthen floor was uncarpeted ; the board was
uncovered by a cloth, and rude massive benches
supplied the place of chairs.

In the centre of the upper table were placed two
chairs more elevated than the rest, for the master
and mistress of the family, who presided over the
scene of hospitality, and from doing so derived
their Saxon title of honour, which signifies 'the
Dividers of Bread.'

To each of these chairs was added a footstool,
curiously carved and inlaid with ivory, which mark

of distinction was peculiar to them. One of these seats was at present occupied by Cedric the Saxon, who, though but in rank a thane. or, as the Normans called him, a franklin, felt at the delay of his evening meal an irritable impatience which might have become an alderman, whether of ancient or of modern times.

It appeared, indeed, from the countenance of this proprietor, that he was of a frank, but hasty and choleric, temper. He was not above the middle stature, but broad-shouldered, long-armed, and powerfully made, like one accustomed to endure the fatigue of war or of the chase; his face was broad, with large blue eyes, open and frank features, fine teeth, and a well-formed head, altogether expressive of that sort of good humour which often lodges with a sudden and hasty temper. Pride and jealousy there was in his eye, for his life had been spent in asserting rights which were constantly liable to invasion; and the prompt, fiery, and resolute disposition of the man had been kept constantly upon the alert by the circumstances of his situation. His long yellow hair was equally divided on the top of his head and upon his brow, and combed down on each side to the length of his shoulders: it had but little tendency to grey, although Cedric was approaching to his sixtieth year.

His dress was a tunic of forest green, furred at the throat and cuffs with what was called minever— a kind of fur inferior in quality to ermine, and formed, it is believed, of the skin of the grey squirrel. This doublet hung unbuttoned over a close dress of scarlet which sate tight to his body; he had breeches of the same, but they did not reach below the lower part of the thigh, leaving the knee exposed. His feet had sandals of the same fashion with the peasants, but of finer materials, and secured in the front with golden clasps. He had bracelets of gold upon his arms, and a broad collar of the same precious metal around his neck. About his waist he wore a richly studded belt, in which was stuck a short, straight, two-edged sword, with a sharp point, so disposed as to hang almost perpendicularly by his side. Behind his seat was hung a scarlet cloth cloak lined with fur, and a cap of the same materials, richly embroidered, which completed the dress of the opulent landholder when he chose to go forth. A short boar-spear, with a broad and bright steel head, also reclined against the back of his chair, which served him, when he walked abroad, for the purposes of a staff or of a weapon, as chance might require.

Several domestics, whose dress held various proportions betwixt the richness of their master's and the coarse and simple attire of Gurth, the swineherd, watched the looks and waited the commands of the Saxon dignitary. Two or three servants of a superior order stood behind their master upon the dais; the rest occupied the lower part of the hall. Other attendants there were of a different description: two or three large and shaggy greyhounds, such as were then employed in hunting the stag and wolf; as many slow-hounds, of a large bony breed, with thick necks, large heads, and long ears; and one or two of the smaller dogs, now called terriers, which waited with impatience the arrival of the supper; but, with the sagacious knowledge of physiognomy peculiar to their race, forbore to intrude upon the moody silence of their master, apprehensive probably of a small white truncheon which lay by Cedric's trencher, for the purpose of repelling the advances of his four-legged dependants. One grisly old wolf-dog alone, with the liberty of an indulged favourite, had planted himself close by the chair of state, and occasionally ventured to solicit notice by putting his large hairy head upon his master's knee, or pushing his nose into his

hand. Even he was repelled by the stern command,
'Down, Balder—down! I am not in the humour
for foolery.'

In fact, Cedric, as we have observed, was in no
very placid state of mind. The Lady Rowena, who
had been absent to attend an evening mass at a
distant church, had but just returned, and was
changing her garments, which had been wetted by
the storm. There were as yet no tidings of Gurth
and his charge, which should long since have been
driven home from the forest; and such was the in-
security of the period as to render it probable that
the delay might be explained by some depredation
of the outlaws, with whom the adjacent forest
abounded, or by the violence of some neighbouring
baron, whose consciousness of strength made him
equally negligent of the laws of property. The
matter was of consequence, for great part of the
domestic wealth of the Saxon proprietors consisted
in numerous herds of swine, especially in forest
land, where those animals easily found their food.

Besides these subjects of anxiety, the Saxon thane
was impatient for the presence of his favourite
clown, Wamba, whose jests, such as they were,
served for a sort of seasoning to his evening meal,
and to the deep draughts of ale and wine with
which he was in the habit of accompanying it. Add
to all this, Cedric had fasted since noon, and his
usual supper hour was long past, a cause of irritation
common to country squires, both in ancient and
modern times. His displeasure was expressed in
broken sentences, partly muttered to himself, partly
addressed to the domestics who stood around; and
particularly to his cupbearer, who offered him from
time to time, as a sedative, a silver goblet filled
with wine—'Why tarries the Lady Rowena?'

'She is but changing her head-gear,' replied a
female attendant, with as much confidence as the
favourite lady's-maid usually answers the master of

a modern family; 'you would not wish her to sit
down to the banquet in her hood and kirtle? and
no lady within the shire can be quicker in arraying
herself than my mistress.'

This undeniable argument produced a sort of
acquiescent 'Umph!' on the part of the Saxon,
with the addition, 'I wish her devotion may choose
fair weather for the next visit to St. John's Kirk.
But what, in the name of ten devils,' continued he,
turning to the cupbearer, and raising his voice, as
if happy to have found a channel into which he
might divert his indignation without fear or control
—'what, in the name of ten devils, keeps Gurth so
long a-field? I suppose we shall have an evil
account of the herd; he was wont to be a faithful
and cautious drudge, and I had destined him for
something better; perchance I might even have
made him one of my warders.'

Oswald, the cupbearer, modestly suggested, 'That
it was scarce an hour since the tolling of the curfew'
—an ill-chosen apology, since it turned upon a
topic so harsh to Saxon ears.

'The foul fiend,' exclaimed Cedric, 'take the
curfew-bell, and the tyrannical bastard by whom
it was devised, and the heartless slave who names
it with a Saxon tongue to a Saxon ear! The
curfew!' he added, pausing —'ay, the curfew, which
compels true men to extinguish their lights, that
thieves and robbers may work their deeds in darkness! Ay, the curfew! Reginald Front-de-Bœuf
and Philip de Malvoisin know the use of the curfew
as well as William the Bastard himself, or e'er a
Norman adventurer that fought at Hastings. I
shall hear, I guess, that my property has been
swept off to save from starving the hungry banditti
whom they cannot support but by theft and robbery. My faithful slave is murdered, and my goods
are taken for a prey; and Wamba—where is

Wamba? Said not some one he had gone forth with Gurth?'

Oswald replied in the affirmative.

'Ay! why, this is better and better! he is carried off too, the Saxon fool, to serve the Norman lord. Fools are we all indeed that serve them, and fitter subjects for their scorn and laughter than if we were born with but half our wits. But I will be avenged,' he added, starting from his chair in impatience at the supposed injury, and catching hold of his boar-spear; 'I will go with my complaint to the great council. I have friends, I have followers; man to man will I appeal the Norman to the lists. Let him come in his plate and his mail, and all that can render cowardice bold: I have sent such a javelin as this through a stronger fence than three of their war shields! Haply they think me old; but they shall find, alone and childless as I am, the blood of Hereward is in the veins of Cedric. Ah, Wilfred, Wilfred!' he exclaimed in a lower tone, 'couldst thou have ruled thine unreasonable passion, thy father had not been left in his age like the solitary oak that throws out its shattered and unprotected branches against the full sweep of the tempest!' The reflection seemed to conjure into sadness his irritated feelings. Replacing his javelin, he resumed his seat, bent his looks downward, and appeared to be absorbed in melancholy reflection.

From his musing, Cedric was suddenly awakened by the blast of a horn, which was replied to by the clamorous yells and barking of all the dogs in the hall, and some twenty or thirty which were quartered in other parts of the building. It cost some exercise of the white truncheon, well seconded by the exertions of the domestics, to silence this canine clamour.

'To the gate, knaves!' said the Saxon, hastily, as soon as the tumult was so much appeased that the dependants could hear his voice. 'See what tidings that horn tells us of: to announce, I ween, some hership and robbery which has been done upon my lands.'

Returning in less than three minutes, a warder announced, 'That the Prior Aymer of Jorvaulx, and the good knight Brian de Bois-Guilbert, commander of the valiant and venerable order of Knights Templars, with a small retinue, requested hospitality and lodging for the night, being on their way to a tournament which was to be held not far from Ashby-de-la-Zouche on the second day from the present.'

'Aymer—the Prior Aymer! Brian de Bois-Guilbert!' muttered Cedric—'Normans both; but Norman or Saxon, the hospitality of Rotherwood must not be impeached: they are welcome, since they have chosen to halt; more welcome would they have been to have ridden further on their way. But it were unworthy to murmur for a night's lodging and a night's food; in the quality of guests, at least, even Normans must suppress their insolence. Go, Hundebert,' he added, to a sort of major-domo who stood behind him with a white wand; 'take six of the attendants and introduce the strangers to the guests' lodging. Look after their horses and mules, and see their train lack nothing. Let them have change of vestments if they require it, and fire, and water to wash, and wine and ale; and bid the cooks add what they hastily can to our evening meal; and let it be put on the board when those strangers are ready to share it. Say to them, Hundebert, that Cedric would himself bid them welcome, but he is under a vow never to step more than three steps from the dais of his own hall to meet any who shares not the blood of Saxon royalty. Begone! see them carefully tended; let them not say in their pride, the Saxon churl has shown at once his poverty and his avarice.'

The major-domo departed with several attendants

to execute his master's commands. 'The Prior Aymer!' repeated Cedric, looking to Oswald, 'the brother, if I mistake not, of Giles de Mauleverer, now lord of Middleham?'

Oswald made a respectful sign of assent. 'His brother sits in the seat, and usurps the patrimony, of a better race—the race of Ulfgar of Middleham; but what Norman lord doth not the same? This Prior is, they say, a free and jovial priest, who loves the wine-cup and the bugle-horn better than bell and book. Good; let him come, he shall be welcome. How named ye the Templar?'

'Brian de Bois-Guilbert.'

'Bois-Guilbert!' said Cedric, still in the musing, half-arguing tone which the habit of living among dependants had accustomed him to employ, and which resembled a man who talks to himself rather than to those around him—'Bois-Guilbert! That name has been spread wide both for good and evil. They say he is valiant as the bravest of his order; but stained with their usual vices—pride, arrogance, cruelty, and voluptuousness—a hard-hearted man, who knows neither fear of earth nor awe of heaven. So say the few warriors who have returned from Palestine. Well, it is but for one night; he shall be welcome too. Oswald, broach the oldest wine-cask; place the best mead, the mightiest ale, the richest morat, the most sparkling cider, the most odoriferous pigments upon the board; fill the largest horns: Templars and abbots love good wines and good measure. Elgitha, let thy Lady Rowena know we shall not this night expect her in the hall, unless such be her especial pleasure.'

'But it will be her especial pleasure,' answered Elgitha, with great readiness, 'for she is ever desirous to hear the latest news from Palestine.'

Cedric darted at the forward damsel a glance of hasty resentment; but Rowena and whatever belonged to her were privileged, and secure from his anger. He only replied, 'Silence, maiden; thy tongue outruns thy discretion. Say my message to thy mistress, and let her do her pleasure. Here, at least, the descendant of Alfred still reigns a princess.'

Elgitha left the apartment.

'Palestine!' repeated the Saxon—'Palestine! how many ears are turned to the tales which dissolute crusaders or hypocritical pilgrims bring from that fatal land! I too might ask—I too might inquire—I too might listen with a beating heart to fables which the wily strollers devise to cheat us into hospitality; but no—the son who has disobeyed me is no longer mine; nor will I concern myself more for his fate than for that of the most worthless among the millions that ever shaped the cross on their shoulder, rushed into excess and blood-guiltiness, and called it an accomplishment of the will of God.'

He knit his brows, and fixed his eyes for an instant on the ground; as he raised them, the folding doors at the bottom of the hall were cast wide, and preceded by the major-domo with his wand, and four domestics bearing blazing torches, the guests of the evening entered the apartment.

CHAPTER IV

With sheep and shaggy goats the porkers bled,
And the proud steer was on the marble spread;
With fire prepared, they deal the morsels round,
Wine rosy bright the brimming goblets crown'd.

Disposed apart, Ulysses shares the treat;
A trivet table and ignobler seat,
The Prince assigns——
                                Odyssey, Book XX.

THE Prior Aymer had taken the opportunity afforded
him of changing his riding robe for one of yet more
costly materials, over which he wore a cope curiously
embroidered. Besides the massive golden signet ring
which marked his ecclesiastical dignity, his fingers,
though contrary to the canon, were loaded with
precious gems; his sandals were of the finest leather
which was imported from Spain; his beard trimmed
to as small dimensions as his order would possibly
permit, and his shaven crown concealed by a scarlet
cap richly embroidered.

The appearance of the Knight Templar was also
changed; and, though less studiously bedecked with
ornament, his dress was as rich, and his appearance
far more commanding, than that of his companion.
He had exchanged his shirt of mail for an under
tunic of dark purple silk, garnished with furs, over
which flowed his long robe of spotless white in ample
folds. The eight-pointed cross of his order was cut
on the shoulder of his mantle in black velvet. The

high cap no longer invested his brows, which were
only shaded by short and thick curled hair of a
raven blackness, corresponding to his unusually
swart complexion. Nothing could be more gracefully majestic than his step and manner, had they
not been marked by a predominant air of haughtiness, easily acquired by the exercise of unresisted
authority.

These two dignified persons were followed by their
respective attendants, and at a more humble distance
by their guide, whose figure had nothing more remarkable than it derived from the usual weeds of a
pilgrim. A cloak or mantle of coarse black serge
enveloped his whole body. It was in shape something like the cloak of a modern hussar, having
similar flaps for covering the arms, and was called
a 'sclaveyn,' or 'sclavonian.' Coarse sandals, bound
with thongs, on his bare feet; a broad and shadowy
hat, with cockle-shells stitched on its brim, and a
long staff shod with iron, to the upper end of which
was attached a branch of palm, completed the
Palmer's attire. He followed modestly the last of
the train which entered the hall, and, observing
that the lower table scarce afforded room sufficient
for the domestics of Cedric and the retinue of his
guests, he withdrew to a settle placed beside, and
almost under, one of the large chimneys, and seemed
to employ himself in drying his garments, until the
retreat of some one should make room at the board,
or the hospitality of the steward should supply him
with refreshments in the place he had chosen apart.

Cedric rose to receive his guests with an air of
dignified hospitality, and, descending from the dais,
or elevated part of his hall, made three steps towards them, and then awaited their approach.

'I grieve,' he said, 'reverend Prior, that my vow
binds me to advance no farther upon this floor of
my fathers, even to receive such guests as you and
this valiant Knight of the Holy Temple. But my

steward has expounded to you the cause of my seeming discourtesy. Let me also pray that you will excuse my speaking to you in my native language, and that you will reply in the same if your knowledge of it permits ; if not, I sufficiently understand Norman to follow your meaning.'

'Vows,' said the Abbot, 'must be unloosed, worthy franklin, or permit me rather to say, worthy thane, though the title is antiquated. Vows are the knots which tie us to Heaven—they are the cords which bind the sacrifice to the horns of the altar— and are therefore, as I said before, to be unloosed and discharged, unless our Holy Mother Church shall pronounce the contrary. And respecting language, I willingly hold communication in that spoken by my respected grandmother, Hilda of Middleham, who died in odour of sanctity, little short, if we may presume to say so, of her glorious namesake, the blessed Saint Hilda of Whitby—God be gracious to her soul !'

When the Prior had ceased what he meant as a conciliatory harangue, his companion said briefly and emphatically, 'I speak ever French, the language of King Richard and his nobles ; but I understand English sufficiently to communicate with the natives of the country.'

Cedric darted at the speaker one of those hasty and impatient glances which comparisons between the two rival nations seldom failed to call forth ; but, recollecting the duties of hospitality, he suppressed further show of resentment, and, motioning with his hand, caused his guests to assume two seats a little lower than his own, but placed close beside him, and gave a signal that the evening meal should be placed upon the board.

While the attendants hastened to obey Cedric's commands, his eye distinguished Gurth, the swineherd, who, with his companion Wamba, had just entered the hall. 'Send these loitering knaves up hither,' said the Saxon, impatiently. And when the culprits came before the dais—'How comes it, villains, that you have loitered abroad so late as this? Hast thou brought home thy charge, sirrah Gurth, or hast thou left them to robbers and marauders?'

'The herd is safe, so please ye,' said Gurth.

'But it does not please me, thou knave,' said Cedric, 'that I should be made to suppose otherwise for two hours, and sit here devising vengeance against my neighbours for wrongs they have not done me. I tell thee, shackles and the prison-house shall punish the next offence of this kind.'

Gurth, knowing his master's irritable temper, attempted no exculpation; but the Jester, who could presume upon Cedric's tolerance, by virtue of his privileges as a fool, replied for them both—'In troth, uncle Cedric, you are neither wise nor reasonable to-night.'

'How, sir!' said his master; 'you shall to the porter's lodge and taste of the discipline there if you give your foolery such license.'

'First let your wisdom tell me,' said Wamba, 'is it just and reasonable to punish one person for the fault of another?'

'Certainly not, fool,' answered Cedric.

'Then why should you shackle poor Gurth, uncle, for the fault of his dog Fangs? for I dare be sworn we lost not a minute by the way, when we had got our herd together, which Fangs did not manage until we heard the vesper-bell.'

'Then hang up Fangs,' said Cedric, turning hastily towards the swineherd, 'if the fault is his, and get thee another dog.'

'Under favour, uncle,' said the Jester, 'that were still somewhat on the bow-hand of fair justice; for it was no fault of Fangs that he was lame and could not gather the herd, but the fault of those that struck off two of his fore-claws, an operation for which, if the poor fellow had been consulted, he would scarce have given his voice.'

'And who dared to lame an animal which belonged to my bondsman?' said the Saxon, kindling in wrath.

'Marry, that did old Hubert,' said Wamba, 'Sir Philip de Malvoisin's keeper of the chase. He caught Fangs strolling in the forest, and said he chased the deer contrary to his master's right, as warden of the walk.'

'The foul fiend take Malvoisin,' answered the Saxon, 'and his keeper both! I will teach them that the wood was disforested in terms of the great Forest Charter. But enough of this. Go to, knave, —go to thy place; and thou, Gurth, get thee another dog, and should the keeper dare to touch it, I will mar his archery; the curse of a coward on my head, if I strike not off the forefinger of his right hand! he shall draw bowstring no more. I crave your pardon, my worthy guests. I am beset here with neighbours that match your infidels, Sir Knight, in Holy Land. But your homely fare is before you; feed, and let welcome make amends for hard fare.'

The feast, however, which was spread upon the board needed no apologies from the lord of the mansion. Swine's flesh, dressed in several modes, appeared on the lower part of the board, as also that of fowls, deer, goats, and hares, and various kinds of fish, together with huge loaves and cakes of bread, and sundry confections made of fruits and honey. The smaller sorts of wild-fowl, of which there was abundance, were not served up in platters, but brought in upon small wooden spits or broaches, and offered by the pages and domestics who bore them to each guest in succession, who cut from them such a portion as he pleased. Beside each person of rank was placed a goblet of silver; the lower board was accommodated with large, drinking-horns.

When the repast was about to commence, the major-domo, or steward, suddenly raising his wand, said aloud—'Forbear! Place for the Lady Rowena.' A side-door at the upper end of the hall now opened behind the banquet table, and Rowena, followed by four female attendants, entered the apartment. Cedric, though surprised, and perhaps not altogether agreeably so, at his ward appearing in public on this occasion, hastened to meet her, and to conduct her, with respectful ceremony, to the elevated seat at his own right hand appropriated to the lady of the mansion. All stood up to receive her; and, replying to their courtesy by a mute gesture of salutation, she moved gracefully forward to assume her place at the board. Ere she had time to do so, the Templar whispered to the Prior, 'I shall wear no collar of gold of yours at the tournament. The Chian wine is your own.'

'Said I not so?' answered the Prior; 'but check your raptures, the franklin observes you.'

Unheeding this remonstrance, and accustomed only to act upon the immediate impulse of his own wishes, Brian de Bois-Guilbert kept his eyes riveted on the Saxon beauty, more striking perhaps to his imagination because differing widely from those of the Eastern sultanas.

Formed in the best proportions of her sex, Rowena was tall in stature, yet not so much so as to attract observation on account of superior height. Her complexion was exquisitely fair, but the noble cast of her head and features prevented the insipidity which sometimes attaches to fair beauties. Her clear blue eye, which sate enshrined beneath a graceful eyebrow of brown, sufficiently marked to give expression to the forehead, seemed capable to kindle as well as melt, to command as well as to beseech. If mildness were the more natural expression of such a combination of features, it was plain that, in the present instance, the exercise of habitual superiority, and the reception of general homage, had given to the Saxon lady a loftier character, which mingled with and qualified that bestowed by nature. Her profuse hair, of a colour betwixt brown and flaxen, was arranged in a fanciful and graceful manner in numerous ringlets, to form which art had probably aided nature. These locks were braided with gems, and being worn at full length, intimated the noble birth and free-born condition of the maiden. A golden chain, to which was attached a small reliquary of the same metal, hung round her neck. She wore bracelets on her arms, which were bare. Her dress was an undergown and kirtle of pale sea-green silk, over which hung a long loose robe, which reached to the ground, having very wide sleeves, which came down, however, very little below the elbow. This robe was crimson, and manufactured out of the very finest wool. A veil of silk, interwoven with gold, was attached to the upper part of it, which could be, at the wearer's pleasure, either drawn over the face and bosom after the Spanish fashion, or disposed as a sort of drapery round the shoulders.

When Rowena perceived the Knight Templar's eyes bent on her with an ardour that, compared with the dark caverns under which they moved, gave them the effect of lighted charcoal, she drew with dignity the veil around her face, as an intimation that the determined freedom of his glance was disagreeable.

Cedric saw the motion and its cause. 'Sir Templar,' said he, 'the cheeks of our Saxon maidens have seen too little of the sun to enable them to bear the fixed glance of a crusader.'

'If I have offended,' replied Sir Brian, 'I crave your pardon—that is, I crave the Lady Rowena's pardon, for my humility will carry me no lower.'

'The Lady Rowena,' said the Prior, 'has punished us all, in chastising the boldness of my friend. Let me hope she will be less cruel to the splendid train which are to meet at the tournament.'

'Our going thither,' said Cedric, 'is uncertain. I love not these vanities, which were unknown to my fathers when England was free.'

'Let us hope, nevertheless,' said the Prior, 'our company may determine you to travel thitherward; when the roads are so unsafe, the escort of Sir Brian de Bois-Guilbert is not to be despised.'

'Sir Prior,' answered the Saxon, 'wheresoever I have travelled in this land, I have hitherto found myself, with the assistance of my good sword and faithful followers, in no respect needful of other aid. At present, if we indeed journey to Ashby-de-la-Zouche, we do so with my noble neighbour and countryman, Athelstane of Coningsburgh, and with such a train as would set outlaws and feudal enemies at defiance. I drink to you, Sir Prior, in this cup of wine, which I trust your taste will approve, and I thank you for your courtesy. Should you be so rigid in adhering to monastic rule,' he added, 'as to prefer your acid preparation of milk, I hope you will not strain courtesy to do me reason.'

'Nay,' said the Priest, laughing, 'it is only in our abbey that we confine ourselves to the *lac dulce* or the *lac acidum* either. Conversing with the world, we use the world's fashion, and therefore I answer your pledge in this honest wine, and leave the weaker liquor to my lay-brother.'

'And I,' said the Templar, filling his goblet, 'drink wassail to the fair Rowena; for since her namesake introduced the word into England, has never been one more worthy of such a tribute. By my faith, I could pardon the unhappy Vortigern, had he half the cause that we now witness for making shipwreck of his honour and his kingdom.'

'I will spare your courtesy, Sir Knight,' said Rowena with dignity, and without unveiling herself; 'or rather I will tax it so far as to require of you the latest news from Palestine, a theme more agreeable to our English ears than the compliments which your French breeding teaches.'

'I have little of importance to say, lady,' answered Sir Brian de Bois-Guilbert, 'excepting the confirmed tidings of a truce with Saladin.'

He was interrupted by Wamba, who had taken his appropriated seat upon a chair the back of which was decorated with two ass's ears, and which was placed about two steps behind that of his master, who, from time to time, supplied him with victuals from his own trencher; a favour, however, which the Jester shared with the favourite dogs, of whom, as we have already noticed, there were several in attendance. Here sat Wamba, with a small table before him, his heels tucked up against the bar of the chair, his cheeks sucked up so as to make his jaws resemble a pair of nut-crackers, and his eyes half-shut, yet watching with alertness every opportunity to exercise his licensed foolery.

'These truces with the infidels,' he exclaimed, without caring how suddenly he interrupted the stately Templar, 'make an old man of me!'

'Go to, knave—how so?' said Cedric, his features prepared to receive favourably the expected jest.

'Because,' answered Wamba, 'I remember three of them in my day, each of which was to endure for the course of fifty years; so that, by computation, I must be at least a hundred and fifty years old.'

'I will warrant you against dying of old age, however,' said the Templar, who now recognised his friend of the forest; 'I will assure you from all deaths but a violent one, if you give such directions to wayfarers as you did this night to the Prior and me.'

'How, sirrah!' said Cedric, 'misdirect travellers? We must have you whipt; you are at least as much rogue as fool.'

'I pray thee, uncle,' answered the Jester, 'let my folly for once protect my roguery. I did but make a mistake between my right hand and my left; and he might have pardoned a greater who took a fool for his counsellor and guide.'

Conversation was here interrupted by the entrance of the porter's page, who announced that there was a stranger at the gate, imploring admittance, and hospitality.

'Admit him,' said Cedric, 'be he who or what he may: a night like that which roars without compels even wild animals to herd with tame, and to seek the protection of man, their mortal foe, rather than perish by the elements. Let his wants be ministered to with all care; look to it, Oswald.'

And the steward left the banqueting-hall to see the commands of his patron obeyed.

CHAPTER V

Hath not a Jew eyes? Hath not a Jew hands, organs,
    dimensions, senses, affections, passions? Fed with the
    same food, hurt with the same weapons, subject to the
    same diseases, healed by the same means, warmed
    and cooled by the same winter and summer, as a
    Christian is?—*Merchant of Venice.*

OSWALD, returning, whispered into the ear of his
master, 'It is a Jew, who calls himself Isaac of
York; is it fit I should marshal him into the
hall?'

'Let Gurth do thine office, Oswald,' said Wamba
with his usual effrontery: 'the swineherd will be a
fit usher to the Jew.'

'St. Mary,' said the Abbot, crossing himself, 'an
unbelieving Jew, and admitted into this presence!'

'A dog Jew,' echoed the Templar, 'to approach
a defender of the Holy Sepulchre?'

'By my faith,' said Wamba, 'it would seem the
Templars love the Jews' inheritance better than
they do their company.'

'Peace, my worthy guests,' said Cedric; 'my
hospitality must not be bounded by your dislikes.
If Heaven bore with the whole nation of stiff-necked
unbelievers for more years than a layman can
number, we may endure the presence of one Jew
for a few hours. But I constrain no man to converse or to feed with him. Let him have a board
and a morsel apart,—unless,' he said smiling, 'these
turban'd strangers will admit his society.'

'Sir Franklin,' answered the Templar, 'my Saracen slaves are true Moslems, and scorn as much as any Christian to hold intercourse with a Jew.'

'Now, in faith,' said Wamba, 'I cannot see that the worshippers of Mahound and Termagaunt have so greatly the advantage over the people once chosen of Heaven.'

'He shall sit with thee, Wamba,' said Cedric; 'the fool and the knave will be well met.'

'The fool,' answered Wamba, raising the relics of a gammon of bacon, 'will take care to erect a bulwark against the knave.'

'Hush,' said Cedric, 'for here he comes.'

Introduced with little ceremony, and advancing with fear and hesitation, and many a bow of deep humility, a tall thin old man, who, however, had lost by the habit of stooping much of his actual height, approached the lower end of the board. His features, keen and regular, with an aquiline nose, and piercing black eyes; his high and wrinkled forehead, and long grey hair and beard, would have been considered as handsome, had they not been the marks of a physiognomy peculiar to a race which, during those dark ages, was alike detested by the credulous and prejudiced vulgar, and persecuted by the greedy and rapacious nobility, and who, perhaps owing to that very hatred and persecution, had adopted a national character in which there was much, to say the least, mean and unamiable.

The Jew's dress, which appeared to have suffered considerably from the storm, was a plain russet cloak of many folds, covering a dark purple tunic. He had large boots lined with fur, and a belt around his waist, which sustained a small knife, together with a case for writing materials, but no weapon. He wore a high square yellow cap of a peculiar fashion, assigned to his nation to distinguish them

from Christians, and which he doffed with great
humility at the door of the hall.

The reception of this person in the hall of Cedric
the Saxon was such as might have satisfied the most
prejudiced enemy of the tribes of Israel. Cedric
himself coldly nodded in answer to the Jew's repeated salutations, and signed to him to take place
at the lower end of the table, where, however, no
one offered to make room for him. On the contrary,
as he passed along the file, casting a timid, suppli-
cating glance, and turning towards each of those
who occupied the lower end of the board, the Saxon
domestics squared their shoulders, and continued to
devour their supper with great perseverance, paying
not the least attention to the wants of the new
guest. The attendants of the Abbot crossed themselves, with looks of pious horror, and the very
heathen Saracens, as Isaac drew near them, curled
up their whiskers with indignation, and laid their
hands on their poniards, as if ready to rid themselves by the most desperate means from the apprehended contamination of his nearer approach.

Probably the same motives which induced Cedric
to open his hall to this son of a rejected people
would have made him insist on his attendants receiving Isaac with more courtesy; but the Abbot
had at this moment engaged him in a most interesting discussion on the breed and character of his
favourite hounds, which he would not have interrupted for matters of much greater importance than
that of a Jew going to bed supperless. While Isaac
thus stood an outcast in the present society, like
his people among the nations, looking in vain for
welcome or resting-place, the Pilgrim, who sat by
the chimney, took compassion upon him, and re-
signed his seat, saying briefly, 'Old man, my
garments are dried, my hunger is appeased; thou
art both wet and fasting.' So saying, he gathered
together and brought to a flame the decaying brands

which lay scattered on the ample hearth ; took from
the larger board a mess of pottage and seethed kid,
placed it upon the small table at which he had himself supped, and, without waiting the Jew's thanks,
went to the other side of the hall, whether from
unwillingness to hold more close communication
with the object of his benevolence, or from a wish
to draw near to the upper end of the table, seemed
uncertain.

Had there been painters in those days capable to
execute such a subject, the Jew, as he bent his
withered form and expanded his chilled and trembling hands over the fire, would have formed no
bad emblematical personification of the Winter
season. Having dispelled the cold, he turned
eagerly to the smoking mess which was placed
before him, and ate with a haste and an apparent
relish that seemed to betoken long abstinence from
food.

Meanwhile the Abbot and Cedric continued their
discourse upon hunting ; the Lady Rowena seemed
engaged in conversation with one of her attendant
females ; and the haughty Templar, whose eye
seemed to wander from the Jew to the Saxon beauty,
revolved in his mind thoughts which appeared
deeply to interest him.

'I marvel, worthy Cedric,' said the Abbot, as
their discourse proceeded, 'that, great as your predilection is for your own manly language, you do
not receive the Norman-French into your favour,
so far at least as the mystery of woodcraft and
hunting is concerned. Surely no tongue is so rich
in the various phrases which the field-sports demand,
or furnishes means to the experienced woodman so
well to express his jovial art.'

'Good Father Aymer,' said the Saxon, 'be it
known to you, I care not for those over-sea refine-
ments, without which I can well enough take my
pleasure in the woods. I can wind my horn, though

I call not the blast either a *recheat* or a *mort*; I can cheer my dogs on the prey, and I can flay and quarter the animal when it is brought down, without using the new-fangled jargon of *curée, arbor, nombles,* and all the babble of the fabulous Sir Tristrem.'

'The French,' said the Templar, raising his voice with the presumptuous and authoritative tone which he used upon all occasions, 'is not only the natural language of the chase, but that of love and of war, in which ladies should be won and enemies defied.'

'Pledge me in a cup of wine, Sir Templar,' said Cedric, 'and fill another to the Abbot; while I look back some thirty years to tell you another tale. As Cedric the Saxon then was, his plain English tale needed no garnish from French troubadours when it was told in the ear of beauty; and the field of Northallerton, upon the day of the Holy Standard, could tell whether the Saxon war-cry was not heard as far within the ranks of the Scottish host as the *cri de guerre* of the boldest Norman baron. To the memory of the brave who fought there! Pledge me, my guests.' He drank deep, and went on with increasing warmth—'Ay, that was a day of cleaving of shields, when a hundred banners were bent forward over the heads of the valiant, and blood flowed round like water, and death was held better than flight. A Saxon bard had called it a feast of the swords—a gathering of the eagles to the prey—the clashing of bills upon shield and helmet, the shouting of battle more joyful than the clamour of a bridal. But our bards are no more,' he said; 'our deeds are lost in those of another race; our language—our very name—is hastening to decay, and none mourns for it save one solitary old man. Cupbearer! knave, fill the goblets. To the strong in arms, Sir Templar, be their race or language

what it will, who now bear them best in Palestine
among the champions of the Cross !'

'It becomes not one wearing this badge to answer,'
said Sir Brian de Bois-Guilbert; 'yet to whom,
besides the sworn champions of the Holy Sepulchre,
can the palm be assigned among the champions of
the Cross?'

'To the Knights Hospitallers,' said the Abbot;
'I have a brother of their order.'

'I impeach not their fame,' said the Templar;
'nevertheless——'

'I think, friend Cedric,' said Wamba, interfering,
'that had Richard of the Lion's Heart been wise
enough to have taken a fool's advice, he might have
staid at home with his merry Englishmen, and left
the recovery of Jerusalem to those same Knights
who had most to do with the loss of it.'

'Were there, then, none in the English army,'
said the Lady Rowena, 'whose names are worthy to
be mentioned with the Knights of the Temple and
of St. John?'

'Forgive me, lady,' replied De Bois-Guilbert;
'the English monarch did indeed bring to Palestine
a host of gallant warriors, second only to those
whose breasts have been the unceasing bulwark of
that blessed land.'

'Second to NONE,' said the Pilgrim, who had stood
near enough to hear, and had listened to this conversation with marked impatience. All turned
towards the spot from whence this unexpected
asseveration was heard. 'I say,' repeated the
Pilgrim in a firm and strong voice, 'that the English
chivalry were second to NONE who ever drew sword
in defence of the Holy Land. I say besides, for I
saw it, that King Richard himself, and five of his
knights, held a tournament after the taking of St.
John-de-Acre, as challengers against all comers. I
say that, on that day, each knight ran three courses,
and cast to the ground three antagonists. I add,

that seven of these assailants were Knights of the Temple ; and Sir Brian de Bois-Guilbert well knows the truth of what I tell you.'

It is impossible for language to describe the bitter scowl of rage which rendered yet darker the swarthy countenance of the Templar. In the extremity of his resentment and confusion, his quivering fingers griped towards the handle of his sword, and perhaps only withdrew from the consciousness that no act of violence could be safely executed in that place and presence. Cedric, whose feelings were all of a right onward and simple kind, and were seldom occupied by more than one object at once, omitted, in the joyous glee with which he heard of the glory of his countrymen, to remark the angry confusion of his guest. ' I would give thee this golden bracelet, Pilgrim,' he said, ' couldst thou tell me the names of those knights who upheld so gallantly the renown of merry England.'

' That will I do blythely,' replied the Pilgrim, ' and without guerdon ; my oath, for a time, prohibits me from touching gold.'

' I will wear the bracelet for you, if you will, friend Palmer,' said Wamba.

' The first in honour as in arms, in renown as in place,' said the Pilgrim, ' was the brave Richard, King of England.'

' I forgive him,' said Cedric—' I forgive him his descent from the tyrant Duke William.'

' The Earl of Leicester was the second,' continued the Pilgrim. ' Sir Thomas Multon of Gilsland was the third.'

' Of Saxon descent, he at least,' said Cedric, with exultation.

' Sir Foulk Doilly the fourth,' proceeded the Pilgrim.

' Saxon also, at least by the mother's side,' continued Cedric, who listened with the utmost eagerness, and forgot, in part at least, his hatred to the

Normans in the common triumph of the King of England and his islanders. 'And who was the fifth?' he demanded.

'The fifth was Sir Edwin Turneham.'

'Genuine Saxon, by the soul of Hengist: shouted Cedric. 'And the sixth?' he continued with eagerness—'how name you the sixth?'

'The sixth,' said the Palmer, after a pause, in which he seemed to recollect himself, 'was a young knight of lesser renown and lower rank, assumed into that honourable company less to aid their enterprise than to make up their number; his name dwells not in my memory.'

'Sir Palmer,' said Sir Brian de Bois-Guilbert, scornfully, 'this assumed forgetfulness, after so much has been remembered, comes too late to serve your purpose. I will myself tell the name of the knight before whose lance fortune and my horse's fault occasioned my falling: it was the Knight of Ivanhoe; nor was there one of the six that, for his years, had more renown in arms. Yet this will I say, and loudly—that were he in England, and durst repeat, in this week's tournament, the challenge of St. John-de-Acre, I, mounted and armed as I now am, would give him every advantage of weapons, and abide the result.'

'Your challenge would be soon answered,' replied the Palmer, 'were your antagonist near you. As the matter is, disturb not the peaceful hall with vaunts of the issue of a conflict which you well know cannot take place. If Ivanhoe ever returns from Palestine, I will be his surety that he meets you.'

'A goodly security!' said the Knight Templar; 'and what do you proffer as a pledge?'

'This reliquary, said the Palmer, taking a small ivory box from his bosom, and crossing himself, 'containing a portion of the true cross, brought from the monastery of Mount Carmel.'

The Prior of Jorvaulx crossed himself and repeated
a paternoster, in which all devoutly joined, excepting
the Jew, the Mahomedans, and the Templar; the
latter of whom, without vailing his bonnet or testi-
fying any reverence for the alleged sanctity of the
relic, took from his neck a gold chain, which he
flung on the board, saying, 'Let Prior Aymer hold
my pledge and that of this nameless vagrant, in
token that, when the Knight of Ivanhoe comes
within the four seas of Britain, he underlies the
challenge of Brian de Bois-Guilbert, which, if he
answer not, I will proclaim him as a coward on the
walls of every Temple court in Europe.'

'It will not need,' said the Lady Rowena, breaking
silence: 'my voice shall be heard, if no other in
this hall is raised, in behalf of the absent Ivanhoe.
I affirm he will meet fairly every honourable challenge. Could my weak warrant add security to the
inestimable pledge of this holy pilgrim, I would
pledge name and fame that Ivanhoe gives this proud
knight the meeting he desires.'

A crowd of conflicting emotions seemed to have
occupied Cedric and kept him silent during this
discussion. Gratified pride, resentment, embarrassment, chased each other over his broad and open
brow, like the shadow of clouds drifting over a
harvest-field; while his attendants, on whom the
name of the sixth knight seemed to produce an
effect almost electrical, hung in suspense upon their
master's looks. But when Rowena spoke, the sound
of her voice seemed to startle him from his silence.

'Lady,' said Cedric, 'this beseems not; were
further pledge necessary, I myself, offended, and
justly offended, as I am, would yet gage my honour
for the honour of Ivanhoe. But the wager of battle
is complete, even according to the fantastic fashions
of Norman chivalry. Is it not, Father Aymer?'

'It is,' replied the Prior; 'and the blessed relic
and rich chain will I bestow safely in the treasury

of our convent, until the decision of this warlike
challenge.'

Having thus spoken, he crossed himself again and
again, and after many genuflections and muttered
prayers, he delivered the reliquary to Brother Ambrose, his attendant monk, while he himself swept
up with less ceremony, but perhaps with no less internal satisfaction, the golden chain, and bestowed
it in a pouch lined with perfumed leather, which
opened under his arm. 'And now, Sir Cedric,' he
said, ' my ears are chiming vespers with the strength
of your good wine : permit us another pledge to the
welfare of the Lady Rowena, and indulge us with
liberty to pass to our repose.'

'By the rood of Bromholme,' said the Saxon,
'you do but small credit to your fame, Sir Prior !
Report speaks you a bonny monk, that would hear
the matin chime ere he quitted his bowl ; and, old
as I am, I feared to hear shame in encountering
you. But, by my faith, a Saxon boy of twelve, in
my time, would not so soon have relinquished his
goblet.'

The Prior had his own reasons, however, for persevering in the course of temperance which he had
adopted. He was not only a professional peacemaker, but from practice a hater of all feuds and
brawls. It was not altogether from a love to his
neighbour, or to himself, or from a mixture of both.
On the present occasion, he had an instinctive apprehension of the fiery temper of the Saxon, and saw
the danger that the reckless and presumptuous spirit
of which his companion had already given so many
proofs might at length produce some disagreeable
explosion. He therefore gently insinuated the in-
capacity of the native of any other country to engage
in the genial conflict of the bowl with the hardy and
strong-headed Saxons ; something he mentioned,
but slightly, about his own holy character, and ended
by pressing his proposal to depart to repose.

The grace-cup was accordingly served round, and
the guests, after making deep obeisance to their
landlord and to the Lady Rowena, arose and mingled
in the hall, while the heads of the family, by separate doors, retired with their attendants.

'Unbelieving dog,' said the Templar to Isaac the
Jew, as he passed him in the throng, 'dost thou
bend thy course to the tournament?'

'I do so propose,' replied Isaac, bowing in all
humility, 'if it please your reverend valour.'

'Ay,' said the Knight, 'to gnaw the bowels of our
nobles with usury, and to gull women and boys with
gauds and toys : I warrant thee store of shekels in
thy Jewish scrip.'

'Not a skekel, not a silver penny, not a halfling,
so help me the God of Abraham!' said the Jew,
clasping his hands. 'I go but to seek the assistance
of some brethren of my tribe to aid me to pay the
fine which the Exchequer of the Jews [1] have imposed
upon me, Father Jacob be my speed! I am an impoverished wretch : the very gaberdine I wear is
borrowed from Reuben of Tadcaster.'

The Templar smiled sourly as he replied, 'Beshrew
thee for a false-hearted liar!' and passing onward,
as if disdaining farther conference, he communed
with his Moslem slaves in a language unknown to the
bystanders. The poor Israelite seemed so staggered
by the address of the military monk, that the Templar
had passed on to the extremity of the hall ere he
raised his head from the humble posture which he
had assumed, so far as to be sensible of his departure. And when he did look around, it was with
the astonished air of one at whose feet a thunderbolt
had just burst, and who hears still the astounding
report ringing in his ears.

The Templar and Prior were shortly after mar-

[1] In those days the Jews were subjected to an Exchequer,
specially dedicated to that purpose, and which laid them
under the most exorbitant impositions.—L. T.

shalled to their sleeping apartments by the steward
and the cupbearer, each attended by two torch-
bearers and two servants carrying refreshments,
while servants of inferior condition indicated to
their retinue and to the other guests their repective
places of repose.

CHAPTER VI

To buy his favour I extend this friendship:
If he will take it, so ; if not, adieu ;
And, for my love, I pray you wrong me not.
Merchant of Venice.

As the Palmer, lighted by a domestic with a torch,
past through the intricate combination of apartments
of this large and irregular mansion, the cupbearer,
coming behind him, whispered in his ear, that if he
had no objection to a cup of good mead in his apartment, there were many domestics in that family who
would gladly hear the news he had brought from
the Holy Land, and particularly that which concerned the Knight of Ivanhoe. Wamba presently
appeared to urge the same request, observing that a
cup after midnight was worth three after curfew.
Without disputing a maxim urged by such grave
authority, the Palmer thanked them for their
courtesy, but observed that he had included in
his religious vow an obligation never to speak in
the kitchen on matters which were prohibited in the
hall.

'That vow,' said Wamba to the cupbearer, 'would
scarce suit a serving-man.'

The cupbearer shrugged up his shoulders in displeasure. 'I thought to have lodged him in the
solere chamber,' said he ; 'but since he is so un-
social to Christians, e'en let him take the next stall
to Isaac the Jew's. Anwold,' said he to the torch-

bearer, 'carry the Pilgrim to the southern cell. I
give you good-night,' he added, 'Sir Palmer, with
small thanks for short courtesy.'

'Good-night, and Our Lady's benison!' said the
Palmer, with composure; and his guide moved
forward.

In a small ante-chamber, into which several doors
opened, and which was lighted by a small iron lamp,
they met a second interruption from the waiting-
maid of Rowena, who, saying in a tone of authority
that her mistress desired to speak with the Palmer,
took the torch from the hand of Anwold, and,
bidding him await her return, made a sign to the
Palmer to follow. Apparently he did not think it
proper to decline this invitation as he had done the
former; for, though his gesture indicated some surprise at the summons, he obeyed it without answer
or remonstrance.

A short passage, and an ascent of seven steps,
each of which was composed of a solid beam of oak,
led him to the apartment of the Lady Rowena,
the rude magnificence of which corresponded to the
respect which was paid to her by the lord of the
mansion. The walls were covered with embroidered
hangings, on which different-coloured silks, interwoven with gold and silver threads, had been
employed, with all the art of which the age was
capable, to represent the sports of hunting and
hawking. The bed was adorned with the same rich
tapestry, and surrounded with curtains dyed with
purple. The seats had also their stained coverings,
and one, which was higher than the rest, was
accommodated with a footstool of ivory, curiously
carved.

No fewer than four silver candelabras, holding
great waxen torches, served to illuminate this
apartment. Yet let not modern beauty envy the
magnificence of a Saxon princess. The walls of the
apartment were so ill finished and so full of crevices,

that the rich hangings shook to the night blast, and, in despite of a sort of screen intended to protect them from the wind, the flame of the torches streamed sideways into the air, like the unfurled pennon of a chieftain. Magnificence there was, with some rude attempt at taste; but of comfort there was little, and, being unknown, it was unmissed.

The Lady Rowena, with three of her attendants standing at her back, and arranging her hair ere she lay down to rest, was seated in the sort of throne already mentioned, and looked as if born to exact general homage. The Pilgrim acknowledged her claim to it by a low genuflection.

'Rise, Palmer,' said she graciously. 'The defender of the absent has a right to favourable reception from all who value truth and honour manhood.' She then said to her train, 'Retire, excepting only Elgitha; I would speak with this holy Pilgrim.'

The maidens, without leaving the apartment, retired to its further extremity, and sat down on a small bench against the wall, where they remained mute as statues, though at such a distance that their whispers could not have interrupted the conversation of their mistress.

'Pilgrim,' said the lady, after a moment's pause, during which she seemed uncertain how to address him, 'you this night mentioned a name—I mean,' she said with a degree of effort, 'the name of Ivanhoe—in the halls where by nature and kindred it should have sounded most acceptably; and yet such is the perverse course of fate, that of many whose hearts must have throbbed at the sound, I only dare ask you where, and in what condition, you left him of whom you spoke? We heard that, having remained in Palestine, on account of his impaired health, after the departure of the English army, he had experienced the persecution of the French faction, to whom the Templars are known to be attached.'

'I know little of the Knight of Ivanhoe,' answered the Palmer, with a troubled voice. 'I would I knew him better, since you, lady, are interested in his fate. He hath, I believe, surmounted the persecution of his enemies in Palestine, and is on the eve of returning to England, where you, lady, must know better than I what is his chance of happiness.'

The Lady Rowena sighed deeply, and asked more particularly when the Knight of Ivanhoe might be expected in his native country, and whether he would not be exposed to great dangers by the road. On the first point, the Palmer professed ignorance; on the second, he said that the voyage might be safely made by the way of Venice and Genoa, and from thence through France to England. 'Ivanhoe,' he said, 'was so well acquainted with the language and manners of the French, that there was no fear of his incurring any hazard during that part of his travels.'

'Would to God,' said the Lady Rowena, 'he were here safely arrived, and able to bear arms in the approaching tourney, in which the chivalry of this land are expected to display their address and valour. Should Athelstane of Coningsburgh obtain the prize, Ivanhoe is like to hear evil tidings when he reaches England. How looked he, stranger, when you last saw him? Had disease laid her hand heavy upon his strength and comeliness?'

'He was darker,' said the Palmer, 'and thinner than when he came from Cyprus in the train of Cœur-de-Lion, and care seemed to sit heavy on his brow; but I approached not his presence, because he is unknown to me.'

'He will,' said the lady, 'I fear, find little in his native land to clear those clouds from his countenance. Thanks, good Pilgrim, for your information concerning the companion of my childhood. Maidens,' she said, 'draw near: offer the sleeping-

cup to this holy man, whom I will no longer detain
from repose.'

One of the maidens presented a silver cup containing a rich mixture of wine and spice, which
Rowena barely put to her lips. It was then offered
to the Palmer, who, after a low obeisance, tasted a
few drops.

'Accept this alms, friend,' continued the lady,
offering a piece of gold, 'in acknowledgment of
thy painful travail, and of the shrines thou hast
visited.'

The Palmer received the boon with another low
reverence, and followed Elgitha out of the apartment.

In the ante-room he found his attendant Anwold,
who, taking the torch from the hand of the waiting-
maid, conducted him with more haste than ceremony
to an exterior and ignoble part of the building,
where a number of small apartments, or rather
cells, served for sleeping-places to the lower order
of domestics, and to strangers of mean degree.

'In which of these sleeps the Jew?' said the
Pilgrim.

'The unbelieving dog,' answered Anwold, 'ken-
nels in the cell next your holiness. St. Dunstan,
how it must be scraped and cleansed ere it be again
fit for a Christian!'

'And where sleeps Gurth, the swineherd?' said
the stranger.

'Gurth,' replied the bondsman, 'sleeps in the cell
on your right, as the Jew in that to your left; you
serve to keep the child of circumcision separate from
the abomination of his tribe. You might have
occupied a more honourable place had you accepted
of Oswald's invitation.'

'It is as well as it is,' said the Palmer; 'the
company, even of a Jew, can hardly spread contamination through an oaken partition.'

So saying, he entered the cabin allotted to him,

and taking the torch from the domestic's hand, thanked him and wished him good-night. Having shut the door of his cell, he placed the torch in a candlestick made of wood, and looked around his sleeping apartment, the furniture of which was of the most simple kind. It consisted of a rude wooden stool, and still ruder hutch or bed-frame, stuffed with clean straw, and accommodated with two or three sheepskins by way of bed-clothes.

The Palmer, having extinguished his torch, threw himself, without taking off any part of his clothes, on this rude couch, and slept, or at least retained his recumbent posture, till the earliest sunbeams found their way through the little grated window, which served at once to admit both air and light to his uncomfortable cell. He then started up, and after repeating his matins and adjusting his dress he left it, and entered that of Isaac the Jew, lifting the latch as gently as he could.

The inmate was lying in troubled slumber upon a couch similar to that on which the Palmer himself had passed the night. Such parts of his dress as the Jew had laid aside on the preceding evening were disposed carefully around his person, as if to prevent the hazard of their being carried off during his slumbers. There was a trouble on his brow amounting almost to agony. His hands and arms moved convulsively, as if struggling with the nightmare; and besides several ejaculations in Hebrew, the following were distinctly heard in the Norman-English, or mixed language of the country: 'For the sake of the God of Abraham, spare an unhappy old man! I am poor, I am penniless; should your irons wrench my limbs asunder, I could not gratify you!'

The Palmer awaited not the end of the Jew's vision, but stirred him with his pilgrim's staff. The touch probably associated, as is usual, with some of the apprehensions excited by his dream; for the old man started up, his grey hair standing almost erect upon his head, and huddling some part of his garments about him, while he held the detached pieces with the tenacious grasp of a falcon, he fixed upon the Palmer his keen black eyes, expressive of wild surprise and of bodily apprehension.

'Fear nothing from me, Isaac,' said the Palmer, 'I come as your friend.'

'The God of Israel requite you,' said the Jew, greatly relieved; 'I dreamed—but Father Abraham be praised, it was but a dream!' Then, collecting himself, he added in his usual tone, 'And what may it be your pleasure to want at so early an hour with the poor Jew?'

'It is to tell you,' said the Palmer, 'that if you leave not this mansion instantly, and travel not with some haste, your journey may prove a dangerous one.'

'Holy father!' said the Jew, 'whom could it interest to endanger so poor a wretch as I am?'

'The purpose you can best guess,' said the Pilgrim; 'but rely on this, that when the Templar crossed the hall yesternight, he spoke to his Mussulman slaves in the Saracen language, which I well understand, and charged them this morning to watch the journey of the Jew, to seize upon him when at a convenient distance from the mansion, and to conduct him to the castle of Philip de Malvoisin or to that of Reginald Front-de-Bœuf.'

It is impossible to describe the extremity of terror which seized upon the Jew at this information, and seemed at once to overpower his whole faculties. His arms fell down to his sides, and his head drooped on his breast, his knees bent under his weight, every nerve and muscle of his frame seemed to collapse and lose its energy, and he sunk at the foot of the Palmer, not in the fashion of one who intentionally stoops, kneels, or prostrates himself to excite compassion, but like a man borne down

on all sides by the pressure of some invisible force,
which crushes him to the earth without the power
of resistance.

'Holy God of Abraham!' was his first exclamation, folding and elevating his wrinkled hands, but
without raising his grey head from the pavement;
'Oh, holy Moses! O, blessed Aaron! the dream is
not dreamed for nought, and the vision cometh not
in vain! I feel their irons already tear my sinews!
I feel the rack pass over my body like the saws, and
harrows, and axes of iron over the men of Rabbah,
and of the cities of the children of Ammon!'

'Stand up, Isaac, and hearken to me,' said the
Palmer, who viewed the extremity of his distress
with a compassion in which contempt was largely
mingled; 'you have cause for your terror, considering how your brethren have been used, in order to
extort from them their hoards, both by princes and
nobles; but stand up, I say, and I will point out to
you the means of escape. Leave this mansion
instantly, while its inmates sleep sound after the
last night's revel. I will guide you by the secret
paths of the forest, known as well to me as to any
forester that ranges it, and I will not leave you till
you are under safe conduct of some chief or baron
going to the tournament, whose good-will you have
probably the means of securing.'

As the ears of Isaac received the hopes of escape
which this speech intimated, he began gradually,
and inch by inch, as it were, to raise himself up
from the ground, until he fairly rested upon his
knees, throwing back his long grey hair and beard,
and fixing his keen black eyes upon the Palmer's
face, with a look expressive at once of hope and
fear, not unmingled with suspicion. But when he
heard the concluding part of the sentence, his
original terror appeared to revive in full force, and
he dropt once more on his face, exclaiming, '*I*
possess the means of securing good-will! Alas!

there is but one road to the favour of a Christian, and how can the poor Jew find it, whom extortions have already reduced to the misery of Lazarus?' Then, as if suspicion had overpowered his other feelings, he suddenly exclaimed, 'For the love of God, young man, betray me not; for the sake of the Great Father who made us all, Jew as well as Gentile, Israelite and Ishmaelite, do me no treason! I have not means to secure the good-will of a Christian beggar, were he rating it at a single penny.' As he spoke these last words, he raised himself and grasped the Palmer's mantle with a look of the most earnest entreaty. The Pilgrim extricated himself, as if there were contamination in the touch.

'Wert thou loaded with all the wealth of thy tribe,' he said, 'what interest have I to injure thee? In this dress I am vowed to poverty, nor do I change it for aught save a horse and a coat of mail. Yet think not that I care for thy company, or propose myself advantage by it; remain here if thou wilt, Cedric the Saxon may protect thee.'

'Alas!' said the Jew, 'he will not let me travel in his train. Saxon or Norman will be equally ashamed of the poor Israelite; and to travel by myself through the domains of Philip de Malvoisin and Reginald Front-de-Bœuf—— Good youth, I will go with you! Let us haste—let us gird up our loins—let us flee! Here is thy staff, why wilt thou tarry?'

'I tarry not,' said the Pilgrim, giving way to the urgency of his companion; 'but I must secure the means of leaving this place; follow me.'

He led the way to the adjoining cell, which, as the reader is apprised, was occupied by Gurth, the swineherd. 'Arise, Gurth,' said the Pilgrim—'arise quickly. Undo the postern gate, and let out the Jew and me.'

Gurth, whose occupation, though now held so mean, gave him as much consequence in Saxon

England as that of Eumæus in Ithaca, was offended at the familiar and commanding tone assumed by the Palmer. 'The Jew leaving Rotherwood,' said he, raising himself on his elbow and looking superciliously at him, without quitting his pallet, 'and travelling in company with the Palmer to boot——'

'I should as soon have dreamt,' said Wamba, who entered the apartment at the instant, 'of his stealing away with a gammon of bacon.'

'Nevertheless,' said Gurth, again laying down his head on the wooden log which served him for a pillow, 'both Jew and Gentile must be content to abide the opening of the great gate; we suffer no visitors to depart by stealth at these unseasonable hours.'

'Nevertheless,' said the Pilgrim, in a commanding tone, 'you will not, I think, refuse me that favour.'

So saying, he stooped over the bed of the recumbent swineherd, and whispered something in his ear in Saxon. Gurth started up as if electrified. The Pilgrim, raising his finger in an attitude as if to express caution, added, 'Gurth, beware; thou art wont to be prudent. I say, undo the postern; thou shalt know more anon.'

With hasty alacrity Gurth obeyed him, while Wamba and the Jew followed, both wondering at the sudden change in the swineherd's demeanour.

'My mule—my mule!' said the Jew, as soon as they stood without the postern.

'Fetch him his mule,' said the Pilgrim; 'and, hearest thou, let me have another, that I may bear him company till he is beyond these parts. I will return it safely to some of Cedric's train at Ashby. And do thou——' he whispered the rest in Gurth's ear.

'Willingly—most willingly shall it be done,' said Gurth, and instantly departed to execute the commission.

'I wish I knew,' said Wamba, when his comrade's

back was turned, 'what you Palmers learn in the
Holy Land.'

'To say our orisons, fool,' answered the Pilgrim,
'to repent our sins, and to mortify ourselves with
fastings, vigils, and long prayers.'

'Something more potent than that,' answered the
Jester; 'for when would repentance or prayer make
Gurth do a courtesy, or fasting or vigil persuade
him to lend you a mule? I trow you might as well
have told his favourite black boar of thy vigils and
penance, and wouldst have gotten as civil an answer.'

'Go to,' said the Pilgrim, 'thou art but a Saxon
fool.'

'Thou sayst well,' said the Jester; 'had I been
born a Norman, as I think thou art, I would have
had luck on my side, and been next door to a wise
man.'

At this moment Gurth appeared on the opposite
side of the moat with the mules. The travellers
crossed the ditch upon a drawbridge of only two
planks' breadth, the narrowness of which was
matched with the straitness of the postern, and with
a little wicket in the exterior palisade, which gave
access to the forest. No sooner had they reached
the mules, than the Jew, with hasty and trembling
hands, secured behind the saddle a small bag of
blue buckram, which he took from under his cloak,
containing, as he muttered, 'a change of raiment—
only a change of raiment.' Then getting upon the
animal with more alacrity and haste than could have
been anticipated from his years, he lost no time in
so disposing of the skirts of his gaberdine as to
conceal completely from observation the burden
which he had thus deposited *en croupe*.

The Pilgrim mounted with more deliberation,
reaching, as he departed, his hand to Gurth, who
kissed it with the utmost possible veneration. The
swineherd stood gazing after the travellers until they
were lost under the boughs of the forest path, when

he was disturbed from his reverie by the voice of
Wamba.

'Knowest thou,' said the Jester, 'my good friend
Gurth, that thou art strangely courteous and most
unwontedly pious on this summer morning? I
would I were a black prior or a barefoot palmer, to
avail myself of thy unwonted zeal and courtesy;
certes, I would make more out of it than a kiss of
the hand.'

'Thou art no fool thus far, Wamba,' answered
Gurth, 'though thou arguest from appearances, and
the wisest of us can do no more. But it is time to
look after my charge.'

So saying, he turned back to the mansion, attended
by the Jester.

Meanwhile the travellers continued to press on
their journey with a despatch which argued the
extremity of the Jew's fears, since persons at his
age are seldom fond of rapid motion. The Palmer,
to whom every path and outlet in the wood appeared
to be familiar, led the way through the most devious
paths, and more than once excited anew the suspicion
of the Israelite that he intended to betray him into
some ambuscade of his enemies.

His doubts might have been indeed pardoned;
for, except perhaps the flying fish, there was no race
existing on the earth, in the air, or the waters, who
were the object of such an unintermitting, general,
and relentless persecution as the Jews of this period.
Upon the slightest and most unreasonable pretences,
as well as upon accusations the most absurd and
groundless, their persons and property were exposed
to every turn of popular fury; for Norman, Saxon,
Dane, and Briton, however adverse these races were
to each other, contended which should look with
greatest detestation upon a people whom it was accounted a point of religion to hate, to revile, to
despise, to plunder, and to persecute. The kings
of the Norman race, and the independent nobles,

who followed their example in all acts of tyranny, maintained against this devoted people a persecution of a more regular, calculated, and self-interested kind. It is a well-known story of King John, that he confined a wealthy Jew in one of the royal castles, and daily caused one of his teeth to be torn out, until, when the jaw of the unhappy Israelite was half disfurnished, he consented to pay a large sum, which it was the tyrant's object to extort from him. The little ready money which was in the country was chiefly in possession of this persecuted people, and the nobility hesitated not to follow the example of their sovereign in wringing it from them by every species of oppression, and even personal torture. Yet the passive courage inspired by the love of gain induced the Jews to dare the various evils to which they were subjected, in consideration of the immense profits which they were enabled to realise in a country naturally so wealthy as England. In spite of every kind of discouragement, and even of the special court of taxations already mentioned, called the Jews' Exchequer, erected for the very purpose of despoiling and distressing them, the Jews increased, multiplied, and accumulated huge sums, which they transferred from one hand to another by means of bills of exchange—an invention for which commerce is said to be indebted to them, and which enabled them to transfer their wealth from land to land, that, when threatened with oppression in one country, their treasure might be secured in another.

The obstinacy and avarice of the Jews being thus in a measure placed in opposition to the fanaticism and tyranny of those under whom they lived, seemed to increase in proportion to the persecution with which they were visited; and the immense wealth they usually acquired in commerce, while it frequently placed them in danger, was at other times used to extend their influence, and to secure

to them a certain degree of protection. On these
terms they lived; and their character, influenced
accordingly, was watchful, suspicious, and timid—
yet obstinate, uncomplying, and skilful in evading
the dangers to which they were exposed.

When the travellers had pushed on at a rapid
rate through many devious paths, the Palmer at
length broke silence.

'That large decayed oak,' he said, 'marks the
boundaries over which Front-de-Bœuf claims authority; we are long since far from those of Malvoisin. There is now no fear of pursuit.'

'May the wheels of their chariots be taken off,'
said the Jew, 'like those of the host of Pharaoh,
that they may drive heavily! But leave me not,
good Pilgrim. Think but of that fierce and savage
Templar, with his Saracen slaves; they will regard
neither territory, nor manner, nor lordship.'

'Our road,' said the Palmer, 'should here
separate; for it beseems not men of my character
and thine to travel together longer than needs must
be. Besides, what succour couldst thou have from
me, a peaceful pilgrim, against two armed heathens?'

'O, good youth,' answered the Jew, 'thou canst
defend me, and I know thou wouldst. Poor as I
am, I will requite it; not with money, for money,
so help me my Father Abraham! I have none;
but——'

'Money and recompense,' said the Palmer, interrupting him, 'I have already said I require not of
thee. Guide thee I can, and, it may be, even in
some sort defend thee; since to protect a Jew
against a Saracen can scarce be accounted unworthy
of a Christian. Therefore, Jew, I will see thee safe
under some fitting escort. We are now not far
from the town of Sheffield, where thou mayest easily
find many of thy tribe with whom to take refuge.'

'The blessing of Jacob be upon thee, good youth!'
said the Jew; 'in Sheffield I can harbour with my

kinsman Zareth, and find some means of travelling forth with safety.'

'Be it so,' said the Palmer; 'at Sheffield then we part, and half an hour's riding will bring us in sight of that town.'

The half hour was spent in perfect silence on both parts; the Pilgrim perhaps disdaining to address the Jew, except in case of absolute necessity, and the Jew not presuming to force a conversation with a person whose journey to the Holy Sepulchre gave a sort of sanctity to his character. They paused on the top of a gently rising bank, and the Pilgrim, pointing to the town of Sheffield, which lay beneath them, repeated the words, 'Here, then, we part.'

'Not till you have had the poor Jew's thanks,' said Isaac; 'for I presume not to ask you to go with me to my kinsman Zareth's, who might aid me with some means of repaying your good offices.'

'I have already said,' answered the Pilgrim, 'that I desire no recompense. If, among the huge list of thy debtors, thou wilt, for my sake, spare the gyves and the dungeon to some unhappy Christian who stands in thy danger, I shall hold this morning's service to thee well bestowed.'

'Stay—stay,' said the Jew, laying hold of his garment; 'something would I do more than this— something for thyself. God knows the Jew is poor —yes, Isaac is the beggar of his tribe—but forgive me should I guess what thou most lackest at this moment.'

'If thou wert to guess truly,' said the Palmer, 'it is what thou canst not supply, wert thou as wealthy as thou sayst thou art poor.'

'As I say!' echoed the Jew. 'O! believe it, I say but the truth; I am a plundered, indebted, distressed man. Hard hands have wrung from me my goods, my money, my ships, and all that I possessed. Yet I can tell thee what thou lackest, and, it may be, supply it too. Thy wish even now is for a horse and armour.'

The Palmer started, and turned suddenly towards the Jew. 'What fiend prompted that guess?' said he, hastily.

'No matter,' said the Jew, smiling, 'so that it be a true one ; and, as I can guess thy want, so I can supply it.'

'But consider,' said the Palmer, 'my character, my dress, my vow.'

'I know you Christians,' replied the Jew, 'and that the noblest of you will take the staff and sandal in superstitious penance, and walk afoot to visit the graves of dead men.'

'Blaspheme not, Jew !' said the Pilgrim, sternly.

'Forgive me,' said the Jew ; 'I spoke rashly. But there dropt words from you last night and this morning that, like sparks from flint, showed the metal within ; and in the bosom of that Palmer's gown is hidden a knight's chain and spurs of gold. They glanced as you stooped over my bed in the morning.'

The Pilgrim could not forbear smiling. 'Were thy garments searched by as curious an eye, Isaac,' said he, 'what discoveries might not be made?'

'No more of that,' said the Jew, changing colour ; and drawing forth his writing materials in haste, as if to stop the conversation, he began to write upon a piece of paper which he supported on the top of his yellow cap, without dismounting from his mule. When he had finished, he delivered the scroll, which was in the Hebrew character, to the Pilgrim, saying, 'In the town of Leicester all men know the rich Jew, Kirjath Jairam of Lombardy ; give him this scroll. He hath on sale six Milan harnesses, the worst would suit a crowned head ; ten goodly steeds, the worst might mount a king, were he to do battle for his throne. Of these he will give thee thy choice, with everything else that can furnish thee forth for the tournament; when it is over, thou wilt return them safely—unless thou shouldst have wherewith to pay their value to the owner.'

'But, Isaac,' said the Pilgrim, smiling, 'dost thou know that in these sports the arms and steed of the knight who is unhorsed are forfeit to his victor? Now I may be unfortunate, and so lose what I cannot replace or repay.'

The Jew looked somewhat astounded at this possibility; but collecting his courage, he replied hastily, 'No—no—no. It is impossible—I will not think so. The blessing of Our Father will be upon thee. Thy lance will be powerful as the rod of Moses.'

So saying, he was turning his mule's head away, when the Palmer, in his turn, took hold of his gaberdine. 'Nay, but, Isaac, thou knowest not all the risk. The steed may be slain, the armour injured; for I will spare neither horse nor man. Besides, those of thy tribe give nothing for nothing; something there must be paid for their use.'

The Jew twisted himself in the saddle, like a man in a fit of the colic; but his better feelings predominated over those which were most familiar to him. 'I care not,' he said—'I care not; let me go. If there is damage, it will cost you nothing; if there is usage money, Kirjath Jairam will forgive it for the sake of his kinsman Isaac. Fare thee well! Yet, hark thee, good youth,' said he, turning about, 'thrust thyself not too forward into this vain hurly-burly: I speak not for endangering the steed and coat of armour, but for the sake of thine own life and limbs.'

'Gramercy for thy caution,' said the Palmer, again smiling; 'I will use thy courtesy frankly, and it will go hard with me but I will requite it.'

They parted, and took different roads for the town of Sheffield.

CHAPTER VII

Knights, with a long retinue of their squires,
In gaudy liveries march and quaint attires;
One laced the helm, another held the lance,
A third the shining buckler did advance.
The courser paw'd the ground with restless feet,
And snorting foam'd and champ'd the golden bit.
The smiths and armourers on palfreys ride,
Files in their hands, and hammers at their side;
And nails for loosen'd spears, and thongs for shields provide.
The yeomen guard the streets in seemly bands;
And clowns come crowding on, with cudgels in their hands.

Palamon and Arcite.

THE condition of the English nation was at this time
sufficiently miserable. King Richard was absent a
prisoner, and in the power of the perfidious and
cruel Duke of Austria. Even the very place of his
captivity was uncertain, and his fate but very imperfectly known to the generality of his subjects,
who were, in the meantime, a prey to every species
of subaltern oppression.

Prince John, in league with Philip of France,
Cœur-de-Lion's mortal enemy, was using every
species of influence with the Duke of Austria to
prolong the captivity of his brother Richard, to
whom he stood indebted for so many favours. In
the meantime, he was strengthening his own faction
in the kingdom, of which he proposed to dispute
the succession, in case of the King's death, with the
legitimate heir, Arthur Duke of Brittany, son of

Geoffrey Plantagenet, the elder brother of John. This usurpation, it is well known, he afterwards effected. His own character being light, profligate, and perfidious, John easily attached to his person and faction not only all who had reason to dread the resentment of Richard for criminal proceedings during his absence, but also the numerous class of 'lawless resolutes' whom the crusades had turned back on their country, accomplished in the vices of the East, impoverished in substance, and hardened in character, and who placed their hopes of harvest in civil commotion.

To these causes of public distress and apprehension must be added the multitude of outlaws who, driven to despair by the oppression of the feudal nobility and the severe exercise of the forest laws, banded together in large gangs, and, keeping possession of the forests and the wastes, set at defiance the justice and magistracy of the country. The nobles themselves, each fortified within his own castle, and playing the petty sovereign over his own dominions, were the leaders of bands scarce less lawless and oppressive than those of the avowed depredators. To maintain these retainers, and to support the extravagance and magnificence which their pride induced them to affect, the nobility borrowed sums of money from the Jews at the most usurious interest, which gnawed into their estates like consuming cankers, scarce to be cured unless when circumstances gave them an opportunity of getting free by exercising upon their creditors some act of unprincipled violence.

Under the various burdens imposed by this unhappy state of affairs, the people of England suffered deeply for the present, and had yet more dreadful cause to fear for the future. To augment their misery, a contagious disorder of a dangerous nature spread through the land; and, rendered more virulent by the uncleanness, the indifferent food, and

the wretched lodging of the lower classes, swept off
many, whose fate the survivors were tempted to
envy, as exempting them from the evils which were
to come.

Yet, amid these accumulated distresses, the poor
as well as the rich, the vulgar as well as the noble,
in the event of a tournament, which was the grand
spectacle of that age, felt as much interested as the
half-starved citizen of Madrid, who has not a real
left to buy provisions for his family, feels in the
issue of a bull-feast. Neither duty nor infirmity
could keep youth or age from such exhibitions.
The passage of arms, as it was called, which was to
take place at Ashby, in the county of Leicester, as
champions of the first renown were to take the field
in the presence of Prince John himself, who was
expected to grace the lists, had attracted universal
attention, and an immense confluence of persons of
all ranks hastened upon the appointed morning to
the place of combat.

The scene was singularly romantic. On the verge
of a wood, which approached to within a mile of the
town of Ashby, was an extensive meadow of the
finest and most beautiful green turf, surrounded on
one side by the forest, and fringed on the other by
straggling oak-trees, some of which had grown to
an immense size. The ground, as if fashioned on
purpose for the martial display which was intended,
sloped gradually down on all sides to a level bottom,
which was inclosed for the lists with strong palisades, forming a space of a quarter of a mile in
length, and about half as broad. The form of the
inclosure was an oblong square, save that the
corners were considerably rounded off, in order to
afford more convenience for the spectators. The
openings for the entry of the combatants were at
the northern and southern extremities of the lists,
accessible by strong wooden gates, each wide enough
to admit two horsemen riding abreast. At each of

these portals were stationed two heralds, attended by six trumpets, as many pursuivants, and a strong body of men-at-arms, for maintaining order, and ascertaining the quality of the knights who proposed to engage in this martial game.

On a platform beyond the southern entrance, formed by a natural elevation of the ground, were pitched five magnificent pavilions, adorned with pennons of russet and black, the chosen colours of the five knights challengers. The cords of the tents were of the same colour. Before each pavilion was suspended the shield of the knight by whom it was occupied, and beside it stood his squire, quaintly disguised as a salvage or silvan man, or in some other fantastic dress, according to the taste of his master and the character he was pleased to assume during the game.[1] The central pavilion, as the place of honour, had been assigned to Brian de Bois-Guilbert, whose renown in all games of chivalry, no less than his connexion with the knights who had undertaken this passage of arms, had occasioned him to be eagerly received into the company of the challengers, and even adopted as their chief and leader, though he had so recently joined them. On one side of his tent were pitched those of Reginald Front-de-Bœuf and Richard [Philip] de Malvoisin, and on the other was the pavilion of Hugh de Grantmesnil, a noble baron in the vicinity, whose ancestor had been Lord High Steward of England in the time of the Conqueror and his son William Rufus. Ralph de Vipont, a knight of St. John of Jerusalem, who had some ancient possessions at a place called Heather, near Ashby-de-la-Zouche, occupied the fifth pavilion. From the entrance into the lists a gently sloping passage, ten yards in breadth, led up to the platform on which the tents

[1] This sort of masquerade is supposed to have occasioned the introduction of supporters into the science of heraldry.

were pitched. It was strongly secured by a palisade
on each side, as was the esplanade in front of the
pavilions, and the whole was guarded by men-at-
arms.

The northern access to the lists terminated in a
similar entrance of thirty feet in breadth, at the
extremity of which was a large inclosed space for
such knights as might be disposed to enter the lists
with the challengers, behind which were placed
tents containing refreshments of every kind for
their accommodation, with armourers, farriers, and
other attendants, in readiness to give their services
wherever they might be necessary.

The exterior of the lists was in part occupied by
temporary galleries, spread with tapestry and carpets,
and accommodated with cushions for the convenience
of those ladies and nobles who were expected to
attend the tournament. A narrow space betwixt
these galleries and the lists gave accommodation for
yeomanry and spectators of a better degree than the
mere vulgar, and might be compared to the pit of a
theatre. The promiscuous multitude arranged themselves upon large banks of turf prepared for the
purpose, which, aided by the natural elevation of
the ground, enabled them to overlook the galleries,
and obtain a fair view into the lists. Besides the
accommodation which these stations afforded, many
hundreds had perched themselves on the branches
of the trees which surrounded the meadow ; and
even the steeple of a country church, at some
distance, was crowded with spectators.

It only remains to notice respecting the general
arrangement, that one gallery in the very centre
of the eastern side of the lists, and consequently
exactly opposite to the spot where the shock of the
combat was to take place, was raised higher than
the others, more richly decorated, and graced by a
sort of throne and canopy, on which the royal arms
were emblazoned. Squires, pages, and yeomen in

rich liveries waited around this place of honour, which was designed for Prince John and his attendants. Opposite to this royal gallery was another, elevated to the same height, on the western side of the lists; and more gaily, if less sumptuously, decorated than that destined for the Prince himself. A train of pages and of young maidens, the most beautiful who could be selected, gaily dressed in fancy habits of green and pink, surrounded a throne decorated in the same colours. Among pennons and flags bearing wounded hearts, burning hearts, bleeding hearts, bows and quivers, and all the commonplace emblems of the triumphs of Cupid, a blazoned inscription informed the spectators that this seat of honour was designed for *La Royne de la Beaulté et des Amours.* But who was to represent the Queen of Beauty and of Love on the present occasion no one was prepared to guess.

Meanwhile, spectators of every description thronged forward to occupy their respective stations, and not without many quarrels concerning those which they were entitled to hold. Some of these were settled by the men-at-arms with brief ceremony; the shafts of their battle axes and pummels of their swords being readily employed as arguments to convince the more refractory. Others, which involved the rival claims of more elevated persons, were determined by the heralds, or by the two marshals of the field, William de Wyvil and Stephen de Martival, who, armed at all points, rode up and down the lists to enforce and preserve good order among the spectators.

Gradually the galleries became filled with knights and nobles, in their robes of peace, whose long and rich-tinted mantles were contrasted with the gayer and more splendid habits of the ladies, who, in a greater proportion than even the men themselves, thronged to witness a sport which one would have thought too bloody and dangerous to afford their sex much pleasure. The lower and interior space was soon filled by substantial yeomen and burghers, and such of the lesser gentry as, from modesty, poverty, or dubious title, durst not assume any higher place. It was of course amongst these that the most frequent disputes for precedence occurred.

'Dog of an unbeliever,' said an old man, whose threadbare tunic bore witness to his poverty, as his sword, and dagger, and golden chain intimated his pretensions to rank—'whelp of a she-wolf! darest thou press upon a Christian, and a Norman gentleman of the blood of Montdidier?'

This rough expostulation was addressed to no other than our acquaintance Isaac, who, richly and even magnificently dressed in a gaberdine ornamented with lace and lined with fur, was endeavouring to make place in the foremost row beneath the gallery for his daughter, the beautiful Rebecca, who had joined him at Ashby, and who was now hanging on her father's arm, not a little terrified by the popular displeasure which seemed generally excited by her parent's presumption. But Isaac, though we have seen him sufficiently timid on other occasions, knew well that at present he had nothing to fear. It was not in places of general resort, or where their equals were assembled, that any avaricious or malevolent noble durst offer him injury. At such meetings the Jews were under the protection of the general law; and if that proved a weak assurance, it usually happened that there were among the persons assembled some barons who, for their own interested motives, were ready to act as their protectors. On the present occasion, Isaac felt more than usually confident, being aware that Prince John was even then in the very act of negotiating a large loan from the Jews of York, to be secured upon certain jewels and lands. Isaac's own share in this transaction was considerable, and he well knew that the Prince's eager desire to bring it to a conclusion would ensure him his protection in the dilemma in which he stood.

Emboldened by these considerations, the Jew pursued his point, and jostled the Norman Christian without respect either to his descent, quality, or religion. The complaints of the old man, however, excited the indignation of the bystanders. One of these, a stout well-set yeoman, arrayed in Lincoln green, having twelve arrows stuck in his belt, with a baldric and badge of silver, and a bow of six feet length in his hand, turned short round, and while his countenance, which his constant exposure to weather had rendered brown as a hazel nut, grew darker with anger, he advised the Jew to remember that all the wealth he had acquired by sucking the blood of his miserable victims had but swelled him like a bloated spider, which might be overlooked while it kept in a corner, but would be crushed if it ventured into the light. The intimation, delivered in Norman-English with a firm voice and a stern aspect, made the Jew shrink back; and he would have probably withdrawn himself altogether from a vicinity so dangerous, had not the attention of every one been called to the sudden entrance of Prince John, who at that moment entered the lists, attended by a numerous and gay train, consisting partly of laymen, partly of churchmen, as light in their dress, and as gay in their demeanour, as their companions. Among the latter was the Prior of Jorvaulx, in the most gallant trim which a dignitary of the church could venture to exhibit. Fur and gold were not spared in his garments; and the point of his boots, out-heroding the preposterous fashion of the time, turned up so very far as to be attached not to his knees merely, but to his very girdle, and effectually prevented him from putting his foot into the stirrup. This, however, was a slight inconvenience to the gallant Abbot, who, perhaps even rejoicing in the opportunity to display his accomplished horsemanship before so many spectators, especially of the fair sex, dispensed with the use of these supports to a timid rider. The rest of Prince John's retinue consisted of the favourite leaders of his mercenary troops, some marauding barons and profligate attendants upon the court, with several Knights Templars and Knights of St. John.

It may be here remarked, that the knights of these two orders were accounted hostile to King Richard, having adopted the side of Philip of France in the long train of disputes which took place in Palestine betwixt that monarch and the lion-hearted King of England. It was the well-known consequence of this discord that Richard's repeated victories had been rendered fruitless, his romantic attempts to besiege Jerusalem disappointed, and the fruit of all the glory which he had acquired had dwindled into an uncertain truce with the Sultan Saladin. With the same policy which had dictated the conduct of their brethren in the Holy Land, the Templars and Hospitallers in England and Normandy attached themselves to the faction of Prince John, having little reason to desire the return of Richard to England, or the succession of Arthur, his legitimate heir. For the opposite reason, Prince John hated and contemned the few Saxon families of consequence which subsisted in England, and omitted no opportunity of mortifying and affronting them; being conscious that his person and pretensions were disliked by them, as well as by the greater part of the English commons, who feared farther innovation upon their rights and liberties from a sovereign of John's licentious and tyrannical disposition.

Attended by this gallant equipage, himself well mounted, and splendidly dressed in crimson and in gold, bearing upon his hand a falcon, and having his head covered by a rich fur bonnet, adorned with a circle of precious stones, from which his long curled hair escaped and overspread his shoulders,

Prince John, upon a grey and high-mettled palfrey, caracoled within the lists at the head of his jovial party, laughing loud with his train, and eyeing with all the boldness of royal criticism the beauties who adorned the lofty galleries.

Those who remarked in the physiognomy of the Prince a dissolute audacity, mingled with extreme haughtiness and indifference to the feelings of others, could not yet deny to his countenance that sort of comeliness which belongs to an open set of features, well formed by nature, modelled by art to the usual rules of courtesy, yet so far frank and honest that they seemed as if they disclaimed to conceal the natural workings of the soul. Such an expression is often mistaken for manly frankness, when in truth it arises from the reckless indifference of a libertine disposition, conscious of superiority of birth, of wealth, or of some other adventitious advantage, totally unconnected with personal merit. To those who did not think so deeply, and they were the greater number by a hundred to one, the splendour of Prince John's *rheno* (*i.e.* fur tippet), the richness of his cloak, lined with the most costly sables, his maroquin boots and golden spurs, together with the grace with which he managed his palfrey, were sufficient to merit clamorous applause.

In his joyous caracole round the lists, the attention of the Prince was called by the commotion, not yet subsided, which had attended the ambitious movement of Isaac towards the higher places of the assembly. The quick eye of Prince John instantly recognised the Jew, but was much more agreeably attracted by the beautiful daughter of Zion, who, terrified by the tumult, clung close to the arm of her aged father.

The figure of Rebecca might indeed have compared with the proudest beauties of England, even though it had been judged by as shrewd a connoisseur as Prince John. Her form was exquisitely

symmetrical, and was shown to advantage by a sort
of Eastern dress, which she wore according to the
fashion of the females of her nation. Her turban
of yellow silk suited well with the darkness of her
complexion. The brilliancy of her eyes, the superb
arch of her eyebrows, her well-formed aquiline nose,
her teeth as white as pearl, and the profusion of her
sable tresses, which, each arranged in its own little
spiral of twisted curls, fell down upon as much of a
lovely neck and bosom as a simarre of the richest
Persian silk, exhibiting flowers in their natural
colours embossed upon a purple ground, permitted
to be visible—all these constituted a combination of
loveliness which yielded not to the most beautiful
of the maidens who surrounded her. It is true, that
of the golden and pearl-studded clasps which closed
her vest from the throat to the waist, the three
uppermost were left unfastened on account of the
heat, which something enlarged the prospect to
which we allude. A diamond necklace, with pen-
dants of inestimable value, were by this means also
made more conspicuous. The feather of an ostrich,
fastened in her turban by an agraffe set with brilliants,
was another distinction of the beautiful Jewess, scoffed
and sneered at by the proud dames who sat above
her, but secretly envied by those who affected to
deride them.

'By the bald scalp of Abraham,' said Prince John,
'yonder Jewess must be the very model of that per-
fection whose charms drove frantic the wisest king
that ever lived! What sayest thou, Prior Aymer?
By the Temple of that wise king, which our wiser
brother Richard proved unable to recover, she is the
very Bride of the Canticles!'

'The Rose of Sharon and the Lily of the Valley,'
answered the Prior, in a sort of snuffling tone;
'but your Grace must remember she is still but a
Jewess.'

'Ay!' added Prince John, without heeding him,

'and there is my Mammon of unrighteousness too—
the Marquis of Marks, the Baron of Byzants, con-
testing for place with penniless dogs, whose threadbare cloaks have not a single cross in their pouches
to keep the devil from dancing there.   By the body
of St. Mark, my prince of supplies, with his lovely
Jewess, shall have a place in the gallery !   What is
she, Isaac ? Thy wife or thy daughter, that Eastern
houri that thou lockest under thy arm as thou wouldst
thy treasure-casket ?'

'My daughter Rebecca, so please your Grace,'
answered Isaac, with a low congee, nothing embarrassed by the Prince's salutation, in which, however, there was at least as much mockery as
courtesy.

'The wiser man thou,' said John, with a peal of
laughter, in which his gay followers obsequiously
joined.   'But, daughter or wife, she should be preferred according to her beauty and thy merits.
Who sits above there ?' he continued, bending his
eye on the gallery.   'Saxon churls, lolling at their
lazy length !   Out upon them ! let them sit close,
and make room for my prince of usurers and his
lovely daughter.   I'll make the hinds know they
must share the high places of the synagogue with
those whom the synagogue properly belongs to.'

Those who occupied the gallery, to whom this
injurious and unpolite speech was addressed, were
the family of Cedric the Saxon, with that of his
ally and kinsman, Athelstane of Coningsburgh, a
personage who, on account of his descent from the
last Saxon monarchs of England, was held in the
highest respect by all the Saxon natives of the north
of England.   But with the blood of this ancient
royal race many of their infirmities had descended
to Athelstane.   He was comely in countenance,
bulky and strong in person, and in the flower of his
age ; yet inanimate in expression, dull-eyed, heavy-
browed, inactive and sluggish in all his motions,

and so slow in resolution, that the soubriquet of one
of his ancestors was conferred upon him, and he
was very generally called Athelstane the Unready.
His friends—and he had many who, as well as
Cedric, were passionately attached to him—contended that this sluggish temper arose not from
want of courage, but from mere want of decision;
others alleged that his hereditary vice of drunkenness had obscured his faculties, never of a very
acute order, and that the passive courage and meek
good-nature which remained behind were merely
the dregs of a character that might have been deserving of praise, but of which all the valuable parts
had flown off in the progress of a long course of
brutal debauchery.

It was to this person, such as we have described
him, that the Prince addressed his imperious command to make place for Isaac and Rebecca. Athelstane, utterly confounded at an order which the
manners and feelings of the times rendered so in-
juriously insulting, unwilling to obey, yet undeter-
mined how to resist, opposed only the *vis inertiæ*
to the will of John; and, without stirring or making
any motion whatever of obedience, opened his large
grey eyes and stared at the Prince with an astonishment which had in it something extremely ludicrous.
But the impatient John regarded it in no such light.

'The Saxon porker,' he said, 'is either asleep or
minds me not. Prick nim with your lance, De
Bracy,' speaking to a knight who rode near him, the
leader of a band of free companions, or *condottieri*;
that is, of mercenaries belonging to no particular
nation, but attached for the time to any prince by
whom they were paid. There was a murmur even
among the attendants of Prince John; but De
Bracy, whose profession freed him from all scruples,
extended his long lance over the space which
separated the gallery from the lists, and would
have executed the commands of the Prince before

Athelstane the Unready had recovered presence of mind sufficient even to draw back his person from the weapon, had not Cedric, as prompt as his companion was tardy, unsheathed, with the speed of lightning, the short sword which he wore, and at a single blow severed the point of the lance from the handle. The blood rushed into the countenance of Prince John. He swore one of his deepest oaths, and was about to utter some threat corresponding in violence, when he was diverted from his purpose, partly by his own attendants, who gathered around him conjuring him to be patient, partly by a general exclamation of the crowd, uttered in loud applause of the spirited conduct of Cedric. The Prince rolled his eyes in indignation, as if to collect some safe and easy victim ; and chancing to encounter the firm glance of the same archer whom we have already noticed, and who seemed to persist in his gesture of applause, in spite of the frowning aspect which the Prince bent upon him, he demanded his reason for clamouring thus.

' I always add my hollo,' said the yeoman, ' when I see a good shot or a gallant blow.'

' Sayst thou?' answered the Prince ; ' then thou canst hit the white thyself, I'll warrant.'

' A woodsman's mark, and at woodsman's distance, I can hit,' answered the yeoman.

' And Wat Tyrrel's mark, at a hundred yards,' said a voice from behind, but by whom uttered could not be discerned.

This allusion to the fate of William Rufus, his grandfather [predecessor], at once incensed and alarmed Prince John. He satisfied himself, however, with commanding the men-at-arms, who surrounded the lists, to keep an eye on the braggart, pointing to the yeoman.

' By St. Grizzel,' he added, ' we will try his own skill, who is so ready to give his voice to the feats of others ! '

'I shall not fly the trial,' said the yeoman, with
the composure which marked his whole deportment.

'Meanwhile, stand up, ye Saxon churls,' said the
fiery Prince; 'for, by the light of Heaven, since I
have said it, the Jew shall have his seat amongst
ye!'

'By no means, an it please your Grace! It is not
fit for such as we to sit with the rulers of the land,'
said the Jew, whose ambition for precedence, though
it had led him to dispute place with the extenuated
and impoverished descendant of the line of Montdidier, by no means stimulated him to an intrusion
upon the privileges of the wealthy Saxons.

'Up, infidel dog, when I command you,' said
Prince John, 'or I will have thy swarthy hide stript
off and tanned for horse-furniture!'

Thus urged, the Jew began to ascend the steep
and narrow steps which led up to the gallery.

'Let me see,' said the Prince, 'who dare stop
him!' fixing his eye on Cedric, whose attitude
intimated his intention to hurl the Jew down headlong.

The catastrophe was prevented by the clown
Wamba, who, springing betwixt his master and
Isaac, and exclaiming, in answer to the Prince's
defiance, 'Marry, that will I!' opposed to the beard
of the Jew a shield of brawn, which he plucked
from beneath his cloak, and with which, doubtless,
he had furnished himself lest the tournament should
have proved longer than his appetite could endure
abstinence. Finding the abomination of his tribe
opposed to his very nose, while the Jester at the
same time flourished his wooden sword above his
head, the Jew recoiled, missed his footing, and
rolled down the steps—an excellent jest to the
spectators, who set up a loud laughter, in which
Prince John and his attendants heartily joined.

'Deal me the prize, cousin Prince,' said Wamba;
'I have vanquished my foe in fair fight with sword

and shield,' he added, brandishing the brawn in one
hand and the wooden sword in the other.

'Who and what art thou, noble champion?' said
Prince John, still laughing.

'A fool by right of descent,' answered the Jester;
'I am Wamba, the son of Witless, who was the son
of Weatherbrain, who was the son of an alderman.'

'Make room for the Jew in front of the lower
ring,' said Prince John, not unwilling, perhaps, to
seize an apology to desist from his original purpose;
'to place the vanquished beside the victor were false
heraldry.'

'Knave upon fool were worse,' answered the
Jester, 'and Jew upon bacon worst of all.'

'Gramercy! good fellow,' cried Prince John,
'thou pleasest me. Here, Isaac, lend me a handful
of byzants

As the Jew, stunned by the request, afraid to
refuse and unwilling to comply, fumbled in the
furred bag which hung by his girdle, and was perhaps endeavouring to ascertain how few coins might
pass for a handful, the Prince stooped from his
jennet and settled Isaac's doubts by snatching the
pouch itself from his side; and flinging to Wamba
a couple of the gold pieces which it contained, he
pursued his career round the lists, leaving the Jew
to the derision of those around him, and himself
receiving as much applause from the spectators as if
he had done some honest and honourable action.

CHAPTER VIII

At this the challenger with fierce defy
His trumpet sounds ; the challenged makes reply.
With clangour rings the field, resounds the vaulted sky.
Their visors closed, their lances in the rest,
Or at the helmet pointed or the crest,
They vanish from the barrier, speed the race,
And spurring see decrease the middle space.
Palamon and Arcite.

In the midst of Prince John's cavalcade, he suddenly
stopt, and, appealing to the Prior of Jorvaulx, declared the principal business of the day had been
forgotten.

'By my halidom,' said he, 'we have neglected,
Sir Prior, to name the fair Sovereign of Love and of
Beauty, by whose white hand the palm is to be dis-
tributed. For my part, I am liberal in my ideas,
and I care not if I give my vote for the black-eyed
Rebecca.'

'Holy Virgin,' answered the Prior, turning up
his eyes in horror, 'a Jewess ! We should deserve
to be stoned out of the lists ; and I am not yet old
enough to be a martyr. Besides, I swear by my
patron saint that she is far inferior to the lovely
Saxon, Rowena.'

'Saxon or Jew,' answered the Prince—'Saxon
or Jew, dog or hog, what matters it ! I say,
name Rebecca, were it only to mortify the Saxon
churls.'

A murmur arose even among his own immediate
attendants.

'This passes a jest, my lord,' said De Bracy; 'no knight here will lay lance in rest if such an insult is attempted.'

'It is the mere wantonness of insult,' said one of the oldest and most important of Prince John's followers, Waldemar Fitzurse, 'and if your Grace attempt it, cannot but prove ruinous to your projects.'

'I entertained you, sir,' said John, reining up his palfrey haughtily, 'for my follower, but not for my counsellor.'

'Those who follow your Grace in the paths which you tread,' said Waldemar, but speaking in a low voice, 'acquire the right of counsellors; for your interest and safety are not more deeply gaged than their own.'

From the tone in which this was spoken, John saw the necessity of acquiescence. 'I did but jest,' he said; 'and you turn upon me like so many adders! Name whom you will, in the fiend's name, and please yourselves.'

'Nay, nay,' said De Bracy, 'let the fair sovereign's throne remain unoccupied until the conqueror shall be named, and then let him choose the lady by whom it shall be filled. It will add another grace to his triumph, and teach fair ladies to prize the love of valiant knights, who can exalt them to such distinction.'

'If Brian de Bois-Guilbert gain the prize,' said the Prior, 'I will gage my rosary that I name the Sovereign of Love and Beauty.'

'Bois-Guilbert,' answered De Bracy, 'is a good lance; but there are others around these lists, Sir Prior, who will not fear to encounter him.'

'Silence, sirs,' said Waldemar, 'and let the Prince assume his seat. The knights and spectators are alike impatient, the time advances, and highly fit it is that the sports should commence.'

Prince John, though not yet a monarch, had in

Waldemar Fitzurse all the inconveniences of a
favourite minister, who, in serving his sovereign,
must always do so in his own way. The Prince
acquiesced, however, although his disposition was
precisely of that kind which is apt to be obstinate
upon trifles, and, assuming his throne, and being
surrounded by his followers, gave signal to the
heralds to proclaim the laws of the tournament,
which were briefly as follows :

First, the five challengers were to undertake all
comers.

Secondly, any knight proposing to combat might,
if he pleased, select a special antagonist from among
the challengers, by touching his shield. If he did
so with the reverse of his lance, the trial of skill
was made with what were called the arms of courtesy,
that is, with lances at whose extremity a piece of
round flat board was fixed, so that no danger was
encountered, save from the shock of the horses and
riders. But if the shield was touched with the
sharp end of the lance, the combat was understood
to be at *outrance*, that is, the knights were to fight
with sharp weapons, as in actual battle.

Thirdly, when the knights present had accomplished their vow, by each of them breaking five
lances, the Prince was to declare the victor in the
first day's tourney, who should receive as prize
a war-horse of exquisite beauty and matchless
strength ; and in addition to this reward of valour,
it was now declared, he should have the peculiar
honour of naming the Queen of Love and Beauty,
by whom the prize should be given on the ensuing
day.

Fourthly, it was announced that, on the second
day, there should be a general tournament, in which
all the knights present, who were desirous to win
praise, might take part ; and being divided into two
bands, of equal numbers, might fight it out manfully
until the signal was given by Prince John to cease

the combat. The elected Queen of Love and Beauty was then to crown the knight, whom the Prince should adjudge to have borne himself best in this second day, with a coronet composed of thin gold plate, cut into the shape of a laurel crown. On this second day the knightly games ceased. But on that which was to follow, feats of archery, of bull-baiting, and other popular amusements were to be practised, for the more immediate amusement of the populace. In this manner did Prince John endeavour to lay the foundation of a popularity which he was perpetually throwing down by some inconsiderate act of wanton aggression upon the feelings and prejudices of the people.

The lists now presented a most splendid spectacle. The sloping galleries were crowded with all that was noble, great, wealthy, and beautiful in the northern and midland parts of England; and the contrast of the various dresses of these dignified spectators rendered the view as gay as it was rich, while the interior and lower space, filled with the substantial burgesses and yeomen of merry England, formed, in their more plain attire, a dark fringe, or border, around this circle of brilliant embroidery, relieving, and at the same time setting off, its splendour.

The heralds finished their proclamation with their usual cry of 'Largesse, largesse, gallant knights!' and gold and silver pieces were showered on them from the galleries, it being a high point of chivalry to exhibit liberality towards those whom the age accounted at once the secretaries and the historians of honour. The bounty of the spectators was acknowledged by the customary shouts of 'Love of ladies—Death of champions—Honour to the generous—Glory to the brave!' To which the more humble spectators added their acclamations, and a numerous band of trumpeters the flourish of their martial instruments. When these sounds had

ceased, the heralds withdrew from the lists in gay
and glittering procession, and none remained within
them save the marshals of the field, who, armed
cap-à-pie, sat on horseback, motionless as statues,
at the opposite ends of the lists.   Meantime, the
inclosed space at the northern extremity of the lists,
large as it was, was now completely crowded with
knights desirous to prove their skill against the
challengers, and, when viewed from the galleries,
presented the appearance of a sea of waving plumage,
intermixed with glistening helmets and tall lances,
to the extremities of which were, in many cases,
attached small pennons of about a span's breadth,
which, fluttering in the air as the breeze caught
them, joined with the restless motion of the feathers
to add liveliness to the scene.

At length the barriers were opened, and five
knights, chosen by lot, advanced slowly into the
area ; a single champion riding in front, and the
other four following in pairs.   All were splendidly
armed, and my Saxon authority (in the Wardour
Manuscript) records at great length their devices,
their colours, and the embroidery of their horse
trappings.   It is unnecessary to be particular on
these subjects.   To borrow lines from a contemporary poet, who has written but too little—

> The knights are dust,
> And their good swords are rust,
> Their souls are with the saints, we trust.

Their escutcheons have long mouldered from the
walls of their castles.   Their castles themselves are
but green mounds and shattered ruins : the place
that once knew them, knows them no more—nay,
many a race since theirs has died out and been
forgotten in the very land which they occupied with
all the authority of feudal proprietors and feudal
lords.   What, then, would it avail the reader to

know their names, or the evanescent symbols of their martial rank?

Now, however, no whit anticipating the oblivion which awaited their names and feats, the champions advanced through the lists, restraining their fiery steeds, and compelling them to move slowly, while, at the same time, they exhibited their paces, together with the grace and dexterity of the riders. As the procession entered the lists, the sound of a wild barbaric music was heard from behind the tents of the challengers, where the performers were concealed. It was of Eastern origin, having been brought from the Holy Land; and the mixture of the cymbals and bells seemed to bid welcome at once, and defiance, to the knights as they advanced. With the eyes of an immense concourse of spectators fixed upon them, the five knights advanced up the platform upon which the tents of the challengers stood, and there separating themselves, each touched slightly, and with the reverse of his lance, the shield of the antagonist to whom he wished to oppose himself. The lower order of spectators in general —nay, many of the higher class, and it is even said several of the ladies—were rather disappointed at the champions choosing the arms of courtesy. For the same sort of persons who, in the present day, applaud most highly the deepest tragedies were then interested in a tournament exactly in proportion to the danger incurred by the champions engaged.

Having intimated their more pacific purpose, the champions retreated to the extremity of the lists, where they remained drawn up in a line; while the challengers, sallying each from his pavilion, mounted their horses, and, headed by Brian de Bois-Guilbert, descended from the platform and opposed themselves individually to the knights who had touched their respective shields.

At the flourish of clarions and trumpets, they started out against each other at full gallop; and such was the superior dexterity or good fortune of the challengers, that those opposed to Bois-Guilbert, Malvoisin, and Front-de-Bœuf rolled on the ground. The antagonist of Grantmesnil, instead of bearing his lance-point fair against the crest or the shield of his enemy, swerved so much from the direct line as to break the weapon athwart the person of his opponent—a circumstance which was accounted more disgraceful than that of being actually unhorsed, because the latter might happen from accident, whereas the former evinced awkwardness and want of management of the weapon and of the horse. The fifth knight alone maintained the honour of his party, and parted fairly with the Knight of St. John, both splintering their lances without advantage on either side.

The shouts of the multitude, together with the acclamations of the heralds and the clangour of the trumpets, announced the triumph of the victors and the defeat of the vanquished. The former retreated to their pavilions, and the latter, gathering themselves up as they could, withdrew from the lists in disgrace and dejection, to agree with their victors concerning the redemption of their arms and their horses, which, according to the laws of the tournament, they had forfeited. The fifth of their number alone tarried in the lists long enough to be greeted by the applauses of the spectators, amongst whom he retreated, to the aggravation, doubtless, of his companions' mortification.

A second and a third party of knights took the field; and although they had various success, yet, upon the whole, the advantage decidedly remained with the challengers, not one of whom lost his seat or swerved from his charge—misfortunes which befell one or two of their antagonists in each encounter. The spirits, therefore, of those opposed to them seemed to be considerably damped by their continued success. Three knights only appeared

on the fourth entry, who, avoiding the shields of
Bois-Guilbert and Front-de-Bœuf, contented themselves with touching those of the three other knights
who had not altogether manifested the same strength
and dexterity. This politic selection did not alter
the fortune of the field : the challengers were still
successful. One of their antagonists was over-
thrown ; and both the others failed in the *attaint*,[1]
that is, in striking the helmet and shield of their
antagonist firmly and strongly, with the lance held
in a direct line, so that the weapon might break
unless the champion was overthrown.

After this fourth encounter, there was a considerable pause ; nor did it appear that any one was
very desirous of renewing the contest. The spectators murmured among themselves ; for, among the
challengers, Malvoisin and Front-de-Bœuf were
unpopular from their characters, and the others,
except Grantmesnil, were disliked as strangers and
foreigners.

But none shared the general feeling of dissatisfac-
tion so keenly as Cedric the Saxon, who saw, in each
advantage gained by the Norman challengers, a
repeated triumph over the honour of England. His
own education had taught him no skill in the games
of chivalry, although, with the arms of his Saxon
ancestors, he had manifested himself, on many
occasions, a brave and determined soldier. He
looked anxiously to Athelstane, who had learned
the accomplishments of the age, as if desiring that
he should make some personal effort to recover the
victory which was passing into the hands of the
Templar and his associates. But, though both stout
of heart and strong of person, Athelstane had a
disposition too inert and unambitious to make the
exertions which Cedric seemed to expect from him.

'The day is against England, my lord,' said

[1] This term of chivalry transferred to the law gives the
phrase of being attainted of treason.

Cedric, in a marked tone; 'are you not tempted to take the lance?'

'I shall tilt to-morrow,' answered Athelstane, 'in the *mêlée*; it is not worth while for me to arm myself to-day.'

Two things displeased Cedric in this speech. It contained the Norman word *mêlée* (to express the general conflict), and it evinced some indifference to the honour of the country; but it was spoken by Athelstane, whom he held in such profound respect that he would not trust himself to canvass his motives or his foibles. Moreover, he had no time to make any remark, for Wamba thrust in his word, observing, 'It was better, though scarce easier, to be the best man among a hundred than the best man of two.'

Athelstane took the observation as a serious compliment; but Cedric, who better understood the Jester's meaning, darted at him a severe and menacing look; and lucky it was for Wamba, perhaps, that the time and place prevented his receiving, notwithstanding his place and service, more sensible marks of his master's resentment.

The pause in the tournament was still uninterrupted, excepting by the voices of the heralds exclaiming—'Love of ladies, splintering of lances! stand forth, gallant knights, fair eyes look upon your deeds!'

The music also of the challengers breathed from time to time wild bursts expressive of triumph or defiance, while the clowns grudged a holiday which seemed to pass away in inactivity; and old knights and nobles lamented in whispers the decay of martial spirit, spoke of the triumphs of their younger days, but agreed that the land did not now supply dames of such transcendent beauty as had animated the jousts of former times. Prince John began to talk to his attendants about making ready the banquet, and the necessity of adjudging the prize to Brian de

Bois-Guilbert, who had, with a single spear, over-thrown two knights and foiled a third.

At length, as the Saracenic music of the chal-lengers concluded one of those long and high flourishes with which they had broken the silence of the lists, it was answered by a solitary trumpet, which breathed a note of defiance from the northern extremity. All eyes were turned to see the new champion which these sounds announced, and no sooner were the barriers opened than he paced into the lists. As far as could be judged of a man sheathed in armour, the new adventurer did not greatly exceed the middle size, and seemed to be rather slender than strongly made. His suit of armour was formed of steel, richly inlaid with gold, and the device on his shield was a young oak-tree pulled up by the roots, with the Spanish word *Desdi-chado*, signifying Disinherited. He was mounted on a gallant black horse, and as he passed through the lists he gracefully saluted the Prince and the ladies by lowering his lance. The dexterity with which he managed his steed, and something of youthful grace which he displayed in his manner, won him the favour of the multitude, which some of the lower classes expressed by calling out, 'Touch Ralph de Vipont's shield—touch the Hospitaller's shield; he has the least sure seat, he is your cheapest bargain.'

The champion, moving onward amid these well-meant hints, ascended the platform by the sloping alley which led to it from the lists, and, to the astonishment of all present, riding straight up to the central pavilion, struck with the sharp end of his spear the shield of Brian de Bois-Guilbert until it rang again. All stood astonished at his presump-tion, but none more than the redoubted Knight whom he had thus defied to mortal combat, and who, little expecting so rude a challenge, was standing carelessly at the door of the pavilion.

'Have you confessed yourself, brother,' said the
Templar, 'and have you heard mass this morning,
that you peril your life so frankly?'

'I am fitter to meet death than thou art,' answered
the Disinherited Knight; for by this name the
stranger had recorded himself in the books of the
tourney.

'Then take your place in the lists,' said Bois-
Guilbert, 'and look your last upon the sun; for
this night thou shalt sleep in paradise.'

'Gramercy for thy courtesy,' replied the Disinherited Knight, 'and to requite it, I advise thee
to take a fresh horse and a new lance, for by my
honour you will need both.'

Having expressed himself thus confidently, he
reined his horse backward down the slope which
he had ascended, and compelled him in the same
manner to move backward through the lists, till he
reached the northern extremity, where he remained
stationary, in expectation of his antagonist. This
feat of horsemanship again attracted the applause of
the multitude.

However incensed at his adversary for the precautions which he recommended, Brian de Bois-
Guilbert did not neglect his advice; for his honour
was too nearly concerned to permit his neglecting
any means which might ensure victory over his
presumptuous opponent. He changed his horse for
a proved and fresh one of great strength and spirit.
He chose a new and tough spear, lest the wood of
the former might have been strained in the previous
encounters he had sustained. Lastly, he laid aside
his shield, which had received some little damage,
and received another from his squires. His first
had only borne the general device of his rider,
representing two knights riding upon one horse, an
emblem expressive of the original humility and
poverty of the Templars, qualities which they had
since exchanged for the arrogance and wealth that

finally occasioned their suppression. Bois-Guilbert's new shield bore a raven in full flight, holding in its claws a skull, and bearing the motto, *Gare le Corbeau*.

When the two champions stood opposed to each other at the two extremities of the lists, the public expectation was strained to the highest pitch. Few augured the possibility that the encounter could terminate well for the Disinherited Knight; yet his courage and gallantry secured the general good wishes of the spectators.

The trumpets had no sooner given the signal, than the champions vanished from their posts with the speed of lightning, and closed in the centre of the lists with the shock of a thunder-bolt. The lances burst into shivers up to the very grasp, and it seemed at the moment that both knights had fallen, for the shock had made each horse recoil backwards upon its haunches. The address of the riders recovered their steeds by use of the bridle and spur; and having glared on each other for an instant with eyes which seemed to flash fire through the bars of their visors, each made a demi-volte, and, retiring to the extremity of the lists, received a fresh lance from the attendants.

A loud shout from the spectators, waving of scarfs and handkerchiefs, and general acclamations, attested the interest taken by the spectators in this encounter—the most equal, as well as the best performed, which had graced the day. But no sooner had the knights resumed their station than the clamour of applause was hushed into a silence so deep and so dead that it seemed the multitude were afraid even to breathe.

A few minutes' pause having been allowed, that the combatants and their horses might recover breath, Prince John with his truncheon signed to the trumpets to sound the onset. The champions a second time sprung from their stations, and closed in the centre of the lists, with the same speed, the same dexterity, the same violence, but not the same equal fortune as before.

In this second encounter, the Templar aimed at the centre of his antagonist's shield, and struck it so fair and forcibly that his spear went to shivers, and the Disinherited Knight reeled in his saddle. On the other hand, that champion had, in the beginning of his career, directed the point of his lance towards Bois-Guilbert's shield, but, changing his aim almost in the moment of encounter, he addressed it to the helmet, a mark more difficult to hit, but which, if attained, rendered the shock more irresistible. Fair and true he hit the Norman on the visor, where his lance's point kept hold of the bars. Yet, even at this disadvantage, the Templar sustained his high reputation; and had not the girths of his saddle burst, he might not have been unhorsed. As it chanced, however, saddle, horse, and man rolled on the ground under a cloud of dust.

To extricate himself from the stirrups and fallen steed was to the Templar scarce the work of a moment; and, stung with madness, both at his disgrace and at the acclamations with which it was hailed by the spectators, he drew his sword and waved it in defiance of his conqueror. The Disinherited Knight sprung from his steed, and also unsheathed his sword. The marshals of the field, however, spurred their horses between them, and reminded them that the laws of the tournament did not, on the present occasion, permit this species of encounter.

'We shall meet again, I trust,' said the Templar, casting a resentful glance at his antagonist; 'and where there are none to separate us.'

'If we do not,' said the Disinherited Knight, 'the fault shall not be mine. On foot or horseback, with spear, with axe, or with sword, I am alike ready to encounter thee.'

More and angrier words would have been exchanged, but the marshals, crossing their lances betwixt them, compelled them to separate. The Disinherited Knight returned to his first station, and Bois-Guilbert to his tent, where he remained for the rest of the day in an agony of despair.

Without alighting from his horse, the conqueror called for a bowl of wine, and opening the beaver, or lower part of his helmet, announced that he quaffed it, 'To all true English hearts, and to the confusion of foreign tyrants.' He then commanded his trumpet to sound a defiance to the challengers, and desired a herald to announce to them that he should make no election, but was willing to encounter them in the order in which they pleased to advance against him.

The gigantic Front-de-Bœuf, armed in sable armour, was the first who took the field. He bore on a white shield a black bull's head, half defaced by the numerous encounters which he had undergone, and bearing the arrogant motto, *Cave, Adsum*. Over this champion the Disinherited Knight obtained a slight but decisive advantage. Both Knights broke their lances fairly, but Front-de-Bœuf, who lost a stirrup in the encounter, was adjudged to have the disadvantage.

In the stranger's third encounter with Sir Philip Malvoisin he was equally successful; striking that baron so forcibly on the casque that the laces of the helmet broke, and Malvoisin, only saved from falling by being unhelmeted, was declared vanquished like his companions.

In his fourth combat with De Grantmesnil the Disinherited Knight showed as much courtesy as he had hitherto evinced courage and dexterity. De Grantmesnil's horse, which was young and violent, reared and plunged in the course of the career so as to disturb the rider's aim, and the stranger, declining to take the advantage which this accident afforded

him, raised his lance, and passing his antagonist
without touching him, wheeled his horse and rode
back again to his own end of the lists, offering his
antagonist, by a herald, the chance of a second
encounter. This De Grantmesnil declined, avowing
himself vanquished as much by the courtesy as by
the address of his opponent.

Ralph de Vipont summed up the list of the
stranger's triumphs, being hurled to the ground
with such force that the blood gushed from his nose
and his mouth, and he was borne senseless from the
lists.

The acclamations of thousands applauded the
unanimous award of the Prince and marshals,
announcing that day's honours to the Disinherited
Knight.

CHAPTER IX

In the midst was seen
A lady of a more majestic mien,
By stature and by beauty mark'd their sovereign Queen.
.   .   .   .

And as in beauty she surpass'd the choir,
So nobler than the rest was her attire ;
A crown of ruddy gold inclosed her brow,
Plain without pomp, and rich without a show ;
A branch of Agnus Castus in her hand,
She bore aloft her symbol of command.

The Flower and the Leaf.

WILLIAM DE WYVIL and Stephen de Martival, the
marshals of the field, were the first to offer their
congratulations to the victor, praying him, at the
same time, to suffer his helmet to be unlaced, or, at
at least, that he would raise his visor ere they conducted him to receive the prize of the day's tourney
from the hands of Prince John. The Disinherited
Knight, with all knightly courtesy, declined their
request, alleging, that he could not at this time
suffer his face to be seen, for reasons which he had
assigned to the heralds when he entered the lists.
The marshals were perfectly satisfied by this reply ;
for amidst the frequent and capricious vows by which
knights were accustomed to bind themselves in the
days of chivalry, there were none more common
than those by which they engaged to remain incognito for a certain space, or until some particular
adventure was achieved. The marshals, therefore,

109

pressed no farther into the mystery of the Disinherited Knight, but, announcing to Prince John
the conqueror's desire to remain unknown, they
requested permission to bring him before his Grace,
in order that he might receive the reward of his
valour.

John's curiosity was excited by the mystery
observed by the stranger; and, being already displeased with the issue of the tournament, in which
the challengers whom he favoured had been successively defeated by one knight, he answered
haughtily to the marshals, 'By the light of Our
Lady's brow, this same knight hath been disinherited
as well of his courtesy as of his lands, since he
desires to appear before us without uncovering his
face. Wot ye, my lords,' he said, turning round to
his train, 'who this gallant can be that bears himself thus proudly?'

'I cannot guess,' answered De Bracy, 'nor did
I think there had been within the four seas that
girth Britain a champion that could bear down
these five knights in one day's jousting. By my
faith, I shall never forget the force with which he
shocked De Vipont. The poor Hospitaller was
hurled from his saddle like a stone from a sling.'

'Boast not of that,' said a Knight of St. John
who was present; 'your Temple champion had no
better luck. I saw your brave lance, Bois-Guilbert,
roll thrice over, grasping his hands full of sand at
every turn.'

De Bracy, being attached to the Templars, would
have replied, but was prevented by Prince John.
'Silence, sirs!' he said; 'what unprofitable debate
have we here?'

'The victor,' said De Wyvil, 'still waits the
pleasure of your Highness.'

'It is our pleasure,' answered John, 'that he do
so wait until we learn whether there is not some
one who can at least guess at his name and quality.

Should he remain there till nightfall, he has had work enough to keep him warm.'

'Your Grace,' said Waldemar Fitzurse, 'will do less than due honour to the victor if you compel him to wait till we tell your Highness that which we cannot know; at least I can form no guess—unless he be one of the good lances who accompanied King Richard to Palestine, and who are now straggling homeward from the Holy Land.'

'It may be the Earl of Salisbury,' said De Bracy; 'he is about the same pitch.'

'Sir Thomas de Multon, the Knight of Gilsland, rather,' said Fitzurse; 'Salisbury is bigger in the bones.' A whisper arose among the train, but by whom first suggested could not be ascertained. 'It might be the King—it might be Richard Cœur-de-Lion himself!'

'Over God's forbode!' said Prince John, involuntarily turning at the same time as pale as death, and shrinking as if blighted by a flash of lightning; 'Waldemar! De Bracy! brave knights and gentlemen, remember your promises, and stand truly by me!'

'Here is no danger impending,' said Waldemar Fitzurse; 'are you so little acquainted with the gigantic limbs of your father's son, as to think they can be held within the circumference of yonder suit of armour? De Wyvil and Martival, you will best serve the Prince by bringing forward the victor to the throne, and ending an error that has conjured all the blood from his cheeks. Look at him more closely,' he continued; 'your Highness will see that he wants three inches of King Richard's height, and twice as much of his shoulder-breadth. The very horse he backs could not have carried the ponderous weight of King Richard through a single course.'

While he was yet speaking, the marshals brought forward the Disinherited Knight to the foot of a

wooden flight of steps, which formed the ascent
from the lists to Prince John's throne. Still dis-
composed with the idea that his brother, so much
injured, and to whom he was so much indebted,
had suddenly arrived in his native kingdom, even
the distinctions pointed out by Fitzurse did not
altogether remove the Prince's apprehensions; and
while, with a short and embarrassed eulogy upon
his valour, he caused to be delivered to him the
war-horse assigned as the prize, he trembled lest
from the barred visor of the mailed form before him
an answer might be returned in the deep and awful
accents of Richard the Lion-hearted.

But the Disinherited Knight spoke not a word in
reply to the compliment of the Prince, which he
only acknowledged with a profound obeisance.

The horse was led into the lists by two grooms
richly dressed, the animal itself being fully accoutred
with the richest war-furniture; which, however,
scarcely added to the value of the noble creature
in the eyes of those who were judges. Laying one
hand upon the pommel of the saddle, the Disinherited Knight vaulted at once upon the back of
the steed without making use of the stirrup, and,
brandishing aloft his lance, rode twice around the
lists, exhibiting the points and paces of the horse
with the skill of a perfect horseman.

The appearance of vanity which might otherwise
have been attributed to this display was removed
by the propriety shown in exhibiting to the best
advantage the princely reward with which he had
been just honoured, and the Knight was again
greeted by the acclamations of all present.

In the meanwhile, the bustling Prior of Jorvaulx
had reminded Prince John, in a whisper, that the
victor must now display his good judgment, instead
of his valour, by selecting from among the beauties
who graced the galleries a lady who should fill the
throne of the Queen of Beauty and of Love, and

deliver the prize of the tourney, upon the ensuing
day. The Prince accordingly made a sign with his
truncheon as the Knight passed him in his second
career around the lists. The Knight turned towards the throne, and, sinking his lance until the
point was within a foot of the ground, remained
motionless, as if expecting John's commands; while
all admired the sudden dexterity with which he
instantly reduced his fiery steed from a state of
violent emotion and high excitation to the stillness
of an equestrian statue.

'Sir Disinherited Knight,' said Prince John,
'since that is the only title by which we can address
you, it is now your duty, as well as privilege, to
name the fair lady who, as Queen of Honour and
of Love, is to preside over next day's festival. If,
as a stranger in our land, you should require the
aid of other judgment to guide your own, we can
only say that Alicia, the daughter of our gallant
knight Waldemar Fitzurse, has at our court been
long held the first in beauty as in place. Nevertheless, it is your undoubted prerogative to confer
on whom you please this crown, by the delivery of
which to the lady of your choice the election of
to-morrow's Queen will be formal and complete.
Raise your lance.'

The Knight obeyed; and Prince John placed
upon its point a coronet of green satin, having
around its edge a circlet of gold, the upper edge
of which was relieved by arrow-points and hearts
placed interchangeably, like the strawberry leaves
and balls upon a ducal crown.

In the broad hint which he dropped respecting the daughter of Waldemar Fitzurse, John had
more than one motive, each the offspring of a mind
which was a strange mixture of carelessness and
presumption with low artifice and cunning. He
wished to banish from the minds of the chivalry
around him his own indecent and unacceptable jest

respecting the Jewess Rebecca ; he was desirous of conciliating Alicia's father, Waldemar, of whom he stood in awe, and who had more than once shown himself dissatisfied during the course of the day's proceedings. He had also a wish to establish himself in the good graces of the lady ; for John was at least as licentious in his pleasures as profligate in his ambition. But besides all these reasons, he was desirous to raise up against the Disinherited Knight, towards whom he already entertained a strong dislike, a powerful enemy in the person of Waldemar Fitzurse, who was likely, he thought, highly to resent the injury done to his daughter in case, as was not unlikely, the victor should make another choice.

And so indeed it proved. For the Disinherited Knight passed the gallery, close to that of the Prince, in which the Lady Alicia was seated in the full pride of triumphant beauty, and pacing forwards as slowly as he had hitherto rode swiftly around the lists, he seemed to exercise his right of examining the numerous fair faces which adorned that splendid circle.

It was worth while to see the different conduct of the beauties who underwent this examination, during the time it was proceeding. Some blushed ; some assumed an air of pride and dignity ; some looked straight forward, and essayed to seem utterly unconscious of what was going on ; some drew back in alarm, which was perhaps affected ; some endeavoured to forbear smiling ; and there were two or three who laughed outright. There were also some who dropped their veils over their charms ; but as the Wardour Manuscript says these were fair ones of ten years' standing, it may be supposed that, having had their full share of such vanities, they were willing to withdraw their claim in order to give a fair chance to the rising beauties of the age.

At length the champion paused beneath the

balcony in which the Lady Rowena was placed, and the expectation of the spectators was excited to the utmost.

It must be owned that, if an interest displayed in his success could have bribed the Disinherited Knight, the part of the lists before which he paused had merited his predilection. Cedric the Saxon, overjoyed at the discomfiture of the Templar, and still more so at the miscarriage of his two malevolent neighbours, Front-de-Bœuf and Malvoisin, had, with his body half-stretched over the balcony, accompanied the victor in each course not with his eyes only, but with his whole heart and soul. The Lady Rowena had watched the progress of the day with equal attention, though without openly betraying the same intense interest. Even the unmoved Athelstane had shown symptoms of shaking off his apathy, when, calling for a huge goblet of museadine, he quaffed it to the health of the Disinherited Knight.

Another group, stationed under the gallery occupied by the Saxons, had shown no less interest in the fate of the day.

'Father Abraham!' said Isaac of York, when the first course was run betwixt the Templar and the Disinherited Knight, 'how fiercely that Gentile rides! Ah, the good horse that was brought all the long way from Barbary, he takes no more care of him than if he were a wild ass's colt; and the noble armour that was worth so many zecchins to Joseph Pareira, the armourer of Milan, besides seventy in the hundred of profits, he cares for it as little as if he had found it in the highways!'

'If he risks his own person and limbs, father,' said Rebecca, 'in doing such a dreadful battle, he can scarce be expected to spare his horse and armour.'

'Child!' replied Isaac, somewhat heated, 'thou knowest not what thou speakest. His neck and

limbs are his own ; but his horse and armour belong
to —— Holy Jacob ! what was I about to say ?
Nevertheless, it is a good youth. See, Rebecca !—
see, he is again about to go up to battle against the
Philistine ! Pray, child—pray for the safety of the
good youth ; and of the speedy horse and the rich
armour. God of my fathers !' he again exclaimed,
'he hath conquered, and the uncircumcised Philistine
hath fallen before his lance, even as Og the King
of Bashan, and Sihon, King of the Amorites, fell
before the sword of our fathers ! Surely he shall
take their gold and their silver, and their war-horses,
and their armour of brass and of steel, for a prey
and for a spoil.'

The same anxiety did the worthy Jew display
during every course that was run, seldom failing to
hazard a hasty calculation concerning the value of
the horse and armour which were forfeited to the
champion upon each new success. There had been
therefore no small interest taken in the success of
the Disinherited Knight by those who occupied the
part of the lists before which he now paused.

Whether from indecision or some other motive
of hesitation, the champion of the day remained
stationary for more than a minute, while the eyes
of the silent audience were riveted upon his motions ;
and then, gradually and gracefully sinking the point
of his lance, he deposited the coronet which it supported at the feet of the fair Rowena. The trumpets
instantly sounded, while the heralds proclaimed the
Lady Rowena the Queen of Beauty and of Love for
the ensuing day, menacing with suitable penalties
those who should be disobedient to her authority.
They then repeated their cry of ' Largesse,' to which
Cedric, in the height of his joy, replied by an ample
donative, and to which Athelstane, though less
promptly, added one equally large.

There was some murmuring among the damsels of
Norman descent, who were as much unused to see

the preference given to a Saxon beauty as the
Norman nobles were to sustain defeat in the games
of chivalry which they themselves had introduced.
But these sounds of disaffection were drowned by
the popular shout of ' Long live the Lady Rowena,
the chosen and lawful Queen of Love and of Beauty ! '
To which many in the lower area added, ' Long live
the Saxon Princess ! long live the race of the im-
mortal Alfred ! '

However unacceptable these sounds might be to
Prince John and to those around him, he saw himself nevertheless obliged to confirm the nomination
of the victor, and accordingly calling to horse, he
left his throne, and mounting his jennet, accompanied by his train, he again entered the lists. The
Prince paused a moment beneath the gallery of the
Lady Alicia, to whom he paid his compliments,
observing, at the same time, to those around him—
' By my halidome, sirs ! if the Knight's feats in arms
have shown that he hath limbs and sinews, his
choice hath no less proved that his eyes are none of
the clearest.'

It was on this occasion, as during his whole life
John's misfortune not perfectly to understand the
characters of those whom he wished to conciliate.
Waldemar Fitzurse was rather offended than pleased
at the Prince stating thus broadly an opinion that
his daughter had been slighted.

' I know no right of chivalry,' he said, ' more
precious or inalienable than that of each free knight
to choose his lady-love by his own judgment. My
daughter courts distinction from no one ; and in her
own character, and in her own sphere, will never fail
to receive the full proportion of that which is her due.'

Prince John replied not ; but, spurring his horse,
as if to give vent to his vexation, he made the animal
bound forward to the gallery where Rowena was
seated, with the crown still at her feet.

' Assume,' he said, ' fair lady, the mark of your

sovereignty, to which none vows homage more
sincerely than ourself, John of Anjou; and if it
please you to-day, with your noble sire and friends,
to grace our banquet in the Castle of Ashby, we
shall learn to know the empress to whose service we
devote to-morrow.'

Rowena remained silent, and Cedric answered for
her in his native Saxon.

'The Lady Rowena,' he said, 'possesses not the
language in which to reply to your courtesy, or to
sustain her part in your festival. I also, and the
noble Athelstane of Coningsburgh, speak only the
language, and practise only the manners, of our
fathers. We therefore decline with thanks your
Highness's courteous invitation to the banquet.
To-morrow, the Lady Rowena will take upon her
the state to which she has been called by the free
election of the victor Knight, confirmed by the
acclamations of the people.'

So saying, he lifted the coronet and placed it upon
Rowena's head, in token of her acceptance of the
temporary authority assigned to her.

'What says he?' said Prince John, affecting not
to understand the Saxon language, in which, however, he was well skilled. The purport of Cedric's
speech was repeated to him in French. 'It is well,'
he said; 'to-morrow we will ourself conduct this
mute sovereign to her seat of dignity. You, at
least, Sir Knight,' he added, turning to the victor,
who had remained near the gallery, 'will this day
share our banquet?'

The Knight, speaking for the first time, in a low
and hurried voice, excused himself by pleading
fatigue, and the necessity of preparing for to-
morrow's encounter.

'It is well,' said Prince John, haughtily; 'although
unused to such refusals, we will endeavour to digest
our banquet as we may, though ungraced by the most
successful in arms and his elected Queen of Beauty.'

So saying, he prepared to leave the lists with his glittering train, and his turning his steed for that purpose was the signal for the breaking up and dispersion of the spectators.

Yet, with the vindictive memory proper to offended pride, especially when combined with conscious want of desert, John had hardly proceeded three paces ere again, turning around, he fixed an eye of stern resentment upon the yeoman who had displeased him in the early part of the day, and issued his commands to the men-at-arms who stood near—'On your life, suffer not that fellow to escape.'

The yeoman stood the angry glance of the Prince with the same unvaried steadiness which had marked his former deportment, saying, with a smile, ' I have no intention to leave Ashby until the day after to-morrow. I must see how Staffordshire and Leicestershire can draw their bows ; the forests of Needwood and Charnwood must rear good archers.'

' I,' said Prince John to his attendants, but not in direct reply—' I will see how he can draw his own ; and woe betide him unless his skill should prove some apology for his insolence !'

' It is full time,' said De Bracy, ' that the *outre-cuidance* of these peasants should be restrained by some striking example.'

Waldemar Fitzurse, who probably thought his patron was not taking the readiest road to popularity, shrugged up his shoulders and was silent. Prince John resumed his retreat from the lists, and the dispersion of the multitude became general.

In various routes, according to the different quarters from which they came, and in groups of various numbers, the spectators were seen retiring over the plain. By far the most numerous part streamed towards the town of Ashby, where many of the distinguished persons were lodged in the castle, and where others found accommodation in the town itself. Among these were most of the knights who had already appeared in the tournament, or who proposed to fight there the ensuing day, and who, as they rode slowly along, talking over the events of the day, were greeted with loud shouts by the populace. The same acclamations were bestowed upon Prince John, although he was indebted for them rather to the splendour of his appearance and train than to the popularity of his character.

A more sincere and more general, as well as a better-merited acclamation, attended the victor of the day, until, anxious to withdraw himself from popular notice, he accepted the accommodation of one of those pavilions pitched at the extremities of the lists, the use of which was courteously tendéred him by the marshals of the field. On his retiring to his tent, many who had lingered in the lists, to look upon and form conjectures concerning him, also dispersed.

The signs and sounds of a tumultuous concourse of men lately crowded together in one place, and agitated by the same passing events, were now exchanged for the distant hum of voices of different groups retreating in all directions, and these speedily died away in silence. No other sounds were heard save the voices of the menials who stripped the galleries of their cushions and tapestry, in order to put them in safety for the night, and wrangled among themselves for the half-used bottles of wine and relics of the refreshment which had been served round to the spectators.

Beyond the precincts of the lists more than one forge was erected ; and these now began to glimmer through the twilight, announcing the toil of the armourers, which was to continue through the whole night, in order to repair or alter the suits of armour to be used again on the morrow.

A strong guard of men-at-arms, renewed at intervals, from two hours to two hours, surrounded the lists, and kept watch during the night.

CHAPTER X

Thus, like the sad presaging raven, that tolls
The sick man's passport in her hollow beak,
And in the shadow of the silent night
Doth shake contagion from her sable wings:
Vex'd and tormented, runs poor Barrabas,
With fatal curses towards these Christians.
Jew of Malta.

The Disinherited Knight had no sooner reached
his pavilion than squires and pages in abundance
tendered their services to disarm him, to bring fresh
attire, and to offer him the refreshment of the bath.
Their zeal on this occasion was perhaps sharpened
by curiosity, since every one desired to know who
the knight was that had gained so many laurels, yet
had refused, even at the command of Prince John,
to lift his visor or to name his name. But their
officious inquisitiveness was not gratified. The Disinherited Knight refused all other assistance save
that of his own squire, or rather yeoman—a clown-
ish-looking man, who, wrapt in a cloak of dark-
coloured felt, and having his head and face half-
buried in a Norman bonnet made of black fur,
seemed to affect the incognito as much as his master.
All others being excluded from the tent, this attendant relieved his master from the more burdensome
parts of his armour, and placed food and wine before
him, which the exertions of the day rendered very
acceptable.

The Knight had scarcely finished a hasty meal

ere his menial announced to him that five men, each
leading a barbed steed, desired to speak with him.
The Disinherited Knight had exchanged his armour
for the long robe usually worn by those of his condition, which, being furnished with a hood, concealed
the features, when such was the pleasure of the
wearer, almost as completely as the visor of the
helmet itself; but the twilight, which was now fast
darkening, would of itself have rendered a disguise
unnecessary, unless to persons to whom the face of
an individual chanced to be particularly well known.

The Disinherited Knight, therefore, stept boldly
forth to the front of his tent, and found in attendance the squires of the challengers, whom he easily
knew by their russet and black dresses, each of
whom led his master's charger, loaded with the
armour in which he had that day fought.

'According to the laws of chivalry,' said the foremost of these men, 'I, Baldwin de Oyley, squire to
the redoubted Knight Brian de Bois-Guilbert, make
offer to you, styling yourself for the present the
Disinherited Knight, of the horse and armour used
by the said Brian de Bois-Guilbert in this day's
passage of arms, leaving it with your nobleness to
retain or to ransom the same, according to your
pleasure; for such is the law of arms.'

The other squires repeated nearly the same
formula, and then stood to await the decision of the
Disinherited Knight.

'To you four, sirs,' replied the Knight, addressing
those who had last spoken, 'and to your honourable
and valiant masters, I have one common reply.
Commend me to the noble knights, your masters,
and say, I should do ill to deprive them of steeds
and arms which can never be used by braver
cavaliers. I would I could here end my message to
these gallant knights; but being, as I term myself,
in truth and earnest the Disinherited, I must be
thus far bound to your masters, that they will, of

their courtesy, be pleased to ransom their steeds and armour, since that which I wear I can hardly term mine own.'

'We stand commissioned, each of us,' answered the squire of Reginald Front-de-Bœuf, 'to offer a hundred zecchins in ransom of these horses and suits of armour.'

'It is sufficient,' said the Disinherited Knight. 'Half the sum my present necessities compel me to accept; of the remaining half, distribute one moiety among yourselves, sir squires, and divide the other half betwixt the heralds and the pursuivants, and minstrels, and attendants.'

The squires, with cap in hand, and low reverences, expressed their deep sense of a courtesy and generosity not often practised, at least upon a scale so extensive. The Disinherited Knight then addressed his discourse to Baldwin, the squire of Brian de Bois-Guilbert. 'From your master,' said he, 'I will accept neither arms nor ransom. Say to him in my name, that our strife is not ended—no, not till we have fought as well with swords as with lances, as well on foot as on horseback. To this mortal quarrel he has himself defied me, and I shall not forget the challenge. Meantime, let him be assured that I hold him not as one of his companions, with whom I can with pleasure exchange courtesies; but rather as one with whom I stand upon terms of mortal defiance.'

'My master,' answered Baldwin, 'knows how to requite scorn with scorn, and blows with blows, as well as courtesy with courtesy. Since you disdain to accept from him any share of the ransom at which you have rated the arms of the other knights, I must leave his armour and his horse here, being well assured that he will never deign to mount the one nor wear the other.'

'You have spoken well, good squire,' said the Disinherited Knight—'well and boldly, as it beseemeth

him to speak who answers for an absent master.
Leave not, however, the horse and armour here.
Restore them to thy master; or, if he scorns to
accept them, retain them, good friend, for thine own
use. So far as they are mine, I bestow them upon
you freely.'

Baldwin made a deep obeisance, and retired with
his companions; and the Disinherited Knight entered
the pavilion.

'Thus far, Gurth,' said he, addressing his attendant, 'the reputation of English chivalry hath not
suffered in my hands.'

'And I,' said Gurth, 'for a Saxon swineherd, have
not ill played the personage of a Norman squire-at-
arms.'

'Yea, but,' answered the Disinherited Knight,
'thou hast ever kept me in anxiety lest thy clownish
bearing should discover thee.'

'Tush!' said Gurth, 'I fear discovery from none,
saving my playfellow, Wamba the Jester, of whom
I could never discover whether he were most knave
or fool. Yet I could scarce choose but laugh, when
my old master passed so near to me, dreaming all
the while that Gurth was keeping his porkers many
a mile off, in the thickets and swamps of Rotherwood. If I am discovered——'

'Enough,' said the Disinherited Knight, 'thou
knowest my promise.'

'Nay, for that matter,' said Gurth, 'I will never
fail my friend for fear of my skin-cutting. I have
a tough hide, that will bear knife or scourge as well
as any boar's hide in my herd.'

'Trust me, I will requite the risk you run for my
love, Gurth,' said the Knight. 'Meanwhile, I pray
you to accept these ten pieces of gold.'

'I am richer,' said Gurth, putting them into his
pouch, 'than ever was swineherd or bondsman.'

'Take this bag of gold to Ashby,' continued his
master, 'and find out Isaac the Jew of York, and

let him pay himself for the horse and arms with
which his credit supplied me.'

'Nay, by St. Dunstan,' replied Gurth, 'that I
will not do.'

'How, knave,' replied his master, 'wilt thou not
obey my commands?'

'So they be honest, reasonable, and Christian
commands,' replied Gurth; 'but this is none of
these. To suffer the Jew to pay himself would be
dishonest, for it would be cheating my master; and
unreasonable, for it were the part of a fool; and
unchristian, since it would be plundering a believer
to enrich an infidel.'

'See him contented, however, thou stubborn
varlet,' said the Disinherited Knight.

'I will do so,' said Gurth, taking the bag under
his cloak and leaving the apartment; 'and it will
go hard,' he muttered, 'but I content him with one-
half of his own asking.' So saying, he departed,
and left the Disinherited Knight to his own per-
plexed ruminations, which, upon more accounts
than it is now possible to communicate to the reader,
were of a nature peculiarly agitating and painful.

We must now change the scene to the village of
Ashby, or rather to a country house in its vicinity
belonging to a wealthy Israelite, with whom Isaac,
his daughter, and retinue had taken up their quarters;
the Jews, it is well known, being as liberal in
exercising the duties of hospitality and charity
among their own people as they were alleged to be
reluctant and churlish in extending them to those
whom they termed Gentiles, and whose treatment
of them certainly merited little hospitality at their
hand.

In an apartment, small indeed, but richly furnished
with decorations of an Oriental taste, Rebecca was
seated on a heap of embroidered cushions, which,
piled along a low platform that surrounded the

chamber, served, like the *estrada* of the Spaniards,
instead of chairs and stools.   She was watching the
motions of her father with a look of anxious and
filial affection, while he paced the apartment with a
dejected mien and disordered step, sometimes clasping his hands together, sometimes casting his eyes
to the roof of the apartment, as one who laboured
under great mental tribulation.   'O, Jacob!' he
exclaimed—'O, all ye twelve Holy Fathers of our
tribe! what a losing venture is this for one who
hath duly kept every jot and tittle of the law of
Moses! Fifty zecchins wrenched from me at one
clutch, and by the talons of a tyrant!'

'But, father,' said Rebecca, 'you seemed to give
the gold to Prince John willingly.'

'Willingly! the blotch of Egypt upon him!
Willingly, saidst thou? Ay, as willingly as when,
in the Gulf of Lyons, I flung over my merchandise
to lighten the ship, while she laboured in the
tempest—robed the seething billows in my choice
silks—perfumed their briny foam with myrrh and
aloes—enriched their caverns with gold and silver
work! And was not that an hour of unutterable
misery, though my own hands made the sacrifice?'

'But it was a sacrifice which Heaven exacted to
save our lives,' answered Rebecca, 'and the God of
our fathers has since blessed your store and your
gettings.'

'Ay,' answered Isaac, 'but if the tyrant lays hold
on them as he did to-day, and compels me to smile
while he is robbing me? O, daughter, disinherited
and wandering as we are, the worst evil which befalls
our race is, that when we are wronged and plundered
all the world laughs around, and we are compelled
to suppress our sense of injury, and to smile tamely
when we would revenge bravely.'

'Think not thus of it, my father,' said Rebecca;
'we also have advantages. These Gentiles, cruel
and oppressive as they are, are in some sort depen-

dent on the dispersed children of Zion, whom they despise and persecute. Without the aid of our wealth they could neither furnish forth their hosts in war nor their triumphs in peace; and the gold which we lend them returns with increase to our coffers. We are like the herb which flourisheth most when it is most trampled on. Even this day's pageant had not proceeded without the consent of the despised Jew, who furnished the means.'

'Daughter,' said Isaac, 'thou hast harped upon another string of sorrow. The goodly steed and the rich armour, equal to the full profit of my adventure with our Kirjath Jairam of Leicester—there is a dead loss too—ay, a loss which swallows up the gains of a week—ay, of the space between two Sabaoths—and yet it may end better than I now think, for 'tis a good youth.'

'Assuredly,' said Rebecca, 'you shall not repent you of requiting the good deed received of the stranger knight.'

'I trust so, daughter,' said Isaac, 'and I trust too in the rebuilding of Zion; but as well do I hope with my own bodily eyes to see the walls and battlements of the new Temple, as to see a Christian, yea, the very best of Christians, repay a debt to a Jew, unless under the awe of the judge and jailor.'

So saying, he resumed his discontented walk through the apartment; and Rebecca, perceiving that her attempts at consolation only served to awaken new subjects of complaint, wisely desisted from her unavailing efforts—a prudential line of conduct, and we recommend to all who set up for comforters and advisers to follow it in the like circumstances.

The evening was now becoming dark, when a Jewish servant entered the apartment and placed upon the table two silver lamps, fed with perfumed oil; the richest wines and the most delicate refreshments were at the same time displayed by another

Israelitish domestic on a small ebony table, inlaid with silver; for, in the interior of their houses, the Jews refused themselves no expensive indulgences. At the same time the servant informed Isaac that a Nazarene (so they termed Christians while conversing among themselves) desired to speak with him. He that would live by traffic must hold himself at the disposal of every one claiming business with him. Isaac at once replaced on the table the untasted glass of Greek wine which he had just raised to his lips, and saying hastily to his daughter, 'Rebecca, veil thyself,' commanded the stranger to be admitted.

Just as Rebecca had dropped over her fine features a screen of silver gauze which reached to her feet, the door opened, and Gurth entered, wrapt in the ample folds of his Norman mantle. His appearance was rather suspicious than prepossessing, especially as, instead of doffing his bonnet, he pulled it still deeper over his rugged brow.

'Art thou Isaac the Jew of York?' said Gurth, in Saxon.

'I am,' replied Isaac, in the same language, for his traffic had rendered every tongue spoken in Britain familiar to him, 'and who art thou?'

'That is not to the purpose,' answered Gurth.

'As much as my name is to thee,' replied Isaac; 'for without knowing thine, how can I hold intercourse with thee?'

'Easily,' answered Gurth; 'I, being to pay money, must know that I deliver it to the right person; thou, who art to receive it, wilt not, I think, care very greatly by whose hands it is delivered.'

'O,' said the Jew, 'you are come to pay monies? Holy Father Abraham! that altereth our relation to each other. And from whom dost thou bring it?'

'From the Disinherited Knight,' said Gurth, 'victor in this day's tournament. It is the price of the armour supplied to him by Kirjath Jairam of Leicester, on thy recommendation. The steed is restored to thy stable. I desire to know the amount of the sum which I am to pay for the armour.'

'I said he was a good youth!' exclaimed Isaac, with joyful exultation. 'A cup of wine will do thee no harm,' he added, filling and handing to the swineherd a richer draught than Gurth had ever before tasted. 'And how much money,' continued Isaac, 'hast thou brought with thee?'

'Holy Virgin!' said Gurth, setting down the cup, 'what nectar these unbelieving dogs drink, while true Christians are fain to quaff ale as muddy and thick as the draff we give to hogs! What money have I brought with me?' continued the Saxon, when he had finished this uncivil ejaculation, 'even but a small sum; something in hand the whilst. What, Isaac! thou must bear a conscience, though it be a Jewish one.'

'Nay, but,' said Isaac, 'thy master has won goodly steeds and rich armours with the strength of his lance and of his right hand—but 'tis a good youth; the Jew will take these in present payment, and render him back the surplus.'

'My master has disposed of them already,' said Gurth.

'Ah! that was wrong,' said the Jew—'that was the part of a fool. No Christian here could buy so many horses and armour; no Jew except myself would give him half the values. But thou hast a hundred zecchins with thee in that bag,' said Isaac, prying under Gurth's cloak, 'it is a heavy one.'

'I have heads for cross-bow bolts in it,' said Gurth, readily.

'Well, then,' said Isaac, panting and hesitating between habitual love of gain and a new-born desire to be liberal in the present instance, 'if I should say that I would take eighty zecchins for the good steed and the rich armour, which leaves me not a guilder's profit, have you money to pay me?'

'Barely,' said Gurth, though the sum demanded

was more reasonable than he expected, 'and it will leave my master nigh penniless. Nevertheless, if such be your least offer, I must be content.'

'Fill thyself another goblet of wine,' said the Jew. 'Ah! eighty zecchins is too little. It leaveth no profit for the usages of the monies; and, besides, the good horse may have suffered wrong in this day's encounter. O, it was a hard and a dangerous meeting! man and steed rushing on each other like wild bulls of Bashan! the horse cannot but have had wrong.'

'And I say,' replied Gurth, 'he is sound, wind and limb; and you may see him now in your stable. And I say, over and above, that seventy zecchins is enough for the armour, and I hope a Christian's word is as good as a Jew's. If you will not take seventy, I will carry this bag (and he shook it till the contents jingled) back to my master.'

'Nay, nay!' said Isaac; 'lay down the talents—the shekels—the eighty zecchins, and thou shalt see I will consider thee liberally.'

Gurth at length complied; and telling out eighty zecchins upon the table, the Jew delivered out to him an acquittance for the horse and suit of armour. The Jew's hand trembled for joy as he wrapped up the first seventy pieces of gold. The last ten he told over with much deliberation, pausing, and saying something as he took each piece from the table and dropt it into his purse. It seemed as if his avarice were struggling with his better nature, and compelling him to pouch zecchin after zecchin, while his generosity urged him to restore some part at least to his benefactor, or as a donation to his agent. His whole speech ran nearly thus:

'Seventy-one, seventy-two—thy master is a good youth—seventy-three—an excellent youth—seventy-four—that piece hath been clipt within the ring—seventy-five—and that looketh light of weight—seventy-six—when thy master wants money, let him come to Isaac of York—seventy-seven—that is, with reasonable security.' Here he made a considerable pause, and Gurth had good hope that the last three pieces might escape the fate of their comrades ; but the enumeration proceeded— 'Seventy-eight—thou art a good fellow—seventy-nine—and deservest something for thyself——'

Here the Jew paused again, and looked at the last zecchin, intending, doubtless, to bestow it upon Gurth. He weighed it upon the tip of his finger, and made it ring by dropping it upon the table. Had it rung too flat, or had it felt a hair's breadth too light, generosity had carried the day ; but, unhappily for Gurth, the chime was full and true, the zecchin plump, newly coined, and a grain above weight. Isaac could not find in his heart to part with it, so dropt it into his purse as if in absence of mind, with the words, 'Eighty completes the tale, and I trust thy master will reward thee handsomely. Surely,' he added, looking earnestly at the bag, 'thou hast more coins in that pouch?'

Gurth grinned, which was his nearest approach to a laugh, as he replied, 'About the same quantity which thou hast just told over so carefully.' He then folded the quittance, and put it under his cap, adding, 'Peril of thy beard, Jew, see that this be full and ample!' He filled himself, unbidden, a third goblet of wine, and left the apartment without ceremony.

'Rebecca,' said the Jew, 'that Ishmaelite hath gone somewhat beyond me. Nevertheless, his master is a good youth ; ay, and I am well pleased that he hath gained shekels of gold and shekels of silver, even by the speed of his horse and by the strength of his lance, which, like that of Goliath the Philistine, might vie with a weaver's beam.'

As he turned to receive Rebecca's answer, he observed that during his chaffering with Gurth she had left the apartment unperceived.

In the meanwhile, Gurth had descended the stair, and, having reached the dark ante-chamber or hall, was puzzling about to discover the entrance, when a figure in white, shown by a small silver lamp which she held in her hand, beckoned him into a side apartment. Gurth had some reluctance to obey the summons. Rough and impetuous as a wild boar where only earthly force was to be apprehended, he had all the characteristic terrors of a Saxon respecting fauns, forest fiends, white women, and the whole of the superstitions which his ancestors had brought with them from the wilds of Germany. He remembered, moreover, that he was in the house of a Jew, a people who, besides the other unamiable qualities which popular report ascribed to them, were supposed to be profound necromancers and cabalists. Nevertheless, after a moment's pause, he obeyed the beckoning summons of the apparition, and followed her into the apartment which she indicated, where he found, to his joyful surprise, that his fair guide was the beautiful Jewess whom he had seen at the tournament, and a short time in her father's apartment.

She asked him the particulars of his transaction with Isaac, which he detailed accurately.

'My father did but jest with thee, good fellow,' said Rebecca; 'he owes thy master deeper kindness than these arms and steed could pay, were their value tenfold. What sum didst thou pay my father even now?'

'Eighty zecchins,' said Gurth, surprised at the question.

'In this purse,' said Rebecca, 'thou wilt find a hundred. Restore to thy master that which is his due, and enrich thyself with the remainder. Haste—begone—stay not to render thanks! and beware how you pass through this crowded town, where thou mayst easily lose both thy burden and thy life. Reuben,' she added, clapping her hands together, 'light forth this stranger, and fail not to draw lock and bar behind him.'

Reuben, a dark-browed and black-bearded Israelite, obeyed her summons, with a torch in his hand; undid the outward door of the house, and conducting Gurth across a paved court, let him out through a wicket in the entrance-gate, which he closed behind him with such bolts and chains as would well have become that of a prison.

'By St. Dunstan,' said Gurth, as he stumbled up the dark avenue, 'this is no Jewess, but an angel from heaven! Ten zecchins from my brave young master—twenty from this pearl of Zion! Oh, happy day! Such another, Gurth, will redeem thy bondage, and make thee a brother as free of thy guild as the best. And then do I lay down my swineherd's horn and staff, and take the freeman's sword and buckler, and follow my young master to the death, without hiding either my face or my name.'

CHAPTER XI

1st Outlaw. Stand, sir, and throw us that you have
   about you ;
If not, we'll make you sit, and rifle you.
   Speed. Sir, we are undone ! these are the villains
That all the travellers do fear so much.
   Val. My friends——
   1st Out. That's not so, sir, we are your euemies.
   2d Out. Peace ! we'll hear him.
   3d Out. Ay, by my beard, will we ;
For he's a proper man.
                              Two Gentlemen of Verona.

The nocturnal adventures of Gurth were not yet
concluded ; indeed, he himself became partly of
that mind when, after passing one or two straggling
houses which stood in the outskirts of the village,
he found himself in a deep lane, running between
two banks overgrown with hazel and holly, while
here and there a dwarf oak flung its arms altogether
across the path. The lane was, moreover, much
rutted and broken up by the carriages which had
recently transported articles of various kinds to the
tournament ; and it was dark, for the banks and
bushes intercepted the light of the harvest moon.

From the village were heard the distant sounds
of revelry, mixed occasionally with loud laughter,
sometimes broken by screams, and sometimes by
wild strains of distant music. All these sounds,
intimating the disorderly state of the town, crowded
with military nobles and their dissolute attendants,
gave Gurth some uneasiness. 'The Jewess was

right,' he said to himself. 'By heaven and St. Dunstan, I would I were safe at my journey's end with all this treasure! Here are such numbers, I will not say of arrant thieves, but of errant knights and errant squires, errant monks and errant minstrels, errant jugglers and errant jesters, that a man with a single merk would be in danger, much more a poor swineherd with a whole bagful of zecchins. Would I were out of the shade of these infernal bushes, that I might at least see any of St. Nicholas's clerks before they spring on my shoulders!'

Gurth accordingly hastened his pace, in order to gain the open common to which the lane led, but was not so fortunate as to accomplish his object. Just as he had attained the upper end of the lane, where the underwood was thickest, four men sprung upon him, even as his fears anticipated, two from each side of the road, and seized him so fast that resistance, if at first practicable, would have been now too late. 'Surrender your charge,' said one of them; 'we are the deliverers of the commonwealth, who ease every man of his burden.'

'You should not ease me of mine so lightly,' muttered Gurth, whose surly honesty could not be tamed even by the pressure of immediate violence, 'had I it but in my power to give three strokes in its defence.'

'We shall see that presently,' said the robber; and, speaking to his companions, he added, 'bring along the knave. I see he would have his head broken as well as his purse cut, and so be let blood in two veins at once.'

Gurth was hurried along agreeably to this mandate, and having been dragged somewhat roughly over the bank on the left-hand side of the lane, found himself in a straggling thicket, which lay betwixt it and the open common. He was compelled to follow his rough conductors into the very depth of this cover, where they stopt unexpectedly in an irregular open space, free in a great measure from trees, and on which, therefore, the beams of the moon fell without much interruption from boughs and leaves. Here his captors were joined by two other persons, apparently belonging to the gang. They had short swords by their sides, and quarter-staves in their hands, and Gurth could now observe that all six wore visors, which rendered their occupation a matter of no question, even had their former proceedings left it in doubt.

'What money hast thou, churl?' said one of the thieves.

'Thirty zecchins of my own property,' answered Gurth, doggedly.

'A forfeit—a forfeit,' shouted the robbers; 'a Saxon hath thirty zecchins, and returns sober from a village! An undeniable and unredeemable forfeit of all he hath about him.'

'I hoarded it to purchase my freedom,' said Gurth.

'Thou art an ass,' replied one of the thieves; 'three quarts of double ale had rendered thee as free as thy master, ay, and freer too, if he be a Saxon like thyself.'

'A sad truth,' replied Gurth; 'but if these same thirty zecchins will buy my freedom from you, unloose my hands and I will pay them to you.'

'Hold,' said one who seemed to exercise some authority over the others; 'this bag which thou bearest, as I can feel through thy cloak, contains more coin than thou hast told us of.'

'It is the good knight my master's,' answered Gurth, 'of which, assuredly, I would not have spoken a word, had you been satisfied with working your will upon mine own property.'

'Thou art an honest fellow,' replied the robber, 'I warrant thee; and we worship not St. Nicholas so devoutly but what thy thirty zecchins may yet escape, if thou deal uprightly with us. Meantime, render up thy trust for the time.   So saying, he took from Gurth's breast the large leathern pouch, in which the purse given him by Rebecca was inclosed, as well as the rest of the zecchins, and then continued his interrogation—'Who is thy master?'

'The Disinherited Knight,' said Gurth.

'Whose good lance,' replied the robber, 'won the prize in to-day's tourney?   What is his name and lineage?'

'It is his pleasure,' answered Gurth, 'that they be concealed; and from me, assuredly, you will learn nought of them.'

'What is thine own name and lineage?'

'To tell that,' said Gurth, 'might reveal my master's.'

'Thou art a saucy groom,' said the robber; 'but of that anon.   How comes thy master by this gold? is it of his inheritance, or by what means hath it accrued to him?'

'By his good lance,' answered Gurth.   'These bags contain the ransom of four good horses and four good suits of armour.'

'How much is there?' demanded the robber.

'Two hundred zecchins.'

'Only two hundred zecchins!' said the bandit; 'your master hath dealt liberally by the vanquished, and put them to a cheap ransom.   Name those who paid the gold.'

Gurth did so.

'The armour and horse of the Templar Brian de Bois-Guilbert—at what ransom were they held? Thou seest thou canst not deceive me.'

'My master,' replied Gurth, 'will take nought from the Templar save his life's-blood.   They are on terms of mortal defiance, and cannot hold courteous intercourse together.'

'Indeed!' repeated the robber, and paused after he had said the word.   'And what wert thou now doing at Ashby with such a charge in thy custody?'

'I went thither to render to Isaac the Jew of York,' replied Gurth, 'the price of a suit of armour with which he fitted my master for this tournament.'

'And how much didst thou pay to Isaac? Methinks, to judge by weight, there is still two hundred zecchins in this pouch.'

'I paid to Isaac,' said the Saxon, 'eighty zecchins, and he restored me a hundred in lieu thereof.'

'How! what!' exclaimed all the robbers at once; 'darest thou trifle with us, that thou tellest such improbable lies?'

'What I tell you,' said Gurth, 'is as true as the moon is in heaven. You will find the just sum in a silken purse within the leathern pouch, and separate from the rest of the gold.'

'Bethink thee, man,' said the Captain, 'thou speakest of a Jew—of an Israelite, as unapt to restore gold as the dry sand of his deserts to return the cup of water which the pilgrim spills upon them.'

'There is no more mercy in them,' said another of the banditti, 'than in an unbribed sheriff's officer.'

'It is, however, as I say,' said Gurth.

'Strike a light instantly,' said the Captain; 'I will examine this said purse; and if it be as this fellow says, the Jew's bounty is little less miraculous than the stream which relieved his fathers in the wilderness.'

A light was procured accordingly, and the robber proceeded to examine the purse. The others crowded around him, and even two who had hold of Gurth relaxed their grasp while they stretched their necks to see the issue of the search. Availing himself of their negligence, by a sudden exertion of strength and activity Gurth shook himself free of their hold, and might have escaped, could he have resolved to leave his master's property behind him. But such was no part of his intention. He wrenched a quarter-staff from one of the fellows, struck down the Captain, who was altogether unaware of his purpose, and had wellnigh repossessed himself of the pouch and treasure. The thieves, however, were too nimble for him, and again secured both the bag and the trusty Gurth.

'Knave!' said the Captain, getting up, 'thou hast broken my head, and with other men of our sort thou wouldst fare the worse for thy insolence. But thou shalt know thy fate instantly. First let us speak of thy master; the knight's matters must go before the squire's, according to the due order of chivalry. Stand thou fast in the meantime; if thou stir again, thou shalt have that will make thee quiet for thy life. Comrades!' he then said, addressing his gang, 'this purse is embroidered with Hebrew characters, and I well believe the yeoman's tale is true. The errant knight, his master, must needs pass us toll-free. He is too like ourselves for us to make booty of him, since dogs should not worry dogs where wolves and foxes are to be found in abundance.'

'Like us!' answered one of the gang; 'I should like to hear how that is made good.'

'Why, thou fool,' answered the Captain, 'is he not poor and disinherited as we are? Doth he not win his substance at the sword's point as we do? Hath he not beaten Front-de-Bœuf and Malvoisin, even as we would beat them if we could? Is he not the enemy to life and death of Brian de Bois-Guilbert, whom we have so much reason to fear? And were all this otherwise, wouldst thou have us show a worse conscience than an unbeliever, a Hebrew Jew?'

'Nay, that were a shame,' muttered the other fellow; 'and yet, when I served in the band of stout old Gandelyn, we had no such scruples of conscience. And this insolent peasant—he too, I warrant me, is to be dismissed scatheless?'

'Not if *thou* canst scathe him,' replied the Captain.

'Here, fellow,' continued he, addressing Gurth, 'canst thou use the staff, that thou startst to it so readily?'

'I think,' said Gurth, 'thou shouldst be best able to reply to that question.'

'Nay, by my troth, thou gavest me a round knock,' replied the Captain; 'do as much for this fellow, and thou shalt pass scot-free; and if thou dost not—why, by my faith, as thou art such a sturdy knave, I think I must pay thy ransom myself. Take thy staff, Miller,' he added, 'and keep thy head; and do you others let the fellow go, and give him a staff—there is light enough to lay on load by.'

The two champions, being alike armed with quarter-staves, stepped forward into the centre of the open space, in order to have the full benefit of the moonlight; the thieves in the meantime laughing, and crying to their comrade, 'Miller! beware thy toll-dish.' The Miller, on the other hand, holding his quarter-staff by the middle, and making it flourish round his head after the fashion which the French call *faire le moulinet*, exclaimed boastfully, 'Come on, churl, an thou darest: thou shalt feel the strength of a miller's thumb!'

'If thou be'st a miller,' answered Gurth, undauntedly, making his weapon play around his head with equal dexterity, 'thou art doubly a thief, and I, as a true man, bid thee defiance.'

So saying, the two champions closed together, and for a few minutes they displayed great equality in strength, courage, and skill, intercepting and returning the blows of their adversary with the most rapid dexterity, while, from the continued clatter of their weapons, a person at a distance might have supposed that there were at least six persons engaged on each side. Less obstinate, and even less dangerous, combats have been described in good heroic verse; but that of Gurth and the Miller must remain unsung, for want of a sacred

poet to do justice to its eventful progress. Yet,
though quarter-staff play be out of date, what we
can in prose we will do for these bold champions.

Long they fought equally, until the Miller began
to lose temper at finding himself so stoutly opposed,
and at hearing the laughter of his companions, who,
as usual in such cases, enjoyed his vexation. This
was not a state of mind favourable to the noble
game of quarter-staff, in which, as in ordinary
cudgel-playing, the utmost coolness is requisite;
and it gave Gurth, whose temper was steady, though
surly, the opportunity of acquiring a decided advantage, in availing himself of which he displayed
great mastery.

The Miller pressed furiously forward, dealing
blows with either end of his weapon alternately,
and striving to come to half-staff distance, while
Gurth defended himself against the attack, keeping
his hands about a yard asunder, and covering himself by shifting his weapon with great celerity, so as
to protect his head and body. Thus did he maintain
the defensive, making his eye, foot, and hand keep
true time, until, observing his antagonist to lose
wind, he darted the staff at his face with his left
hand; and, as the Miller endeavoured to parry the
thrust, he slid his right hand down to his left, and
with the full swing of the weapon struck his
opponent on the left side of the head, who instantly
measured his length upon the green sward.

'Well and yeomanly done!' shouted the robbers:
'fair play and Old England for ever! The Saxon
has saved both his purse and his hide, and the
Miller has met his match.'

'Thou mayst go thy ways, my friend,' said the
Captain, addressing Gurth, in special confirmation
of the general voice, 'and I will cause two of my
comrades to guide thee by the best way to thy
master's pavilion, and to guard thee from night-
walkers that might have less tender consciences

than ours; for there is many one of them upon the amble in such a night as this. Take heed, however,' he added sternly; 'remember thou hast refused to tell thy name; ask not after ours, nor endeavour to discover who or what we are, for, if thou makest such an attempt, thou wilt come by worse fortune than has yet befallen thee.'

Gurth thanked the Captain for his courtesy, and promised to attend to his recommendation. Two of the outlaws, taking up their quarter-staves, and desiring Gurth to follow close in the rear, walked roundly forward along a bye-path, which traversed the thicket and the broken ground adjacent to it. On the very verge of the thicket two men spoke to his conductors, and receiving an answer in a whisper, withdrew into the wood, and suffered them to pass unmolested. This circumstance induced Gurth to believe both that the gang was strong in numbers, and that they kept regular guards around their place of rendezvous.

When they arrived on the open heath, where Gurth might have had some trouble in finding his road, the thieves guided him straight forward to the top of a little eminence, whence he could see, spread beneath him in the moonlight, the palisades of the lists, the glimmering pavilions pitched at either end, with the pennons which adorned them fluttering in the moonbeam, and from which could be heard the hum of the song with which the sentinels were beginning their night-watch.

Here the thieves stopt.

'We go with you no farther,' said they; 'it were not safe that we should do so. Remember the warning that you have received: keep secret what has this night befallen you, and you will have no room to repent it; neglect what is now told you, and the Tower of London shall not protect you against our revenge.'

'Good-night to you, kind sirs,' said Gurth; 'I

shall remember your orders, and trust that there is no offence in wishing you a safer and an honester trade.'

Thus they parted, the outlaws returning in the direction from whence they had come, and Gurth proceeding to the tent of his master, to whom, notwithstanding the injunction he had received, he communicated the whole adventures of the evening.

The Disinherited Knight was filled with astonishment, no less at the generosity of Rebecca, by which, however, he resolved he would not profit, than that of the robbers, to whose profession such a quality seemed totally foreign. His course of reflections upon these singular circumstances was, however, interrupted by the necessity for taking repose, which the fatigue of the preceding day and the propriety of refreshing himself for the morrow's encounter rendered alike indispensable.

The knight, therefore, stretched himself for repose upon a rich couch with which the tent was provided ; and the faithful Gurth, extending his hardy limbs upon a bear-skin which formed a sort of carpet to the pavilion, laid himself across the opening of the tent, so that no one could enter without awakening him.

CHAPTER XII

The heralds left their pricking up and down,
Now ringen trumpets loud and clarion.
There is no more to say, but east and west,
In go the speares sadly in the rest,
In goth the sharp spur into the side,
There see men who can just and who can ride ;
There shiver shaftes upon shieldes thick,
He feeleth through the heart-spone the prick ;
Up springen speares, twenty feet in height,
Out go the swordes to the silver bright ;
The helms they to-hewn and to-shred ;
Out bursts the blood with stern streames red.
                                        CHAUCER.

MORNING arose in unclouded splendour, and ere the
sun was much above the horizon the idlest or the
most eager of the spectators appeared on the common, moving to the lists as to a general centre, in
order to secure a favourable situation for viewing
the continuation of the expected games.

The marshals and their attendants appeared next
on the field, together with the heralds, for the
purpose of receiving the names of the knights who
intended to just, with the side which each chose to
espouse. This was a necessary precaution, in order
to secure equality betwixt the two bodies who should
be opposed to each other.

According to due formality, the Disinherited
Knight was to be considered as leader of the one
body, while Brian de Bois-Guilbert, who had been
rated as having done second-best in the preceding

day, was named first champion of the other band.
Those who had concurred in the challenge adhered
to his party, of course, excepting only Ralph de
Vipont, whom his fall had rendered unfit so soon
to put on his armour. There was no want of distinguished and noble candidates to fill up the ranks
on either side.

In fact, although the general tournament, in which
all knights fought at once, was more dangerous than
single encounters, they were, nevertheless, more
frequented and practised by the chivalry of the age.
Many knights, who had not sufficient confidence in
their own skill to defy a single adversary of high
reputation, were, nevertheless, desirous of displaying their valour in the general combat, where
they might meet others with whom they were
more upon an equality. On the present occasion,
about fifty knights were inscribed as desirous of
combating upon each side, when the marshals declared that no more could be admitted, to the
disappointment of several who were too late in
preferring their claim to be included.

About the hour of ten o'clock the whole plain was
crowded with horsemen, horsewomen, and foot-pas-
sengers, hastening to the tournament; and shortly
after, a grand flourish of trumpets announced Prince
John and his retinue, attended by many of those
knights who meant to take share in the game, as
well as others who had no such intention.

About the same time arrived Cedric the Saxon,
with the Lady Rowena, unattended, however, by
Athelstane. This Saxon lord had arrayed his tall
and strong person in armour, in order to take his
place among the combatants; and, considerably to
the surprise of Cedric, had chosen to enlist himself
on the part of the Knight Templar. The Saxon,
indeed, had remonstrated strongly with his friend
upon the injudicious choice he had made of his
party; but he had only received that sort of answer

usually given by those who are more obstinate in
following their own course than strong in justifying it.

His best, if not his only, reason for adhering to
the party of Brian de Bois-Guilbert, Athelstane had
the prudence to keep to himself. Though his apathy
of disposition prevented his taking any means to
recommend himself to the Lady Rowena, he was,
nevertheless, by no means insensible to her charms,
and considered his union with her as a matter
already fixed beyond doubt by the assent of Cedric
and her other friends. It had therefore been with
smothered displeasure that the proud though indolent Lord of Coningsburgh beheld the victor of the
preceding day select Rowena as the object of that
honour which it became his privilege to confer. In
order to punish him for a preference which seemed
to interfere with his own suit, Athelstane, confident
of his strength, and to whom his flatterers, at least,
ascribed great skill in arms, had determined not
only to deprive the Disinherited Knight of his
powerful succour, but, if an opportunity should
occur, to make him feel the weight of his battle-
axe.

De Bracy, and other knights attached to Prince
John, in obedience to a hint from him, had joined
the party of the challengers, John being desirous to
secure, if possible, the victory to that side. On the
other hand, many other knights, both English and
Norman, natives and strangers, took part against
the challengers, the more readily that the opposite
band was to be led by so distinguished a champion
as the Disinherited Knight had approved himself.

As soon as Prince John observed that the destined
Queen of the day had arrived upon the field, assuming that air of courtesy which sat well upon him
when he was pleased to exhibit it, he rode forward
to meet her, doffed his bonnet, and, alighting from
his horse, assisted the Lady Rowena from her saddle,
while his followers uncovered at the same time, and

one of the most distinguished dismounted to hold her palfrey.

'It is thus,' said Prince John, 'that we set the dutiful example of loyalty to the Queen of Love and Beauty, and are ourselves her guide to the throne which she must this day occupy. Ladies,' he said, 'attend your Queen, as you wish in your turn to be distinguished by like honours.'

So saying, the Prince marshalled Rowena to the seat of honour opposite his own, while the fairest and most distinguished ladies present crowded after her to obtain places as near as possible to their temporary sovereign.

No sooner was Rowena seated than a burst of music, half-drowned by the shouts of the multitude, greeted her new dignity. Meantime, the sun shone fierce and bright upon the polished arms of the knights of either side, who crowded the opposite extremities of the lists, and held eager conference together concerning the best mode of arranging their line of battle and supporting the conflict.

The heralds then proclaimed silence until the laws of the tourney should be rehearsed. These were calculated in some degree to abate the dangers of the day—a precaution the more necessary as the conflict was to be maintained with sharp swords and pointed lances.

The champions were therefore prohibited to thrust with the sword, and were confined to striking. A knight, it was announced, might use a mace or battle-axe at pleasure; but the dagger was a prohibited weapon. A knight unhorsed might renew the fight on foot with any other on the opposite side in the same predicament; but mounted horsemen were in that case forbidden to assail him. When any knight could force his antagonist to the extremity of the lists, so as to touch the palisade with his person or arms, such opponent was obliged to yield himself vanquished, and his armour and horse were placed at the disposal of the conqueror. A knight thus overcome was not permitted to take farther share in the combat. If any combatant was struck down, and unable to recover his feet, his squire or page might enter the lists and drag his master out of the press; but in that case the knight was adjudged vanquished, and his arms and horse declared forfeited. The combat was to cease as soon as Prince John should throw down his leading staff, or truncheon—another precaution usually taken to prevent the unnecessary effusion of blood by the too long endurance of a sport so desperate. Any knight breaking the rules of the tournament, or otherwise transgressing the rules of honourable chivalry, was liable to be stript of his arms, and, having his shield reversed, to be placed in that posture astride upon the bars of the palisade, and exposed to public derision, in punishment of his unknightly conduct. Having announced these precautions, the heralds concluded with an exhortation to each good knight to do his duty, and to merit favour from the Queen of Beauty and Love.

This proclamation having been made, the heralds withdrew to their stations. The knights, entering at either end of the lists in long procession, arranged themselves in a double file, precisely opposite to each other, the leader of each party being in the centre of the foremost rank, a post which he did not occupy until each had carefully arranged the ranks of his party, and stationed every one in his place.

It was a goodly, and at the same time an anxious, sight to behold so many gallant champions, mounted bravely and armed richly, stand ready prepared for an encounter so formidable, seated on their war-saddles like so many pillars of iron, and awaiting the signal of encounter with the same ardour as their generous steeds, which, by neighing and pawing the ground, gave signal of their impatience.

As yet the knights held their long lances upright,

their bright points glancing to the sun, and the streamers with which they were decorated fluttering over the plumage of the helmets. Thus they remained while the marshals of the field surveyed their ranks with the utmost exactness, lest either party had more or fewer than the appointed number. The tale was found exactly complete. The marshals then withdrew from the lists, and William de Wyvil, with a voice of thunder, pronounced the signal words—'*Laissez aller!*' The trumpets sounded as he spoke; the spears of the champions were at once lowered and placed in the rests; the spurs were dashed into the flanks of the horses; and the two foremost ranks of either party rushed upon each other in full gallop, and met in the middle of the lists with a shock the sound of which was heard at a mile's distance. The rear rank of each party advanced at a slower pace to sustain the defeated, and follow up the success of the victors, of their party.

The consequences of the encounter were not instantly seen, for the dust raised by the trampling of so many steeds darkened the air, and it was a minute ere the anxious spectators could see the fate of the encounter. When the fight became visible, half the knights on each side were dismounted— some by the dexterity of their adversary's lance; some by the superior weight and strength of opponents, which had borne down both horse and man; some lay stretched on earth as if never more to rise; some had already gained their feet, and were closing hand to hand with those of their antagonists who were in the same predicament; and several on both sides, who had received wounds by which they were disabled, were stopping their blood by their scarfs, and endeavouring to extricate themselves from the tumult. The mounted knights, whose lances had been almost all broken by the fury of the encounter, were now closely engaged with their swords, shouting their war-cries, and exchanging buffets, as if honour and life depended on the issue of the combat.

The tumult was presently increased by the advance of the second rank on either side, which, acting as a reserve, now rushed on to aid their companions. The followers of Brian de Bois-Guilbert shouted— '*Ha! Beau-seant! Beau-seant!*'[1] For the Temple! For the Temple!' The opposite party shouted in answer—'*Desdichado! Desdichado!*' which watch-word they took from the motto upon their leader's shield.

The champions thus encountering each other with the utmost fury, and with alternate success, the tide of battle seemed to flow now toward the southern, now toward the northern, extremity of the lists, as the one or the other party prevailed. Meantime the clang of the blows and the shouts of the combatants mixed fearfully with the sound of the trumpets, and drowned the groans of those who fell, and lay rolling defenceless beneath the feet of the horses. The splendid armour of the combatants was now defaced with dust and blood, and gave way at every stroke of the sword and battle-axe. The gay plumage, shorn from the crests, drifted upon the breeze like snowflakes. All that was beautiful and graceful in the martial array had disappeared, and what was now visible was only calculated to awake terror or compassion.

Yet such is the force of habit, that not only the vulgar spectators, who are naturally attracted by sights of horror, but even the ladies of distinction, who crowded the galleries, saw the conflict with a thrilling interest certainly, but without a wish to withdraw their eyes from a sight so terrible. Here

---

[1] *Beau-seant* was the name of the Templars' banner, which was half black, half white, to intimate, it is said, that they were candid and fair towards Christians, but black and terrible towards infidels.

and there, indeed, a fair cheek might turn pale, or a faint scream might be heard, as a lover, a brother, or a husband was struck from his horse. But, in general, the ladies around encouraged the combatants, not only by clapping their hands and waving their veils and kerchiefs, but even by exclaiming, 'Brave lance! Good sword!' when any successful thrust or blow took place under their observation.

Such being the interest taken by the fair sex in this bloody game, that of the men is the more easily understood. It showed itself in loud acclamations upon every change of fortune, while all eyes were so riveted on the lists that the spectators seemed as if they themselves had dealt and received the blows which were there so freely bestowed. And between every pause was heard the voice of the heralds, exclaiming, 'Fight on, brave knights! Man dies, but glory lives! Fight on; death is better than defeat! Fight on, brave knights! for bright eyes behold your deeds!'

Amid the varied fortunes of the combat, the eyes of all endeavoured to discover the leaders of each band, who, mingling in the thick of the fight, encouraged their companions both by voice and example. Both displayed great feats of gallantry, nor did either Bois-Guilbert or the Disinherited Knight find in the ranks opposed to them a champion who could be termed their unquestioned match. They repeatedly endeavoured to single out each other, spurred by mutual animosity, and aware that the fall of either leader might be considered as decisive of victory. Such, however, was the crowd and confusion that, during the earlier part of the conflict, their efforts to meet were unavailing, and they were repeatedly separated by the eagerness of their followers, each of whom was anxious to win honour by measuring his strength against the leader of the opposite party.

But when the field became thin by the numbers on either side who had yielded themselves vanquished, had been compelled to the extremity of the lists, or been otherwise rendered incapable of continuing the strife, the Templar and the Disinherited Knight at length encountered hand to hand, with all the fury that mortal animosity, joined to rivalry of honour, could inspire. Such was the address of each in parrying and striking, that the spectators broke forth into a unanimous and involuntary shout, expressive of their delight and admiration.

But at this moment the party of the Disinherited Knight had the worst; the gigantic arm of Front-de-Bœuf on the one flank, and the ponderous strength of Athelstane on the other, bearing down and dispersing those immediately exposed to them. Finding themselves freed from their immediate antagonists, it seems to have occurred to both these knights at the same instant that they would render the most decisive advantage to their party by aiding the Templar in his contest with his rival. Turning their horses, therefore, at the same moment, the Norman spurred against the Disinherited Knight on the one side and the Saxon on the other. It was utterly impossible that the object of this unequal and unexpected assault could have sustained it, had he not been warned by a general cry from the spectators, who could not but take interest in one exposed to such disadvantage.

'Beware! beware! Sir Disinherited!' was shouted so universally that the knight became aware of his danger; and striking a full blow at the Templar, he reined back his steed in the same moment, so as to escape the charge of Athelstane and Front-de-Bœuf. These knights, therefore, their aim being thus eluded, rushed from opposite sides betwixt the object of their attack and the Templar, almost running their horses against each other ere they could stop their career. Recovering their horses, however, and wheeling them round, the whole three pursued their united purpose of bearing to the earth the Disinherited Knight.

Nothing could have saved him except the remarkable strength and activity of the noble horse which he had won on the preceding day.

This stood him in the more stead, as the horse of Bois-Guilbert was wounded, and those of Front-de-Bœuf and Athelstane were both tired with the weight of their gigantic masters, clad in complete armour, and with the preceding exertions of the day. The masterly horsemanship of the Disinherited Knight, and the activity of the noble animal which he mounted, enabled him for a few minutes to keep at sword's point his three antagonists, turning and wheeling with the agility of a hawk upon the wing, keeping his enemies as far separate as he could, and rushing now against the one, now against the other, dealing sweeping blows with his sword, without waiting to receive those which were aimed at him in return.

But although the lists rang with the applauses of his dexterity, it was evident that he must at last be overpowered ; and the nobles around Prince John implored him with one voice to throw down his warder, and to save so brave a knight from the disgrace of being overcome by odds.

'Not I, by the light of Heaven !' answered Prince John ; 'this same springal, who conceals his name and despises our proffered hospitality, hath already gained one prize, and may now afford to let others have their turn.' As he spoke thus, an unexpected incident changed the fortune of the day.

There was among the ranks of the Disinherited Knight a champion in black armour, mounted on a black horse, large of size, tall, and to all appearance powerful and strong, like the rider by whom he was mounted. This knight, who bore on his shield no

device of any kind, had hitherto evinced very little
interest in the event of the fight, beating off with
seeming ease those combatants who attacked him,
but neither pursuing his advantages nor himself
assailing any one. In short, he had hitherto acted
the part rather of a spectator than of a party in
the tournament, a circumstance which procured him
among the spectators the name of *Le Noir Faineant*,
or the Black Sluggard.

At once this knight seemed to throw aside his
apathy, when he discovered the leader of his party
so hard bested ; for, setting spurs to his horse,
which was quite fresh, he came to his assistance
like a thunderbolt, exclaiming, in a voice like a
trumpet-call, '*Desdichado*, to the rescue !' It was
high time ; for, while the Disinherited Knight was
pressing upon the Templar, Front-de-Bœuf had got
nigh to him with his uplifted sword ; but ere the
blow could descend, the Sable Knight dealt a stroke
on his head, which, glancing from the polished
helmet, lighted with violence scarcely abated on the
chamfron of the steed, and Front-de-Bœuf rolled on
the ground, both horse and man equally stunned
by the fury of the blow. *Le Noir Faineant* then
turned his horse upon Athelstane of Coningsburgh ;
and his own sword having been broken in his encounter with Front-de-Bœuf, he wrenched from the
hand of the bulky Saxon the battle-axe which he
wielded, and, like one familiar with the use of the
weapon, bestowed him such a blow upon the crest
that Athelstane also lay senseless on the field.
Having achieved this double feat, for which he was
the more highly applauded that it was totally unexpected from him, the knight seemed to resume the
sluggishness of his character, returning calmly to
the northern extremity of the lists, leaving his leader
to cope as he best could with Brian de Bois-Guilbert.
This was no longer matter of so much difficulty
as formerly. The Templar's horse had bled much,

and gave way under the shock of the Disinherited Knight's charge. Brian de Bois-Guilbert rolled on the field, encumbered with the stirrup, from which he was unable to draw his foot. His antagonist sprung from horseback, waved his fatal sword over the head of his adversary, and commanded him to yield himself; when Prince John, more moved by the Templar's dangerous situation than he had been by that of his rival, saved him the mortification of confessing himself vanquished, by casting down his warder and putting an end to the conflict.

It was, indeed, only the relics and embers of the fight which continued to burn; for of the few knights who still continued in the lists, the greater part had, by tacit consent, forborne the conflict for some time, leaving it to be determined by the strife of the leaders.

The squires, who had found it a matter of danger and difficulty to attend their masters during the engagement, now thronged into the lists to pay their dutiful attendance to the wounded, who were removed with the utmost care and attention to the neighbouring pavilions, or to the quarters prepared for them in the adjoining village.

Thus ended the memorable field of Ashby-de-la-Zouche, one of the most gallantly contested tournaments of that age; for although only four knights, including one who was smothered by the heat of his armour, had died upon the field, yet upwards of thirty were desperately wounded, four or five of whom never recovered. Several more were disabled for life; and those who escaped best carried the marks of the conflict to the grave with them. Hence it is always mentioned in the old records as the 'gentle and joyous passage of arms of Ashby.'

It being now the duty of Prince John to name the knight who had done best, he determined that the honour of the day remained with the knight whom the popular voice had termed *Le Noir Faineant*.

It was pointed out to the Prince, in impeachment of this decree, that the victory had been in fact won by the Disinherited Knight, who, in the course of the day, had overcome six champions with his own hand, and who had finally unhorsed and struck down the leader of the opposite party. But Prince John adhered to his own opinion, on the ground that the Disinherited Knight and his party had lost the day but for the powerful assistance of the Knight of the Black Armour, to whom, therefore, he persisted in awarding the prize.

To the surprise of all present, however, the knight thus preferred was nowhere to be found. He had left the lists immediately when the conflict ceased, and had been observed by some spectators to move down one of the forest glades with the same slow pace and listless and indifferent manner which had procured him the epithet of the Black Sluggard. After he had been summoned twice by sound of trumpet and proclamation of the heralds, it became necessary to name another to receive the honours which had been assigned to him. Prince John had now no further excuse for resisting the claim of the Disinherited Knight, whom, therefore, he named the champion of the day.

Through a field slippery with blood and encumbered with broken armour and the bodies of slain and wounded horses, the marshals of the lists again conducted the victor to the foot of Prince John's throne.

'Disinherited Knight,' said Prince John, 'since by that title only you will consent to be known to us, we a second time award to you the honours of this tournament, and announce to you your right to claim and receive from the hands of the Queen of Love and Beauty the chaplet of honour which your valour has justly deserved.'

The Knight bowed low and gracefully, but returned no answer.

While 'the trumpets sounded, while the heralds strained their voices in proclaiming honour to the brave and glory to the victor, while ladies waved their silken kerchiefs and embroidered veils, and while all ranks joined in a clamorous shout of exultation, the marshals conducted the Disinherited Knight across the lists to the foot of that throne of honour which was occupied by the Lady Rowena.

On the lower step of this throne the champion was made to kneel down. Indeed, his whole action since the fight had ended seemed rather to have been upon the impulse of those around him than from his own free will; and it was observed that he tottered as they guided him the second time across the lists. Rowena, descending from her station with a graceful and dignified step, was about to place the chaplet which she held in her hand upon the helmet of the champion, when the marshals exclaimed with one voice, 'It must not be thus; his head must be bare.' The knight muttered faintly a few words, which were lost in the hollow of his helmet; but their purport seemed to be a desire that his casque might not be removed.

Whether from love of form or from curiosity, the marshals paid no attention to his expressions of reluctance, but unhelmed him by cutting the laces of his casque, and undoing the fastening of his gorget. When the helmet was removed, the well-formed yet sun-burnt features of a young man of twenty-five were seen, amidst a profusion of short fair hair. His countenance was as pale as death, and marked in one or two places with streaks of blood.

Rowena had no sooner beheld him than she uttered a faint shriek; but at once summoning up the energy of her disposition, and compelling herself, as it were, to proceed, while her frame yet trembled with the violence of sudden emotion, she placed upon the drooping head of the victor the

splendid chaplet which was the destined reward of
the day, and pronounced in a clear and distinct
tone these words : 'I bestow on thee this chaplet,
Sir Knight, as the meed of valour assigned to this
day's victor.' Here she paused a moment, and then
firmly added, 'And upon brows more worthy could
a wreath of chivalry never be placed !'

The knight stooped his head and kissed the hand
of the lovely Sovereign by whom his valour had
been rewarded ; and then, sinking yet farther forward, lay prostrate at her feet.

There was a general consternation. Cedric, who
had been struck mute by the sudden appearance of
his banished son, now rushed forward, as if to separate him from Rowena. But this had been already
accomplished by the marshals of the field, who,
guessing the cause of Ivanhoe's swoon, had hastened
to undo his armour, and found that the head of a
lance had penetrated his breastplate and inflicted a
wound in his side.

CHAPTER XIII

'Heroes, approach!' Atrides thus aloud;
'Stand forth distinguish'd from the circling crowd,
Ye who by skill or manly force may claim
Your rivals to surpass and merit fame.
This cow, worth twenty oxen, is decreed
For him who farthest sends the winged reed.'

Iliad.

THE name of Ivanhoe was no sooner pronounced than it flew from mouth to mouth with all the celerity with which eagerness could convey and curiosity receive it. It was not long ere it reached the circle of the Prince, whose brow darkened as he heard the news. Looking around him, however, with an air of scorn, 'My lords,' said he, 'and especially you, Sir Prior, what think ye of the doctrine the learned tell us concerning innate attractions and antipathies? Methinks that I felt the presence of my brother's minion, even when I least guessed whom yonder suit of armour inclosed.'

'Front-de-Bœuf must prepare to restore his fief of Ivanhoe,' said De Bracy, who, having discharged his part honourably in the tournament, had laid his shield and helmet aside, and again mingled with the Prince's retinue.

'Ay,' answered Waldemar Fitzurse, 'this gallant is likely to reclaim the castle and manor which Richard assigned to him, and which your Highness's generosity has since given to Front-de-Bœuf.'

'Front-de-Bœuf,' replied John, 'is a man more

willing to swallow three manors such as Ivanhoe than to disgorge one of them. For the rest, sirs, I hope none here will deny my right to confer the fiefs of the crown upon the faithful followers who are around me, and ready to perform the usual military service, in the room of those who have wandered to foreign countries, and can neither render homage nor service when called upon.'

The audience were too much interested in the question not to pronounce the Prince's assumed right altogether indubitable. 'A generous Prince! a most noble Lord, who thus takes upon himself the task of rewarding his faithful followers!'

Such were the words which burst from the train, expectants all of them of similar grants at the expense of King Richard's followers and favourites, if indeed they had not as yet received such. Prior Aymer also assented to the general proposition, observing, however, 'That the blessed Jerusalem could not indeed be termed a foreign country. She was *communis mater*—the mother of all Christians. But he saw not,' he declared, 'how the Knight of Ivanhoe could plead any advantage from this, since he (the Prior) was assured that the crusaders under Richard had never proceeded much farther than Askalon, which, as all the world knew, was a town of the Philistines, and entitled to none of the privileges of the Holy City.'

Waldemar, whose curiosity had led him towards the place where Ivanhoe had fallen to the ground, now returned. 'The gallant,' said he, 'is likely to give your Highness little disturbance, and to leave Front-de-Bœuf in the quiet possession of his gains; he is severely wounded.'

'Whatever becomes of him,' said Prince John, 'he is victor of the day; and were he tenfold our enemy, or the devoted friend of our brother, which is perhaps the same, his wounds must be looked to; our own physician shall attend him.'

A stern smile curled the Prince's lip as he spoke. Waldemar Fitzurse hastened to reply that Ivanhoe was already removed from the lists, and in the custody of his friends.

'I was somewhat afflicted,' he said, 'to see the grief of the Queen of Love and Beauty, whose sovereignty of a day this event has changed into mourning. I am not a man to be moved by a woman's lament for her lover, but this same Lady Rowena suppressed her sorrow with such dignity of manner that it could only be discovered by her folded hands and her tearless eye, which trembled as it remained fixed on the lifeless form before her.'

'Who is this Lady Rowena,' said Prince John, 'of whom we have heard so much?'

'A Saxon heiress of large possessions,' replied the Prior Aymer; 'a rose of loveliness, and a jewel of wealth; the fairest among a thousand, a bundle of myrrh, and a cluster of camphire.'

'We shall cheer her sorrows,' said Prince John, 'and amend her blood, by wedding her to a Norman. She seems a minor, and must therefore be at our royal disposal in marriage. How sayst thou, De Bracy? What thinkst thou of gaining fair lands and livings, by wedding a Saxon, after the fashion of the followers of the Conqueror?'

'If the lands are to my liking, my lord,' answered De Bracy, 'it will be hard to displease me with a bride; and deeply will I hold myself bound to your Highness for a good deed, which will fulfil all promises made in favour of your servant and vassal.'

'We will not forget it,' said Prince John; 'and that we may instantly go to work, command our seneschal presently to order the attendance of the Lady Rowena and her company—that is, the rude churl her guardian, and the Saxon ox whom the Black Knight struck down in the tournament—upon this evening's banquet. De Bigot,' he added to his seneschal, 'thou wilt word this our second summons

so courteously as to gratify the pride of these
Saxons, and make it impossible for them again to
refuse ; although, by the bones of Becket, courtesy
to them is casting pearls before swine.'

Prince John had proceeded thus far, and was about
to give the signal for retiring from the lists, when
a small billet was put into his hand.

'From whence?' said Prince John, looking at the
person by whom it was delivered.

'From foreign parts, my lord, but from whence
I know not,' replied his attendant.   'A Frenchman
brought it hither, who said he had ridden night and
day to put it into the hands of your Highness.'

The Prince looked narrowly at the superscription,
and then at the seal, placed so as to secure the flox-
silk with which the billet was surrounded, and which
bore the impression of three fleurs-de-lis.   John
then opened the billet with apparent agitation,
which visibly and greatly increased when he had
perused the contents, which were expressed in these
words—

'Take heed to yourself, for the Devil is un-
chained !'

The Prince turned as pale as death, looked first
on the earth, and then up to heaven, like a man
who has received news that sentence of execution
has been passed upon him.   Recovering from the
first effects of his surprise, he took Waldemar
Fitzurse and De Bracy aside, and put the billet
into their hands successively.   'It means,' he
added, in a faltering voice, 'that my brother
Richard has obtained his freedom.'

'This may be a false alarm or a forged letter,'
said De Bracy.

'It is France's own hand and seal,' replied Prince
John.

'It is time, then,' said Fitzurse, 'to draw our
party to a head, either at York or some other
centrical place.   A few days later, and it will be

indeed too late. Your Highness must break short this present mummery.'

'The yeomen and commons,' said De Bracy, 'must not be dismissed discontented, for lack of their share in the sports.'

'The day,' said Waldemar, 'is not yet very far spent; let the archers shoot a few rounds at the target, and the prize be adjudged. This will be an abundant fulfilment of the Prince's promises, so far as this herd of Saxon serfs is concerned.'

'I thank thee, Waldemar,' said the Prince; 'thou remindest me, too, that I have a debt to pay to that insolent peasant who yesterday insulted our person. Our banquet also shall go forward to-night as we proposed. Were this my last hour of power, it should be an hour sacred to revenge and to pleasure; let new cares come with to-morrow's new day.'

The sound of the trumpets soon recalled those spectators who had already begun to leave the field; and proclamation was made that Prince John, suddenly called by high and peremptory public duties, held himself obliged to discontinue the entertainments of to-morrow's festival; nevertheless, that, unwilling so many good yeomen should depart without a trial of skill, he was pleased to appoint them, before leaving the ground, presently to execute the competition of archery intended for the morrow. To the best archer a prize was to be awarded, being a bugle-horn, mounted with silver, and a silken baldric richly ornamented with a medallion of St. Hubert, the patron of silvan sport.

More than thirty yeomen at first presented themselves as competitors, several of whom were rangers and under-keepers in the royal forests of Needwood and Charnwood. When, however, the archers understood with whom they were to be matched, upwards of twenty withdrew themselves from the contest, unwilling to encounter the dishonour of

almost certain defeat. For in those days the skill
of each celebrated marksman was as well known for
many miles round him as the qualities of a horse
trained at Newmarket are familiar to those who
frequent that well-known meeting.

The diminished list of competitors for silvan fame
still amounted to eight. Prince John stepped from
his royal seat to view more nearly the persons of
these chosen yeomen, several of whom wore the
royal livery. Having satisfied his curiosity by this
investigation, he looked for the object of his resentment, whom he observed standing on the same spot,
and with the same composed countenance which he
had exhibited upon the preceding day.

'Fellow,' said Prince John, 'I guessed by thy
insolent babble thou wert no true lover of the long-
bow, and I see thou darest not adventure thy skill
among such merry men as stand yonder.'

'Under favour, sir,' replied the yeoman, 'I have
another reason for refraining to shoot, besides the
fearing discomfiture and disgrace.'

'And what is thy other reason?' said Prince
John, who, for some cause which perhaps he could
not himself have explained, felt a painful curiosity
respecting this individual.

'Because,' replied the woodsman, 'I know not if
these yeomen and I are used to shoot at the same
marks; and because, moreover, I know not how
your Grace might relish the winning of a third prize
by one who has unwittingly fallen under your
displeasure.'

Prince John coloured as he put the question,
'What is thy name, yeoman?'

'Locksley,' answered the yeoman.

'Then, Locksley,' said Prince John, 'thou shalt
shoot in thy turn, when these yeomen have displayed their skill. If thou carriest the prize, I will
add to it twenty nobles; but if thou losest it, thou
shalt be stript of thy Lincoln green and scourged

out of the lists with bowstrings, for a wordy and insolent braggart.'

'And how if I refuse to shoot on such a wager?' said the yeoman. 'Your Grace's power, supported, as it is, by so many men-at-arms, may indeed easily strip and scourge me, but cannot compel me to bend or to draw my bow.'

'If thou refusest my fair proffer,' said the Prince, 'the provost of the lists shall cut thy bowstring, break thy bow and arrows, and expel thee from the presence as a faint-hearted craven.'

'This is no fair chance you put on me, proud Prince,' said the yeoman, 'to compel me to peril myself against the best archers of Leicester and Staffordshire, under the penalty of infamy if they should overshoot me. Nevertheless, I will obey your pleasure.'

'Look to him close, men-at-arms,' said Prince John, 'his heart is sinking; I am jealous lest he attempt to escape the trial. And do you, good fellows, shoot boldly round; a buck and a butt of wine are ready for your refreshment in yonder tent, when the prize is won.'

A target was placed at the upper end of the southern avenue which led to the lists. The contending archers took their station in turn, at the bottom of the southern access; the distance between that station and the mark allowing full distance for what was called a shot at rovers. The archers having previously determined by lot their order of precedence, were to shoot each three shafts in succession. The sports were regulated by an officer of inferior rank, termed the provost of the games; for the high rank of the marshals of the lists would have been held degraded had they condescended to superintend the sports of the yeomanry.

One by one the archers, stepping forward, delivered their shafts yeomanlike and bravely. Of twenty-four arrows shot in succession, ten were fixed in the target, and the others ranged so near it that, considering the distance of the mark, it was accounted good archery. Of the ten shafts which hit the target, two within the inner ring were shot by Hubert, a forester in the service of Malvoisin, who was accordingly pronounced victorious.

'Now, Locksley,' said Prince John to the bold yeoman, with a bitter smile, 'wilt thou try conclusions with Hubert, or wilt thou yield up bow, baldric, and quiver to the provost of the sports?'

'Sith it be no better,' said Locksley, 'I am content to try my fortune; on condition that when I have shot two shafts at yonder mark of Hubert's, he shall be bound to shoot one at that which I shall propose.'

'That is but fair,' answered Prince John, 'and it shall not be refused thee. If thou dost beat this braggart, Hubert, I will fill the bugle with silver pennies for thee.'

'A man can but do his best,' answered Hubert; 'but my grandsire drew a good long bow at Hastings, and I trust not to dishonour his memory.'

The former target was now removed, and a fresh one of the same size placed in its room. Hubert, who, as victor in the first trial of skill, had the right to shoot first, took his aim with great deliberation, long measuring the distance with his eye, while he held in his hand his bended bow, with the arrow placed on the string. At length he made a step forward, and raising the bow at the full stretch of his left arm, till the centre or grasping-place was nigh level with his face, he drew his bowstring to his ear. The arrow whistled through the air, and lighted within the inner ring of the target, but not exactly in the centre.

'You have not allowed for the wind, Hubert,' said his antagonist, bending his bow, 'or that had been a better shot.'

So saying, and without showing the least anxiety

to pause upon his aim, Locksley stept to the appointed station, and shot his arrow as carelessly in appearance as if he had not even looked at the mark. He was speaking almost at the instant that the shaft left the bowstring, yet it alighted in the target two inches nearer to the white spot which marked the centre than that of Hubert.

'By the light of Heaven!' said Prince John to Hubert, 'an thou suffer that runagate knave to overcome thee, thou art worthy of the gallows!'

Hubert had but one set speech for all occasions. 'An your Highness were to hang me,' he said, 'a man can but do his best. Nevertheless, my grandsire drew a good bow——'

'The foul fiend on thy grandsire and all his generation!' interrupted John. 'Shoot, knave, and shoot thy best, or it shall be the worse for thee!'

Thus exhorted, Hubert resumed his place, and not neglecting the caution which he had received from his adversary, he made the necessary allowance for a very light air of wind which had just arisen, and shot so successfully that his arrow alighted in the very centre of the target.

'A Hubert! a Hubert!' shouted the populace, more interested in a known person than in a stranger. 'In the clout!—in the clout! a Hubert for ever!'

'Thou canst not mend that shot, Locksley,' said the Prince, with an insulting smile.

'I will notch his shaft for him, however,' replied Locksley.

And letting fly his arrow with a little more precaution than before, it lighted right upon that of his competitor, which it split to shivers. The people who stood around were so astonished at his wonderful dexterity that they could not even give vent to their surprise in their usual clamour. 'This must be the devil, and no man of flesh and blood,' whispered the yeomen to each other; 'such archery was never seen since a bow was first bent in Britain.'

'And now,' said Locksley, 'I will crave your Grace's permission to plant such a mark as is used in the North Country; and welcome every brave yeoman who shall try a shot at it to win a smile from the bonny lass he loves best.'

He then turned to leave the lists. 'Let your guards attend me,' he said, 'if you please; I go but to cut a rod from the next willow-bush.'

Prince John made a signal that some attendants should follow him in case of his escape; but the cry of 'Shame! shame!' which burst from the multitude induced him to alter his ungenerous purpose.

Locksley returned almost instantly with a willow wand about six feet in length, perfectly straight, and rather thicker than a man's thumb. He began to peel this with great composure, observing at the same time that to ask a good woodsman to shoot at a target so broad as had hitherto been used was to put shame upon his skill. 'For his own part,' he said, 'and in the land where he was bred, men would as soon take for their mark King Arthur's round table, which held sixty knights around it. A child of seven years old,' he said, 'might hit yonder target with a headless shaft; but,' added he, walking deliberately to the other end of the lists, and sticking the willow wand upright in the ground, 'he that hits that rod at fivescore yards, I call him an archer fit to bear both bow and quiver before a king, an it were the stout King Richard himself.'

'My grandsire,' said Hubert, 'drew a good bow at the battle of Hastings, and never shot at such a mark in his life—and neither will I. If this yeoman can cleave that rod, I give him the bucklers; or rather, I yield to the devil that is in his jerkin, and not to any human skill; a man can but do his best, and I will not shoot where I am sure to miss.

I might as well shoot at the edge of our parson's whittle, or at a wheat straw, or at a sunbeam, as at a twinkling white streak which I can hardly see.'

'Cowardly dog!' said Prince John. 'Sirrah Locksley, do thou shoot; but if thou hittest such a mark, I will say thou art the first man ever did so. Howe'er it be, thou shalt not crow over us with a mere show of superior skill.'

'I will do my best, as Hubert says,' answered Locksley; 'no man can do more.'

So saying, he again bent his bow, but on the present occasion looked with attention to his weapon, and changed the string, which he thought was no longer truly round, having been a little frayed by the two former shots. He then took his aim with some deliberation, and the multitude awaited the event in breathless silence. The archer vindicated their opinion of his skill: his arrow split the willow rod against which it was aimed. A jubilee of acclamations followed; and even Prince John, in admiration of Locksley's skill, lost for an instant his dislike to his person. 'These twenty nobles,' he said, 'which, with the bugle, thou hast fairly won, are thine own; we will make them fifty if thou wilt take livery and service with us as a yeoman of our body-guard, and be near to our person. For never did so strong a hand bend a bow or so true an eye direct a shaft.'

'Pardon me, noble Prince,' said Locksley; 'but I have vowed that, if ever I take service, it should be with your royal brother King Richard. These twenty nobles I leave to Hubert, who has this day drawn as brave a bow as his grandsire did at Hastings. Had his modesty not refused the trial, he would have hit the wand as well as I.'

Hubert shook his head as he received with reluctance the bounty of the stranger; and Locksley, anxious to escape further observation, mixed with the crowd, and was seen no more.

The victorious archer would not perhaps have escaped John's attention so easily, had not that Prince had other subjects of anxious and more important meditation pressing upon his mind at that instant. He called upon his chamberlain as he gave the signal for retiring from the lists, and commanded him instantly to gallop to Ashby and seek out Isaac the Jew. 'Tell the dog,' he said, 'to send me, before sundown, two thousand crowns. He knows the security; but thou mayst show him this ring for a token. The rest of the money must be paid at York within six days. If he neglects, I will have the unbelieving villain's head. Look that thou pass him not on the way; for the circumcised slave was displaying his stolen finery amongst us.'

So saying, the Prince resumed his horse, and returned to Ashby, the whole crowd breaking up and dispersing upon his retreat.

CHAPTER XIV

In rough magnificence array'd,
When ancient chivalry display'd
The pomp of her heroic games,
And crested chiefs and tissued dames
Assembled, at the clarion's call,
In some proud castle's high arch'd hall.

WARTON.

PRINCE JOHN held his high festival in the Castle of
Ashby. This was not the same building of which
the stately ruins still interest the traveller, and
which was erected at a later period by the Lord
Hastings, High Chamberlain of England, one of
the first victims of the tyranny of Richard the Third,
and yet better known as one of Shakspeare's characters than by his historical fame. The castle and
town of Ashby, at this time, belonged to Roger de
Quincy, Earl of Winchester, who, during the period
of our history, was absent in the Holy Land. Prince
John, in the meanwhile, occupied his castle, and
disposed of his domains without scruple; and seeking at present to dazzle men's eyes by his hospitality
and magnificence, had given orders for great preparations, in order to render the banquet as splendid
as possible.

The purveyors of the Prince, who exercised on
this and other occasions the full authority of royalty,
had swept the country of all that could be collected
which was esteemed fit for their master's table.
Guests also were invited in great numbers; and in

the necessity in which he then found himself of
courting popularity, Prince John had extended his
invitation to a few distinguished Saxon and Danish
families, as well as to the Norman nobility and
gentry of the neighbourhood. However despised
and degraded on ordinary occasions, the great
numbers of the Anglo-Saxons must necessarily
render them formidable in the civil commotions
which seemed approaching, and it was an obvious
point of policy to secure popularity with their
leaders.

It was accordingly the Prince's intention, which
he for some time maintained, to treat these unwonted guests with a courtesy to which they had
been little accustomed. But although no man with
less scruple made his ordinary habits and feelings
bend to his interest, it was the misfortune of this
Prince that his levity and petulance were perpetually
breaking out, and undoing all that had been gained
by his previous dissimulation.

Of this fickle temper he gave a memorable example in Ireland, when sent thither by his father,
Henry the Second, with the purpose of buying
golden opinions of the inhabitants of that new and
important acquisition to the English crown. Upon
this occasion the Irish chieftains contended which
should first offer to the young Prince their loyal
homage and the kiss of peace. But, instead of receiving their salutations with courtesy, John and
his petulant attendants could not resist the temptation of pulling the long beards of the Irish chieftains
—a conduct which, as might have been expected,
was highly resented by these insulted dignitaries,
and produced fatal consequences to the English
domination in Ireland. It is necessary to keep
these inconsistencies of John's character in view,
that the reader may understand his conduct during
the present evening.

In execution of the resolution which he had

formed during his cooler moments, Prince John received Cedric and Athelstane with distinguished courtesy, and expressed his disappointment, without resentment, when the indisposition of Rowena was alleged by the former as a reason for her not attending upon his gracious summons. Cedric and Athelstane were both dressed in the ancient Saxon garb, which, although not unhandsome in itself, and in the present instance composed of costly materials, was so remote in shape and appearance from that of the other guests that Prince John took great credit to himself with Waldemar Fitzurse for refraining from laughter at a sight which the fashion of the day rendered ridiculous. Yet, in the eye of sober judgment, the short close tunic and long mantle of the Saxons was a more graceful, as well as a more convenient, dress than the garb of the Normans, whose under-garment was a long doublet, so loose as to resemble a shirt or waggoner's frock, covered by a cloak of scanty dimensions, neither fit to defend the wearer from cold or from rain, and the only purpose of which appeared to be to display as much fur, embroidery, and jewellery work as the ingenuity of the tailor could contrive to lay upon it. The Emperor Charlemagne, in whose reign they were first introduced, seems to have been very sensible of the inconveniences arising from the fashion of this garment. 'In Heaven's name,' said he, 'to what purpose serve these abridged cloaks? If we are in bed they are no cover, on horseback they are no protection from the wind and rain, and when seated they do not guard our legs from the damp or the frost.'

Nevertheless, spite of this imperial objurgation, the short cloaks continued in fashion down to the time of which we treat, and particularly among the princes of the house of Anjou. They were therefore in universal use among Prince John's courtiers; and the long mantle, which formed the upper

garment of the Saxons, was held in proportional
derision.

The guests were seated at a table which groaned
under the quantity of good cheer. The numerous
cooks who attended on the Prince's progress, having
exerted all their art in varying the forms in which
the ordinary provisions were served up, had succeeded almost as well as the modern professors of
the culinary art in rendering them perfectly unlike
their natural appearance. Besides these dishes of
domestic origin, there were various delicacies brought
from foreign parts, and a quantity of rich pastry,
as well as of the simnel bread and wastel cakes,
which were only used at the tables of the highest
nobility. The banquet was crowned with the richest
wines, both foreign and domestic.

But, though luxurious, the Norman nobles were
not, generally speaking, an intemperate race.
While indulging themselves in the pleasures of the
table, they aimed at delicacy, but avoided excess,
and were apt to attribute gluttony and drunkenness
to the vanquished Saxons, as vices peculiar to their
inferior station. Prince John, indeed, and those
who courted his pleasure by imitating his foibles,
were apt to indulge to excess in the pleasures of
the trencher and the goblet ; and indeed it is well
known that his death was occasioned by a surfeit
upon peaches and new ale. His conduct, however,
was an exception to the general manners of his
countrymen.

With sly gravity, interrupted only by private
signs to each other, the Norman knights and nobles
beheld the ruder demeanour of Athelstane and
Cedric at a banquet to the form and fashion of which
they were unaccustomed. And while their manners
were thus the subject of sarcastic observation, the
untaught Saxons unwittingly transgressed several
of the arbitrary rules established for the regulation
of society. Now, it is well known that a man may

with more impunity be guilty of an actual breach
either of real good breeding or of good morals, than
appear ignorant of the most minute point of fashion-
able etiquette. Thus Cedric, who dried his hands
with a towel, instead of suffering the moisture to
exhale by waving them gracefully in the air, incurred more ridicule than his companion Athelstane,
when he swallowed to his own single share the
whole of a large pasty composed of the most exquisite foreign delicacies, and termed at that time
a 'karum pie.' When, however, it was discovered,
by a serious cross-examination, that the thane of
Coningsburgh—or franklin, as the Normans termed
him—had no idea what he had been devouring, and
that he had taken the contents of the 'karum pie'
for larks and pigeons, whereas they were in fact
beccaficoes and nightingales, his ignorance brought
him in for an ample share of the ridicule which
would have been more justly bestowed on his
gluttony.

The long feast had at length its end ; and, while
the goblet circulated freely, men talked of the feats
of the preceding tournament—of the unknown
victor in the archery games, of the Black Knight,
whose self-denial had induced him to withdraw from
the honours he had won, and of the gallant Ivanhoe,
who had so dearly bought the honours of the day.
The topics were treated with military frankness,
and the jest and laugh went round the hall. The
brow of Prince John alone was overclouded during
these discussions ; some overpowering care seemed
agitating his mind, and it was only when he received
occasional hints from his attendants that he seemed
to take interest in what was passing around him.
On such occasions he would start up, quaff a cup of
wine as if to raise his spirits, and then mingle in
the conversation by some observation made abruptly
or at random.

'We drink this beaker,' said he, 'to the health

of Wilfred of Ivanhoe, champion of this passage of arms, and grieve that his wound renders him absent from our board. Let all fill to the pledge, and especially Cedric of Rotherwood, the worthy father of a son so promising.'

'No, my lord,' replied Cedric, standing up, and placing on the table his untasted cup, 'I yield not the name of son to the disobedient youth who at once despises my commands and relinquishes the manners and customs of his fathers.'

''Tis impossible,' cried Prince John, with well-feigned astonishment, 'that so gallant a knight should be an unworthy or disobedient son!'

'Yet, my lord,' answered Cedric, 'so it is with this Wilfred. He left my homely dwelling to mingle with the gay nobility of your brother's court, where he learned to do those tricks of horsemanship which you prize so highly. He left it contrary to my wish and command; and in the days of Alfred that would have been termed disobedience—ay, and a crime severely punishable.'

'Alas!' replied Prince John, with a deep sigh of affected sympathy, 'since your son was a follower of my unhappy brother, it need not be inquired where or from whom he learned the lesson of filial disobedience.'

Thus spake Prince John, wilfully forgetting that, of all the sons of Henry the Second, though no one was free from the charge, he himself had been most distinguished for rebellion and ingratitude to his father.

'I think,' said he, after a moment's pause, 'that my brother proposed to confer upon his favourite the rich manor of Ivanhoe.'

'He did endow him with it,' answered Cedric; 'nor is it my least quarrel with my son that he stooped to hold, as a feudal vassal, the very domains which his fathers possessed in free and independent right.'

'We shall then have your willing sanction, good Cedric,' said Prince John, ' to confer this fief upon a person whose dignity will not be diminished by holding land of the British crown. Sir Reginald Front-de-Bœuf,' he said, turning towards that baron, ' I trust you will so keep the goodly barony of Ivanhoe that Sir Wilfred shall not incur his father's farther displeasure by again entering upon that fief.'

'By St. Anthony!' answered the black-browed giant, ' I will consent that your Highness shall hold me a Saxon, if either Cedric or Wilfred, or the best that ever bore English blood, shall wrench from me the gift with which your Highness has graced me.'

'Whoever shall call thee Saxon, Sir Baron,' replied Cedric, offended at a mode of expression by which the Normans frequently expressed their habitual contempt of the English, ' will do thee an honour as great as it is undeserved.'

Front-de-Bœuf would have replied, but Prince John's petulance and levity got the start.

'Assuredly,' said he, ' my lords, the noble Cedric speaks truth ; and his race may claim precedence over us as much in the length of their pedigrees as in the longitude of their cloaks.'

'They go before us indeed in the field, as deer before dogs,' said Malvoisin.

'And with good right may they go before us ; forget not,' said the Prior Aymer, ' the superior decency and decorum of their manners.'

'Their singular abstemiousness and temperance,' said De Bracy, forgetting the plan which promised him a Saxon bride.

'Together with the courage and conduct,' said Brian de Bois-Guilbert, 'by which they distinguished themselves at Hastings and elsewhere.'

While, with smooth and smiling cheek, the courtiers, each in turn, followed their Prince's example, and aimed a shaft of ridicule at Cedric,

the face of the Saxon became inflamed with passion,
and he glanced his eyes fiercely from one to another,
as if the quick succession of so many injuries had
prevented his replying to them in turn ; or, like a
baited bull, who, surrounded by his tormentors, is
at a loss to choose from among them the immediate
object of his revenge. At length he spoke, in a
voice half-choked with passion ; and, addressing
himself to Prince John as the head and front of the
offence which he had received, ' Whatever,' he said,
' have been the follies and vices of our race, a Saxon
would have been held *nidering* (the most emphatic
term for abject worthlessness) who should in his
own hall, and while his own wine-cup passed, have
treated, or suffered to be treated, an unoffending
guest as your Highness has this day beheld me
used ; and whatever was the misfortune of our
fathers on the field of Hastings, those may at least
be silent (here he looked at Front-de-Bœuf and the
Templar) who have within these few hours once and
again lost saddle and stirrup before the lance of a
Saxon.'

' By my faith, a biting jest !' said Prince John.
' How like you it, sirs ? Our Saxon subjects rise in
spirit and courage, become shrewd in wit and bold
in bearing, in these unsettled times. What say ye,
my lords ? By this good light, I hold it best to take
our galleys and return to Normandy in time.'

' For fear of the Saxons ?' said De Bracy, laughing. ' We should need no weapon but our hunting
spears to bring these boars to bay.'

' A truce with your raillery, Sir Knights,' said
Fitzurse ; ' and it were well,' he added, addressing
the Prince, ' that your Highness should assure the
worthy Cedric there is no insult intended him by
jests which must sound but harshly in the ear of a
stranger.'

' Insult !' answered Prince John, resuming his

courtesy of demeanour; 'I trust it will not be
thought that I could mean or permit any to be
offered in my presence. Here! I fill my cup to
Cedric himself, since he refuses to pledge his son's
health.'

The cup went round amid the well-dissembled
applause of the courtiers, which, however, failed to
make the impression on the mind of the Saxon that
had been designed. He was not naturally acute of
perception, but those too much undervalued his
understanding who deemed that this flattering
compliment would obliterate the sense of the prior
insult. He was silent, however, when the royal
pledge again passed round, 'To Sir Athelstane of
Coningsburgh.'

The knight made his obeisance, and showed his
sense of the honour by draining a huge goblet in
answer to it.

'And now, sirs,' said Prince John, who began to
be warmed with the wine which he had drank,
'having done justice to our Saxon guests, we will
pray of them some requital to our courtesy. Worthy
thane,' he continued, addressing Cedric, 'may we
pray you to name to us some Norman whose mention
may least sully your mouth, and to wash down with
a goblet of wine all bitterness which the sound may
leave behind it?'

Fitzurse arose while Prince John spoke, and
gliding behind the seat of the Saxon, whispered to
him not to omit the opportunity of putting an end
to unkindness betwixt the two races by naming
Prince John. The Saxon replied not to this politic
insinuation, but, rising up, and filling his cup to the
brim, he addressed Prince John in these words:
'Your Highness has required that I should name a
Norman deserving to be remembered at our banquet.
This, perchance, is a hard task, since it calls on the
slave to sing the praises of the master—upon the vanquished, while pressed by all the evils of conquest,

to sing the praises of the conqueror. Yet I *will*
name a Norman—the first in arms and in place—
the best and the noblest of his race. And the lips
that shall refuse to pledge me to his well-earned
fame, I term false and dishonoured, and will so
maintain them with my life. I quaff this goblet to
the health of Richard the Lion-hearted !'

Prince John, who had expected that his own
name would have closed the Saxon's speech, started
when that of his injured brother was so unexpectedly
introduced. He raised mechanically the wine-cup
to his lips, then instantly set it down, to view the
demeanour of the company at this unexpected proposal, which many of them felt it as unsafe to oppose
as to comply with. Some of them, ancient and
experienced courtiers, closely imitated the example
of the Prince himself, raising the goblet to their
lips, and again replacing it before them. There
were many who, with a more generous feeling,
exclaimed, 'Long live King Richard ! and may he
be speedily restored to us !' And some few,
among whom were Front-de-Bœuf and the Templar,
in sullen disdain suffered their goblets to stand untasted before them. But no man ventured directly
to gainsay a pledge filled to the health of the reigning monarch.

Having enjoyed his triumph for about a minute,
Cedric said to his companion, 'Up, noble Athelstane ! we have remained here long enough, since
we have requited the hospitable courtesy of Prince
John's banquet. Those who wish to know further of
our rude Saxon manners must henceforth seek us in
the homes of our fathers, since we have seen enough
of royal banquets and enough of Norman courtesy.'

So saying, he arose and left the banqueting-room,
followed by Athelstane, and by several other guests,
who, partaking of the Saxon lineage, held themselves insulted by the sarcasms of Prince John and
his courtiers.

'By the bones of St. Thomas,' said Prince John, as they retreated, 'the Saxon churls have borne off the best of the day, and have retreated with triumph !'

'*Conclamatum est, poculatum est,*' said Prior Aymer : 'we have drunk and we have shouted, it were time we left our wine flagons.'

'The monk hath some fair penitent to shrive to-night, that he is in such a hurry to depart,' said De Bracy.

'Not so, Sir Knight,' replied the Abbot; 'but I must move several miles forward this evening upon my homeward journey.'

'They are breaking up,' said the Prince in a whisper to Fitzurse; 'their fears anticipate the event, and this coward Prior is the first to shrink from me.'

'Fear not, my lord,' said Waldemar; 'I will show him such reasons as shall induce him to join us when we hold our meeting at York. Sir Prior,' he said, 'I must speak with you in private before you mount your palfrey.'

The other guests were now fast dispersing, with the exception of those immediately attached to Prince John's faction and his retinue.

'This, then, is the result of your advice,' said the Prince, turning an angry countenance upon Fitzurse; 'that I should be bearded at my own board by a drunken Saxon churl, and that, on the mere sound of my brother's name, men should fall off from me as if I had the leprosy?'

'Have patience, sir,' replied his counsellor; 'I might retort your accusation, and blame the inconsiderate levity which foiled my design, and misled your own better judgment. But this is no time for recrimination. De Bracy and I will instantly go among these shuffling cowards and convince them they have gone too far to recede.'

'It will be in vain,' said Prince John, pacing the

apartment with disordered steps, and expressing himself with an agitation to which the wine he had drank partly contributed—'it will be in vain; they have seen the handwriting on the wall—they have marked the paw of the lion in the sand—they have heard his approaching roar shake the wood; nothing will reanimate their courage.'

'Would to God,' said Fitzurse to De Bracy, 'that aught could reanimate his own! His brother's very name is an ague to him. Unhappy are the counsellors of a prince who wants fortitude and perseverance alike in good and in evil!'

CHAPTER XV

And yet he thinks—ha, ha, ha, ha—he thinks
I am the tool and servant of his will.
Well, let it be; through all the maze of trouble
His plots and base oppression must create,
I'll shape myself a way to higher things,
And who will say 'tis wrong?

Basil, a Tragedy.

No spider ever took more pains to repair the shattered meshes of his web than did Waldemar Fitzurse to reunite and combine the scattered members of Prince John's cabal. Few of these were attached to him from inclination, and none from personal regard. It was therefore necessary that Fitzurse should open to them new prospects of advantage, and remind them of those which they at present enjoyed. To the young and wild nobles he held out the prospect of unpunished license and uncontrolled revelry, to the ambitious that of power, and to the covetous that of increased wealth and extended domains. The leaders of the mercenaries received a donation in gold—an argument the most persuasive to their minds, and without which all others would have proved in vain. Promises were still more liberally distributed than money by this active agent; and, in fine, nothing was left undone that could determine the wavering or animate the disheartened. The return of King Richard he spoke of as an event altogether beyond the reach of probability; yet, when he observed, from the

183

doubtful looks and uncertain answers which he received, that this was the apprehension by which the minds of his accomplices were most haunted, he boldly treated that event, should it really take place, as one which ought not to alter their political calculations.

'If Richard returns,' said Fitzurse, 'he returns to enrich his needy and impoverished crusaders at the expense of those who did not follow him to the Holy Land. He returns to call to a fearful reckoning those who, during his absence, have done aught that can be construed offence or encroachment upon either the laws of the land or the privileges of the crown. He returns to avenge upon the Orders of the Temple and the Hospital the preference which they showed to Philip of France during the wars in the Holy Land. He returns, in fine, to punish as a rebel every adherent of his brother Prince John. Are ye afraid of his power?' continued the artful confidant of that Prince; 'we acknowledge him a strong and valiant knight; but these are not the days of King Arthur, when a champion could encounter an army. If Richard indeed comes back, it must be alone, unfollowed, unfriended. The bones of his gallant army have whitened the sands of Palestine. The few of his followers who have returned have straggled hither like this Wilfred of Ivanhoe, beggared and broken men. And what talk ye of Richard's right of birth?' he proceeded, in answer to those who objected scruples on that head. 'Is Richard's title of primogeniture more decidedly certain than that of Duke Robert of Normandy, the Conqueror's eldest son? And yet William the Red and Henry, his second and third brothers, were successively preferred to him by the voice of the nation. Robert had every merit which can be pleaded for Richard: he was a bold knight, a good leader, generous to his friends and to the church, and, to crown the whole, a crusader and a conqueror of the Holy Sepulchre; and yet he died a blind and miserable prisoner in the Castle of Cardiff, because he opposed himself to the will of the people, who chose that he should not rule over them. It is our right,' he said, 'to choose from the blood royal the prince who is best qualified to hold the supreme power—that is,' said he, correcting himself, 'him whose election will best promote the interests of the nobility. In personal qualifications,' he added, 'it was possible that Prince John might be inferior to his brother Richard; but when it was considered that the latter returned with the sword of vengeance in his hand, while the former held out rewards, immunities, privileges, wealth, and honours, it could not be doubted which was the king whom in wisdom the nobility were called on to support.'

These, and many more arguments, some adapted to the peculiar circumstances of those whom he addressed, had the expected weight with the nobles of Prince John's faction. Most of them consented to attend the proposed meeting at York, for the purpose of making general arrangements for placing the crown upon the head of Prince John.

It was late at night when, worn out and exhausted with his various exertions, however gratified with the result, Fitzurse, returning to the Castle of Ashby, met with De Bracy, who had exchanged his banqueting garments for a short green kirtle, with hose of the same cloth and colour, a leathern cap or head-piece, a short sword, a horn slung over his shoulder, a long-bow in his hand, and a bundle of arrows stuck in his belt. Had Fitzurse met this figure in an outer apartment, he would have passed him without notice, as one of the yeomen of the guard; but finding him in the inner hall, he looked at him with more attention, and recognised the Norman knight in the dress of an English yeoman.

'What mummery is this, De Bracy?' said Fitzurse, somewhat angrily; 'is this a time for

Christmas gambols and quaint maskings, when the
fate of our master, Prince John, is on the very
verge of decision? Why hast thou not been, like
me, among these heartless cravens whom the very
name of King Richard terrifies, as it is said to do
the children of the Saracens?'

'I have been attending to mine own business,'
answered De Bracy, calmly, 'as you, Fitzurse, have
been minding yours.'

'I minding mine own business!' echoed Waldemar; 'I have been engaged in that of Prince John,
our joint patron.'

'As if thou hadst any other reason for that,
Waldemar,' said De Bracy, 'than the promotion
of thine own individual interest! Come, Fitzurse,
we know each other: ambition is thy pursuit,
pleasure is mine, and they become our different
ages. Of Prince John thou thinkest as I do—that
he is too weak to be a determined monarch, too
tyrannical to be an easy monarch, too insolent and
presumptuous to be a popular monarch, and too
fickle and timid to be long a monarch of any kind.
But he is a monarch by whom Fitzurse and De
Bracy hope to rise and thrive; and therefore you
aid him with your policy, and I with the lances of
my Free Companions.'

'A hopeful auxiliary,' said Fitzurse, impatiently,
'playing the fool in the very moment of utter
necessity. What on earth dost thou purpose by
this absurd disguise at a moment so urgent?'

'To get me a wife,' answered De Bracy, coolly,
'after the manner of the tribe of Benjamin.'

'The tribe of Benjamin!' said Fitzurse. 'I com-
prehend thee not.'

'Wert thou not in presence yestereven,' said De
Bracy, 'when we heard the Prior Aymer tell us a
tale in reply to the romance which was sung by the
minstrel? He told how, long since in Palestine,
a deadly feud arose between the tribe of Benjamin

and the rest of the Israelitish nation; and how they cut to pieces wellnigh all the chivalry of that tribe; and how they swore by our blessed Lady that they would not permit those who remained to marry in their lineage; and how they became grieved for their vow, and sent to consult his holiness the Pope how they might be absolved from it; and how, by the advice of the Holy Father, the youth of the tribe of Benjamin carried off from a superb tournament all the ladies who were there present, and thus won them wives without the consent either of their brides or their brides' families.'

'I have heard the story,' said Fitzurse, 'though either the Prior or thou hast made some singular alterations in date and circumstances.'

'I tell thee,' said De Bracy, 'that I mean to purvey me a wife after the fashion of the tribe of Benjamin; which is as much as to say, that in this same equipment I will fall upon that herd of Saxon bullocks who have this night left the castle, and carry off from them the lovely Rowena.'

'Art thou mad, De Bracy?' said Fitzurse. 'Bethink thee that, though the men be Saxons, they are rich and powerful, and regarded with the more respect by their countrymen that wealth and honour are but the lot of few of Saxon descent.'

'And should belong to none,' said De Bracy; 'the work of the Conquest should be completed.'

'This is no time for it at least,' said Fitzurse; 'the approaching crisis renders the favour of the multitude indispensable, and Prince John cannot refuse justice to any one who injures their favourites.'

'Let him grant it if he dare,' said De Bracy; 'he will soon see the difference betwixt the support of such a lusty lot of spears as mine and that of a heartless mob of Saxon churls. Yet I mean no immediate discovery of myself. Seem I not in this garb as bold a forester as ever blew horn? The

blame of the violence shall rest with the outlaws
of the Yorkshire forests. I have sure spies on the
Saxons' motions. To-night they sleep in the convent of St. Wittol, or Withold, or whatever they
call that churl of a Saxon saint, at Burton-on-Trent.
Next day's march brings them within our reach,
and, falcon-ways, we swoop on them at once. Presently after I will appear in mine own shape, play
the courteous knight, rescue the unfortunate and
afflicted fair one from the hands of the rude
ravishers, conduct her to Front-de-Bœuf's castle,
or to Normandy, if it should be necessary, and
produce her not again to her kindred until she be
the bride and dame of Maurice de Bracy.'

'A marvellously sage plan,' said Fitzurse, 'and,
as I think, not entirely of thine own device. Come,
be frank, De Bracy, who aided thee in the invention? and who is to assist in the execution?
for, as I think, thine own band lies as far off as
York.'

'Marry, if thou must needs know,' said De Bracy,
'it was the Templar Brian de Bois-Guilbert that
shaped out the enterprise, which the adventure of
the men of Benjamin suggested to me. He is to
aid me in the onslaught, and he and his followers
will personate the outlaws, from whom my valorous
arm is, after changing my garb, to rescue the lady.'

'By my halidome,' said Fitzurse, 'the plan was
worthy of your united wisdom! and thy prudence,
De Bracy, is most especially manifested in the
project of leaving the lady in the hands of thy
worthy confederate. Thou mayst, I think, succeed
in taking her from her Saxon friends, but how thou
wilt rescue her afterwards from the clutches of Bois-
Guilbert seems considerably more doubtful. He is
a falcon well accustomed to pounce on a partridge
and to hold his prey fast.'

'He is a Templar,' said De Bracy, 'and cannot
therefore rival me in my plan of wedding this

heiress; and to attempt aught dishonourable against the intended bride of De Bracy—— By Heaven! were he a whole chapter of his order in his single person, he dared not do me such an injury!'

'Then, since nought that I can say,' said Fitzurse, 'will put this folly from thy imagination, for well I know the obstinacy of thy disposition, at least waste as little time as possible; let not thy folly be lasting as well as untimely.'

'I tell thee,' answered De Bracy, 'that it will be the work of a few hours, and I shall be at York at the head of my daring and valorous fellows, as ready to support any bold design as thy policy can be to form one. But I hear my comrades assembling, and the steeds stamping and neighing in the outer court. Farewell. I go, like a true knight, to win the smiles of beauty.'

'Like a true knight!' repeated Fitzurse, looking after him; 'like a fool, I should say, or like a child, who will leave the most serious and needful occupation to chase the down of the thistle that drives past him. But it is with such tools that I must work—and for whose advantage? For that of a Prince as unwise as he is profligate, and as likely to be an ungrateful master as he has already proved a rebellious son and an unnatural brother. But he—he too is but one of the tools with which I labour; and, proud as he is, should he presume to separate his interest from mine, this is a secret which he shall soon learn.'

The meditations of the statesman were here interrupted by the voice of the Prince from an interior apartment calling out, 'Noble Waldemar Fitzurse!' and, with bonnet doffed, the future Chancellor, for to such high preferment did the wily Norman aspire, hastened to receive the orders of the future sovereign.

CHAPTER XVI

Far in a wild, unknown to public view,
From youth to age a reverend hermit grew;
The moss his bed, the cave his humble cell,
His food the fruits, his drink the crystal well;
Remote from man, with God he pass'd his days,
Prayer all his business, all his pleasure praise.

PARNELL.

THE reader cannot have forgotten that the event of
the tournament was decided by the exertions of an
unknown knight, whom, on account of the passive
and indifferent conduct which he had manifested on
the former part of the day, the spectators had entitled *Le Noir Faineant*. This knight had left the
field abruptly when the victory was achieved; and
when he was called upon to receive the reward of
his valour he was nowhere to be found. In the
meantime, while summoned by heralds and by
trumpets, the knight was holding his course north-
ward, avoiding all frequented paths, and taking the
shortest road through the woodlands. He paused
for the night at a small hostelry lying out of the
ordinary route, where, however, he obtained from a
wandering minstrel news of the event of the tourney.

On the next morning the knight departed early,
with the intention of making a long journey; the
condition of his horse, which he had carefully spared
during the preceding morning, being such as enabled
him to travel far without the necessity of much repose. Yet his purpose was baffled by the devious

paths through which he rode, so that when evening closed upon him he only found himself on the frontiers of the West Riding of Yorkshire. By this time both horse and man required refreshment, and it became necessary, moreover, to look out for some place in which they might spend the night, which was now fast approaching.

The place where the traveller found himself seemed unpropitious for obtaining either shelter or refreshment, and he was likely to be reduced to the usual expedient of knights errant, who, on such occasions, turned their horses to graze, and laid themselves down to meditate on their lady-mistress, with an oak-tree for a canopy. But the Black Knight either had no mistress to meditate upon, or, being as indifferent in love as he seemed to be in war, was not sufficiently occupied by passionate reflections upon her beauty and cruelty to be able to parry the effects of fatigue and hunger, and suffer love to act as a substitute for the solid comforts of a bed and supper. He felt dissatisfied, therefore, when, looking around, he found himself deeply involved in woods, through which indeed there were many open glades and some paths, but such as seemed only formed by the numerous herds of cattle which grazed in the forest, or by the animals of chase, and the hunters who made prey of them.

The sun, by which the knight had chiefly directed his course, had now sunk behind the Derbyshire hills on his left, and every effort which he might make to pursue his journey was as likely to lead him out of his road as to advance him on his route. After having in vain endeavoured to select the most beaten path, in hopes it might lead to the cottage of some herdsman or the silvan lodge of a forester, and having repeatedly found himself totally unable to determine on a choice, the knight resolved to trust to the sagacity of his horse, experience having on former occasions made him acquainted with the wonderful talent possessed by these animals for extricating themselves and their riders on such emergencies.

The good steed, grievously fatigued with so long a day's journey under a rider cased in mail, had no sooner found, by the slackened reins, that he was abandoned to his own guidance, than he seemed to assume new strength and spirit; and whereas formerly he had scarce replied to the spur otherwise than by a groan, he now, as if proud of the confidence reposed in him, pricked up his ears, and assumed, of his own accord, a more lively motion. The path which the animal adopted rather turned off from the course pursued by the knight during the day; but as the horse seemed confident in his choice, the rider abandoned himself to his discretion.

He was justified by the event, for the footpath soon after appeared a little wider and more worn, and the tinkle of a small bell gave the knight to understand that he was in the vicinity of some chapel or hermitage.

Accordingly, he soon reached an open plat of turf, on the opposite side of which a rock, rising abruptly from a gently sloping plain, offered its grey and weather-beaten front to the traveller. Ivy mantled its sides in some places, and in others oaks and holly bushes, whose roots found nourishment in the cliffs of the crag, waved over the precipices below, like the plumage of the warrior over his steel helmet, giving grace to that whose chief expression was terror. At the bottom of the rock, and leaning, as it were, against it, was constructed a rude hut, built chiefly of the trunks of trees felled in the neighbouring forest, and secured against the weather by having its crevices stuffed with moss mingled with clay. The stem of a young fir-tree lopped of its branches, with a piece of wood tied across near the top, was planted upright by the door, as a rude emblem of the holy cross. At a little distance on the right hand, a fountain of the purest water trickled out of the rock, and was received in a hollow stone, which labour had formed into a rustic basin. Escaping from thence, the stream murmured down the descent by a channel which its course had long worn, and so wandered through the little plain to lose itself in the neighbouring wood.

Beside this fountain were the ruins of a very small chapel, of which the roof had partly fallen in. The building, when entire, had never been above sixteen feet long by twelve feet in breadth, and the roof, low in proportion, rested upon four concentric arches which sprung from the four corners of the building, each supported upon a short and heavy pillar. The ribs of two of these arches remained, though the roof had fallen down betwixt them; over the others it remained entire. The entrance to this ancient place of devotion was under a very low round arch, ornamented by several courses of that zig-zag moulding, resembling sharks' teeth, which appears so often in the more ancient Saxon architecture. A belfry rose above the porch on four small pillars, within which hung the green and weather-beaten bell, the feeble sounds of which had been some time before heard by the Black Knight.

The whole peaceful and quiet scene lay glimmering in twilight before the eyes of the traveller, giving him good assurance of lodging for the night; since it was a special duty of those hermits who dwelt in the woods to exercise hospitality towards benighted or bewildered passengers.

Accordingly, the knight took no time to consider minutely the particulars which we have detailed, but thanking St. Julian, the patron of travellers, who had sent him good harbourage, he leaped from his horse and assailed the door of the hermitage with the butt of his lance, in order to arouse attention and gain admittance.

It was some time before he obtained any answer,
and the reply, when made, was unpropitious.

'Pass on, whosoever thou art,' was the answer
given by a deep hoarse voice from within the hut,
'and disturb not the servant of God and St. Dunstan
in his evening devotions.'

'Worthy father,' answered the knight, 'here is a
poor wanderer bewildered in these woods, who gives
thee the opportunity of exercising thy charity and
hospitality.'

'Good brother,' replied the inhabitant of the
hermitage, 'it has pleased Our Lady and St.
Dunstan to destine me for the object of those
virtues, instead of the exercise thereof. I have no
provisions here which even a dog would share with
me, and a horse of any tenderness of nurture would
despise my couch; pass therefore on thy way, and
God speed thee.'

'But how,' replied the knight, 'is it possible for
me to find my way through such a wood as this,
when darkness is coming on? I pray you, reverend
father, as you are a Christian, to undo your door,
and at least point out to me my road.'

'And I pray you, good Christian brother,' replied
the anchorite, 'to disturb me no more. You have
already interrupted one *pater*, two *aves*, and a *credo*,
which I, miserable sinner that I am, should, according to my vow, have said before moonrise.'

'The road—the road!' vociferated the knight;
'give me directions for the road, if I am to expect
no more from thee.'

'The road,' replied the hermit, 'is easy to hit.
The path from the wood leads to a morass, and
from thence to a ford, which, as the rains have
abated, may now be passable. When thou hast
crossed the ford, thou wilt take care of thy footing
up the left bank, as it is somewhat precipitous, and
the path, which hangs over the river, has lately, as I
learn—for I seldom leave the duties of my chapel—

given way in sundry places. Thou wilt then keep straight forward——'

'A broken path—a precipice—a ford—and a morass!' said the knight, interrupting him. 'Sir Hermit, if you were the holiest that ever wore beard or told bead, you shall scarce prevail on me to hold this road to-night. I tell thee, that thou, who livest by the charity of the country—ill deserved, as I doubt it is—hast no right to refuse shelter to the wayfarer when in distress. Either open the door quickly, or, by the rood, I will beat it down and make entry for myself.'

'Friend wayfarer,' replied the hermit, 'be not importunate; if thou puttest me to use the carnal weapon in mine own defence, it will be e'en the worse for you.'

At this moment a distant noise of barking and growling, which the traveller had for some time heard, became extremely loud and furious, and made the knight suppose that the hermit, alarmed by his threat of making forcible entry, had called the dogs, who made this clamour to aid him in his defence, out of some inner recess in which they had been kennelled. Incensed at this preparation on the hermit's part for making good his inhospitable purpose, the knight struck the door so furiously with his foot that posts as well as staples shook with violence.

The anchorite, not caring again to expose his door to a similar shock, now called out aloud, 'Patience—patience; spare thy strength, good traveller, and I will presently undo the door, though, it may be, my doing so will be little to thy pleasure.'

The door accordingly was opened; and the hermit, a large, strong-built man, in his sackcloth gown and hood, girt with a rope of rushes, stood before the knight. He had in one hand a lighted torch, or link, and in the other a baton of crab-tree, so thick and heavy that it might well be termed a club. Two large shaggy dogs, half greyhound, half mastiff, stood ready to rush upon the traveller as soon as the door should be opened. But when the torch glanced upon the lofty crest and golden spurs of the knight who stood without, the hermit, altering probably his original intentions, repressed the rage of his auxiliaries, and, changing his tone to a sort of churlish courtesy, invited the knight to enter his hut, making excuse for his unwillingness to open his lodge after sunset, by alleging the multitude of robbers and outlaws who were abroad, and who gave no honour to Our Lady or St. Dunstan, nor to those holy men who spent life in their service.

'The poverty of your cell, good father,' said the knight, looking around him, and seeing nothing but a bed of leaves, a crucifix rudely carved in oak, a missal, with a rough-hewn table and two stools, and one or two clumsy articles of furniture—'the poverty of your cell should seem a sufficient defence against any risk of thieves, not to mention the aid of two trusty dogs, large and strong enough, I think, to pull down a stag, and, of course, to match with most men.'

'The good keeper of the forest,' said the hermit, 'hath allowed me the use of these animals to protect my solitude until the times shall mend.'

Having said this, he fixed his torch in a twisted branch of iron which served for a candlestick ; and placing the oaken trivet before the embers of the fire, which he refreshed with some dry wood, he placed a stool upon one side of the table, and beckoned to the knight to do the same upon the other.

They sat down, and gazed with great gravity at each other, each thinking in his heart that he had seldom seen a stronger or more athletic figure than was placed opposite to him.

'Reverend hermit,' said the knight, after looking long and fixedly at his host, ' were it not to interrupt your devout meditations, I would pray to know three things of your holiness ; first, where I am to put my horse ? secondly, what I can have for supper ? thirdly, where I am to take up my couch for the night ?'

' I will reply to you,' said the hermit, ' with my finger, it being against my rule to speak by words where signs can answer the purpose.' So saying, he pointed successively to two corners of the hut. 'Your stable,' said he, ' is there ; your bed there ; and,' reaching down a platter with two handfuls of parched pease upon it from the neighbouring shelf, and placing it upon the table, he added, ' your supper is here.'

The knight shrugged his shoulders, and leaving the hut, brought in his horse, which in the interim he had fastened to a tree, unsaddled him with much attention, and spread upon the steed's weary back his own mantle.

The hermit was apparently somewhat moved to compassion by the anxiety as well as address which the stranger displayed in tending his horse ; for, muttering something about provender left for the keeper's palfrey, he dragged out of a recess a bundle of forage, which he spread before the knight's charger, and immediately afterwards shook down a quantity of dried fern in the corner which he had assigned for the rider's couch. The knight returned him thanks for his courtesy ; and, this duty done, both resumed their seats by the table, whereon stood the trencher of pease placed between them. The hermit, after a long grace, which had once been Latin, but of which original language few traces remained, excepting here and there the long rolling termination of some word or phrase, set example to his guest by modestly putting into a very large mouth, furnished with teeth which might

have ranked with those of a boar both in sharpness
and whiteness, some three or four dried pease, a
miserable grist, as it seemed, for so large and able
a mill.

The knight, in order to follow so laudable an
example, laid aside his helmet, his corslet, and the
greater part of his armour, and showed to the hermit
a head thick-curled with yellow hair, high features,
blue eyes, remarkably bright and sparkling, a
mouth well formed, having an upper lip clothed
with mustachoes darker than his hair, and bearing
altogether the look of a bold, daring, and enter-
prising man, with which his strong form well
corresponded.

The hermit, as if wishing to answer to the confidence of his guest, threw back his cowl, and
showed a round bullet head belonging to a man in the
prime of life. His close-shaven crown, surrounded
by a circle of stiff curled black hair, had something
the appearance of a parish pinfold begirt by its high
hedge. The features expressed nothing of monastic
austerity or of ascetic privations; on the contrary,
it was a bold bluff countenance, with broad black
eyebrows, a well-turned forehead, and cheeks as
round and vermilion as those of a trumpeter, from
which descended a long and curly black beard. Such
a visage, joined to the brawny form of the holy
man, spoke rather of sirloins and haunches than of
pease and pulse. This incongruity did not escape
the guest. After he had with great difficulty
accomplished the mastication of a mouthful of the
dried pease, he found it absolutely necessary to
request his pious entertainer to furnish him with
some liquor; who replied to his request by placing
before him a large can of the purest water from the
fountain.

'It is from the well of St. Dunstan,' said he, 'in
which, betwixt sun and sun, he baptized five hundred heathen Danes and Britons—blessed be his

name!' And applying his black beard to the
pitcher, he took a draught much more moderate in
quantity than his encomium seemed to warrant.

'It seems to me, reverend father,' said the
knight, 'that the small morsels which you eat,
together with this holy but somewhat thin beverage,
have thriven with you marvellously. You appear a
man more fit to win the ram at a wrestling-match,
or the ring at a bout at quarter-staff, or the bucklers
at a sword-play, than to linger out your time in
this desolate wilderness, saying masses, and living
upon parched pease and cold water.'

'Sir Knight,' answered the hermit, 'your
thoughts, like those of the ignorant laity, are
according to the flesh. It has pleased Our Lady
and my patron saint to bless the pittance to which
I restrain myself, even as the pulse and water was
blessed to the children Shadrach, Meshech, and
Abednego, who drank the same rather than defile
themselves with the wine and meats which were
appointed them by the King of the Saracens.'

'Holy father,' said the knight, 'upon whose
countenance it hath pleased Heaven to work such a
miracle, permit a sinful layman to crave thy name?'

'Thou mayst call me,' answered the hermit, 'the
Clerk of Copmanhurst, for so I am termed in these
parts. They add, it is true, the epithet holy, but
I stand not upon that, as being unworthy of such
addition. And now, valiant knight, may I pray ye
for the name of my honourable guest?'

'Truly,' said the knight, 'Holy Clerk of Copmanhurst, men call me in these parts the Black Knight;
many, sir, add to it the epithet of Sluggard, whereby I am no way ambitious to be distinguished.'

The hermit could scarcely forbear from smiling
at his guest's reply.

'I see,' said he, 'Sir Sluggish Knight, that thou
art a man of prudence and of counsel; and, moreover, I see that my poor monastic fare likes thee

not, accustomed, perhaps, as thou hast been to the
license of courts and of camps, and the luxuries of
cities ; and now I bethink me, Sir Sluggard, that
when the charitable keeper of this forest-walk left
these dogs for my protection, and also those bundles
of forage, he left me also some food, which, being
unfit for my use, the very recollection of it had
escaped me amid my more weighty meditations.'

'I dare be sworn he did so,' said the knight ; 'I
was convinced that there was better food in the
cell, Holy Clerk, since you first doffed your cowl.
Your keeper is ever a jovial fellow ; and none who
beheld thy grinders contending with these pease,
and thy throat flooded with this ungenial element,
could see thee doomed to such horse-provender and
horse-beverage (pointing to the provisions upon the
table), and refrain from mending thy cheer. Let
us see the keeper's bounty, therefore, without
delay.'

The hermit cast a wistful look upon the knight,
in which there was a sort of comic expression of
hesitation, as if uncertain how far he should act
prudently in trusting his guest. There was, however, as much of bold frankness in the knight's
countenance as was possible to be expressed by
features. His smile, too, had something in it
irresistibly comic, and gave an assurance of faith
and loyalty, with which his host could not refrain
from sympathising.

After exchanging a mute glance or two, the
hermit went to the further side of the hut, and
opened a hutch, which was concealed with great
care and some ingenuity. Out of the recesses of a
dark closet, into which this aperture gave admittance, he brought a large pasty, baked in a pewter
platter of unusual dimensions. This mighty dish
he placed before his guest, who, using his poniard
to cut it open, lost no time in making himself acquainted with its contents.

'How long is it since the good keeper has been here?' said the knight to his host, after having swallowed several hasty morsels of this reinforcement to the hermit's good cheer.

'About two months,' answered the father, hastily.

'By the true Lord,' answered the knight, 'everything in your hermitage is miraculous, Holy Clerk! for I would have been sworn that the fat buck which furnished this venison had been running on foot within the week.'

The hermit was somewhat discountenanced by this observation; and, moreover, he made but a poor figure while gazing on the diminution of the pasty, on which his guest was making desperate inroads—a warfare in which his previous profession of abstinence left him no pretext for joining.

'I have been in Palestine, Sir Clerk,' said the knight, stopping short of a sudden, 'and I bethink me it is a custom there that every host who entertains a guest shall assure him of the wholesomeness of his food by partaking of it along with him. Far be it from me to suspect so holy a man of aught inhospitable; nevertheless, I will be highly bound to you would you comply with this Eastern custom.'

'To ease your unnecessary scruples, Sir Knight, I will for once depart from my rule,' replied the hermit. And as there were no forks in those days, his clutches were instantly in the bowels of the pasty.

The ice of ceremony being once broken, it seemed matter of rivalry between the guest and the entertainer which should display the best appetite; and although the former had probably fasted longest, yet the hermit fairly surpassed him.

'Holy Clerk,' said the knight, when his hunger was appeased, 'I would gage my good horse yonder against a zecchin, that that same honest keeper to whom we are obliged for the venison has left thee a stoup of wine, or a runlet of canary, or some such trifle, by way of ally to this noble pasty. This would be a circumstance, doubtless, totally unworthy to dwell in the memory of so rigid an anchorite; yet, I think, were you to search yonder crypt once more, you would find that I am right in my conjecture.'

The hermit only replied by a grin; and returning to the hutch, he produced a leathern bottle, which might contain about four quarts. He also brought forth two large drinking cups, made out of the horn of the urus, and hooped with silver. Having made this goodly provision for washing down the supper, he seemed to think no farther ceremonious scruple necessary on his part; but filling both cups, and saying, in the Saxon fashion, ' *Waes hael*,' Sir Sluggish Knight!' he emptied his own at a draught.

' *Drinc hael*, Holy Clerk of Copmanhurst!' answered the warrior, and did his host reason in a similar brimmer.

'Holy Clerk,' said the stranger, after the first cup was thus swallowed, 'I cannot but marvel that a man possessed of such thews and sinews as thine, and who therewithal shows the talent of so goodly a trencherman, should think of abiding by himself in this wilderness. In my judgment, you are fitter to keep a castle or a fort, eating of the fat and drinking of the strong, than to live here upon pulse and water, or even upon the charity of the keeper. At least, were I as thou, I should find myself both disport and plenty out of the king's deer. There is many a goodly herd in these forests, and a buck will never be missed that goes to the use of St. Dunstan's chaplain.'

'Sir Sluggish Knight,' replied the Clerk, 'these are dangerous words, and I pray you to forbear them. I am true hermit to the king and law, and were I to spoil my liege's game, I should be sure of the prison, and, an my gown saved me not, were in some peril of hanging.'

'Nevertheless, were I as thou,' said the knight, 'I would take my walk by moonlight, when foresters and keepers were warm in bed, and ever and anon —as I pattered my prayers—I would let fly a shaft among the herds of dun deer that feed in the glades. Resolve me, Holy Clerk, hast thou never practised such a pastime?'

'Friend Sluggard,' answered the hermit, 'thou hast seen all that can concern thee of my house-keeping, and something more than he deserves who takes up his quarters by violence. Credit me, it is better to enjoy the good which God sends thee, than to be impertinently curious how it comes. Fill thy cup, and welcome; and do not, I pray thee, by further impertinent inquiries, put me to show that thou couldst hardly have made good thy lodging had I been earnest to oppose thee.'

'By my faith,' said the knight, 'thou makest me more curious than ever! Thou art the most mysterious hermit I ever met; and I will know more of thee ere we part. As for thy threats, know, holy man, thou speakest to one whose trade it is to find out danger wherever it is to be met with.'

'Sir Sluggish Knight, I drink to thee,' said the hermit, 'respecting thy valour much, but deeming wondrous slightly of thy discretion. If thou wilt take equal arms with me, I will give thee, in all friendship and brotherly love, such sufficing penance and complete absolution that thou shalt not for the next twelve months sin the sin of excess of curiosity.'

The knight pledged him, and desired him to name his weapons.

'There is none,' replied the hermit, 'from the scissors of Dalilah and the tenpenny nail of Jael to the scimitar of Goliath, at which I am not a match for thee. But, if I am to make the election, what sayst thou, good friend, to these trinkets?'

Thus speaking, he opened another hutch, and took out from it a couple of broadswords and

bucklers, such as were used by the yeomanry of
the period. The knight, who watched his motions,
observed that this second place of concealment was
furnished with two or three good long-bows, a cross-
bow, a bundle of bolts for the latter, and half a
dozen sheaves of arrows for the former. A harp,
and other matters of a very uncanonical appearance,
were also visible when this dark recess was opened.

'I promise thee, brother Clerk,' said he, 'I will
ask thee no more offensive questions. The contents
of that cupboard are an answer to all my inquiries;
and I see a weapon there (here he stooped and took
out the harp) on which I would more gladly prove
my skill with thee than at the sword and buckler.'

'I hope, Sir Knight,' said the hermit, 'thou hast
given no good reason for thy surname of the Sluggard. I do promise thee, I suspect thee grievously.
Nevertheless, thou art my guest, and I will not put
thy manhood to the proof without thine own free
will. Sit thee down, then, and fill thy cup; let us
drink, sing, and be merry. If thou knowest ever a
good lay, thou shalt be welcome to a nook of pasty
at Copmanhurst so long as I serve the chapel of
St. Dunstan, which, please God, shall be till I
change my grey covering for one of green turf.
But come, fill a flagon, for it will crave some time
to tune the harp; and nought pitches the voice and
sharpens the ear like a cup of wine. For my part,
I love to feel the grape at my very finger-ends
before they make the harp-strings tinkle.'

CHAPTER XVII

At eve, within yon studious nook,
I ope my brass-embossed book,
Portray'd with many a holy deed
Of martyrs crown'd with heavenly meed;
Then, as my taper waxes dim,
Chant, ere I sleep, my measured hymn.

. . . .

Who but would cast his pomp away,
To take my staff and amice grey,
And to the world's tumultuous stage,
Prefer the peaceful HERMITAGE?

WARTON.

NOTWITHSTANDING the prescription of the genial hermit, with which his guest willingly complied, he found it no easy matter to bring the harp to harmony.

'Methinks, holy father,' said he, 'the instrument wants one string, and the rest have been somewhat misused.'

'Ay, mark'st thou that?' replied the hermit; 'that shows thee a master of the craft. Wine and wassail,' he added, gravely casting up his eyes—'all the fault of wine and wassail! I told Allan-a-Dale, the northern minstrel, that he would damage the harp if he touched it after the seventh cup, but he would not be controlled. Friend, I drink to thy successful performance.'

So saying, he took off his cup with much gravity, at the same time shaking his head at the intemperance of the Scottish harper.

The knight, in the meantime, had brought the strings into some order, and, after a short prelude, asked his host whether he would choose a *sirvente* in the language of *oc*, or a *lai* in the language of *oui*, or a *virelai*, or a ballad in the vulgar English.

'A ballad—a ballad,' said the hermit, 'against all the *ocs* and *ouis* of France. Downright English am I, Sir Knight, and downright English was my patron St. Dunstan, and scorned *oc* and *oui*, as he would have scorned the parings of the devil's hoof; downright English alone shall be sung in this cell.'

'I will assay, then,' said the knight, 'a ballad composed by a Saxon gleeman, whom I knew in Holy Land.'

It speedily appeared that, if the knight was not a complete master of the minstrel art, his taste for it had at least been cultivated under the best instructors Art had taught him to soften the faults of a voice which had little compass, and was naturally rough rather than mellow, and, in short, had done all that culture can do in supplying natural deficiencies. His performance, therefore, might have been termed very respectable by abler judges than the hermit, especially as the knight threw into the notes now a degree of spirit, and now of plaintive enthusiasm, which gave force and energy to the verses which he sung.

THE CRUSADER'S RETURN

High deeds achieved of knightly fame,
From Palestine the champion came ;
The cross upon his shoulders borne
Battle and blast had dimm'd and torn.
Each dint upon his batter'd shield
Was token of a foughten field ;
And thus, beneath his lady's bower,
He sung, as fell the twilight hour :—

'Joy to the fair!—thy knight behold,
Return'd from yonder land of gold.
No wealth he brings, nor wealth can need
Save his good arms and battle-steed,
His spurs, to dash against a foe,
His lance and sword to lay him low;
Such all the trophies of his toil,
Such—and the hope of Tekla's smile!

'Joy to the fair! whose constant knight
Her favour fired to feats of might;
Unnoted shall she not remain,
Where meet the bright and noble train;
Minstrel shall sing and herald tell—
"Mark yonder maid of beauty well,
'Tis she for whose bright eyes was won
The listed field at Askalon!

'"Note well her smile! it edged the blade
Which fifty wives to widows made,
When, vain his strength and Mahound's spell,
Iconium's turban'd soldan fell.
Seest thou her locks, whose sunny glow
Half shows, half shades, her neck of snow?
Twines not of them one golden thread,
But for its sake a Paynim bled."

'Joy to the fair!—my name unknown,
Each deed and all its praise thine own;
Then, oh! unbar this churlish gate,
The night dew falls, the hour is late.
Inured to Syria's glowing breath,
I feel the north breeze chill as death;
Let grateful love quell maiden shame,
And grant him bliss who brings thee fame.'

During this performance, the hermit demeaned himself much like a first-rate critic of the present day at a new opera. He reclined back upon his seat with his eyes half shut: now folding his hands and twisting his thumbs, he seemed absorbed in attention, and anon, balancing his expanded palms, he gently flourished them in time to the music. At one or two favourite cadences he threw in a little

assistance of his own, where the knight's voice
seemed unable to carry the air so high as his
worshipful taste approved. When the song was
ended, the anchorite emphatically declared it a
good one, and well sung.

'And yet,' said he, 'I think my Saxon countrymen had herded long enough with the Normans to
fall into the tone of their melancholy ditties. What
took the honest knight from home? or what could
he expect but to find his mistress agreeably engaged
with a rival on his return, and his serenade, as they
call it, as little regarded as the caterwauling of a
cat in the gutter? Nevertheless, Sir Knight, I
drink this cup to thee, to the success of all true
lovers. I fear you are none,' he added, on observing
that the knight, whose brain began to be heated
with these repeated draughts, qualified his flagon
from the water pitcher.

'Why,' said the knight, 'did you not tell me that
this water was from the well of your blessed patron,
St. Dunstan?'

'Ay, truly,' said the hermit, 'and many a hundred
of pagans did he baptize there, but I never heard
that he drank any of it. Everything should be put
to its proper use in this world. St. Dunstan knew,
as well as any one, the prerogatives of a jovial
friar.'

And so saying, he reached the harp, and entertained his guest with the following characteristic
song, to a sort of derry-down chorus,[1] appropriate
to an old English ditty :—

THE BAREFOOTED FRIAR

I'll give thee, good fellow, a twelvemonth or twain,
To search Europe through, from Byzantium to Spain;
But ne'er shall you find, should you search till you tire'
So happy a man as the Barefooted Friar.

Your knight for his lady pricks forth in career,
And is brought home at evensong prick'd through with a
    spear;
I confess him in haste—for his lady desires
No comfort on earth save the Barefooted Friar's.

Your monarch! Pshaw! many a prince has been known
To barter his robes for our cowl and our gown;
But which of us e'er felt the idle desire
To exchange for a crown the grey hood of a Friar!

The Friar has walk'd out, and where'er he has gone,
The land and its fatness is mark'd for his own;
He can roam where he lists, he can stop when he tires,
For every man's house is the Barefooted Friar's.

He's expected at noon, and no wight till he comes
May profane the great chair, or the porridge of plums;
For the best of the cheer, and the seat by the fire,
Is the undenied right of the Barefooted Friar.

He's expected at night, and the pasty's made hot,
They broach the brown ale, and they fill the black pot,
And the goodwife would wish the goodman in the mire,
Ere he lack'd a soft pillow, the Barefooted Friar.

Long flourish the sandal, the cord, and the cope,
The dread of the devil and trust of the Pope;
For to gather life's roses, unscathed by the briar,
Is granted alone to the Barefooted Friar.

'By my troth,' said the knight, 'thou hast sung well and lustily, and in high praise of thine order. And, talking of the devil, Holy Clerk, are you not afraid that he may pay you a visit during some of your uncanonical pastimes?'

'I uncanonical!' answered the hermit; 'I scorn the charge—I scorn it with my heels! I serve the duty of my chapel duly and truly. Two masses daily, morning and evening, primes, noons, and vespers, *aves, credos, paters*——'

'Excepting moonlight nights, when the venison is in season,' said his guest.

'*Exceptis excipiendis*,' replied the hermit, 'as our

old abbot taught me to say, when impertinent laymen should ask me if I kept every punctilio of mine
order.'

'True, holy father,' said the knight; 'but the
devil is apt to keep an eye on such exceptions; he
goes about, thou knowest, like a roaring lion.'

'Let him roar here if he dares,' said the Friar;
'a touch of my cord will make him roar as loud as
the tongs of St. Dunstan himself did. I never
feared man, and I as little fear the devil and his
imps. St. Dunstan, St. Dubric, St. Winibald, St.
Winifred, St. Swibert, St. Willick, not forgetting
St. Thomas à Kent and my own poor merits to
speed,—I defy every devil of them, come cut and
long tail. But to let you into a secret, I never
speak upon such subjects, my friend, until after
morning vespers.'

He changed the conversation: fast and furious
grew the mirth of the parties, and many a song was
exchanged betwixt them, when their revels were
interrupted by a loud knocking at the door of the
hermitage.

The occasion of this interruption we can only
explain by resuming the adventures of another set
of our characters; for, like old Ariosto, we do not
pique ourselves upon continuing uniformly to keep
company with any one personage of our drama.

CHAPTER XVIII

Away! our journey lies through dell and dingle,
Where the blithe fawn trips by its timid mother,
Where the broad oak, with intercepting boughs,
Chequers the sunbeam in the greensward alley—
Up and away! for lovely paths are these
To tread, when the glad Sun is on his throne;
Less pleasant, and less safe, when Cynthia's lamp
With doubtful glimmer lights the dreary forest.
                                    Ettrick Forest.

When Cedric the Saxon saw his son drop down
senseless in the lists at Ashby, his first impulse was
to order him into the custody and care of his own
attendants; but the words choked in his throat.
He could not bring himself to acknowledge, in
presence of such an assembly, the son whom he had
renounced and disinherited. He ordered, however,
Oswald to keep an eye upon him; and directed that
officer, with two of his serfs, to convey Ivanhoe to
Ashby as soon as the crowd had dispersed. Oswald,
however, was anticipated in this good office. The
crowd dispersed, indeed, but the knight was nowhere
to be seen.

It was in vain that Cedric's cupbearer looked
around for his young master: he saw the bloody
spot on which he had lately sunk down, but himself
he saw no longer; it seemed as if the fairies had
conveyed him from the spot. Perhaps Oswald—for
the Saxons were very superstitious—might have
adopted some such hypothesis to account for Ivanhoe's disappearance, had he not suddenly cast his

eye upon a person attired like a squire, in whom he recognised the features of his fellow-servant Gurth. Anxious concerning his master's fate, and in despair at his sudden disappearance, the translated swine-herd was searching for him everywhere, and had neglected, in doing so, the concealment on which his own safety depended. Oswald deemed it his duty to secure Gurth, as a fugitive of whose fate his master was to judge.

Renewing his inquiries concerning the fate of Ivanhoe, the only information which the cupbearer could collect from the bystanders was, that the knight had been raised with care by certain well-attired grooms, and placed in a litter belonging to a lady among the spectators, which had immediately transported him out of the press. Oswald, on receiving this intelligence, resolved to return to his master for farther instructions, carrying along with him Gurth, whom he considered in some sort as a deserter from the service of Cedric.

The Saxon had been under very intense and agonising apprehensions concerning his son, for nature had asserted her rights, in spite of the patriotic stoicism which laboured to disown her. But no sooner was he informed that Ivanhoe was in careful, and probably in friendly, hands than the paternal anxiety, which had been excited by the dubiety of his fate, gave way anew to the feeling of injured pride and resentment at what he termed Wilfred's filial disobedience. 'Let him wander his way,' said he ; 'let those leech his wounds for whose sake he encountered them. He is fitter to do the juggling tricks of the Norman chivalry than to maintain the fame and honour of his English ancestry with the glaive and brown-bill, the good old weapons of his country.'

'If to maintain the honour of ancestry,' said Rowena, who was present, 'it is sufficient to be wise in council and brave in execution, to be boldest among the bold, and gentlest among the gentle, I know no voice, save his father's——'

'Be silent, Lady Rowena! on this subject only I hear you not. Prepare yourself for the Prince's festival: we have been summoned thither with unwonted circumstance of honour and of courtesy, such as the haughty Normans have rarely used to our race since the fatal day of Hastings. Thither will I go, were it only to show these proud Normans how little the fate of a son who could defeat their bravest can affect a Saxon.'

'Thither,' said Rowena, 'do I NOT go; and I pray you to beware, lest what you mean for courage and constancy shall be accounted hardness of heart.'

'Remain at home then, ungrateful lady,' answered Cedric; 'thine is the hard heart, which can sacrifice the weal of an oppressed people to an idle and unauthorised attachment. I seek the noble Athelstane, and with him attend the banquet of John of Anjou.'

He went accordingly to the banquet, of which we have already mentioned the principal events. Immediately upon retiring from the castle, the Saxon thanes, with their attendants, took horse; and it was during the bustle which attended their doing so that Cedric for the first time cast his eyes upon the deserter Gurth. The noble Saxon had returned from the banquet, as we have seen, in no very placid humour, and wanted but a pretext for wreaking his anger upon some one. 'The gyves!' he said—'the gyves! Oswald—Hundebert! Dogs and villains! why leave ye the knave unfettered?'

Without daring to remonstrate, the companions of Gurth bound him with a halter, as the readiest cord which occurred. He submitted to the operation without remonstrance, except that, darting a reproachful look at his master, he said, 'This comes of loving your flesh and blood better than mine own.'

'To horse, and forward!' said Cedric.

'It is indeed full time,' said the noble Athelstane; 'for, if we ride not the faster, the worthy Abbot Waltheoff's preparations for a rere-supper [1] will be altogether spoiled.'

The travellers, however, used such speed as to reach the convent of St. Withold's before the apprehended evil took place. The Abbot, himself of ancient Saxon descent, received the noble Saxons with the profuse and exuberant hospitality of their nation, wherein they indulged to a late, or rather an early, hour; nor did they take leave of their reverend host the next morning until they had shared with him a sumptuous refection.

As the cavalcade left the court of the monastery, an incident happened somewhat alarming to the Saxons, who, of all people of Europe, were most addicted to a superstitious observance of omens, and to whose opinions can be traced most of those notions upon such subjects still to be found among our popular antiquities. For the Normans being a mixed race, and better informed according to the information of the times, had lost most of the superstitious prejudices which their ancestors had brought from Scandinavia, and piqued themselves upon thinking freely on such topics.

In the present instance, the apprehension of impending evil was inspired by no less respectable a prophet than a large lean black dog, which, sitting upright, howled most piteously as the foremost riders left the gate, and presently afterwards, barking wildly, and jumping to and fro, seemed bent upon attaching itself to the party.

'I like not that music, father Cedric,' said Athelstane; for by this title of respect he was accustomed to address him.

---

[1] A rere-supper was a night-meal, and sometimes signified a collation which was given at a late hour, after the regular supper had made its appearance.—L. T.

'Nor I either, uncle,' said Wamba; 'I greatly fear we shall have to pay the piper.'

'In my mind,' said Athelstane, upon whose memory the Abbot's good ale—for Burton was already famous for that genial liquor—had made a favourable impression—'in my mind we had better turn back and abide with the Abbot until the afternoon. It is unlucky to travel where your path is crossed by a monk, a hare, or a howling dog, until you have eaten your next meal.'

'Away!' said Cedric, impatiently; 'the day is already too short for our journey. For the dog, I know it to be the cur of the runaway slave Gurth, a useless fugitive like its master.'

So saying, and rising at the same time in his stirrups, impatient at the interruption of his journey, he launched his javelin at poor Fangs; for Fangs it was, who, having traced his master thus far upon his stolen expedition, had here lost him, and was now, in his uncouth way, rejoicing at his reappearance. The javelin inflicted a wound upon the animal's shoulder, and narrowly missed pinning him to the earth; and Fangs fled howling from the presence of the enraged thane. Gurth's heart swelled within him; for he felt this meditated slaughter of his faithful adherent in a degree much deeper than the harsh treatment he had himself received. Having in vain attempted to raise his hand to his eyes, he said to Wamba, who, seeing his master's ill-humour, had prudently retreated to the rear, 'I pray thee, do me the kindness to wipe my eyes with the skirt of thy mantle; the dust offends me, and these bonds will not let me help myself one way or another.'

Wamba did him the service he required, and they rode side by side for some time, during which Gurth maintained a moody silence. At length he could repress his feelings no longer.

'Friend Wamba,' said he, 'of all those who are

fools enough to serve Cedric, thou alone hast
dexterity enough to make thy folly acceptable to
him. Go to him, therefore, and tell him that
neither for love nor fear will Gurth serve him
longer. He may strike the head from me, he may
scourge me, he may load me with irons, but henceforth he shall never compel me either to love or to
obey him. Go to him, then, and tell him that
Gurth the son of Beowulph renounces his service.'

'Assuredly,' said Wamba, 'fool as I am, I shall
not do your fool's errand. Cedric hath another
javelin stuck into his girdle, and thou knowest he
does not always miss his mark.'

'I care not,' replied Gurth, 'how soon he makes
a mark of me. Yesterday he left Wilfred, my
young master, in his blood. To-day he has striven
to kill before my face the only other living creature
that ever showed me kindness. By St. Edmund,
St. Dunstan, St. Withold, St. Edward the Confessor,
and every other Saxon saint in the calendar (for
Cedric never swore by any that was not of Saxon
lineage, and all his household had the same limited
devotion), I will never forgive him!'

'To my thinking now,' said the Jester, who was
frequently wont to act as peacemaker in the family,
' our master did not propose to hurt Fangs, but only
to affright him. For, if you observed, he rose in
his stirrups, as thereby meaning to overcast the
mark; and so he would have done, but Fangs
happening to bound up at the very moment, received
a scratch, which I will be bound to heal with a
penny's breadth of tar.'

'If I thought so,' said Gurth—'if I could but
think so; but no, I saw the javelin was well aimed;
I heard it whizz through the air with all the wrath-
ful malevolence of him who cast it, and it quivered
after it had pitched in the ground, as if with regret
for having missed its mark. By the hog dear to
St. Anthony, I renounce him!'

And the indignant swineherd resumed his sullen silence, which no efforts of the Jester could again induce him to break.

Meanwhile Cedric and Athelstane, the leaders of the troop, conversed together on the state of the land, on the dissensions of the royal family, on the feuds and quarrels among the Norman nobles, and on the chance which there was that the oppressed Saxons might be able to free themselves from the yoke of the Normans, or at least to elevate themselves into national consequence and independence, during the civil convulsions which were likely to ensue. On this subject Cedric was all animation. The restoration of the independence of his race was the idol of his heart, to which he had willingly sacrificed domestic happiness and the interests of his own son. But, in order to achieve this great revolution in favour of the native English, it was necessary that they should be united among themselves, and act under an acknowledged head. The necessity of choosing their chief from the Saxon blood-royal was not only evident in itself, but had been made a solemn condition by those whom Cedric had entrusted with his secret plans and hopes. Athelstane had this quality at least; and though he had few mental accomplishments or talents to recommend him as a leader, he had still a goodly person, was no coward, had been accustomed to martial exercises, and seemed willing to defer to the advice of counsellors more wise than himself. Above all, he was known to be liberal and hospitable, and believed to be good-natured. But whatever pretensions Athelstane had to be considered as head of the Saxon confederacy, many of that nation were disposed to prefer to his the title of the Lady Rowena, who drew her descent from Alfred, and whose father having been a chief renowned for wisdom, courage, and generosity, his memory was highly honoured by his oppressed countrymen.

It would have been no difficult thing for Cedric,
had he been so disposed, to have placed himself at
the head of a third party, as formidable at least as
any of the others. To counterbalance their royal
descent, he had courage, activity, energy, and,
above all, that devoted attachment to the cause
which had procured him the epithet of THE SAXON,
and his birth was inferior to none, excepting only
that of Athelstane and his ward. These qualities,
however, were unalloyed by the slightest shade of
selfishness; and, instead of dividing yet further his
weakened nation by forming a faction of his own,
it was a leading part of Cedric's plan to extinguish
that which already existed by promoting a marriage
betwixt Rowena and Athelstane. An obstacle occurred to this his favourite project in the mutual
attachment of his ward and his son; and hence the
original cause of the banishment of Wilfred from
the house of his father.

This stern measure Cedric had adopted in hopes
that, during Wilfred's absence, Rowena might
relinquish her preference; but in this hope he was
disappointed—a disappointment which might be
attributed in part to the mode in which his ward
had been educated. Cedric, to whom the name of
Alfred was as that of a deity, had treated the sole
remaining scion of that great monarch with a degree
of observance such as, perhaps, was in those days
scarce paid to an acknowledged princess. Rowena's
will had been in almost all cases a law to his household; and Cedric himself, as if determined that her
sovereignty should be fully acknowledged within
that little circle at least, seemed to take a pride in
acting as the first of her subjects. Thus trained in
the exercise not only of free will but despotic
authority, Rowena was, by her previous education,
disposed both to resist and to resent any attempt to
control her affections, or dispose of her hand contrary
to her inclinations, and to assert her independence

in a case in which even those females who have been trained up to obedience and subjection are not infrequently apt to dispute the authority of guardians and parents. The opinions which she felt strongly she avowed boldly; and Cedric, who could not free himself from his habitual deference to her opinions, felt totally at a loss how to enforce his authority of guardian.

It was in vain that he attempted to dazzle her with the prospect of a visionary throne. Rowena, who possessed strong sense, neither considered his plan as practicable nor as desirable, so far as she was concerned, could it have been achieved. Without attempting to conceal her avowed preference of Wilfred of Ivanhoe, she declared that, were that favoured knight out of question, she would rather take refuge in a convent than share a throne with Athelstane, whom, having always despised, she now began, on account of the trouble she received on his account, thoroughly to detest.

Nevertheless, Cedric, whose opinion of women's constancy was far from strong, persisted in using every means in his power to bring about the proposed match, in which he conceived he was rendering an important service to the Saxon cause. The sudden and romantic appearance of his son in the lists at Ashby he had justly regarded as almost a death's blow to his hopes. His paternal affection, it is true, had for an instant gained the victory over pride and patriotism; but both had returned in full force, and under their joint operation he was now bent upon making a determined effort for the union of Athelstane and Rowena, together with expediting those other measures which seemed necessary to forward the restoration of Saxon independence.

On this last subject he was now labouring with Athelstane, not without having reason, every now and then, to lament, like Hotspur, that he should have moved such a dish of skimmed milk to so

honourable an action.   Athelstane, it is true, was
vain enough, and loved to have his ears tickled with
tales of his high descent, and of his right by inheritance to homage and sovereignty.   But his petty
vanity was sufficiently gratified by receiving this
homage at the hands of his immediate attendants
and of the Saxons who approached him.   If he had
the courage to encounter danger, he at least hated
the trouble of going to seek it ; and while he agreed
in the general principles laid down by Cedric concerning the claim of the Saxons to independence,
and was still more easily convinced of his own title
to reign over them when that independence should
be attained, yet when the means of asserting these
rights came to be discussed, he was still Athelstane
the Unready—slow, irresolute, procrastinating, and
unenterprising.   The warm and impassioned ex-
hortations of Cedric had as little effect upon his
impassive temper as red-hot balls alighting in the
water, which produce a little sound and smoke, and
are instantly extinguished.

If, leaving this task, which might be compared to
spurring a tired jade, or to hammering upon cold
iron, Cedric fell back to his ward Rowena, he
received little more satisfaction from conferring
with her.   For, as his presence interrupted the
discourse between the lady and her favourite attendant upon the gallantry and fate of Wilfred, Elgitha
failed not to revenge both her mistress and herself
by recurring to the overthrow of Athelstane in the
lists, the most disagreeable subject which could
greet the ears of Cedric.   To this sturdy Saxon,
therefore, the day's journey was fraught with all
manner of displeasure and discomfort ; so that he
more than once internally cursed the tournament,
and him who had proclaimed it, together with his
own folly in ever thinking of going thither.

At noon, upon the motion of Athelstane, the
travellers paused in a woodland shade by a fountain,

to repose their horses and partake of some provisions, with which the hospitable Abbot had loaded a sumpter mule. Their repast was a pretty long one; and these several interruptions rendered it impossible for them to hope to reach Rotherwood without travelling all night, a conviction which induced them to proceed on their way at a more hasty pace than they had hitherto used.

to repose their horses and partake of some provisions with which the hospitable Abbot had loaded
a sumpter mule. Their scouts, &c. [faded text]
[faded text, obscured lines]

CHAPTER XIX

A train of armed men, some noble dame
Escorting (so their scatter'd words discover'd,
As unperceived I hung upon their rear),
Are close at hand, and mean to pass the night
Within the castle.

Orra, a Tragedy.

THE travellers had now reached the verge of the
wooded country, and were about to plunge into its
recesses, held dangerous at that time from the
number of outlaws whom oppression and poverty
had driven to despair, and who occupied the forests
in such large bands as could easily bid defiance to
the feeble police of the period. From these rovers,
however, notwithstanding the lateness of the hour,
Cedric and Athelstane accounted themselves secure,
as they had in attendance ten servants, besides
Wamba and Gurth, whose aid could not be counted
upon, the one being a jester and the other a captive.
It may be added, that in travelling thus late through
the forest, Cedric and Athelstane relied on their
descent and character as well as their courage.
The outlaws, whom the severity of the forest laws
had reduced to this roving and desperate mode of
life, were chiefly peasants and yeomen of Saxon
descent, and were generally supposed to respect the
persons and property of their countrymen.

As the travellers journeyed on their way, they
were alarmed by repeated cries for assistance; and
when they rode up to the place from whence they

came, they were surprised to find a horse-litter
placed upon the ground, beside which sat a young
woman, richly dressed in the Jewish fashion, while
an old man, whose yellow cap proclaimed him to
belong to the same nation, walked up and down
with gestures expressive of the deepest despair, and
wrung his hands as if affected by some strange
disaster.

To the inquiries of Athelstane and Cedric, the
old Jew could for some time only answer by in-
voking the protection of all the patriarchs of the
Old Testament successively against the sons of
Ishmael, who were coming to smite them, hip and
thigh, with the edge of the sword. When he began
to come to himself out of this agony of terror, Isaac
of York (for it was our old friend) was at length
able to explain that he had hired a body-guard of
six men at Ashby, together with mules for carrying
the litter of a sick friend. This party had undertaken to escort him as far as Doncaster. They had
come thus far in safety; but, having received information from a wood-cutter that there was a
strong band of outlaws lying in wait in the woods
before them, Isaac's mercenaries had not only taken
flight, but had carried off with them the horses
which bore the litter, and left the Jew and his
daughter without the means either of defence or of
retreat, to be plundered, and probably murdered,
by the banditti, whom they expected every moment
would bring down upon them. 'Would it but
please your valours,' added Isaac, in a tone of deep
humiliation, 'to permit the poor Jews to travel
under your safeguard, I swear by the tables of our
Law that never has favour been conferred upon a
child of Israel since the days of our captivity which
shall be more gratefully acknowledged.'

'Dog of a Jew!' said Athelstane, whose memory
was of that petty kind which stores up trifles of all
kinds, but particularly trifling offences, 'dost not

remember how thou didst beard us in the gallery at
the tilt-yard? Fight or flee, or compound with the
outlaws as thou dost list, ask neither aid nor company from us; and if they rob only such as thee,
who rob all the world, I, for mine own share, shall
hold them right honest folk.'

Cedric did not assent to the severe proposal of
his companion. 'We shall do better,' said he, 'to
leave them two of our attendants and two horses
to convey them back to the next village. It will
diminish our strength but little; and with your
good sword, noble Athelstane, and the aid of those
who remain, it will be light work for us to face
twenty of those runagates.'

Rowena, somewhat alarmed by the mention of outlaws in force, and so near them, strongly seconded
the proposal of her guardian. But Rebecca, suddenly quitting her dejected posture, and making her
way through the attendants to the palfrey of the
Saxon lady, knelt down, and, after the Oriental
fashion in addressing superiors, kissed the hem of
Rowena's garment. Then rising and throwing back
her veil, she implored her in the great name of the
God whom they both worshipped, and by that
revelation of the Law upon Mount Sinai in which
they both believed, that she would have compassion
upon them, and suffer them to go forward under
their safeguard. 'It is not for myself that I pray
this favour,' said Rebecca; 'nor is it even for that
poor old man. I know, that to wrong and to spoil
our nation is a light fault, if not a merit, with the
Christians; and what is it to us whether it be done
in the city, in the desert, or in the field? But it is
in the name of one dear to many, and dear even to
you, that I beseech you to let this sick person be
transported with care and tenderness under your
protection. For, if evil chance him, the last moment
of your life would be embittered with regret for
denying that which I ask of you.'

The noble and solemn air with which Rebecca made this appeal gave it double weight with the fair Saxon.

'The man is old and feeble,' she said to her guardian, 'the maiden young and beautiful, their friend sick and in peril of his life; Jews though they be, we cannot as Christians leave them in this extremity. Let them unload two of the sumpter mules and put the baggage behind two of the serfs. The mules may transport the litter, and we have led horses for the old man and his daughter.'

Cedric readily assented to what she proposed, and Athelstane only added the condition, 'That they should travel in the rear of the whole party, where Wamba,' he said, 'might attend them with his shield of boar's brawn.'

'I have left my shield in the tilt-yard,' answered the Jester, 'as has been the fate of many a better knight than myself.'

Athelstane coloured deeply, for such had been his own fate on the last day of the tournament; while Rowena, who was pleased in the same proportion, as if to make amends for the brutal jest of her unfeeling suitor, requested Rebecca to ride by her side.

'It were not fit I should do so,' answered Rebecca, with proud humility, 'where my society might be held a disgrace to my protectress.'

By this time the change of baggage was hastily achieved; for the single word 'outlaws' rendered every one sufficiently alert, and the approach of twilight made the sound yet more impressive. Amid the bustle, Gurth was taken from horseback, in the course of which removal he prevailed upon the Jester to slack the cord with which his arms were bound. It was so negligently refastened, perhaps intentionally, on the part of Wamba, that Gurth found no difficulty in freeing his arms altogether from bondage, and then, gliding into the thicket, he made his escape from the party.

The bustle had been considerable, and it was
some time before Gurth was missed; for, as he was
to be placed for the rest of the journey behind a
servant, every one supposed that some other of his
companions had him under his custody, and when
it began to be whispered among them that Gurth
had actually disappeared, they were under such
immediate expectation of an attack from the outlaws that it was not held convenient to pay much
attention to the circumstance.

The path upon which the party travelled was now
so narrow as not to admit, with any sort of convenience, above two riders abreast, and began to
descend into a dingle, traversed by a brook whose
banks were broken, swampy, and overgrown with
dwarf willows. Cedric and Athelstane, who were
at the head of their retinue, saw the risk of being
attacked at this pass; but neither of them having
had much practice in war, no better mode of pre-
venting the danger occurred to them than that they
should hasten through the defile as fast as possible.
Advancing, therefore, without much order, they
had just crossed the brook with a part of their
followers, when they were assailed in front, flank,
and rear at once, with an impetuosity to which, in
their confused and ill-prepared condition, it was
impossible to offer effectual resistance. The shout
of 'A white dragon!—a white dragon! St. George
for merry England!' war-cries adopted by the
assailants, as belonging to their assumed character
of Saxon outlaws, was heard on every side, and on
every side enemies appeared with a rapidity of
advance and attack which seemed to multiply their
numbers.

Both the Saxon chiefs were made prisoners at the
same moment, and each under circumstances expressive of his character. Cedric, the instant that
an enemy appeared, launched at him his remaining
javelin, which, taking better effect than that which

he had hurled at Fangs, nailed the man against an oak-tree that happened to be close behind him. Thus far successful, Cedric spurred his horse against a second, drawing his sword at the same time, and striking with such inconsiderate fury that his weapon encountered a thick branch which hung over him, and he was disarmed by the violence of his own blow. He was instantly made prisoner, and pulled from his horse by two or three of the banditti who crowded around him. Athelstane shared his captivity, his bridle having been seized and he himself forcibly dismounted long before he could draw his weapon or assume any posture of effectual defence.

The attendants, embarrassed with baggage, surprised and terrified at the fate of their masters, fell an easy prey to the assailants; while the Lady Rowena, in the centre of the cavalcade, and the Jew and his daughter in the rear, experienced the same misfortune.

Of all the train none escaped except Wamba, who showed upon the occasion much more courage than those who pretended to greater sense. He possessed himself of a sword belonging to one of the domestics, who was just drawing it with a tardy and irresolute hand, laid it about him like a lion, drove back several who approached him, and made a brave though ineffectual attempt to succour his master. Finding himself overpowered, the Jester at length threw himself from his horse, plunged into the thicket, and, favoured by the general confusion, escaped from the scene of action.

Yet the valiant Jester, as soon as he found himself safe, hesitated more than once whether he should not turn back and share the captivity of a master to whom he was sincerely attached.

'I have heard men talk of the blessings of freedom,' he said to himself, 'but I wish any wise man would teach me what use to make of it now that I have it.'

As he pronounced these words aloud, a voice very near him called out in a low and cautious tone, 'Wamba!' and at the same time a dog, which he recognised to be Fangs, jumped up and fawned upon him. 'Gurth!' answered Wamba with the same caution, and the swineherd immediately stood before him.

'What is the matter?' said he, eagerly; 'what mean these cries and that clashing of swords?'

'Only a trick of the times,' said Wamba; 'they are all prisoners.'

'Who are prisoners?' exclaimed Gurth, impatiently.

'My lord, and my lady, and Athelstane, and Hundebert, and Oswald.'

'In the name of God!' said Gurth, 'how came they prisoners? and to whom?'

'Our master was too ready to fight,' said the Jester, 'and Athelstane was not ready enough, and no other person was ready at all. And they are prisoners to green cassocks and black visors. And they lie all tumbled about on the green, like the crab-apples that you shake down to your swine. And I would laugh at it,' said the honest Jester, 'if I could for weeping.' And he shed tears of unfeigned sorrow.

Gurth's countenance kindled. 'Wamba,' he said, 'thou hast a weapon, and thy heart was ever stronger than thy brain; we are only two, but a sudden attack from men of resolution will do much; follow me!'

'Whither? and for what purpose?' said the Jester.

'To rescue Cedric.'

'But you have renounced his service but now,' said Wamba.

'That,' said Gurth, 'was but while he was fortunate; follow me!'

As the Jester was about to obey, a third person

suddenly made his appearance and commanded them both to halt. From his dress and arms, Wamba would have conjectured him to be one of those outlaws who had just assailed his master; but, besides that he wore no mask, the glittering baldric across his shoulder, with the rich bugle-horn which it supported, as well as the calm and commanding expression of his voice and manner, made him, notwithstanding the twilight, recognise Locksley, the yeoman who had been victorious, under such disadvantageous circumstances, in the contest for the prize of archery.

'What is the meaning of all this,' said he, 'or who is it that rifle, and ransom, and make prisoners in these forests?'

'You may look at their cassocks close by,' said Wamba, 'and see whether they be thy children's coats or no; for they are as like thine own as one green pea-cod is to another.'

'I will learn that presently,' answered Locksley; 'and I charge ye, on peril of your lives, not to stir from the place where ye stand, until I have returned. Obey me, and it shall be the better for you and your masters. Yet stay, I must render myself as like these men as possible.'

So saying, he unbuckled his baldric with the bugle, took a feather from his cap, and gave them to Wamba; then drew a vizard from his pouch, and repeating his charges to them to stand fast, went to execute his purposes of reconnoitring.

'Shall we stand fast, Gurth?' said Wamba, 'or shall we e'en give him leg-bail? In my foolish mind, he had all the equipage of a thief too much in readiness to be himself a true man.'

'Let him be the devil,' said Gurth, 'an he will. We can be no worse of waiting his return. If he belong to that party, he must already have given them the alarm, and it will avail nothing either to fight or fly. Besides, I have late experience that

arrant thieves are not the worst men in the world
to have to deal with.'

The yeoman returned in the course of a few
minutes.

'Friend Gurth,' he said, 'I have mingled among
yon men, and have learnt to whom they belong,
and whither they are bound. There is, I think, no
chance that they will proceed to any actual violence
against their prisoners. For three men to attempt
them at this moment were little else than madness;
for they are good men of war, and have, as such,
placed sentinels to give the alarm when any one
approaches. But I trust soon to gather such a
force as may act in defiance of all their precautions.
You are both servants, and, as I think, faithful
servants, of Cedric the Saxon, the friend of the
rights of Englishmen. He shall not want English
hands to help him in this extremity. Come, then,
with me, until I gather more aid.'

So saying, he walked through the wood at a
great pace, followed by the jester and the swineherd. It was not consistent with Wamba's humour
to travel long in silence.

'I think,' said he, looking at the baldric and
bugle which he still carried, 'that I saw the arrow
shot which won this gay prize, and that not so long
since as Christmas.'

'And I,' said Gurth, 'could take it on my halidome that I have heard the voice of the good yeoman
who won it, by night as well as by day, and that
the moon is not three days older since I did so.'

'Mine honest friends,' replied the yeoman, 'who
or what I am is little to the present purpose; should
I free your master, you will have reason to think
me the best friend you have ever had in your lives.
And whether I am known by one name or another,
or whether I can draw a bow as well or better than
a cow-keeper, or whether it is my pleasure to walk
in sunshine or by moonlight, are matters which, as

they do not concern you, so neither need ye busy yourselves respecting them.'

'Our heads are in the lion's mouth,' said Wamba, in a whisper to Gurth, 'get them out how we can.'

'Hush—be silent,' said Gurth. 'Offend him not by thy folly, and I trust sincerely that all will go well.'

CHAPTER XX

When autumn nights were long and drear,
And forest walks were dark and dim,
How sweet on the...

To waked Morrow's Hymn.

It was after three hours' good walking that the servants of Cedric, with their mysterious guide, arrived at a small opening in the forest, in the centre of which grew an oak-tree of enormous magnitude, throwing its twisted branches in every direction. Beneath this tree four or five yeomen lay stretched on the ground, while another, as sentinel, walked to and fro in the moonlight shade.

Upon hearing the sound of feet approaching, the watch instantly gave the alarm, and the sleepers as suddenly started up and bent their bows. Six arrows placed on the string were pointed towards the quarter from which the travellers approached, when their guide, being recognised, was welcomed with every token of respect and attachment, and all signs and fears of a rough reception at once subsided.

'Where is the Miller?' was his first question.

'On the road toward Rotherham.'

'With how many?' demanded the leader, for such he appeared to be.

they do not concern you, or neither could you busy
yourselves respecting them.'
'Our heads are in the lion's mouth,' said Gurth,
in a whisper to Wamba, 'get them out how we can.'
'Hush—be silent,' said Gurth. 'Offend him not
by thy folly; and I trust sincerely that all will go
well.'

CHAPTER XX

When autumn nights were long and drear,
  And forest walks were dark and dim,
How sweetly on the pilgrim's ear
  Was wont to steal the hermit's hymn!

Devotion borrows Music's tone,
  And Music took Devotion's wing;
And, like the bird that hails the sun,
  They soar to heaven, and soaring sing.
        The Hermit of St. Clement's Well.

IT was after three hours' good walking that the
servants of Cedric, with their mysterious guide,
arrived at a small opening in the forest, in the
centre of which grew an oak-tree of enormous
magnitude, throwing its twisted branches in every
direction. Beneath this tree four or five yeomen
lay stretched on the ground, while another, as
sentinel, walked to and fro in the moonlight shade.

Upon hearing the sound of feet approaching, the
watch instantly gave the alarm, and the sleepers as
suddenly started up and bent their bows. Six
arrows placed on the string were pointed towards
the quarter from which the travellers approached,
when their guide, being recognised, was welcomed
with every token of respect and attachment, and all
signs and fears of a rough reception at once subsided.

'Where is the Miller?' was his first question.

'On the road towards Rotherham.'

'With how many?' demanded the leader, for
such he seemed to be.

'With six men, and good hope of booty, if it please St. Nicholas.'

'Devoutly spoken,' said Locksley; 'and where is Allan-a-Dale?'

'Walked up towards the Watling Street to watch for the Prior of Jorvaulx.'

'That is well thought on also,' replied the Captain; 'and where is the Friar?'

'In his cell.'

'Thither will I go,' said Locksley. 'Disperse and seek your companions. Collect what force you can, for there's game afoot that must be hunted hard, and will turn to bay. Meet me here by daybreak. And, stay,' he added, 'I have forgotten what is most necessary of the whole. Two of you take the road quickly towards Torquilstone, the castle of Front-de-Bœuf. A set of gallants, who have been masquerading in such guise as our own, are carrying a band of prisoners thither. Watch them closely, for even if they reach the castle before we collect our force, our honour is concerned to punish them, and we will find means to do so. Keep a close watch on them, therefore; and despatch one of your comrades, the lightest of foot, to bring the news of the yeomen thereabout.'

They promised implicit obedience, and departed with alacrity on their different errands. In the meanwhile, their leader and his two companions, who now looked upon him with great respect, as well as some fear, pursued their way to the chapel of Copmanhurst.

When they had reached the little moonlight glade, having in front the reverend though ruinous chapel and the rude hermitage, so well suited to ascetic devotion, Wamba whispered to Gurth, 'If this be the habitation of a thief, it makes good the old proverb, "The nearer the church the farther from God." And by my cockscomb,' he added, 'I think it be even so. Hearken but to the black sanctus which they are singing in the hermitage!'

In fact, the anchorite and his guest were performing, at the full extent of their very powerful lungs, an old drinking song, of which this was the burden:

> 'Come, trowl the brown bowl to me,
>   Bully boy, bully boy,
> Come, trowl the brown bowl to me.
>   Ho! jolly Jenkin, I spy a knave in drinking,
> Come, trowl the brown bowl to me.'

'Now, that is not ill sung,' said Wamba, who had thrown in a few of his own flourishes to help out the chorus. 'But who, in the saint's name, ever expected to have heard such a jolly chant come from out a hermit's cell at midnight!'

'Marry, that should I,' said Gurth, 'for the jolly clerk of Copmanhurst is a known man, and kills half the deer that are stolen in this walk. Men say that the keeper has complained to his official, and that he will be stripped of his cowl and cope altogether if he keep not better order.'

While they were thus speaking, Locksley's loud and repeated knocks had at length disturbed the anchorite and his guest. 'By my beads,' said the hermit, stopping short in a grand flourish, 'here come more benighted guests. I would not for my cowl that they found us in this goodly exercise. All men have their enemies, good Sir Sluggard; and there be those malignant enough to construe the hospitable refreshment which I have been offering to you, a weary traveller, for the matter of three short hours, into sheer drunkenness and debauchery, vices alike alien to my profession and my disposition.'

'Base calumniators!' replied the knight; 'I would I had the chastising of them. Nevertheless, Holy Clerk, it is true that all have their enemies; and there be those in this very land whom I would rather speak to through the bars of my helmet than barefaced.'

'Get thine iron pot on thy head then, friend Sluggard, as quickly as thy nature will permit,' said the hermit, 'while I remove these pewter flagons, whose late contents run strangely in mine own pate; and to drown the clatter—for, in faith, I feel somewhat unsteady—strike into the tune which thou hearest me sing. It is no matter for the words; I scarce know them myself.'

So saying, he struck up a thundering *De profundis clamavi*, under cover of which he removed the apparatus of their banquet; while the knight, laughing heartily, and arming himself all the while, assisted his host with his voice from time to time as his mirth permitted.

'What devil's matins are you after at this hour?' said a voice from without.

'Heaven forgive you, Sir Traveller!' said the hermit, whose own noise, and perhaps his nocturnal potations, prevented from recognising accents which were tolerably familiar to him. 'Wend on your way, in the name of God and St. Dunstan, and disturb not the devotions of me and my holy brother.'

'Mad priest,' answered the voice from without, 'open to Locksley!'

'All's safe—all's right,' said the hermit to his companion.

'But who is he?' said the Black Knight; 'it imports me much to know.'

'Who is he!' answered the hermit; 'I tell thee he is a friend.'

'But what friend?' answered the knight; 'for he may be friend to thee and none of mine?'

'What friend!' replied the hermit; 'that, now, is one of the questions that is more easily asked than answered. What friend! why, he is, now that I bethink me a little, the very same honest keeper I told thee of a while since.'

'Ay, as honest a keeper as thou art a pious hermit,' replied the knight, 'I doubt it not. But undo the door to him before he beat it from its hinges.'

The dogs, in the meantime, which had made a dreadful baying at the commencement of the disturbance, seemed now to recognise the voice of him who stood without; for, totally changing their manner, they scratched and whined at the door, as if interceding for his admission. The hermit speedily unbolted his portal, and admitted Locksley, with his two companions.

'Why, hermit,' was the yeoman's first question as soon as he beheld the knight, 'what boon companion hast thou here?'

'A brother of our order,' replied the Friar, shaking his head; 'we have been at our orisons all night.'

'He is a monk of the church militant, I think,' answered Locksley; 'and there be more of them abroad. I tell thee, Friar, thou must lay down the rosary and take up the quarter-staff; we shall need every one of our merry men, whether clerk or layman. But,' he added, taking him a step aside, 'art thou mad? to give admittance to a knight thou dost not know? Hast thou forgot our articles?'

'Not know him!' replied the Friar, boldly, 'I know him as well as the beggar knows his dish.'

'And what is his name, then?' demanded Locksley.

'His name,' said the hermit—'his name is Sir Anthony of Scrabelstone; as if I would drink with a man, and did not know his name!'

'Thou hast been drinking more than enough, Friar,' said the woodsman, 'and, I fear, prating more than enough too.'

'Good yeoman,' said the knight, coming forward, 'be not wroth with my merry host. He did but afford me the hospitality which I would have compelled from him if he had refused it.'

'Thou compel!' said the Friar; 'wait but till I have changed this grey gown for a green cassock, and if I make not a quarter-staff ring twelve upon thy pate, I am neither true clerk nor good woodsman.'

While he spoke thus, he stript off his gown, and appeared in a close black buckram doublet and drawers, over which he speedily did on a cassock of green and hose of the same colour. 'I pray thee, truss my points,' said he to Wamba, 'and thou shalt have a cup of sack for thy labour.'

'Gramercy for thy sack,' said Wamba; 'but think'st thou it is lawful for me to aid you to transmew thyself from a holy hermit into a sinful forester?'

'Never fear,' said the hermit; 'I will but confess the sins of my green cloak to my grey friar's frock, and all shall be well again.'

'Amen!' answered the Jester. 'A broadcloth penitent should have a sackcloth confessor, and your frock may absolve my motley doublet into the bargain.'

So saying, he accommodated the Friar with his assistance in tying the endless number of points, as the laces which attached the hose to the doublet were then termed.

While they were thus employed, Locksley led the knight a little apart, and addressed him thus: 'Deny it not, Sir Knight, you are he who decided the victory to the advantage of the English against the strangers on the second day of the tournament at Ashby.'

'And what follows if you guess truly, good yeoman?' replied the knight.

'I should in that case hold you,' replied the yeoman, 'a friend to the weaker party.'

'Such is the duty of a true knight at least,' replied the Black Champion; 'and I would not willingly that there were reason to think otherwise of me.'

'But for my purpose,' said the yeoman, 'thou shouldst be as well a good Englishman as a good knight; for that which I have to speak of concerns, indeed, the duty of every honest man, but is more especially that of a true-born native of England.'

'You can speak to no one,' replied the knight, 'to whom England, and the life of every Englishman, can be dearer than to me.'

'I would willingly believe so,' said the woodsman, 'for never had this country such need to be supported by those who love her. Hear me, and I will tell thee of an enterprise in which, if thou be'st really that which thou seemest, thou mayst take an honourable part. A band of villains, in the disguise of better men than themselves, have made themselves master of the person of a noble Englishman, called Cedric the Saxon, together with his ward and his friend Athelstane of Coningsburgh, and have transported them to a castle in this forest called Torquilstone. I ask of thee, as a good knight and a good Englishman, wilt thou aid in their rescue?'

'I am bound by my vow to do so,' replied the knight; 'but I would willingly know who you are, who request my assistance in their behalf?'

'I am,' said the forester, 'a nameless man; but I am the friend of my country, and of my country's friends. With this account of me you must for the present remain satisfied, the more especially since you yourself desire to continue unknown. Believe, however, that my word, when pledged, is as inviolate as if I wore golden spurs.'

'I willingly believe it,' said the knight; 'I have been accustomed to study men's countenances, and I can read in thine honesty and resolution. I will, therefore, ask thee no further questions, but aid thee in setting at freedom these oppressed captives; which done, I trust we shall part better acquainted, and well satisfied with each other.'

'So,' said Wamba to Gurth; for the Friar being now fully equipped, the Jester, having approached to the other side of the hut, had heard the conclusion of the conversation, 'so we have got a new ally? I trust the valour of the knight will be truer metal than the religion of the hermit or the honesty of the yeoman; for this Locksley looks like a born deer-stealer, and the priest like a lusty hypocrite.'

'Hold thy peace, Wamba,' said Gurth; 'it may all be as thou dost guess; but were the horned devil to rise and proffer me his assistance to set at liberty Cedric and the Lady Rowena, I fear I should hardly have religion enough to refuse the foul fiend's offer, and bid him get behind me.'

The Friar was now completely accoutred as a yeoman, with sword and buckler, bow and quiver, and a strong partizan over his shoulder. He left his cell at the head of the party, and, having carefully locked the door, deposited the key under the threshold.

'Art thou in condition to do good service, Friar,' said Locksley, 'or does the brown bowl still run in thy head?'

'Not more than a draught of St. Dunstan's fountain will allay,' answered the priest; 'something there is of a whizzing in my brain, and of instability in my legs, but you shall presently see both pass away.'

So saying, he stepped to the stone basin, in which the waters of the fountain as they fell formed bubbles which danced in the white moonlight, and took so long a draught as if he had meant to exhaust the spring.

'When didst thou drink as deep a draught of water before, Holy Clerk of Copmanhurst?' said the Black Knight.

'Never since my wine butt leaked, and let out its liquor by an illegal vent,' replied the Friar, 'and so left me nothing to drink but my patron's bounty here.'

Then plunging his hands and head into the fountain, he washed from them all marks of the midnight revel.

Thus refreshed and sobered, the jolly priest twirled his heavy partizan round his head with three fingers, as if he had been balancing a reed, exclaiming at the same time, 'Where be those false ravishers who carry off wenches against their will? May the foul fiend fly off with me, if I am not man enough for a dozen of them.'

'Swearest thou, Holy Clerk?' said the Black Knight.

'Clerk me no clerks,' replied the transformed priest; 'by St. George and the Dragon, I am no longer a shaveling than while my frock is on my back. When I am cased in my green cassock, I will drink, swear, and woo a lass with any blythe forester in the West Riding.'

'Come on, Jack Priest,' said Locksley, 'and be silent; thou art as noisy as a whole convent on a holy eve, when the Father Abbot has gone to bed. Come on you, too, my masters, tarry not to talk of it—I say, come on; we must collect all our forces, and few enough we shall have, if we are to storm the castle of Reginald Front-de-Bœuf.'

'What! is it Front-de-Bœuf,' said the Black Knight, 'who has stopt on the king's highway the king's liege subjects? Is he turned thief and oppressor?'

'Oppressor he ever was,' said Locksley.

'And for thief,' said the priest, 'I doubt if ever he were even half so honest a man as many a thief of my acquaintance.'

'Move on, priest, and be silent,' said the yeoman; 'it were better you led the way to the place of rendezvous than say what should be left unsaid, both in decency and prudence.'

CHAPTER XXI

Alas, how many hours and years have past,
Since human forms have round this table sate,
Or lamp, or taper, on its surface gleam'd!
Methinks, I hear the sound of time long pass'd
Still murmuring o'er us, in the lofty void
Of these dark arches, like the ling'ring voices
Of those who long within their graves have slept.
                                    Orra, a Tragedy.

WHILE these measures were taking in behalf of
Cedric and his companions, the armed men by
whom the latter had been seized hurried their captives along towards the place of security where they
intended to imprison them. But darkness came on
fast, and the paths of the wood seemed but imperfectly known to the marauders. They were compelled to make several long halts, and once or twice
to return on their road to resume the direction which
they wished to pursue. The summer morn had
dawned upon them ere they could travel in full
assurance that they held the right path. But confidence returned with light, and the cavalcade now
moved rapidly forward. Meanwhile, the following
dialogue took place between the two leaders of the
banditti :—

'It is time thou shouldst leave us, Sir Maurice,'
said the Templar to De Bracy, 'in order to prepare
the second part of thy mystery. Thou art next,
thou knowest, to act the Knight Deliverer.'

'I have thought better of it,' said De Bracy ; 'I
241

will not leave thee till the prize is fairly deposited
in Front-de-Bœuf's castle. There will I appear
before the Lady Rowena in mine own shape, and
trust that she will set down to the vehemence of my
passion the violence of which I have been guilty.'

'And what has made thee change thy plan, De
Bracy?' replied the Knight Templar.

'That concerns thee nothing,' answered his
companion.

'I would hope, however, Sir Knight,' said the
Templar, 'that this alteration of measures arises
from no suspicion of my honourable meaning, such
as Fitzurse endeavoured to instil into thee?'

'My thoughts are my own,' answered De Bracy;
'the fiend laughs, they say, when one thief robs
another; and we know, that were he to spit fire and
brimstone instead, it would never prevent a Templar
from following his bent.'

'Or the leader of a Free Company,' answered the
Templar, 'from dreading at the hands of a comrade
and friend the injustice he does to all mankind.'

'This is unprofitable and perilous recrimination,'
answered De Bracy; 'suffice it to say, I know the
morals of the Temple Order, and I will not give
thee the power of cheating me out of the fair prey
for which I have run such risks.'

'Psha,' replied the Templar, 'what hast thou to
fear? Thou knowest the vows of our order.'

'Right well,' said De Bracy, 'and also how they
are kept. Come, Sir Templar, the laws of gallantry
have a liberal interpretation in Palestine, and this
is a case in which I will trust nothing to your
conscience.'

'Hear the truth, then,' said the Templar; 'I care
not for your blue-eyed beauty. There is in that
train one who will make me a better mate.'

'What! wouldst thou stoop to the waiting
damsel?' said De Bracy.

'No, Sir Knight,' said the Templar, haughtily.

'To the waiting-woman will I not stoop. I have a prize among the captives as lovely as thine own.'

'By the mass, thou meanest the fair Jewess!' said De Bracy.

'And if I do,' said Bois-Guilbert, 'who shall gainsay me?'

'No one that I know,' said De Bracy, 'unless it be your vow of celibacy or a check of conscience for an intrigue with a Jewess.'

'For my vow,' said the Templar, 'our Grand Master hath granted me a dispensation. And for my conscience, a man that has slain three hundred Saracens need not reckon up every little failing, like a village girl at her first confession upon Good Friday eve.'

'Thou knowest best thine own privileges,' said De Bracy. 'Yet, I would have sworn thy thought had been more on the old usurer's money-bags than on the black eyes of the daughter.'

'I can admire both,' answered the Templar; 'besides, the old Jew is but half-prize. I must share his spoils with Front-de-Bœuf, who will not lend us the use of his castle for nothing. I must have something that I can term exclusively my own by this foray of ours, and I have fixed on the lovely Jewess as my peculiar prize. But, now thou knowest my drift, thou wilt resume thine own original plan, wilt thou not? Thou hast nothing, thou seest, to fear from my interference.'

'No,' replied De Bracy, 'I will remain beside my prize. What thou sayst is passing true, but I like not the privileges acquired by the dispensation of the Grand Master, and the merit acquired by the slaughter of three hundred Saracens. You have too good a right to a free pardon to render you very scrupulous about peccadilloes.'

While this dialogue was proceeding, Cedric was endeavouring to wring out of those who guarded him an avowal of their character and purpose. 'You

should be Englishmen,' said he; 'and yet, sacred
Heaven! you prey upon your countrymen as if you
were very Normans. You should be my neighbours,
and, if so, my friends; for which of my English
neighbours have reason to be otherwise? I tell ye,
yeomen, that even those among ye who have been
branded with outlawry have had from me protection;
for I have pitied their miseries, and curst the
oppression of their tyrannic nobles. What, then,
would you have of me? or in what can this violence
serve ye? Ye are worse than brute beasts in your
actions, and will you imitate them in their very
dumbness?'

It was in vain that Cedric expostulated with his
guards, who had too many good reasons for their
silence to be induced to break it either by his wrath
or his expostulations. They continued to hurry
him along, travelling at a very rapid rate, until, at
the end of an avenue of huge trees, arose Torquilstone, now the hoary and ancient castle of Reginald
Front-de-Bœuf. It was a fortress of no great size,
consisting of a donjon, or large and high square
tower, surrounded by buildings of inferior height,
which were encircled by an inner courtyard. Around
the exterior wall was a deep moat, supplied with
water from a neighbouring rivulet. Front-de-Bœuf,
whose character placed him often at feud with his
enemies, had made considerable additions to the
strength of his castle, by building towers upon the
outward wall, so as to flank it at every angle. The
access, as usual in castles of the period, lay through
an arched barbican, or outwork, which was terminated and defended by a small turret at each corner.

Cedric no sooner saw the turrets of Front-de-
Bœuf's castle raise their grey and moss-grown
battlements, glimmering in the morning sun above
the wood by which they were surrounded, than he
instantly augured more truly concerning the cause
of his misfortune.

'I did injustice,' he said, 'to the thieves and outlaws of these woods, when I supposed such banditti
to belong to their bands; I might as justly have
confounded the foxes of these brakes with the raven-
ing wolves of France. Tell me, dogs, is it my life
or my wealth that your master aims at? Is it too
much that two Saxons, myself and the noble Athelstane, should hold land in the country which was
once the patrimony of our race? Put us, then, to
death, and complete your tyranny by taking our
lives, as you began with our liberties. If the Saxon
Cedric cannot rescue England, he is willing to die
for her. Tell your tyrannical master, I do only
beseech him to dismiss the Lady Rowena in honour
and safety. She is a woman, and he need not dread
her; and with us will die all who dare fight in her
cause.'

The attendants remained as mute to this address
as to the former, and they now stood before the gate
of the castle. De Bracy winded his horn three
times, and the archers and crossbow men, who
had manned the wall upon seeing their approach,
hastened to lower the drawbridge and admit them.
The prisoners were compelled by their guards to
alight, and were conducted to an apartment where
a hasty repast was offered them, of which none but
Athelstane felt any inclination to partake. Neither
had the descendant of the Confessor much time to
do justice to the good cheer placed before them, for
their guards gave him and Cedric to understand
that they were to be imprisoned in a chamber apart
from Rowena. Resistance was vain; and they were
compelled to follow to a large room, which, rising
on clumsy Saxon pillars, resembled those refectories
and chapter-houses which may be still seen in the
most ancient parts of our most ancient monasteries.

The Lady Rowena was next separated from her
train, and conducted, with courtesy, indeed, but still
without consulting her inclination, to a distant

apartment. The same alarming distinction was
conferred on Rebecca, in spite of her father's entreaties, who offered even money, in this extremity
of distress, that she might be permitted to abide
with him. 'Base unbeliever,' answered one of his
guards, 'when thou hast seen thy lair, thou wilt not
wish thy daughter to partake it.' And, without
farther discussion, the old Jew was forcibly dragged
off in a different direction from the other prisoners.
The domestics, after being carefully searched and
disarmed, were confined in another part of the
castle; and Rowena was refused even the comfort
she might have derived from the attendance of her
handmaiden Elgitha.

The apartment in which the Saxon chiefs were
confined, for to them we turn our first attention,
although at present used as a sort of guard-room,
had formerly been the great hall of the castle. It
was now abandoned to meaner purposes, because
the present lord, among other conditions to the
convenience, security, and beauty of his baronial
residence, had erected a new and noble hall, whose
vaulted roof was supported by lighter and more
elegant pillars, and fitted up with that higher
degree of ornament which the Normans had already
introduced into architecture.

Cedric paced the apartment, filled with indignant
reflections on the past and on the present, while
the apathy of his companion served, instead of
patience and philosophy, to defend him against
everything save the inconvenience of the present
moment; and so little did he feel even this last,
that he was only from time to time roused to a
reply by Cedric's animated and impassioned appeal
to him.

'Yes,' said Cedric, half speaking to himself and
half addressing himself to Athelstane, 'it was in
this very hall that my [grand-]father feasted with
Torquil Wolfganger, when he entertained the

valiant and unfortunate Harold, then advancing against the Norwegians, who had united themselves to the rebel Tosti. It was in this hall that Harold returned the magnanimous answer to the ambassador of his rebel brother. Oft have I heard my father kindle as he told the tale. The envoy of Tosti was admitted, when this ample room could scarce contain the crowd of noble Saxon leaders who were quaffing the blood-red wine around their monarch.'

'I hope,' said Athelstane, somewhat moved by this part of his friend's discourse, 'they will not forget to send us some wine and refections at noon : we had scarce a breathing-space allowed to break our fast, and I never have the benefit of my food when I eat immediately after dismounting from horseback, though the leeches recommend that practice.'

Cedric went on with his story without noticing this interjectional observation of his friend.

'The envoy of Tosti,' he said, 'moved up the hall, undismayed by the frowning countenances of all around him, until he made his obeisance before the throne of King Harold.'

'"What terms," he said, "Lord King, hath thy brother Tosti to hope, if he should lay down his arms and crave peace at thy hands?"

'"A brother's love," cried the generous Harold, "and the fair earldom of Northumberland."

'"But should Tosti accept these terms," continued the envoy, "what lands shall be assigned to his faithful ally, Hardrada, King of Norway?"

'"Seven feet of English ground," answered Harold, fiercely, "or, as Hardrada is said to be a giant, perhaps we may allow him twelve inches more."

'The hall rung with acclamations, and cup and horn was filled to the Norwegian, who should be speedily in possession of his English territory.'

'I could have pledged him with all my soul,' said Athelstane, 'for my tongue cleaves to my palate.

'The baffled envoy,' continued Cedric, pursuing with animation his tale, though it interested not the listener, 'retreated, to carry to Tosti and his ally the ominous answer of his injured brother. It was then that the distant towers of York and the bloody streams of the Derwent beheld that direful conflict, in which, after displaying the most undaunted valour, the King of Norway and Tosti both fell, with ten thousand of their bravest followers. Who would have thought that, upon the proud day when this battle was won, the very gale which waved the Saxon banners in triumph was filling the Norman sails, and impelling them to the fatal shores of Sussex? Who would have thought that Harold, within a few brief days, would himself possess no more of his kingdom than the share which he allotted in his wrath to the Norwegian invader? Who would have thought that you, noble Athelstane—that you, descended of Harold's blood, and that I, whose father was not the worst defender of the Saxon crown, should be prisoners to a vile Norman, in the very hall in which our ancestors held such high festival?'

'It is sad enough,' replied Athelstane; 'but I trust they will hold us to a moderate ransom. At any rate, it cannot be their purpose to starve us outright; and yet, although it is high noon, I see no preparations for serving dinner. Look up at the window, noble Cedric, and judge by the sunbeams if it is not on the verge of noon.'

'It may be so,' answered Cedric; 'but I cannot look on that stained lattice without its awakening other reflections than those which concern the passing moment or its privations. When that window was wrought, my noble friend, our hardy fathers knew not the art of making glass, or of staining it.

The pride of Wolfganger's father brought an artist from Normandy to adorn his hall with this new species of emblazonment, that breaks the golden light of God's blessed day into so many fantastic hues. The foreigner came here poor, beggarly, cringing, and subservient, ready to doff his cap to the meanest native of the household. He returned pampered and proud to tell his rapacious countrymen of the wealth and the simplicity of the Saxon nobles—a folly, oh Athelstane! foreboded of old, as well as foreseen by those descendants of Hengist and his hardy tribes who retained the simplicity of their manners. We made these strangers our bosom friends, our confidential servants; we borrowed their artists and their arts, and despised the honest simplicity and hardihood with which our brave ancestors supported themselves; and we became enervated by Norman arts long ere we fell under Norman arms. Far better was our homely diet, eaten in peace and liberty, than the luxurious dainties, the love of which hath delivered us as bondsmen to the foreign conqueror!'

'I should,' replied Athelstane, 'hold very humble diet a luxury at present; and it astonishes me, noble Cedric, that you can bear so truly in mind the memory of past deeds, when it appeareth you forget the very hour of dinner.'

'It is time lost,' muttered Cedric apart and impatiently, 'to speak to him of aught else but that which concerns his appetite! The soul of Hardicanute hath taken possession of him, and he hath no pleasure save to fill, to swill, and to call for more. Alas!' said he, looking at Athelstane with compassion, 'that so dull a spirit should be lodged in so goodly a form! Alas! that such an enterprise as the regeneration of England should turn on a hinge so imperfect! Wedded to Rowena, indeed, her nobler and more generous soul may yet awake the better nature which is torpid within him. Yet how should this be, while Rowena, Athelstane, and I myself remain the prisoners of this brutal marauder, and have been made so perhaps from a sense of the dangers which our liberty might bring to the usurped power of his nation?'

While the Saxon was plunged in these painful reflections, the door of their prison opened and gave entrance to a sewer, holding his white rod of office. This important person advanced into the chamber with a grave pace, followed by four attendants, bearing in a table covered with dishes, the sight and smell of which seemed to be an instant compensation to Athelstane for all the inconvenience he had undergone. The persons who attended on the feast were masked and cloaked.

'What mummery is this?' said Cedric; 'think you that we are ignorant whose prisoners we are, when we are in the castle of your master? Tell him,' he continued, willing to use this opportunity to open a negotiation for his freedom—'tell your master, Reginald Front-de-Bœuf, that we know no reason he can have for withholding our liberty, excepting his unlawful desire to enrich himself at our expense. Tell him that we yield to his rapacity, as in similar circumstances we should do to that of a literal robber. Let him name the ransom at which he rates our liberty, and it shall be paid, providing the exaction is suited to our means.'

The sewer made no answer, but bowed his head.

'And tell Sir Reginald Front-de-Bœuf,' said Athelstane, 'that I send him my mortal defiance, and challenge him to combat with me, on foot or horseback, at any secure place, within eight days after our liberation; which, if he be a true knight, he will not, under these circumstances, venture to refuse or to delay.'

'I shall deliver to the knight your defiance,' answered the sewer; 'meanwhile I leave you to your food.'

The challenge of Athelstane was delivered with no good grace; for a large mouthful, which required the exercise of both jaws at once, added to a natural hesitation, considerably damped the effect of the bold defiance it contained. Still, however, his speech was hailed by Cedric as an incontestable token of reviving spirit in his companion, whose previous indifference had begun, notwithstanding his respect for Athelstane's descent, to wear out his patience. But he now cordially shook hands with him in token of his approbation, and was somewhat grieved when Athelstane observed, 'That he would fight a dozen such men as Front-de-Bœuf, if by so doing he could hasten his departure from a dungeon where they put so much garlic into their pottage.' Notwithstanding this intimation of a relapse into the apathy of sensuality, Cedric placed himself opposite to Athelstane, and soon showed that, if the distresses of his country could banish the recollection of food while the table was uncovered, yet no sooner were the victuals put there than he proved that the appetite of his Saxon ancestors had descended to him along with their other qualities.

The captives had not long enjoyed their refreshment, however, ere their attention was disturbed even from this most serious occupation by the blast of a horn winded before the gate. It was repeated three times, with as much violence as if it had been blown before an enchanted castle by the destined knight at whose summons halls and towers, barbican and battlement, were to roll off like a morning vapour. The Saxons started from the table and hastened to the window. But their curiosity was disappointed; for these outlets only looked upon the court of the castle, and the sound came from beyond its precincts. The summons, however, seemed of importance, for a considerable degree of bustle instantly took place in the castle.

CHAPTER XXII

My daughter! O my ducats! O my daughter!
  . . . O my Christian ducats!
Justice—the Law—my ducats and my daughter!
                              Merchant of Venice.

LEAVING the Saxon chiefs to return to their banquet
as soon as their ungratified curiosity should permit
them to attend to the calls of their half-satiated
appetite, we have to look in upon the yet more
severe imprisonment of Isaac of York. The poor
Jew had been hastily thrust into a dungeon-vault of
the castle, the floor of which was deep beneath the
level of the ground, and very damp, being lower
than even the moat itself. The only light was
received through one or two loopholes far above
the reach of the captive's hand. These apertures
admitted, even at mid-day, only a dim and uncertain
light, which was changed for utter darkness long
before the rest of the castle had lost the blessing of
day. Chains and shackles, which had been the
portion of former captives, from whom active exertions to escape had been apprehended, hung rusted
and empty on the walls of the prison, and in the
rings of one of those sets of fetters there remained
two mouldering bones, which seemed to have been
once those of the human leg, as if some prisoner
had been left not only to perish there, but to be
consumed to a skeleton.

At one end of this ghastly apartment was a large
fire-grate, over the top of which were stretched
some transverse iron bars, half-devoured with rust.

The whole appearance of the dungeon might have appalled a stouter heart than that of Isaac, who, nevertheless, was more composed under the imminent pressure of danger than he had seemed to be while affected by terrors of which the cause was as yet remote and contingent. The lovers of the chase say that the hare feels more agony during the pursuit of the greyhounds than when she is struggling in their fangs.[1] And thus it is probable that the Jews, by the very frequency of their fear on all occasions, had their minds in some degree prepared for every effort of tyranny which could be practised upon them ; so that no aggression, when it had taken place, could bring with it that surprise which is the most disabling quality of terror. Neither was it the first time that Isaac had been placed in circumstances so dangerous. He had therefore experience to guide him, as well as hope that he might again, as formerly, be delivered as a prey from the fowler. Above all, he had upon his side the unyielding obstinacy of his nation, and that unbending resolution with which Israelites have been frequently known to submit to the uttermost evils which power and violence can inflict upon them, rather than gratify their oppressors by granting their demands.

In this humour of passive resistance, and with his garment collected beneath him to keep his limbs from the wet pavement, Isaac sat in a corner of his dungeon, where his folded hands, his dishevelled hair and beard, his furred cloak and high cap, seen by the wiry and broken light, would have afforded a study for Rembrandt, had that celebrated painter existed at the period. The Jew remained without altering his position for nearly three hours, at the expiry of which steps were heard on the dungeon

[1] *Nota Bene.*—We by no means warrant the accuracy of this piece of natural history, which we give on the authority of the Wardour MS.—L. T.

stair. The bolts screamed as they were withdrawn,
the hinges creaked as the wicket opened, and Reginald Front-de-Bœuf, followed by the two Saracen
slaves of the Templar, entered the prison.

Front-de-Bœuf, a tall and strong man, whose life
had been spent in public war or in private feuds
and broils, and who had hesitated at no means of
extending his feudal power, had features corresponding to his character, and which strongly
expressed the fiercer and more malignant passions
of the mind. The scars with which his visage was
seamed would, on features of a different cast, have
excited the sympathy and veneration due to the
marks of honourable valour; but, in the peculiar
case of Front-de-Bœuf, they only added to the
ferocity of his countenance, and to the dread which
his presence inspired. This formidable baron was
clad in a leathern doublet, fitted close to his body,
which was frayed and soiled with the stains of his
armour. He had no weapon, excepting a poniard
at his belt, which served to counterbalance the
weight of the bunch of rusty keys that hung at
his right side.

The black slaves who attended Front-de-Bœuf
were stripped of their gorgeous apparel, and attired
in jerkins and trowsers of coarse linen, their sleeves
being tucked up above the elbow, like those of
butchers when about to exercise their function in
the slaughter-house. Each had in his hand a small
pannier; and, when they entered the dungeon,
they stopt at the door until Front-de-Bœuf himself
carefully locked and double-locked it. Having
taken this precaution, he advanced slowly up the
apartment towards the Jew, upon whom he kept
his eye fixed, as if he wished to paralyse him with
his glance, as some animals are said to fascinate
their prey. It seemed, indeed, as if the sullen and
malignant eye of Front-de-Bœuf possessed some
portion of that supposed power over his unfortunate

prisoner. The Jew sate with his mouth agape, and his eyes fixed on the savage baron with such earnestness of terror that his frame seemed literally to shrink together, and to diminish in size while encountering the fierce Norman's fixed and baleful gaze. The unhappy Isaac was deprived not only of the power of rising to make the obeisance which his terror dictated, but he could not even doff his cap, or utter any word of supplication; so strongly was he agitated by the conviction that tortures and death were impending over him.

On the other hand, the stately form of the Norman appeared to dilate in magnitude, like that of the eagle, which ruffles up its plumage when about to pounce on its defenceless prey. He paused within three steps of the corner in which the unfortunate Jew had now, as it were, coiled himself up into the smallest possible space, and made a sign for one of the slaves to approach. The black satellite came forward accordingly, and, producing from his basket a large pair of scales and several weights, he laid them at the feet of Front-de-Bœuf, and again retired to the respectful distance at which his companion had already taken his station.

The motions of these men were slow and solemn, as if there impended over their souls some preconception of horror and of cruelty. Front-de-Bœuf himself opened the scene by thus addressing his ill-fated captive.

'Most accursed dog of an accursed race,' he said, awaking with his deep and sullen voice the sullen echoes of his dungeon-vault, 'seest thou these scales?'

The unhappy Jew returned a feeble affirmative.

'In these very scales shalt thou weigh me out,' said the relentless Baron, 'a thousand silver pounds, after the just measure and weight of the Tower of London.'

'Holy Abraham!' returned the Jew, finding voice
through the very extremity of his danger, 'heard
man ever such a demand? Who ever heard, even
in a minstrel's tale, of such a sum as a thousand
pounds of silver? What human sight was ever
blessed with the vision of such a mass of treasure?
Not within the walls of York, ransack my house and
that of all my tribe, wilt thou find the tithe of that
huge sum of silver that thou speakest of.'

'I am reasonable,' answered Front-de-Bœuf, 'and
if silver be scant, I refuse not gold. At the rate of
a mark of gold for each six pounds of silver, thou
shalt free thy unbelieving carcass from such punishment as thy heart has never even conceived.'

'Have mercy on me, noble knight!' exclaimed
Isaac; 'I am old, and poor, and helpless. It were
unworthy to triumph over me. It is a poor deed to
crush a worm.'

'Old thou mayst be,' replied the knight; 'more
shame to their folly who have suffered thee to grow
grey in usury and knavery. Feeble thou mayst be,
for when had a Jew either heart or hand? But rich
it is well known thou art.'

'I swear to you, noble knight,' said the Jew, 'by
all which I believe, and by all which we believe in
common——'

'Perjure not thyself,' said the Norman, interrupting him, 'and let not thine obstinacy seal thy
doom, until thou hast seen and well considered the
fate that awaits thee. Think not I speak to thee
only to excite thy terror, and practise on the base
cowardice thou hast derived from thy tribe. I swear
to thee by that which thou dost NOT believe, by the
Gospel which our church teaches, and by the keys
which are given her to bind and to loose, that my
purpose is deep and peremptory. This dungeon is
no place for trifling. Prisoners ten thousand times
more distinguished than thou have died within these
walls, and their fate hath never been known! But

for thee is reserved a long and lingering death, to which theirs were luxury.'

He again made a signal for the slaves to approach, and spoke to them apart, in their own language ; for he also had been in Palestine, where, perhaps, he had learnt his lesson of cruelty. The Saracens produced from their baskets a quantity of charcoal, a pair of bellows, and a flask of oil. While the one struck a light with a flint and steel, the other disposed the charcoal in the large rusty grate which we have already mentioned, and exercised the bellows until the fuel came to a red glow.

'Seest thou, Isaac,' said Front-de-Bœuf, 'the range of iron bars above that glowing charcoal? On that warm couch thou shalt lie, stripped of thy clothes as if thou wert to rest on a bed of down. One of these slaves shall maintain the fire beneath thee, while the other shall anoint thy wretched limbs with oil, lest the roast should burn. Now, choose betwixt such a scorching bed and the payment of a thousand pounds of silver ; for, by the head of my father, thou hast no other option.'

'It is impossible,' exclaimed the miserable Jew— 'it is impossible that your purpose can be real ! The good God of nature never made a heart capable of exercising such cruelty !'

'Trust not to that, Isaac,' said Front-de-Bœuf, 'it were a fatal error. Dost thou think that I, who have seen a town sacked, in which thousands of my Christian countrymen perished by sword, by flood, and by fire, will blench from my purpose for the outcries or screams of one single wretched Jew? Or thinkest thou that these swarthy slaves, who have neither law, country, nor conscience, but their master's will—who use the poison, or the stake, or the poniard, or the cord, at his slightest wink— thinkest thou that *they* will have mercy, who do not even understand the language in which it is asked?

Be wise, old man ; discharge thyself of a portion of
thy superfluous wealth ; repay to the hands of a
Christian a part of what thou hast acquired by the
usury thou hast practised on those of his religion.
Thy cunning may soon swell out once more thy
shrivelled purse, but neither leech nor medicine
can restore thy scorched hide and flesh wert thou
once stretched on these bars. Tell down thy ransom,
I say, and rejoice that at such rate thou canst redeem thee from a dungeon the secrets of which few
have returned to tell. I waste no more words with
thee : choose between thy dross and thy flesh and
blood, and as thou choosest, so shall it be.'

'So may Abraham, Jacob, and all the fathers
of our people assist me,' said Isaac, 'I cannot
make the choice, because I have not the means
of satisfying your exorbitant demand !'

'Seize him and strip him, slaves,' said the knight,
' and let the fathers of his race assist him if they can.'

The assistants, taking their directions more from
the Baron's eye and his hand than his tongue, once
more stepped forward, laid hands on the unfortunate
Isaac, plucked him up from the ground, and, holding
him between them, waited the hard-hearted Baron's
farther signal. The unhappy Jew eyed their countenances and that of Front-de-Bœuf, in hope of
discovering some symptoms of relenting ; but that
of the Baron exhibited the same cold, half-sullen,
half-sarcastic smile which had been the prelude to
his cruelty ; and the savage eyes of the Saracens,
rolling gloomily under their dark brows, acquiring
a yet more sinister expression by the whiteness of
the circle which surrounds the pupil, evinced rather
the secret pleasure which they expected from the
approaching scene than any reluctance to be its
directors or agents. The Jew then looked at the
glowing furnace over which he was presently to be
stretched, and seeing no chance of his tormentor's
relenting, his resolution gave way.

'I will pay,' he said, 'the thousand pounds of silver. That is,' he added, after a moment's pause, 'I will pay it with the help of my brethren; for I must beg as a mendicant at the door of our synagogue ere I make up so unheard-of a sum. When and where must it be delivered?'

'Here,' replied Front-de-Bœuf—'here it must be delivered; weighed it must be—weighed and told down on this very dungeon floor. Thinkest thou I will part with thee until thy ransom is secure?'

'And what is to be my surety,' said the Jew, 'that I shall be at liberty after this ransom is paid?'

'The word of a Norman noble, thou pawnbroking slave,' answered Front-de-Bœuf—'the faith of a Norman nobleman, more pure than the gold and silver of thee and all thy tribe.'

'I crave pardon, noble lord,' said Isaac, timidly, 'but wherefore should I rely wholly on the word of one who will trust nothing to mine?'

'Because thou canst not help it, Jew,' said the knight, sternly. 'Wert thou now in thy treasure-chamber at York, and were I craving a loan of thy shekels, it would be thine to dictate the time of payment and the pledge of security. This is *my* treasure-chamber. Here I have thee at advantage, nor will I again deign to repeat the terms on which I grant thee liberty.'

The Jew groaned deeply. 'Grant me,' he said, 'at least, with my own liberty, that of the companions with whom I travel. They scorned me as a Jew, yet they pitied my desolation, and because they tarried to aid me by the way a share of my evil hath come upon them; moreover, they may contribute in some sort to my ransom.'

'If thou meanest yonder Saxon churls,' said Front-de-Bœuf, 'their ransom will depend upon other terms than thine. Mind thine own concerns, Jew, I warn thee, and meddle not with those of others.'

'I am, then,' said Isaac, 'only to be set at liberty, together with mine wounded friend?'

'Shall I twice recommend it,' said Front-de-Bœuf, 'to a son of Israel, to meddle with his own concerns, and leave those of others alone? Since thou hast made thy choice, it remains but that thou payest down thy ransom, and that at a short day.'

'Yet hear me,' said the Jew, 'for the sake of that very wealth which thou wouldst obtain at the expense of thy——' here he stopt short, afraid of irritating the savage Norman. But Front-de-Bœuf only laughed, and himself filled up the blank at which the Jew had hesitated. 'At the expense of my conscience, thou wouldst say, Isaac; speak it out—I tell thee, I am reasonable. I can bear the reproaches of a loser, even when that loser is a Jew. Thou wert not so patient, Isaac, when thou didst invoke justice against Jacques Fitzdotterel, for calling thee a usurious blood-sucker, when thy exactions had devoured his patrimony.'

'I swear by the Talmud,' said the Jew, 'that your valour has been misled in that matter. Fitzdotterel drew his poniard upon me in mine own chamber, because I craved him for mine own silver. The term of payment was due at the Passover.'

'I care not what he did,' said Front-de-Bœuf; 'the question is, when shall I have mine own?— when shall I have the shekels, Isaac?'

'Let my daughter Rebecca go forth to York,' answered Isaac, 'with your safe-conduct, noble knight, and so soon as man and horse can return, the treasure——' here he groaned deeply, but added, after the pause of a few seconds—'the treasure shall be told down on this very floor.'

'Thy daughter!' said Front-de-Bœuf, as if surprised, 'by heavens, Isaac, I would I had known of this. I deemed that yonder black-browed girl had been thy concubine, and I gave her to be a hand-maiden to Sir Brian de Bois-Guilbert, after the fashion of patriarchs and heroes of the days of old, who set us in these matters a wholesome example.'

The yell which Isaac raised at this unfeeling communication made the very vault to ring, and astounded the two Saracens so much that they let go their hold of the Jew. He availed himself of his enlargement to throw himself on the pavement and clasp the knees of Front-de-Bœuf.

'Take all that you have asked,' said he, 'Sir Knight; take ten times more—reduce me to ruin and to beggary, if thou wilt,—nay, pierce me with thy poniard, broil me on that furnace; but spare my daughter, deliver her in safety and honour. As thou art born of woman, spare the honour of a helpless maiden. She is the image of my deceased Rachael—she is the last of six pledges of her love. Will you deprive a widowed husband of his sole remaining comfort? Will you reduce a father to wish that his only living child were laid beside her dead mother, in the tomb of our fathers?'

'I would,' said the Norman, somewhat relenting, 'that I had known of this before. I thought your race had loved nothing save their money-bags.'

'Think not so vilely of us, Jews though we be,' said Isaac, eager to improve the moment of apparent sympathy; 'the hunted fox, the tortured wild-cat loves its young—the despised and persecuted race of Abraham love their children!'

'Be it so,' said Front-de-Bœuf; 'I will believe it in future, Isaac, for thy very sake. But it aids us not now; I cannot help what has happened, or what is to follow: my word is passed to my comrade in arms, nor would I break it for ten Jews and Jewesses to boot. Besides, why shouldst thou think evil is to come to the girl, even if she became Bois-Guilbert's booty?'

'There will—there must!' exclaimed Isaac, wringing his hands in agony; 'when did Templars breathe aught but cruelty to men and dishonour to women!'

'Dog of an infidel,' said Front-de-Bœuf, with
sparkling eyes, and not sorry, perhaps, to seize a
pretext for working himself into a passion, 'blaspheme not the Holy Order of the Temple of Zion,
but take thought instead to pay me the ransom thou
hast promised, or woe betide thy Jewish throat!'

'Robber and villain!' said the Jew, retorting the
insults of his oppressor with passion, which, however
impotent, he now found it impossible to bridle, 'I
will pay thee nothing—not one silver penny will I
pay thee—unless my daughter is delivered to me in
safety and honour!'

'Art thou in thy senses, Israelite?' said the
Norman, sternly; 'has thy flesh and blood a charm
against heated iron and scalding oil?'

'I care not!' said the Jew, rendered desperate
by paternal affection; 'do thy worst. My daughter
is my flesh and blood, dearer to me a thousand times
than those limbs which thy cruelty threatens. No
silver will I give thee, unless I were to pour it
molten down thy avaricious throat; no, not a silver
penny will I give thee, Nazarene, were it to save
thee from the deep damnation thy whole life has
merited! Take my life if thou wilt, and say the
Jew, amidst his tortures, knew how to disappoint
the Christian.'

'We shall see that,' said Front-de-Bœuf; 'for by
the blessed rood, which is the abomination of thy
accursed tribe, thou shalt feel the extremities of fire
and steel! Strip him, slaves, and chain him down
upon the bars.'

In spite of the feeble struggles of the old man,
the Saracens had already torn from him his upper
garment, and were proceeding totally to disrobe
him, when the sound of a bugle, twice [thrice]
winded without the castle, penetrated even to the
recesses of the dungeon, and immediately after loud
voices were heard calling for Sir Reginald Front-
de-Bœuf. Unwilling to be found engaged in his

hellish occupation, the savage Baron gave the slaves a signal to restore Isaac's garment, and quitting the dungeon with his attendants, he left the Jew to thank God for his own deliverance, or to lament over his daughter's captivity and probable fate, as his personal or parental feelings might prove strongest.

CHAPTER XXIII

Nay, if the gentle spirit of moving words
Can no way change you to a milder form,
I'll woo you, like a soldier, at arms' end,
And love you 'gainst the nature of love, force you.
                                    Two Gentlemen of Verona.

The apartment to which the Lady Rowena had been introduced was fitted up with some rude attempts at ornament and magnificence, and her being placed there might be considered as a peculiar mark of respect not offered to the other prisoners. But the wife of Front-de-Bœuf, for whom it had been originally furnished, was long dead, and decay and neglect had impaired the few ornaments with which her taste had adorned it. The tapestry hung down from the walls in many places, and in others was tarnished and faded under the effects of the sun, or tattered and decayed by age. Desolate, however, as it was, this was the apartment of the castle which had been judged most fitting for the accommodation of the Saxon heiress; and here she was left to meditate upon her fate, until the actors in this nefarious drama had arranged the several parts which each of them was to perform. This had been settled in a council held by Front-de-Bœuf, De Bracy, and the Templar, in which, after a long and warm debate concerning the several advantages which each insisted upon deriving from his peculiar share in this audacious enterprise, they had at length determined the fate of their unhappy prisoners.

It was about the hour of noon, therefore, when
De Bracy, for whose advantage the expedition had
been first planned, appeared to prosecute his views
upon the hand and possessions of the Lady Rowena.
The interval had not entirely been bestowed in
holding council with his confederates, for De Bracy
had found leisure to decorate his person with all the
foppery of the times. His green cassock and vizard
were now flung aside. His long luxuriant hair was
trained to flow in quaint tresses down his richly
furred cloak. His beard was closely shaved, his
doublet reached to the middle of his leg, and the
girdle which secured it, and at the same time supported his ponderous sword, was embroidered and
embossed with gold work. We have already noticed
the extravagant fashion of the shoes at this period,
and the points of Maurice de Bracy's might have
challenged the prize of extravagance with the gayest,
being turned up and twisted like the horns of a
ram. Such was the dress of a gallant of the period ;
and, in the present instance, that effect was aided
by the handsome person and good demeanour of the
wearer, whose manners partook alike of the grace
of a courtier and the frankness of a soldier.

He saluted Rowena by doffing his velvet bonnet,
garnished with a golden brooch, representing St.
Michael trampling down the Prince of Evil. With
this, he gently motioned the lady to a seat ; and, as
she still retained her standing posture, the knight
ungloved his right hand, and motioned to conduct
her thither. But Rowena declined, by her gesture,
the proffered compliment, and replied, 'If I be in
the presence of my jailor, Sir Knight—nor will circumstances allow me to think otherwise—it best
becomes his prisoner to remain standing till she
learns her doom.'

'Alas ! fair Rowena,' returned De Bracy, 'you
are in presence of your captive, not your jailor ;
and it is from your fair eyes that De Bracy must

receive that doom which you fondly expect from him.'

'I know you not, sir,' said the lady, drawing herself up with all the pride of offended rank and beauty —'I know you not; and the insolent familiarity with which you apply to me the jargon of a troubadour forms no apology for the violence of a robber.'

'To thyself, fair maid,' answered De Bracy, in his former tone—'to thine own charms be ascribed whate'er I have done which passed the respect due to her whom I have chosen queen of my heart and loadstar of my eyes.'

'I repeat to you, Sir Knight, that I know you not, and that no man wearing chain and spurs ought thus to intrude himself upon the presence of an unprotected lady.'

'That I am unknown to you,' said De Bracy, 'is indeed my misfortune; yet let me hope that De Bracy's name has not been always unspoken when minstrels or heralds have praised deeds of chivalry, whether in the lists or in the battlefield.'

'To heralds and to minstrels, then, leave thy praise, Sir Knight,' replied Rowena, 'more suiting for their mouths than for thine own; and tell me which of them shall record in song, or in book of tourney, the memorable conquest of this night, a conquest obtained over an old man, followed by a few timid hinds; and its booty, an unfortunate maiden transported against her will to the castle of a robber?'

'You are unjust, Lady Rowena,' said the knight, biting his lips in some confusion, and speaking in a tone more natural to him than that of affected gallantry which he had at first adopted; 'yourself free from passion, you can allow no excuse for the frenzy of another, although caused by your own beauty.'

'I pray you, Sir Knight,' said Rowena, 'to cease a language so commonly used by strolling minstrels

that it becomes not the mouth of knights or nobles.
Certes, you constrain me to sit down, since you
enter upon such commonplace terms, of which each
vile crowder hath a stock that might last from hence
to Christmas.'

'Proud damsel,' said De Bracy, incensed at finding his gallant style procured him nothing but contempt —'proud damsel, thou shalt be as proudly
encountered. Know, then, that I have supported
my pretensions to your hand in the way that best
suited thy character. It is meeter for thy humour
to be wooed with bow and bill than in set terms and
in courtly language.'

'Courtesy of tongue,' said Rowena, 'when it is
used to veil churlishness of deed, is but a knight's
girdle around the breast of a base clown. I wonder
not that the restraint appears to gall you: more it
were for your honour to have retained the dress and
language of an outlaw than to veil the deeds of
one under an affectation of gentle language and
demeanour.'

'You counsel well, lady,' said the Norman; 'and
in the bold language which best justifies bold action,
I tell thee, thou shalt never leave this castle, or
thou shalt leave it as Maurice de Bracy's wife. I
am not wont to be baffled in my enterprises, nor
needs a Norman noble scrupulously to vindicate his
conduct to the Saxon maiden whom he distinguishes
by the offer of his hand. Thou art proud, Rowena,
and thou art the fitter to be my wife. By what
other means couldst thou be raised to high honour
and to princely place, saving by my alliance? How
else wouldst thou escape from the mean precincts
of a country grange, where Saxons herd with the
swine which form their wealth, to take thy seat,
honoured as thou shouldst be, and shalt be, amid
all in England that is distinguished by beauty or
dignified by power?'

'Sir Knight,' replied Rowena, 'the grange which

you contemn hath been my shelter from infancy;
and, trust me, when I leave it—should that day ever
arrive—it shall be with one who has not learnt to
despise the dwelling and manners in which I have
been brought up.'

'I guess your meaning, lady,' said De Bracy,
'though you may think it lies too obscure for my
apprehension. But dream not that Richard Cœur-
de-Lion will ever resume his throne, far less that
Wilfred of Ivanhoe, his minion, will ever lead thee
to his footstool, to be there welcomed as the bride
of a favourite. Another suitor might feel jealousy
while he touched this string; but my firm purpose
cannot be changed by a passion so childish and so
hopeless. Know, lady, that this rival is in my
power, and that it rests but with me to betray the
secret of his being within the castle to Front-de-
Bœuf, whose jealousy will be more fatal than mine.'

'Wilfred here!' said Rowena, in disdain; 'that
is as true as that Front-de-Bœuf is his rival.'

De Bracy looked at her steadily for an instant.
'Wert thou really ignorant of this?' said he; 'didst
thou not know that Wilfred of Ivanhoe travelled in
the litter of the Jew?—a meet conveyance for the
crusader whose doughty arm was to reconquer the
Holy Sepulchre!' And he laughed scornfully.

'And if he is here,' said Rowena, compelling herself to a tone of indifference, though trembling with
an agony of apprehension which she could not
suppress, 'in what is he the rival of Front-de-Bœuf?
or what has he to fear beyond a short imprisonment and an honourable ransom, according to the
use of chivalry?'

'Rowena,' said De Bracy, 'art thou, too, deceived
by the common error of thy sex, who think there
can be no rivalry but that respecting their own
charms? Knowest thou not there is a jealousy of
ambition and of wealth, as well as of love; and that
this our host, Front-de-Bœuf, will push from his

road him who opposes his claim to the fair barony
of Ivanhoe as readily, eagerly, and unscrupulously
as if he were preferred to him by some blue-eyed
damsel? But smile on my suit, lady, and the
wounded champion shall have nothing to fear from
Front-de-Bœuf, whom else thou mayst mourn for,
as in the hands of one who has never shown compassion.'

'Save him, for the love of Heaven!' said Rowena,
her firmness giving way under terror for her lover's
impending fate.

'I can—I will—it is my purpose,' said De Bracy;
'for, when Rowena consents to be the bride of De
Bracy, who is it shall dare to put forth a violent
hand upon her kinsman—the son of her guardian—
the companion of her youth? But it is thy love
must buy his protection. I am not romantic fool
enough to further the fortune, or avert the fate, of
one who is likely to be a successful obstacle between
me and my wishes. Use thine influence with me in
his behalf, and he is safe; refuse to employ it,
Wilfred dies, and thou thyself art not the nearer to
freedom.'

'Thy language,' answered Rowena, 'hath in its
indifferent bluntness something which cannot be
reconciled with the horrors it seems to express. I
believe not that thy purpose is so wicked, or thy
power so great.'

'Flatter thyself, then, with that belief,' said De
Bracy, 'until time shall prove it false. Thy lover
lies wounded in this castle—thy preferred lover.
He is a bar betwixt Front-de-Bœuf and that which
Front-de-Bœuf loves better than either ambition or
beauty. What will it cost beyond the blow of a
poniard, or the thrust of a javelin, to silence his
opposition for ever? Nay, were Front-de-Bœuf
afraid to justify a deed so open, let the leech but
give his patient a wrong draught, let the chamberlain, or the nurse who tends him, but pluck the

pillow from his head, and Wilfred, in his present
condition, is sped without the effusion of blood.
Cedric also——'

'And Cedric also,' said Rowena, repeating his
words—'my noble—my generous guardian ! I deserved the evil I have encountered, for forgetting
his fate even in that of his son !'

'Cedric's fate also depends upon thy determination,' said De Bracy, 'and I leave thee to form it.'

Hitherto, Rowena had sustained her part in this
trying scene with undismayed courage, but it was
because she had not considered the danger as
serious and imminent. Her disposition was naturally that which physiognomists consider as proper
to fair complexions—mild, timid, and gentle ; but
it had been tempered, and, as it were, hardened, by
the circumstances of her education. Accustomed
to see the will of all, even of Cedric himself—
sufficiently arbitrary with others—give way before
her wishes, she had acquired that sort of courage
and self-confidence which arises from the habitual
and constant deference of the circle in which we
move. She could scarce conceive the possibility of
her will being opposed, far less that of its being
treated with total disregard.

Her haughtiness and habit of domination was,
therefore, a fictitious character, induced over that
which was natural to her, and it deserted her when
her eyes were opened to the extent of her own
danger, as well as that of her lover and her
guardian ; and when she found her will, the slightest expression of which was wont to command
respect and attention, now placed in opposition to
that of a man of a strong, fierce, and determined
mind, who possessed the advantage over her, and
was resolved to use it, she quailed before him.

After casting her eyes around, as if to look for
the aid which was nowhere to be found, and after a
few broken interjections, she raised her hands to

heaven, and burst into a passion of uncontrolled
vexation and sorrow. It was impossible to see so
beautiful a creature in such extremity without feeling for her, and De Bracy was not unmoved, though
he was yet more embarrassed than touched. He
had, in truth, gone too far to recede; and yet, in
Rowena's present condition, she could not be acted
on either by argument or threats. He paced the
apartment to and fro, now vainly exhorting the
terrified maiden to compose herself, now hesitating
concerning his own line of conduct.

'If,' thought he, 'I should be moved by the tears
and sorrow of this disconsolate damsel, what should
I reap but the loss of those fair hopes for which I
have encountered so much risk, and the ridicule of
Prince John and his jovial comrades? And yet,'
he said to himself, 'I feel myself ill framed for the
part which I am playing. I cannot look on so fair
a face while it is disturbed with agony, or on those
eyes when they are drowned in tears. I would she
had retained her original haughtiness of disposition,
or that I had a larger share of Front-de-Bœuf's
thrice-tempered hardness of heart!'

Agitated by these thoughts, he could only bid
the unfortunate Rowena be comforted, and assure
her that as yet she had no reason for the excess of
despair to which she was now giving way. But in
this task of consolation De Bracy was interrupted
by the horn, 'hoarse-winded blowing far and keen,'
which had at the same time alarmed the other
inmates of the castle, and interrupted their several
plans of avarice and of license. Of them all, perhaps, De Bracy least regretted the interruption;
for his conference with the Lady Rowena had
arrived at a point where he found it equally difficult
to prosecute or to resign his enterprise.

And here we cannot but think it necessary to
offer some better proof than the incidents of an idle
tale to vindicate the melancholy representation of

manners which has been just laid before the reader. It is grievous to think that those valiant barons, to whose stand against the crown the liberties of England were indebted for their existence, should themselves have been such dreadful oppressors, and capable of excesses contrary not only to the laws of England, but to those of nature and humanity. But, alas! we have only to extract from the industrious Henry one of those numerous passages which he has collected from contemporary historians, to prove that fiction itself can hardly reach the dark reality of the horrors of the period.

The description given by the author of the *Saxon Chronicle* of the cruelties exercised in the reign of King Stephen by the great barons and lords of castles, who were all Normans, affords a strong proof of the excesses of which they were capable when their passions were inflamed. 'They grievously oppressed the poor people by building castles; and when they were built, they filled them with wicked men, or rather devils, who seized both men and women who they imagined had any money, threw them into prison, and put them to more cruel tortures than the martyrs ever endured. They suffocated some in mud, and suspended others by the feet, or the head, or the thumbs, kindling fires below them. They squeezed the heads of some with knotted cords till they pierced their brains, while they threw others into dungeons swarming with serpents, snakes, and toads.' But it would be cruel to put the reader to the pain of perusing the remainder of this description.[1]

As another instance of these bitter fruits of conquest, and perhaps the strongest that can be quoted, we may mention, that the Empress Matilda, though a daughter of the King of Scotland, and afterwards both Queen of England and Empress of Germany, the daughter, the wife, and the mother of monarchs,

[1] Henry's *Hist.*, edit. 1805, vol. vii. p. 346.

was obliged, during her early residence for education in England, to assume the veil of a nun, as the only means of escaping the licentious pursuit of the Norman nobles. This excuse she stated before a great council of the clergy of England, as the sole reason for her having taken the religious habit. The assembled clergy admitted the validity of the plea, and the notoriety of the circumstances upon which it was founded; giving thus an indubitable and most remarkable testimony to the existence of that disgraceful license by which that age was stained. It was a matter of public knowledge, they said, that after the conquest of King William, his Norman followers, elated by so great a victory, acknowledged no law but their own wicked pleasure, and not only despoiled the conquered Saxons of their lands and their goods, but invaded the honour of their wives and of their daughters with the most unbridled license; and hence it was then common for matrons and maidens of noble families to assume the veil, and take shelter in convents, not as called thither by the vocation of God, but solely to preserve their honour from the unbridled wickedness of man.

Such and so licentious were the times, as announced by the public declaration of the assembled clergy, recorded by Eadmer; and we need add nothing more to vindicate the probability of the scenes which we have detailed, and are about to detail, upon the more apocryphal authority of the Wardour MS.

CHAPTER XXIV

I'll woo her as the lion woos his bride.
                                        Douglas.

WHILE the scenes we have described were passing
in other parts of the castle, the Jewess Rebecca
awaited her fate in a distant and sequestered turret.
Hither she had been led by two of her disguised
ravishers, and on being thrust into the little cell,
she found herself in the presence of an old sibyl,
who kept murmuring to herself a Saxon rhyme, as
if to beat time to the revolving dance which her
spindle was performing upon the floor. The hag
raised her head as Rebecca entered, and scowled
at the fair Jewess with the malignant envy with
which old age and ugliness, when united with evil
conditions, are apt to look upon youth and beauty.

'Thou must up and away, old house-cricket,'
said one of the men ; ' our noble master commands
it. Thou must e'en leave this chamber to a fairer
guest.'

'Ay,' grumbled the hag, ' even thus is service
requited. I have known when my bare word would
have cast the best man-at-arms among ye out of
saddle and out of service ; and now must I up and
away at the command of every groom such as
thou.'

'Good Dame Urfried,' said the other man, ' stand
not to reason on it, but up and away. Lords' hests
must be listened to with a quick ear. Thou hast
had thy day, old dame, but thy sun has long been
274

set. Thou art now the very emblem of an old war-horse turned out on the barren heath; thou hast had thy paces in thy time, but now a broken amble is the best of them. Come, amble off with thee.'

'Ill omens dog ye both!' said the old woman; 'and a kennel be your burying-place! May the evil demon Zernebock tear me limb from limb, if I leave my own cell ere I have spun out the hemp on my distaff!'

'Answer it to our lord, then, old house-fiend,' said the man, and retired, leaving Rebecca in company with the old woman, upon whose presence she had been thus unwillingly forced.

'What devil's deed have they now in the wind?' said the old hag, murmuring to herself, yet from time to time casting a sidelong and malignant glance at Rebecca; 'but it is easy to guess. Bright eyes, black locks, and a skin like paper, ere the priest stains it with his black unguent! Ay, it is easy to guess why they send her to this lone turret, whence a shriek could no more be heard than at the depth of five hundred fathoms beneath the earth. Thou wilt have owls for thy neighbours, fair one; and their screams will be heard as far, and as much regarded, as thine own. Outlandish, too,' she said, marking the dress and turban of Rebecca. 'What country art thou of?—a Saracen or an Egyptian? Why dost not answer? Thou canst weep, canst thou not speak?'

'Be not angry, good mother,' said Rebecca.

'Thou needst say no more,' replied Urfried; 'men know a fox by the train, and a Jewess by her tongue.'

'For the sake of mercy,' said Rebecca, 'tell me what I am to expect as the conclusion of the violence which hath dragged me hither! Is it my life they seek, to atone for my religion? I will lay it down cheerfully.'

'Thy life, minion!' answered the sibyl; 'what

would taking thy life pleasure them? Trust me,
thy life is in no peril. Such usage shalt thou have
as was once thought good enough for a noble
Saxon maiden. And shall a Jewess like thee repine
because she hath no better? Look at me. I was as
young and twice as fair as thou, when Front-de-
Bœuf, father of this Reginald, and his Normans,
stormed this castle. My father and his seven sons
defended their inheritance from story to story,
from chamber to chamber. There was not a room,
not a step of the stair, that was not slippery with
their blood. They died—they died every man;
and ere their bodies were cold, and ere their blood
was dried, I had become the prey and the scorn of
the conqueror!'

'Is there no help? Are there no means of
escape?' said Rebecca. 'Richly—richly would I
requite thine aid.'

'Think not of it,' said the hag; 'from hence
there is no escape but through the gates of death;
and it is late—late,' she added, shaking her grey
head, 'ere these open to us. Yet it is comfort to
think that we leave behind us on earth those who
shall be wretched as ourselves. Fare thee well,
Jewess! Jew or Gentile, thy fate would be the
same; for thou hast to do with them that have
neither scruple nor pity. Fare thee well, I say.
My thread is spun out; thy task is yet to begin.'

'Stay! stay! for Heaven's sake!' said Rebecca—
'stay, though it be to curse and to revile me; thy
presence is yet some protection.'

'The presence of the mother of God were no
protection,' answered the old woman. 'There she
stands,' pointing to a rude image of the Virgin
Mary, 'see if she can avert the fate that awaits
thee.'

She left the room as she spoke, her features
writhed into a sort of sneering laugh, which made
them seem even more hideous than their habitual

frown. She locked the door behind her, and Rebecca might hear her curse every step for its steepness, as slowly and with difficulty she descended the turret stair.

Rebecca was now to expect a fate even more dreadful than that of Rowena; for what probability was there that either softness or ceremony would be used towards one of her oppressed race, whatever shadow of these might be preserved towards a Saxon heiress? Yet had the Jewess this advantage, that she was better prepared by habits of thought, and by natural strength of mind, to encounter the dangers to which she was exposed. Of a strong and observing character, even from her earliest years, the pomp and wealth which her father displayed within his walls, or which she witnessed in the houses of other wealthy Hebrews, had not been able to blind her to the precarious circumstances under which they were enjoyed. Like Damocles at his celebrated banquet, Rebecca perpetually beheld, amid that gorgeous display, the sword which was suspended over the heads of her people by a single hair. These reflections had tamed and brought down to a pitch of sounder judgment a temper which, under other circumstances, might have waxed haughty, supercilious, and obstinate.

From her father's example and injunctions, Rebecca had learnt to bear herself courteously towards all who approached her. She could not indeed imitate his excess of subservience, because she was a stranger to the meanness of mind and to the constant state of timid apprehension by which it was dictated; but she bore herself with a proud humility, as if submitting to the evil circumstances in which she was placed as the daughter of a despised race, while she felt in her mind the consciousness that she was entitled to hold a higher rank from her merit than the arbitrary despotism of religious prejudice permitted her to aspire to.

Thus prepared to expect adverse circumstances, she had acquired the firmness necessary for acting under them. Her present situation required all her presence of mind, and she summoned it up accordingly.

Her first care was to inspect the apartment; but it afforded few hopes either of escape or protection. It contained neither secret passage nor trap-door, and, unless where the door by which she had entered joined the main building, seemed to be circumscribed by the round exterior wall of the turret. The door had no inside bolt or bar. The single window opened upon an embattled space surmounting the turret, which gave Rebecca, at first sight, some hopes of escaping; but she soon found it had no communication with any other part of the battlements, being an isolated bartizan, or balcony, secured, as usual, by a parapet, with embrasures, at which a few archers might be stationed for defending the turret, and flanking with their shot the wall of the castle on that side.

There was therefore no hope but in passive fortitude, and in that strong reliance on Heaven natural to great and generous characters. Rebecca, however erroneously taught to interpret the promises of Scripture to the chosen people of Heaven, did not err in supposing the present to be their hour of trial, or in trusting that the children of Zion would be one day called in with the fulness of the Gentiles. In the meanwhile, all around her showed that their present state was that of punishment and probation, and that it was their especial duty to suffer without sinning. Thus prepared to consider herself as the victim of misfortune, Rebecca had early reflected upon her own state, and schooled her mind to meet the dangers which she had probably to encounter.

The prisoner trembled, however, and changed colour, when a step was heard on the stair, and the door of the turret-chamber slowly opened, and a tall man, dressed as one of those banditti to whom they owed their misfortune, slowly entered, and shut the door behind him; his cap, pulled down upon his brows, concealed the upper part of his face, and he held his mantle in such a manner as to muffle the rest. In this guise, as if prepared for the execution of some deed, at the thought of which he was himself ashamed, he stood before the affrighted prisoner; yet, ruffian as his dress bespoke him, he seemed at a loss to express what purpose had brought him thither, so that Rebecca, making an effort upon herself, had time to anticipate his explanation. She had already unclasped two costly bracelets and a collar, which she hastened to proffer to the supposed outlaw, concluding naturally that to gratify his avarice was to bespeak his favour.

'Take these,' she said, 'good friend, and for God's sake be merciful to me and my aged father! These ornaments are of value, yet are they trifling to what he would bestow to obtain our dismissal from this castle free and uninjured.'

'Fair flower of Palestine,' replied the outlaw, 'these pearls are orient, but they yield in whiteness to your teeth; the diamonds are brilliant, but they cannot match your eyes; and ever since I have taken up this wild trade, I have made a vow to prefer beauty to wealth.'

'Do not do yourself such wrong,' said Rebecca; 'take ransom, and have mercy! Gold will purchase you pleasure; to misuse us could only bring thee remorse. My father will willingly satiate thy utmost wishes; and if thou wilt act wisely, thou mayst purchase with our spoils thy restoration to civil society—mayst obtain pardon for past errors, and be placed beyond the necessity of committing more.'

'It is well spoken,' replied the outlaw in French, finding it difficult probably to sustain in Saxon a conversation which Rebecca had opened in that language; 'but know, bright lily of the vale of Baca! that thy father is already in the hands of a powerful alchemist, who knows how to convert into gold and silver even the rusty bars of a dungeon grate. The venerable Isaac is subjected to an alembic which will distil from him all he holds dear, without any assistance from my requests or thy entreaty. Thy ransom must be paid by love and beauty, and in no other coin will I accept it.'

'Thou art no outlaw,' said Rebecca, in the same language in which he addressed her; 'no outlaw had refused such offers. No outlaw in this land uses the dialect in which thou hast spoken. Thou art no outlaw, but a Norman—a Norman, noble perhaps in birth. O, be so in thy actions, and cast off this fearful mask of outrage and violence!'

'And thou, who canst guess so truly,' said Brian de Bois-Guilbert, dropping the mantle from his face, 'art no true daughter of Israel, but in all save youth and beauty a very witch of Endor. I am not an outlaw then, fair rose of Sharon. And I am one who will be more prompt to hang thy neck and arms with pearls and diamonds, which so well become them, than to deprive thee of these ornaments.'

'What wouldst thou have of me,' said Rebecca, 'if not my wealth? We can have nought in common between us; you are a Christian, I am a Jewess. Our union were contrary to the laws alike of the church and the synagogue.'

'It were so, indeed,' replied the Templar, laughing. 'Wed with a Jewess! *Despardieux!* Not if she were the Queen of Sheba! And know, besides, sweet daughter of Zion, that were the most Christian king to offer me his most Christian daughter, with Languedoc for a dowry, I could not wed her. It is against my vow to love any maiden, otherwise than *par amours*, as I will love thee. I am a Templar. Behold the cross of my holy order.'

'Darest thou appeal to it,' said Rebecca, 'on an occasion like the present?'

'And if I do so,' said the Templar, 'it concerns not thee, who art no believer in the blessed sign of our salvation.'

'I believe as my fathers taught,' said Rebecca; 'and may God forgive my belief if erroneous! But you, Sir Knight, what is *yours*, when you appeal without scruple to that which you deem most holy, even while you are about to transgress the most solemn of your vows as a knight and as a man of religion?'

'It is gravely and well preached, O daughter of Sirach!' answered the Templar; 'but, gentle Ecclesiastica, thy narow Jewish prejudices make thee blind to our high privilege. Marriage were an enduring crime on the part of a Templar; but what lesser folly I may practise, I shall speedily be absolved from at the next preceptory of our order. Not the wisest of monarchs, not his father, whose examples you must needs allow are weighty, claimed wider privileges than we poor soldiers of the Temple of Zion have won by our zeal in its defence. The protectors of Solomon's temple may claim license by the example of Solomon.'

'If thou readest the Scripture,' said the Jewess, 'and the lives of the saints, only to justify thine own license and profligacy, thy crime is like that of him who extracts poison from the most healthful and necessary herbs.'

The eyes of the Templar flashed fire at this reproof. 'Hearken,' he said, 'Rebecca; I have hitherto spoken mildly to thee, but now my language shall be that of a conqueror. Thou art the captive of my bow and spear, subject to my will by the laws of all nations; nor will I abate an inch of my right, or abstain from taking by violence what thou refusest to entreaty or necessity.'

'Stand back,' said Rebecca—'stand back, and

hear me ere thou offerest to commit a sin so deadly! My strength thou mayst indeed overpower, for God made women weak, and trusted their defence to man's generosity. But I will proclaim thy villainy, Templar, from one end of Europe to the other. I will owe to the superstition of thy brethren what their compassion might refuse me. Each preceptory —each chapter of thy order, shall learn that, like a heretic, thou hast sinned with a Jewess. Those who tremble not at thy crime will hold thee accursed for having so far dishonoured the cross thou wearest as to follow a daughter of my people.'

'Thou art keen-witted, Jewess,' replied the Templar, well aware of the truth of what she spoke, and that the rules of his order condemned in the most positive manner, and under high penalties, such intrigues as he now prosecuted, and that in some instances even degradation had followed upon it—'thou art sharp-witted,' he said; 'but loud must be thy voice of complaint if it is heard beyond the iron walls of this castle; within these, murmurs, laments, appeals to justice, and screams for help die alike silent away. One thing only can save thee, Rebecca. Submit to thy fate, embrace our religion, and thou shalt go forth in such state that many a Norman lady shall yield as well in pomp as in beauty to the favourite of the best lance among the defenders of the Temple.'

'Submit to my fate!' said Rebecca; 'and, sacred Heaven! to what fate? Embrace thy religion! and what religion can it be that harbours such a villain? *Thou* the best lance of the Templars! Craven knight!—forsworn priest! I spit at thee, and I defy thee. The God of Abraham's promise hath opened an escape to his daughter—even from this abyss of infamy!'

As she spoke, she threw open the latticed window which led to the bartizan, and in an instant after stood on the very verge of the parapet, with not the slightest screen between her and the tremendous depth below. Unprepared for such a desperate effort, for she had hitherto stood perfectly motionless, Bois-Guilbert had neither time to intercept nor to stop her. As he offered to advance, she exclaimed, 'Remain where thou art, proud Templar, or at thy choice advance!—one foot nearer, and I plunge myself from the precipice; my body shall be crushed out of the very form of humanity upon the stones of that courtyard ere it become the victim of thy brutality!'

As she spoke this, she clasped her hands and extended them towards heaven, as if imploring mercy on her soul before she made the final plunge. The Templar hesitated, and a resolution which had never yielded to pity or distress gave way to his admiration of her fortitude. 'Come down,' he said, 'rash girl! I swear by earth, and sea, and sky, I will offer thee no offence.'

'I will not trust thee, Templar,' said Rebecca; 'thou hast taught me better how to estimate the virtues of thine order. The next preceptory would grant thee absolution for an oath the keeping of which concerned nought but the honour or the dishonour of a miserable Jewish maiden.'

'You do me injustice,' exclaimed the Templar, fervently; 'I swear to you by the name which I bear—by the cross on my bosom—by the sword on my side—by the ancient crest of my fathers do I swear, I will do thee no injury whatsoever! If not for thyself, yet for thy father's sake forbear! I will be his friend, and in this castle he will need a powerful one.'

'Alas!' said Rebecca, 'I know it but too well. Dare I trust thee?'

'May my arms be reversed and my name dishonoured,' said Brian de Bois-Guilbert, 'if thou shalt have reason to complain of me! Many a law, many a commandment have I broken, but my word never.'

'I will then trust thee,' said Rebecca, 'thus far'; and she descended from the verge of the battlement, but remained standing close by one of the embrasures, or *machicolles*, as they were then called. 'Here,' she said, 'I take my stand. Remain where thou art, and if thou shalt attempt to diminish by one step the distance now between us, thou shalt see that the Jewish maiden will rather trust her soul with God than her honour to the Templar!'

While Rebecca spoke thus, her high and firm resolve, which corresponded so well with the expressive beauty of her countenance, gave to her looks, air, and manner a dignity that seemed more than mortal. Her glance quailed not, her cheek blanched not, for the fear of a fate so instant and so horrible; on the contrary, the thought that she had her fate at her command, and could escape at will from infamy to death, gave a yet deeper colour of carnation to her complexion, and a yet more brilliant fire to her eye. Bois-Guilbert, proud himself and high-spirited, thought he had never beheld beauty so animated and so commanding.

'Let there be peace between us, Rebecca,' he said.

'Peace, if thou wilt,' answered Rebecca—'peace; but with this space between.'

'Thou needst no longer fear me,' said Bois-Guilbert.

'I fear thee not,' replied she, 'thanks to him that reared this dizzy tower so high that nought could fall from it and live. Thanks to him, and to the God of Israel! I fear thee not.'

'Thou dost me injustice,' said the Templar; 'by earth, sea, and sky, thou dost me injustice! I am not naturally that which you have seen me—hard, selfish, and relentless. It was woman that taught me cruelty, and on woman therefore I have exercised it; but not upon such as thou. Hear me, Rebecca. Never did knight take lance in his hand with a

heart more devoted to the lady of his love than
Brian de Bois-Guilbert. She, the daughter of a
petty baron, who boasted for all his domains but a
ruinous tower and an unproductive vineyard, and
some few leagues of the barren Landes of Bourdeaux,
her name was known wherever deeds of arms were
done, known wider than that of many a lady's that
had a county for a dowry. Yes,' he continued,
pacing up and down the little platform, with an
animation in which he seemed to lose all consciousness of Rebecca's presence—'yes, my deeds, my
danger, my blood made the name of Adelaide de
Montemare known from the court of Castile to that
of Byzantium. And how was I requited? When
I returned with my dear-bought honours, purchased
by toil and blood, I found her wedded to a Gascon
squire, whose name was never heard beyond the
limits of his own paltry domain! Truly did I love
her, and bitterly did I revenge me of her broken
faith! But my vengeance has recoiled on myself.
Since that day I have separated myself from life and
its ties. My manhood must know no domestic
home, must be soothed by no affectionate wife.
My age must know no kindly hearth. My grave
must be solitary, and no offspring must outlive
me, to bear the ancient name of Bois-Guilbert.
At the feet of my superior I have laid down the
right of self-action — the privilege of independence. The Templar, a serf in all but the name,
can possess neither lands nor goods, and lives,
moves, and breathes but at the will and pleasure
of another.'

'Alas!' said Rebecca, 'what advantages could
compensate for such an absolute sacrifice?'

'The power of vengeance, Rebecca,' replied the
Templar, 'and the prospects of ambition.'

'An evil recompense,' said Rebecca, 'for the
surrender of the rights which are dearest to
humanity.'

'Say not so, maiden,' answered the Templar;
'revenge is a feast for the gods! And if they have
reserved it, as priests tell us, to themselves, it is
because they hold it an enjoyment too precious for
the possession of mere mortals. And ambition! it
is a temptation which could disturb even the bliss
of Heaven itself.' He paused a moment, and then
added, 'Rebecca! she who could prefer death to
dishonour must have a proud and a powerful soul.
Mine thou must be! Nay, start not,' he added, 'it
must be with thine own consent, and on thine own
terms. Thou must consent to share with me hopes
more extended that can be viewed from the throne
of a monarch! Hear me ere you answer, and judge
ere you refuse. The Templar loses, as thou hast
said, his social rights, his power of free agency, but
he becomes a member and a limb of a mighty body,
before which thrones already tremble—even as the
single drop of rain which mixes with the sea becomes
an individual part of that resistless ocean which
undermines rocks and ingulphs royal armadas. Such
a swelling flood is that powerful league. Of this
mighty order I am no mean member, but already
one of the chief commanders, and may well aspire
one day to hold the batoon of Grand Master. The
poor soldiers of the Temple will not alone place
their foot upon the necks of kings; a hemp-sandall'd
monk can do that. Our mailed step shall ascend
their throne, our gauntlet shall wrench the sceptre
from their gripe. Not the reign of your vainly-
expected Messiah offers such power to your dispersed
tribes as my ambition may aim at. I have sought
but a kindred spirit to share it, and I have found
such in thee.'

'Sayest thou this to one of my people?' answered
Rebecca. 'Bethink thee——'

'Answer me not,' said the Templar, 'by urging
the difference of our creeds; within our secret con-
claves we hold these nursery tales in derision. Think

not we long remained blind to the idiotical folly of our founders, who forswore every delight of life for the pleasure of dying martyrs by hunger, by thirst, and by pestilence, and by the swords of savages, while they vainly strove to defend a barren desert, valuable only in the eyes of superstition. Our order soon adopted bolder and wider views, and found out a better indemnification for our sacrifices. Our immense possessions in every kingdom of Europe, our high military fame, which brings within our circle the flower of chivalry from every Christian clime—these are dedicated to ends of which our pious founders little dreamed, and which are equally concealed from such weak spirits as embrace our order on the ancient principles, and whose superstition makes them our passive tools. But I will not further withdraw the veil of our mysteries. That bugle-sound announces something which may require my presence. Think on what I have said. Farewell! I do not say forgive me the violence I have threatened, for it was necessary to the display of thy character. Gold can be only known by the application of the touchstone. I will soon return, and hold further conference with thee.'

He re-entered the turret-chamber, and descended the stair, leaving Rebecca scarcely more terrified at the prospect of the death to which she had been so lately exposed, than at the furious ambition of the bold bad man in whose power she found herself so unhappily placed. When she entered the turret-chamber, her first duty was to return thanks to the God of Jacob for the protection which He had afforded her, and to implore its continuance for her and for her father. Another name glided into her petition; it was that of the wounded Christian, whom fate had placed in the hands of bloodthirsty men, his avowed enemies. Her heart indeed checked her, as if, even in communing with the Deity in prayer, she mingled in her devotions the recollection

of one with whose fate hers could have no alliance—
a Nazarene, and an enemy to her faith. But the
petition was already breathed, nor could all the
narrow prejudices of her sect induce Rebecca to
wish it recalled.

CHAPTER XXV

A damn'd cramp piece of penmanship as ever I saw in my life!—*She Stoops to Conquer.*

WHEN the Templar reached the hall of the castle, he found De Bracy already there. 'Your love-suit,' said De Bracy, 'hath, I suppose, been disturbed, like mine, by this obstreperous summons. But you have come later and more reluctantly, and therefore I presume your interview has proved more agreeable than mine.'

'Has your suit, then, been unsuccessfully paid to the Saxon heiress?' said the Templar.

'By the bones of Thomas à Becket,' answered De Bracy, 'the Lady Rowena must have heard that I cannot endure the sight of women's tears.'

'Away!' said the Templar; 'thou a leader of a Free Company, and regard a woman's tears! A few drops sprinkled on the torch of love make the flame blaze the brighter.'

'Gramercy for the few drops of thy sprinkling,' replied De Bracy; 'but this damsel hath wept enough to extinguish a beacon-light. Never was such wringing of hands and such overflowing of eyes, since the days of St. Niobe, of whom Prior Aymer told us.[1] A water-fiend hath possessed the fair Saxon.'

[1] I wish the Prior had also informed them when Niobe was sainted. Probably during that enlightened period when

Pan to Moses lent his pagan horn.

L. T.

'A legion of fiends have occupied the bosom of
the Jewess,' replied the Templar; 'for I think no
single one, not even Apollyon himself, could have
inspired such indomitable pride and resolution. But
where is Front-de-Bœuf? That horn is sounded
more and more clamorously.'

'He is negotiating with the Jew, I suppose,'
replied De Bracy, coolly; 'probably the howls of
Isaac have drowned the blast of the bugle. Thou
mayst know, by experience, Sir Brian, that a Jew
parting with his treasures on such terms as our
friend Front-de-Bœuf is like to offer will raise a
clamour loud enough to be heard over twenty horns
and trumpets to boot. But we will make the vassals
call him.'

They were soon after joined by Front-de-Bœuf,
who had been disturbed in his tyrannic cruelty in
the manner with which the reader is acquainted,
and had only tarried to give some necessary directions.

'Let us see the cause of this cursed clamour,'
said Front-de-Bœuf; 'here is a letter, and, if I
mistake not, it is in Saxon.'

He looked at it, turning it round and round as if
he had really some hopes of coming at the meaning
by inverting the position of the paper, and then
handed it to De Bracy.

'It may be magic spells for aught I know,' said
De Bracy, who possessed his full proportion of the
ignorance which characterised the chivalry of the
period. 'Our chaplain attempted to teach me to
write,' he said, 'but all my letters were formed like
spear-heads and sword-blades, and so the old shaveling gave up the task.'

'Give it me,' said the Templar. 'We have that
of the priestly character, that we have some knowledge to enlighten our valour.'

'Let us profit by your most reverend knowledge,
then,' said De Bracy; 'what says the scroll?'

'It is a formal letter of defiance,' answered the Templar; 'but, by our Lady of Bethlehem, if it be not a foolish jest, it is the most extraordinary cartel that ever was sent across the drawbridge of a baronial castle.'

'Jest!' said Front-de-Bœuf, 'I would gladly know who dares jest with me in such a matter! Read it, Sir Brian.'

The Templar accordingly read it as follows:—

'I, Wamba, the son of Witless, jester to a noble and freeborn man, Cedric of Rotherwood, called the Saxon: and I, Gurth, the son of Beowulph, the swineherd——'

'Thou art mad,' said Front-de-Bœuf, interrupting the reader.

'By St. Luke, it is so set down,' answered the Templar. Then resuming his task, he went on— 'I, Gurth, the son of Beowulph, swineherd unto the said Cedric, with the assistance of our allies and confederates, who make common cause with us in this our feud, namely, the good knight, called for the present *Le Noir Fainéant*, and the stout yeoman, Robert Locksley, called Cleave-the-Wand, do you, Reginald Front-de-Bœuf, and your allies and accomplices whomsoever, to wit, that whereas you have, without cause given or feud declared, wrongfully and by mastery seized upon the person of our lord and master the said Cedric; also upon the person of a noble and freeborn damsel, the Lady Rowena of Hargottstandstede; also upon the person of a noble and freeborn man, Athelstane of Coningsburgh; also upon the persons of certain freeborn men, their *cnichts*; also upon certain serfs, their born bondsmen; also upon a certain Jew, named Isaac of York, together with his daughter, a Jewess, and certain horses and mules: which noble persons, with their *cnichts* and slaves, and also with the horses and mules, Jew and Jewess beforesaid, were all in peace with his Majesty, and travelling as

liege subjects upon the king's highway; therefore
we require and demand that the said noble persons,
namely, Cedric of Rotherwood, Rowena of Hargottstandstede, Athelstane of Coningsburgh, with their
servants, *cnichts*, and followers, also the horses and
mules, Jew and Jewess aforesaid, together with all
goods and chattels to them pertaining, be, within
an hour after the delivery hereof, delivered to us,
or to those whom we shall appoint to receive the
same, and that untouched and unharmed in body
and goods. Failing of which, we do pronounce to
you, that we hold ye as robbers and traitors, and
will wager our bodies against ye in battle, siege, or
otherwise, and do our utmost to your annoyance
and destruction. Wherefore may God have you in
His keeping. Signed by us upon the eve of St.
Withold's day, under the great trysting oak in the
Harthill Walk, the above being written by a holy
man, clerk to God, our Lady, and St. Dunstan, in
the chapel of Copmanhurst.'

At the bottom of this document was scrawled, in
the first place, a rude sketch of a cock's head and
comb, with a legend expressing this hieroglyphic to
be the sign-manual of Wamba, son of Witless.
Under this respectable emblem stood a cross, stated
to be the mark of Gurth, the son of Beowulph.
Then was written, in rough bold characters, the
words *Le Noir Faineant*. And, to conclude the
whole, an arrow, neatly enough drawn, was described as the mark of the yeoman Locksley.

The knights heard this uncommon document
read from end to end, and then gazed upon each
other in silent amazement, as being utterly at a loss
to know what it could portend. De Bracy was the
first to break silence by an uncontrollable fit of
laughter, wherein he was joined, though with more
moderation, by the Templar. Front-de-Bœuf, on
the contrary, seemed impatient of their ill-timed
jocularity.

'I give you plain warning,' he said, 'fair sirs, that you had better consult how to bear yourselves under these circumstances, than give way to such misplaced merriment.'

'Front-de-Bœuf has not recovered his temper since his late overthrow,' said De Bracy to the Templar; 'he is cowed at the very idea of a cartel, though it come but from a fool and a swineherd.'

'By St. Michael,' answered Front-de-Bœuf, 'I would thou couldst stand the whole brunt of this adventure thyself, De Bracy. These fellows dared not have acted with such inconceivable impudence, had they not been supported by some strong bands. There are enough of outlaws in this forest to resent my protecting the deer. I did but tie one fellow, who was taken red-handed and in the fact, to the horns of a wild stag, which gored him to death in five minutes, and I had as many arrows shot at me as there were launched against yonder target at Ashby. Here, fellow,' he added, to one of his attendants, 'hast thou sent out to see by what force this precious challenge is to be supported?'

'There are at least two hundred men assembled in the woods,' answered a squire who was in attendance.

'Here is a proper matter!' said Front-de-Bœuf; 'this comes of lending you the use of my castle, that cannot manage your undertaking quietly, but you must bring this nest of hornets about my ears!'

'Of hornets!' said De Bracy, 'of stingless drones rather; a band of lazy knaves, who take to the wood and destroy the venison rather than labour for their maintenance.'

'Stingless!' replied Front-de-Bœuf; 'fork-headed shafts of a cloth-yard in length, and these shot within the breadth of a French crown, are sting enough.'

'For shame, Sir Knight!' said the Templar.

'Let us summon our people and sally forth upon them. One knight—ay, one man-at-arms, were enough for twenty such peasants.'

'Enough, and too much,' said De Bracy; 'I should only be ashamed to couch lance against them.'

'True,' answered Front-de-Bœuf; 'were they black Turks or Moors, Sir Templar, or the craven peasants of France, most valiant De Bracy; but these are English yeomen, over whom we shall have no advantage, save what we may derive from our arms and horses, which will avail us little in the glades of the forest. Sally, saidst thou? We have scarce men enough to defend the castle. The best of mine are at York; so is all your band, De Bracy; and we have scarcely twenty, besides the handful that were engaged in this mad business.'

'Thou dost not fear,' said the Templar, 'that they can assemble in force sufficient to attempt the castle?'

'Not so, Sir Brian,' answered Front-de-Bœuf. 'These outlaws have indeed a daring captain; but without machines, scaling ladders, and experienced leaders, my castle may defy them.'

'Send to thy neighbours,' said the Templar; 'let them assemble their people and come to the rescue of three knights, besieged by a jester and a swineherd in the baronial castle of Reginald Front-de-Bœuf!'

'You jest, Sir Knight,' answered the baron; 'but to whom should I send? Malvoisin is by this time at York with his retainers, and so are my other allies; and so should I have been, but for this infernal enterprise.'

'Then send to York and recall our people,' said De Bracy. 'If they abide the shaking of my standard, or the sight of my Free Companions, I will give them credit for the boldest outlaws ever bent bow in greenwood.'

'And who shall bear such a message?' said Front-de-Bœuf; 'they will beset every path, and rip the errand out of his bosom. I have it,' he added, after pausing for a moment. 'Sir Templar, thou canst write as well as read, and if we can but find the writing materials of my chaplain, who died a twelvemonth since in the midst of his Christmas carousals——

'So please ye,' said the squire, who was still in attendance, 'I think old Urfried has them somewhere in keeping, for love of the confessor. He was the last man, I have heard her tell, who ever said aught to her which man ought in courtesy to address to maid or matron.'

'Go, search them out, Engelred,' said Front-de-Bœuf; 'and then, Sir Templar, thou shalt return an answer to this bold challenge.'

'I would rather do it at the sword's point than at that of the pen,' said Bois-Guilbert: 'but be it as you will.'

He sat down accordingly, and indited, in the French language, an epistle of the following tenor :—

'Sir Reginald Front-de-Bœuf, with his noble and knightly allies and confederates, receive no defiances at the hands of slaves, bondsmen, or fugitives. If the person calling himself the Black Knight have indeed a claim to the honours of chivalry, he ought to know that he stands degraded by his present association, and has no right to ask reckoning at the hands of good men of noble blood. Touching the prisoners we have made, we do in Christian charity require you to send a man of religion to receive their confession and reconcile them with God ; since it is our fixed intention to execute them this morning before noon, so that their heads, being placed on the battlements, shall show to all men how lightly we esteem those who have bestirred themselves in their rescue. Wherefore, as above, we require you to send a priest to reconcile them to

God, in doing which you shall render them the last earthly service.'

This letter, being folded, was delivered to the squire, and by him to the messenger who waited without, as the answer to that which he had brought.

The yeoman, having thus accomplished his mission, returned to the headquarters of the allies, which were for the present established under a venerable oak-tree, about three arrow-flights distant from the castle. Here Wamba and Gurth, with their allies the Black Knight and Locksley, and the jovial hermit, awaited with impatience an answer to their summons. Around, and at a distance from them, were seen many a bold yeoman, whose silvan dress and weather-beaten countenances showed the ordinary nature of their occupation. More than two hundred had already assembled, and others were fast coming in. Those whom they obeyed as leaders were only distinguished from the others by a feather in the cap, their dress, arms, and equipments being in all other respects the same.

Besides these bands, a less orderly and a worse-armed force, consisting of the Saxon inhabitants of the neighbouring township, as well as many bondsmen and servants from Cedric's extensive estate, had already arrived, for the purpose of assisting in his rescue. Few of these were armed otherwise than with such rustic weapons as necessity sometimes converts to military purposes. Boar-spears, scythes, flails, and the like, were their chief arms; for the Normans, with the usual policy of conquerors, were jealous of permitting to the vanquished Saxons the possession or the use of swords and spears. These circumstances rendered the assistance of the Saxons far from being so formidable to the besieged as the strength of the men themselves, their superior numbers, and the animation inspired by a just cause, might otherwise well have made them. It was to the leaders of this motley army that the letter of the Templar was now delivered.

Reference was at first made to the chaplain for an exposition of its contents

'By the crook of St. Dunstan,' said that worthy ecclesiastic, 'which hath brought more sheep within the sheepfold than the crook of e'er another saint in Paradise, I swear that I cannot expound unto you this jargon, which, whether it be French or Arabic, is beyond my guess.'

He then gave the letter to Gurth, who shook his head gruffly, and passed it to Wamba. The Jester looked at each of the four corners of the paper with such a grin of affected intelligence as a monkey is apt to assume upon similar occasions, then cut a caper, and gave the letter to Locksley.

'If the long letters were bows, and the short letters broad arrows, I might know something of the matter,' said the brave yeoman; 'but as the matter stands, the meaning is as safe, for me, as the stag that's at twelve miles' distance.'

'I must be clerk, then,' said the Black Knight; and taking the letter from Locksley, he first read it over to himself, and then explained the meaning in Saxon to his confederates.

'Execute the noble Cedric!' exclaimed Wamba; 'by the rood, thou must be mistaken, Sir Knight.'

'Not I, my worthy friend,' replied the knight; 'I have explained the words as they are here set down.'

'Then, by St. Thomas of Canterbury,' replied Gurth, 'we will have the castle, should we tear it down with our hands!'

'We have nothing else to tear it with,' replied Wamba; 'but mine are scarce fit to make mammocks of freestone and mortar.'

''Tis but a contrivance to gain time,' said Locksley; 'they dare not do a deed for which I could exact a fearful penalty.'

'I would,' said the Black Knight, 'there were some one among us who could obtain admission into the castle, and discover how the case stands with the besieged. Methinks, as they require a confessor to be sent, this holy hermit might at once exercise his pious vocation and procure us the information we desire.'

'A plague on thee and thy advice!' said the pious hermit; 'I tell thee, Sir Slothful Knight, that when I doff my friar's frock, my priesthood, my sanctity, my very Latin, are put off along with it; and when in my green jerkin I can better kill twenty deer than confess one Christian.'

'I fear,' said the Black Knight—'I fear greatly there is no one here that is qualified to take upon him, for the nonce, this same character of father confessor?'

All looked on each other, and were silent.

'I see,' said Wamba, after a short pause, 'that the fool must be still the fool, and put his neck in the venture which wise men shrink from. You must know, my dear cousins and countrymen, that I wore russet before I wore motley, and was bred to be a friar, until a brain-fever came upon me and left me just wit enough to be a fool. I trust, with the assistance of the good hermit's frock, together with the priesthood, sanctity, and learning which are stitched into the cowl of it, I shall be found qualified to administer both worldly and ghostly comfort to our worthy master Cedric and his companions in adversity.'

'Hath he sense enough, thinkst thou?' said the Black Knight, addressing Gurth.

'I know not,' said Gurth; 'but if he hath not, it will be the first time he hath wanted wit to turn his folly to account.'

'On with the frock, then, good fellow,' quoth the Knight, 'and let thy master send us an account of their situation within the castle. Their numbers must be few, and it is five to one they may be accessible by a sudden and bold attack. Time wears—away with thee.'

'And, in the, meantime,' said Locksley, 'we will beset the place so closely that not so much as a fly shall carry news from thence. So that, my good friend,' he continued, addressing Wamba, 'thou mayst assure these tyrants that whatever violence they exercise on the persons of their prisoners shall be most severely repaid upon their own.'

'*Pax vobiscum*,' said Wamba, who was now muffled in his religious disguise.

And so saying, he imitated the solemn and stately deportment of a friar, and departed to execute his mission.

CHAPTER XXVI

The hottest horse will oft be cool,
    The dullest will show fire;
The friar will often play the fool,
    The fool will play the friar.
                              Old Song.

WHEN the Jester, arrayed in the cowl and frock of the hermit, and having his knotted cord twisted round his middle, stood before the portal of the castle of Front-de-Bœuf, the warder demanded of him his name and errand.

'*Pax vobiscum*,' answered the Jester, 'I am a poor brother of the Order of St. Francis, who come hither to do my office to certain unhappy prisoners now secured within this castle.'

'Thou art a bold friar,' said the warder, 'to come hither, where, saving our own drunken confessor, a cock of thy feather hath not crowed these twenty years.'

'Yet I pray thee, do mine errand to the lord of the castle,' answered the pretended friar; 'trust me, it will find good acceptance with him, and the cock shall crow, that the whole castle shall hear him.'

'Gramercy,' said the warder; 'but if I come to shame for leaving my post upon thine errand, I will try whether a friar's grey gown be proof against a grey-goose shaft.'

With this threat he left his turret, and carried to the hall of the castle his unwonted intelligence, that a holy friar stood before the gate and demanded instant admission. With no small wonder he received his master's commands to admit the holy man immediately; and, having previously manned the entrance to guard against surprise, he obeyed, without further scruple, the commands which he had received. The hare-brained self-conceit which had emboldened Wamba to undertake this dangerous office was scarce sufficient to support him when he found himself in the presence of a man so dreadful, and so much dreaded, as Reginald Front-de-Bœuf, and he brought out his '*Pax vobiscum*,' to which he, in a good measure, trusted for supporting his character, with more anxiety and hesitation than had hitherto accompanied it. But Front-de-Bœuf was accustomed to see men of all ranks tremble in his presence, so that the timidity of the supposed father did not give him any cause of suspicion. 'Who and whence art thou, priest?' said he.

'*Pax vobiscum*,' reiterated the Jester, 'I am a poor servant of St. Francis, who, travelling through this wilderness, have fallen among thieves as Scripture hath it—*quidam viator incidit in latrones*—which thieves have sent me unto this castle in order to do my ghostly office on two persons condemned by your honourable justice.'

'Ay, right,' answered Front-de-Bœuf; 'and canst thou tell me, holy father, the number of those banditti?'

'Gallant sir,' answered the Jester, '*nomen illis legio*—their name is legion.'

'Tell me in plain terms what numbers there are, or, priest, thy cloak and cord will ill protect thee.'

'Alas!' said the supposed friar, '*cor meum eructavit*, that is to say, I was like to burst with fear! but I conceive they may be, what of yeomen, what of commons, at least five hundred men.'

'What!' said the Templar, who came into the hall that moment, 'muster the wasps so thick here?

It is time to stifle such a mischievous brood.' Then
taking Front-de-Bœuf aside, 'Knowest thou the
priest?'

'He is a stranger from a distant convent,' said
Front-de-Bœuf; 'I know him not.'

'Then trust him not with thy purpose in words,'
answered the Templar. 'Let him carry a written
order to De Bracy's company of Free Companions,
to repair instantly to their master's aid. In the
meantime, and that the shaveling may suspect
nothing, permit him to go freely about his task
of preparing these Saxon hogs for the slaughter-
house.'

'It shall be so,' said Front-de-Bœuf. And he
forthwith appointed a domestic to conduct Wamba
to the apartment where Cedric and Athelstane were
confined.

The impatience of Cedric had been rather enhanced than diminished by his confinement. He
walked from one end of the hall to the other, with
the attitude of one who advances to charge an
enemy, or to storm the breach of a beleaguered
place, sometimes ejaculating to himself, sometimes
addressing Athelstane, who stoutly and stoically
awaited the issue of the adventure, digesting, in
the meantime, with great composure, the liberal
meal which he had made at noon, and not greatly
interesting himself about the duration of his captivity, which he concluded would, like all earthly
evils, find an end in Heaven's good time.

'*Pax vobiscum*,' said the Jester, entering the
apartment; 'the blessing of St. Dunstan, St. Denis,
St. Duthoc, and all other saints whatsoever, be
upon ye and about ye.'

'Enter freely,' answered Cedric to the supposed
friar; 'with what intent art thou come hither?'

'To bid you prepare yourselves for death,'
answered the Jester.

'It is impossible!' replied Cedric, starting.

'Fearless and wicked as they are, they dare not attempt such open and gratuitous cruelty!'

'Alas!' said the Jester, 'to restrain them by their sense of humanity is the same as to stop a runaway horse with a bridle of silk thread. Bethink thee, therefore, noble Cedric, and you also, gallant Athelstane, what crimes you have committed in the flesh; for this very day will ye be called to answer at a higher tribunal.'

'Hearest thou this, Athelstane?' said Cedric. 'We must rouse up our hearts to this last action, since better it is we should die like men than live like slaves.'

'I am ready,' answered Athelstane, 'to stand the worst of their malice, and shall walk to my death with as much composure as ever I did to my dinner.'

'Let us then unto our holy gear, father,' said Cedric.

'Wait yet a moment, good uncle,' said the Jester, in his natural tone; 'better look long before you leap in the dark.'

'By my faith,' said Cedric, 'I should know that voice!'

'It is that of your trusty slave and jester,' answered Wamba, throwing back his cowl. 'Had you taken a fool's advice formerly, you would not have been here at all. Take a fool's advice now, and you will not be here long.'

'How mean'st thou, knave?' answered the Saxon.

'Even thus,' replied Wamba; 'take thou this frock and cord, which are all the orders I ever had, and march quietly out of the castle, leaving me your cloak and girdle to take the long leap in thy stead.'

'Leave thee in my stead!' said Cedric, astonished at the proposal; 'why, they would hang thee, my poor knave.'

'E'en let them do as they are permitted,' said

Wamba; 'I trust—no disparagement to your birth
—that the son of Witless may hang in a chain with
as much gravity as the chain hung upon his ancestor
the alderman.'

'Well, Wamba,' answered Cedric, 'for one thing
will I grant thy request. And that is, if thou wilt
make the exchange of garments with Lord Athelstane instead of me.'

'No, by St. Dunstan,' answered Wamba; 'there
were little reason in that. Good right there is that
the son of Witless should suffer to save the son of
Hereward; but little wisdom there were in his
dying for the benefit of one whose fathers were
strangers to his.'

'Villain,' said Cedric, 'the fathers of Athelstane
were monarchs of England!'

'They might be whomsoever they pleased,'
replied Wamba; 'but my neck stands too straight
upon my shoulders to have it twisted for their sake.
Wherefore, good my master, either take my proffer
yourself or suffer me to leave this dungeon as free
as I entered.'

'Let the old tree wither,' continued Cedric, 'so
the stately hope of the forest be preserved. Save
the noble Athelstane, my trusty Wamba! it is the
duty of each who has Saxon blood in his veins.
Thou and I will abide together the utmost rage
of our injurious oppressors, while he, free and safe,
shall arouse the awakened spirits of our countrymen
to avenge us.'

'Not so, father Cedric,' said Athelstane, grasping
his hand, for, when roused to think or act, his
deeds and sentiments were not unbecoming his high
race—'not so,' he continued; 'I would rather
remain in this hall a week without food save the
prisoner's stinted loaf, or drink save the prisoner's
measure of water, than embrace the opportunity to
escape which the slave's untaught kindness has
purveyed for his master.'

'You are called wise men, sirs,' said the Jester, 'and I a crazed fool; but, uncle Cedric and cousin Athelstane, the fool shall decide this controversy for ye, and save ye the trouble of straining courtesies any farther. I am like John-a-Duck's mare, that will let no man mount her but John-a-Duck. I came to save my master, and if he will not consent, basta! I can but go away home again. Kind service cannot be chucked from hand to hand like a shuttle-cock or stool-ball. I'll hang for no man but my own born master.'

'Go, then, noble Cedric,' said Athelstane, 'neglect not this opportunity. Your presence without may encourage friends to our rescue; your remaining here would ruin us all.'

'And is there any prospect, then, of rescue from without?' said Cedric, looking to the Jester.

'Prospect, indeed!' echoed Wamba; 'let me tell you, when you fill my cloak, you are wrapped in a general's cassock. Five hundred men are there without, and I was this morning one of their chief leaders. My fool's cap was a casque, and my bauble a truncheon. Well, we shall see what good they will make by exchanging a fool for a wise man. Truly, I fear they will lose in valour what they may gain in discretion. And so farewell, master, and be kind to poor Gurth and his dog Fangs; and let my cockscomb hang in the hall at Rotherwood, in memory that I flung away my life for my master, like a faithful—fool.' The last word came out with a sort of double expression, betwixt jest and earnest.

The tears stood in Cedric's eyes. 'Thy memory shall be preserved,' he said, 'while fidelity and affection have honour upon earth! But that I trust I shall find the means of saving Rowena, and thee, Athelstane, and thee also, my poor Wamba, thou shouldst not overbear me in this matter.'

The exchange of dress was now accomplished, when a sudden doubt struck Cedric.

'I know no language,' he said, 'but my own, and
a few words of their mincing Norman. How shall
I bear myself like a reverend brother?'

'The spell lies in two words,' replied Wamba.
'*Pax vobiscum* will answer all queries. If you go
or come, eat or drink, bless or ban, *Pax vobiscum*
carries you through it all. It is as useful to a friar
as a broomstick to a witch, or a wand to a conjurer.
Speak it but thus, in a deep grave tone—*Pax
vobiscum*—it is irresistible. Watch and ward, knight
and squire, foot and horse, it acts as a charm upon
them all. I think, if they bring me out to be
hanged to-morrow, as is much to be doubted they
may, I will try its weight upon the finisher of the
sentence.'

'If such prove the case,' said his master, 'my
religious orders are soon taken—*Pax vobiscum*. I
trust I shall remember the password. Noble Athelstane, farewell; and farewell, my poor boy, whose
heart might make amends for a weaker head; I will
save you, or return and die with you. The royal
blood of our Saxon kings shall not be spilt while
mine beats in my veins; nor shall one hair fall
from the head of the kind knave who risked himself
for his master, if Cedric's peril can prevent it.
Farewell.'

'Farewell, noble Cedric,' said Athelstane; 'remember, it is the true part of a friar to accept
refreshment, if you are offered any.'

'Farewell, uncle,' added Wamba; 'and remember
Pax vobiscum.'

Thus exhorted, Cedric sallied forth upon his expedition; and it was not long ere he had occasion
to try the force of that spell which his Jester had
recommended as omnipotent. In a low-arched and
dusky passage, by which he endeavoured to work
his way to the hall of the castle, he was interrupted
by a female form.

'*Pax vobiscum!*' said the pseudo friar, and was

endeavouring to hurry past, when a soft voice replied, ' *Et vobis; quæso, domine reverendissime, pro misericordia vestra.* '

' I am somewhat deaf,' replied Cedric, in good Saxon, and at the same time muttered to himself, ' A curse on the fool and his *Pax vobiscum!* I have lost my javelin at the first cast.'

It was, however, no unusual thing for a priest of those days to be deaf of his Latin ear, and this the person who now addressed Cedric knew full well.

' I pray you of dear love, reverend father,' she replied in his own language, ' that you will deign to visit with your ghostly comfort a wounded prisoner of this castle, and have such compassion upon him and us as thy holy office teaches. Never shall good deed so highly advantage thy convent.'

' Daughter,' answered Cedric, much embarrassed, ' my time in this castle will not permit me to exercise the duties of mine office. I must presently forth : there is life and death upon my speed.'

' Yet, father, let me entreat you by the vow you have taken on you,' replied the suppliant, ' not to leave the oppressed and endangered without counsel or succour.'

' May the fiend fly away with me, and leave me in Ifrin with the souls of Odin and of Thor !' answered Cedric, impatiently, and would probably have proceeded in the same tone of total departure from his spiritual character, when the colloquy was interrupted by the harsh voice of Urfried, the old crone of the turret.

' How, minion,' said she to the female speaker, ' is this the manner in which you requite the kindness which permitted thee to leave thy prison-cell yonder ? Puttest thou the reverend man to use ungracious language to free himself from the importunities of a Jewess ?'

' A Jewess !' said Cedric, availing himself of the information to get clear of their interruption. ' Let me pass, woman! stop me not at your peril. I am fresh from my holy office, and would avoid pollution.'

'Come this way, father,' said the old hag, 'thou art a stranger in this castle, and canst not leave it without a guide. Come hither, for I would speak with thee. And you, daughter of an accursed race, go to the sick man's chamber, and tend him until my return; and woe betide you if you again quit it without my permission!'

Rebecca retreated. Her importunities had prevailed upon Urfried to suffer her to quit the turret, and Urfried had employed her services where she herself would most gladly have paid them, by the bedside of the wounded Ivanhoe. With an understanding awake to their dangerous situation, and prompt to avail herself of each means of safety which occurred, Rebecca had hoped something from the presence of a man of religion, who, she learned from Urfried, had penetrated into this godless castle. She watched the return of the supposed ecclesiastic, with the purpose of addressing him, and interesting him in favour of the prisoners; with what imperfect success the reader has been just acquainted.

CHAPTER XXVII

Fond wretch! and what canst thou relate,
  But deeds of sorrow, shame, and sin?
Thy deeds are proved—thou know'st thy fate;
  But come, thy tale! begin—begin.

. . . .

But I have griefs of other kind,
  Troubles and sorrows more severe;
Give me to ease my tortured mind,
  Lend to my woes a patient ear;
And let me, if I may not find
  A friend to help, find one to hear.
                    CRABBE's *Hall of Justice.*

WHEN Urfried had with clamours and menaces
driven Rebecca back to the apartment from which
she had sallied, she proceeded to conduct the unwilling Cedric into a small apartment, the door of
which she heedfully secured. Then fetching from
a cupboard a stoup of wine and two flagons, she
placed them on the table, and said in a tone rather
asserting a fact than asking a question, 'Thou art
Saxon, father. Deny it not,' she continued, observing that Cedric hastened not to reply; 'the
sounds of my native language are sweet to mine
ears, though seldom heard save from the tongues of
the wretched and degraded serfs on whom the proud
Normans impose the meanest drudgery of this
dwelling. Thou art a Saxon, father—a Saxon, and,
save as thou art a servant of God, a freeman. Thine
accents are sweet in mine ear.'

'Do not Saxon priests visit this castle, then?'
replied Cedric; 'it were, methinks, their duty to

comfort the outcast and oppressed children of the soil.'

'They come not; or if they come, they better love to revel at the boards of their conquerors,' answered Urfried, 'than to hear the groans of their countrymen; so, at least, report speaks of them, of myself I can say little. This castle, for ten years, has opened to no priest save the debauched Norman chaplain who partook the nightly revels of Front-de-Bœuf, and he has been long gone to render an account of his stewardship. But thou art a Saxon —a Saxon priest, and I have one question to ask of thee.'

'I am a Saxon,' answered Cedric, 'but unworthy, surely, of the name of priest. Let me begone on my way. I swear I will return, or send one of our fathers more worthy to hear your confession.'

'Stay yet a while,' said Urfried; 'the accents of the voice which thou hearest now will soon be choked with the cold earth, and I would not descend to it like the beast I have lived. But wine must give me strength to tell the horrors of my tale.' She poured out a cup, and drank it with a frightful avidity, which seemed desirous of draining the last drop in the goblet. 'It stupifies,' she said, looking upwards as she finished her draught, 'but it cannot cheer. Partake it, father, if you would hear my tale without sinking down upon the pavement.' Cedric would have avoided pledging her in this ominous conviviality, but the sign which she made to him expressed impatience and despair. He complied with her request, and answered her challenge in a large wine-cup; she then proceeded with her story, as if appeased by his complaisance.

'I was not born,' she said, 'father, the wretch that thou now seest me. I was free, was happy, was honoured, loved, and was beloved. I am now a slave, miserable and degraded, the sport of my masters' passions while I had yet beauty, the object of their contempt, scorn, and hatred, since it has passed away. Dost thou wonder, father, that I should hate mankind, and, above all, the race that has wrought this change in me? Can the wrinkled decrepit hag before thee, whose wrath must vent itself in impotent curses, forget she was once the daughter of the noble thane of Torquilstone, before whose frown a thousand vassals trembled?'

'Thou the daughter of Torquil Wolfganger!' said Cedric, receding as he spoke; 'thou—thou— the daughter of that noble Saxon, my father's friend and companion in arms!'

'Thy father's friend!' echoed Urfried; 'then Cedric called the Saxon stands before me, for the noble Hereward of Rotherwood had but one son, whose name is well known among his countrymen. But if thou art Cedric of Rotherwood, why this religious dress? hast thou too despaired of saving thy country, and sought refuge from oppression in the shade of the convent?'

'It matters not who I am,' said Cedric; 'proceed, unhappy woman, with thy tale of horror and guilt! Guilt there must be; there is guilt even in thy living to tell it.'

'There is — there is,' answered the wretched woman, 'deep, black, damning guilt—guilt that lies like a load at my breast—guilt that all the penitential fires of hereafter cannot cleanse. Yes, in these halls, stained with the noble and pure blood of my father and my brethren—in these very halls, to have lived the paramour of their murderer, the slave at once and the partaker of his pleasures, was to render every breath which I drew of vital air a crime and a curse.'

'Wretched woman!' exclaimed Cedric. 'And while the friends of thy father—while each true Saxon heart, as it breathed a requiem for his soul, and those of his valiant sons, forgot not in their prayers the murdered Ulrica—while all mourned

and honoured the dead, thou hast lived to merit
our hate and execration—lived to unite thyself with
the vile tyrant who murdered thy nearest and
dearest, who shed the blood of infancy rather than
a male of the noble house of Torquil Wolfganger
should survive—with him hast thou lived to unite
thyself, and in the bands of lawless love !'

'In lawless bands, indeed, but not in those of
love !' answered the hag; 'love will sooner visit
the regions of eternal doom than those unhallowed
vaults.   No ; with that at least I cannot reproach
myself : hatred to Front-de-Bœuf and his race
governed my soul most deeply, even in the hour
of his guilty endearments.'

'You hated him, and yet you lived,' replied
Cedric ; 'wretch ! was there no poniard—no knife
—no bodkin ! Well was it for thee, since thou
didst prize such an existence, that the secrets of a
Norman castle are like those of the grave.   For
had I but dreamed of the daughter of Torquil living
in foul communion with the murderer of her father,
the sword of a true Saxon had found thee out even
in the arms of thy paramour !'

'Wouldst thou indeed have done this justice to
the name of Torquil ?' said Ulrica, for we may now
lay aside her assumed name of Urfried ; 'thou art
then the true Saxon report speaks thee ! for even
within these accursed walls, where, as thou well
sayest, guilt shrouds itself in inscrutable mystery—
even there has the name of Cedric been sounded ;
and I, wretched and degraded, have rejoiced to
think that there yet breathed an avenger of our
unhappy nation. I also have had my hours of
vengeance. I have fomented the quarrels of our
foes, and heated drunken revelry into murderous
broil. I have seen their blood flow—I have heard
their dying groans ! Look on me, Cedric ; are
there not still left on this foul and faded face some
traces of the features of Torquil ?'

'Ask me not of them, Ulrica,' replied Cedric, in a tone of grief mixed with abhorrence; 'these traces form such a resemblance as arises from the grave of the dead when a fiend has animated the lifeless corpse.'

'Be it so,' answered Ulrica; 'yet wore these fiendish features the mask of a spirit of light when they were able to set at variance the elder Front-de-Bœuf and his son Reginald! The darkness of hell should hide what followed; but revenge must lift the veil, and darkly intimate what it would raise the dead to speak aloud. Long had the smouldering fire of discord glowed between the tyrant father and his savage son; long had I nursed, in secret, the unnatural hatred; it blazed forth in an hour of drunken wassail, and at his own board fell my oppressor by the hand of his own son: such are the secrets these vaults conceal! Rend asunder, ye accursed arches,' she added, looking up towards the roof, 'and bury in your fall all who are conscious of the hideous mystery!'

'And thou, creature of guilt and misery,' said Cedric, 'what became thy lot on the death of thy ravisher?'

'Guess it, but ask it not. Here—here I dwelt, till age, premature age, has stamped its ghastly features on my countenance—scorned and insulted where I was once obeyed, and compelled to bound the revenge which had once such ample scope to the efforts of petty malice of a discontented menial, or the vain or unheeded curses of an impotent hag; condemned to hear from my lonely turret the sounds of revelry in which I once partook, or the shrieks and groans of new victims of oppression.'

'Ulrica,' said Cedric, 'with a heart which still, I fear, regrets the lost reward of thy crimes, as much as the deeds by which thou didst acquire that meed, how didst thou dare to address thee to one who wears this robe? Consider, unhappy woman, what could the sainted Edward himself do for thee, were he here in bodily presence? The royal Confessor was endowed by Heaven with power to cleanse the ulcers of the body; but only God Himself can cure the leprosy of the soul.'

'Yet, turn not from me, stern prophet of wrath,' she exclaimed, 'but tell me, if thou canst, in what shall terminate these new and awful feelings that burst on my solitude. Why do deeds, long since done, rise before me in new and irresistible horrors? What fate is prepared beyond the grave for her to whom God has assigned on earth a lot of such unspeakable wretchedness? Better had I turn to Woden, Hertha, and Zernebock, to Mista, and to Skogula, the gods of our yet unbaptized ancestors, than endure the dreadful anticipations which have of late haunted my waking and my sleeping hours!'

'I am no priest,' said Cedric, turning with disgust from this miserable picture of guilt, wretchedness, and despair—'I am no priest, though I wear a priest's garment.'

'Priest or layman,' answered Ulrica, 'thou art the first I have seen for twenty years by whom God was feared or man regarded; and dost thou bid me despair?'

'I bid thee repent,' said Cedric. 'Seek to prayer and penance, and mayest thou find acceptance! But I cannot, I will not, longer abide with thee.'

'Stay yet a moment!' said Ulrica; 'leave me not now, son of my father's friend, lest the demon who has governed my life should tempt me to avenge myself of thy hard-hearted scorn. Thinkest thou, if Front-de-Bœuf found Cedric the Saxon in his castle, in such a disguise, that thy life would be a long one? Already his eye has been upon thee like a falcon on his prey.'

'And be it so,' said Cedric; 'and let him tear me with beak and talons, ere my tongue say one word which my heart doth not warrant. I will die a

Saxon—true in word, open in deed. I bid thee
avaunt! touch me not, stay me not! The sight of
Front-de-Bœuf himself is less odious to me than
thou, degraded and degenerate as thou art.'

'Be it so,' said Ulrica, no longer interrupting
him; 'go thy way, and forget, in the insolence of
thy superiority, that the wretch before thee is the
daughter of thy father's friend. Go thy way; if I
am separated from mankind by my sufferings—
separated from those whose aid I might most justly
expect—not less will I be separated from them in
my revenge! No man shall aid me, but the ears of
all men shall tingle to hear of the deed which I shall
dare to do! Farewell! thy scorn has burst the last
tie which seemed yet to unite me to my kind—a
thought that my woes might claim the compassion
of my people.'

'Ulrica,' said Cedric, softened by this appeal,
'hast thou borne up and endured to live through so
much guilt and so much misery, and wilt thou now
yield to despair when thine eyes are opened to thy
crimes, and when repentance were thy fitter occupation?'

'Cedric,' answered Ulrica, 'thou little knowest
the human heart. To act as I have acted, to think
as I have thought, requires the maddening love of
pleasure, mingled with the keen appetite of revenge,
the proud consciousness of power—draughts too
intoxicating for the human heart to bear, and yet
retain the power to prevent. Their force has long
passed away. Age has no pleasures, wrinkles have
no influence, revenge itself dies away in impotent
curses. Then comes remorse, with all its vipers,
mixed with vain regrets for the past and despair for
the future! Then, when all other strong impulses
have ceased, we become like the fiends in hell, who
may feel remorse, but never repentance. But thy
words have awakened a new soul within me. Well
hast thou said, all is possible for those who dare to

die! Thou hast shown me the means of revenge, and be assured I will embrace them. It has hitherto shared this wasted bosom with other and with rival passions; henceforward it shall possess me wholly, and thou thyself shalt say that, whatever was the life of Ulrica, her death well became the daughter of the noble Torquil. There is a force without beleaguering this accursed castle; hasten to lead them to the attack, and when thou shalt see a red flag wave from the turret on the eastern angle of the donjon, press the Normans hard: they will then have enough to do within, and you may win the wall in spite both of bow and mangonel. Begone, I pray thee; follow thine own fate, and leave me to mine.'

Cedric would have inquired farther into the purpose which she thus darkly announced, but the stern voice of Front-de-Bœuf was heard exclaiming, 'Where tarries this loitering priest? By the scallop-shell of Compostella, I will make a martyr of him, if he loiters here to hatch treason among my domestics!'

'What a true prophet,' said Ulrica, 'is an evil conscience! But heed him not; out and to thy people. Cry your Saxon onslaught; and let them sing their war-song of Rollo, if they will, vengeance shall bear a burden to it.'

As she thus spoke, she vanished through a private door, and Reginald Front-de-Bœuf entered the apartment. Cedric, with some difficulty, compelled himself to make obeisance to the haughty Baron, who returned his courtesy with a slight inclination of the head.

'Thy penitents, father, have made a long shrift: it is the better for them, since it is the last they shall ever make. Hast thou prepared them for death?'

'I found them,' said Cedric, in such French as he could command, 'expecting the worst, from the moment they knew into whose power they had fallen.'

'How now, Sir Friar,' replied Front-de-Bœuf, 'thy speech, methinks, smacks of a Saxon tongue?'

'I was bred in the convent of St. Withold of Burton,' answered Cedric.

'Ay?' said the Baron; 'it had been better for thee to have been a Norman, and better for my purpose too; but need has no choice of messengers. That St. Withold's of Burton is a howlet's nest worth the harrying. The day will soon come that the frock shall protect the Saxon as little as the mail-coat.'

'God's will be done,' said Cedric, in a voice tremulous with passion, which Front-de-Bœuf imputed to fear.

'I see,' said he, 'thou dreamest already that our men-at-arms are in thy refectory and thy ale-vaults. But do me one cast of thy holy office, and, come what list of others, thou shalt sleep as safe in thy cell as a snail within his shell of proof.'

'Speak your commands,' said Cedric, with suppressed emotion.

'Follow me through this passage, then, that I may dismiss thee by the postern.'

And as he strode on his way before the supposed friar, Front-de-Bœuf thus schooled him in the part which he desired he should act.

'Thou seest, Sir Friar, yon herd of Saxon swine, who have dared to environ this castle of Torquilstone. Tell them whatever thou hast a mind of the weakness of this fortalice, or aught else that can detain them before it for twenty-four hours. Meantime bear thou this scroll. But soft—canst read, Sir Priest?'

'Not a jot I,' answered Cedric, 'save on my breviary; and then I know the characters, because I have the holy service by heart, praised be Our Lady and St. Withold!'

'The fitter messenger for my purpose. Carry thou this scroll to the castle of Philip de Malvoisin; say it cometh from me, and is written by the Templar Brian de Bois-Guilbert, and that I pray him to send it to York with all the speed man and horse can make. Meanwhile, tell him to doubt nothing, he shall find us whole and sound behind our battlement. Shame on it, that we should be compelled to hide thus by a pack of runagates, who are wont to fly even at the flash of our pennons and the tramp of our horses! I say to thee, priest, contrive some cast of thine art to keep the knaves where they are, until our friends bring up their lances. My vengeance is awake, and she is a falcon that slumbers not till she has been gorged.'

'By my patron saint,' said Cedric, with deeper energy than became his character, 'and by every saint who has lived and died in England, your commands shall be obeyed! Not a Saxon shall stir from before these walls, if I have art and influence to detain them there.'

'Ha!' said Front-de-Bœuf, 'thou changest thy tone, Sir Priest, and speakest brief and bold, as if thy heart were in the slaughter of the Saxon herd; and yet thou art thyself of kindred to the swine?'

Cedric was no ready practiser of the art of dissimulation, and would at this moment have been much the better of a hint from Wamba's more fertile brain. But necessity, according to the ancient proverb, sharpens invention, and he muttered something under his cowl concerning the men in question being excommunicated outlaws both to church and to kingdom.

'*Despardieux*,' answered Front-de-Bœuf, 'thou hast spoken the very truth: I forgot that the knaves can strip a fat abbot as well as if they had been born south of yonder salt channel. Was it not he of St. Ives whom they tied to an oak-tree, and compelled to sing a mass while they were rifling his mails and his wallets? No, by Our Lady, that jest was played by Gualtier of Middleton, one of our own companions-at-arms. But they were Saxons who robbed the chapel at St. Bees of cup, candlestick, and chalice, were they not?'

'They were godless men,' answered Cedric.

'Ay, and they drank out all the good wine and ale that lay in store for many a secret carousal, when ye pretend ye are but busied with vigils and primes! Priest, thou art bound to revenge such sacrilege.'

'I am indeed bound to vengeance,' murmured Cedric; 'St. Withold knows my heart.'

Front-de-Bœuf, in the meanwhile, led the way to a postern, where, passing the moat on a single plank, they reached a small barbican, or exterior defence, which communicated with the open field by a well-fortified sallyport.

'Begone, then; and if thou wilt do mine errand, and if thou return hither when it is done, thou shalt see Saxon flesh cheap as ever was hog's in the shambles of Sheffield. And, hark thee, thou seemest to be a jolly confessor; come hither after the onslaught, and thou shalt have as much Malvoisie as would drench thy whole convent.'

'Assuredly we shall meet again,' answered Cedric.

'Something in hand the whilst,' continued the Norman; and, as they parted at the postern door, he thrust into Cedric's reluctant hand a gold byzant, adding, 'Remember, I will flay off both cowl and skin if thou failest in thy purpose.'

'And full leave will I give thee to do both,' answered Cedric, leaving the postern, and striding forth over the free field with a joyful step, 'if, when we meet next, I deserve not better at thine hand.' Turning then back towards the castle, he threw the piece of gold towards the donor, exclaiming at the same time, 'False Norman, thy money perish with thee!'

Front-de-Bœuf heard the words imperfectly, but the action was suspicious. 'Archers,' he called to the warders on the outward battlements, 'send me an arrow through yon monk's frock! Yet stay,' he said, as his retainers were bending their bows, 'it avails not; we must thus far trust him since we have no better shift. I think he dares not betray me; at the worst I can but treat with these Saxon dogs whom I have safe in kennel. Ho! Giles jailor, let them bring Cedric of Rotherwood before me, and the other churl, his companion—him I mean of Coningsburgh—Athelstane there, or what call they him? Their very names are an encumbrance to a Norman knight's mouth, and have, as it were, a flavour of bacon. Give me a stoup of wine, as jolly Prince John said, that I may wash away the relish; place it in the armoury, and thither lead the prisoners.'

His commands were obeyed; and, upon entering that Gothic apartment, hung with many spoils won by his own valour and that of his father, he found a flagon of wine on the massive oaken table, and the two Saxon captives under the guard of four of his dependants. Front-de-Bœuf took a long draught of wine, and then addressed his prisoners; for the manner in which Wamba drew the cap over his face, the change of dress, the gloomy and broken light, and the Baron's imperfect acquaintance with the features of Cedric, who avoided his Norman neighbours, and seldom stirred beyond his own domains, prevented him from discovering that the most important of his captives had made his escape.

'Gallants of England,' said Front-de-Bœuf, 'how relish ye your entertainment at Torquilstone? Are ye yet aware what your *surquedy* and *outrecuidance* [1] merit, for scoffing at the entertainment of a prince of the house of Anjou? Have ye forgotten how

---

[1] *Surquedy* and *outrecuidance*—insolence and presumption.

ye requited the unmerited hospitality of the royal
John? By God and St. Denis, an ye pay not the
richer ransom, I will hang ye up by the feet from
the iron bars of these windows, till the kites and
hooded crows have made skeletons of you! Speak
out, ye Saxon dogs—what bid ye for your worthless
lives? How say you, you of Rotherwood?'

'Not a doit I,' answered poor Wamba; 'and for
hanging up by the feet, my brain has been topsy-
turvy, they say, ever since the biggin was bound
first round my head; so turning me upside down
may peradventure restore it again.'

'St. Genevieve!' said Front-de-Bœuf, 'what have
we got here?'

And with the back of his hand he struck Cedric's
cap from the head of the Jester, and throwing open
his collar, discovered the fatal badge of servitude,
the silver collar round his neck.

'Giles—Clement—dogs and varlets!' exclaimed
the furious Norman, 'what have you brought me
here?'

'I think I can tell you,' said De Bracy, who just
entered the apartment. 'This is Cedric's clown,
who fought so manful a skirmish with Isaac of York
about a question of precedence.'

'I shall settle it for them both,' replied Front-
de-Bœuf; 'they shall hang on the same gallows,
unless his master and this boar of Coningsburgh
will pay well for their lives. Their wealth is the
least they can surrender; they must also carry off
with them the swarms that are besetting the castle,
subscribe a surrender of their pretended immunities,
and live under us as serfs and vassals; too happy
if, in the new world that is about to begin, we leave
them the breath of their nostrils. Go,' said he to
two of his attendants, 'fetch me the right Cedric
hither, and I pardon your error for once; the
rather that you but mistook a fool for a Saxon
franklin.'

' Ay, but,' said Wamba, ' your chivalrous excellency will find there are more fools than franklins among us.'

' What means the knave?' said Front-de-Bœuf, looking towards his followers, who, lingering and loth, faltered forth their belief that, if this were not Cedric who was there in presence, they knew not what was become of him.

' Saints of Heaven!' exclaimed De Bracy, ' he must have escaped in the monk's garments!'

' Fiends of hell!' echoed Front-de-Bœuf, ' it was then the boar of Rotherwood whom I ushered to the postern, and dismissed with my own hands! And thou,' he said to Wamba, ' whose folly could overreach the wisdom of idiots yet more gross than thyself—I will give thee holy orders—I will shave thy crown for thee! Here, let them tear the scalp from his head, and then pitch him headlong from the battlements. Thy trade is to jest, canst thou jest now?'

' You deal with me better than your word, noble knight,' whimpered forth poor Wamba, whose habits of buffoonery were not to be overcome even by the immediate prospect of death; ' if you give me the red cap you propose, out of a simple monk you will make a cardinal.'

' The poor wretch,' said De Bracy, ' is resolved to die in his vocation. Front-de-Bœuf, you shall not slay him. Give him to me to make sport for my Free Companions. How sayst thou, knave? Wilt thou take heart of grace, and go to the wars with me?'

' Ay, with my master's leave,' said Wamba; ' for, look you, I must not slip collar (and he touched that which he wore) without his permission.'

' Oh, a Norman saw will soon cut a Saxon collar,' said De Bracy.

' Ay, noble sir,' said Wamba, ' and thence goes the proverb—

Norman saw on English oak,
　On English neck a Norman yoke;
Norman spoon in English dish,
　And England ruled as Normans wish;
Blythe world to England never will be more,
　Till England's rid of all the four.'

'Thou dost well, De Bracy,' said Front-de-Bœuf,
'to stand there listening to a fool's jargon, when
destruction is gaping for us! Seest thou not we
are overreached, and that our proposed mode of
communicating with our friends without has been
disconcerted by this same motley gentleman thou
art so fond to brother? What views have we to
expect but instant storm?'

'To the battlements then,' said De·Bracy; 'when
didst thou ever see me the graver for the thoughts
of battle? Call the Templar yonder, and let him
fight but half so well for his life as he has done for
his order. Make thou to the walls thyself with thy
huge body. Let me do my poor endeavour in my
own way, and I tell thee the Saxon outlaws may as
well attempt to scale the clouds as the castle of
Torquilstone; or, if you will treat with the banditti,
why not employ the mediation of this worthy
franklin, who seems in such deep contemplation of
the wine-flagon? Here, Saxon,' he continued, addressing Athelstane, and handing the cup·to him,
'rinse thy throat with that noble liquor, and rouse
up thy soul to say what thou wilt do for thy
liberty.'

'What a man of mould may,' answered Athelstane, 'providing it be what a man of manhood
ought. Dismiss me free, with my companions, and
I will pay a ransom of a thousand marks.'

'And wilt moreover assure us the retreat of that
scum of mankind who are swarming around the
castle, contrary to God's peace and the king's?'
said Front-de-Bœuf.

'In so far as I can,' answered Athelstane, 'I will

withdraw them ; and I fear not but that my father Cedric will do his best to assist me.'

'We are agreed then,' said Front-de-Bœuf, 'thou and they are to be set at freedom, and peace is to be on both sides, for payment of a thousand marks. It is a trifling ransom, Saxon, and thou wilt owe gratitude to the moderation which accepts of it in exchange of your persons. But mark, this extends not to the Jew Isaac.'

'Nor to the Jew Isaac's daughter,' said the Templar, who had now joined them.

'Neither,' said Front-de-Bœuf, 'belong to this Saxon's company.'

'I were unworthy to be called Christian, if they did,' replied Athelstane ; 'deal with the unbelievers as ye list.'

'Neither does the ransom include the Lady Rowena,' said De Bracy. 'It shall never be said I was scared out of a fair prize without striking a blow for it.'

'Neither,' said Front-de-Bœuf, 'does our treaty refer to this wretched Jester, whom I retain, that I may make him an example to every knave who turns jest into earnest.'

'The Lady Rowena,' answered Athelstane, with the most steady countenance, 'is my affianced bride. I will be drawn by wild horses before I consent to part with her. The slave Wamba has this day saved the life of my father Cedric. I will lose mine ere a hair of his head be injured.'

'Thy affianced bride ! The Lady Rowena the affianced bride of a vassal like thee !' said De Bracy. 'Saxon, thou dreamest that the days of thy seven kingdoms are returned again. I tell thee, the princes of the house of Anjou confer not their wards on men of such lineage as thine.'

'My lineage, proud Norman,' replied Athelstane, 'is drawn from a source more pure and ancient than that of a beggarly Frenchman, whose living is won by selling the blood of the thieves whom he assembles under his paltry standard. Kings were my ancestors, strong in war and wise in council, who every day feasted in their hall more hundreds than thou canst number individual followers; whose names have been sung by minstrels, and their laws recorded by Witenagemotes; whose bones were interred amid the prayers of saints, and over whose tombs minsters have been builded.'

'Thou hast it, De Bracy,' said Front-de-Bœuf, well pleased with the rebuff which his companion had received; 'the Saxon hath hit thee fairly.'

'As fairly as a captive can strike,' said De Bracy, with apparent carelessness; 'for he whose hands are tied should have his tongue at freedom. But thy glibness of reply, comrade,' rejoined he, speaking to Athelstane, 'will not win the freedom of the Lady Rowena.'

To this Athelstane, who had already made a longer speech than was his custom to do on any topic, however interesting, returned no answer. The conversation was interrupted by the arrival of a menial, who announced that a monk demanded admittance at the postern gate.

'In the name of St. Bennet, the prince of these bull-beggars,' said Front-de-Bœuf, 'have we a real monk this time, or another impostor? Search him, slaves; for an ye suffer a second impostor to be palmed upon you, I will have your eyes torn out, and hot coals put into the sockets.'

'Let me endure the extremity of your anger, my lord,' said Giles, 'if this be not a real shaveling. Your squire Jocelyn knows him well, and will vouch him to be Brother Ambrose, a monk in attendance upon the Prior of Jorvaulx.'

'Admit him,' said Front-de-Bœuf; 'most likely he brings us news from his jovial master. Surely the devil keeps holiday, and the priests are relieved from duty, that they are strolling thus wildly through the country. Remove these prisoners; and, Saxon, think on what thou hast heard.'

'I claim,' said Athelstane, 'an honourable imprisonment, with due care of my board and of my couch, as becomes my rank, and as is due to one who is in treaty for ransom. Moreover, I hold him that deems himself the best of you bound to answer to me with his body for this aggression on my freedom. This defiance hath already been sent to thee by thy sewer; thou underliest it, and art bound to answer me. There lies my glove.'

'I answer not the challenge of my prisoner,' said Front-de-Bœuf, 'nor shalt thou, Maurice de Bracy. Giles,' he continued, 'hang the franklin's glove upon the tine of yonder branched antlers; there shall it remain until he is a free man. Should he then presume to demand it, or to affirm he was unlawfully made my prisoner, by the belt of St. Christopher, he will speak to one who hath never refused to meet a foe on foot or on horseback, alone or with his vassals at his back!'

The Saxon prisoners were accordingly removed, just as they introduced the monk Ambrose, who appeared to be in great perturbation.

'This is the real *Deus vobiscum*,' said Wamba, as he passed the reverend brother; 'the others were but counterfeits.'

'Holy Mother!' said the monk, as he addressed the assembled knights, 'I am at last safe and in Christian keeping!'

'Safe thou art,' replied De Bracy, 'and for Christianity, here is the stout Baron Reginald Front-de-Bœuf, whose utter abomination is a Jew; and the good Knight Templar, Brian de Bois-Guilbert, whose trade is to slay Saracens. If these are not good marks of Christianity, I know no other which they bear about them.'

'Ye are friends and allies of our reverend father

in God, Aymer, Prior of Jorvaulx,' said the monk, without noticing the tone of De Bracy's reply; 'ye owe him aid both by knightly faith and holy charity; for what saith the blessed St. Augustin, in his treatise *De Civitate Dei*——'

'What saith the devil!' interrupted Front-de-Bœuf; 'or rather what dost *thou* say, Sir Priest? We have little time to hear texts from the holy fathers.'

'*Sancta Maria!*' ejaculated Father Ambrose, 'how prompt to ire are these unhallowed laymen! But be it known to you, brave knights, that certain murderous caitiffs, casting behind them fear of God and reverence of His church, and not regarding the bull of the holy see, *Si quis, suadente Diabolo*——'

'Brother priest,' said the Templar, 'all this we know or guess at; tell us plainly, is thy master, the Prior, made prisoner, and to whom?'

'Surely,' said Ambrose, 'he is in the hands of the men of Belial, infesters of these woods, and contemners of the holy text, "Touch not mine anointed, and do my prophets nought of evil."'

'Here is a new argument for our swords, sirs,' said Front-de-Bœuf, turning to his companions; 'and so, instead of reaching us any assistance, the Prior of Jorvaulx requests aid at our hands? A man is well helped of these lazy churchmen when he hath most to do! But speak out, priest, and say at once what doth thy master expect from us?'

'So please you,' said Ambrose, 'violent hands having been imposed on my reverend superior, contrary to the holy ordinance which I did already quote, and the men of Belial having rifled his mails and budgets, and stripped him of two hundred marks of pure refined gold, they do yet demand of him a large sum beside, ere they will suffer him to depart from their uncircumcised hands. Wherefore the reverend father in God prays you, as his dear

friends, to rescue him, either by paying down the
ransom at which they hold him, or by force of
arms, at your best discretion.'

'The foul fiend quell the Prior!' said Front-de-
Bœuf; 'his morning's draught has been a deep one.
When did thy master hear of a Norman baron
unbuckling his purse to relieve a churchman, whose
bags are ten times as weighty as ours? And how
can we do aught by valour to free him, that are
cooped up here by ten times our number, and expect
an assault every moment?'

'And that was what I was about to tell you,'
said the monk, 'had your hastiness allowed me
time. But, God help me, I am old, and these foul
onslaughts distract an aged man's brain. Nevertheless, it is of verity that they assemble a camp,
and raise a bank against the walls of this castle.'

'To the battlements!' cried De Bracy, 'and let
us mark what these knaves do without'; and so
saying, he opened a latticed window which led to a
sort of bartizan or projecting balcony, and immediately called from thence to those in the apartment—'St. Denis, but the old monk hath brought
true tidings! They bring forward mantelets and
pavisses, and the archers muster on the skirts of
the wood like a dark cloud before a hail-storm.'

Reginald Front-de-Bœuf also looked out upon the
field, and immediately snatched his bugle; and after
winding a long and loud blast, commanded his men
to their posts on the walls.

'De Bracy, look to the eastern side where the
walls are lowest. Noble Bois-Guilbert, thy trade
hath well taught thee how to attack and defend,
look thou to the western side. I myself will take
post at the barbican. Yet, do not confine your
exertions to any one spot, noble friends! We must
this day be everywhere, and multiply ourselves,
were it possible, so as to carry by our presence

succour and relief wherever the attack is hottest. Our numbers are few, but activity and courage may supply that defect, since we have only to do with rascal clowns.'

'But, noble knights,' exclaimed Father Ambrose, amidst the bustle and confusion occasioned by the preparations for defence, 'will none of ye hear the message of the reverend father in God, Aymer, Prior of Jorvaulx? I beseech thee to hear me, noble Sir Reginald!'

'Go patter thy petitions to Heaven,' said the fierce Norman, 'for we on earth have no time to listen to them. Ho! there, Anselm! see that seething pitch and oil are ready to pour on the heads of these audacious traitors. Look that the cross-bowmen lack not bolts. Fling abroad my banner with the old bull's head; the knaves shall soon find with whom they have to do this day!'

'But, noble sir,' continued the monk, persevering in his endeavours to draw attention, 'consider my vow of obedience, and let me discharge myself of my superior's errand.'

'Away with this prating dotard,' said Front-de-Bœuf; 'lock him up in the chapel to tell his beads till the broil be over. It will be a new thing to the saints in Torquilstone to hear aves and paters; they have not been so honoured, I trow, since they were cut out of stone.'

'Blaspheme not the holy saints, Sir Reginald,' said De Bracy, 'we shall have need of their aid to-day before yon rascal rout disband.'

'I expect little aid from their hand,' said Front-de-Bœuf, 'unless we were to hurl them from the battlements on the heads of the villains. There is a huge lumbering St. Christopher yonder, sufficient to bear a whole company to the earth.'

The Templar had in the meantime been looking out on the proceedings of the besiegers, with rather more attention than the brutal Front-de-Bœuf or his giddy companion.

'By the faith of mine order,' he said, 'these men approach with more touch of discipline than could have been judged, however they come by it. See ye how dexterously they avail themselves of every cover which a tree or bush affords, and shun exposing themselves to the shot of our cross-bows? I spy neither banner nor pennon among them, and yet will I gage my golden chain that they are led on by some noble knight or gentleman, skilful in the practice of wars.'

'I espy him,' said De Bracy; 'I see the waving of a knight's crest, and the gleam of his armour. See yon tall man in the black mail, who is busied marshalling the farther troop of the rascaille yeomen; by St. Denis, I hold him to be the same whom we called *Le Noir Faineant*, who overthrew thee, Front-de-Bœuf, in the lists at Ashby.'

'So much the better,' said Front-de-Bœuf, 'that he comes here to give me my revenge. Some hilding fellow he must be, who dared not stay to assert his claim to the tourney prize which chance had assigned him. I should in vain have sought for him where knights and nobles seek their foes, and right glad am I he hath here shown himself among yon villain yeomanry.'

The demonstrations of the enemy's immediate approach cut off all farther discourse. Each knight repaired to his post, and at the head of the few followers whom they were able to muster, and who were in numbers inadequate to defend the whole extent of the walls, they awaited with calm determination the threatened assault.

CHAPTER XXVIII

The wandering race, sever'd from other men,
Boast yet their intercourse with human arts ;
The seas, the woods, the deserts, which they haunt.
Find them acquainted with their secret treasures ;
And unregarded herbs, and flowers, and blossoms,
Display undreamt-of powers when gather'd by them.
The Jew.

OUR history must needs retrograde for the space of
a few pages, to inform the reader of certain passages
material to his understanding the rest of this important narrative. His own intelligence may indeed
have easily anticipated that, when Ivanhoe sunk
down, and seemed abandoned by all the world, it
was the importunity of Rebecca which prevailed on
her father to have the gallant young warrior transported from the lists to the house which, for the
time, the Jews inhabited in the suburbs of Ashby.

It would not have been difficult to have persuaded
Isaac to this step in any other circumstances, for
his disposition was kind and grateful. But he had
also the prejudices and scrupulous timidity of his
persecuted people, and those were to be conquered.

'Holy Abraham !' he exclaimed, 'he is a good
youth, and my heart bleeds to see the gore trickle
down his rich embroidered hacqueton, and his
corslet of goodly price ; but to carry him to our
house ! damsel, hast thou well considered ? He is
a Christian, and by our law we may not deal with
the stranger and Gentile, save for the advantage of
our commerce.'

'Speak not so, my dear father,' replied Rebecca; 'we may not indeed mix with them in banquet and in jollity; but in wounds and in misery, the Gentile becometh the Jew's brother.'

'I would I knew what the Rabbi Jacob ben Tudela would opine on it,' replied Isaac; 'nevertheless, the good youth must not bleed to death. Let Seth and Reuben bear him to Ashby.'

'Nay, let them place him in my litter,' said Rebecca; 'I will mount one of the palfreys.'

'That were to expose thee to the gaze of those dogs of Ishmael and of Edom,' whispered Isaac, with a suspicious glance towards the crowd of knights and squires. But Rebecca was already busied in carrying her charitable purpose into effect, and listed not what he said, until Isaac, seizing the sleeve of her mantle, again exclaimed, in a hurried voice—'Beard of Aaron! what if the youth perish! If he die in our custody, shall we not be held guilty of his blood, and be torn to pieces by the multitude?'

'He will not die, my father,' said Rebecca, gently extricating herself from the grasp of Isaac—'he will not die unless we abandon him; and if so, we are indeed answerable for his blood to God and to man.'

'Nay,' said Isaac, releasing his hold, 'it grieveth me as much to see the drops of his blood as if they were so many golden byzants from mine own purse; and I well know that the lessons of Miriam, daughter of the Rabbi Manasses of Byzantium, whose soul is in Paradise, have made thee skilful in the art of healing, and that thou knowest the craft of herbs and the force of elixirs. Therefore, do as thy mind giveth thee: thou art a good damsel—a blessing, and a crown, and a song of rejoicing unto me and unto my house, and unto the people of my fathers.'

The apprehensions of Isaac, however, were not ill founded; and the generous and grateful benevolence of his daughter exposed her, on her return to Ashby, to the unhallowed gaze of Brian de Bois-Guilbert. The Templar twice passed and repassed them on the road, fixing his bold and ardent look on the beautiful Jewess; and we have already seen the consequences of the admiration which her charms excited, when accident threw her into the power of that unprincipled voluptuary.

Rebecca lost no time in causing the patient to be transported to their temporary dwelling, and proceeded with her own hands to examine and to bind up his wounds. The youngest reader of romances and romantic ballads must recollect how often the females, during the dark ages, as they are called, were initiated into the mysteries of surgery, and how frequently the gallant knight submitted the wounds of his person to her cure whose eyes had yet more deeply penetrated his heart.

But the Jews, both male and female, possessed and practised the medical science in all its branches, and the monarchs and powerful barons of the time frequently committed themselves to the charge of some experienced sage among this despised people when wounded or in sickness. The aid of the Jewish physicians was not the less eagerly sought after, though a general belief prevailed among the Christians that the Jewish rabbins were deeply acquainted with the occult sciences, and particularly with the cabalistical art, which had its name and origin in the studies of the sages of Israel. Neither did the rabbins disown such acquaintance with supernatural arts, which added nothing—for what could add aught?—to the hatred with which their nation was regarded, while it diminished the contempt with which that malevolence was mingled. A Jewish magician might be the subject of equal abhorrence with a Jewish usurer, but he could not be equally despised. It is, besides, probable, considering the wonderful cures they are said to have performed, that the Jews possessed some secrets of the healing art peculiar to themselves, and which, with the exclusive spirit arising out of their condition, they took great care to conceal from the Christians amongst whom they dwelt.

The beautiful Rebecca had been heedfully brought up in all the knowledge proper to her nation, which her apt and powerful mind had retained, arranged, and enlarged, in the course of a progress beyond her years, her sex, and even the age in which she lived. Her knowledge of medicine and of the healing art had been acquired under an aged Jewess, the daughter of one of their most celebrated doctors, who loved Rebecca as her own child, and was believed to have communicated to her secrets which had been left to herself by her sage father at the same time, and under the same circumstances. The fate of Miriam had indeed been to fall a sacrifice to the fanaticism of the times ; but her secrets had survived in her apt pupil.

Rebecca, thus endowed with knowledge as with beauty, was universally revered and admired by her own tribe, who almost regarded her as one of those gifted women mentioned in the sacred history. Her father himself, out of reverence for her talents, which involuntarily mingled itself with his unbounded affection, permitted the maiden a greater liberty than was usually indulged to those of her sex by the habits of her people, and was, as we have just seen, frequently guided by her opinion, even in preference to his own.

When Ivanhoe reached the habitation of Isaac, he was still in a state of unconsciousness, owing to the profuse loss of blood which had taken place during his exertions in the lists. Rebecca examined the wound, and having applied to it such vulnerary remedies as her art prescribed, informed her father that if fever could be averted, of which the great bleeding rendered her little apprehensive, and if the healing balsam of Miriam retained its virtue,

there was nothing to fear for his guest's life, and
that he might with safety travel to York with them
on the ensuing day. Isaac looked a little blank at
this annunciation. His charity would willingly have
stopped short at Ashby, or at most would have left
the wounded Christian to be tended in the house
where he was residing at present, with an assurance
to the Hebrew to whom it belonged that all expenses should be duly discharged. To this, however, Rebecca opposed many reasons, of which we
shall only mention two that had peculiar weight
with Isaac. The one was, that she would on no
account put the phial of precious balsam into the
hands of another physician even of her own tribe,
lest that valuable mystery should be discovered ;
the other, that this wounded knight, Wilfred of
Ivanhoe, was an intimate favourite of Richard Cœur-
de-Lion, and that, in case the monarch should
return, Isaac, who had supplied his brother John
with treasure to prosecute his rebellious purposes,
would stand in no small need of a powerful protector
who enjoyed Richard's favour.

'Thou art speaking but sooth, Rebecca,' said
Isaac, giving way to these weighty arguments : ' it
were an offending of Heaven to betray the secrets
of the blessed Miriam ; for the good which Heaven
giveth is not rashly to be squandered upon others,
whether it be talents of gold and shekels of silver,
or whether it be the secret mysteries of a wise
physician ; assuredly they should be preserved to
those to whom Providence hath vouchsafed them.
And him whom the Nazarenes of England call the
Lion's Heart—assuredly it were better for me to
fall into the hands of a strong lion of Idumea than
into his, if he shall have got assurance of my dealing
with his brother. Wherefore I will lend ear to thy
counsel, and this youth shall journey with us unto
York, and our house shall be as a home to him until
his wounds shall be healed. And if he of the Lion

Heart shall return to the land, as is now noised
abroad, then shall this Wilfred of Ivanhoe be unto
me as a wall of defence, when the king's displeasure
shall burn high against thy father. And if he doth
not return, this Wilfred may natheless repay us our
charges when he shall gain treasure by the strength
of his spear and of his sword, even as he did yesterday and this day also. For the youth is a good
youth, and keepeth the day which he appointeth,
and restoreth that which he borroweth, and suc-
coureth the Israelite, even the child of my father's
house, when he is encompassed by strong thieves
and sons of Belial.'

It was not until evening was nearly closed that
Ivanhoe was restored to consciousness of his situation. He awoke from a broken slumber, under the
confused impressions which are naturally attendant
on the recovery from a state of insensibility. He
was unable for some time to recall exactly to
memory the circumstances which had preceded his
fall in the lists, or to make out any connected chain
of the events in which he had been engaged upon
the yesterday. A sense of wounds and injury,
joined to great weakness and exhaustion, was
mingled with the recollection of blows dealt and
received, of steeds rushing upon each other, over-
throwing and overthrown, of shouts and clashing of
arms, and all the heady tumult of a confused fight.
An effort to draw aside the curtain of his couch
was in some degree successful, although rendered
difficult by the pain of his wound.

To his great surprise, he found himself in a room
magnificently furnished, but having cushions instead
of chairs to rest upon, and in other respects partaking so much of Oriental costume that he began
to doubt whether he had not, during his sleep, been
transported back again to the land of Palestine.
The impression was increased when, the tapestry
being drawn aside, a female form, dressed in a rich

habit, which partook more of the Eastern taste than that of Europe, glided through the door which it concealed, and was followed by a swarthy domestic.

As the wounded knight was about to address this fair apparition, she imposed silence by placing her slender finger upon her ruby lips, while the attendant, approaching him, proceeded to uncover Ivanhoe's side, and the lovely Jewess satisfied herself that the bandage was in its place, and the wound doing well. She performed her task with a graceful and dignified simplicity and modesty, which might, even in more civilised days, have served to redeem it from whatever might seem repugnant to female delicacy. The idea of so young and beautiful a person engaged in attendance on a sick-bed, or in dressing the wound of one of a different sex, was melted away and lost in that of a beneficent being contributing her effectual aid to relieve pain, and to avert the stroke of death. Rebecca's few and brief directions were given in the Hebrew language to the old domestic ; and he, who had been frequently her assistant in similar cases, obeyed them without reply.

The accents of an unknown tongue, however harsh they might have sounded when uttered by another, had, coming from the beautiful Rebecca, the romantic and pleasing effect which fancy ascribes to the charms pronounced by some beneficent fairy, unintelligible, indeed, to the ear, but from the sweetness of utterance and benignity of aspect which accompanied them touching and affecting to the heart. Without making an attempt at further question, Ivanhoe suffered them in silence to take the measures they thought most proper for his recovery ; and it was not until those were completed, and this kind physician about to retire, that his curiosity could no longer be suppressed. 'Gentle maiden,' he began in the Arabian tongue, with which his Eastern travels had rendered him

familiar, and which he thought most likely to be
understood by the turbaned and caftaned damsel
who stood before him—' I pray you, gentle maiden,
of your courtesy——'

But here he was interrupted by his fair physician,
a smile which she could scarce suppress dimpling
for an instant a face whose general expression was
that of contemplative melancholy. 'I am of England, Sir Knight, and speak the English tongue,
although my dress and my lineage belong to
another climate.'

'Noble damsel——' again the Knight of Ivanhoe
began, and again Rebecca hastened to interrupt him.

'Bestow not on me, Sir Knight,' she said, 'the
epithet of noble. It is well you should speedily
know that your handmaiden is a poor Jewess, the
daughter of that Isaac of York to whom you were
so lately a good and kind lord. It well becomes
him and those of his household to render to you
such careful tendance as your present state necessarily demands.'

I know not whether the fair Rowena would have
been altogether satisfied with the species of emotion
with which her devoted knight had hitherto gazed
on the beautiful features, and fair form, and lustrous
eyes of the lovely Rebecca—eyes whose brilliancy
was shaded, and, as it were, mellowed, by the
fringe of her long silken eyelashes, and which a
minstrel would have compared to the evening star
darting its rays through a bower of jessamine. But
Ivanhoe was too good a Catholic to retain the same
class of feelings towards a Jewess. This Rebecca
had foreseen, and for this very purpose she had
hastened to mention her father's name and lineage;
yet—for the fair and wise daughter of Isaac was not
without a touch of female weakness—she could not
but sigh internally when the glance of respectful
admiration, not altogether unmixed with tenderness, with which Ivanhoe had hitherto regarded his

unknown benefactress, was exchanged at once for a manner cold, composed, and collected, and fraught with no deeper feeling than that which expressed a grateful sense of courtesy received from an unexpected quarter, and from one of an inferior race. It was not that Ivanhoe's former carriage expressed more than that general devotional homage which youth always pays to beauty; yet it was mortifying that one word should operate as a spell to remove poor Rebecca, who could not be supposed altogether ignorant of her title to such homage, into a degraded class, to whom it could not be honourably rendered.

But the gentleness and candour of Rebecca's nature imputed no fault to Ivanhoe for sharing in the universal prejudices of his age and religion. On the contrary, the fair Jewess, though sensible her patient now regarded her as one of a race of reprobation, with whom it was disgraceful to hold any beyond the most necessary intercourse, ceased not to pay the same patient and devoted attention to his safety and convalescence. She informed him of the necessity they were under of removing to York, and of her father's resolution to transport him thither, and tend him in his own house until his health should be restored. Ivanhoe expressed great repugnance to this plan, which he grounded on unwillingness to give farther trouble to his benefactors.

'Was there not,' he said, 'in Ashby, or near it, some Saxon franklin, or even some wealthy peasant, who would endure the burden of a wounded countryman's residence with him until he should be again able to bear his armour? Was there no convent of Saxon endowment, where he could be received? Or could he not be transported as far as Burton, where he was sure to find hospitality with Waltheoff, the Abbot of St. Withold's, to whom he was related?'

'Any, the worst of these harbourages,' said Rebecca, with a melancholy smile, 'would unquestionably be more fitting for your residence than the abode of a despised Jew; yet, Sir Knight, unless you would dismiss your physician, you cannot change your lodging. Our nation, as you well know, can cure wounds, though we deal not in inflicting them; and in our own family, in particular, are secrets which have been handed down since the days of Solomon, and of which you have already experienced the advantages. No Nazarene— I crave your forgiveness, Sir Knight—no Christian leech, within the four seas of Britain, could enable you to bear your corslet within a month.'

'And how soon wilt *thou* enable me to brook it?' said Ivanhoe, impatiently.

'Within eight days, if thou wilt be patient and conformable to my directions,' replied Rebecca.

'By Our Blessed Lady,' said Wilfred, 'if it be not a sin to name her here, it is no time for me or any true knight to be bedridden; and if thou accomplish thy promise, maiden, I will pay thee with my casque full of crowns, come by them as I may.'

'I will accomplish my promise,' said Rebecca, 'and thou shalt bear thine armour on the eighth day from hence, if thou wilt grant me but one boon in the stead of the silver thou dost promise me.'

'If it be within my power, and such as a true Christian knight may yield to one of thy people,' replied Ivanhoe, 'I will grant thy boon blythely and thankfully.'

'Nay,' answered Rebecca, 'I will but pray of thee to believe henceforward that a Jew may do good service to a Christian, without desiring other guerdon than the blessing of the Great Father who made both Jew and Gentile.'

'It were sin to doubt it, maiden,' replied Ivanhoe; 'and I repose myself on thy skill without further scruple or question, well trusting you will enable me to bear my corslet on the eighth day. And now, my kind leech, let me inquire of the news abroad. What of the noble Saxon Cedric and his household? what of the lovely Lady——' He stopt, as if unwilling to speak Rowena's name in the house of a Jew—'Of her, I mean, who was named Queen of the tournament?'

'And who was selected by you, Sir Knight, to hold that dignity, with judgment which was admired as much as your valour,' replied Rebecca.

The blood which Ivanhoe had lost did not prevent a flush from crossing his cheek, feeling that he had incautiously betrayed his deep interest in Rowena by the awkward attempt he had made to conceal it.

'It was less of her I would speak,' said he, 'than of Prince John; and I would fain know somewhat of a faithful squire, and why he now attends me not?'

'Let me use my authority as a leech,' answered Rebecca, 'and enjoin you to keep silence, and avoid agitating reflections, whilst I apprise you of what you desire to know. Prince John hath broken off the tournament, and set forward in all haste towards York, with the nobles, knights, and churchmen of his party, after collecting such sums as they could wring, by fair means or foul, from those who are esteemed the wealthy of the land. It is said he designs to assume his brother's crown.'

'Not without a blow struck in its defence,' said Ivanhoe, raising himself upon the couch, 'if there were but one true subject in England. I will fight for Richard's title with the best of them—ay, one to two, in his just quarrel!'

'But that you may be able to do so,' said Rebecca, touching his shoulder with her hand, 'you must now observe my directions, and remain quiet.'

'True, maiden,' said Ivanhoe, 'as quiet as these disquieted times will permit. And of Cedric and his household?'

'His steward came but brief while since,' said the Jewess, 'panting with haste, to ask my father for certain monies, the price of wool the growth of Cedric's flocks, and from him I learned that Cedric and Athelstane of Coningsburgh had left Prince John's lodging in high displeasure, and were about to set forth on their return homeward.'

'Went any lady with them to the banquet?' said Wilfred.

'The Lady Rowena,' said Rebecca, answering the question with more precision than it had been asked—'the Lady Rowena went not to the Prince's feast, and, as the steward reported to us, she is now on her journey back to Rotherwood with her guardian Cedric. And touching your faithful squire Gurth——'

'Ha!' exclaimed the knight, 'knowest thou his name? But thou dost,' he immediately added, 'and well thou mayst, for it was from thy hand, and, as I am now convinced, from thine own generosity of spirit, that he received but yesterday a hundred zecchins.'

'Speak not of that,' said Rebecca, blushing deeply; 'I see how easy it is for the tongue to betray what the heart would gladly conceal.'

'But this sum of gold,' said Ivanhoe, gravely, 'my honour is concerned in repaying it to your father.'

'Let it be as thou wilt,' said Rebecca, 'when eight days have passed away; but think not, and speak not, now of aught that may retard thy recovery.'

'Be it so, kind maiden,' said Ivanhoe; 'I were most ungrateful to dispute thy commands. But one word of the fate of poor Gurth, and I have done with questioning thee.'

'I grieve to tell thee, Sir Knight,' answered the Jewess, 'that he is in custody by the order of Cedric.' And then observing the distress which

her communication gave to Wilfred, she instantly
added, 'But the steward Oswald said, that if
nothing occurred to renew his master's displeasure
against him, he was sure that Cedric would pardon
Gurth, a faithful serf, and one who stood high in
favour, and who had but committed this error out
of the love which he bore to Cedric's son. And he
said, moreover, that he and his comrades, and
especially Wamba, the Jester, were resolved to
warn Gurth to make his escape by the way, in case
Cedric's ire against him could not be mitigated.'

'Would to God they may keep their purpose!'
said Ivanhoe; 'but it seems as if I were destined
to bring ruin on whomsoever hath shown kindness
to me. My king, by whom I was honoured and
distinguished—thou seest that the brother most
indebted to him is raising his arms to grasp his
crown; my regard hath brought restraint and
trouble on the fairest of her sex; and now my
father in his mood may slay this poor bondsman,
but for his love and loyal service to me! Thou
seest, maiden, what an ill-fated wretch thou dost
labour to assist; be wise, and let me go, ere the
misfortunes which track my footsteps like slot-
hounds shall involve thee also in their pursuit.'

'Nay,' said Rebecca, 'thy weakness and thy grief,
Sir Knight, make thee miscalculate the purposes of
Heaven. Thou hast been restored to thy country
when it most needed the assistance of a strong hand
and a true heart, and thou hast humbled the pride
of thine enemies and those of thy king, when their
horn was most highly exalted; and for the evil
which thou hast sustained, seest thou not that
Heaven has raised thee a helper and a physician,
even among the most despised of the land? Therefore, be of good courage, and trust that thou art
preserved for some marvel which thine arm shall
work before this people. Adieu; and having taken
the medicine which I shall send thee by the hand

of Reuben, compose thyself again to rest, that thou
mayst be the more able to endure the journey on
the succeeding day.'

Ivanhoe was convinced by the reasoning, and
obeyed the directions, of Rebecca. The draught
which Reuben administered was of a sedative and
narcotic quality, and secured the patient sound and
undisturbed slumbers. In the morning his kind
physician found him entirely free from feverish
symptoms, and fit to undergo the fatigue of a
journey.

He was deposited in the horse-litter which had
brought him from the lists, and every precaution
taken for his travelling with ease. In one circumstance only even the entreaties of Rebecca were
unable to secure sufficient attention to the accommodation of the wounded knight. Isaac, like the
enriched traveller of Juvenal's *Tenth Satire*, had
ever the fear of robbery before his eyes, conscious
that he would be alike accounted fair game by the
marauding Norman noble and by the Saxon outlaw.
He therefore journeyed at a great rate, and made
short halts and shorter repasts, so that he passed
by Cedric and Athelstane, who had several hours
the start of him, but who had been delayed by their
protracted feasting at the convent of St. Withold's.
Yet such was the virtue of Miriam's balsam, or such
the strength of Ivanhoe's constitution, that he did
not sustain from the hurried journey that inconvenience which his kind physician had apprehended.

In another point of view, however, the Jew's
haste proved somewhat more than good speed. The
rapidity with which he insisted on travelling bred
several disputes between him and the party whom
he had hired to attend him as a guard. These men
were Saxons, and not free by any means from the
national love of ease and good living which the
Normans stigmatised as laziness and gluttony.
Reversing Shylock's position, they had accepted

the employment in hopes of feeding upon the wealthy Jew, and were very much displeased when they found themselves disappointed by the rapidity with which he insisted on their proceeding. They remonstrated also upon the risk of damage to their horses by these forced marches. Finally, there arose betwixt Isaac and his satellites a deadly feud concerning the quantity of wine and ale to be allowed for consumption at each meal. And thus it happened, that when the alarm of danger approached, and that which Isaac feared was likely to come upon him, he was deserted by the discontented mercenaries, on whose protection he had relied without using the means necessary to secure their attachment.

In this deplorable condition, the Jew, with his daughter and her wounded patient, were found by Cedric, as has already been noticed, and soon afterwards fell into the power of De Bracy and his confederates. Little notice was at first taken of the horse-litter, and it might have remained behind but for the curiosity of De Bracy, who looked into it under the impression that it might contain the object of his enterprise, for Rowena had not unveiled herself. But De Bracy's astonishment was considerable when he discovered that the litter contained a wounded man, who, conceiving himself to have fallen into the power of Saxon outlaws, with whom his name might be a protection for himself and his friends, frankly avowed himself to be Wilfred of Ivanhoe.

The ideas of chivalrous honour, which, amidst his wildness and levity, never utterly abandoned De Bracy, prohibited him from doing the knight any injury in his defenceless condition, and equally interdicted his betraying him to Front-de-Bœuf, who would have had no scruples to put to death, under any circumstances, the rival claimant of the fief of Ivanhoe. On the other hand, to liberate a suitor preferred by the Lady Rowena, as the events of the tournament, and indeed Wilfred's previous banishment from his father's house, had made matter of notoriety, was a pitch far above the flight of De Bracy's generosity. A middle course betwixt good and evil was all which he found himself capable of adopting, and he commanded two of his own squires to keep close by the litter, and to suffer no one to approach it. If questioned, they were directed by their master to say that the empty litter of the Lady Rowena was employed to transport one of their comrades who had been wounded in the scuffle. On arriving at Torquilstone, while the Knight Templar and the lord of that castle were each intent upon their own schemes, the one on the Jew's treasure, and the other on his daughter, De Bracy's squires conveyed Ivanhoe, still under the name of a wounded comrade, to a distant apartment. This explanation was accordingly returned by these men to Front-de-Bœuf, when he questioned them why they did not make for the battlements upon the alarm.

'A wounded companion!' he replied in great wrath and astonishment. 'No wonder that churls and yeomen wax so presumptuous as even to lay leaguer before castles, and that clowns and swine-herds send defiances to nobles, since men-at-arms have turned sick men's nurses, and Free Companions are grown keepers of dying folks' curtains, when the castle is about to be assailed. To the battlements, ye loitering villains!' he exclaimed, raising his stentorian voice till the arches around rung again—'to the battlements, or I will splinter your bones with this truncheon!'

The men sulkily replied, 'That they desired nothing better than to go to the battlements, providing Front-de-Bœuf would bear them out with their master, who had commanded them to tend the dying man.'

'The dying man, knaves!' rejoined the baron;
'I promise thee, we shall all be dying men an we
stand not to it the more stoutly. But I will relieve
the guard upon this caitiff companion of yours.
Here, Urfried—hag—fiend of a Saxon witch—
hearest me not? Tend me this bedridden fellow,
since he must needs be tended, whilst these knaves
use their weapons. Here be two arblasts, comrades, with windlaces and quarrells —to the barbican
with you, and see you drive each bolt through a
Saxon brain.'

The men, who, like most of their description,
were fond of enterprise and detested inaction, went
joyfully to the scene of danger as they were commanded, and thus the charge of Ivanhoe was transferred to Urfried, or Ulrica. But she, whose brain
was burning with remembrance of injuries and with
hopes of vengeance, was readily induced to devolve
upon Rebecca the care of her patient.

CHAPTER XXIX

Ascend the watch-tower yonder, valiant soldier,
Look on the field, and say how goes the battle.
                              SCHILLER'S *Maid of Orleans.*

A MOMENT of peril is often also a moment of open-hearted kindness and affection. We are thrown off our guard by the general agitation of our feelings, and betray the intensity of those which, at more tranquil periods, our prudence at least conceals, if it cannot altogether suppress them. In finding herself once more by the side of Ivanhoe, Rebecca was astonished at the keen sensation of pleasure which she experienced, even at a time when all around them both was danger, if not despair. As she felt his pulse, and inquired after his health, there was a softness in her touch and in her accents, implying a kinder interest than she would herself have been pleased to have voluntarily expressed. Her voice faltered and her hand trembled, and it was only the cold question of Ivanhoe, 'Is it you, gentle maiden?' which recalled her to herself, and re-minded her the sensations which she felt were not and could not be mutual. A sigh escaped, but it was scarce audible; and the questions which she asked the knight concerning his state of health were put in the tone of calm friendship. Ivanhoe answered her hastily that he was, in point of health, as well, and better, than he could have expected. 'Thanks,' he said, 'dear Rebecca, to thy helpful skill.'

348

'He calls me *dear* Rebecca,' said the maiden to herself, 'but it is in the cold and careless tone which ill suits the word. His war-horse, his hunting hound, are dearer to him than the despised Jewess!'

'My mind, gentle maiden,' continued Ivanhoe, 'is more disturbed by anxiety than my body with pain. From the speeches of these men who were my warders just now, I learn that I am a prisoner, and, if I judge aright of the loud hoarse voice which even now despatched them hence on some military duty, I am in the castle of Front-de-Bœuf. If so, how will this end, or how can I protect Rowena and my father?'

'He names not the Jew or Jewess,' said Rebecca, internally; 'yet what is our portion in him, and how justly am I punished by Heaven for letting my thoughts dwell upon him!' She hastened after this brief self-accusation to give Ivanhoe what information she could; but it amounted only to this, that the Templar Bois-Guilbert and the Baron Front-de-Bœuf were commanders within the castle; that it was beleaguered from without, but by whom she knew not. She added, that there was a Christian priest within the castle who might be possessed of more information.

'A Christian priest!' said the knight, joyfully; 'fetch him hither, Rebecca, if thou canst. Say a sick man desires his ghostly counsel—say what thou wilt, but bring him; something I must do or attempt, but how can I determine until I know how matters stand without?'

Rebecca, in compliance with the wishes of Ivanhoe, made that attempt to bring Cedric into the wounded knight's chamber which was defeated, as we have already seen, by the interference of Urfried, who had been also on the watch to intercept the supposed monk. Rebecca retired to communicate to Ivanhoe the result of her errand.

They had not much leisure to regret the failure of this source of intelligence, or to contrive by what means it might be supplied; for the noise within the castle, occasioned by the defensive preparations, which had been considerable for some time, now increased into tenfold bustle and clamour. The heavy yet hasty step of the men-at-arms traversed the battlements, or resounded on the narrow and winding passages and stairs which led to the various bartizans and points of defence. The voices of the knights were heard, animating their followers, or directing means of defence, while their commands were often drowned in the clashing of armour, or the clamorous shouts of those whom they addressed. Tremendous as these sounds were, and yet more terrible from the awful event which they presaged, there was a sublimity mixed with them which Rebecca's high-toned mind could feel even in that moment of terror. Her eye kindled, although the blood fled from her cheeks; and there was a strong mixture of fear, and of a thrilling sense of the sublime, as she repeated, half-whispering to herself, half-speaking to her companion, the sacred text— 'The quiver rattleth—the glittering spear and the shield—the noise of the captains and the shouting!'

But Ivanhoe was like the war-horse of that sublime passage, glowing with impatience at his inactivity, and with his ardent desire to mingle in the affray of which these sounds were the introduction. 'If I could but drag myself,' he said, 'to yonder window, that I might see how this brave game is like to go! If I had but bow to shoot a shaft, or battle-axe to strike were it but a single blow for our deliverance! It is in vain—it is in vain—I am alike nerveless and weaponless!'

'Fret not thyself, noble knight,' answered Rebecca, 'the sounds have ceased of a sudden; it may be they join not battle.'

'Thou knowest nought of it,' said Wilfred,

impatiently; 'this dead pause only shows that the men are at their posts on the walls, and expecting an instant attack; what we have heard was but the distant muttering of the storm: it will burst anon in all its fury. Could I but reach yonder window!'

'Thou wilt but injure thyself by the attempt, noble knight,' replied his attendant. Observing his extreme solicitude, she firmly added, 'I myself will stand at the lattice, and describe to you as I can what passes without.'

'You must not—you shall not!' exclaimed Ivanhoe. 'Each lattice, each aperture, will be soon a mark for the archers; some random shaft——'

'It shall be welcome!' murmured Rebecca, as with firm pace she ascended two or three steps, which led to the window of which they spoke.

'Rebecca—dear Rebecca!' exclaimed Ivanhoe, 'this is no maiden's pastime; do not expose thyself to wounds and death, and render me for ever miserable for having given the occasion; at least, cover thyself with yonder ancient buckler, and show as little of your person at the lattice as may be.'

Following with wonderful promptitude the directions of Ivanhoe, and availing herself of the protection of the large ancient shield, which she placed against the lower part of the window, Rebecca, with tolerable security to herself, could witness part of what was passing without the castle, and report to Ivanhoe the preparations which the assailants were making for the storm. Indeed, the situation which she thus obtained was peculiarly favourable for this purpose, because, being placed on an angle of the main building, Rebecca could not only see what passed beyond the precincts of the castle, but also commanded a view of the outwork likely to be the first object of the meditated assault. It was an exterior fortification of no great height or strength, intended to protect the postern-gate, through which Cedric had been recently dismissed by Front-de-Bœuf. The castle moat divided this species of barbican from the rest of the fortress, so that, in case of its being taken, it was easy to cut off the communication with the main building, by withdrawing the temporary bridge. In the outwork was a sallyport corresponding to the postern of the castle, and the whole was surrounded by a strong palisade. Rebecca could observe, from the number of men placed for the defence of this post, that the besieged entertained apprehensions for its safety; and from the mustering of the assailants in a direction nearly opposite to the outwork, it seemed no less plain that it had been selected as a vulnerable point of attack.

These appearances she hastily communicated to Ivanhoe, and added, 'The skirts of the wood seem lined with archers, although only a few are advanced from its dark shadow.'

'Under what banner?' asked Ivanhoe.

'Under no ensign of war which I can observe,' answered Rebecca.

'A singular novelty,' muttered the knight, 'to advance to storm such a castle without pennon or banner displayed! Seest thou who they be that act as leaders?'

'A knight, clad in sable armour, is the most conspicuous,' said the Jewess; 'he alone is armed from head to heel, and seems to assume the direction of all around him.'

'What device does he bear on his shield?' replied Ivanhoe.

'Something resembling a bar of iron, and a padlock painted blue on the black shield.'

'A fetterlock and shackle-bolt azure,' said Ivanhoe; 'I know not who may bear the device, but well I ween it might now be mine own. Canst thou not see the motto?'

'Scarce the device itself at this distance,' replied

Rebecca; 'but when the sun glances fair upon his shield it shows as I tell you.'

'Seem there no other leaders?' exclaimed the anxious inquirer.

'None of mark and distinction that I can behold from this station,' said Rebecca; 'but doubtless the other side of the castle is also assailed. They appear even now preparing to advance—God of Zion protect us! What a dreadful sight! Those who advance first bear huge shields and defences made of plank; the others follow, bending their bows as they come on. They raise their bows! God of Moses, forgive the creatures Thou hast made!'

Her description was here suddenly interrupted by the signal for assault, which was given by the blast of a shrill bugle, and at once answered by a flourish of the Norman trumpets from the battlements, which, mingled with the deep and hollow clang of the nakers (a species of kettle-drum), retorted in notes of defiance the challenge of the enemy. The shouts of both parties augmented the fearful din, the assailants crying, 'St. George for merry England!' and the Normans answering them with loud cries of '*En avant De Bracy! Beau-seant! Beau-seant! Front-de-Bœuf à la rescousse!*' according to the war-cries of their different commanders.

It was not, however, by clamour that the contest was to be decided, and the desperate efforts of the assailants were met by an equally vigorous defence on the part of the besieged. The archers, trained by their woodland pastimes to the most effective use of the long-bow, shot, to use the appropriate phrase of the time, so 'wholly together,' that no point at which a defender could show the least part of his person escaped their cloth-yard shafts. By this heavy discharge, which continued as thick and sharp as hail, while, notwithstanding, every arrow had its individual aim, and flew by scores together against each embrasure and opening in the parapets, as well as at every window where a defender either occasionally had post, or might be suspected to be stationed—by this sustained discharge, two or three of the garrison were slain and several others wounded. But, confident in their armour of proof, and in the cover which their situation afforded, the followers of Front-de-Bœuf and his allies showed an obstinacy in defence proportioned to the fury of the attack, and replied with the discharge of their large cross-bows, as well as with their long-bows, slings, and other missile weapons, to the close and continued shower of arrows; and, as the assailants were necessarily but indifferently protected, did considerably more damage than they received at their hand. The whizzing of shafts and of missiles on both sides was only interrupted by the shouts which arose when either side inflicted or sustained some notable loss.

'And I must lie here like a bedridden monk,' exclaimed Ivanhoe, 'while the game that gives me freedom or death is played out by the hand of others! Look from the window once again, kind maiden, but beware that you are not marked by the archers beneath. Look out once more, and tell me if they yet advance to the storm.'

With patient courage, strengthened by the interval which she had employed in mental devotion, Rebecca again took post at the lattice, sheltering herself, however, so as not to be visible from beneath.

'What dost thou see, Rebecca?' again demanded the wounded knight.

'Nothing but the cloud of arrows flying so thick as to dazzle mine eyes, and to hide the bowmen who shoot them.'

'That cannot endure,' said Ivanhoe; 'if they press not right on to carry the castle by pure force of arms, the archery may avail but little against stone walls and bulwarks. Look for the Knight of the Fetterlock, fair Rebecca, and see how he bears himself; for as the leader is, so will his followers be.'

'I see him not,' said Rebecca.

'Foul craven!' exclaimed Ivanhoe; 'does he blench from the helm when the wind blows highest?'

'He blenches not!—he blenches not!' said Rebecca, 'I see him now; he leads a body of men close under the outer barrier of the barbican. They pull down the piles and palisades; they hew down the barriers with axes. His high black plume floats abroad over the throng, like a raven over the field of the slain. They have made a breach in the barriers—they rush in—they are thrust back! Front-de-Bœuf heads the defenders; I see his gigantic form above the press. They throng again to the breach, and the pass is disputed hand to hand, and man to man. God of Jacob! it is the meeting of two fierce tides—the conflict of two oceans moved by adverse winds!'

She turned her head from the lattice, as if unable longer to endure a sight so terrible.

'Look forth again, Rebecca,' said Ivanhoe, mistaking the cause of her retiring; 'the archery must in some degree have ceased, since they are now fighting hand to hand. Look again, there is now less danger.'

Rebecca again looked forth, and almost immediately exclaimed, 'Holy prophets of the law! Front-de-Bœuf and the Black Knight fight hand to hand on the breach, amid the roar of their followers, who watch the progress of the strife. Heaven strike with the cause of the oppressed and of the captive!' She then uttered a loud shriek, and exclaimed, 'He is down!—he is down!'

'Who is down?' cried Ivanhoe; 'for our dear Lady's sake, tell me which has fallen?'

'The Black Knight,' answered Rebecca, faintly ;
then instantly again shouted with joyful eagerness
—' But no—but no ! the name of the Lord of Hosts
be blessed ! he is on foot again, and fights as if
there were twenty men's strength in his single arm.
His sword is broken—he snatches an axe from a
yeoman—he presses Front-de-Bœuf with blow on
blow. The giant stoops and totters like an oak
under the steel of the woodman—he falls—he
falls !'

'Front-de-Bœuf?' exclaimed Ivanhoe.

'Front-de-Bœuf,' answered the Jewess. 'His
men rush to the rescue, headed by the haughty
Templar ; their united force compels the champion
to pause. They drag Front-de-Bœuf within the
walls.'

'The assailants have won the barriers, have they
not?' said Ivanhoe.

'They have—they have !' exclaimed Rebecca ;
'and they press the besieged hard upon the outer
wall ; some plant ladders, some swarm like bees,
and endeavour to ascend upon the shoulders of each
other ; down go stones, beams, and trunks of trees
upon their heads, and as fast as they bear the
wounded to the rear, fresh men supply their places
in the assault. Great God ! hast Thou given men
Thine own image that it should be thus cruelly
defaced by the hands of their brethren !'

'Think not of that,' said Ivanhoe ; 'this is no
time for such thoughts. Who yield? who push
their way?'

'The ladders are thrown down,' replied Rebecca,
shuddering ; 'the soldiers lie grovelling under them
like crushed reptiles. The besieged have the better.'

'St. George strike for us !' exclaimed the knight ;
'do the false yeomen give way?'

'No !' exclaimed Rebecca, 'they bear themselves
right yeomanly. The Black Knight approaches the
postern with his huge axe ; the thundering blows

which he deals, you may hear them above all the din and shouts of the battle. Stones and beams are hailed down on the bold champion: he regards them no more than if they were thistle-down or feathers!'

'By St. John of Acre,' said Ivanhoe, raising himself joyfully on his couch, 'methought there was but one man in England that might do such a deed!'

'The postern gate shakes,' continued Rebecca— 'it crashes—it is splintered by his blows—they rush in—the outwork is won. Oh God! they hurl the defenders from the battlements—they throw them into the moat. O men, if ye be indeed men, spare them that can resist no longer!'

'The bridge—the bridge which communicates with the castle—have they won that pass?' exclaimed Ivanhoe.

'No,' replied Rebecca; 'the Templar has destroyed the plank on which they crossed; few of the defenders escaped with him into the castle—the shrieks and cries which you hear tell the fate of the others. Alas! I see it is still more difficult to look upon victory than upon battle.'

'What do they now, maiden?' said Ivanhoe; 'look forth yet again—this is no time to faint at bloodshed.'

'It is over for the time,' answered Rebecca; 'our friends strengthen themselves within the outwork which they have mastered, and it affords them so good a shelter from the foemen's shot that the garrison only bestow a few bolts on it from interval to interval, as if rather to disquiet than effectually to injure them.'

'Our friends,' said Wilfred, 'will surely not abandon an enterprise so gloriously begun and so happily attained. O no! I will put my faith in the good knight whose axe hath rent heart-of-oak and bars of iron. Singular,' he again muttered to himself, 'if there be two who can do a deed of such derring-do! A fetterlock, and a shackle-bolt on a field sable—what may that mean? Seest thou nought else, Rebecca, by which the Black Knight may be distinguished?'

'Nothing,' said the Jewess; 'all about him is black as the wing of the night raven. Nothing can I spy that can mark him further; but having once seen him put forth his strength in battle, methinks I could know him again among a thousand warriors. He rushes to the fray as if he were summoned to a banquet. There is more than mere strength—there seems as if the whole soul and spirit of the champion were given to every blow which he deals upon his enemies. God assoilzie him of the sin of bloodshed! It is fearful, yet magnificent, to behold how the arm and heart of one man can triumph over hundreds.'

'Rebecca,' said Ivanhoe, 'thou hast painted a hero; surely they rest but to refresh their force, or to provide the means of crossing the moat. Under such a leader as thou hast spoken this knight to be, there are no craven fears, no cold-blooded delays, no yielding up a gallant emprize, since the difficulties which render it arduous render it also glorious. I swear by the honour of my house—I vow by the name of my bright lady-love, I would endure ten years' captivity to fight one day by that good knight's side in such a quarrel as this!'

'Alas!' said Rebecca, leaving her station at the window, and approaching the couch of the wounded knight, 'this impatient yearning after action—this struggling with and repining at your present weakness, will not fail to injure your returning health. How couldst thou hope to inflict wounds on others, ere that be healed which thou thyself hast received?'

'Rebecca,' he replied, 'thou knowest not how impossible it is for one trained to actions of chivalry to remain passive as a priest, or a woman, when

they are acting deeds of honour around him. The
love of battle is the food upon which we live—the
dust of the *mêlée* is the breath of our nostrils ! We
live not—we wish not to live—longer than while
we are victorious and renowned. Such, maiden,
are the laws of chivalry to which we are sworn,
and to which we offer all that we hold dear.'

'Alas !' said the fair Jewess, 'and what is it,
valiant knight, save an offering of sacrifice to a
demon of vain glory, and a passing through the
fire to Moloch ? What remains to you as the prize
of all the blood you have spilled, of all the travail
and pain you have endured, of all the tears which
your deeds have caused, when death hath broken
the strong man's spear, and overtaken the speed
of his war-horse ?'

'What remains ?' cried Ivanhoe. 'Glory, maiden
—glory ! which gilds our sepulchre and embalms
our name.'

'Glory !' continued Rebecca ; 'alas ! is the rusted
mail which hangs as a hatchment over the champion's dim and mouldering tomb, is the defaced
sculpture of the inscription which the ignorant
monk can hardly read to the inquiring pilgrim—
are these sufficient rewards for the sacrifice of every
kindly affection, for a life spent miserably that ye
may make others miserable ? Or is there such
virtue in the rude rhymes of a wandering bard,
that domestic love, kindly affection, peace and
happiness, are so wildly bartered, to become the
hero of those ballads which vagabond minstrels sing
to drunken churls over their evening ale ?'

'By the soul of Hereward !' replied the knight,
impatiently, 'thou speakest, maiden, of thou
knowest not what. Thou wouldst quench the pure
light of chivalry, which alone distinguishes the
noble from the base, the gentle knight from the
churl and the savage ; which rates our life far,
far beneath the pitch of our honour, raises us

victorious over pain, toil, and suffering, and teaches us to fear no evil but disgrace. Thou art no Christian, Rebecca; and to thee are unknown those high feelings which swell the bosom of a noble maiden when her lover hath done some deed of emprize which sanctions his flame. Chivalry! Why, maiden, she is the nurse of pure and high affection, the stay of the oppressed, the redresser of grievances, the curb of the power of the tyrant. Nobility were but an empty name without her, and liberty finds the best protection in her lance and her sword.'

'I am, indeed,' said Rebecca, 'sprung from a race whose courage was distinguished in the defence of their own land, but who warred not, even while yet a nation, save at the command of the Deity, or in defending their country from oppression. The sound of the trumpet wakes Judah no longer, and her despised children are now but the unresisting victims of hostile and military oppression. Well hast thou spoken, Sir Knight: until the God of Jacob shall raise up for His chosen people a second Gideon, or a new Maccabeus, it ill beseemeth the Jewish damsel to speak of battle or of war.'

The high-minded maiden concluded the argument in a tone of sorrow, which deeply expressed her sense of the degradation of her people, embittered perhaps by the idea that Ivanhoe considered her as one not entitled to interfere in a case of honour, and incapable of entertaining or expressing sentiments of honour and generosity.

'How little he knows this bosom,' she said, 'to imagine that cowardice or meanness of soul must needs be its guests, because I have censured the fantastic chivalry of the Nazarenes! Would to Heaven that the shedding of mine own blood, drop by drop, could redeem the captivity of Judah! Nay, would to God it could avail to set free my father, and this his benefactor, from the chains of

the oppressor! The proud Christian should then
see whether the daughter of God's chosen people
dared not to die as bravely as the vainest Nazarene
maiden, that boasts her descent from some petty
chieftain of the rude and frozen north!'

She then looked towards the couch of the wounded
knight.

'He sleeps,' she said; 'nature exhausted by
sufferance and the waste of spirits, his wearied
frame embraces the first moment of temporary
relaxation to sink into slumber. Alas! is it a
crime that I should look upon him, when it may
be for the last time? When yet but a short space,
and those fair features will be no longer animated
by the bold and buoyant spirit which forsakes them
not even in sleep! When the nostril shall be dis-
tended, the mouth agape, the eyes fixed and blood-
shot; and when the proud and noble knight may
be trodden on by the lowest caitiff of this accursed
castle, yet stir not when the heel is lifted up against
him! And my father!—oh, my father! evil is it
with his daughter, when his grey hairs are not
remembered because of the golden locks of youth!
What know I but that these evils are the messengers
of Jehovah's wrath to the unnatural child who
thinks of a stranger's captivity before a parent's?
who forgets the desolation of Judah, and looks
upon the comeliness of a Gentile and a stranger?
But I will tear this folly from my heart, though
every fibre bleed as I rend it away!'

She wrapped herself closely in her veil, and sat
down at a distance from the couch of the wounded
knight, with her back turned towards it, fortifying,
or endeavouring to fortify, her mind not only
against the impending evils from without, but also
against those treacherous feelings which assailed
her from within.

CHAPTER XXX

Approach the chamber, look upon his bed,
His is the passing of no peaceful ghost,
Which, as the lark arises to the sky,
'Mid morning's sweetest breeze and softest dew,
Is wing'd to heaven by good men's sighs and tears!
Anselm parts otherwise.

Old Play.

DURING the interval of quiet which followed the first success of the besiegers, while the one party was preparing to pursue their advantage and the other to strengthen their means of defence, the Templar and De Bracy held brief counsel together in the hall of the castle.

'Where is Front-de-Bœuf?' said the latter, who had superintended the defence of the fortress on the other side; 'men say he hath been slain.'

'He lives,' said the Templar, coolly—'lives as yet; but had he worn the bull's head of which he bears the name, and ten plates of iron to fence it withal, he must have gone down before yonder fatal axe. Yet a few hours, and Front-de-Bœuf is with his fathers—a powerful limb lopped off Prince John's enterprise.'

'And a brave addition to the kingdom of Satan,' said De Bracy; 'this comes of reviling saints and angels, and ordering images of holy things and holy men to be flung down on the heads of these rascaille yeomen.'

'Go to, thou art a fool,' said the Templar; 'thy

superstition is upon a level with Front-de-Bœuf's
want of faith; neither of you can render a reason
for your belief or unbelief.'

'*Benedicite*, Sir Templar,' replied De Bracy, 'I
pray you to keep better rule with your tongue when
I am the theme of it. By the Mother of Heaven,
I am a better Christian man than thou and thy
fellowship; for the bruit goeth shrewdly out, that
the most holy order of the Temple of Zion nurseth
not a few heretics within its bosom, and that Sir
Brian de Bois-Guilbert is of the number.'

'Care not thou for such reports,' said the Templar;
'but let us think of making good the castle. How
fought these villain yeomen on thy side?'

'Like fiends incarnate,' said De Bracy. 'They
swarmed close up to the walls, headed, as I think,
by the knave who won the prize at the archery, for
I knew his horn and baldric. And this is old
Fitzurse's boasted policy, encouraging these malapert knaves to rebel against us! Had I not been
armed in proof, the villain had marked me down
seven times with as little remorse as if I had been
a buck in season. He told every rivet on my
armour with a cloth-yard shaft, that rapped against
my ribs with as little compunction as if my bones
had been of iron. But that I wore a shirt of Spanish
mail under my plate-coat, I had been fairly sped.'

'But you maintained your post?' said the Templar.
'We lost the outwork on our part.'

'That is a shrewd loss,' said De Bracy; 'the
knaves will find cover there to assault the castle
more closely, and may, if not well watched, gain
some unguarded corner of a tower, or some forgotten
window, and so break in upon us. Our numbers
are too few for the defence of every point, and the
men complain that they can nowhere show themselves, but they are the mark for as many arrows
as a parish-butt on a holyday even. Front-de-Bœuf
is dying too, so we shall receive no more aid from

his bull's head and brutal strength. How think
you, Sir Brian, were we not better make a virtue of
necessity, and compound with the rogues by delivering up our prisoners?'

'How!' exclaimed the Templar; 'deliver up our
prisoners, and stand an object alike of ridicule and
execration, as the doughty warriors who dared by a
night-attack to possess themselves of the persons of
a party of defenceless travellers, yet could not make
good a strong castle against a vagabond troop of
outlaws, led by swineherds, jesters, and the very
refuse of mankind? Shame on thy counsel, Maurice
de Bracy! The ruins of this castle shall bury both
my body and my shame, ere I consent to such base
and dishonourable composition.'

'Let us to the walls, then,' said De Bracy, carelessly; 'that man never breathed, be he Turk or
Templar, who held life at lighter rate than I do.
But I trust there is no dishonour in wishing I had
here some two scores of my gallant troop of Free
Companions? Oh, my brave lances! if ye knew
but how hard your captain were this day bested,
how soon should I see my banner at the head of
your clump of spears! And how short while
would these rabble villains stand to endure your
encounter!'

'Wish for whom thou wilt,' said the Templar,
'but let us make what defence we can with the
soldiers who remain. They are chiefly Front-de-
Bœuf's followers, hated by the English for a thousand
acts of insolence and oppression.'

'The better,' said De Bracy; 'the rugged slaves
will defend themselves to the last drop of their
blood, ere they encounter the revenge of the peasants
without. Let us up and be doing, then, Brian de
Bois-Guilbert; and, live or die, thou shalt see
Maurice de Bracy bear himself this day as a gentleman of blood and lineage.'

'To the walls!' answered the Templar; and they

both ascended the battlements to do all that skill could dictate, and manhood accomplish, in defence of the place. They readily agreed that the point of greatest danger was that opposite to the outwork of which the assailants had possessed themselves. The castle, indeed, was divided from that barbican by the moat, and it was impossible that the besiegers could assail the postern door, with which the outwork corresponded, without surmounting that obstacle; but it was the opinion both of the Templar and De Bracy that the besiegers, if governed by the same policy their leader had already displayed, would endeavour, by a formidable assault, to draw the chief part of the defenders' observation to this point, and take measures to avail themselves of every negligence which might take place in the defence elsewhere. To guard against such an evil, their numbers only permitted the knights to place sentinels from space to space along the walls in communication with each other, who might give the alarm whenever danger was threatened. Meanwhile, they agreed that De Bracy should command the defence at the postern, and the Templar should keep with him a score of men or thereabouts as a body of reserve, ready to hasten to any other point which might be suddenly threatened. The loss of the barbican had also this unfortunate effect, that, notwithstanding the superior height of the castle walls, the besieged could not see from them, with the same precision as before, the operations of the enemy; for some straggling underwood approached so near the sallyport of the outwork that the assailants might introduce into it whatever force they thought proper, not only under cover, but even without the knowledge of the defenders. Utterly uncertain, therefore, upon what point the storm was to burst, De Bracy and his companion were under the necessity of providing against every possible contingency, and their followers, however brave, experienced the anxious dejection of mind incident to men inclosed by enemies, who possessed the power of choosing their time and mode of attack.

Meanwhile, the lord of the beleaguered and endangered castle lay upon a bed of bodily pain and mental agony. He had not the usual resource of bigots in that superstitious period, most of whom were wont to atone for the crimes they were guilty of by liberality to the church, stupifying by this means their terrors by the idea of atonement and forgiveness; and although the refuge which success thus purchased was no more like to the peace of mind which follows on sincere repentance than the turbid stupefaction procured by opium resembles healthy and natural slumbers, it was still a state of mind preferable to the agonies of awakened remorse. But among the vices of Front-de-Bœuf, a hard and griping man, avarice was predominant; and he preferred setting church and churchmen at defiance to purchasing from them pardon and absolution at the price of treasure and of manors. Nor did the Templar, an infidel of another stamp, justly characterise his associate when he said Front-de-Bœuf could assign no cause for his unbelief and contempt for the established faith; for the baron would have alleged that the church sold her wares too dear, that the spiritual freedom which she put up to sale was only to be bought, like that of the chief captain of Jerusalem, 'with a great sum,' and Front-de-Bœuf preferred denying the virtue of the medicine to paying the expense of the physician.

But the moment had now arrived when earth and all his treasures were gliding from before his eyes, and when the savage baron's heart, though hard as a nether millstone, became appalled as he gazed forward into the waste darkness of futurity. The fever of his body aided the impatience and agony of his mind, and his death-bed exhibited a mixture of the newly-awakened feelings of horror combating with the fixed and inveterate obstinacy of his disposition—a fearful state of mind, only to be equalled in those tremendous regions where there are complaints without hope, remorse without repentance, a dreadful sense of present agony, and a presentiment that it cannot cease or be diminished !

'Where be these dog-priests now,' growled the baron, 'who set such price on their ghostly mummery?—where be all those unshod Carmelites, for whom old Front-de-Bœuf founded the convent of St. Anne, robbing his heir of many a fair rood of meadow, and many a fat field and close—where be the greedy hounds now? Swilling, I warrant me, at the ale, or playing their juggling tricks at the bedside of some miserly churl. Me, the heir of their founder—me, whom their foundation binds them to pray for—me—ungrateful villains as they are ! they suffer to die like the houseless dog on yonder common, unshriven and unhouseled ! Tell the Templar to come hither ; he is a priest, and may do something. But no ! as well confess myself to the devil as to Brian de Bois-Guilbert, who recks neither of Heaven nor of Hell. I have heard old men talk of prayer—prayer by their own voice—such need not to court or to bribe the false priest. But I—I dare not !'

'Lives Reginald Front-de-Bœuf,' said a broken and shrill voice close by his bedside, 'to say there is that which he dares not ?'

The evil conscience and the shaken nerves of Front-de-Bœuf heard, in this strange interruption to his soliloquy, the voice of one of those demons who, as the superstition of the times believed, beset the beds of dying men, to distract their thoughts, and turn them from the meditations which concerned their eternal welfare. He shuddered and drew himself together ; but, instantly summoning

up his wonted resolution, he exclaimed, 'Who is
there? what art thou, that darest to echo my words
in a tone like that of the night-raven? Come before
my couch that I may see thee.'

'I am thine evil angel, Reginald Front-de-Bœuf,'
replied the voice.

'Let me behold thee then in thy bodily shape, if
thou be'st indeed a fiend,' replied the dying knight;
'think not that I will blench from thee. By the
eternal dungeon, could I but grapple with these
horrors that hover round me as I have done with
mortal dangers, Heaven or Hell should never say
that I shrunk from the conflict!'

'Think on thy sins, Reginald Front-de-Bœuf,'
said the almost unearthly voice—'on rebellion, on
rapine, on murder! Who stirred up the licentious
John to war against his grey-headed father—against
his generous brother?'

'Be thou fiend, priest, or devil,' replied Front-de-
Bœuf, 'thou liest in thy throat! Not I stirred
John to rebellion—not I alone; there were fifty
knights and barons, the flower of the midland
counties, better men never laid lance in rest. And
must I answer for the fault done by fifty? False
fiend, I defy thee! Depart, and haunt my couch
no more. Let me die in peace if thou be mortal;
if thou be a demon, thy time is not yet come.'

'In peace thou shalt NOT die,' repeated the voice;
'even in death shalt thou think on thy murders—
on the groans which this castle has echoed—on the
blood that is engrained in its floors!'

'Thou canst not shake me by thy petty malice,'
answered Front-de-Bœuf, with a ghastly and constrained laugh. 'The infidel Jew—it was merit
with Heaven to deal with him as I did, else wherefore are men canonised who dip their hands in the
blood of Saracens? The Saxon porkers whom I
have slain—they were the foes of my country, and
of my lineage, and of my liege lord. Ho! ho!

thou seest there is no crevice in my coat of plate.
Art thou fled? art thou silenced?'

'No, foul parricide!' replied the voice; 'think
of thy father!—think of his death!—think of his
banquet-room flooded with his gore, and that poured
forth by the hand of a son!'

'Ha!' answered the Baron, after a long pause,
'an thou knowest that, thou art indeed the Author
of Evil, and as omniscient as the monks call thee!
That secret I deemed locked in my own breast,
and in that of one besides—the temptress, the
partaker of my guilt. Go, leave me, fiend! and
seek the Saxon witch Ulrica, who alone could tell
thee what she and I alone witnessed. Go, I say,
to her, who washed the wounds, and straighted the
corpse, and gave to the slain'man the outward show
of one parted in time and in the course of nature.
Go to her; she was my temptress, the foul provoker,
the more foul rewarder, of the deed; let her, as well
as I, taste of the tortures which anticipate Hell!'

'She already tastes them,' said Ulrica, stepping
before the couch of Front-de-Bœuf; 'she hath long
drunken of this cup, and its bitterness is now
sweetened to see that thou dost partake it. Grind
not thy teeth, Front-de-Bœuf—roll not thine eyes
—clench not thy hand, nor shake it at me with
that gesture of menace! The hand which, like
that of thy renowned ancestor who gained thy
name, could have broken with one stroke the skull
of a mountain-bull, is now unnerved and powerless
as mine own!'

'Vile, murderous hag!' replied Front-de-Bœuf—
'detestable screech-owl! it is then thou who ar'
come to exult over the ruins thou hast assisted to
lay low?'

'Ay, Reginald Front-de-Bœuf,' answered she, 'it
is Ulrica!—it is the daughter of the murdered
Torquil Wolfganger!—it is the sister of his
slaughtered sons! it is she who demands of thee,

and of thy father's house, father and kindred, name and fame—all that she has lost by the name of Front-de-Bœuf! Think of my wrongs, Front-de-Bœuf, and answer me if I speak not truth. Thou hast been my evil angel, and I will be thine: I will dog thee till the very instant of dissolution!'

'Detestable fury!' exclaimed Front-de-Bœuf, 'that moment shalt thou never witness. Ho! Giles, Clement, and Eustace! St. Maur and Stephen! seize this damned witch, and hurl her from the battlements headlong; she has betrayed us to the Saxon! Ho! St. Maur! Clement! false-hearted knaves, where tarry ye?'

'Call on them again, valiant baron,' said the hag, with a smile of grisly mockery; 'summon thy vassals around thee, doom them that loiter to the scourge and the dungeon. But know, mighty chief,' she continued, suddenly changing her tone, 'thou shalt have neither answer, nor aid, nor obedience at their hands. Listen to these horrid sounds,' for the din of the recommenced assault and defence now rung fearfully loud from the battlements of the castle; 'in that war-cry is the downfall of thy house. The blood-cemented fabric of Front-de-Bœuf's power totters to the foundation, and before the foes he most despised! The Saxon, Reginald!—the scorned Saxon assails thy walls! Why liest thou here, like a worn-out hind, when the Saxon storms thy place of strength?'

'Gods and fiends!' exclaimed the wounded knight. 'O, for one moment's strength, to drag myself to the *mêlée*, and perish as becomes my name!'

'Think not of it, valiant warrior!' replied she; 'thou shalt die no soldier's death, but perish like the fox in his den, when the peasants have set fire to the cover around it.'

'Hateful hag! thou liest!' exclaimed Front-de-Bœuf; 'my followers bear them bravely—my walls are strong and high—my comrades in arms fear not a whole host of Saxons, were they headed by Hengist and Horsa! The war-cry of the Templar and of the Free Companions rises high over the conflict! And by mine honour, when we kindle the blazing beacon for joy of our defence, it shall consume thee, body and bones; and I shall live to hear thou art gone from earthly fires to those of that Hell which never sent forth an incarnate fiend more utterly diabolical!'

'Hold thy belief,' replied Ulrica, 'till the proof reach thee. But no!' she said, interrupting herself, 'thou shalt know even now the doom which all thy power, strength, and courage is unable to avoid, though it is prepared for thee by this feeble hand. Markest thou the smouldering and suffocating vapour which already eddies in sable folds through the chamber? Didst thou think it was but the darkening of thy bursting eyes, the difficulty of thy cumbered breathing? No! Front-de-Bœuf, there is another cause. Rememberest thou the magazine of fuel that is stored beneath these apartments?'

'Woman!' he exclaimed with fury, 'thou hast not set fire to it? By Heaven, thou hast, and the castle is in flames!'

'They are fast rising at least,' said Ulrica, with frightful composure; 'and a signal shall soon wave to warn the besiegers to press hard upon those who would extinguish them. Farewell, Front-de-Bœuf! May Mista, Skogula, and Zernebock, gods of the ancient Saxons—fiends, as the priests now call them—supply the place of comforters at your dying bed, which Ulrica now relinquishes! But know, if it will give thee comfort to know it, that Ulrica is bound to the same dark coast with thyself, the companion of thy punishment as the companion of thy guilt. And now, parricide, farewell for ever! May each stone of this vaulted roof find a tongue to echo that title into thine ear!'

So saying, she left the apartment; and Front-de-
Bœuf could hear the crash of the ponderous key as
she locked and double-locked the door behind her,
thus cutting off the most slender chance of escape.
In the extremity of agony, he shouted upon his servants and allies—'Stephen and St. Maur! Clement
and Giles! I burn here unaided! To the rescue—
to the rescue, brave Bois-Guilbert, valiant De
Bracy! It is Front-de-Bœuf who calls! It is your
master, ye traitor squires! Your ally—your brother
in arms, ye perjured and faithless knights! All
the curses due to traitors upon your recreant heads,
do you abandon me to perish thus miserably! They
hear me not—they cannot hear me—my voice is
lost in the din of battle. The smoke rolls thicker
and thicker, the fire has caught upon the floor
below. O, for one draught of the air of heaven,
were it to be purchased by instant annihilation!'
And in the mad frenzy of despair, the wretch now
shouted with the shouts of the fighters, now
muttered curses on himself, on mankind, and on
Heaven itself. 'The red fire flashes through the
thick smoke!' he exclaimed; 'the demon marches
against me under the banner of his own element.
Foul spirit, avoid! I go not with thee without my
comrades—all, all are thine that garrison these
walls. Thinkest thou Front-de-Bœuf will be singled
out to go alone? No; the infidel Templar, the
licentious De Bracy, Ulrica, the foul murdering
strumpet, the men who aided my enterprises, the
dog Saxons and accursed Jews who are my prisoners
—all, all shall attend me—a goodly fellowship as
ever took the downward road. Ha, ha, ha!' and
he laughed in his frenzy till the vaulted roof rang
again. 'Who laughed there?' exclaimed Front-
de-Bœuf, in altered mood, for the noise of the
conflict did not prevent the echoes of his own mad
laughter from returning upon his ear—'who laughed
there? Ulrica, was it thou? Speak, witch, and I

forgive thee; for only thou or the Fiend of Hell himself could have laughed at such a moment. Avaunt—avaunt——!'

But it were impious to trace any farther the picture of the blasphemer and parricide's death-bed.

tongue that, he only think on the friend of Hell
himself could have laughed at such a moment.

Again—again!

But it were impious to describe any further the
picture of the blasphemer and parricide death-
bed.

CHAPTER XXXI

Once more unto the breach, dear friends, once more,
Or close the wall up with our English dead.
. . . And you, good yeomen,
Whose limbs were made in England, show us here
The mettle of your pasture—let us swear
That you are worth your breeding.

King Henry V.

CEDRIC, although not greatly confident in Ulrica's
message, omitted not to communicate her promise
to the Black Knight and Locksley. They were
well pleased to find they had a friend within the
place, who might, in the moment of need, be able
to facilitate their entrance, and readily agreed with
the Saxon that a storm, under whatever disad-
vantages, ought to be attempted, as the only means
of liberating the prisoners now in the hands of the
cruel Front-de-Bœuf.

'The royal blood of Alfred is endangered,' said
Cedric.

'The honour of a noble lady is in peril,' said the
Black Knight.

'And, by the St. Christopher at my baldric,' said
the good yeoman, 'were there no other cause than
the safety of that poor faithful knave, Wamba, I
would jeopard a joint ere a hair of his head were
hurt.'

'And so would I,' said the Friar ; 'what, sirs !
I trust well that a fool—I mean, d'ye see me, sirs,
a fool that is free of his guild and master of his

craft, and can give as much relish and flavour to a cup of wine as ever a flitch of bacon can—I say, brethren, such a fool shall never want a wise clerk to pray for or fight for him at a strait, while I can say a mass or flourish a partizan.'

And with that he made his heavy halberd to play around his head as a shepherd boy flourishes his light crook.

'True, holy clerk,' said the Black Knight—'true as if St. Dunstan himself had said it. And now, good Locksley, were it not well that noble Cedric should assume the direction of this assault?'

'Not a jot I,' returned Cedric; 'I have never been wont to study either how to take or how to hold out those abodes of tyrannic power which the Normans have erected in this groaning land. I will fight among the foremost; but my honest neighbours well know I am not a trained soldier in the discipline of wars or the attack of strongholds.'

'Since it stands thus with noble Cedric,' said Locksley, 'I am most willing to take on me the direction of the archery; and ye shall hang me up on my own trysting-tree an the defenders be permitted to show themselves over the walls without being stuck with as many shafts as there are cloves in a gammon of bacon at Christmas.'

'Well said, stout yeoman,' answered the Black Knight; 'and if I be thought worthy to have a charge in these matters, and can find among these brave men as many as are willing to follow a true English knight, for so I may surely call myself, I am ready, with such skill as my experience has taught me, to lead them to the attack of these walls.'

The parts being thus distributed to the leaders, they commenced the first assault, of which the reader has already heard the issue.

When the barbican was carried, the Sable Knight

sent notice of the happy event to Locksley, request-
ing him at the same time to keep such a strict
observation on the castle as might prevent the defenders from combining their force for a sudden
sally, and recovering the outwork which they had
lost.   This the knight was chiefly desirous of avoiding, conscious that the men whom he led, being
hasty and untrained volunteers, imperfectly armed
and unaccustomed to discipline, must, upon any
sudden attack, fight at great disadvantage with
the veteran soldiers of the Norman knights, who
were well provided with arms both defensive and
offensive ; and who, to match the zeal and high
spirit of the besiegers, had all the confidence which
arises from perfect discipline and the habitual use
of weapons.

The knight employed the interval in causing to
be constructed a sort of floating bridge, or long
raft, by means of which he hoped to cross the moat
in despite of the resistance of the enemy.   This
was a work of some time, which the leaders the
less regretted, as it gave Ulrica leisure to execute
her plan of diversion in their favour, whatever that
might be.

When the raft was completed, the Black Knight
addressed the besiegers : 'It avails not waiting here
longer, my friends ; the sun is descending to the
west, and I have that upon my hands which will
not permit me to tarry with you another day.
Besides, it will be a marvel if the horsemen come
not upon us from York, unless we speedily accomplish our purpose.   Wherefore, one of ye go to
Locksley, and bid him commence a discharge of
arrows on the opposite side of the castle, and move
forward as if about to assault it ; and you, true
English hearts, stand by me, and be ready to thrust
the raft endlong over the moat whenever the postern
on our side is thrown open.   Follow me boldly
across, and aid me to burst yon sallyport in the

main wall of the castle. As many of you as like
not this service, or are but ill armed to meet it, do
you man the top of the outwork, draw your bowstrings to your ears, and mind you quell with your
shot whatever shall appear to man the rampart.
Noble Cedric, wilt thou take the direction of those
which remain?'

'Not so, by the soul of Hereward!' said the
Saxon; 'lead I cannot; but may posterity curse
me in my grave, if I follow not with the foremost
wherever thou shalt point the way. The quarrel
is mine, and well it becomes me to be in the van
of the battle.'

'Yet, bethink thee, noble Saxon,' said the knight,
'thou hast neither hauberk, nor corslet, nor aught
but that light helmet, target, and sword.'

'The better!' answered Cedric; 'I shall be the
lighter to climb these walls. And—forgive the
boast, Sir Knight—thou shalt this day see the naked
breast of a Saxon as boldly presented to the battle
as ever ye beheld the steel corslet of a Norman.'

'In the name of God, then,' said the knight,
'fling open the door, and launch the floating
bridge.'

The portal, which led from the inner wall of the
barbican to the moat, and which corresponded with
a sallyport in the main wall of the castle, was now
suddenly opened; the temporary bridge was then
thrust forward, and soon flashed in the waters,
extending its length between the castle and outwork, and forming a slippery and precarious passage
for two men abreast to cross the moat. Well aware
of the importance of taking the foe by surprise, the
Black Knight, closely followed by Cedric, threw
himself upon the bridge, and reached the opposite
side. Here he began to thunder with his axe upon
the gate of the castle, protected in part from the
shot and stones cast by the defenders by the ruins
of the former drawbridge, which the Templar had

demolished in his retreat from the barbican, leaving the counterpoise still attached to the upper part of the portal. The followers of the knight had no such shelter; two were instantly shot with cross-bow bolts, and two more fell into the moat; the others retreated back into the barbican.

The situation of Cedric and of the Black Knight was now truly dangerous, and would have been still more so but for the constancy of the archers in the barbican, who ceased not to shower their arrows upon the battlements, distracting the attention of those by whom they were manned, and thus afford-ing a respite to their two chiefs from the storm of missiles which must otherwise have overwhelmed them. But their situation was eminently perilous, and was becoming more so with every moment.

'Shame on ye all!' cried De Bracy to the soldiers around him; 'do ye call yourselves cross-bowmen, and let these two dogs keep their station under the walls of the castle? Heave over the coping stones from the battlement, an better may not be. Get pickaxe and levers, and down with that huge pinnacle!' pointing to a heavy piece of stone carved-work that projected from the parapet.

At this moment the besiegers caught sight of the red flag upon the angle of the tower which Ulrica had described to Cedric. The stout yeoman Locksley was the first who was aware of it, as he was hasting to the outwork, impatient to see the progress of the assault.

'St. George!' he cried—'Merry St. George for England! To the charge, bold yeomen! why leave ye the good knight and noble Cedric to storm the pass alone? Make in, mad priest, show thou canst fight for thy rosary—make in, brave yeomen!—the castle is ours, we have friends within. See yonder flag, it is the appointed signal—Torquilstone is ours! Think of honour—think of spoil! One effort, and the place is ours!'

With that he bent his good bow, and sent a shaft right through the breast of one of the men-at-arms, who, under De Bracy's direction, was loosening a fragment from one of the battlements to precipitate on the heads of Cedric and the Black Knight. A second soldier caught from the hands of the dying man the iron crow with which he heaved at and had loosened the stone pinnacle, when, receiving an arrow through his headpiece, he dropped from the battlements into the moat a dead man. The men-at-arms were daunted, for no armour seemed proof against the shot of this tremendous archer.

'Do you give ground, base knaves!' said De Bracy; '*Mount joye Saint Denis!* Give me the lever!'

And, snatching it up, he again assailed the loosened pinnacle, which was of weight enough, if thrown down, not only to have destroyed the remnant of the drawbridge which sheltered the two foremost assailants, but also to have sunk the rude float of planks over which they had crossed. All saw the danger, and the boldest, even the stout Friar himself, avoided setting foot on the raft. Thrice did Locksley bend his shaft against De Bracy, and thrice did his arrow bound back from the knight's armour of proof.

'Curse on thy Spanish steel-coat!' said Locksley, 'had English smith forged it, these arrows had gone through, an as if it had been silk or sendal.' He then began to call out, 'Comrades! friends! noble Cedric! bear back and let the ruin fall.'

His warning voice was unheard, for the din which the knight himself occasioned by his strokes upon the postern would have drowned twenty war-trumpets. The faithful Gurth indeed sprung forward on the planked bridge, to warn Cedric of his impending fate, or to share it with him. But his warning would have come too late; the massive pinnacle already tottered, and De Bracy, who still heaved at his task, would have accomplished it, had not the voice of the Templar sounded close in his ear:

'All is lost, De Bracy; the castle burns.'

'Thou art mad to say so!' replied the knight.

It is all in a light flame on the western side. I have striven in vain to extinguish it.'

With the stern coolness which formed the basis of his character, Brian de Bois-Guilbert communicated this hideous intelligence, which was not so calmly received by his astonished comrade.

'Saints of Paradise!' said De Bracy; 'what is to be done? I vow to St. Nicholas of Limoges a candlestick of pure gold——'

'Spare thy vow,' said the Templar, 'and mark me. Lead thy men down, as if to a sally; throw the postern gate open. There are but two men who occupy the float, fling them into the moat, and push across for the barbican. I will charge from the main gate, and attack the barbican on the outside; and if we can regain that post, be assured we shall defend ourselves until we are relieved, or at least till they grant us fair quarter.'

'It is well thought upon,' said De Bracy; 'I will play my part. Templar, thou wilt not fail me?'

'Hand and glove, I will not!' said Bois-Guilbert. 'But haste thee, in the name of God!'

De Bracy hastily drew his men together, and rushed down to the postern gate, which he caused instantly to be thrown open. But scarce was this done ere the portentous strength of the Black Knight forced his way inward in despite of De Bracy and his followers. Two of the foremost instantly fell, and the rest gave way notwithstanding all their leader's efforts to stop them.

'Dogs!' said De Bracy, 'will ye let *two* men win our only pass for safety?'

'He is the devil!' said a veteran man-at-arms,

bearing back from the blows of their sable antagonist.

'And if he be the devil,' replied De Bracy, 'would you fly from him into the mouth of hell? The castle burns behind us, villains!—let despair give you courage, or let me forward! I will cope with this champion myself.'

And well and chivalrous did De Bracy that day maintain the fame he had acquired in the civil wars of that dreadful period. The vaulted passage to which the postern gave entrance, and in which these two redoubted champions were now fighting hand to hand, rung with the furious blows which they dealt each other, De Bracy with his sword, the Black Knight with his ponderous axe. At length the Norman received a blow which, though its force was partly parried by his shield, for otherwise never more would De Bracy have again moved limb, descended yet with such violence on his crest that he measured his length on the paved floor.

'Yield thee, De Bracy,' said the Black Champion, stooping over him, and holding against the bars of his helmet the fatal poniard with which the knights despatched their enemies, and which was called the dagger of mercy—'yield thee, Maurice de Bracy, rescue or no rescue, or thou art but a dead man.'

'I will not yield,' replied De Bracy, faintly, 'to an unknown conqueror. Tell me thy name, or work thy pleasure on me; it shall never be said that Maurice de Bracy was prisoner to a nameless churl.'

The Black Knight whispered something into the ear of the vanquished.

'I yield me to be true prisoner, rescue or no rescue,' answered the Norman, exchanging his tone of stern and determined obstinacy for one of deep though sullen submission.

'Go to the barbican,' said the victor, in a tone of authority, 'and there wait my further orders.'

'Yet first let me say,' said De Bracy, 'what it imports thee to know. Wilfred of Ivanhoe is wounded and a prisoner, and will perish in the burning castle without present help.'

'Wilfred of Ivanhoe!' exclaimed the Black Knight—'prisoner, and perish! The life of every man in the castle shall answer it if a hair of his head be singed. Show me his chamber!'

'Ascend yonder winding stair,' said De Bracy; 'it leads to his apartment. Wilt thou not accept my guidance?' he added, in a submissive voice.

'No. To the barbican, and there wait my orders. I trust thee not, De Bracy.'

During this combat and the brief conversation which ensued, Cedric, at the head of a body of men, among whom the Friar was conspicuous, had pushed across the bridge as soon as they saw the postern open, and drove back the dispirited and despairing followers of De Bracy, of whom some asked quarter, some offered vain resistance, and the greater part fled towards the courtyard. De Bracy himself arose from the ground, and cast a sorrowful glance after his conqueror. 'He trusts me not!' he repeated; 'but have I deserved his trust?' He then lifted his sword from the floor, took off his helmet in token of submission, and, going to the barbican, gave up his sword to Locksley, whom he met by the way.

As the fire augmented, symptoms of it became soon apparent in the chamber where Ivanhoe was watched and tended by the Jewess Rebecca. He had been awakened from his brief slumber by the noise of the battle; and his attendant, who had, at his anxious desire, again placed herself at the window to watch and report to him the fate of the attack, was for some time prevented from observing either by the increase of the smouldering and stifling vapour. At length the volumes of smoke which rolled into the apartment, the cries for water, which were heard even above the din of the battle, made them sensible of the progress of this new danger.

'The castle burns,' said Rebecca—'it burns! What can we do to save ourselves?'

'Fly, Rebecca, and save thine own life,' said Ivanhoe, 'for no human aid can avail me.'

'I will not fly,' answered Rebecca; 'we will be saved or perish together. And yet, great God! my father—my father, what will be his fate?'

At this moment the door of the apartment flew open, and the Templar presented himself—a ghastly figure, for his gilded armour was broken and bloody, and the plume was partly shorn away, partly burnt from his casque. 'I have found thee,' said he to Rebecca; 'thou shalt prove I will keep my word to share weal and woe with thee. There is but one path to safety: I have cut my way through fifty dangers to point it to thee; up, and instantly follow me!'

'Alone,' answered Rebecca, 'I will not follow thee. If thou wert born of woman—if thou hast but a touch of human charity in thee—if thy heart be not hard as thy breastplate—save my aged father —save this wounded knight!'

'A knight,' answered the Templar, with his characteristic calmness—'a knight, Rebecca, must encounter his fate, whether it meet him in the shape of sword or flame; and who recks how or where a Jew meets with his?'

'Savage warrior,' said Rebecca, 'rather will I perish in the flames than accept safety from thee!'

'Thou shalt not choose, Rebecca; once didst thou foil me, but never mortal did so twice.'

So saying, he seized on the terrified maiden, who filled the air with her shrieks, and bore her out of the room in his arms, in spite of her cries, and without regarding the menaces and defiance which

Ivanhoe thundered against him. 'Hound of the
Temple—stain to thine order—set free the damsel!
Traitor of Bois-Guilbert, it is Ivanhoe commands
thee! Villain, I will have thy heart's blood!'

'I had not found thee, Wilfred,' said the Black
Knight, who at that instant entered the apartment,
'but for thy shouts.'

'If thou be'st true knight,' said Wilfred, 'think
not of me—pursue yon ravisher—save the Lady
Rowena—look to the noble Cedric!'

'In their turn,' answered he of the Fetterlock,
'but thine is first.'

And seizing upon Ivanhoe, he bore him off with
as much ease as the Templar had carried off Rebecca,
rushed with him to the postern, and having there
delivered his burden to the care of two yeomen,
he again entered the castle to assist in the rescue
of the other prisoners.

One turret was now in bright flames, which flashed
out furiously from window and shot-hole. But in
other parts the great thickness of the walls and the
vaulted roofs of the apartments resisted the progress
of the flames, and there the rage of man still
triumphed, as the scarce more dreadful element
held mastery elsewhere; for the besiegers pursued
the defenders of the castle from chamber to chamber,
and satiated in their blood the vengeance which had
long animated them against the soldiers of the
tyrant Front-de-Bœuf. Most of the garrison resisted
to the uttermost; few of them asked quarter; none
received it. The air was filled with groans and
clashing of arms; the floors were slippery with the
blood of despairing and expiring wretches.

Through this scene of confusion, Cedric rushed in
quest of Rowena, while the faithful Gurth, following
him closely through the *mêlée*, neglected his own
safety while he strove to avert the blows that were
aimed at his master. The noble Saxon was so
fortunate as to reach his ward's apartment just as

she had abandoned all hope of safety, and, with a crucifix clasped in agony to her bosom, sat in expectation of instant death. He committed her to the charge of Gurth, to be conducted in safety to the barbican, the road to which was now cleared of the enemy, and not yet interrupted by the flames. This accomplished, the loyal Cedric hastened in quest of his friend Athelstane, determined, at every risk to himself, to save that last scion of Saxon royalty. But ere Cedric penetrated as far as the old hall in which he had himself been a prisoner, the inventive genius of Wamba had procured liberation for himself and his companion in adversity.

When the noise of the conflict announced that it was at the hottest, the Jester began to shout, with the utmost power of his lungs, 'St. George and the dragon! Bonny St. George for merry England! The castle is won!' And these sounds he rendered yet more fearful by banging against each other two or three pieces of rusty armour which lay scattered around the hall.

A guard, which had been stationed in the outer or ante-room, and whose spirits were already in a state of alarm, took fright at Wamba's clamour, and, leaving the door open behind them, ran to tell the Templar that foemen had entered the old hall. Meantime the prisoners found no difficulty in making their escape into the ante-room, and from thence into the court of the castle, which was now the last scene of contest. Here sat the fierce Templar, mounted on horseback, surrounded by several of the garrison both on horse and foot, who had united their strength to that of this renowned leader, in order to secure the last chance of safety and retreat which remained to them. The draw-bridge had been lowered by his orders, but the passage was beset; for the archers, who had hitherto only annoyed the castle on that side by their missiles, no sooner saw the flames breaking out, and the bridge lowered, than they thronged to the entrance, as well to prevent the escape of the garrison as to secure their own share of booty ere the castle should be burnt down. On the other hand, a party of the besiegers, who had entered by the postern, were now issuing out into the courtyard, and attacking with fury the remnant of the defenders, who were thus assaulted on both sides at once.

Animated, however, by despair, and supported by the example of their indomitable leader, the remaining soldiers of the castle fought with the utmost valour; and, being well armed, succeeded more than once in driving back the assailants, though much inferior in numbers. Rebecca, placed on horseback before one of the Templar's Saracen slaves, was in the midst of the little party; and Bois-Guilbert, notwithstanding the confusion of the bloody fray, showed every attention to her safety. Repeatedly he was by her side, and, neglecting his own defence, held before her the fence of his triangular steel-plated shield; and anon starting from his position by her, he cried his war-cry, dashed forward, struck to earth the most forward of the assailants, and was on the same instant once more at her bridle rein.

Athelstane, who, as the reader knows, was slothful, but not cowardly, beheld the female form whom the Templar protected thus sedulously, and doubted not that it was Rowena whom the knight was carrying off, in despite of all resistance which could be offered.

'By the soul of St. Edward,' he said, 'I will rescue her from yonder over-proud knight, and he shall die by my hand!'

'Think what you do!' cried Wamba; 'hasty hand catches frog for fish; by my bauble, yonder is none of my Lady Rowena, see but her long dark locks! Nay, an ye will not know black from white, ye may be leader, but I will be no follower; no

bones of mine shall be broken unless I know for
whom. And you without armour too! Bethink
you, silk bonnet never kept out steel blade. Nay,
then, if wilful will to water, wilful must drench.
Deus vobiscum, most doughty Athelstane!' he concluded, loosening the hold which he had hitherto
kept upon the Saxon's tunic.

To snatch a mace from the pavement, on which it
lay beside one whose dying grasp had just relinquished it, to rush on the Templar's band, and
to strike in quick succession to the right and left,
levelling a warrior at each blow, was, for Athelstane's great strength, now animated with unusual
fury, but the work of a single moment; he was
soon within two yards of Bois-Guilbert, whom he
defied in his loudest tone.

'Turn, false-hearted Templar! let go her whom
thou art unworthy to touch; turn, limb of a band
of murdering and hypocritical robbers!'

'Dog!' said the Templar, grinding his teeth,
'I will teach thee to blaspheme the holy order of
the Temple of Zion'; and with these words, half-
wheeling his steed, he made a demi-courbette towards
the Saxon, and rising in the stirrups, so as to take
full advantage of the descent of the horse, he discharged a fearful blow upon the head of Athelstane.

Well said Wamba, that silken bonnet keeps out
no steel blade! So trenchant was the Templar's
weapon, that it shore asunder, as it had been a
willow twig, the tough and plaited handle of the
mace, which the ill-fated Saxon reared to parry
the blow, and, descending on his head, levelled
him with the earth.

'*Ha! Beau-seant!*' exclaimed Bois-Guilbert, 'thus
be it to the maligners of the Temple knights!'
Taking advantage of the dismay which was spread
by the fall of Athelstane, and calling aloud, 'Those
who would save themselves, follow me!' he pushed
across the drawbridge, dispersing the archers who

would have intercepted them. He was followed by
his Saracens, and some five or six men-at-arms, who
had mounted their horses. The Templar's retreat
was rendered perilous by the numbers of arrows shot
off at him and his party; but this did not prevent
him from galloping round to the barbican, of which,
according to his previous plan, he supposed it
possible De Bracy might have been in possession.

'De Bracy! De Bracy!' he shouted, 'art thou
there?'

'I am here,' replied De Bracy, 'but I am a
prisoner.'

'Can I rescue thee?' cried Bois-Guilbert.

'No,' replied De Bracy; 'I have rendered me,
rescue or no rescue. I will be true prisoner. Save
thyself; there are hawks abroad. Put the seas
betwixt you and England; I dare not say more.'

'Well,' answered the Templar; 'an thou wilt
tarry there, remember I have redeemed word and
glove. Be the hawks where they will, methinks the
walls of the preceptory of Templestowe will be cover
sufficient, and thither will I, like heron to her
haunt.'

Having thus spoken, he galloped off with his
followers.

Those of the castle who had not gotten to horse,
still continued to fight desperately with the besiegers,
after the departure of the Templar, but rather in
despair of quarter than that they entertained any
hope of escape. The fire was spreading rapidly
through all parts of the castle, when Ulrica, who
had first kindled it, appeared on a turret, in the
guise of one of the ancient furies, yelling forth a
war-song, such as was of yore raised on the field of
battle by the scalds of the yet heathen Saxons. Her
long dishevelled grey hair flew back from her uncovered head; the inebriating delight of gratified
vengeance contended in her eyes with the fire of
insanity; and she brandished the distaff which she

held in her hand, as if she had been one of the Fatal Sisters who spin and abridge the thread of human life. Tradition has preserved some wild strophes of the barbarous hymn which she chanted wildly amid that scene of fire and of slaughter :—

Whet the bright steel,
Sons of the White Dragon!
Kindle the torch,
Daughter of Hengist!
The steel glimmers not for the carving of the banquet,
It is hard, broad, and sharply pointed;
The torch goeth not to the bridal chamber,
It steams and glitters blue with sulphur.
Whet the steel, the raven croaks!
Light the torch, Zernebock is yelling!
Whet the steel, sons of the Dragon!
Kindle the torch, daughter of Hengist!

The black cloud is low over the thane's castle;
The eagle screams—he rides on its bosom.
Scream not, grey rider of the sable cloud,
Thy banquet is prepared!
The maidens of Valhalla look forth,
The race of Hengist will send them guests.
Shake your black tresses, maidens of Valhalla!
And strike your loud timbrels for joy!
Many a haughty step bends to your halls,
Many a helmed head.
Dark sits the evening upon the thane's castle,
The black clouds gather round;
Soon shall they be red as the blood of the valiant!
The destroyer of forests shall shake his red crest against
    them.
He, the bright consumer of palaces,
Broad waves he his blazing banner;
Red, wide, and dusky,
Over the strife of the valiant:
His joy is in the clashing swords and broken bucklers;
He loves to lick the hissing blood as it bursts warm from
    the wound!

All must perish!
The sword cleaveth the helmet;
The strong armour is pierced by the lance;
Fire devoureth the dwelling of princes;

> Engines break down the fences of the battle.
> All must perish !
> The race of Hengist is gone—
> The name of Horsa is no more !
> Shrink not then from your doom, sons of the sword !
> Let your blades drink blood like wine ;
> Feast ye in the banquet of slaughter,
> By the light of the blazing halls !
> Strong be your swords while your blood is warm,
> And spare neither for pity nor fear,
> For vengeance hath but an hour ;
> Strong hate itself shall expire !
> I also must perish !

The towering flames had now surmounted every obstruction, and rose to the evening skies one huge and burning beacon, seen far and wide through the adjacent country. Tower after tower crashed down, with blazing roof and rafter ; and the combatants were driven from the courtyard. The vanquished, of whom very few remained, scattered and escaped into the neighbouring wood. The victors, assembling in large bands, gazed with wonder, not unmixed with fear, upon the flames, in which their own ranks and arms glanced dusky red. The maniac figure of the Saxon Ulrica was for a long time visible on the lofty stand she had chosen, tossing her arms abroad with wild exultation, as if she reigned empress of the conflagration which she had raised. At length, with a terrific crash, the whole turret gave way, and she perished in the flames which had consumed her tyrant. An awful pause of horror silenced each murmur of the armed spectators, who, for the space of several minutes, stirred not a finger, save to sign the cross. The voice of Locksley was then heard— 'Shout, yeomen ! the den of tyrants is no more ! Let each bring his spoil to our chosen place of rendezvous at the trysting-tree in the Harthill Walk ; for there at break of day will we make just partition among our own bands, together with our worthy allies in this great deed of vengeance.'

CHAPTER XXXII

Trust me, each state must have its policies:
Kingdoms have edicts, cities have their charters;
Even the wild outlaw, in his forest-walk,
Keeps yet some touch of civil discipline;
For not since Adam wore his verdant apron,
Hath man with man in social union dwelt,
But laws were made to draw that union closer.

Old Play.

THE daylight had dawned upon the glades of the oak forest. The green boughs glittered with all their pearls of dew. The hind led her fawn from the covert of high fern to the more open walks of the greenwood, and no huntsman was there to watch or intercept the stately hart, as he paced at the head of the antlered herd.

The outlaws were all assembled around the trysting-tree in the Harthill Walk, where they had spent the night in refreshing themselves after the fatigues of the siege—some with wine, some with slumber, many with hearing and recounting the events of the day, and computing the heaps of plunder which their success had placed at the disposal of their chief.

The spoils were indeed very large; for, notwithstanding that much was consumed, a great deal of plate, rich armour, and splendid clothing had been secured by the exertions of the dauntless outlaws, who could be appalled by no danger when such rewards were in view. Yet so strict were the laws of their society, that no one ventured to appropriate any part of the booty, which was brought into one common mass, to be at the disposal of their leader.

The place of rendezvous was an aged oak ; not, however, the same to which Locksley had conducted Gurth and Wamba in the earlier part of the story, but one which was the centre of a silvan amphitheatre, within half a mile of the demolished castle of Torquilstone.   Here Locksley assumed his seat— a throne of turf erected under the twisted branches of the huge oak, and the silvan followers were gathered around him.   He assigned to the Black Knight a seat at his right hand, and to Cedric a place upon his left.

'Pardon my freedom, noble sirs,' he said, 'but in these glades I am monarch : they are my kingdom ; and these my wild subjects would reck but little of my power, were I, within my own dominions, to yield place to mortal man.   Now, sirs, who hath seen our chaplain? where is our curtal friar?   A mass amongst Christian men best begins a busy morning.'   No one had seen the clerk of Copmanhurst.   'Over God's forbode !'   said the outlaw chief, 'I trust the jolly priest hath but abidden by the wine-pot a thought too late.   Who saw him since the castle was ta'en?'

'I,' quoth the Miller, 'marked him busy about the door of a cellar, swearing by each saint in the calendar he would taste the smack of Front-de-Bœuf's Gascoigne wine.'

'Now, the saints, as many as there be of them,' said the captain, 'forefend, lest he has drunk too deep of the wine-butts, and perished by the fall of the castle !   Away, Miller !   take with you enow of men, seek the place where you last saw him, throw water from the moat on the scorching ruins ; I will have them removed stone by stone ere I lose my curtal friar.'

The numbers who hastened to execute this duty, considering that an interesting division of spoil was about to take place, showed how much the troop had at heart the safety of their spiritual father.

'Meanwhile, let us proceed,' said Locksley; 'for when this bold deed shall be sounded abroad, the bands of De Bracy, of Malvoisin, and other allies of Front-de-Bœuf, will be in motion against us, and it were well for our safety that we retreat from the vicinity. Noble Cedric,' he said, turning to the Saxon, 'that spoil is divided into two portions; do thou make choice of that which best suits thee, to recompense thy people who were partakers with us in this adventure.'

'Good yeoman,' said Cedric, 'my heart is oppressed with sadness. The noble Athelstane of Coningsburgh is no more—the last sprout of the sainted Confessor! Hopes have perished with him which can never return! A sparkle hath been quenched by his blood which no human breath can again rekindle! My people, save the few who are now with me, do but tarry my presence to transport his honoured remains to their last mansion. The Lady Rowena is desirous to return to Rotherwood, and must be escorted by a sufficient force. I should, therefore, ere now have left this place; and I waited, not to share the booty, for, so help me God and St. Withold! as neither I nor any of mine will touch the value of a liard—I waited but to render my thanks to thee and to thy bold yeomen, for the life and honour ye have saved.'

'Nay, but,' said the chief outlaw, 'we did but half the work at most; take of the spoil what may reward your own neighbours and followers.'

'I am rich enough to reward them from mine own wealth,' answered Cedric.

'And some,' said Wamba, 'have been wise enough to reward themselves; they do not march off empty-handed altogether. We do not all wear motley.'

'They are welcome,' said Locksley; 'our laws bind none but ourselves.'

'But thou, my poor knave,' said Cedric, turning about and embracing his Jester, 'how shall I reward thee, who feared not to give thy body to chains and death instead of mine? All forsook me, when the poor fool was faithful!'

A tear stood in the eye of the rough thane as he spoke—a mark of feeling which even the death of Athelstane had not extracted; but there was something in the half-instinctive attachment of his clown that waked his nature more keenly than even grief itself.

'Nay,' said the Jester, extricating himself from his master's caress, 'if you pay my service with the water of your eye, the Jester must weep for company, and then what becomes of his vocation? But, uncle, if you would indeed pleasure me, I pray you to pardon my playfellow Gurth, who stole a week from your service to bestow it on your son.'

'Pardon him!' exclaimed Cedric; 'I will both pardon and reward him. Kneel down, Gurth.' The swineherd was in an instant at his master's feet. 'THEOW and ESNE art thou no longer,' said Cedric, touching him with a wand; 'FOLKFREE and SACLESS art thou in town and from town, in the forest as in the field. A hide of land I give to thee in my steads of Walbrugham, from me and mine to thee and thine aye and for ever; and God's malison on his head who this gainsays!'

No longer a serf but a freeman and a landholder, Gurth sprung upon his feet, and twice bounded aloft to almost his own height from the ground.

'A smith and a file,' he cried, 'to do away the collar from the neck of a freeman! Noble master! doubled is my strength by your gift, and doubly will I fight for you! There is a free spirit in my breast. I am a man changed to myself and all around. Ha, Fangs!' he continued, for that faithful cur, seeing his master thus transported, began to jump upon him to express his sympathy, 'knowest thou thy master still?'

'Ay,' said Wamba, 'Fangs and I still know thee, Gurth, though we must needs abide by the collar; it is only thou art likely to forget both us and thyself.'

'I shall forget myself indeed ere I forget thee, true comrade,' said Gurth; 'and were freedom fit for thee, Wamba, the master would not let thee want it.'

'Nay,' said Wamba, 'never think I envy thee, brother Gurth; the serf sits by the hall fire when the freeman must forth to the field of battle. And what saith Aldhelm of Malmsbury—"Better a fool at a feast than a wise man at a fray."'

The tramp of horses was now heard, and the Lady Rowena appeared, surrounded by several riders, and a much stronger party of footmen, who joyfully shook their pikes and clashed their brownbills for joy of her freedom. She herself, richly attired, and mounted on a dark chestnut palfrey, had recovered all the dignity of her manner, and only an unwonted degree of paleness showed the sufferings she had undergone. Her lovely brow, though sorrowful, bore on it a cast of reviving hope for the future, as well as of grateful thankfulness for the past deliverance. She knew that Ivanhoe was safe, and she knew that Athelstane was dead. The former assurance filled her with the most sincere delight; and if she did not absolutely rejoice at the latter, she might be pardoned for feeling the full advantage of being freed from further persecution on the only subject in which she had ever been contradicted by her guardian Cedric.

As Rowena bent her steed towards Locksley's seat, that bold yeoman, with all his followers, rose to receive her, as if by a general instinct of courtesy. The blood rose to her cheeks as, courteously waving her hand, and bending so low that her beautiful and loose tresses were for an instant mixed with the flowing mane of her palfrey, she expressed in few but apt words her obligations and her gratitude to Locksley and her other deliverers. 'God bless you, brave men,' she concluded—'God and Our Lady bless you and requite you for gallantly perilling yourselves in the cause of the oppressed! If any of you should hunger, remember Rowena has food; if you should thirst, she has many a butt of wine and brown ale; and if the Normans drive ye from these walks, Rowena has forests of her own, where her gallant deliverers may range at full freedom, and never ranger ask whose arrow hath struck down the deer.'

'Thanks, gentle lady,' said Locksley—'thanks from my company and myself. But to have saved you requites itself. We who walk the greenwood do many a wild deed, and the Lady Rowena's deliverance may be received as an atonement.'

Again bowing from her palfrey, Rowena turned to depart; but pausing a moment, while Cedric, who was to attend her, was also taking his leave, she found herself unexpectedly close by the prisoner De Bracy. He stood under a tree in deep meditation, his arms crossed upon his breast, and Rowena was in hopes she might pass him unobserved. He looked up, however, and, when aware of her presence, a deep flush of shame suffused his handsome countenance. He stood a moment most irresolute; then, stepping forward, took her palfrey by the rein and bent his knee before her.

'Will the Lady Rowena deign to cast an eye on a captive knight—on a dishonoured soldier?'

'Sir Knight,' answered Rowena, 'in enterprises such as yours, the real dishonour lies not in failure, but in success.'

'Conquest, lady, should soften the heart,' answered De Bracy; 'let me but know that the Lady Rowena forgives the violence occasioned by an ill-fated passion, and she shall soon learn that De Bracy knows how to serve her in nobler ways.'

'I forgive you, Sir Knight,' said Rowena, 'as a Christian.'

'That means,' said Wamba, 'that she does not forgive him at all.'

'But I can never forgive the misery and desolation your madness has occasioned,' continued Rowena.

'Unloose your hold on the lady's rein,' said Cedric, coming up. 'By the bright sun above us, but it were shame, I would pin thee to the earth with my javelin; but be well assured, thou shalt smart, Maurice de Bracy, for thy share in this foul deed.'

'He threatens safely who threatens a prisoner,' said De Bracy; 'but when had a Saxon any touch of courtesy?'

Then retiring two steps backward, he permitted the lady to move on.

Cedric, ere they departed, expressed his peculiar gratitude to the Black Champion, and earnestly entreated him to accompany him to Rotherwood.

'I know,' he said, 'that ye errant knights desire to carry your fortunes on the point of your lance, and reck not of land or goods; but war is a changeful mistress, and a home is sometimes desirable even to the champion whose trade is wandering. Thou hast earned one in the halls of Rotherwood, noble knight. Cedric has wealth enough to repair the injuries of fortune, and all he has is his deliverer's. Come, therefore, to Rotherwood, not as a guest, but as a son or brother.'

'Cedric has already made me rich,' said the Knight; 'he has taught me the value of Saxon virtue. To Rotherwood will I come, brave Saxon, and that speedily; but, as now, pressing matters of moment detain me from your halls. Peradventure, when I come hither, I will ask such a boon as will put even thy generosity to the test.'

'It is granted ere spoken out,' said Cedric, striking his ready hand into the gauntleted palm of the Black Knight—'it is granted already, were it to affect half my fortune.'

'Gage not thy promise so lightly,' said the Knight of the Fetterlock; 'yet well I hope to gain the boon I shall ask. Meanwhile, adieu.'

'I have but to say,' added the Saxon, 'that, during the funeral rites of the noble Athelstane, I shall be an inhabitant of the halls of his castle of Coningsburgh. They will be open to all who choose to partake of the funeral banqueting; and—I speak in name of the noble Edith, mother of the fallen prince—they will never be shut against him who laboured so bravely, though unsuccessfully, to save Athelstane from Norman chains and Norman steel.'

'Ay, ay,' said Wamba, who had resumed his attendance on his master, 'rare feeding there will be; pity that the noble Athelstane cannot banquet at his own funeral. But he,' continued the Jester, lifting up his eyes gravely, 'is supping in Paradise, and doubtless does honour to the cheer.'

'Peace, and move on,' said Cedric, his anger at this untimely jest being checked by the recollection of Wamba's recent services. Rowena waved a graceful adieu to him of the Fetterlock, the Saxon bade God speed him, and on they moved through a wide glade of the forest.

They had scarce departed, ere a sudden procession moved from under the greenwood branches, swept slowly round the silvan amphitheatre, and took the same direction with Rowena and her followers. The priests of a neighbouring convent, in expectation of the ample donation, or 'soul-scat,' which Cedric had propined, attended upon the car in which the body of Athelstane was laid, and sang hymns as it was sadly and slowly borne on the shoulders of his vassals to his castle of Coningsburgh, to be there deposited in the grave of Hengist, from whom the deceased derived his long descent. Many of his vassals had assembled at the news of his death, and followed the bier with all the external marks, at least, of dejection and sorrow. Again the outlaws arose, and paid the same rude and spontaneous homage to death which they had so lately rendered to beauty: the slow chant and mournful step of the priests brought back to their remembrance such of their comrades as had fallen in the yesterday's affray. But such recollections dwell not long with those who lead a life of danger and enterprise, and ere the sound of the death-hymn had died on the wind, the outlaws were again busied in the distribution of their spoil.

'Valiant knight,' said Locksley to the Black Champion, 'without whose good heart and mighty arm our enterprise must altogether have failed, will it please you to take from that mass of spoil whatever may best serve to pleasure you, and to remind you of this my trysting-tree?'

'I accept the offer,' said the Knight, 'as frankly as it is given; and I ask permission to dispose of Sir Maurice de Bracy at my own pleasure.'

'He is thine already,' said Locksley, 'and well for him! else the tyrant had graced the highest bough of this oak, with as many of his Free Companions as we could gather hanging thick as acorns around him. But he is thy prisoner, and he is safe, though he had slain my father.'

'De Bracy,' said the Knight, 'thou art free—depart. He whose prisoner thou art scorns to take mean revenge for what is past. But beware of the future, lest a worse thing befall thee. Maurice de Bracy, I say BEWARE!'

De Bracy bowed low and in silence, and was about to withdraw, when the yeomen burst at once into a shout of execration and derision. The proud knight instantly stopped, turned back, folded his arms, drew up his form to its full height, and exclaimed, 'Peace, ye yelping curs! who open upon a cry which ye followed not when the stag was at bay. De Bracy scorns your censure as he would disdain your applause. To your brakes and caves, ye outlawed thieves! and be silent when aught knightly or noble is but spoken within a league of your fox-earths.'

This ill-timed defiance might have procured for De Bracy a volley of arrows, but for the hasty and imperative interference of the outlaw chief. Meanwhile, the knight caught a horse by the rein, for several which had been taken in the stables of Front-de-Bœuf stood accoutred around, and were a valuable part of the booty. He threw himself upon the saddle, and galloped off through the wood.

When the bustle occasioned by this incident was somewhat composed, the chief outlaw took from his neck the rich horn and baldric which he had recently gained at the strife of archery near Ashby.

'Noble knight,' he said to him of the Fetterlock, 'if you disdain not to grace by your acceptance a bugle which an English yeoman has once worn, this I will pray you to keep as a memorial of your gallant bearing; and if ye have aught to do, and, as happeneth oft to a gallant knight, ye chance to be hard bested in any forest between Trent and Tees, wind three mots upon the horn thus, *Wa-sa-hoa!* and it may well chance ye shall find helpers and rescue.'

He then gave breath to the bugle, and winded once and again the call which he described, until the Knight had caught the notes.

'Gramercy for the gift, bold yeoman,' said the Knight; 'and better help than thine and thy rangers would I never seek, were it at my utmost need.' And then in his turn he winded the call till all the greenwood rang.

'Well blown and clearly,' said the yeoman;

'beshrew me an thou knowest not as much of woodcraft as of war! Thou hast been a striker of deer in thy day, I warrant. Comrades, mark these three mots, it is the call of the Knight of the Fetterlock; and he who hears it, and hastens not to serve him at his need, I will have him scourged out of our band with his own bowstring.'

'Long live our leader!' shouted the yeomen, 'and long live the Black Knight of the Fetterlock! May he soon use our service to prove how readily it will be paid.'

Locksley now proceeded to the distribution of the spoil, which he performed with the most laudable impartiality. A tenth part of the whole was set apart for the church and for pious uses; a portion was next allotted to a sort of public treasury; a part was assigned to the widows and children of those who had fallen, or to be expended in masses for the souls of such as had left no surviving family. The rest was divided amongst the outlaws, according to their rank and merit; and the judgment of the chief, on all such doubtful questions as occurred, was delivered with great shrewdness, and received with absolute submission. The Black Knight was not a little surprised to find that men in a state so lawless were nevertheless among themselves so regularly and equitably governed, and all that he observed added to his opinion of the justice and judgment of their leader.

When each had taken his own proportion of the booty, and while the treasurer, accompanied by four tall yeomen, was transporting that belonging to the state to some place of concealment or of security, the portion devoted to the church still remained unappropriated.

'I would,' said the leader, 'we could hear tidings of our joyous chaplain; he was never wont to be absent when meat was to be blessed, or spoil to be parted; and it is his duty to take care of these the tithes of our successful enterprise. It may be the office has helped to cover some of his canonical irregularities. Also, I have a holy brother of his a prisoner at no great distance, and I would fain have the Friar to help me to deal with him in due sort. I greatly misdoubt the safety of the bluff priest.'

'I were right sorry for that,' said the Knight of the Fetterlock, 'for I stand indebted to him for the joyous hospitality of a merry night in his cell. Let us to the ruins of the castle; it may be we shall there learn some tidings of him.'

While they thus spoke, a loud shout among the yeomen announced the arrival of him for whom they feared, as they learned from the stentorian voice of the Friar himself, long before they saw his burly person.

'Make room, my merry men!' he exclaimed— 'room for your godly father and his prisoner. Cry welcome once more. I come, noble leader, like an eagle with my prey in my clutch.' And making his way through the ring, amidst the laughter of all around, he appeared in majestic triumph, his huge partizan in one hand, and in the other a halter, one end of which was fastened to the neck of the unfortunate Isaac of York, who, bent down by sorrow and terror, was dragged on by the victorious priest, who shouted aloud, 'Where is Allan-a-Dale, to chronicle me in a ballad, or if it were but a lay? By St. Hermangild, the jingling crowder is ever out of the way where there is an apt theme for exalting valour!'

'Curtal priest,' said the captain, 'thou hast been at a wet mass this morning, as early as it is. In the name of St. Nicholas, whom hast thou got here?'

'A captive to my sword and to my lance, noble captain,' replied the clerk of Copmanhurst—'to my bow and to my halberd, I should rather say; and yet I have redeemed him by my divinity from a worse captivity. Speak, Jew—have I not ransomed thee from Sathanas?—have I not taught thee thy *credo*, thy *pater*, and thine *Ave Maria?* Did I not spend the whole night in drinking to thee, and in expounding of mysteries?'

'For the love of God!' ejaculated the poor Jew, 'will no one take me out of the keeping of this mad —I mean this holy man?'

'How's this, Jew?' said the Friar, with a menacing aspect; 'dost thou recant, Jew? Bethink thee, if thou dost relapse into thine infidelity, though thou art not so tender as a suckling pig—I would I had one to break my fast upon—thou art not too tough to be roasted! Be conformable, Isaac, and repeat the words after me. *Ave Maria!*——'

'Nay, we will have no profanation, mad priest,' said Locksley; 'let us rather hear where you found this prisoner of thine.'

'By St. Dunstan,' said the Friar, 'I found him where I sought for better ware! I did step into the cellarage to see what might be rescued there; for though a cup of burnt wine, with spice, be an evening's draught for an emperor, it were waste, methought, to let so much good liquor be mulled at once; and I had caught up one runlet of sack, and was coming to call more aid among these lazy knaves, who are ever to seek when a good deed is to be done, when I was avised of a strong door. "Aha!" thought I, "here is the choicest juice of all in this secret crypt; and the knave butler, being disturbed in his vocation, hath left the key in the door." In therefore I went, and found just nought besides a commodity of rusted chains and this dog of a Jew, who presently rendered himself my prisoner, rescue or no rescue. I did but refresh myself after the fatigue of the action with the unbeliever with one humming cup of sack, and was proceeding to lead forth my captive, when, crash after crash, as with wild thunder-dint and levin-fire, down toppled

the masonry of an outer tower—marry beshrew their
hands that built it not the firmer !—and blocked up
the passage. The roar of one falling tower followed
another. I gave up thought of life ; and deeming
it a dishonour to one of my profession to pass out of
this world in company with a Jew, I heaved up my
halberd to beat his brains out ; but I took pity on
his grey hairs, and judged it better to lay down the
partizan, and take up my spiritual weapon for his
conversion. And truly, by the blessing of St.
Dunstan, the seed has been sown in good soil ; only
that, with speaking to him of mysteries through the
whole night, and being in a manner fasting—for
the few draughts of sack which I sharpened my
wits with were not worth marking—my head is wellnigh dizzied, I trow. But I was clean exhausted.
Gilbert and Wibbald know in what state they found
me— quite and clean exhausted.'

'We can bear witness,' said Gilbert ; 'for when
we had cleared away the ruin, and by St. Dunstan's
help lighted upon the dungeon stair, we found the
runlet of sack half-empty, the Jew half-dead, and
the Friar more than half—exhausted, as he calls it.'

'Ye be knaves ! ye lie !' retorted the offended
Friar ; 'it was you and your gormandising companions that drank up the sack, and called it your
morning draught. I am a pagan, an I kept it not
for the captain's own throat. But what recks it ?
The Jew is converted, and understands all I have
told him, very nearly, if not altogether, as well as
myself.'

'Jew,' said the captain, 'is this true ? Hast thou
renounced thine unbelief ?'

'May I so find mercy in your eyes,' said the Jew,
'as I know not one word which the reverend prelate
spake to me all this fearful night. Alas ! I was so
distraught with agony, and fear, and grief, that had
our holy father Abraham come to preach to me, he
had found but a deaf listener.'

'Thou liest, Jew, and thou knowest thou dost,' said the Friar; 'I will remind thee but of one word of our conference: thou didst promise to give all thy substance to our holy order.'

'So help me the promise, fair sirs,' said Isaac, even more alarmed than before, 'as no such sounds ever crossed my lips! Alas! I am an aged beggar'd man—I fear me a childless; have ruth on me, and let me go!'

'Nay,' said the Friar, 'if thou dost retract vows made in favour of holy church, thou must do penance.'

Accordingly, he raised his halberd, and would have laid the staff of it lustily on the Jew's shoulders, had not the Black Knight stopped the blow, and thereby transferred the holy clerk's resentment to himself.

'By St. Thomas of Kent,' said he, 'an I buckle to my gear, I will teach thee, sir lazy lover, to mell with thine own matters, maugre thine iron case there!'

'Nay, be not wroth with me,' said the Knight; 'thou knowest I am thy sworn friend and comrade.'

'I know no such thing,' answered the Friar; 'and defy thee for a meddling coxcomb!'

'Nay, but,' said the Knight, who seemed to take a pleasure in provoking his quondam host, 'hast thou forgotten how, that for my sake—for I say nothing of the temptation of the flagon and the pasty—thou didst break thy vow of fast and vigil?'

'Truly, friend,' said the Friar, clenching his huge fist, 'I will bestow a buffet on thee.'

'I accept of no such presents,' said the Knight: 'I am content to take thy cuff as a loan, but I will repay thee with usury as deep as ever thy prisoner there exacted in his traffic.'

'I will prove that presently,' said the Friar.

'Hola!' cried the captain, 'what art thou after, mad Friar—brawling beneath our trysting-tree?'

'No brawling,' said the Knight; 'it is but a friendly interchange of courtesy. Friar, strike an thou darest; I will stand thy blow, if thou wilt stand mine.'

'Thou hast the advantage with that iron pot on thy head,' said the churchman; 'but have at thee. Down thou goest, an thou wert Goliath of Gath in his brazen helmet.'

The Friar bared his brawny arm up to the elbow, and putting his full strength to the blow, gave the Knight a buffet that might have felled an ox. But his adversary stood firm as a rock. A loud shout was uttered by all the yeomen around; for the clerk's cuff was proverbial amongst them, and there were few who, in jest or earnest, had not had occasion to know its vigour.

'Now, priest,' said the Knight, pulling off his gauntlet, 'if I had vantage on my head, I will have none on my hand; stand fast as a true man.'

'*Genam meam dedi vapulatori*—I have given my cheek to the smiter,' said the priest; 'an thou canst stir me from the spot, fellow, I will freely bestow on thee the Jew's ransom.'

So spoke the burly priest, assuming, on his part, high defiance. But who may resist his fate? The buffet of the Knight was given with such strength and good-will that the Friar rolled head over heels upon the plain, to the great amazement of all the spectators. But he arose neither angry nor crestfallen.

'Brother,' said he to the Knight, 'thou shouldst have used thy strength with more discretion. I had mumbled but a lame mass an thou hadst broken my jaw, for the piper plays ill that wants the nether chops. Nevertheless, there is my hand, in friendly witness that I will exchange no more cuffs with thee, having been a loser by the barter. End now all unkindness. Let us put the Jew to ransom, since the leopard will not change his spots, and a Jew he will continue to be.'

'The priest,' said Clement, 'is not half so confident of the Jew's conversion since he received that buffet on the ear.'

'Go to, knave, what pratest thou of conversions? What, is there no respect?—all masters and no men? I tell thee, fellow, I was somewhat totty when I received the good knight's blow, or I had kept my ground under it. But an thou gibest more of it, thou shalt learn I can give as well as take.'

'Peace all!' said the captain. 'And thou, Jew, think of thy ransom; thou needest not to be told that thy race are held to be accursed in all Christian communities, and trust me that we cannot endure thy presence among us. Think, therefore, of an offer, while I examine a prisoner of another cast.'

'Were many of Front-de-Bœuf's men taken?' demanded the Black Knight.

'None of note enough to be put to ransom,' answered the captain; 'a set of hilding fellows there were, whom we dismissed to find them a new master; enough had been done for revenge and profit; the bunch of them were not worth a cardecu. The prisoner I speak of is better booty—a jolly monk riding to visit his leman, an I may judge by his horse-gear and wearing apparel. Here cometh the worthy prelate, as pert as a pyet.' And between two yeomen was brought before the silvan throne of the outlaw chief our old friend, Prior Aymer of Jorvaulx.

CHAPTER XXXIII

Flower of warriors,
How is't with Titus Lartius?
Marcius. As with a man busied about decrees,
Condemning some to death and some to exile,
Ransoming him or pitying, threatening the other.

Coriolanus.

THE captive Abbot's features and manners exhibited a whimsical mixture of offended pride, and deranged foppery, and bodily terror.

'Why, how now, my masters?' said he, with a voice in which all three emotions were blended. 'What order is this among ye? Be ye Turks or Christians, that handle a churchman? Know ye what it is, *manus imponere in servos Domini?* Ye have plundered my mails, torn my cope of curious cut lace, which might have served a cardinal. Another in my place would have been at his *excommunicabo vos;* but I am placable, and if ye order forth my palfreys, release my brethren, and restore my mails, tell down with all speed an hundred crowns to be expended in masses at the high altar of Jorvaulx Abbey, and make your vow to eat no venison until next Pentecost, it may be you shall hear little more of this mad frolic.'

'Holy father,' said the chief outlaw, 'it grieves me to think that you have met with such usage from any of my followers as calls for your fatherly reprehension.'

'Usage!' echoed the priest, encouraged by the mild tone of the silvan leader; 'it were usage fit for no hound of good race, much less for a Christian, far less for a priest, and least of all for the prior of the holy community of Jorvaulx. Here is a profane and drunken minstrel, called Allan-a-Dale—*nebulo quidam*—who has menaced me with corporal punishment—nay, with death itself, an I pay not down four hundred crowns of ransom, to the boot of all the treasure he hath already robbed me of—gold chains and gymmal rings to an unknown value; besides what is broken and spoiled among their rude hands, such as my pouncet-box and silver crisping-tongs.'

'It is impossible that Allan-a-Dale can have thus treated a man of your reverend bearing,' replied the captain.

'It is true as the gospel of St. Nicodemus,' said the Prior; 'he swore, with many a cruel north-country oath, that he would hang me up on the highest tree in the greenwood.'

'Did he so in very deed? Nay, then, reverend father, I think you had better comply with his demands, for Allan-a-Dale is the very man to abide by his word when he has so pledged it.' [1]

'You do but jest with me,' said the astounded Prior, with a forced laugh; 'and I love a good jest with all my heart. But, ha! ha! ha! when the mirth has lasted the livelong night, it is time to be grave in the morning.'

'And I am as grave as a father confessor,' replied the outlaw; 'you must pay a round ransom, Sir Prior, or your convent is likely to be called to a new election; for your place will know you no more.'

'Are ye Christians,' said the Prior, 'and hold this language to a churchman?'

---

[1] A commissary is said to have received similar consolation from a certain commander-in-chief, to whom he complained that a general officer had used some such threat towards him as that in the text.

'Christians ! ay, marry are we, and have divinity among us to boot,' answered the outlaw. ' Let our buxom chaplain stand forth, and expound to this reverend father the texts which concern this matter.'

The Friar, half-drunk, half-sober, had huddled a friar's frock over his green cassock, and now summoning together whatever scraps of learning he had acquired by rote in former days—' Holy father,' said he, ' *Deus faciat salvam benignitatem vestram*—you are welcome to the greenwood.'

' What profane mummery is this ? ' said the Prior. ' Friend, if thou be'st indeed of the church, it were a better deed to show me how I may escape from these men's hands than to stand ducking and grinning here like a morris-dancer.'

'Truly, reverend father,' said the Friar, ' I know but one mode in which thou mayst escape. This is St. Andrew's day with us : we are taking our tithes.'

' But not of the church, then, I trust, my good brother ? ' said the Prior.

' Of church and lay,' said the Friar ; ' and therefore, Sir Prior, *facite vobis amicos de mammone iniquitatis*—make yourselves friends of the mammon of unrighteousness, for no other friendship is like to serve your turn.'

' I love a jolly woodsman at heart,' said the Prior, softening his tone ; ' come, ye must not deal too hard with me. I can well of woodcraft, and can wind a horn clear and lustily, and hollo till every oak rings again. Come, ye must not deal too hard with me.'

' Give him a horn,' said the outlaw ; ' we will prove the skill he boasts of.'

The Prior Aymer winded a blast accordingly. The captain shook his head.

' Sir Prior,' he said, ' thou blowest a merry note, but it may not ransom thee ; we cannot afford, as the legend on a good knight's shield hath it, to set thee free for a blast. Moreover, I have found thee :

thou art one of those who, with new French graces
and tra-li-ras, disturb the ancient English bugle
notes. Prior, that last flourish on the recheat hath
added fifty crowns to thy ransom, for corrupting
the true old manly blasts of venerie.'

'Well, friend,' said the Abbot, peevishly, 'thou
art ill to please with thy woodcraft. I pray thee
be more conformable in this matter of my ransom.
At a word—since I must needs, for once, hold a
candle to the devil—what ransom am I to pay for
walking on Watling Street without having fifty men
at my back?'

'Were it not well,' said the lieutenant of the
gang apart to the captain, 'that the Prior should
name the Jew's ransom, and the Jew name the
Prior's?'

'Thou art a mad knave,' said the captain, 'but
thy plan transcends! Here, Jew, step forth.
Look at that holy Father Aymer, Prior of the rich
Abbey of Jorvaulx, and tell us at what ransom we
should hold him? Thou knowest the income of
his convent, I warrant thee.'

'O, assuredly,' said Isaac. 'I have trafficked with
the good fathers, and bought wheat and barley, and
fruits of the earth, and also much wool. O, it is
a rich abbey-stede, and they do live upon the fat,
and drink the sweet wines upon the lees, these good
fathers of Jorvaulx. Ah, if an outcast like me had
such a home to go to, and such incomings by the
year and by the month, I would pay much gold and
silver to redeem my captivity.'

'Hound of a Jew!' exclaimed the Prior, 'no one
knows better than thy own cursed self that our
holy house of God is indebted for the finishing of
our chancel——'

'And for the storing of your cellars in the last
season with the due allowance of Gascon wine,'
interrupted the Jew; 'but that—that is small
matters.'

'Hear the infidel dog!' said the churchman;
'he jangles as if our holy community did come
under debts for the wines we have a license to drink
propter necessitatem et ad frigus depellendum. The
circumcised villain blasphemeth the holy church,
and Christian men listen and rebuke him not!'

'All this helps nothing,' said the leader. 'Isaac,
pronounce what he may pay, without flaying both
hide and hair.'

'An six hundred crowns,' said Isaac, 'the good
Prior might well pay to your honoured valours,
and never sit less soft in his stall.'

'Six hundred crowns,' said the leader, gravely;
'I am contented—thou hast well spoken, Isaac—
six hundred crowns. It is a sentence, Sir Prior.'

'A sentence!—a sentence!' exclaimed the band;
'Solomon had not done it better.'

'Thou hearest thy doom, Prior,' said the leader.

'Ye are mad, my masters,' said the Prior; 'where
am I to find such a sum? If I sell the very pyx
and candlesticks on the altar at Jorvaulx, I shall
scarce raise the half; and it will be necessary for
that purpose that I go to Jorvaulx myself; ye may
retain as borrows[1] my two priests.'

'That will be but blind trust,' said the outlaw;
'we will retain thee, Prior, and send them to fetch
thy ransom. Thou shalt not want a cup of wine
and a collop of venison the while; and if thou lovest
woodcraft, thou shalt see such as your north country
never witnessed.'

'Or, if so please you,' said Isaac, willing to curry
favour with the outlaws, 'I can send to York for
the six hundred crowns, out of certain monies in
my hands, if so be that the most reverend Prior
present will grant me a quittance.'

'He shall grant thee whatever thou dost list,
Isaac,' said the captain; 'and thou shalt lay down

[1] *Borghs* or *borrows* signifies pledge. Hence our word to
borrow, because we pledge ourselves to restore what is lent.

the redemption money for Prior Aymer as well as for thyself.'

'For myself! ah, courageous sirs,' said the Jew, 'I am a broken and impoverished man; a beggar's staff must be my portion through life, supposing I were to pay you fifty crowns.'

'The Prior shall judge of that matter,' replied the captain. 'How say you, Father Aymer? Can the Jew afford a good ransom?'

'*Can* he afford a ransom?' answered the Prior. 'Is he not Isaac of York, rich enough to redeem the captivity of the ten tribes of Israel who were led into Assyrian bondage? I have seen but little of him myself, but our cellarer and treasurer have dealt largely with him, and report says that his house at York is so full of gold and silver as is a shame in any Christian land. Marvel it is to all living Christian hearts that such gnawing adders should be suffered to eat into the bowels of the state, and even of the holy church herself, with foul usuries and extortions.'

'Hold, father,' said the Jew, 'mitigate and assuage your choler. I pray of your reverence to remember that I force my monies upon no one. But when churchman and layman, prince and prior, knight and priest, come knocking to Isaac's door, they borrow not his shekels with these uncivil terms. It is then, "Friend Isaac, will you pleasure us in this matter, and our day shall be truly kept, so God sa' me?"—and "Kind Isaac, if ever you served man, show yourself a friend in this need!" And when the day comes, and I ask my own, then what hear I but "Damned Jew," and "The curse of Egypt on your tribe," and all that may stir up the rude and uncivil populace against poor strangers!'

'Prior,' said the captain, 'Jew though he be, he hath in this spoken well. Do thou, therefore, name his ransom, as he named thine, without farther rude terms.'

'None but *latro famosus* — the interpretation whereof,' said the Prior, 'will I give at some other time and tide—would place a Christian prelate and an unbaptized Jew upon the same bench. But since ye require me to put a price upon this caitiff, I tell you openly that ye will wrong yourselves if you take from him a penny under a thousand crowns.'

'A sentence!—a sentence!' exclaimed the chief outlaw.

'A sentence!—a sentence!' shouted his assessors; 'the Christian has shown his good nurture, and dealt with us more generously than the Jew.'

'The God of my fathers help me!' said the Jew; 'will ye bear to the ground an impoverished creature? I am this day childless, and will ye deprive me of the means of livelihood?'

'Thou wilt have the less to provide for, Jew, if thou art childless,' said Aymer.

'Alas! my lord,' said Isaac, 'your law permits you not to know how the child of our bosom is entwined with the strings of our heart. O Rebecca! daughter of my beloved Rachael! were each leaf on that tree a zecchin, and each zecchin mine own, all that mass of wealth would I give to know whether thou art alive, and escaped the hands of the Nazarene!'

'Was not thy daughter dark-haired?' said one of the outlaws; 'and wore she not a veil of twisted sendal, broidered with silver?'

'She did!—she did!' said the old man, trembling with eagerness, as formerly with fear. 'The blessing of Jacob be upon thee! canst thou tell me aught of her safety?'

'It was she, then,' said the yeoman, 'who was carried off by the proud Templar, when he broke through our ranks on yester-even. I had drawn my bow to send a shaft after him, but spared him even for the sake of the damsel, who I feared might take harm from the arrow.'

'Oh!' answered the Jew, 'I would to God thou hadst shot, though the arrow had pierced her bosom! Better the tomb of her fathers than the dishonourable couch of the licentious and savage Templar. Ichabod! Ichabod! the glory hath departed from my house!'

'Friends,' said the chief, looking round, 'the old man is but a Jew, natheless his grief touches me. Deal uprightly with us, Isaac: will paying this ransom of a thousand crowns leave thee altogether penniless?'

Isaac, recalled to think of his worldly goods, the love of which, by dint of inveterate habit, contended even with his parental affection, grew pale, stammered, and could not deny there might be some small surplus.

'Well, go to, what though there be,' said the outlaw, 'we will not reckon with thee too closely. Without treasure thou mayst as well hope to redeem thy child from the clutches of Sir Brian de Bois-Guilbert as to shoot a stag-royal with a headless shaft. We will take thee at the same ransom with Prior Aymer, or rather at one hundred crowns lower, which hundred crowns shall be mine own peculiar loss, and not light upon this worshipful community; and so we shall avoid the heinous offence of rating a Jew merchant as high as a Christian prelate, and thou wilt have six [five] hundred crowns remaining to treat for thy daughter's ransom. Templars love the glitter of silver shekels as well as the sparkle of black eyes. Hasten to make thy crowns chink in the ear of De Bois-Guilbert, ere worse comes of it. Thou wilt find him, as our scouts have brought notice, at the next preceptory house of his order. Said I well, my merry mates?'

The yeomen expressed their wonted acquiescence in their leader's opinion; and Isaac, relieved of one half of his apprehensions, by learning that his daughter lived, and might possibly be ransomed, threw himself at the feet of the generous outlaw, and, rubbing his beard against his buskins, sought to kiss the hem of his green cassock. The captain drew himself back, and extricated himself from the Jew's grasp, not without some marks of contempt.

'Nay, beshrew thee, man, up with thee! I am English born, and love no such Eastern prostrations. Kneel to God, and not to a poor sinner like me.'

'Ay, Jew,' said Prior Aymer, 'kneel to God, as represented in the servant of His altar, and who knows, with thy sincere repentance and due gifts to the shrine of St. Robert, what grace thou mayst acquire for thyself and thy daughter Rebecca? I grieve for the maiden, for she is of fair and comely countenance: I beheld her in the lists of Ashby. Also Brian de Bois-Guilbert is one with whom I may do much: bethink thee how thou mayst deserve my good word with him.'

'Alas! alas!' said the Jew, 'on every hand the spoilers arise against me: I am given as a prey unto the Assyrian, and a prey unto him of Egypt.'

'And what else should be the lot of thy accursed race?' answered the Prior; 'for what saith Holy Writ, *verbum Domini projecerunt, et sapientia est nulla in eis*—they have cast forth the Word of the Lord, and there is no wisdom in them—*propterea dabo mulieres eorum exteris*—I will give their women to strangers, that is to the Templar, as in the present matter—*et thesauros eorum hæredibus alienis* —and their treasures to others, as in the present case to these honest gentlemen.'

Isaac groaned deeply, and began to wring his hands, and to relapse into his state of desolation and despair. But the leader of the yeomen led him aside.

'Advise thee well, Isaac,' said Locksley, 'what thou wilt do in this matter; my counsel to thee is to make a friend of this churchman. He is vain, Isaac, and he is covetous; at least he needs money to supply his profusion. Thou canst easily gratify his greed; for think not that I am blinded by thy pretexts of poverty. I am intimately acquainted, Isaac, with the very iron chest in which thou dost keep thy money-bags. What! know I not the great stone beneath the apple-tree, that leads into the vaulted chamber under thy garden at York?' The Jew grew as pale as death. 'But fear nothing from me,' continued the yeoman, 'for we are of old acquainted. Dost thou not remember the sick yeoman whom thy fair daughter Rebecca redeemed from the gyves at York, and kept him in thy house till his health was restored, when thou didst dismiss him recovered, and with a piece of money? Usurer as thou art, thou didst never place coin at better interest than that poor silver mark, for it has this day saved thee five hundred crowns.'

'And thou art he whom we called Diccon Bend-the-Bow?' said Isaac; 'I thought ever I knew the accent of thy voice.'

'I am Bend-the-Bow,' said the captain, 'and Locksley, and have a good name besides all these.'

'But thou art mistaken, good Bend-the-Bow, concerning that same vaulted apartment. So help me Heaven, as there is nought in it but some merchandises which I will gladly part with to you—one hundred yards of Lincoln green to make doublets to thy men, and a hundred staves of Spanish yew to make bows, and one hundred silken bowstrings, tough, round, and sound—these will I send thee for thy good-will, honest Diccon, an thou wilt keep silence about the vault, my good Diccon.'

'Silent as a dormouse,' said the outlaw; 'and never trust me but I am grieved for thy daughter. But I may not help it. The Templar's lances are too strong for my archery in the open field; they would scatter us like dust. Had I but known it was Rebecca when she was borne off, something might have been done; but now thou must needs

proceed by policy. Come, shall I treat for thee
with the Prior?'

'In God's name, Diccon, an thou canst, aid me
to recover the child of my bosom!'

'Do not thou interrupt me with thine ill-timed
avarice,' said the outlaw, 'and I will deal with him
in thy behalf.'

He then turned from the Jew, who followed him,
however, as closely as his shadow.

'Prior Aymer,' said the captain, 'come apart with
me under this tree. Men say thou dost love wine
and a lady's smile better than beseems thy order,
Sir Priest; but with that I have nought to do. I
have heard, too, thou dost love a brace of good dogs
and a fleet horse, and it may well be that, loving
things which are costly to come by, thou hatest not
a purse of gold. But I have never heard that thou
didst love oppression or cruelty. Now, here is Isaac
willing to give thee the means of pleasure and
pastime in a bag containing one hundred marks
of silver, if thy intercession with thine ally the
Templar shall avail to procure the freedom of his
daughter.'

'In safety and honour, as when taken from me,'
said the Jew, 'otherwise it is no bargain.'

'Peace, Isaac,' said the outlaw, 'or I give up
thine interest. What say you to this my purpose,
Prior Aymer?'

'The matter,' quoth the Prior, 'is of a mixed
condition; for, if I do a good deed on the one
hand, yet, on the other, it goeth to the vantage
of a Jew, and in so much is against my conscience.
Yet, if the Israelite will advantage the church by
giving me somewhat over to the building of our
dortour,[1] I will take it on my conscience to aid
him in the matter of his daughter.'

'For a score of marks to the dortour,' said the
outlaw—'Be still, I say, Isaac!—or for a brace of

---

[1] *Dortour*, or dormitory.

silver candlesticks to the altar, we will not stand with you.'

'Nay, but, good Diccon Bend-the-Bow,' said Isaac, endeavouring to interpose.

'Good Jew—good beast—good earthworm!' said the yeoman, losing patience; 'an thou dost go on to put thy filthy lucre in the balance with thy daughter's life and honour, by Heaven, I will strip thee of every maravedi thou hast in the world before three days are out!'

Isaac shrunk together, and was silent.

'And what pledge am I to have for all this?' said the Prior.

'When Isaac returns successful through your mediation,' said the outlaw, 'I swear by St. Hubert, I will see that he pays thee the money in good silver, or I will reckon with him for it in such sort, he had better have paid twenty such sums.'

'Well then, Jew,' said Aymer, 'since I must needs meddle in this matter, let me have the use of thy writing-tablets—though, hold—rather than use thy pen, I would fast for twenty-four hours, and where shall I find one?'

'If your holy scruples can dispense with using the Jew's tablets, for the pen I can find a remedy,' said the yeoman; and, bending his bow, he aimed his shaft at a wild goose which was soaring over their heads, the advanced guard of a phalanx of his tribe, which were winging their way to the distant and solitary fens of Holderness. The bird came fluttering down, transfixed with the arrow.

'There, Prior,' said the captain, 'are quills enow to supply all the monks of Jorvaulx for the next hundred years, an they take not to writing chronicles.'

The Prior sat down, and at great leisure indited an epistle to Brian de Bois-Guilbert, and having carefully sealed up the tablets, delivered them to the Jew, saying, 'This will be thy safe-conduct to the preceptory of Templestowe, and, as I think, is most likely to accomplish the delivery of thy daughter, if it be well backed with proffers of advantage and commodity at thine own hand; for, trust me well, the good knight Bois-Guilbert is of their confraternity that do nought for nought.'

'Well, Prior,' said the outlaw, 'I will detain thee no longer here than to give the Jew a quittance for the six hundred crowns at which thy ransom is fixed—I accept of him for my paymaster; and if I hear that ye boggle at allowing him in his accompts the sum so paid by him, St. Mary refuse me, an I burn not the abbey over thine head, though I hang ten years the sooner!'

With a much worse grace than that wherewith he had penned the letter to Bois-Guilbert, the Prior wrote an acquittance, discharging Isaac of York of six hundred crowns, advanced to him in his need for acquittal of his ransom, and faithfully promising to hold true compt with him for that sum.

'And now,' said Prior Aymer, 'I will pray you of restitution of my mules and palfreys, and the freedom of the reverend brethren attending upon me, and also of the gymmal rings, jewels, and fair vestures of which I have been despoiled, having now satisfied you for my ransom as a true prisoner.'

'Touching your brethren, Sir Prior,' said Locksley, 'they shall have present freedom, it were unjust to detain them; touching your horses and mules, they shall also be restored, with such spending-money as may enable you to reach York, for it were cruel to deprive you of the means of journeying. But as concerning rings, jewels, chains, and what else, you must understand that we are men of tender consciences, and will not yield to a venerable man like yourself, who should be dead to the vanities of this life, the strong temptation to break the rule of his foundation, by wearing rings, chains, or other vain gauds.'

'Think what you do, my masters,' said the Prior,
'ere you put your hand on the church's patrimony.
These things are *inter res sacras*, and I wot not what
judgment might ensue were they to be handled by
laical hands.'

'I will take care of that, reverend Prior,' said the
hermit of Copmanhurst; 'for I will wear them
myself.'

'Friend, or brother,' said the Prior, in answer to
this solution of his doubts, 'if thou hast really taken
religious orders, I pray thee to look how thou wilt
answer to thine official for the share thou hast taken
in this day's work.'

'Friend Prior,' returned the hermit, 'you are to
know that I belong to a little diocese where I am
my own diocesan, and care as little for the Bishop
of York as I do for the Abbot of Jorvaulx, the Prior,
and all the convent.'

'Thou art utterly irregular,' said the Prior—'one
of those disorderly men who, taking on them the
sacred character without due cause, profane the holy
rites, and endanger the souls of those who take
counsel at their hands; *lapides pro pane condonantes
iis*, giving them stones instead of bread, as the
Vulgate hath it.'

'Nay,' said the Friar, 'an my brain-pan could
have been broken by Latin, it had not held so long
together. I say, that easing a world of such mis-
proud priests as thou art of their jewels and their
gimcracks is a lawful spoiling of the Egyptians.'

'Thou be'st a hedge-priest,' said the Prior, in
great wrath, '*excommunicabo vos.*'

'Thou be'st thyself more like a thief and a heretic,'
said the Friar, equally indignant; 'I will pouch up
no such affront before my parishioners as thou
thinkest it not shame to put upon me, although I
be a reverend brother to thee. *Ossa ejus perfringam*,
I will break your bones, as the Vulgate hath it.'

'Hola!' cried the captain, 'come the reverend
brethren to such terms? Keep thine assurance of
peace, Friar. Prior, an thou hast not made thy
peace perfect with God, provoke the Friar no
further. Hermit, let the reverend father depart in
peace, as a ransomed man.'

The yeomen separated the incensed priests, who
continued to raise their voices, vituperating each
other in bad Latin, which the Prior delivered the
more fluently, and the hermit with the greater
vehemence. The Prior at length recollected himself
sufficiently to be aware that he was compromising
his dignity by squabbling with such a hedge-priest
as the outlaw's chaplain, and being joined by his
attendants, rode off with considerably less pomp,
and in a much more apostolical condition, so far
as worldly matters were concerned, than he had
exhibited before this rencounter.

It remained that the Jew should produce some
security for the ransom which he was to pay on the
Prior's account, as well as upon his own. He gave,
accordingly, an order sealed with his signet, to a
brother of his tribe at York, requiring him to pay
to the bearer the sum of a thousand [eleven hundred]
crowns, and to deliver certain merchandises specified
in the note.

'My brother Sheva,' he said, groaning deeply,
'hath the key of my warehouses.'

'And of the vaulted chamber,' whispered Locksley.

'No, no—may Heaven forefend!' said Isaac; 'evil
is the hour that let any one whomsoever into that
secret!'

'It is safe with me,' said the outlaw, 'so be that
this thy scroll produce the sum therein nominated
and set down. But what now, Isaac? art dead?
art stupefied? hath the payment of a thousand
crowns put thy daughter's peril out of thy mind?'

The Jew started to his feet—'No, Diccon, no;
I will presently set forth. Farewell, thou whom

I may not call good, and dare not, and will not, call evil.'

Yet, ere Isaac departed, the outlaw chief bestowed on him this parting advice: 'Be liberal of thine offers, Isaac, and spare not thy purse for thy daughter's safety. Credit me, that the gold thou shalt spare in her cause will hereafter give thee as much agony as if it were poured molten down thy throat.'

Isaac acquiesced with a deep groan, and set forth on his journey, accompanied by two tall foresters, who were to be his guides, and at the same time his guards, through the wood.

The Black Knight, who had seen with no small interest these various proceedings, now took his leave of the outlaw in turn; nor could he avoid expressing his surprise at having witnessed so much of civil policy amongst persons cast out from all the ordinary protection and influence of the laws.

'Good fruit, Sir Knight,' said the yeoman, 'will sometimes grow on a sorry tree; and evil times are not always productive of evil alone and unmixed. Amongst those who are drawn into this lawless state, there are, doubtless, numbers who wish to exercise its license with some moderation, and some who regret, it may be, that they are obliged to follow such a trade at all.'

'And to one of those,' said the Knight, 'I am now, I presume, speaking?'

'Sir Knight,' said the outlaw, 'we have each our secret. You are welcome to form your judgment of me, and I may use my conjectures touching you, though neither of our shafts may hit the mark they are shot at. But as I do not pray to be admitted into your mystery, be not offended that I preserve my own.'

'I crave pardon, brave outlaw,' said the Knight, 'your reproof is just. But it may be we shall meet hereafter with less of concealment on either side. Meanwhile we part friends, do we not?'

'There is my hand upon it,' said Locksley; 'and I will call it the hand of a true Englishman, though an outlaw for the present.'

'And there is mine in return,' said the Knight, 'and I hold it honoured by being clasped with yours. For he that does good, having the unlimited power to do evil, deserves praise not only for the good which he performs, but for the evil which he forbears. Fare thee well, gallant outlaw!'

Thus parted that fair fellowship; and he of the Fetterlock, mounting upon his strong war-horse, rode off through the forest.

CHAPTER XXXIV

King John. I'll tell thee what, my friend,
He is a very serpent in my way;
And wheresoe'er this foot of mine doth tread,
He lies before me. Dost thou understand me?
                                                    King John.

THERE was brave feasting in the Castle of York,
to which Prince John had invited those nobles, pre-
lates, and leaders by whose assistance he hoped
to carry through his ambitious projects upon his
brother's throne. Waldemar Fitzurse, his able and
politic agent, was at secret work among them, tem-
pering all to that pitch of courage which was necessary in making an open declaration of their purpose.
But their enterprise was delayed by the absence of
more than one main limb of the confederacy. The
stubborn and daring, though brutal, courage of
Front-de-Bœuf; the buoyant spirits and bold bearing of De Bracy; the sagacity, martial experience,
and renowned valour of Brian de Bois-Guilbert,
were important to the success of their conspiracy;
and, while cursing in secret their unnecessary and
unmeaning absence, neither John nor his adviser
dared to proceed without them. Isaac the Jew also
seemed to have vanished, and with him the hope of
certain sums of money, making up the subsidy for
which Prince John had contracted with that Israelite and his brethren. This deficiency was likely
to prove perilous in an emergency so critical.

It was on the morning after the fall of Torquilstone, that a confused report began to spread abroad

in the city of York that De Bracy and Bois-Guilbert,
with their confederate Front-de-Bœuf, had been
taken or slain. Waldemar brought the rumour to
Prince John, announcing, that he feared its truth
the more that they had set out with a small attendance, for the purpose of committing an assault on
the Saxon Cedric and his attendants. At another
time the Prince would have treated this deed of
violence as a good jest; but now that it interfered
with and impeded his own plans, he exclaimed
against the perpetrators, and spoke of the broken
laws, and the infringement of public order and of
private property, in a tone which might have become
King Alfred.

'The unprincipled marauders!' he said; 'were
I ever to become monarch of England, I would hang
such transgressors over the drawbridges of their
own castles.'

'But to become monarch of England,' said his
Ahithophel, coolly, 'it is necessary not only that
your Grace should endure the transgressions of
these unprincipled marauders, but that you should
afford them your protection, notwithstanding your
laudable zeal for the laws they are in the habit of
infringing. We shall be finely helped, if the churl
Saxons should have realised your Grace's vision of
converting feudal drawbridges into gibbets; and
yonder bold-spirited Cedric seemeth one to whom
such an imagination might occur. Your Grace is
well aware, it will be dangerous to stir without
Front-de-Bœuf, De Bracy, and the Templar; and
yet we have gone too far to recede with safety.'

Prince John struck his forehead with impatience,
and then began to stride up and down the apartment.

'The villains,' he said—'the base, treacherous
villains, to desert me at this pinch!'

'Nay, say rather the feather-pated, giddy mad-
men,' said Waldemar, 'who must be toying with
follies when such business was in hand.'

'What is to be done?' said the Prince, stopping short before Waldemar.

'I know nothing which can be done,' answered his counsellor, 'save that which I have already taken order for. I came not to bewail this evil chance with your Grace until I had done my best to remedy it.'

'Thou art ever my better angel, Waldemar,' said the Prince; 'and when I have such a chancellor to advise withal, the reign of John will be renowned in our annals. What hast thou commanded?'

'I have ordered Louis Winkelbrand, De Bracy's lieutenant, to cause his trumpet sound to horse, and to display his banner, and to set presently forth towards the castle of Front-de-Bœuf, to do what yet may be done for the succour of our friends.'

Prince John's face flushed with the pride of a spoilt child, who has undergone what it conceives to be an insult.

'By the face of God!' he said, 'Waldemar Fitzurse, much hast thou taken upon thee! and over malapert thou wert to cause trumpet to blow, or banner to be raised, in a town where ourselves were in presence, without our express command.'

'I crave your Grace's pardon,' said Fitzurse, internally cursing the idle vanity of his patron; 'but when time pressed, and even the loss of minutes might be fatal, I judged it best to take this much burden upon me, in a matter of such importance to your Grace's interest.'

'Thou art pardoned, Fitzurse,' said the Prince, gravely; 'thy purpose hath atoned for thy hasty rashness. But whom have we here? De Bracy himself, by the rood! and in strange guise doth he come before us.'

It was indeed De Bracy, 'bloody with spurring, fiery red with speed.' His armour bore all the marks of the late obstinate fray, being broken, defaced, and stained with blood in many places, and covered with clay and dust from the crest to the spur. Undoing his helmet, he placed it on the table, and stood a moment as if to collect himself before he told his news.

'De Bracy,' said Prince John, 'what means this? Speak, I charge thee! Are the Saxons in rebellion?'

'Speak, De Bracy,' said Fitzurse, almost in the same moment with his master, 'thou wert wont to be a man. Where is the Templar? where Front-de-Bœuf?'

'The Templar is fled,' said De Bracy; 'Front-de-Bœuf you will never see more. He has found a red grave among the blazing rafters of his own castle, and I alone am escaped to tell you.'

'Cold news,' said Waldemar, 'to us, though you speak of fire and conflagration.'

'The worst news is not yet said,' answered De Bracy; and, coming up to Prince John, he uttered in a low and emphatic tone—'Richard is in England; I have seen and spoken with him.'

Prince John turned pale, tottered, and caught at the back of an oaken bench to support himself, much like to a man who receives an arrow in his bosom.

'Thou ravest, De Bracy,' said Fitzurse; 'it cannot be.'

'It is as true as truth itself,' said De Bracy; 'I was his prisoner, and spoke with him.'

'With Richard Plantagenet, sayest thou?' continued Fitzurse.

'With Richard Plantagenet,' replied De Bracy —'with Richard Cœur-de-Lion—with Richard of England.'

'And thou wert his prisoner?' said Waldemar; 'he is then at the head of a power?'

'No; only a few outlawed yeomen were around him, and to these his person is unknown. I heard him say he was about to depart from them. He

joined them only to assist at the storming of Torquilstone.'

'Ay,' said Fitzurse, 'such is indeed the fashion
of Richard — a true knight - errant he, and will
wander in wild adventure, trusting the prowess of
his single arm, like any Sir Guy or Sir Bevis, while
the weighty affairs of his kingdom slumber, and his
own safety is endangered. What dost thou propose
to do, De Bracy?'

'I? I offered Richard the service of my Free
Lances, and he refused them. I will lead them to
Hull, seize on shipping, and embark for Flanders ;
thanks to the bustling times, a man of action will
always find employment. And thou, Waldemar,
wilt thou take lance and shield, and lay down thy
policies, and wend along with me, and share the
fate which God sends us ?'

'I am too old, Maurice, and I have a daughter,'
answered Waldemar.

'Give her to me, Fitzurse, and I will maintain
her as fits her rank, with the help of lance and
stirrup,' said De Bracy.

'Not so,' answered Fitzurse ; 'I will take sanctuary in this church of St. Peter ; the Archbishop
is my sworn brother.'

During this discourse, Prince John had gradually
awakened from the stupor into which he had been
thrown by the unexpected intelligence, and had
been attentive to the conversation which passed
betwixt his followers. 'They fall off from me,' he
said to himself: 'they hold no more by me than a
withered leaf by the bough when a breeze blows on
it ! Hell and fiends ! can I shape no means for
myself when I am deserted by these cravens ?' He
paused, and there was an expression of diabolical
passion in the constrained laugh with which he at
length broke in on their conversation.

'Ha, ha, ha ! my good lords, by the light of Our
Lady's brow, I held ye sage men, bold men, ready-

witted men, loving things which are costly to come
by ; yet ye throw down wealth, honour, pleasure,
all that our noble game promised you, at the moment
it might be won by one bold cast !'

'I understand you not,' said De Bracy. 'As
soon as Richard's return is blown abroad, he will
be at the head of an army, and all is then over with
us. I would counsel you, my lord, either to fly to
France or take the protection of the Queen Mother.'

'I seek no safety for myself,' said Prince John,
haughtily ; 'that I could secure by a word spoken
to my brother. But although you, De Bracy, and
you, Waldemar Fitzurse, are so ready to abandon me,
I should not greatly delight to see your heads
blackening on Clifford's gate yonder. Thinkest
thou, Waldemar, that the wily Archbishop will not
suffer thee to be taken from the very horns of the
altar, would it make his peace with King Richard?
And forgettest thou, De Bracy, that Robert Estoteville lies betwixt thee and Hull with all his forces,
and that the Earl of Essex is gathering his followers?
If we had reason to fear these levies even before
Richard's return, trowest thou there is any doubt
now which party their leaders will take ? Trust me,
Estoteville alone has strength enough to drive all
thy Free Lances into the Humber.' Waldemar
Fitzurse and De Bracy looked in each other's faces
with blank dismay. 'There is but one road to
safety,' continued the Prince, and his brow grew
black as midnight : 'this object of our terror
journeys alone ; he must be met withal.'

'Not by me,' said De Bracy, hastily ; 'I was his
prisoner, and he took me to mercy. I will not
harm a feather in his crest.'

'Who spoke of harming him?' said Prince John,
with a hardened laugh ; 'the knave will say next
that I meant he should slay him ! No—a prison
were better ; and whether in Britain or Austria,
what matters it ? Things will be but as they were

when we commenced our enterprise. It was founded on the hope that Richard would remain a captive in Germany. Our uncle [relative] Robert lived and died in the castle of Cardiff.'

'Ay, but,' said Waldemar, 'your sire [ancestor] Henry sate more firm in his seat than your Grace can. I say the best prison is that which is made by the sexton: no dungeon like a church-vault! I have said my say.'

'Prison or tomb,' said De Bracy, 'I wash my hands of the whole matter.'

'Villain!' said Prince John, 'thou wouldst not bewray our counsel?'

'Counsel was never bewrayed by me,' said De Bracy, haughtily, 'nor must the name of villain be coupled with mine!'

'Peace, Sir Knight!' said Waldemar; 'and you, good my lord, forgive the scruples of valiant De Bracy; I trust I shall soon remove them.'

'That passes your eloquence, Fitzurse,' replied the knight.

'Why, good Sir Maurice,' rejoined the wily politician, 'start not aside like a scared steed, without, at least, considering the object of your terror. This Richard—but a day since, and it would have been thy dearest wish to have met him hand to hand in the ranks of battle; a hundred times I have heard thee wish it.'

'Ay,' said De Bracy, 'but that was, as thou sayest, hand to hand, and in the ranks of battle! Thou never heardest me breathe a thought of assaulting him alone, and in a forest.'

'Thou art no good knight if thou dost scruple at it,' said Waldemar. 'Was it in battle that Lancelot de Lac and Sir Tristram won renown? or was it not by encountering gigantic knights under the shade of deep and unknown forests?'

'Ay, but I promise you,' said De Bracy, 'that neither Tristram nor Lancelot would have been

match, hand to hand, for Richard Plantagenet, and
I think it was not their wont to take odds against
a single man.'

'Thou art mad, De Bracy: what is it we propose
to thee, a hired and retained captain of Free Companions, whose swords are purchased for Prince
John's service? Thou art apprised of our enemy,
and then thou scruplest, though thy patron's fortunes, those of thy comrades, thine own, and the
life and honour of every one amongst us, be at
stake!'

'I tell you,' said De Bracy, sullenly, 'that he gave
me my life. True, he sent me from his presence,
and refused my homage, so far I owe him neither
favour nor allegiance; but I will not lift hand
against him.'

'It needs not; send Louis Winkelbrand and a
score of thy lances.'

'Ye have sufficient ruffians of your own,' said De
Bracy; 'not one of mine shall budge on such an
errand.'

'Art thou so obstinate, De Bracy?' said Prince
John; 'and wilt thou forsake me, after so many
protestations of zeal for my service?'

'I mean it not,' said De Bracy; 'I will abide by
you in aught that becomes a knight, whether in the
lists or in the camp; but this highway practice
comes not within my vow.'

'Come hither, Waldemar,' said Prince John.
'An unhappy prince am I. My father, King Henry,
had faithful servants. He had but to say that he
was plagued with a factious priest, and the blood of
Thomas-a-Becket, saint though he was, stained the
steps of his own altar. Tracy, Morville, Brito,
loyal and daring subjects, your names, your spirit,
are extinct! and although Reginald Fitzurse hath
left a son, he hath fallen off from his father's fidelity
and courage.'

IVANHOE

433

'He has fallen off from neither,' said Waldemar Fitzurse; 'and since it may not better be, I will take on me the conduct of this perilous enterprise. Dearly, however, did my father purchase the praise of a zealous friend; and yet did his proof of loyalty to Henry fall far short of what I am about to afford; for rather would I assail a whole calendar of saints than put spear in rest against Cœur-de-Lion. De Bracy, to thee I must trust to keep up the spirits of the doubtful, and to guard Prince John's person. If you receive such news as I trust to send you, our enterprise will no longer wear a doubtful aspect. Page,' he said, 'hie to my lodgings, and tell my armourer to be there in readiness; and bid Stephen Wetheral, Broad Thoresby, and the Three Spears of Spyinghow come to me instantly; and let the scout-master, Hugh Bardon, attend me also. Adieu, my Prince, till better times.' Thus speaking, he left the apartment.

'He goes to make my brother prisoner,' said Prince John to De Bracy, 'with as little touch of compunction as if it but concerned the liberty of a Saxon franklin. I trust he will observe our orders, and use our dear Richard's person with all due respect.'

De Bracy only answered by a smile.

'By the light of Our Lady's brow,' said Prince John, 'our orders to him were most precise, though it may be you heard them not, as we stood together in the oriel window. Most clear and positive was our charge that Richard's safety should be cared for, and woe to Waldemar's head if he transgress it!'

'I had better pass to his lodgings,' said De Bracy, 'and make him fully aware of your Grace's pleasure; for, as it quite escaped my ear, it may not perchance have reached that of Waldemar.'

'Nay, nay,' said Prince John, impatiently, 'I promise thee he heard me; and, besides, I have farther occupation for thee. Maurice, come hither; let me lean on thy shoulder.'

They walked a turn through the hall in this familiar posture, and Prince John, with an air of the most confidential intimacy, proceeded to say, 'What thinkest thou of this Waldemar Fitzurse, my De Bracy? He trusts to be our Chancellor. Surely we will pause ere we give an office so high to one who shows evidently how little he reverences our blood, by his so readily undertaking this enterprise against Richard. Thou dost think, I warrant, that thou hast lost somewhat of our regard by thy boldly declining this unpleasing task. But no, Maurice! I rather honour thee for thy virtuous constancy. There are things most necessary to be done, the perpetrator of which we neither love nor honour; and there may be refusals to serve us which shall rather exalt in our estimation those who deny our request. The arrest of my unfortunate brother forms no such good title to the high office of Chancellor as thy chivalrous and courageous denial establishes in thee to the truncheon of High Marshal. Think of this, De Bracy, and begone to thy charge.'

'Fickle tyrant!' muttered De Bracy, as he left the presence of the Prince; 'evil luck have they who trust thee. Thy Chancellor, indeed! He who hath the keeping of thy conscience shall have an easy charge, I trow. But High Marshal of England! that,' he said, extending his arm, as if to grasp the baton of office, and assuming a loftier stride along the ante-chamber—'that is indeed a prize worth playing for!'

De Bracy had no sooner left the apartment than Prince John summoned an attendant.

'Bid Hugh Bardon, our scout-master, come hither, as soon as he shall have spoken with Waldemar Fitzurse.'

The scout-master arrived after a brief delay,

during which John traversed the apartment with unequal and disordered steps.

'Bardon,' said he, 'what did Waldemar desire of thee?'

'Two resolute men, well acquainted with these northern wilds, and skilful in tracking the tread of man and horse.'

'And thou hast fitted him?'

'Let your Grace never trust me else,' answered the master of the spies. 'One is from Hexhamshire; he is wont to trace the Tynedale and Teviotdale thieves, as a bloodhou follows the slot of a hurt deer. The other is Yorkshire bred, and has twanged his bowstring right oft in merry Sherwood; he knows each glade and dingle, copse and highwood, betwixt this and Richmond.'

'Tis well,' said the Prince. 'Goes Waldemar forth with them?'

'Instantly,' said Bardon.

'With what attendance?' asked John, carelessly.

'Broad Thoresby goes with him, and Wetheral, whom they call, for his cruelty, Stephen Steel-Heart; and three northern men-at-arms that belonged to Ralph Middleton's gang; they are called the Spears of Spyinghow.'

'Tis well,' said Prince John; then added, after a moment's pause, 'Bardon, it imports our service that thou keep a strict watch on Maurice de Bracy, so that he shall not observe it, however. And let us know of his motions from time to time, with whom he converses, what he proposeth. Fail not in this, as thou wilt be answerable.'

Hugh Bardon bowed, and retired.

'If Maurice betrays me,' said Prince John—'if he betrays me, as his bearing leads me to fear, I will have his head, were Richard thundering at the gates of York.'

CHAPTER XXXV

Arouse the tiger of Hyrcanian deserts,
Strive with the half-starved lion for his prey ;
Lesser the risk, than rouse the slumbering fire
Of wild fanaticism.

Anonymous.

OUR tale now returns to Isaac of York. Mounted
upon a mule, the gift of the outlaw, with two tall
yeomen to act as his guard and guides, the Jew had
set out for the preceptory of Templestowe, for the
purpose of negotiating his daughter's redemption.
The preceptory was but a day's journey from the
demolished castle of Torquilstone, and the Jew had
hoped to reach it before nightfall ; accordingly,
having dismissed his guides at the verge of the
forest, and rewarded them with a piece of silver, he
began to press on with such speed as his weariness
permitted him to exert. But his strength failed
him totally ere he had reached within four miles of
the Temple court ; racking pains shot along his back
and through his limbs, and the excessive anguish
which he felt at heart being now augmented by
bodily suffering, he was rendered altogether incapable of proceeding farther than a small market-
town, where dwelt a Jewish rabbi of his tribe,
eminent in the medical profession, and to whom
Isaac was well known. Nathan ben Israel received
his suffering countryman with that kindness which
the law prescribed, and which the Jews practised to
each other. He insisted on his betaking himself to
repose, and used such remedies as were then in

most repute to check the progress of the fever which terror, fatigue, ill-usage, and sorrow had brought upon the poor old Jew.

On the morrow, when Isaac proposed to arise and pursue his journey, Nathan remonstrated against his purpose, both as his host and as his physician. 'It might cost him,' he said, 'his life.' But Isaac replied, 'That more than life and death depended upon his going that morning to Templestowe.'

'To Templestowe!' said his host with surprise; again felt his pulse, and then muttered to himself, 'His fever is abated, yet seems his mind somewhat alienated and disturbed.'

'And why not to Templestowe?' answered his patient. 'I grant thee, Nathan, that it is a dwelling of those to whom the despised Children of the Promise are a stumbling-block and an abomination; yet thou knowest that pressing affairs of traffic sometimes carry us among these bloodthirsty Nazarene soldiers, and that we visit the preceptories of the Templars, as well as the commanderies of the Knights Hospitallers, as they are called.'

'I know it well,' said Nathan; 'but wottest thou that Lucas de Beaumanoir, the chief of their order, and whom they term Grand Master, is now himself at Templestowe?'

'I know it not,' said Isaac; 'our last letters from our brethren at Paris advised us that he was at that city, beseeching Philip for aid against the Sultan Saladine.'

'He hath since come to England, unexpected by his brethren,' said Ben Israel; 'and he cometh among them with a strong and outstretched arm to correct and to punish. His countenance is kindled in anger against those who have departed from the vow which they have made, and great is the fear of those sons of Belial. Thou must have heard of his name?'

'It is well known unto me,' said Isaac: 'the
Gentiles deliver this Lucas Beaumanoir as a man
zealous to slaying for every point of the Nazarene
law; and our brethren have termed him a fierce
destroyer of the Saracens, and a cruel tyrant to the
Children of the Promise.'

'And truly have they termed him,' said Nathan
the physician. 'Other Templars may be moved
from the purpose of their heart by pleasure, or
bribed by promise of gold and silver; but Beaumanoir is of a different stamp—hating sensuality,
despising treasure, and pressing forward to that
which they call the crown of martyrdom—the God
of Jacob speedily send it unto him, and unto them
all! Specially hath this proud man extended his
glove over the children of Judah, as holy David
over Edom, holding the murder of a Jew to be an
offering of as sweet savour as the death of a Saracen.
Impious and false things has he said even of the
virtues of our medicines, as if they were the devices
of Satan—the Lord rebuke him!'

'Nevertheless,' said Isaac, 'I must present myself
at Templestowe, though he hath made his face like
unto a fiery furnace seven times heated.'

He then explained to Nathan the pressing cause
of his journey. The Rabbi listened with interest,
and testified his sympathy after the fashion of his
people, rending his clothes, and saying, 'Ah, my
daughter!—ah, my daughter! Alas! for the beauty
of Zion! Alas! for the captivity of Israel!'

'Thou seest,' said Isaac, 'how it stands with me,
and that I may not tarry. Peradventure, the
presence of this Lucas Beaumanoir, being the chief
man over them, may turn Brian de Bois-Guilbert
from the ill which he doth meditate, and that he
may deliver to me my beloved daughter Rebecca.'

'Go thou,' said Nathan ben Israel, 'and be wise,
for wisdom availed Daniel in the den of lions into
which he was cast; and may it go well with thee,

even as thine heart wisheth. Yet, if thou canst, keep thee from the presence of the Grand Master, for to do foul scorn to our people is his morning and evening delight. It may be, if thou couldst speak with Bois-Guilbert in private, thou shalt the better prevail with him ; for men say that these accursed Nazarenes are not of one mind in the preceptory—may their counsels be confounded and brought to shame ! But do thou, brother, return to me as if it were to the house of thy father, and bring me word how it has sped with thee ; and well do I hope thou wilt bring with thee Rebecca, even the scholar of the wise Miriam, whose cures the Gentiles slandered as if they had been wrought by necromancy.'

Isaac accordingly bade his friend farewell, and about an hour's riding brought him before the preceptory of Templestowe.

This establishment of the Templars was seated amidst fair meadows and pastures, which the devotion of the former preceptor had bestowed upon their order. It was strong and well fortified, a point never neglected by these knights, and which the disordered state of England rendered peculiarly necessary. Two halberdiers, clad in black, guarded the drawbridge, and others, in the same sad livery, glided to and fro upon the walls with a funereal pace, resembling spectres more than soldiers. The inferior officers of the order were thus dressed, ever since their use of white garments, similar to those of the knights and esquires, had given rise to a combination of certain false brethren in the mountains of Palestine, terming themselves Templars, and bringing great dishonour on the order. A knight was now and then seen to cross the court in his long white cloak, his head depressed on his breast, and his arms folded. They passed each other, if they chanced to meet, with a slow, solemn, and mute greeting ; for such was the rule of their order, quoting thereupon the holy texts, 'In many words thou shalt not avoid sin,' and 'Life and death are in the power of the tongue.' In a word, the stern, ascetic rigour of the Temple discipline, which had been so long exchanged for prodigal and licentious indulgence, seemed at once to have revived at Templestowe under the severe eye of Lucas Beaumanoir.

Isaac paused at the gate, to consider how he might seek entrance in the manner most likely to bespeak favour; for he was well aware that to his unhappy race the reviving fanaticism of the order was not less dangerous than their unprincipled licentiousness; and that his religion would be the object of hate and persecution in the one case, as his wealth would have exposed him in the other to the extortions of unrelenting oppression.

Meantime, Lucas Beaumanoir walked in a small garden belonging to the preceptory, included within the precincts of its exterior fortification, and held sad and confidential communication with a brother of his order, who had come in his company from Palestine.

The Grand Master was a man advanced in age, as was testified by his long grey beard, and the shaggy grey eyebrows, overhanging eyes of which, however, years had been unable to quench the fire. A formidable warrior, his thin and severe features retained the soldier's fierceness of expression; an ascetic bigot, they were no less marked by the emaciation of abstinence, and the spiritual pride of the self-satisfied devotee. Yet with these severer traits of physiognomy, there was mixed somewhat striking and noble, arising, doubtless, from the great part which his high office called upon him to act among monarchs and princes, and from the habitual exercise of supreme authority over the valiant and high-born knights who were united by

the rules of the order. His stature was tall, and
his gait, undepressed by age and toil, was erect and
stately. His white mantle was shaped with severe
regularity, according to the rule of St. Bernard
himself, being composed of what was then called
burrel cloth, exactly fitted to the size of the wearer,
and bearing on the left shoulder the octangular
cross peculiar to the order, formed of red cloth.
No vair or ermine decked this garment; but in
respect of his age, the Grand Master, as permitted
by the rules, wore his doublet lined and trimmed
with the softest lambskin, dressed with the wool
outwards, which was the nearest approach he could
regularly make to the use of fur, then the greatest
luxury of dress. In his hand he bore that singular
abacus, or staff of office, with which Templars are
usually represented, having at the upper end a
round plate, on which was engraved the cross of
the order, inscribed within a circle or orle, as
heralds term it. His companion, who attended on
this great personage, had nearly the same dress
in all respects, but his extreme deference towards
his superior showed that no other equality subsisted between them. The preceptor, for such
he was in rank, walked not in a line with the
Grand Master, but just so far behind that Beaumanoir could speak to him without turning round
his head.

'Conrade,' said the Grand Master, 'dear companion of my battles and my toils, to thy faithful
bosom alone I can confide my sorrows. To thee
alone can I tell how oft, since I came to this
kingdom, I have desired to be dissolved and to be
with the just. Not one object in England hath met
mine eye which it could rest upon with pleasure,
save the tombs of our brethren, beneath the massive
roof of our Temple Church in yonder proud capital.
"O, valiant Robert de Ros!" did I exclaim internally, as I gazed upon these good soldiers of the

cross, where they lie sculptured on their sepulchres
—" O, worthy William de Mareschal! open your
marble cells, and take to your repose a weary
brother, who would rather strive with a hundred
thousand pagans than witness the decay of our holy
order!'"

'It is but true,' answered Conrade Mont-Fitchet
—' it is but too true; and the irregularities of our
brethren in England are even more gross than those
in France.'

'Because they are more wealthy,' answered the
Grand Master. 'Bear with me, brother, although
I should something vaunt myself. Thou knowest
the life I have led, keeping each point of my order,
striving with devils embodied and disembodied,
striking down the roaring lion, who goeth about
seeking whom he may devour, like a good knight
and devout priest, wheresoever I met with him,
even as blessed St. Bernard hath prescribed to us
in the forty-fifth capital of our rule, *Ut leo semper
feriatur.* But, by the Holy Temple! the zeal
which hath devoured my substance and my life,
yea, the very nerves and marrow of my bones—by
that very Holy Temple I swear to thee, that save
thyself and some few that still retain the ancient
severity of our order, I look upon no brethren whom
I can bring my soul to embrace under that holy
name. What say our statutes, and how do our
brethren observe them? They should wear no
vain or worldly ornament, no crest upon their
helmet, no gold upon stirrup or bridle-bit; yet
who now go pranked out so proudly and so gaily
as the poor soldiers of the Temple? They are
forbidden by our statutes to take one bird by means
of another, to shoot beasts with bow or arblast, to
halloo to a hunting-horn, or to spur the horse after
game; but now, at hunting and hawking, and each
idle sport of wood and river, who so prompt as the

Templars in all these fond vanities? They are forbidden to read, save what their superior permitted, or listen to what is read, save such holy things as may be recited aloud during the hours of refection; but lo! their ears are at the command of idle minstrels, and their eyes study empty romaunts. They were commanded to extirpate magic and heresy; lo! they are charged with studying the accursed cabalistical secrets of the Jews, and the magic of the paynim Saracens. Simpleness of diet was prescribed to them—roots, pottage, gruels, eating flesh but thrice a-week, because the accustomed feeding on flesh is a dishonourable corruption of the body; and behold, their tables groan under delicate fare. Their drink was to be water; and now, to drink like a Templar is the boast of each jolly boon companion. This very garden, filled as it is with curious herbs and trees sent from the Eastern climes, better becomes the harem of an unbelieving emir than the plot which Christian monks should devote to raise their homely pot-herbs. And O, Conrade! well it were that the relaxation of discipline stopped even here! Well thou knowest that we were forbidden to receive those devout women who at the beginning were associated as sisters of our order, because, saith the forty-sixth chapter, the Ancient Enemy hath, by female society, withdrawn many from the right path to paradise. Nay, in the last capital, being, as it were, the copestone which our blessed founder placed on the pure and undefiled doctrine which he had enjoined, we are prohibited from offering, even to our sisters and our mothers, the kiss of affection: *ut omnium mulierum fugiantur oscula.* I shame to speak—I shame to think—of the corruptions which have rushed in upon us even like a flood. The souls of our pure founders, the spirits of Hugh de Payen and Godfrey de St. Omer, and of the blessed seven who first joined in dedicating their lives to

the service of the Temple, are disturbed even in the
enjoyment of paradise itself. I have seen them,
Conrade, in the visions of the night: their sainted
eyes shed tears for the sins and follies of their
brethren, and for the foul and shameful luxury in
which they wallow. "Beaumanoir," they say,
"thou slumberest; awake! There is a stain in
the fabric of the Temple, deep and foul as that left
by the streaks of leprosy on the walls of the infected
houses of old.[1] The soldiers of the Cross, who
should shun the glance of a woman as the eye of a
basilisk, live in open sin, not with the females of
their own race only, but with the daughters of the
accursed heathen, and more accursed Jew. Beaumanoir, thou sleepest; up, and avenge our cause!
Slay the sinners, male and female! Take to thee
the brand of Phineas!" The vision fled, Conrade,
but as I awaked I could still hear the clank of their
mail, and see the waving of their white mantles.
And I will do according to their word: I WILL
purify the fabric of the Temple; and the unclean
stones in which the plague is, I will remove and
cast out of the building.'

'Yet bethink thee, reverend father,' said Mont-
Fitchet, 'the stain hath become engrained by time
and consuetude; let thy reformation be cautious,
as it is just and wise.'

'No, Mont-Fitchet,' answered the stern old man,
'it must be sharp and sudden; the order is on the
crisis of its fate. The sobriety, self-devotion, and
piety of our predecessors made us powerful friends;
our presumption, our wealth, our luxury have raised
up against us mighty enemies. We must cast away
these riches, which are a temptation to princes; we
must lay down that presumption, which is an offence
to them; we must reform that license of manners,
which is a scandal to the whole Christian world!
Or—mark my words—the order of the Temple will

---

[1] See the 13th chapter of Leviticus.

be utterly demolished, and the place thereof shall no more be known among the nations.'

'Now may God avert such a calamity!' said the preceptor.

'Amen,' said the Grand Master, with solemnity, 'but we must deserve His aid. I tell thee, Conrade, that neither the powers in Heaven, nor the powers on earth, will longer endure the wickedness of this generation. My intelligence is sure—the ground on which our fabric is reared is already undermined, and each addition we make to the structure of our greatness will only sink it the sooner in the abyss. We must retrace our steps, and show ourselves the faithful champions of the Cross, sacrificing to our calling not alone our blood and our lives, not alone our lusts and our vices, but our ease, our comforts, and our natural affections, and act as men convinced that many a pleasure which may be lawful to others is forbidden to the vowed soldier of the Temple.'

At this moment a squire, clothed in a threadbare vestment—for the aspirants after this holy order wore during their noviciate the cast-off garments of the knights—entered the garden, and, bowing profoundly before the Grand Master, stood silent, awaiting his permission ere he presumed to tell his errand.

'Is it not more seemly,' said the Grand Master, 'to see this Damian, clothed in the garments of Christian humility, thus appear with reverend silence before his superior, than but two days since, when the fond fool was decked in a painted coat, and jangling as pert and as proud as any popinjay? Speak, Damian, we permit thee. What is thine errand?'

'A Jew stands without the gate, noble and reverend father,' said the squire, 'who prays to speak with brother Brian de Bois-Guilbert.'

'Thou wert right to give me knowledge of it,' said the Grand Master; 'in our presence a preceptor is but as a common compeer of our order, who may not walk according to his own will, but to that of his Master, even according to the text, "In the hearing of the ear he hath obeyed me." It imports us especially to know of this Bois-Guilbert's proceedings,' said he, turning to his companion.

'Report speaks him brave and valiant,' said Conrade.

'And truly is he so spoken of,' said the Grand Master; 'in our valour only we are not degenerated from our predecessors, the heroes of the Cross. But brother Brian came into our order a moody and disappointed man, stirred, I doubt me, to take our vows and to renounce the world, not in sincerity of soul, but as one whom some touch of light discontent had driven into penitence. Since then he hath become an active and earnest agitator, a murmurer, and a machinator, and a leader amongst those who impugn our authority; not considering that the rule is given to the Master even by the symbol of the staff and the rod—the staff to support the infirmities of the weak, the rod to correct the faults of delinquents. Damian,' he continued, 'lead the Jew to our presence.'

The squire departed with a profound reverence, and in a few minutes returned, marshalling in Isaac of York. No naked slave, ushered into the presence of some mighty prince, could approach his judgment-seat with more profound reverence and terror than that with which the Jew drew near to the presence of the Grand Master. When he had approached within the distance of three yards, Beaumanoir made a sign with his staff that he should come no farther. The Jew kneeled down on the earth, which he kissed in token of reverence; then rising, stood before the Templars, his hands folded on his bosom, his head bowed on his breast, in all the submission of Oriental slavery.

'Damian,' said the Grand Master, 'retire, and
have a guard ready to await our sudden call; and
suffer no one to enter the garden until we shall
leave it.' The squire bowed and retreated. 'Jew,'
continued the haughty old man, 'mark me. It
suits not our condition to hold with thee long
communication, nor do we waste words or time
upon any one. Wherefore be brief in thy answers
to what questions I shall ask thee, and let thy
words be of truth; for if thy tongue doubles with
me, I will have it torn from thy misbelieving
jaws.'

The Jew was about to reply; but the Grand
Master went on—

'Peace, unbeliever! not a word in our presence,
save in answer to our questions. What is thy
business with our brother Brian de Bois-Guilbert?'

Isaac gasped with terror and uncertainty. To
tell his tale might be interpreted into scandalising
the order; yet, unless he told it, what hope could
he have of achieving his daughter's deliverance?
Beaumanoir saw his mortal apprehension, and condescended to give him some assurance.

'Fear nothing,' he said, 'for thy wretched person,
Jew, so thou dealest uprightly in this matter. I
demand again to know from thee thy business with
Brian de Bois-Guilbert?'

'I am bearer of a letter,' stammered out the Jew,
'so please your reverend valour, to that good knight,
from Prior Aymer of the Abbey of Jorvaulx.'

'Said I not these were evil times, Conrade?' said
the Master. 'A Cistercian prior sends a letter to
a soldier of the Temple, and can find no more fitting
messenger than an unbelieving Jew. Give me the
letter.'

The Jew, with trembling hands, undid the folds
of his Armenian cap, in which he had deposited the
Prior's tablets for the greater security, and was
about to approach, with hand extended and body

crouched, to place it within the reach of his grim
interrogator.

'Back, dog!' said the Grand Master; 'I touch
not misbelievers, save with the sword. Conrade,
take thou the letter from the Jew and give it
to me.'

Beaumanoir, being thus possessed of the tablets,
inspected the outside carefully, and then proceeded
to undo the packthread which secured its folds.
'Reverend father,' said Conrade, interposing, though
with much deference, 'wilt thou break the seal?'

'And will I not?' said Beaumanoir, with a frown.
'Is it not written in the forty-second capital, *De
Lectione Literarum*, that a Templar shall not receive
a letter, no not from his father, without communicating the same to the Grand Master, and reading
it in his presence?'

He then perused the letter in haste, with an
expression of surprise and horror; read it over
again more slowly; then holding it out to Conrade
with one hand, and slightly striking it with the
other, exclaimed—'Here is goodly stuff for one
Christian man to write to another, and both members, and no inconsiderable members, of religious
professions! When,' said he solemnly, and looking
upward, 'wilt Thou come with Thy fanners to purge
the thrashing-floor?'

Mont-Fitchet took the letter from his superior,
and was about to peruse it. 'Read it aloud, Conrade,' said the Grand Master; 'and do thou (to
Isaac) attend to the purport of it, for we will
question thee concerning it.'

Conrade read the letter, which was in these words:
'Aymer, by divine grace, prior of the Cistercian
house of St. Mary's of Jorvaulx, to Sir Brian de
Bois-Guilbert, a knight of the holy order of the
Temple, wisheth health, with the bounties of King
Bacchus and of my Lady Venus. Touching our
present condition, dear brother, we are a captive in

the hands of certain lawless and godless men, who
have not feared to detain our person, and put us to
ransom; whereby we have also learned of Front-
de-Bœuf's misfortune, and that thou hast escaped
with that fair Jewish sorceress whose black eyes
have bewitched thee. We are heartily rejoiced of
thy safety; nevertheless, we pray thee to be on thy
guard in the matter of this second Witch of Endor;
for we are privately assured that your Great Master,
who careth not a bean for cherry cheeks and black
eyes, comes from Normandy to diminish your mirth
and amend your misdoings. Wherefore we pray
you heartily to beware, and to be found watching,
even as the Holy Text hath it, *Invenientur vigilantes.*
And the wealthy Jew her father, Isaac of York,
having prayed of me letters in his behalf, I gave him
these, earnestly advising, and in a sort entreating,
that you do hold the damsel to ransom, seeing he
will pay you from his bags as much as may find fifty
damsels upon safer terms, whereof I trust·to have
my part when we make merry together, as true
brothers, not forgetting the wine-cup. For what
saith the text, *Vinum lætificat cor hominis;* and
again, *Rex delectabitur pulchritudine tua.*

'Till which merry meeting, we wish you farewell.
Given from this den of thieves, about the hour of
matins,

'AYMER PR. S. M. JORVOLCIENCIS.

'*Postscriptum.*—Truly your golden chain hath not
long abidden with me, and will now sustain, around
the neck of an outlaw deer-stealer, the whistle
wherewith he calleth on his hounds.'

'What sayest thou to this, Conrade?' said the
Grand Master. 'Den of thieves! and a fit residence
is a den of thieves for such a prior. No wonder
that the hand of God is upon us, and that in the
Holy Land we lose place by place, foot by foot,

before the infidels, when we have such churchmen
as this Aymer. And what meaneth he, I trow, by
"this second Witch of Endor"?' said he to his
confidant, something apart.

Conrade was better acquainted, perhaps by
practice, with the jargon of gallantry than was his
superior; and he expounded the passage which
embarrassed the Grand Master to be a sort of
language used by worldly men towards those whom
they loved *par amours;* but the explanation did not
satisfy the bigoted Beaumanoir.

'There is more in it than thou dost guess, Conrade; thy simplicity is no match for this deep abyss
of wickedness. This Rebecca of York was a pupil
of that Miriam of whom thou hast heard. Thou
shalt hear the Jew own it even now.' Then turning
to Isaac, he said aloud, 'Thy daughter, then, is
prisoner with Brian de Bois-Guilbert?'

'Ay, reverend valorous sir,' stammered poor
Isaac, 'and whatsoever ransom a poor man may pay
for her deliverance——'

'Peace!' said the Grand Master. 'This thy
daughter hath practised the art of healing, hath
she not?'

'Ay, gracious sir,' answered the Jew, with more
confidence; 'and knight and yeoman, squire and
vassal, may bless the goodly gift which Heaven
hath assigned to her. Many a one can testify that
she hath recovered them by her art, when every
other human aid hath proved vain; but the blessing
of the God of Jacob was upon her.'

Beaumanoir turned to Mont-Fitchet with a grim
smile. 'See, brother,' he said, 'the deceptions of
the devouring Enemy! Behold the baits with which
he fishes for souls, giving a poor space of earthly
life in exchange for eternal happiness hereafter.
Well said our blessed rule, *Semper percutiatur leo
vorans.* Upon the lion! Down with the destroyer!'
said he, shaking aloft his mystic abacus, as if in

defiance of the powers of darkness. 'Thy daughter
worketh the cures, I doubt not,' thus he went on to
address the Jew, 'by words and sigils, and periapts,
and other cabalistical mysteries.'

'Nay, reverend and brave knight,' answered
Isaac, 'but in chief measure by a balsam of marvellous virtue.'

'Where had she that secret?' said Beaumanoir.

'It was delivered to her,' answered Isaac, reluctantly, 'by Miriam, a sage matron of our tribe.'

'Ah, false Jew!' said the Grand Master; 'was it
not from that same witch Miriam, the abomination
of whose enchantments have been heard of throughout every Christian land?' exclaimed the Grand
Master, crossing himself. 'Her body was burnt
at a stake, and her ashes were scattered to the four
winds; and so be it with me and mine order, if I
do not as much to her pupil, and more also! I will
teach her to throw spell and incantation over the
soldiers of the blessed Temple! There, Damian,
spurn this Jew from the gate; shoot him dead if he
oppose or turn again. With his daughter we will
deal as the Christian law and our own high office
warrant.'

Poor Isaac was hurried off accordingly, and ex-
pelled from the preceptory, all his entreaties, and
even his offers, unheard and disregarded. He could
do no better than return to the house of the Rabbi,
and endeavour, through his means, to learn how
his daughter was to be disposed of. He had hitherto
feared for her honour; he was now to tremble for
her life. Meanwhile, the Grand Master ordered to
his presence the preceptor of Templestowe.

CHAPTER XXXVI

Say not my art is fraud: all live by seeming.
The beggar begs with it, and the gay courtier
Gains land and title, rank and rule, by seeming;
The clergy scorn it not; and the bold soldier
Will eke with it his service. All admit it,
All practise it; and he who is content
With showing what he is shall have small credit
In church, or camp, or state. So wags the world.
Old Play.

ALBERT MALVOISIN, president, or, in the language
of the order, preceptor of the establishment of
Templestowe, was brother to that Philip Malvoisin
who has been already occasionally mentioned in
this history, and was, like that baron, in close
league with Brian de Bois-Guilbert.

Amongst dissolute and unprincipled men, of
whom the Temple order included but too many,
Albert of Templestowe might be distinguished; but
with this difference from the audacious Bois-Guilbert,
that he knew how to throw over his vices and his
ambition the veil of hypocrisy, and to assume in
his exterior the fanaticism which he internally
despised. Had not the arrival of the Grand Master
been so unexpectedly sudden, he would have seen
nothing at Templestowe which might have appeared
to argue any relaxation of discipline. And, even
although surprised, and to a certain extent detected,
Albert Malvoisin listened with such respect and
apparent contrition to the rebuke of his superior,
and made such haste to reform the particulars he

censured—succeeded, in fine, so well in giving an
air of ascetic devotion to a family which had been
lately devoted to license and pleasure, that Lucas
Beaumanoir began to entertain a higher opinion of
the preceptor's morals than the first appearance of
the establishment had inclined him to adopt.

But these favourable sentiments on the part of
the Grand Master were greatly shaken by the intelligence that Albert had received within a house
of religion the Jewish captive, and, as was to be
feared, the paramour of a brother of the order; and
when Albert appeared before him he was regarded
with unwonted sternness.

'There is in this mansion, dedicated to the purposes of the holy order of the Temple,' said the
Grand Master, in a severe tone, 'a Jewish woman,
brought hither by a brother of religion, by your
connivance, Sir Preceptor.'

Albert Malvoisin was overwhelmed with confusion; for the unfortunate Rebecca had been confined in a remote and secret part of the building,
and every precaution used to prevent her residence
there from being known. He read in the looks of
Beaumanoir ruin to Bois-Guilbert and to himself,
unless he should be able to avert the impending
storm.

'Why are you mute?' continued the Grand
Master.

'Is it permitted to me to reply?' answered the
preceptor, in a tone of the deepest humility, although
by the question he only meant to gain an instant's
space for arranging his ideas.

'Speak, you are permitted,' said the Grand Master
—'speak, and say, knowest thou the capital of our
holy rule—*De commilitonibus Templi in sancta civitate, qui cum miserrimis mulieribus versantur, propter
oblectationem carnis?* [1]

[1] The edict which he quotes is against communication with
women of light character.

'Surely, most reverend father,' answered the preceptor, 'I have not risen to this office in the order, being ignorant of one of its most important prohibitions.'

'How comes it, then, I demand of thee once more, that thou hast suffered a brother to bring a paramour, and that paramour a Jewish sorceress, into this holy place, to the stain and pollution thereof?'

'A Jewish sorceress!' echoed Albert Malvoisin, 'good angels guard us!'

'Ay, brother, a Jewish sorceress,' said the Grand Master, sternly. 'I have said it. Darest thou deny that this Rebecca, the daughter of that wretched usurer Isaac of York, and the pupil of the foul witch Miriam, is now—shame to be thought or spoken!—lodged within this thy preceptory?'

'Your wisdom, reverend father,' answered the preceptor, 'hath rolled away the darkness from my understanding. Much did I wonder that so good a knight as Brian de Bois-Guilbert seemed so fondly besotted on the charms of this female, whom I received into this house merely to place a bar betwixt their growing intimacy, which else might have been cemented at the expense of the fall of our valiant and religious brother.'

'Hath nothing, then, as yet passed betwixt them in breach of his vow?' demanded the Grand Master.

'What! under this roof?' said the preceptor, crossing himself; 'St. Magdalene and the ten thousand virgins forbid! No! if I have sinned in receiving her here, it was in the erring thought that I might thus break off our brother's besotted devotion to this Jewess, which seemed to me so wild and unnatural, that I could not but ascribe it to some touch of insanity, more to be cured by pity than reproof. But, since your reverend wisdom hath discovered this Jewish quean to be a sorceress, perchance it may account fully for his enamoured folly.'

'It doth!—it doth!' said Beaumanoir. 'See, brother Conrade, the peril of yielding to the first devices and blandishments of Satan! We look upon woman only to gratify the lust of the eye, and to take pleasure in what men call her beauty; and the Ancient Enemy, the devouring lion, obtains power over us, to complete, by talisman and spell, a work which was begun by idleness and folly. It may be that our brother Bois-Guilbert does in this matter deserve rather pity than severe chastisement, rather the support of the staff than the strokes of the rod; and that our admonitions and prayers may turn him from his folly, and restore him to his brethren.'

'It were deep pity,' said Conrade Mont-Fitchet, 'to lose to the order one of its best lances, when the holy community most requires the aid of its sons. Three hundred Saracens hath this Brian de Bois-Guilbert slain with his own hand.'

'The blood of these accursed dogs,' said the Grand Master, 'shall be a sweet and acceptable offering to the saints and angels whom they despise and blaspheme; and with their aid will we counteract the spells and charms with which our brother is entwined as in a net. He shall burst the bands of this Dalilah as Sampson burst the two new cords with which the Philistines had bound him, and shall slaughter the infidels, even heaps upon heaps. But concerning this foul witch, who hath flung her enchantments over a brother of the Holy Temple, assuredly she shall die the death.'

'But the laws of England——' said the preceptor, who, though delighted that the Grand Master's resentment, thus fortunately averted from himself and Bois-Guilbert, had taken another direction, began now to fear he was carrying it too far.

'The laws of England,' interrupted Beaumanoir, 'permit and enjoin each judge to execute justice within his own jurisdiction. The most petty baron

may arrest, try, and condemn a witch found within
his own domain. And shall that power be denied
to the Grand Master of the Temple within a preceptory of his order? No! we will judge and
condemn. The witch shall be taken out of the
land, and the wickedness thereof shall be for-
given. Prepare the castle hall for the trial of
the sorceress.'

Albert Malvoisin bowed and retired, not to give
directions for preparing the hall, but to seek out
Brian de Bois-Guilbert, and communicate to him
how matters were likely to terminate. It was not
long ere he found him, foaming with indignation
at a repulse he had anew sustained from the fair
Jewess. 'The unthinking,' he said—'the ungrateful, to scorn him who, amidst blood and flames,
would have saved her life at the risk of his own!
By Heaven, Malvoisin! I abode until roof and
rafters crackled and crashed around me. I was the
butt of a hundred arrows; they rattled on mine
armour like hailstones against a latticed casement,
and the only use I made of my shield was for her
protection. This did I endure for her; and now
the self-willed girl upbraids me that I did not leave
her to perish, and refuses me not only the slightest
proof of gratitude, but even the most distant hope
that ever she will be brought to grant any. The
devil, that possessed her race with obstinacy, has
concentrated its full force in her single person!'

'The devil,' said the preceptor, 'I think, possessed you both. How oft have I preached to you
caution, if not continence? Did I not tell you that
there were enough willing Christian damsels to be
met with, who would think it sin to refuse so brave
a knight *le don d'amoureux merci*, and you must
needs anchor your affection on a wilful, obstinate
Jewess! By the mass, I think old Lucas Beaumanoir guesses right, when he maintains she hath
cast a spell over you.'

'Lucas Beaumanoir!' said Bois-Guilbert, reproachfully. 'Are these your precautions, Malvoisin? Hast thou suffered the dotard to learn that Rebecca is in the preceptory?'

'How could I help it?' said the preceptor. 'I neglected nothing that could keep secret your mystery; but it is betrayed, and whether by the devil or no, the devil only can tell. But I have turned the matter as I could; you are safe if you renounce Rebecca. You are pitied—the victim of magical delusion. She is a sorceress, and must suffer as such.'

'She shall not, by Heaven!' said Bois-Guilbert.

'By Heaven, she must and will!' said Malvoisin. 'Neither you nor any one else can save her. Lucas Beaumanoir hath settled that the death of a Jewess will be a sin-offering sufficient to atone for all the amorous indulgences of the Knights Templars; and thou knowest he hath both the power and will to execute so reasonable and pious a purpose.'

'Will future ages believe that such stupid bigotry ever existed!' said Bois-Guilbert, striding up and down the apartment.

'What they may believe, I know not,' said Malvoisin, calmly; 'but I know well, that in this our day clergy and laymen, take ninety-nine to the hundred, will cry "Amen" to the Grand Master's sentence.'

'I have it,' said Bois-Guilbert. 'Albert, thou art my friend. Thou must connive at her escape, Malvoisin, and I will transport her to some place of greater security and secrecy.'

'I cannot, if I would,' replied the preceptor: 'the mansion is filled with the attendants of the Grand Master, and others who are devoted to him. And, to be frank with you, brother, I would not embark with you in this matter, even if I could hope to bring my bark to haven. I have risked enough already for your sake. I have no mind to

encounter a sentence of degradation, or even to lose
my preceptory, for the sake of a painted piece of
Jewish flesh and blood.   And you, if you will be
guided by my counsel, will give up this wild-goose
chase, and fly your hawk at some other game.
Think, Bois-Guilbert; thy present rank, thy future
honours, all depend on thy place in the order.
Shouldst thou adhere perversely to thy passion for
this Rebecca, thou wilt give Beaumanoir the power
of expelling thee, and he will not neglect it.   He
is jealous of the truncheon which he holds in his
trembling gripe, and he knows thou stretchest thy
bold hand towards it.   Doubt not he will ruin thee,
if thou affordest him a pretext so fair as thy protection of a Jewish sorceress.   Give him his scope
in this matter, for thou canst not control him.
When the staff is in thine own firm grasp, thou
mayest caress the daughters of Judah, or burn
them, as may best suit thine own humour.'

'Malvoisin,' said Bois-Guilbert, 'thou art a cold-
blooded——'

'Friend,' said the preceptor, hastening to fill up
the blank, in which Bois-Guilbert would probably
have placed a worse word—'a cold-blooded friend
I am, and therefore more fit to give thee advice.   I
tell thee once more, that thou canst not save Rebecca.   I tell thee once more, thou canst but perish
with her.   Go hie thee to the Grand Master; throw
thyself at his feet and tell him——'

'Not at his feet, by Heaven! but to the dotard's
very beard will I say——'

'Say to him, then, to his beard,' continued Malvoisin, coolly, 'that you love this captive Jewess to
distraction; and the more thou dost enlarge on thy
passion, the greater will be his haste to end it by
the death of the fair enchantress; while thou, taken
in flagrant delict by the avowal of a crime contrary
to thine oath, canst hope no aid of thy brethren, and
must exchange all thy brilliant visions of ambition

and power, to lift perhaps a mercenary spear in some of the petty quarrels between Flanders and Burgundy.'

'Thou speakest the truth, Malvoisin,' said Brian de Bois-Guilbert, after a moment's reflection. 'I will give the hoary bigot no advantage over me; and for Rebecca, she hath not merited at my hand that I should expose rank and honour for her sake. I will cast her off; yes, I will leave her to her fate, unless——'

'Qualify not thy wise and necessary resolution,' said Malvoisin; 'women are but the toys which amuse our lighter hours; ambition is the serious business of life. Perish a thousand such frail baubles as this Jewess, before thy manly step pause in the brilliant career that lies stretched before thee! For the present we part, nor must we be seen to hold close conversation; I must order the hall for his judgment-seat.'

'What!' said Bois-Guilbert, 'so soon?'

'Ay,' replied the preceptor, 'trial moves rapidly on when the judge has determined the sentence beforehand.'

'Rebecca,' said Bois-Guilbert, when he was left alone, 'thou art like to cost me dear. Why cannot I abandon thee to thy fate, as this calm hypocrite recommends? One effort will I make to save thee; but beware of ingratitude! for, if I am again repulsed, my vengeance shall equal my love. The life and honour of Bois-Guilbert must not be hazarded, where contempt and reproaches are his only reward.'

The preceptor had hardly given the necessary orders, when he was joined by Conrade Mont-Fitchet, who acquainted him with the Grand Master's resolution to bring the Jewess to instant trial for sorcery.

'It is surely a dream,' said the preceptor; 'we have many Jewish physicians, and we call them not wizards though they work wonderful cures.'

'The Grand Master thinks otherwise,' said Mont-Fitchet; 'and, Albert, I will be upright with thee: wizard or not, it were better that this miserable damsel die than that Brian de Bois-Guilbert should be lost to the order, or the order divided by internal dissension. Thou knowest his high rank, his fame in arms; thou knowest the zeal with which many of our brethren regard him; but all this will not avail him with our Grand Master, should he consider Brian as the accomplice, not the victim, of this Jewess. Were the souls of the twelve tribes in her single body, it were better she suffered alone than that Bois-Guilbert were partner in her destruction.'

'I have been working him even now to abandon her,' said Malvoisin; 'but still, are there grounds enough to condemn this Rebecca for sorcery? Will not the Grand Master change his mind when he sees that the proofs are so weak?'

'They must be strengthened, Albert,' replied Mont-Fitchet—'they must be strengthened. Dost thou understand me?'

'I do,' said the preceptor, 'nor do I scruple to do aught for advancement of the order; but there is little time to find engines fitting.'

'Malvoisin, they *must* be found,' said Conrade; 'well will it advantage both the order and thee. This Templestowe is a poor preceptory; that of Maison-Dieu is worth double its value. Thou knowest my interest with our old chief; find those who can carry this matter through, and thou art preceptor of Maison-Dieu in the fertile Kent. How sayst thou?'

'There is,' replied Malvoisin, 'among those who came hither with Bois-Guilbert, two fellows whom I well know; servants they were to my brother Philip de Malvoisin, and passed from his service to that of Front-de-Bœuf. It may be they know something of the witcheries of this woman.'

'Away, seek them out instantly; and hark thee,

if a byzant or two will sharpen their memory, let
them not be wanting.'

'They would swear the mother that bore them a
sorceress for a zecchin,' said the preceptor.

'Away, then,' said Mont-Fitchet; 'at noon the
affair will proceed. I have not seen our senior in
such earnest preparation since he condemned to the
stake Hamet Alfagi, a convert who relapsed to the
Moslem faith.'

The ponderous castle-bell had tolled the point of
noon, when Rebecca heard a trampling of feet upon
the private stair which led to her place of confinement. The noise announced the arrival of several
persons, and the circumstance rather gave her joy;
for she was more afraid of the solitary visits of the
fierce and passionate Bois-Guilbert than of any evil
that could befall her besides. The door of the
chamber was unlocked, and Conrade and the preceptor Malvoisin entered, attended by four warders
clothed in black, and bearing halberds.

'Daughter of an accursed race!' said the preceptor, 'arise and follow us.'

'Whither,' said Rebecca, 'and for what purpose?'

'Damsel,' answered Conrade, 'it is not for thee
to question, but to obey. Nevertheless, be it known
to thee, that thou art to be brought before the
tribunal of the Grand Master of our holy order,
there to answer for thine offences.'

'May the God of Abraham be praised!' said
Rebecca, folding her hands devoutly; 'the name of
a judge, though an enemy to my people, is to me
as the name of a protector. Most willingly do I
follow thee; permit me only to wrap my veil
around my head.'

They descended the stair with slow and solemn
step, traversed a long gallery, and, by a pair of
folding-doors placed at the end, entered the great
hall in which the Grand Master had for the time
established his court of justice.

The lower part of this ample apartment was filled with squires and yeomen, who made way, not without some difficulty, for Rebecca, attended by the preceptor and Mont-Fitchet, and followed by the guard of halberdiers, to move forward to the seat appointed for her. As she passed through the crowd, her arms folded and her head depressed, a scrap of paper was thrust into her hand, which she received almost unconsciously, and continued to hold without examining its contents. The assurance that she possessed some friend in this awful assembly gave her courage to look around, and to mark into whose presence she had been conducted. She gazed, accordingly, upon the scene, which we shall endeavour to describe in the next chapter.

CHAPTER XXXVII

Stern was the law which bade its vot'ries leave
At human woes with human hearts to grieve ;
Stern was the law, which at the winning wile
Of frank and harmless mirth forbade to smile ;
But sterner still, when high the iron rod
Of tyrant power she shook, and call'd that power of God.
                                            The Middle Ages.

THE tribunal, erected for the trial of the innocent
and unhappy Rebecca, occupied the dais or elevated
part of the upper end of the great hall—a platform
which we have already described as the place of
honour, destined to be occupied by the most distinguished inhabitants or guests of an ancient
mansion.

On an elevated seat, directly before the accused,
sat the Grand Master of the Temple, in full and
ample robes of flowing white, holding in his hand
the mystic staff which bore the symbol of the order.
At his feet was placed a table, occupied by two
scribes, chaplains of the order, whose duty it was to
reduce to formal record the proceedings of the day.
The black dresses, bare scalps, and demure looks of
these churchmen formed a strong contrast to the
warlike appearance of the knights who attended,
either as residing in the preceptory or as come
thither to attend upon their Grand Master. The
preceptors, of whom there were four present, occupied seats lower in height, and somewhat drawn
back behind that of their superior ; and the knights

who enjoyed no such rank in the order were placed
on benches still lower, and preserving the same distance from the preceptors as these from the Grand
Master. Behind them, but still upon the dais or
elevated portion of the hall, stood the esquires of
the order, in white dresses of an inferior quality.

The whole assembly wore an aspect of the most
profound gravity; and in the faces of the knights
might be perceived traces of military daring, united
with the solemn carriage becoming men of a religious
profession, and which, in the presence of their Grand
Master, failed not to sit upon every brow.

The remaining and lower part of the hall was
filled with guards, holding partizans, and with other
attendants whom curiosity had drawn thither to see
at once a Grand Master and a Jewish sorceress.
By far the greater part of those inferior persons
were, in one rank or other, connected with the
order, and were accordingly distinguished by their
black dresses. But peasants from the neighbouring
country were not refused admittance; for it was the
pride of Beaumanoir to render the edifying spectacle
of the justice which he administered as public as
possible. His large blue eyes seemed to expand as
he gazed around the assembly, and his countenance
appeared elated by the conscious dignity and
imaginary merit of the part which he was about
to perform. A psalm, which he himself accompanied
with a deep mellow voice, which age had not
deprived of its powers, commenced the proceedings
of the day; and the solemn sounds, *Venite, exultemus
Domino,* so often sung by the Templars before
engaging with earthly adversaries, was judged by
Lucas most appropriate to introduce the approaching
triumph, for such he deemed it, over the powers of
darkness. The deep prolonged notes, raised by a
hundred masculine voices accustomed to combine in
the choral chant, arose to the vaulted roof of the
hall, and rolled on amongst its arches with the

pleasing yet solemn sound of the rushing of mighty
waters.

When the sounds ceased, the Grand Master
glanced his eye slowly around the circle, and
observed that the seat of one of the preceptors was
vacant. Brian de Bois-Guilbert, by whom it had
been occupied, had left his place, and was now
standing near the extreme corner of one of the
benches occupied by the knights companions of
the Temple, one hand extending his long mantle,
so as in some degree to hide his face; while the
other held his cross-handled sword, with the point
of which, sheathed as it was, he was slowly drawing
lines upon the oaken floor.

'Unhappy man!' said the Grand Master, after
favouring him with a glance of compassion. 'Thou
seest, Conrade, how this holy work distresses him.
To this can the light look of woman, aided by the
Prince of the Powers of this world, bring a valiant
and worthy knight! Seest thou he cannot look
upon us; he cannot look upon her; and who knows
by what impulse from his tormentor his hand forms
these cabalistic lines upon the floor? It may be our
life and safety are thus aimed at; but we spit at and
defy the foul enemy. *Semper Leo percutiatur!*'

This was communicated apart to his confidential
follower, Conrade Mont-Fitchet. The Grand Master
then raised his voice and addressed the assembly.

'Reverend and valiant men, knights, preceptors,
and companions of this holy order, my brethren and
my children! you also, well-born and pious esquires,
who aspire to wear this Holy Cross! and you also,
Christian brethren, of every degree!—be it known
to you, that it is not defect of power in us which
hath occasioned the assembling of this congregation;
for, however unworthy in our person, yet to us is
committed, with this batoon, full power to judge
and to try all that regards the weal of this our holy
order. Holy St. Bernard, in the rule of our

knightly and religious profession, hath said, in the
fifty-ninth capital,[1] that he would not that brethren
be called together in council, save at the will and
command of the Master; leaving it free to us, as
to those more worthy fathers who have preceded us
in this our office, to judge as well of the occasion
as of the time and place in which a chapter of the
whole order, or of any part thereof, may be con-
voked. Also, in all such chapters, it is our duty to
hear the advice of our brethren, and to proceed
according to our own pleasure. But when the
raging wolf hath made an inroad upon the flock,
and carried off one member thereof, it is the duty
of the kind shepherd to call his comrades together,
that with bows and slings they may quell the invader,
according to our well-known rule, that the lion is
ever to be beaten down. We have therefore
summoned to our presence a Jewish woman, by
name Rebecca, daughter of Isaac of York—a woman
infamous for sortileges and for witcheries; whereby
she hath maddened the blood, and besotted the
brain, not of a churl, but of a knight; not of a
secular knight, but of one devoted to the service of
the Holy Temple; not of a knight companion, but
of a preceptor of our order, first in honour as in
place. Our brother, Brian de Bois-Guilbert, is well
known to ourselves, and to all degrees who now
hear me, as a true and zealous champion of the
Cross, by whose arm many deeds of valour have
been wrought in the Holy Land, and the holy places
purified from pollution by the blood of those infidels
who defiled them. Neither have our brother's
sagacity and prudence been less in repute among
his brethren than his valour and discipline; inso-
much that knights, both in eastern and western
lands, have named De Bois-Guilbert as one who may

---

[1] The reader is again referred to the rules of the poor
military brotherhood of the Temple, which occur in the
Works of St. Bernard.—L. T.

well be put in nomination as successor to this batoon, when it shall please Heaven to release us from the toil of bearing it. If we were told that such a man, so honoured, and so honourable, suddenly casting away regard for his character, his vows, his brethren, and his prospects, had associated to himself a Jewish damsel, wandered in this lewd company through solitary places, defended her person in preference to his own, and, finally, was so utterly blinded and besotted by his folly, as to bring her even to one of our own preceptories, what should we say but that the noble knight was possessed by some evil demon, or influenced by some wicked spell? If we could suppose it otherwise, think not rank, valour, high repute, or any earthly consideration, should prevent us from visiting him with punishment, that the evil thing might be removed, even according to the text, *Auferte malum ex robis*. For various and heinous are the acts of transgression against the rule of our blessed order in this lamentable history. 1st, He hath walked according to his proper will, contrary to capital 33, *Quod nullus juxta propriam voluntatem incedat*. 2d, He hath held communication with an excommunicated person, capital 57, *Ut fratres non participent cum excommunicatis*, and therefore hath a portion in *Anathema Maranatha*. 3d, He hath conversed with strange women, contrary to the capital, *Ut fratres non conversentur cum extraneis mulieribus*. 4th, He hath not avoided, nay, he hath, it is to be feared, solicited, the kiss of woman, by which, saith the last rule of our renowned order, *Ut fugiantur oscula*, the soldiers of the Cross are brought into a snare. For which heinous and multiplied guilt, Brian de Bois-Guilbert should be cut off and cast out from our congregation, were he the right hand and right eye thereof.'

He paused. A low murmur went through the assembly. Some of the younger part, who had been inclined to smile at the statute *De osculis fugiendis*, became now grave enough, and anxiously waited what the Grand Master was next to propose.

'Such,' he said, 'and so great should indeed be the punishment of a Knight Templar who wilfully offended against the rules of his order in such weighty points. But if, by means of charms and of spells, Satan had obtained dominion over the knight, perchance because he cast his eyes too lightly upon a damsel's beauty, we are then rather to lament than chastise his backsliding; and, imposing on him only such penance as may purify him from his iniquity, we are to turn the full edge of our indignation upon the accursed instrument, which had so wellnigh occasioned his utter falling away. Stand forth, therefore, and bear witness, ye who have witnessed these unhappy doings, that we may judge of the sum and bearing thereof; and judge whether our justice may be satisfied with the punishment of this infidel woman, or if we must go on, with a bleeding heart, to the further proceeding against our brother.'

Several witnesses were called upon to prove the risks to which Bois-Guilbert exposed himself in endeavouring to save Rebecca from the blazing castle, and his neglect of his personal defence in attending to her safety. The men gave these details with the exaggerations common to vulgar minds which have been strongly excited by any remarkable event, and their natural disposition to the marvellous was greatly increased by the satisfaction which their evidence seemed to afford to the eminent person for whose information it had been delivered. Thus the dangers which Bois-Guilbert surmounted, in themselves sufficiently great, became portentous in their narrative. The devotion of the knight to Rebecca's defence was exaggerated beyond the bounds not only of discretion, but even of the most frantic excess of chivalrous zeal; and his deference to what she said, even although her language was often severe and

upbraiding, was painted as carried to an excess
which, in a man of his haughty temper, seemed
almost preternatural.

The preceptor of Templestowe was then called on
to describe the manner in which Bois-Guilbert and
the Jewess arrived at the preceptory. The evidence
of Malvoisin was skilfully guarded. But while he
apparently studied to spare the feelings of Bois-
Guilbert, he threw in, from time to time, such hints
as seemed to infer that he laboured under some
temporary alienation of mind, so deeply did he
appear to be enamoured of the damsel whom he
brought along with him. With sighs of penitence,
the preceptor avowed his own contrition for having
admitted Rebecca and her lover within the walls of
the preceptory. 'But my defence,' he concluded,
'has been made in my confession to our most
reverend father the Grand Master; he knows my
motives were not evil, though my conduct may have
been irregular. Joyfully will I submit to any
penance he shall assign me.'

'Thou hast spoken well, brother Albert,' said
Beaumanoir; 'thy motives were good, since thou
didst judge it right to arrest thine erring brother in
his career of precipitate folly. But thy conduct
was wrong; as he that would stop a runaway steed,
and seizing by the stirrup instead of the bridle,
receiveth injury himself, instead of accomplishing
his purpose. Thirteen paternosters are assigned by
our pious founder for matins, and nine for vespers;
be those services doubled by thee. Thrice a-week are
Templars permitted the use of flesh; but do thou
keep fast for all the seven days. This do for six
weeks to come, and thy penance is accomplished.'

With a hypocritical look of the deepest submission, the preceptor of Templestowe bowed to
the ground before his superior, and resumed his
seat.

'Were it not well, brethren,' said the Grand

Master, 'that we examine something into the former
life and conversation of this woman, specially that
we may discover whether she be one likely to use
magical charms and spells, since the truths which
we have heard may well incline us to suppose that
in this unhappy course our erring brother has been
acted upon by some infernal enticement and delusion?'

Herman of Goodalricke was the fourth preceptor
present; the other three were Conrade, Malvoisin,
and Bois-Guilbert himself. Herman was an ancient
warrior, whose face was marked with scars inflicted
by the sabre of the Moslemah, and had great rank
and consideration among his brethren. He arose
and bowed to the Grand Master, who instantly
granted him license of speech. 'I would crave to
know, most reverend father, of our valiant brother,
Brian de Bois-Guilbert, what he says to these
wondrous accusations, and with what eye he himself
now regards his unhappy intercourse with this Jewish
maiden?'

'Brian de Bois-Guilbert,' said the Grand Master,
'thou hearest the question which our brother of
Goodalricke desirest thou shouldst answer. I command thee to reply to him.'

Bois-Guilbert turned his head towards the Grand
Master when thus addressed, and remained silent.

'He is possessed by a dumb devil,' said the Grand
Master. 'Avoid thee, Sathanas! Speak, Brian de
Bois-Guilbert, I conjure thee, by this symbol of our
holy order.'

Bois-Guilbert made an effort to suppress his rising
scorn and indignation, the expression of which, he
was well aware, would have little availed him.
'Brian de Bois-Guilbert,' he answered, 'replies
not, most reverend father, to such wild and vague
charges. If his honour be impeached, he will defend it with his body, and with that sword which
has often fought for Christendom.'

'We forgive thee, brother Brian,' said the Grand Master; 'though that thou hast boasted thy warlike achievements before us is a glorifying of thine own deeds, and cometh of the Enemy, who tempteth us to exalt our own worship. But thou hast our pardon, judging thou speakest less of thine own suggestion than from the impulse of him whom, by Heaven's leave, we will quell and drive forth from our assembly.' A glance of disdain flashed from the dark fierce eyes of Bois-Guilbert, but he made no reply. 'And now,' pursued the Grand Master, 'since our brother of Goodalricke's question has been thus imperfectly answered, pursue we our quest, brethren, and with our patron's assistance we will search to the bottom this mystery of iniquity. Let those who have aught to witness of the life and conversation of this Jewish woman stand forth before us.'

There was a bustle in the lower part of the hall, and when the Grand Master inquired the reason, it was replied, there was in the crowd a bedridden man, whom the prisoner had restored to the perfect use of his limbs, by a miraculous balsam.

The poor peasant, a Saxon by birth, was dragged forward to the bar, terrified at the penal consequences which he might have incurred by the guilt of having been cured of the palsy by a Jewish damsel. Perfectly cured he certainly was not, for he supported himself forward on crutches to give evidence. Most unwilling was his testimony, and given with many tears; but he admitted that two years since, when residing at York, he was suddenly afflicted with a sore disease, while labouring for Isaac the rich Jew, in his vocation of a joiner; that he had been unable to stir from his bed until the remedies applied by Rebecca's directions, and especially a warming and spicy-smelling balsam, had in some degree restored him to the use of his limbs. Moreover, he said, she had given him a pot

of that precious ointment, and furnished him with
a piece of money withal, to return to the house of
his father, near to Templestowe. 'And may it
please your gracious reverence,' said the man, 'I
cannot think the damsel meant harm by me, though
she hath the ill hap to be a Jewess; for even when
I used her remedy, I said the pater and the creed,
and it never operated a whit less kindly.'

'Peace, slave,' said the Grand Master, 'and begone! It well suits brutes like thee to be tampering
and trinketing with hellish cures, and to be giving
your labour to the sons of mischief. I tell thee,
the fiend can impose diseases for the very purpose
of removing them, in order to bring into credit
some diabolical fashion of cure. Hast thou that
unguent of which thou speakest?'

The peasant, fumbling in his bosom with a
trembling hand, produced a small box, bearing
some Hebrew characters on the lid, which was,
with most of the audience, a sure proof that the
devil had stood apothecary. Beaumanoir, after
crossing himself, took the box into his hand, and,
learned in most of the Eastern tongues, read with
ease the motto on the lid—'The Lion of the Tribe
of Judah hath conquered.' 'Strange powers of
Sathanas,' said he, 'which can convert Scripture
into blasphemy, mingling poison with our necessary
food! Is there no leech here who can tell us the
ingredients of this mystic unguent?'

Two mediciners, as they called themselves, the
one a monk, the other a barber, appeared, and
avouched they knew nothing of the materials, excepting that they savoured of myrrh and camphire,
which they took to be Oriental herbs. But with
the true professional hatred to a successful prac-
titioner of their art, they insinuated that, since the
medicine was beyond their own knowledge, it must
necessarily have been compounded from an unlawful
and magical pharmacopœia; since they themselves,

though no conjurors, fully understood every branch of their art, so far as it might be exercised with the good faith of a Christian. When this medical research was ended, the Saxon peasant desired humbly to have back the medicine which he had found so salutary; but the Grand Master frowned severely at the request. 'What is thy name, fellow?' said he to the cripple.

'Higg, the son of Snell,' answered the peasant.

'Then, Higg, son of Snell,' said the Grand Master, 'I tell thee, it is better to be bedridden than to accept the benefit of unbelievers' medicine that thou mayest arise and walk; better to despoil infidels of their treasure by the strong hand than to accept of them benevolent gifts, or do them service for wages. Go thou, and do as I have said.'

'Alack,' said the peasant, 'an it shall not displease your reverence, the lesson comes too late for me, for I am but a maimed man; but I will tell my two brethren, who serve the rich rabbi Nathan ben Samuel [Israel], that your mastership says it is more lawful to rob him than to render him faithful service.'

'Out with the prating villain!' said Beaumanoir, who was not prepared to refute this practical application of his general maxim.

Higg, the son of Snell, withdrew into the crowd, but, interested in the fate of his benefactress, lingered until he should learn her doom, even at the risk of again encountering the frown of that severe judge, the terror of which withered his very heart within him.

At this period of the trial, the Grand Master commanded Rebecca to unveil herself. Opening her lips for the first time, she replied patiently, but with dignity, 'That it was not the wont of the daughters of her people to uncover their faces when alone in an assembly of strangers.' The sweet tones of her voice, and the softness of her reply, impressed

on the audience a sentiment of pity and sympathy.
But Beaumanoir, in whose mind the suppression of
each feeling of humanity which could interfere with
his imagined duty was a virtue of itself, repeated
his commands that his victim should be unveiled.
The guards were about to remove her veil accordingly, when she stood up before the Grand Master,
and said, 'Nay, but for the love of your own
daughters—alas,' she said, recollecting herself, 'ye
have no daughters!—yet for the remembrance of
your mothers, for the love of your sisters, and of
female decency, let me not be thus handled in your
presence : it suits not a maiden to be disrobed by
such rude grooms. I will obey you,' she added,
with an expression of patient sorrow in her voice,
which had almost melted the heart of Beaumanoir
himself; 'ye are elders among your people, and at
your command I will show the features of an ill-
fated maiden.'

She withdrew her veil, and looked on them with
a countenance in which bashfulness contended with
dignity. Her exceeding beauty excited a murmur
of surprise, and the younger knights told each other
with their eyes, in silent correspondence, that Brian's
best apology was in the power of her real charms,
rather than of her imaginary witchcraft. But Higg,
the son of Snell, felt most deeply the effect produced by the sight of the countenance of his benefactress. 'Let me go forth,' he said to the warders
at the door of the hall—'let me go forth ! To look
at her again will kill me, for I have had a share in
murdering her.'

'Peace, poor man,' said Rebecca, when she heard
his exclamation ; 'thou hast done me no harm by
speaking the truth ; thou canst not aid me by thy
complaints or lamentations. Peace, I pray thee ;
go home and save thyself.'

Higg was about to be thrust out by the compassion
of the warders, who were apprehensive lest his

clamorous grief should draw upon them reprehension, and upon himself punishment. But he promised to be silent, and was permitted to remain. The two men-at-arms, with whom Albert Malvoisin had not failed to communicate upon the import of their testimony, were now called forward. Though both were hardened and inflexible villains, the sight of the captive maiden, as well as her excelling beauty, at first appeared to stagger them; but an expressive glance from the preceptor of Templestowe restored them to their dogged composure; and they delivered, with a precision which would have seemed suspicious to more impartial judges, circumstances either altogether fictitious or trivial, and natural in themselves, but rendered pregnant with suspicion by the exaggerated manner in which they were told, and the sinister commentary which the witnesses added to the facts. The circumstances of their evidence would have been, in modern days, divided into two classes—those which were immaterial and those which were actually and physically impossible. But both were, in those ignorant and superstitious times, easily credited as proofs of guilt. The first class set forth that Rebecca was heard to mutter to herself in an unknown tongue; that the songs she sung by fits were of a strangely sweet sound, which made the ears of the hearer tingle and his heart throb; that she spoke at times to herself, and seemed to look upward for a reply; that her garments were of a strange and mystic form, unlike those of women of good repute; that she had rings impressed with cabalistical devices, and that strange characters were broidered on her veil. All these circumstances, so natural and so trivial, were gravely listened to as proofs, or at least as affording strong suspicions, that Rebecca had unlawful correspondence with mystical powers.

But there was less equivocal testimony, which the credulity of the assembly, or of the greater part, greedily swallowed, however incredible. One of the soldiers had seen her work a cure upon a wounded man brought with them to the castle of Torquilstone. 'She did,' he said, 'make certain signs upon the wound, and repeated certain mysterious words, which he blessed God he understood not, when the iron head of a square cross-bow bolt disengaged itself from the wound, the bleeding was stanched, the wound was closed, and the dying man was, within the quarter of an hour, walking upon the ramparts, and assisting the witness in managing a mangonel, or machine for hurling stones.' This legend was probably founded upon the fact that Rebecca had attended on the wounded Ivanhoe when in the castle of Torquilstone. But it was the more difficult to dispute the accuracy of the witness, as, in order to produce real evidence in support of his verbal testimony, he drew from his pouch the very bolt-head which, according to his story, had been miraculously extracted from the wound; and as the iron weighed a full ounce, it completely confirmed the tale, however marvellous.

His comrade had been a witness from a neighbouring battlement of the scene betwixt Rebecca and Bois-Guilbert, when she was upon the point of precipitating herself from the top of the tower. Not to be behind his companion, this fellow stated that he had seen Rebecca perch herself upon the parapet of the turret, and there take the form of a milk-white swan, under which appearance she flitted three times round the castle of Torquilstone; then again settle on the turret, and once more assume the female form.

Less than one half of this weighty evidence would have been sufficient to convict any old woman, poor and ugly, even though she had not been a Jewess. United with that fatal circumstance, the body of proof was too weighty for Rebecca's youth, though combined with the most exquisite beauty.

The Grand Master had collected the suffrages, and now in a solemn tone demanded of Rebecca what she had to say against the sentence of condemnation which he was about to pronounce.

'To invoke your pity,' said the lovely Jewess, with a voice somewhat tremulous with emotion, 'would, I am aware, be as useless as I should hold it mean. To state, that to relieve the sick and wounded of another religion cannot be displeasing to the acknowledged Founder of both our faiths, were also unavailing; to plead, that many things which these men—whom may Heaven pardon!—have spoken against me are impossible, would avail me but little, since you believe in their possibility; and still less would it advantage me to explain that the peculiarities of my dress, language, and manners are those of my people—I had wellnigh said of my country, but, alas! we have no country. Nor will I even vindicate myself at the expense of my oppressor, who stands there listening to the fictions and surmises which seem to convert the tyrant into the victim. God be judge between him and me! but rather would I submit to ten such deaths as your pleasure may denounce against me than listen to the suit which that man of Belial has urged upon me—friendless, defenceless, and his prisoner. But he is of your own faith, and his lightest affirmance would weigh down the most solemn protestations of the distressed Jewess. I will not therefore return to himself the charge brought against me; but to himself—yes, Brian de Bois-Guilbert, to thyself I appeal, whether these accusations are not false? as monstrous and calumnious as they are deadly?'

There was a pause; all eyes turned to Brian de Bois-Guilbert. He was silent.

'Speak,' she said, 'if thou art a man; if thou art a Christian, speak! I conjure thee, by the habit which thou dost wear—by the name thou dost inherit—by the knighthood thou dost vaunt—by

the honour of thy mother—by the tomb and the
bones of thy father—I conjure thee to say, are these
things true?'

'Answer her, brother,' said the Grand Master,
'if the Enemy with whom thou dost wrestle will
give thee power.'

In fact, Bois-Guilbert seemed agitated by contending passions, which almost convulsed his features,
and it was with a constrained voice that at last he replied, looking to Rebecca—'The scroll!—the scroll!'

'Ay,' said Beaumanoir, 'this is indeed testimony!
The victim of her witcheries can only name the fatal
scroll, the spell inscribed on which is, doubtless, the
pause of his silence.'

But Rebecca put another interpretation on the
words extorted as it were from Bois-Guilbert, and
glancing her eye upon the slip of parchment which
she continued to hold in her hand, she read written
thereupon in the Arabian character, 'Demand a
champion!' The murmuring commentary which
ran through the assembly at the strange reply of
Bois-Guilbert gave Rebecca leisure to examine and
instantly to destroy the scroll unobserved. When
the whisper had ceased, the Grand Master spoke.

'Rebecca, thou canst derive no benefit from the
evidence of this unhappy knight, for whom, as we
well perceive, the Enemy is yet too powerful.
Hast thou aught else to say?'

'There is yet one chance of life left to me,' said
Rebecca, 'even by your own fierce laws. Life has
been miserable—miserable, at least, of late—but I
will not cast away the gift of God while He affords
me the means of defending it. I deny this charge:
I maintain my innocence, and I declare the falsehood of this accusation. I challenge the privilege
of trial by combat, and will appear by my champion.'

'And who, Rebecca,' replied the Grand Master,
'will lay lance in rest for a sorceress? who will be
the champion of a Jewess?'

'God will raise me up a champion,' said Rebecca. 'It cannot be that in merry England, the hospitable, the generous, the free, where so many are ready to peril their lives for honour, there will not be found one to fight for justice. But it is enough that I challenge the trial by combat: there lies my gage.'

She took her embroidered glove from her hand, and flung it down before the Grand Master with an air of mingled simplicity and dignity which excited universal surprise and admiration.

CHAPTER XXXVIII

There I throw my gage,
To prove it on thee to the extremest point
Of martial daring.

Richard II.

EVEN Lucas Beaumanoir himself was affected by the mien and appearance of Rebecca. He was not originally a cruel or even a severe man ; but with passions by nature cold, and with a high, though mistaken, sense of duty, his heart had been gradually hardened by the ascetic life which he pursued, the supreme power which he enjoyed, and the supposed necessity of subduing infidelity and eradicating heresy which he conceived peculiarly incumbent on him. His features relaxed in their usual severity as he gazed upon the beautiful creature before him, alone, unfriended, and defending herself with so much spirit and courage. He crossed himself twice, as doubting whence arose the unwonted softening of a heart which on such occasions used to resemble in hardness the steel of his sword. At length he spoke.

'Damsel,' he said, 'if the pity I feel for thee arise from any practice thine evil arts have made on me, great is thy guilt. But I rather judge it the kinder feelings of nature, which grieves that so goodly a form should be a vessel of perdition. Repent, my daughter, confess thy witchcrafts, turn thee from thine evil faith, embrace this holy emblem, and all shall yet be well with thee here and hereafter. In some sisterhood of the strictest order

shalt thou have time for prayer and fitting penance,
and that repentance not to be repented of. This do
and live: what has the law of Moses done for thee
that thou shouldst die for it?'

'It was the law of my fathers,' said Rebecca; 'it
was delivered in thunders and in storms upon the
mountain of Sinai, in cloud and in fire. This, if ye
are Christians, ye believe. It is, you say, recalled;
but so my teachers have not taught me.'

'Let our chaplain,' said Beaumanoir, 'stand forth,
and tell this obstinate infidel——'

'Forgive the interruption,' said Rebecca, meekly;
'I am a maiden, unskilled to dispute for my religion;
but I can die for it, if it be God's will. Let me pray
your answer to my demand of a champion.'

'Give me her glove,' said Beaumanoir. 'This is
indeed,' he continued, as he looked at the flimsy
texture and slender fingers, 'a slight and frail gage
for a purpose so deadly! Seest thou, Rebecca, as
this thin and light glove of thine is to one of our
heavy steel gauntlets, so is thy cause to that of the
Temple, for it is our order which thou hast defied.'

'Cast my innocence into the scale,' answered
Rebecca, 'and the glove of silk shall outweigh the
glove of iron.'

'Then thou dost persist in thy refusal to confess
thy guilt, and in that bold challenge which thou
hast made?'

'I do persist, noble sir,' answered Rebecca.

'So be it then, in the name of Heaven,' said the
Grand Master; 'and may God show the right!'

'Amen,' replied the preceptors around him, and
the word was deeply echoed by the whole assembly.

'Brethren,' said Beaumanoir, 'you are aware that
we might well have refused to this woman the benefit
of the trial by combat; but, though a Jewess and
an unbeliever, she is also a stranger and defenceless,
and God forbid that she should ask the benefit of
our mild laws and that it should be refused to her.

Moreover, we are knights and soldiers as well as men of religion, and shame it were to us, upon any pretence, to refuse proffered combat. Thus, therefore, stands the case. Rebecca, the daughter of Isaac of York, is, by many frequent and suspicious circumstances, defamed of sorcery practised on the person of a noble knight of our holy order, and hath challenged the combat in proof of her innocence. To whom, reverend brother, is it your opinion that we should deliver the gage of battle, naming him, at the same time, to be our champion on the field?'

'To Brian de Bois-Guilbert, whom it chiefly concerns,' said the preceptor of Goodalricke, 'and who, moreover, best knows how the truth stands in this matter.'

'But if,' said the Grand Master, 'our brother Brian be under the influence of a charm or a spell— we speak but for the sake of precaution, for to the arm of none of our holy order would we more willingly confide this or a more weighty cause.'

'Reverend father,' answered the preceptor of Goodalricke, 'no spell can affect the champion who comes forward to fight for the judgment of God.'

'Thou sayest right, brother,' said the Grand Master. 'Albert Malvoisin, give this gage of battle to Brian de Bois-Guilbert. It is our charge to thee, brother,' he continued, addressing himself to Bois-Guilbert, 'that thou do thy battle manfully, nothing doubting that the good cause shall triumph. And do thou, Rebecca, attend, that we assign thee the third day from the present to find a champion.'

'That is but brief space,' answered Rebecca, 'for a stranger, who is also of another faith, to find one who will do battle, wagering life and honour for her cause, against a knight who is called an approved soldier.'

'We may not extend it,' answered the Grand Master; 'the field must be foughten in our own presence, and divers weighty causes call us on the fourth day from hence.'

'God's will be done!' said Rebecca; 'I put my trust in Him, to whom an instant is as effectual to save as a whole age.'

'Thou hast spoken well, damsel,' said the Grand Master; 'but well know we who can array himself like an angel of light. It remains but to name a fitting place of combat, and, if it so hap, also of execution. Where is the preceptor of this house?'

Albert Malvoisin, still holding Rebecca's glove in his hand, was speaking to Bois-Guilbert very earnestly, but in a low voice.

'How!' said the Grand Master, 'will he not receive the gage?'

'He will—he doth, most reverend father,' said Malvoisin, slipping the glove under his own mantle. 'And for the place of combat, I hold the fittest to be the lists of St. George belonging to this preceptory, and used by us for military exercise.'

'It is well,' said the Grand Master. 'Rebecca, in those lists shalt thou produce thy champion; and if thou failest to do so, or if thy champion shall be discomfited by the judgment of God, thou shalt then die the death of a sorceress, according to doom. Let this our judgment be recorded, and the record read aloud that no one may pretend ignorance.'

One of the chaplains who acted as clerks to the chapter immediately engrossed the order in a huge volume, which contained the proceedings of the Templar Knights when solemnly assembled on such occasions; and when he had finished writing, the other read aloud the sentence of the Grand Master, which, when translated from the Norman-French in which it was couched, was expressed as follows:—

'Rebecca, a Jewess, daughter of Isaac of York, being attainted of sorcery, seduction, and other damnable practices, practised on a knight of the

most holy order of the Temple of Zion, doth deny
the same, and saith that the testimony delivered
against her this day is false, wicked, and disloyal;
and that by lawful *essoine* [1] of her body, as being
unable to combat in her own behalf, she doth offer,
by a champion instead thereof, to avouch her case,
he performing his loyal devoir in all knightly sort,
with such arms as to gage of battle do fully apper-
tain, and that at her peril and cost. And therewith
she proffered her gage. And the gage having been
delivered to the noble lord and knight, Brian de
Bois-Guilbert, of the holy order of the Temple of
Zion, he was appointed to do this battle in behalf of
his order and himself, as injured and impaired by
the practices of the appellant. Wherefore the most
reverend father and puissant lord, Lucas Marquis of
Beaumanoir, did allow of the said challenge, and of
the said *essoine* of the appellant's body, and assigned
the third day for the said combat, the place being the
inclosure called the lists of St. George, near to the
preceptory of Templestowe. And the Grand Master
appointed the appellant to appear there by her
champion, on pain of doom, as a person convicted
of sorcery or seduction; and also the defendant so
to appear, under the penalty of being held and
adjudged recreant in case of default; and the noble
lord and most reverend father aforesaid appointed
the battle to be done in his own presence, and
according to all that is commendable and profitable
in such a case. And may God aid the just cause!'

'Amen!' said the Grand Master; and the word
was echoed by all around. Rebecca spoke not, but
she looked up to Heaven, and, folding her hands,
remained for a minute without change of attitude.
She then modestly reminded the Grand Master that
she ought to be permitted some opportunity of free

---

[1] *Essoine* signifies excuse, and here relates to the appellant's
privilege of appearing by her champion, in excuse of her own
person on account of her sex.

communication with her friends, for the purpose of making her condition known to them, and procuring, if possible, some champion to fight in her behalf.

'It is just and lawful,' said the Grand Master; 'choose what messenger thou shalt trust, and he shall have free communication with thee in thy prison-chamber.'

'Is there,' said Rebecca, 'any one here who, either for love of a good cause or for ample hire, will do the errand of a distressed being?'

All were silent; for none thought it safe, in the presence of the Grand Master, to avow any interest in the calumniated prisoner, lest he should be suspected of leaning towards Judaism. Not even the prospect of reward, far less any feelings of compassion alone, could surmount this apprehension.

Rebecca stood for a few moments in indescribable anxiety, and then exclaimed, 'Is it really thus? And in English land am I to be deprived of the poor chance of safety which remains to me, for want of an act of charity which would not be refused to the worst criminal?'

Higg, the son of Snell, at length replied, 'I am but a maimed man, but that I can at all stir or move was owing to her charitable assistance. I will do thine errand,' he added, addressing Rebecca, 'as well as a crippled object can, and happy were my limbs fleet enough to repair the mischief done by my tongue. Alas! when I boasted of thy charity, I little thought I was leading thee into danger!'

'God,' said Rebecca, 'is the disposer of all. He can turn back the captivity of Judah, even by the weakest instrument. To execute His message the snail is as sure a messenger as the falcon. Seek out Isaac of York—here is that will pay for horse and man—let him have this scroll. I know not if it be of Heaven the spirit which inspires me, but most truly do I judge that I am not to die this death, and

that a champion will be raised up for me.   Farewell !
Life and death are in thy haste.'

The peasant took the scroll, which contained only
a few lines in Hebrew.   Many of the crowd would
have dissuaded him from touching a document so
suspicious ; but Higg was resolute in the service of
his benefactress.   'She had saved his body,' he said,
'and he was confident she did not mean to peril his
soul.'

'I will get me,' he said, 'my neighbour Buthan's
good capul, and I will be at York within as brief
space as man and beast may.'

But, as it fortuned, he had no occasion to go so
far, for within a quarter of a mile from the gate of
the preceptory he met with two riders, whom, by
their dress and their huge yellow caps, he knew to
be Jews ; and, on approaching more nearly, discovered that one of them was his ancient employer,
Isaac of York.   The other was the Rabbi ben Samuel
[Israel] ; and both had approached as near to the
preceptory as they dared, on hearing that the Grand
Master had summoned a chapter for the trial of a
sorceress.

'Brother ben Samuel,' said Isaac, 'my soul is
disquieted, and I wot not why.   This charge of
necromancy is right often used for cloaking evil
practices on our people.'

'Be of good comfort, brother,' said the physician ;
'thou canst deal with the Nazarenes as one possessing the mammon of unrighteousness, and canst
therefore purchase immunity at their hands : it
rules the savage minds of those ungodly men, even
as the signet of the mighty Solomon was said to
command the evil genii.   But what poor wretch
comes hither upon his crutches, desiring, as I think,
some speech of me ?   Friend,' continued the physician,
addressing Higg, the son of Snell, 'I refuse thee
not the aid of mine art, but I relieve not with one
asper those who beg for alms upon the highway.

Out upon thee ! Hast thou the palsy in thy legs ?
then let thy hands work for thy livelihood ; for,
albeit thou be'st unfit for a speedy post, or for a
careful shepherd, or for the warfare, or for the
service of a hasty master, yet there be occupa-
tions—— How now, brother ?' said he, interrupting his harangue to look towards Isaac, who had
but glanced at the scroll which Higg offered, when,
uttering a deep groan, he fell from his mule like a
dying man, and lay for a minute insensible.

The Rabbi now dismounted in great alarm, and
hastily applied the remedies which his art suggested
for the recovery of his companion. He had even
taken from his pocket a cupping apparatus, and was
about to proceed to phlebotomy, when the object of
his anxious solicitude suddenly revived ; but it was
to dash his cap from his head, and to throw dust on
his grey hairs. The physician was at first inclined
to ascribe this sudden and violent emotion to the
effects of insanity ; and, adhering to his original
purpose, began once again to handle his implements.
But Isaac soon convinced him of his error.

'Child of my sorrow,' he said, 'well shouldst thou
be called Benoni, instead of Rebecca ! Why should
thy death bring down my grey hairs to the grave,
till, in the bitterness of my heart, I curse God and
die !'

'Brother,' said the Rabbi, in great surprise, 'art
thou a father in Israel, and dost thou utter words
like unto these ? I trust that the child of thy house
yet liveth ?'

'She liveth,' answered Isaac ; 'but it is as Daniel,
who was called Belteshazzar, even when within the
den of the lions. She is captive unto those men of
Belial, and they will wreak their cruelty upon her,
sparing neither for her youth nor her comely favour.
O ! she was as a crown of green palms to my grey
locks ; and she must wither in a night, like the
gourd of Jonah ! Child of my love !—child of my

old age !—oh, Rebecca, daughter of Rachael! the
darkness of the shadow of death hath encompassed
thee.'

'Yet read the scroll,' said the Rabbi; 'peradventure it may be that we may yet find out a way
of deliverance.'

'Do thou read, brother,' answered Isaac, 'for
mine eyes are as a fountain of water.'

The physician read, but in their native language,
the following words :—

'To Isaac, the son of Adonikam, whom the
Gentiles call Isaac of York, peace and the blessing
of the promise be multiplied unto thee ! My father,
I am as one doomed to die for that which my soul
knoweth not, even for the crime of witchcraft. My
father, if a strong man can be found to do battle
for my cause with sword and spear, according to
the custom of the Nazarenes, and that within the
lists of Templestowe, on the third day from this
time, peradventure our fathers' God will give him
strength to defend the innocent, and her who hath
none to help her. But if this may not be, let the
virgins of our people mourn for me as for one cast
off, and for the hart that is stricken by the hunter,
and for the flower which is cut down by the scythe
of the mower. Wherefore look now what thou
doest, and whether there be any rescue. One
Nazarene warrior might indeed bear arms in my
behalf, even Wilfred, son of Cedric, whom the
Gentiles call Ivanhoe. But he may not yet endure
the weight of his armour. Nevertheless, send the
tidings unto him, my father ; for he hath favour
among the strong men of his people, and as he was
our companion in the house of bondage, he may find
some one to do battle for my sake. And say unto
him—even unto him—even unto Wilfred, the son of
Cedric, that if Rebecca live, or if Rebecca die, she
liveth or dieth wholly free of the guilt she is charged
withal. And if it be the will of God that thou shalt

be deprived of thy daughter, do not thou tarry, old man, in this land of bloodshed and cruelty; but betake thyself to Cordova, where thy brother liveth in safety, under the shadow of the throne, even of the throne of Boabdil the Saracen; for less cruel are the cruelties of the Moors unto the race of Jacob than the cruelties of the Nazarenes of England.'

Isaac listened with tolerable composure while Ben Samuel [Israel] read the letter, and then again resumed the gestures and exclamations of Oriental sorrow, tearing his garments, besprinkling his head with dust, and ejaculating, 'My daughter! my daughter! flesh of my flesh, and bone of my bone!'

'Yet,' said the Rabbi, 'take courage, for this grief availeth nothing. Gird up thy loins, and seek out this Wilfred, the son of Cedric. It may be he will help thee with counsel or with strength; for the youth hath favour in the eyes of Richard, called of the Nazarenes Cœur-de-Lion, and the tidings that he hath returned are constant in the land. It may be that he may obtain his letter, and his signet, commanding these men of blood, who take their name from the Temple to the dishonour thereof, that they proceed not in their purposed wickedness.'

'I will seek him out,' said Isaac, 'for he is a good youth, and hath compassion for the exile of Jacob. But he cannot bear his armour, and what other Christian shall do battle for the oppressed of Zion?'

'Nay, but,' said the Rabbi, 'thou speakest as one that knoweth not the Gentiles. With gold shalt thou buy their valour, even as with gold thou buyest thine own safety. Be of good courage, and do thou set forward to find out this Wilfred of Ivanhoe. I will also up and be doing, for great sin it were to leave thee in thy calamity. I will hie me to the city of York, where many warriors and strong men are assembled, and doubt not I will find among them some one who will do battle for thy daughter: for gold is their god, and for riches will they pawn

their lives as well as their lands. Thou wilt fulfil,
my brother, such promise as I may make unto them
in thy name?'

'Assuredly, brother,' said Isaac, 'and Heaven be
praised that raised me up a comforter in my misery!
Howbeit, grant them not their full demand at once,
for thou shalt find it the quality of this accursed
people that they will ask pounds, and peradventure
accept of ounces. Nevertheless be it as thou willest,
for I am distracted in this thing, and what would
my gold avail me if the child of my love should
perish!'

'Farewell,' said the physician, 'and may it be to
thee as thy heart desireth.'

They embraced accordingly, and departed on their
several roads. The crippled peasant remained for
some time looking after them.

'These dog Jews!' said he; 'to take no more
notice of a free guild-brother than if I were a bond
slave or a Turk, or a circumcised Hebrew like themselves! They might have flung me a mancus or
two, however. I was not obliged to bring their
unhallowed scrawls, and run the risk of being
bewitched, as more folks than one told me. And
what care I for the bit of gold that the wench gave
me, if I am to come to harm from the priest next
Easter at confession, and be obliged to give him
twice as much to make it up with him, and be called
the Jew's flying post all my life, as it may hap, into
the bargain? I think I was bewitched in earnest
when I was beside that girl! But it was always so
with Jew or Gentile, whosoever came near her:
none could stay when she had an errand to go;
and still, whenever I think of her, I would give
shop and tools to save her life.'

CHAPTER XXXIX

O maid, unrelenting and cold as thou art,
My bosom is proud as thine own.
                                        SEWARD.

IT was in the twilight of the day when her trial, if
it could be called such, had taken place, that a low
knock was heard at the door of Rebecca's prison-
chamber. It disturbed not the inmate, who was then
engaged in the evening prayer recommended by her
religion, and which concluded with a hymn we have
ventured thus to translate into English :—

When Israel, of the Lord beloved,
    Out of the land of bondage came,
Her fathers' God before her moved,
    An awful guide, in smoke and flame
By day, along the astonish'd lands
    The cloudy pillar glided slow ;
By night, Arabia's crimson'd sands
    Return'd the fiery column's glow.

There rose the choral hymn of praise,
    And trump and timbrel answer'd keen,
And Zion's daughters pour'd their lays,
    With priest's and warrior's voice between.
No portents now our foes amaze,
    Forsaken Israel wanders lone ;
Our fathers would not know THY ways,
    And THOU hast left them to their own.

But, present still, though now unseen,
    When brightly shines the prosperous day
Be thoughts of THEE a cloudy screen
    To temper the deceitful ray.

And oh, when stoops on Judah's path
    In shade and storm the frequent night,
Be THOU, long-suffering, slow to wrath,
    A burning and a shining light!

Our harps we left by Babel's streams,
    The tyrant's jest, the Gentile's scorn;
No censer round our altar beams,
    And mute our timbrel, trump, and horn.
But THOU hast said, the blood of goat,
    The flesh of rams, I will not prize;
A contrite heart, an humble thought,
    Are Mine accepted sacrifice.

When the sounds of Rebecca's devotional hymn had died away in silence, the low knock at the door was again renewed. 'Enter,' she said, 'if thou art a friend; and if a foe, I have not the means of refusing thy entrance.'

'I am,' said Brian de Bois-Guilbert, entering the apartment, 'friend or foe, Rebecca, as the event of this interview shall make me.'

Alarmed at the sight of this man, whose licentious passion she considered as the root of her misfortunes, Rebecca drew backward with a cautious and alarmed, yet not a timorous, demeanour into the farthest corner of the apartment, as if determined to retreat as far as she could, but to stand her ground when retreat became no longer possible. She drew herself into an attitude not of defiance, but of resolution, as one that would avoid provoking assault, yet was resolute to repel it, being offered, to the utmost of her power.

'You have no reason to fear me, Rebecca,' said the Templar; 'or, if I must so qualify my speech, you have at least *now* no reason to fear me.'

'I fear you not, Sir Knight,' replied Rebecca, although her short-drawn breath seemed to belie the heroism of her accents; 'my trust is strong, and I fear thee not.'

'You have no cause,' answered Bois-Guilbert,

gravely; 'my former frantic attempts you have not now to dread. Within your call are guards over whom I have no authority. They are designed to conduct you to death, Rebecca, yet would not suffer you to be insulted by any one, even by me, were my frenzy—for frenzy it is—to urge me so far.'

'May Heaven be praised!' said the Jewess; 'death is the least of my apprehensions in this den of evil.'

'Ay,' replied the Templar, 'the idea of death is easily received by the courageous mind, when the road to it is sudden and open. A thrust with a lance, a stroke with a sword, were to me little; to you, a spring from a dizzy battlement, a stroke with a sharp poniard, has no terrors, compared with what either thinks disgrace. Mark me—I say this—perhaps mine own sentiments of honour are not less fantastic, Rebecca, than thine are; but we know alike how to die for them.'

'Unhappy man,' said the Jewess; 'and art thou condemned to expose thy life for principles of which thy sober judgment does not acknowledge the solidity? Surely this is a parting with your treasure for that which is not bread. But deem not so of me. Thy resolution may fluctuate on the wild and changeful billows of human opinion; but mine is anchored on the Rock of Ages.'

'Silence, maiden,' answered the Templar; 'such discourse now avails but little. Thou art condemned to die not a sudden and easy death, such as misery chooses and despair welcomes, but a slow, wretched, protracted course of torture, suited to what the diabolical bigotry of these men calls thy crime.'

'And to whom—if such my fate—to whom do I owe this?' said Rebecca; 'surely only to him who, for a most selfish and brutal cause, dragged me hither, and who now, for some unknown purpose of his own, strives to exaggerate the wretched fate to which he exposed me.'

'Think not,' said the Templar, 'that I have so exposed thee; I would have bucklered thee against such danger with my own bosom, as freely as ever I exposed it to the shafts which had otherwise reached thy life.'

'Had thy purpose been the honourable protection of the innocent,' said Rebecca, 'I had thanked thee for thy care; as it is, thou hast claimed merit for it so often that I tell thee life is worth nothing to me, preserved at the price which thou wouldst exact for it.'

'Truce with thine upbraidings, Rebecca,' said the Templar; 'I have my own cause of grief, and brook not that thy reproaches should add to it.'

'What is thy purpose, then, Sir Knight?' said the Jewess; 'speak it briefly. If thou hast aught to do save to witness the misery thou hast caused, let me know it; and then, if so it please you, leave me to myself. The step between time and eternity is short but terrible, and I have few moments to prepare for it.'

'I perceive, Rebecca,' said Bois-Guilbert, 'that thou dost continue to burden me with the charge of distresses which most fain would I have prevented.'

'Sir Knight,' said Rebecca, 'I would avoid reproaches; but what is more certain than that I owe my death to thine unbridled passion?'

'You err—you err,' said the Templar, hastily, 'if you impute what I could neither foresee nor prevent to my purpose or agency. Could I guess the unexpected arrival of yon dotard, whom some flashes of frantic valour, and the praises yielded by fools to the stupid self-torments of an ascetic, have raised for the present above his own merits, above common sense, above me, and above the hundreds of our order who think and feel as men free from such silly and fantastic prejudices as are the grounds of his opinions and actions?'

'Yet,' said Rebecca, 'you sate a judge upon me;

innocent—most innocent—as you knew me to be, you concurred in my condemnation; and, if I aright understood, are yourself to appear in arms to assert my guilt, and assure my punishment.'

'Thy patience, maiden,' replied the Templar. 'No race knows so well as thine own tribes how to submit to the time, and so to trim their bark as to make advantage even of an adverse wind.'

'Lamented be the hour,' said Rebecca, 'that has taught such art to the House of Israel! but adversity bends the heart as fire bends the stubborn steel, and those who are no longer their own governors, and the denizens of their own free independent state, must crouch before strangers. It is our curse, Sir Knight, deserved, doubtless, by our own misdeeds and those of our fathers; but you—you who boast your freedom as your birthright, how much deeper is your disgrace when you stoop to soothe the prejudices of others, and that against your own conviction?'

'Your words are bitter, Rebecca,' said Bois-Guilbert, pacing the apartment with impatience, 'but I came not hither to bandy reproaches with you. Know that Bois-Guilbert yields not to created man, although circumstances may for a time induce him to alter his plan. His will is the mountain stream, which may indeed be turned for a little space aside by the rock, but fails not to find its course to the ocean. That scroll which warned thee to demand a champion, from whom couldst thou think it came, if not from Bois-Guilbert? In whom else couldst thou have excited such interest?'

'A brief respite from instant death,' said Rebecca, 'which will little avail me. Was this all thou couldst do for one on whose head thou hast heaped sorrow, and whom thou hast brought near even to the verge of the tomb?'

'No, maiden,' said Bois-Guilbert, 'this was *not* all that I purposed. Had it not been for the

accursed interference of yon fanatical dotard, and
the fool of Goodalricke, who, being a Templar,
affects to think and judge according to the ordinary
rules of humanity, the office of the champion defender had devolved, not on a preceptor, but on a
companion of the order. Then I myself—such was
my purpose—had, on the sounding of the trumpet,
appeared in the lists as thy champion, disguised
indeed in the fashion of a roving knight, who seeks
adventures to prove his shield and spear; and then,
let Beaumanoir have chosen not one but two or
three of the brethren here assembled, I had not
doubted to cast them out of the saddle with my
single lance. Thus, Rebecca, should thine innocence have been avouched, and to thine own
gratitude would I have trusted for the reward of
my victory.'

'This, Sir Knight,' said Rebecca, 'is but idle
boasting—a brag of what you would have done had
you not found it convenient to do otherwise. You
received my glove, and my champion, if a creature
so desolate can find one, must encounter your lance
in the lists; yet you would assume the air of my
friend and protector!'

'Thy friend and protector,' said the Templar,
gravely, 'I will yet be; but mark at what risk,
or rather at what certainty, of dishonour; and then
blame me not if I make my stipulations before I
offer up all that I have hitherto held dear, to save
the life of a Jewish maiden.'

'Speak,' said Rebecca; 'I understand thee not.'

'Well, then,' said Bois-Guilbert, 'I will speak
as freely as ever did doting penitent to his ghostly
father, when placed in the tricky confessional.
Rebecca, if I appear not in these lists I lose fame
and rank—lose that which is the breath of my
nostrils, the esteem, I mean, in which I am held
by my brethren, and the hopes I have of succeeding
to that mighty authority which is now wielded by

the bigoted dotard Lucas de Beaumanoir, but of
which I should make a far different use. Such is
my certain doom, except I appear in arms against
thy cause. Accursed be he of Goodalricke, who
baited this trap for me! and doubly accursed Albert
de Malvoisin, who withheld me from the resolution
I had formed of hurling back the glove at the face
of the superstitious and superannuated fool who
listened to a charge so absurd, and against a creature
so high in mind and so lovely in form as thou art!'

'And what now avails rant or flattery?' answered
Rebecca. 'Thou hast made thy choice between
causing to be shed the blood of an innocent woman,
or of endangering thine own earthly state and earthly
hopes. What avails it to reckon together? thy
choice is made.'

'No, Rebecca,' said the knight, in a softer tone,
and drawing nearer towards her, 'my choice is NOT
made; nay, mark, it is thine to make the election.
If I appear in the lists, I must maintain my name in
arms; and if I do so, championed or unchampioned,
thou diest by the stake and faggot, for there lives
not the knight who hath coped with me in arms on
equal issue or on terms of vantage, save Richard
Cœur-de-Lion and his minion of Ivanhoe. Ivanhoe,
as thou well knowest, is unable to bear his corslet,
and Richard is in a foreign prison. If I appear,
then thou diest, even although thy charms should
instigate some hot-headed youth to enter the lists
in thy defence.'

'And what avails repeating this so often?' said
Rebecca.

'Much,' replied the Templar; 'for thou must
learn to look at thy fate on every side.'

'Well, then, turn the tapestry,' said the Jewess,
'and let me see the other side.'

'If I appear,' said Bois-Guilbert, 'in the fatal
lists, thou diest by a slow and cruel death, in pain
such as they say is destined to the guilty hereafter.

2 K

But if I appear not, then am I a degraded and
dishonoured knight, accused of witchcraft and of
communion with infidels : the illustrious name which
has grown yet more so under my wearing becomes
a hissing and a reproach. I lose fame—I lose
honour—I lose the prospect of such greatness as
scarce emperors attain to ; I sacrifice mighty ambition—I destroy schemes built as high as the
mountains with which heathens say their heaven
was once nearly scaled ; and yet, Rebecca,' he
added, throwing himself at her feet, 'this greatness
will I sacrifice—this fame will I renounce—this
power will I forego, even now when it is half within
my grasp, if thou wilt say, " Bois-Guilbert, I receive
thee for my lover." '

'Think not of such foolishness, Sir Knight,'
answered Rebecca, 'but hasten to the Regent, the
Queen Mother, and to Prince John ; they cannot,
in honour to the English crown, allow of the proceedings of your Grand Master. So shall you give
me protection without sacrifice on your part, or the
pretext of requiring any requital from me.'

'With these I deal not,' he continued, holding
the train of her robe—'it is thee only I address ;
and what can counterbalance thy choice ? Bethink
thee, were I a fiend, yet death is a worse, and it is
death who is my rival.'

'I weigh not these evils,' said Rebecca, afraid to
provoke the wild knight, yet equally determined
neither to endure his passion nor even feign to
endure it. 'Be a man, be a Christian ! If indeed
thy faith recommends that mercy which rather your
tongues than your actions pretend, save me from
this dreadful death, without seeking a requital
which would change thy magnanimity into base
barter.'

'No, damsel !' said the proud Templar, springing up, 'thou shalt not thus impose on me : if I
renounce present fame and future ambition, I

renounce it for thy sake, and we will escape in
company. Listen to me, Rebecca,' he said, again
softening his tone; 'England—Europe—is not the
world. There are spheres in which we may act,
ample enough even for my ambition. We will go
to Palestine, where Conrade Marquis of Montserrat
is my friend—a friend free as myself from the doting
scruples which fetter our free-born reason: rather
with Saladin will we league ourselves than endure
the scorn of the bigots whom we contemn. I will
form new paths to greatness,' he continued, again
traversing the room with hasty strides: 'Europe
shall hear the loud step of him she has driven from
her sons! Not the millions whom her crusaders
send to slaughter can do so much to defend Palestine; not the sabres of the thousands and ten
thousands of Saracens can hew their way so deep
into that land for which nations are striving, as
the strength and policy of me and those brethren
who, in despite of yonder old bigot, will adhere to
me in good and evil. Thou shalt be a queen,
Rebecca: on Mount Carmel shall we pitch the
throne which my valour will gain for you, and I
will exchange my long-desired batoon for a sceptre!'

'A dream,' said Rebecca—'an empty vision of
the night, which, were it a waking reality, affects
me not. Enough, that the power which thou
mightest acquire I will never share; nor hold I so
light of country or religious faith as to esteem him
who is willing to barter these ties, and cast away
the bonds of the order of which he is a sworn
member, in order to gratify an unruly passion for
the daughter of another people. Put not a price
on my deliverance, Sir Knight—sell not a deed of
generosity—protect the oppressed for the sake of
charity, and not for a selfish advantage. Go to the
throne of England; Richard will listen to my appeal
from these cruel men.'

'Never, Rebecca!' said the Templar, fiercely.

'If I renounce my order, for thee alone will I renounce it. Ambition shall remain mine, if thou refuse my love; I will not be fooled on all hands. Stoop my crest to Richard?—ask a boon of that heart of pride? Never, Rebecca, will I place the order of the Temple at his feet in my person. I may forsake the order; I never will degrade or betray it.'

'Now God be gracious to me,' said Rebecca, 'for the succour of man is wellnigh hopeless!'

'It is indeed,' said the Templar; 'for, proud as thou art, thou hast in me found thy match. If I enter the lists with my spear in rest, think not any human consideration shall prevent my putting forth my strength; and think then upon thine own fate— to die the dreadful death of the worst of criminals— to be consumed upon a blazing pile—dispersed to the elements of which our strange forms are so mystically composed—not a relic left of that graceful frame, from which we could say this lived and moved! Rebecca, it is not in woman to sustain this prospect—thou wilt yield to my suit.'

'Bois-Guilbert,' answered the Jewess, 'thou knowest not the heart of woman, or hast only conversed with those who are lost to her best feelings. I tell thee, proud Templar, that not in thy fiercest battles hast thou displayed more of thy vaunted courage than has been shown by woman when called upon to suffer by affection or duty. I am myself a woman, tenderly nurtured, naturally fearful of danger, and impatient of pain; yet, when we enter those fatal lists, thou to fight and I to suffer, I feel the strong assurance within me that my courage shall mount higher than thine. Farewell. I waste no more words on thee; the time that remains on earth to the daughter of Jacob must be otherwise spent: she must seek the Comforter, who may hide His face from His people, but who ever opens His ear to the cry of those who seek Him in sincerity and in truth.'

'We part then thus?' said the Templar, after a short pause; 'would to Heaven that we had never met, or that thou hadst been noble in birth and Christian in faith! Nay, by Heaven! when I gaze on thee, and think when and how we are next to meet, I could even wish myself one of thine own degraded nation; my hand conversant with ingots and shekels, instead of spear and shield; my head bent down before each petty noble, and my look only terrible to the shivering and bankrupt debtor —this could I wish, Rebecca, to be near to thee in life, and to escape the fearful share I must have in thy death.'

'Thou hast spoken the Jew,' said Rebecca, 'as the persecution of such as thou art has made him. Heaven in ire has driven him from his country, but industry has opened to him the only road to power and to influence which oppression has left unbarred. Read the ancient history of the people of God, and tell me if those by whom Jehovah wrought such marvels among the nations were then a people of misers and of usurers! And know, proud knight, we number names amongst us to which your boasted northern nobility is as the gourd compared with the cedar—names that ascend far back to those high times when the Divine Presence shook the mercy-seat between the cherubim, and which derive their splendour from no earthly prince, but from the awful Voice which bade their fathers be nearest of the congregation to the Vision. Such were the princes of the House of Jacob.'

Rebecca's colour rose as she boasted the ancient glories of her race, but faded as she added, with a sigh, 'Such *were* the princes of Judah, now such no more! They are trampled down like the shorn grass, and mixed with the mire of the ways. Yet are there those among them who shame not such high descent, and of such shall be the daughter of Isaac the son of Adonikam! Farewell! I envy not thy blood-won honours; I envy not thy barbarous descent from Northern heathens; I envy thee not thy faith, which is ever in thy mouth but never in thy heart nor in thy practice.'

'There is a spell on me, by Heaven!' said Bois-Guilbert. 'I almost think yon besotted skeleton spoke truth, and that the reluctance with which I part from thee hath something in it more than is natural. Fair creature!' he said, approaching near her, but with great respect, 'so young, so beautiful, so fearless of death! and yet doomed to die, and with infamy and agony. Who would not weep for thee? The tear, that has been a stranger to these eyelids for twenty years, moistens them as I gaze on thee. But it must be—nothing may now save thy life. Thou and I are but the blind instruments of some irresistible fatality, that hurries us along, like goodly vessels driving before the storm, which are dashed against each other, and so perish. Forgive me, then, and let us part at least as friends part. I have assailed thy resolution in vain, and mine own is fixed as the adamantine decrees of fate.'

'Thus,' said Rebecca, 'do men throw on fate the issue of their own wild passions. But I do forgive thee, Bois-Guilbert, though the author of my early death. There are noble things which cross over thy powerful mind; but it is the garden of the sluggard, and the weeds have rushed up, and conspired to choke the fair and wholesome blossom.'

'Yes,' said the Templar, 'I am, Rebecca, as thou hast spoken me, untaught, untamed: and proud that, amidst a shoal of empty fools and crafty bigots, I have retained the pre-eminent fortitude that places me above them. I have been a child of battle from my youth upward, high in my views, steady and inflexible in pursuing them. Such must I remain—proud, inflexible, and unchanging; and of this the world shall have proof. But thou forgivest me, Rebecca?'

'As freely as ever victim forgave her executioner.'

'Farewell, then,' said the Templar, and left the apartment.

The preceptor Albert waited impatiently in an adjacent chamber the return of Bois-Guilbert.

'Thou hast tarried long,' he said; 'I have been as if stretched on red-hot iron with very impatience. What if the Grand Master, or his spy Conrade, had come hither? I had paid dear for my complaisance. But what ails thee, brother? Thy step totters, thy brow is as black as night. Art thou well, Bois-Guilbert?'

'Ay,' answered the Templar, 'as well as the wretch who is doomed to die within an hour. Nay, by the rood, not half so well; for there be those in such state who can lay down life like a cast-off garment. By Heaven, Malvoisin, yonder girl hath wellnigh unmanned me. I am half resolved to go to the Grand Master, abjure the order to his very teeth, and refuse to act the brutality which his tyranny has imposed on me.'

'Thou art mad,' answered Malvoisin; 'thou mayst thus indeed utterly ruin thyself, but canst not even find a chance thereby to save the life of this Jewess, which seems so precious in thine eyes. Beaumanoir will name another of the order to defend his judgment in thy place, and the accused will as assuredly perish as if thou hadst taken the duty imposed on thee.'

''Tis false; I will myself take arms in her behalf,' answered the Templar, haughtily; 'and should I do so, I think, Malvoisin, that thou knowest not one of the order who will keep his saddle before the point of my lance.'

'Ay, but thou forgettest,' said the wily adviser, 'thou wilt have neither leisure nor opportunity to execute this mad project. Go to Lucas Beaumanoir, and say thou hast renounced thy vow of obedience, and see how long the despotic old man will leave

thee in personal freedom. The words shall scarce
have left thy lips, ere thou wilt either be an hundred
feet under ground, in the dungeon of the preceptory,
to abide trial as a recreant knight; or, if his opinion
holds concerning thy possession, thou wilt be enjoy-
ing straw, darkness, and chains in some distant
convent cell, stunned with exorcisms, and drenched
with holy water, to expel the foul fiend which hath
obtained dominion over thee. Thou must to the
lists, Brian, or thou art a lost and dishonoured man.'

'I will break forth and fly,' said Bois-Guilbert—
'fly to some distant land, to which folly and fanaticism have not yet found their way. No drop of the
blood of this most excellent creature shall be spilled
by my sanction.'

'Thou canst not fly,' said the preceptor: 'thy
ravings have excited suspicion, and thou wilt not be
permitted to leave the preceptory. Go and make
the essay: present thyself before the gate, and
command the bridge to be lowered, and mark what
answer thou shalt receive. Thou art surprised and
offended; but is it not the better for thee? Wert
thou to fly, what would ensue but the reversal of
thy arms, the dishonour of thine ancestry, the
degradation of thy rank? Think on it. Where
shall thine old companions in arms hide their heads
when Brian de Bois-Guilbert, the best lance of the
Templars, is proclaimed recreant, amid the hisses of
the assembled people? What grief will be at the
Court of France! With what joy will the haughty
Richard hear the news, that the knight that set him
hard in Palestine, and wellnigh darkened his renown, has lost fame and honour for a Jewish girl,
whom he could not even save by so costly a sacrifice!'

'Malvoisin,' said the Knight, 'I thank thee—
thou hast touched the string at which my heart
most readily thrills! Come of it what may, recreant
shall never be added to the name of Bois-Guilbert.
Would to God, Richard, or any of his vaunting

minions of England, would appear in these lists! But they will be empty—no one will risk to break a lance for the innocent, the forlorn.'

'The better for thee, if it prove so,' said the preceptor; 'if no champion appears, it is not by thy means that this unlucky damsel shall die, but by the doom of the Grand Master, with whom rests all the blame, and who will count that blame for praise and commendation.'

'True,' said Bois-Guilbert; 'if no champion appears, I am but a part of the pageant, sitting indeed on horseback in the lists, but having no part in what is to follow.'

'None whatever,' said Malvoisin—'no more than the armed image of St. George when it makes part of a procession.'

'Well, I will resume my resolution,' replied the haughty Templar. 'She has despised me—repulsed me—reviled me; and wherefore should I offer up for her whatever of estimation I have in the opinion of others? Malvoisin, I will appear in the lists.'

He left the apartment hastily as he uttered these words, and the preceptor followed, to watch and confirm him in his resolution; for in Bois-Guilbert's fame he had himself a strong interest, expecting much advantage from his being one day at the head of the order, not to mention the preferment of which Mont-Fitchet had given him hopes, on condition he would forward the condemnation of the unfortunate Rebecca. Yet although, in combating his friend's better feelings, he possessed all the advantage which a wily, composed, selfish disposition has over a man agitated by strong and contending passions, it required all Malvoisin's art to keep Bois-Guilbert steady to the purpose he had prevailed on him to adopt. He was obliged to watch him closely to prevent his resuming his purpose of flight, to intercept his communication with the Grand Master, lest he should come to an open rupture with his superior, and to renew, from time to time, the various arguments by which he endeavoured to show that, in appearing as champion on this occasion, Bois-Guilbert, without either accelerating or ensuring the fate of Rebecca, would follow the only course by which he could save himself from degradation and disgrace.

CHAPTER XL

Shadows avaunt!—Richard's himself again.
Richard III.

WHEN the Black Knight—for it becomes necessary to resume the train of his adventures—left the trysting-tree of the generous outlaw, he held his way straight to a neighbouring religious house, of small extent and revenue, called the priory of St. Botolph, to which the wounded Ivanhoe had been removed when the castle was taken, under the guidance of the faithful Gurth and the magnanimous Wamba. It is unnecessary at present to mention what took place in the interim betwixt Wilfred and his deliverer; suffice it to say that, after long and grave communication, messengers were despatched by the prior in several directions, and that on the succeeding morning the Black Knight was about to set forth on his journey, accompanied by the jester, Wamba, who attended as his guide.

'We will meet,' he said to Ivanhoe, 'at Coningsburgh, the castle of the deceased Athelstane, since there thy father Cedric holds the funeral feast for his noble relation. I would see your Saxon kindred together, Sir Wilfred, and become better acquainted with them than heretofore. Thou also wilt meet me; and it shall be my task to reconcile thee to thy father.'

So saying, he took an affectionate farewell of Ivanhoe, who expressed an anxious desire to attend upon his deliverer. But the Black Knight would not listen to the proposal.

'Rest this day; thou wilt have scarce strength enough to travel on the next. I will have no guide with me but honest Wamba, who can play priest or fool as I shall be most in the humour.'

'And I,' said Wamba, 'will attend you with all my heart. I would fain see the feasting at the funeral of Athelstane; for, if it be not full and frequent, he will rise from the dead to rebuke cook, sewer, and cupbearer; and that were a sight worth seeing. Always, Sir Knight, I will trust your valour with making my excuse to my master Cedric, in case mine own wit should fail.'

'And how should my poor valour succeed, Sir Jester, when thy light wit halts? resolve me that.'

'Wit, Sir Knight,' replied the Jester, 'may do much. He is a quick, apprehensive knave, who sees his neighbour's blind side, and knows how to keep the lee-gage when his passions are blowing high. But valour is a sturdy fellow, that makes all split. He rows against both wind and tide, and makes way notwithstanding; and, therefore, good Sir Knight, while I take advantage of the fair weather in our noble master's temper, I will expect you to bestir yourself when it grows rough.'

'Sir Knight of the Fetterlock, since it is your pleasure so to be distinguished,' said Ivanhoe, 'I fear me you have chosen a talkative and a troublesome fool to be your guide. But he knows every path and alley in the woods as well as e'er a hunter who frequents them; and the poor knave, as thou hast partly seen, is as faithful as steel.'

'Nay,' said the Knight, 'an he have the gift of showing my road, I shall not grumble with him that he desires to make it pleasant. Fare thee well, kind Wilfred; I charge thee not to attempt to travel till to-morrow at earliest.'

So saying, he extended his hand to Ivanhoe, who

pressed it to his lips, took leave of the prior, mounted his horse, and departed, with Wamba for his companion. Ivanhoe followed them with his eyes until they were lost in the shades of the surrounding forest, and then returned into the convent.

But shortly after matin-song he requested to see the prior. The old man came in haste, and inquired anxiously after the state of his health.

'It is better,' he said, 'than my fondest hope could have anticipated; either my wound has been slighter than the effusion of blood led me to suppose, or this balsam hath wrought a wonderful cure upon it. I feel already as if I could bear my corslet; and so much the better, for thoughts pass in my mind which render me unwilling to remain here longer in inactivity.'

'Now, the saints forbid,' said the prior, 'that the son of the Saxon Cedric should leave our convent ere his wounds were healed! It were shame to our profession were we to suffer it.'

'Nor would I desire to leave your hospitable roof, venerable father,' said Ivanhoe, 'did I not feel myself able to endure the journey, and compelled to undertake it.'

'And what can have urged you to so sudden a departure?' said the prior.

'Have you never, holy father,' answered the knight, 'felt an apprehension of approaching evil, for which you in vain attempted to assign a cause? Have you never found your mind darkened, like the sunny landscape, by the sudden cloud, which augurs a coming tempest? And thinkest thou not that such impulses are deserving of attention, as being the hints of our guardian spirits that danger is impending?'

'I may not deny,' said the prior, crossing himself, 'that such things have been, and have been of Heaven; but then such communications have had a visibly useful scope and tendency. But thou,

wounded as thou art, what avails it thou shouldst
follow the steps of him whom thou couldst not aid,
were he to be assaulted?'

'Prior,' said Ivanhoe, 'thou dost mistake—I am
stout enough to exchange buffets with any who will
challenge me to such a traffic. But were it otherwise, may I not aid him, were he in danger, by other
means than by force of arms? It is but too well
known that the Saxons love not the Norman race,
and who knows what may be the issue if he break
in upon them when their hearts are irritated by the
death of Athelstane, and their heads heated by the
carousal in which they will indulge themselves?
I hold his entrance among them at such a moment
most perilous, and I am resolved to share or avert
the danger; which, that I may the better do, I
would crave of thee the use of some palfrey whose
pace may be softer than that of my *destrier*.'[1]

'Surely,' said the worthy churchman; 'you shall
have mine own ambling jennet, and I would it
ambled as easy for your sake as that of the abbot of
St. Alban's. Yet this will I say for Malkin, for so
I call her, that unless you were to borrow a ride on
the juggler's steed that paces a hornpipe amongst
the eggs, you could not go a journey on a creature
so gentle and smooth-paced. I have composed
many a homily on her back, to the edification of
my brethren of the convent and many poor Christian
souls.'

'I pray you, reverend father,' said Ivanhoe, 'let
Malkin be got ready instantly, and bid Gurth attend
me with mine arms.'

'Nay but, fair sir,' said the prior, 'I pray you to
remember that Malkin hath as little skill in arms
as her master, and that I warrant not her enduring
the sight or weight of your full panoply. O, Malkin,
I promise you, is a beast of judgment, and will contend against any undue weight. I did but borrow

[1] *Destrier*—war-horse.

the *Fructus Temporum* from the priest of St. Bee's,
and I promise you she would not stir from the gate
until I had exchanged the huge volume for my little
breviary.'

'Trust me, holy father,' said Ivanhoe, 'I will
not distress her with too much weight; and if she
calls a combat with me, it is odds but she has the
worst.'

This reply was made while Gurth was buckling
on the knight's heels a pair of large gilded spurs,
capable of convincing any restive horse that his best
safety lay in being conformable to the will of his
rider.

The deep and sharp rowels with which Ivanhoe's
heels were now armed began to make the worthy
prior repent of his courtesy, and ejaculate, 'Nay
but, fair sir, now I bethink me, my Malkin abideth
not the spur. Better it were that you tarry for the
mare of our maniciple down at the grange, which
may be had in little more than an hour, and cannot
but be tractable, in respect that she draweth much
of our winter firewood, and eateth no corn.'

'I thank you, reverend father, but will abide by
your first offer, as I see Malkin is already led forth
to the gate. Gurth shall carry mine armour; and
for the rest, rely on it that, as I will not overload
Malkin's back, she shall not overcome my patience.
And now, farewell!'

Ivanhoe now descended the stairs more hastily
and easily than his wound promised, and threw
himself upon the jennet, eager to escape the importunity of the prior, who stuck as closely to his side
as his age and fatness would permit, now singing
the praises of Malkin, now recommending caution
to the knight in managing her.

'She is at the most dangerous period for maidens
as well as mares,' said the old man, laughing at his
own jest, 'being barely in her fifteenth year.'

Ivanhoe, who had other web to weave than to

stand canvassing a palfrey's paces with its owner,
lent but a deaf ear to the prior's grave advices and
facetious jests, and having leapt on his mare, and
commanded his squire (for such Gurth now called
himself) to keep close by his side, he followed the
track of the Black Knight into the forest, while
the prior stood at the gate of the convent looking
after him, and ejaculating, 'St. Mary! how prompt
and fiery be these men of war! I would I had not
trusted Malkin to his keeping, for, crippled as I am
with the cold rheum, I am undone if aught but
good befalls her. And yet,' said he, recollecting
himself, 'as I would not spare my own old and
disabled limbs in the good cause of Old England,
so Malkin must e'en run her hazard on the same
venture; and it may be they will think our poor
house worthy of some munificent guerdon; or, it
may be, they will send the old prior a pacing nag.
And if they do none of these, as great men will
forget little men's service, truly I shall hold me
well repaid in having done that which is right.
And it is now well-nigh the fitting time to summon
the brethren to breakfast in the refectory. Ah! I
doubt they obey that call more cheerily than the
bells for primes and matins.'

So the prior of St. Botolph's hobbled back again
into the refectory, to preside over the stock-fish
and ale which were just serving out for the friars'
breakfast. Pursy and important, he sat him down
at the table, and many a dark word he threw out
of benefits to be expected to the convent, and high
deeds of service done by himself, which at another
season would have attracted observation. But as
the stock-fish was highly salted, and the ale reasonably powerful, the jaws of the brethren were too
anxiously employed to admit of their making much
use of their ears; nor do we read of any of the
fraternity who was tempted to speculate upon the
mysterious hints of their superior, except Father

Diggory, who was severely afflicted by the tooth-
ache, so that he could only eat on one side of his
jaws.

In the meantime, the Black Champion and his
guide were pacing at their leisure through the
recesses of the forest; the good Knight whiles
humming to himself the lay of some enamoured
troubadour, sometimes encouraging by questions
the prating disposition of his attendant, so that
their dialogue formed a whimsical mixture of song
and jest, of which we would fain give our readers
some idea. You are then to imagine this Knight,
such as we have already described him, strong of
person, tall, broad-shouldered, and large of bone,
mounted on his mighty black charger, which seemed
made on purpose to bear his weight, so easily he
paced forward under it, having the visor of his
helmet raised, in order to admit freedom of breath,
yet keeping the beaver, or under part, closed, so
that his features could be but imperfectly distinguished. But his ruddy, embrowned cheek-bones
could be plainly seen, and the large and bright blue
eyes, that flashed from under the dark shade of the
raised visor; and the whole gesture and look of
the champion expressed careless gaiety and fearless
confidence— a mind which was unapt to apprehend
danger, and prompt to defy it when most imminent,
yet with whom danger was a familiar thought, as
with one whose trade was war and adventure.
The Jester wore his usual fantastic habit, but
late accidents had led him to adopt a good cutting
falchion, instead of his wooden sword, with a targe
to match it; of both which weapons he had, notwithstanding his profession, shown himself a skilful
master during the storming of Torquilstone. Indeed, the infirmity of Wamba's brain consisted
chiefly in a kind of impatient irritability, which suffered him not long to remain quiet in any posture,

or adhere to any certain train of ideas, although he
was for a few minutes alert enough in performing
any immediate task, or in apprehending any immediate topic.   On horseback, therefore, he was perpetually swinging himself backwards and forwards,
now on the horse's ears, then anon on the very
rump of the animal ; now hanging both his legs on
one side, and now sitting with his face to the tail,
moping, mowing, and making a thousand apish
gestures, until his palfrey took his freaks so much
to heart as fairly to lay him at his length on the
green grass—an incident which greatly amused the
Knight, but compelled his companion to ride more
steadily thereafter.

At the point of their journey at which we take
them up, this joyous pair were engaged in singing
a virelai, as it was called, in which the clown bore
a mellow burden to the better-instructed Knight of
the Fetterlock.   And thus run the ditty :—

> Anna Marie, love, up is the sun,
> Anna Marie, love, morn is begun,
> Mists are dispersing, love, birds singing free,
> Up in the morning, love, Anna Marie.
> Anna Marie, love, up in the morn,
> The hunter is winding blythe sounds on his horn,
> The echo rings merry from rock and from tree,
> 'Tis time to arouse thee, love, Anna Marie.

WAMBA.

> O Tybalt, love, Tybalt, awake me not yet,
> Around my soft pillow while softer dreams flit,
> For what are the joys that in waking we prove,
> Compared with these visions, O, Tybalt, my love?
> Let the birds to the rise of the mist carol shrill,
> Let the hunter blow out his loud horn on the hill,
> Softer sounds, softer pleasures, in slumber I prove,—
> But think not I dreamt of thee, Tybalt, my love.

' A dainty song,' said Wamba, when they had
finished their carol, ' and I swear by my bauble, a
pretty moral !   I used to sing it with Gurth, once

my playfellow, and now, by the grace of God and
his master, no less than a freeman ; and we once
came by the cudgel for being so entranced by the
melody that we lay in bed two hours after sunrise,
singing the ditty betwixt sleeping and waking : my
bones ache at thinking of the tune ever since.
Nevertheless, I have played the part of Anna Marie
to please you, fair sir.'

The Jester next struck into another carol, a sort
of comic ditty, to which the Knight, catching up
the tune, replied in the like manner.

KNIGHT and WAMBA.

There came three merry men from south, west, and north,
  Ever more sing the roundelay ;
To win the Widow of Wycombe forth,
  And where was the widow might say them nay ?

The first was a knight, and from Tynedale he came,
  Ever more sing the roundelay ;
And his fathers, God save us, were men of great fame,
  And where was the widow might say him nay ?

Of his father the laird, of his uncle the squire,
  He boasted in rhyme and in roundelay ;
She bade him go bask by his sea-coal fire,
  For she was the widow would say him nay.

WAMBA.

The next that came forth, swore by blood and by nails,
  Merrily sing the roundelay ;
Hur's a gentleman, God wot, and hur's lineage was of Wales,
  And where was the widow might say him nay ?

Sir David ap Morgan ap Griffith ap Hugh
  Ap Tudor ap Rhice, quoth his roundelay ;
She said that one widow for so many was too few,
  And she bade the Welshman wend his way.

But then next came a yeoman, a yeoman of Kent,
  Jollily singing his roundelay ;
He spoke to the widow of living and rent,
  And where was the widow could say him nay ?

Both.

So the knight and the squire were both left in the mire,
    There for to sing their roundelay ;
For a yeoman of Kent, with his yearly rent,
    There never was a widow could say him nay.

'I would, Wamba,' said the Knight, 'that our
host of the trysting-tree, or the jolly Friar, his
chaplain, heard this thy ditty in praise of our bluff
yeoman.'

'So would not I,' said Wamba, 'but for the horn
that hangs at your baldric.'

'Ay,' said the Knight, 'this is a pledge of
Locksley's goodwill, though I am not like to need
it. Three mots on this bugle will, I am assured,
bring round, at our need, a jolly band of yonder
honest yeomen.'

'I would say, Heaven forefend,' said the Jester,
'were it not that that fair gift is a pledge they
would let us pass peaceably.'

'Why, what meanest thou?' said the Knight ;
'thinkest thou that but for this pledge of fellowship
they would assault us?'

'Nay, for me I say nothing,' said Wamba ; 'for
green trees have ears as well as stone walls. But
canst thou construe me this, Sir Knight? When is
thy wine-pitcher and thy purse better empty than
full?'

'Why, never, I think,' replied the Knight.

'Thou never deservest to have a full one in thy
hand, for so simple an answer! Thou hadst best
empty thy pitcher ere thou pass it to a Saxon, and
leave thy money at home ere thou walk in the
greenwood.'

'You hold our friends for robbers, then?' said
the Knight of the Fetterlock.

'You hear me not say so, fair sir,' said Wamba.
'It may relieve a man's steed to take off his mail
when he hath a long journey to make ; and, certes,
it may do good to the rider's soul to ease him of

that which is the root of evil; therefore will I give no hard names to those who do such services. Only I would wish my mail at home, and my purse in my chamber, when I meet with these good fellows, because it might save them some trouble.'

'*We* are bound to pray for them, my friend, notwithstanding the fair character thou dost afford them.'

'Pray for them with all my heart,' said Wamba; 'but in the town, not in the greenwood, like the abbot of St. Bee's, whom they caused to say mass with an old hollow oak-tree for his stall.'

'Say as thou list, Wamba,' replied the Knight, 'these yeomen did thy master Cedric yeomanly service at Torquilstone.'

'Ay, truly,' answered Wamba; 'but that was in the fashion of their trade with Heaven.'

'Their trade, Wamba! how mean you by that?' replied his companion.

'Marry, thus,' said the Jester. 'They make up a balanced account with Heaven, as our old cellarer used to call his ciphering, as fair as Isaac the Jew keeps with his debtors, and, like him, give out a very little, and take large credit for doing so; reckoning, doubtless, on their own behalf the sevenfold usury which the blessed text hath promised to charitable loans.'

'Give me an example of your meaning, Wamba; I know nothing of ciphers or rates of usage,' answered the Knight.

'Why,' said Wamba, 'an your valour be so dull, you will please to learn that those honest fellows balance a good deed with one not quite so laudable, as a crown given to a begging friar with an hundred byzants taken from a fat abbot, or a wench kissed in the greenwood with the relief of a poor widow.'

'Which of these was the good deed, which was the felony?' interrupted the Knight.

'A good gibe! a good gibe!' said Wamba;

'keeping witty company sharpeneth the apprehension. You said nothing so well, Sir Knight, I will be sworn, when you held drunken vespers with the bluff hermit. But to go on.—The merry men of the forest set off the building of a cottage with the burning of a castle, the thatching of a choir against the robbing of a church, the setting free a poor prisoner against the murder of a proud sheriff, or, to come nearer to our point, the deliverance of a Saxon franklin against the burning alive of a Norman baron. Gentle thieves they are, in short, and courteous robbers; but it is ever the luckiest to meet with them when they are at the worst.'

'How so, Wamba?' said the Knight.

'Why, then they have some compunction, and are for making up matters with Heaven. But when they have struck an even balance, Heaven help them with whom they next open the account! The travellers who first met them after their good service at Torquilstone would have a woeful flaying. And yet,' said Wamba, coming close up to the Knight's side, 'there be companions who are far more dangerous for travellers to meet than yonder outlaws.'

'And who may they be, for you have neither bears nor wolves, I trow?' said the Knight.

'Marry, sir, but we have Malvoisin's men-at-arms,' said Wamba; 'and let me tell you that, in time of civil war, a halfscore of these is worth a band of wolves at any time. They are now expecting their harvest, and are reinforced with the soldiers that escaped from Torquilstone; so that, should we meet with a band of them, we are like to pay for our feats of arms. Now, I pray you, Sir Knight, what would you do if we met two of them?'

'Pin the villains to the earth with my lance, Wamba, if they offered us any impediment.'

'But what if there were four of them?'

'They should drink of the same cup,' answered the Knight.

'What if six,' continued Wamba, 'and we as we now are, barely two; would you not remember Locksley's horn?'

'What! sound for aid,' exclaimed the Knight, 'against a score of such rascaille as these, whom one good knight could drive before him, as the wind drives the withered leaves?'

'Nay, then,' said Wamba, 'I will pray you for a close sight of that same horn that hath so powerful a breath.'

The Knight undid the clasp of the baldric, and indulged his fellow-traveller, who immediately hung the bugle round his own neck.

'Tra-lira-la,' said he, whistling the notes; 'nay, I know my gamut as well as another.'

'How mean you, knave?' said the Knight; 'restore me the bugle.'

'Content you, Sir Knight, it is in safe keeping. When valour and folly travel, folly should bear the horn, because she can blow the best.'

'Nay but, rogue,' said the Black Knight, 'this exceedeth thy license. Beware ye tamper not with my patience.'

'Urge me not with violence, Sir Knight,' said the Jester, keeping at a distance from the impatient champion, 'or folly will show a clean pair of heels, and leave valour to find out his way through the wood as best he may.'

'Nay, thou hast hit me there,' said the Knight; 'and, sooth to say, I have little time to jangle with thee. Keep the horn an thou wilt, but let us proceed on our journey.'

'You will not harm me, then?' said Wamba.

'I tell thee no, thou knave!'

'Ay, but pledge me your knightly word for it,' continued Wamba, as he approached with great caution.

'My knightly word I pledge; only come on with thy foolish self.'

'Nay, then, valour and folly are once more boon companions,' said the Jester, coming up frankly to the Knight's side; 'but, in truth, I love not such buffets as that you bestowed on the burly Friar, when his holiness rolled on the green like a king of the nine-pins. And now that folly wears the horn, let valour rouse himself and shake his mane; for, if I mistake not, there are company in yonder brake that are on the look-out for us.'

'What makes thee judge so?' said the Knight.

'Because I have twice or thrice noticed the glance of a morrion from amongst the green leaves. Had they been honest men, they had kept the path. But yonder thicket is a choice chapel for the clerks of St. Nicholas.'

'By my faith,' said the Knight, closing his visor, 'I think thou be'st in the right on't.'

And in good time did he close it, for three arrows flew at the same instant from the suspected spot against his head and breast, one of which would have penetrated to the brain, had it not been turned aside by the steel visor. The other two were averted by the gorget, and by the shield which hung around his neck.

'Thanks, trusty armourer,' said the Knight. 'Wamba, let us close with them,' and he rode straight to the thicket. He was met by six or seven men-at-arms, who ran against him with their lances at full career. Three of the weapons struck against him, and splintered with as little effect as if they had been driven against a tower of steel. The Black Knight's eyes seemed to flash fire even through the aperture of his visor. He raised himself in his stirrups with an air of inexpressible dignity, and exclaimed, 'What means this, my masters!' The men made no other reply than by drawing their swords and attacking him on every side, crying, 'Die, tyrant!'

'Ha! St. Edward! Ha! St. George!' said the

Black Knight, striking down a man at every invocation; 'have we traitors here?'

His opponents, desperate as they were, bore back from an arm which carried death in every blow, and it seemed as if the terror of his single strength was about to gain the battle against such odds, when a knight, in blue armour, who had hitherto kept himself behind the other assailants, spurred forward with his lance, and taking aim, not at the rider but at the steed, wounded the noble animal mortally.

'That was a felon stroke!' exclaimed the Black Knight, as the steed fell to the earth, bearing his rider along with him.

And at this moment Wamba winded the bugle, for the whole had passed so speedily that he had not time to do so sooner. The sudden sound made the murderers bear back once more, and Wamba, though so imperfectly weaponed, did not hesitate to rush in and assist the Black Knight to rise.

'Shame on ye, false cowards!' exclaimed he in the blue harness, who seemed to lead the assailants, 'do ye fly from the empty blast of a horn blown by a jester?'

Animated by his words, they attacked the Black Knight anew, whose best refuge was now to place his back against an oak, and defend himself with his sword. The felon knight, who had taken another spear, watching the moment when his formidable antagonist was most closely pressed, galloped against him in hopes to nail him with his lance against the tree, when his purpose was again intercepted by Wamba. The Jester, making up by agility the want of strength, and little noticed by the men-at-arms, who were busied in their more important object, hovered on the skirts of the fight, and effectually checked the fatal career of the Blue Knight, by hamstringing his horse with a stroke of his sword. Horse and man went to the ground; yet the situation of the Knight of the Fetterlock

continued very precarious, as he was pressed close
by several men completely armed, and began to be
fatigued by the violent exertions necessary to defend
himself on so many points at nearly the same
moment, when a grey-goose shaft suddenly stretched
on the earth one of the most formidable of his
assailants, and a band of yeomen broke forth from
the glade, headed by Locksley and the jovial Friar,
who, taking ready and effectual part in the fray,
soon disposed of the ruffians, all of whom lay on
the spot dead or mortally wounded. The Black
Knight thanked his deliverers with a dignity they
had not observed in his former bearing, which
hitherto had seemed rather that of a blunt, bold
soldier than of a person of exalted rank.

'It concerns me much,' he said, 'even before I
express my full gratitude to my ready friends, to
discover, if I may, who have been my unprovoked
enemies. Open the visor of that Blue Knight,
Wamba, who seems the chief of these villains.'

The Jester instantly made up to the leader of the
assassins, who, bruised by his fall, and entangled
under the wounded steed, lay incapable either of
flight or resistance.

'Come, valiant sir,' said Wamba, 'I must be
your armourer as well as your equerry. I have
dismounted you, and now I will unhelm you.'

So saying, with no very gentle hand he undid the
helmet of the Blue Knight, which, rolling to a
distance on the grass, displayed to the Knight of the
Fetterlock grizzled locks, and a countenance he did
not expect to have seen under such circumstances.

'Waldemar Fitzurse!' he said in astonishment:
'what could urge one of thy rank and seeming
worth to so foul an undertaking?'

'Richard,' said the captive knight, looking up to
him, 'thou knowest little of mankind, if thou
knowest not to what ambition and revenge can lead
every child of Adam.'

'Revenge! answered the Black Knight; 'I never wronged thee. On me thou hast nought to revenge.'

'My daughter, Richard, whose alliance thou didst scorn—was that no injury to a Norman, whose blood is noble as thine own?'

'Thy daughter!' replied the Black Knight. 'A proper cause of enmity, and followed up to a bloody issue! Stand back, my masters, I would speak to him alone. And now, Waldemar Fitzurse, say me the truth: confess who set thee on this traitorous deed.'

'Thy father's son,' answered Waldemar, 'who, in so doing, did but avenge on thee thy disobedience to thy father.'

Richard's eyes sparkled with indignation, but his better nature overcame it. He pressed his hand against his brow, and remained an instant gazing on the face of the humbled baron, in whose features pride was contending with shame.

'Thou dost not ask thy life, Waldemar?' said the King.

'He that is in the lion's clutch,' answered Fitzurse, 'knows it were needless.'

'Take it, then, unasked,' said Richard; 'the lion preys not on prostrate carcasses. Take thy life, but with this condition, that in three days thou shalt leave England, and go to hide thine infamy in thy Norman castle, and that thou wilt never mention the name of John of Anjou as connected with thy felony. If thou art found on English ground after the space I have allotted thee, thou diest; or if thou breathest aught that can attaint the honour of my house, by St. George! not the altar itself shall be a sanctuary. I will hang thee out to feed the ravens from the very pinnacle of thine own castle. Let this knight have a steed, Locksley, for I see your yeomen have caught those which were running loose, and let him depart unharmed.'

'But that I judge I listen to a voice whose be-nests must not be disputed,' answered the yeoman, 'I would send a shaft after the skulking villain that should spare him the labour of a long journey.'

'Thou bearest an English heart, Locksley,' said the Black Knight, 'and well dost judge thou art the more bound to obey my behest: I am Richard of England!'

At these words, pronounced in a tone of majesty suited to the high rank, and no less distinguished character, of Cœur-de-Lion, the yeomen at once kneeled down before him, and at the same time tendered their allegiance, and implored pardon for their offences.

'Rise, my friends,' said Richard, in a gracious tone, looking on them with a countenance in which his habitual good-humour had already conquered the blaze of hasty resentment, and whose features retained no mark of the late desperate conflict, ex-cepting the flush arising from exertion—'arise,' he said, 'my friends! Your misdemeanours, whether in forest or field, have been atoned by the loyal services you rendered my distressed subjects before the walls of Torquilstone, and the rescue you have this day afforded to your sovereign. Arise, my liegemen, and be good subjects in future. And thou, brave Locksley——'

'Call me no longer Locksley, my Liege, but know me under the name which, I fear, fame hath blown too widely not to have reached even your royal ears: I am Robin Hood of Sherwood Forest.'

'King of outlaws, and Prince of good fellows!' said the King, 'who hath not heard a name that has been borne as far as Palestine? But be assured, brave outlaw, that no deed done in our absence, and in the turbulent times to which it hath given rise, shall be remembered to thy disadvantage.'

'True says the proverb,' said Wamba, interposing

his word, but with some abatement of his usual petulance—

> 'When the cat is away,
> The mice will play.'

'What, Wamba, art thou there?' said Richard; 'I have been so long of hearing thy voice, I thought thou hadst taken flight.'

'I take flight!' said Wamba; 'when do you ever find folly separated from valour? There lies the trophy of my sword, that good grey gelding, whom I heartily wish upon his legs again, conditioning his master lay there houghed in his place. It is true, I gave a little ground at first, for a motley jacket does not brook lance-heads as a steel doublet will. But if I fought not at sword's point, you will grant me that I sounded the onset.'

'And to good purpose, honest Wamba,' replied the King. 'Thy good service shall not be forgotten.'

'*Confiteor! confiteor!*' exclaimed, in a submissive tone, a voice near the King's side; 'my Latin will carry me no farther, but I confess my deadly treason, and pray leave to have absolution before I am led to execution!'

Richard looked around, and beheld the jovial Friar on his knees, telling his rosary, while his quarter-staff, which had not been idle during the skirmish, lay on the grass beside him. His countenance was gathered so as he thought might best express the most profound contrition, his eyes being turned up, and the corners of his mouth drawn down, as Wamba expressed it, like the tassels at the mouth of a purse. Yet this demure affectation of extreme penitence was whimsically belied by a ludicrous meaning which lurked in his huge features, and seemed to pronounce his fear and repentance alike hypocritical.

'For what art thou cast down, mad priest?' said Richard: 'art thou afraid thy diocesan should

learn how truly thou dost serve Our Lady and St.
Dunstan? Tush, man! fear it not; Richard of
England betrays no secrets that pass over the
flagon.'

'Nay, most gracious sovereign,' answered the
hermit, well known to the curious in penny histories
of Robin Hood by the name of Friar Tuck, 'it is
not the crosier I fear, but the sceptre. Alas! that
my sacrilegious fist should ever have been applied
to the ear of the Lord's anointed!'

'Ha! ha!' said Richard, 'sits the wind there?
In truth, I had forgotten the buffet, though mine
ear sung after it for a whole day. But if the cuff
was fairly given, I will be judged by the good men
around, if it was not as well repaid; or, if thou
thinkest I still owe thee aught, and will stand forth
for another counterbuff——'

'By no means,' replied Friar Tuck, 'I had mine
own returned, and with usury: may your Majesty
ever pay your debts as fully!'

'If I could do so with cuffs,' said the King, 'my
creditors should have little reason to complain of
an empty exchequer.'

'And yet,' said the Friar, resuming his demure,
hypocritical countenance, 'I know not what penance
I ought to perform for that most sacrilegious
blow——!'

'Speak no more of it, brother,' said the King;
'after having stood so many cuffs from paynims and
misbelievers, I were void of reason to quarrel with
the buffet of a clerk so holy as he of Copmanhurst.
Yet, mine honest Friar, I think it would be best
both for the church and thyself that I should procure a license to unfrock thee, and retain thee as a
yeoman of our guard, serving in care of our person,
as formerly in attendance upon the altar of St.
Dunstan.'

'My Liege,' said the Friar, 'I humbly crave your
pardon; and you would readily grant my excuse,

did you but know how the sin of laziness has beset
me. St. Dunstan—may he be gracious to us!—
stands quiet in his niche, though I should forget
my orisons in killing a fat buck; I stay out of my
cell sometimes a night, doing I wot not what—St.
Dunstan never complains—a quiet master he is,
and a peaceful, as ever was made of wood. But to
be a yeoman in attendance on my sovereign the
King—the honour is great, doubtless—yet, if I
were but to step aside to comfort a widow in one
corner, or to kill a deer in another, it would be,
"Where is the dog priest?" says one. "Who
has seen the accursed Tuck?" says another. "The
unfrocked villain destroys more venison than half
the country besides," says one keeper; "And is
hunting after every shy doe in the country!" quoth
a second. In fine, good my Liege, I pray you to
leave me as you found me; or, if in aught you
desire to extend your benevolence to me, that I
may be considered as the poor clerk of St. Dunstan's
cell in Copmanhurst, to whom any small donation
will be most thankfully acceptable.'

'I understand thee,' said the King, 'and the
holy clerk shall have a grant of vert and venison
in my woods of Wharncliffe. Mark, however, I
will but assign thee three bucks every season; but
if that do not prove an apology for thy slaying
thirty, I am no Christian knight nor true king.'

'Your Grace may be well assured,' said the Friar,
'that, with the grace of St. Dunstan, I shall find
the way of multiplying your most bounteous gift.'

'I nothing doubt it, good brother,' said the
King; 'and as venison is but dry food, our cellarer
shall have orders to deliver to thee a butt of sack,
a runlet of Malvoisie, and three hogsheads of ale
of the first strike, yearly. If that will not quench
thy thirst, thou must come to court, and become
acquainted with my butler.'

'But for St. Dunstan?' said the Friar——

'A cope, a stole, and an altar-cloth shalt thou also have,' continued the King, crossing himself. 'But we may not turn our game into earnest, lest God punish us for thinking more on our follies than on His honour and worship.'

'I will answer for my patron,' said the priest, joyously.

'Answer for thyself, Friar,' said King Richard, something sternly; but immediately stretching out his hand to the hermit, the latter, somewhat abashed, bent his knee, and saluted it. 'Thou dost less honour to my extended palm than to my clenched fist,' said the monarch; 'thou didst only kneel to the one, and to the other didst prostrate thyself.'

But the Friar, afraid perhaps of again giving offence by continuing the conversation in too jocose a style—a false step to be particularly guarded against by those who converse with monarchs—bowed profoundly, and fell into the rear.

At the same time, two additional personages appeared on the scene.

CHAPTER XLI

All hail to the lordlings of high degree,
Who live not more happy, though greater than we!
      Our pastimes to see,
      Under every green tree,
In all the gay woodland, right welcome ye be.
                                        MACDONALD.

THE new-comers were Wilfred of Ivanhoe, on the prior of Botolph's palfrey, and Gurth, who attended him, on the knight's own war-horse. The astonishment of Ivanhoe was beyond bounds when he saw his master besprinkled with blood, and six or seven dead bodies lying around in the little glade in which the battle had taken place. Nor was he less surprised to see Richard surrounded by so many silvan attendants, the outlaws, as they seemed to be, of the forest, and a perilous retinue therefore for a prince. He hesitated whether to address the King as the Black Knight-errant, or in what other manner to demean himself towards him. Richard saw his embarrassment.

'Fear not, Wilfred,' he said, 'to address Richard Plantagenet as himself, since thou seest him in the company of true English hearts, although it may be they have been urged a few steps aside by warm English blood.'

'Sir Wilfred of Ivanhoe,' said the gallant outlaw, stepping forward, 'my assurances can add nothing to those of our sovereign; yet, let me say somewhat proudly, that of men who have suffered much, he hath not truer subjects than those who now stand around him.'

'I cannot doubt it, brave man,' said Wilfred, 'since thou art of the number. But what mean these marks of death and danger—these slain men, and the bloody armour of my Prince?'

'Treason hath been with us, Ivanhoe,' said the King; 'but, thanks to these brave men, treason hath met its meed. But, now I bethink me, thou too art a traitor,' said Richard, smiling—'a most disobedient traitor; for were not our orders positive that thou shouldst repose thyself at St. Botolph's until thy wound was healed?'

'It is healed,' said Ivanhoe—'it is not of more consequence than the scratch of a bodkin. But why—oh why, noble Prince, will you thus vex the hearts of your faithful servants, and expose your life by lonely journeys and rash adventures, as if it were of no more value than that of a mere knight-errant, who has no interest on earth but what lance and sword may procure him?'

'And Richard Plantagenet,' said the King, 'desires no more fame than his good lance and sword may acquire him; and Richard Plantagenet is prouder of achieving an adventure, with only his good sword, and his good arm to speed, than if he led to battle an host of an hundred thousand armed men.'

'But your kingdom, my Liege,' said Ivanhoe— 'your kingdom is threatened with dissolution and civil war; your subjects menaced with every species of evil, if deprived of their sovereign in some of those dangers which it is your daily pleasure to incur, and from which you have but this moment narrowly escaped.'

'Ho! ho! my kingdom and my subjects!' answered Richard, impatiently; 'I tell thee, Sir Wilfred, the best of them are most willing to repay my follies in kind. For example, my very faithful servant, Wilfred of Ivanhoe, will not obey my positive commands, and yet reads his king a homily, because he does not walk exactly by his advice. Which of us has most reason to upbraid the other? Yet forgive me, my faithful Wilfred. The time I have spent, and am yet to spend, in concealment is, as I explained to thee at St. Botolph's, necessary to give my friends and faithful nobles time to assemble their forces, that, when Richard's return is announced, he should be at the head of such a force as enemies shall tremble to face, and thus subdue the meditated treason, without even unsheathing a sword. Estoteville and Bohun will not be strong enough to move forward to York for twenty-four hours. I must have news of Salisbury from the south, and of Beauchamp in Warwickshire, and of Multon and Percy in the north. The Chancellor must make sure of London. Too sudden an appearance would subject me to dangers other than my lance and sword, though backed by the bow of bold Robin, or the quarter-staff of Friar Tuck, and the horn of the sage Wamba, may be able to rescue me from.'

Wilfred bowed in submission, well knowing how vain it was to contend with the wild spirit of chivalry which so often impelled his master upon dangers which he might easily have avoided, or rather, which it was unpardonable in him to have sought out. The young knight sighed, therefore, and held his peace; while Richard, rejoiced at having silenced his counsellor, though his heart acknowledged the justice of the charge he had brought against him, went on in conversation with Robin Hood. 'King of outlaws,' he said, 'have you no refreshment to offer to your brother sovereign? for these dead knaves have found me both in exercise and appetite.'

'In troth,' replied the outlaw, 'for I scorn to lie to your Grace, our larder is chiefly supplied with——' He stopped, and was somewhat embarrassed.

'With venison, I suppose?' said Richard, gaily;
'better food at need there can be none; and truly,
if a king will not remain at home and slay his own
game, methinks he should not brawl too loud if he
finds it killed to his hand.'

'If your Grace, then,' said Robin, 'will again
honour with your presence one of Robin Hood's
places of rendezvous, the venison shall not be lack-
ing; and a stoup of ale, and it may be a cup of
reasonably good wine, to relish it withal.'

The outlaw accordingly led the way, followed by
the buxom monarch, more happy, probably, in this
chance meeting with Robin Hood and his foresters
than he would have been in again assuming his
royal state, and presiding over a splendid circle of
peers and nobles. Novelty in society and adventure
were the zest of life to Richard Cœur-de-Lion, and
it had its highest relish when enhanced by dangers
encountered and surmounted. In the lion-hearted
king, the brilliant, but useless, character of a knight
of romance was in a great measure realised and
revived; and the personal glory which he acquired
by his own deeds of arms was far more dear to his
excited imagination than that which a course of
policy and wisdom would have spread around his
government. Accordingly, his reign was like the
course of a brilliant and rapid meteor, which shoots
along the face of heaven, shedding around an unnecessary and portentous light, which is instantly
swallowed up by universal darkness; his feats of
chivalry furnishing themes for bards and minstrels,
but affording none of those solid benefits to his
country on which history loves to pause, and hold
up as an example to posterity. But in his present
company Richard showed to the greatest imaginable
advantage. He was gay, good-humoured, and fond
of manhood in every rank of life.

Beneath a huge oak-tree the silvan repast was
hastily prepared for the King of England, sur-

rounded by men outlaws to his government, but who now formed his court and his guard. As the flagon went round, the rough foresters soon lost their awe for the presence of Majesty. The song and the jest were exchanged, the stories of former deeds were told with advantage; and at length, and while boasting of their successful infraction of the laws, no one recollected they were speaking in presence of their natural guardian. The merry king, nothing heeding his dignity any more than his company, laughed, quaffed, and jested among the jolly band. The natural and rough sense of Robin Hood led him to be desirous that the scene should be closed ere anything should occur to disturb its harmony, the more especially that he observed Ivanhoe's brow clouded with anxiety. 'We are honoured,' he said to Ivanhoe, apart, 'by the presence of our gallant sovereign; yet I would not that he dallied with time which the circumstances of his kingdom may render precious.'

'It is well and wisely spoken, brave Robin Hood,' said Wilfred, apart; 'and know, moreover, that they who jest with Majesty, even in its gayest mood, are but toying with the lion's whelp, which, on slight provocation, uses both fangs and claws.'

'You have touched the very cause of my fear,' said the outlaw. 'My men are rough by practice and nature; the King is hasty as well as good-humoured; nor know I how soon cause of offence may arise, or how warmly it may be received; it is time this revel were broken off.'

'It must be by your management then, gallant yeoman,' said Ivanhoe; 'for each hint I have essayed to give him serves only to induce him to prolong it.'

'Must I so soon risk the pardon and favour of my sovereign?' said Robin Hood, pausing for an instant; 'but, by St. Christopher, it shall be so. I were undeserving his grace did I not peril it for his good. Here, Scathlock, get thee behind yonder thicket, and wind me a Norman blast on thy bugle, and without an instant's delay, on peril of your life.'

Scathlock obeyed his captain, and in less than five minutes the revellers were startled by the sound of his horn.

'It is the bugle of Malvoisin,' said the Miller, starting to his feet, and seizing his bow. The Friar dropped the flagon, and grasped his quarter-staff. Wamba stopt short in the midst of a jest, and betook himself to sword and target. All the others stood to their weapons.

Men of their precarious course of life change readily from the banquet to the battle; and to Richard the exchange seemed but a succession of pleasure. He called for his helmet and the most cumbrous parts of his armour, which he had laid aside; and while Gurth was putting them on, he laid his strict injunctions on Wilfred, under pain of his highest displeasure, not to engage in the skirmish which he supposed was approaching.

'Thou hast fought for me a hundred times, Wilfred, and I have seen it. Thou shalt this day look on, and see how Richard will fight for his friend and liegeman.'

In the meantime, Robin Hood had sent off several of his followers in different directions, as if to reconnoitre the enemy; and when he saw the company effectually broken up, he approached Richard, who was now completely armed, and, kneeling down on one knee, craved pardon of his sovereign.

'For what, good yeoman?' said Richard, somewhat impatiently. 'Have we not already granted thee a full pardon for all transgressions? Thinkest thou our word is a feather, to be blown backward and forward between us? Thou canst not have had time to commit any new offence since that time?'

'Ay, but I have though,' answered the yeoman,

'if it be an offence to deceive my prince for his own advantage. The bugle you have heard was none of Malvoisin's, but blown by my direction, to break off the banquet, lest it trenched upon hours of dearer import than to be thus dallied with.'

He then rose from his knee, folded his arms on his bosom, and, in a manner rather respectful than submissive, awaited the answer of the King, like one who is conscious he may have given offence, yet is confident in the rectitude of his motive. The blood rushed in anger to the countenance of Richard; but it was the first transient emotion, and his sense of justice instantly subdued it.

'The King of Sherwood,' he said, 'grudges his venison and his wine-flask to the King of England! It is well, bold Robin! but when you come to see me in merry London, I trust to be a less niggard host. Thou art right, however, good fellow. Let us therefore to horse and away. Wilfred has been impatient this hour. Tell me, bold Robin, hast thou never a friend in thy band, who, not content with advising, will needs direct thy motions, and look miserable when thou dost presume to act for thyself?'

'Such a one,' said Robin, 'is my lieutenant, Little John, who is even now absent on an expedition as far as the borders of Scotland; and I will own to your Majesty that I am sometimes displeased by the freedom of his counsels; but, when I think twice, I cannot be long angry with one who can have no motive for his anxiety save zeal for his master's service.'

'Thou art right, good yeoman,' answered Richard; 'and if I had Ivanhoe, on the one hand, to give grave advice, and recommend it by the sad gravity of his brow, and thee, on the other, to trick me into what thou thinkest my own good, I should have as little the freedom of mine own will as any king in Christendom or Heathenesse. But come,

sirs, let us merrily on to Coningsburgh, and think
no more on't.'

Robin Hood assured them that he had detached
a party in the direction of the road they were to
pass, who would not fail to discover and apprise
them of any secret ambuscade; and that he had
little doubt they would find the ways secure, or,
if otherwise, would receive such timely notice of
the danger as would enable them to fall back on a
strong troop of archers, with which he himself
proposed to follow on the same route.

The wise and attentive precautions adopted for
his safety touched Richard's feelings, and removed
any slight grudge which he might retain on account
of the deception the outlaw captain had practised
upon him. He once more extended his hand to
Robin Hood, assured him of his full pardon and
future favour, as well as his firm resolution to
restrain the tyrannical exercise of the forest rights
and other oppressive laws, by which so many English yeomen were driven into a state of rebellion.
But Richard's good intentions towards the bold
outlaw were frustrated by the King's untimely
death; and the Charter of the Forest was extorted
from the unwilling hands of King John when he
succeeded to his heroic brother. As for the rest
of Robin Hood's career, as well as the tale of his
treacherous death, they are to be found in those
black-letter garlands, once sold at the low and easy
rate of one halfpenny—

Now cheaply purchased at their weight in gold.

The outlaw's opinion proved true; and the King,
attended by Ivanhoe, Gurth, and Wamba, arrived
without any interruption within view of the Castle
of Coningsburgh, while the sun was yet in the
horizon.

There are few more beautiful or striking scenes
in England than are presented by the vicinity of

this ancient Saxon fortress. The soft and gentle
river Don sweeps through an amphitheatre, in which
cultivation is richly blended with woodland, and on
a mount ascending from the river, well defended by
walls and ditches, rises this ancient edifice, which,
as its Saxon name implies, was, previous to the
Conquest, a royal residence of the kings of England.
The outer walls have probably been added by the
Normans, but the inner keep bears token of very
great antiquity. It is situated on a mount at one
angle of the inner court, and forms a complete
circle of perhaps twenty-five feet in diameter. The
wall is of immense thickness, and is propped or
defended by six huge external buttresses, which
project from the circle, and rise up against the sides
of the tower as if to strengthen or to support it.
These massive buttresses are solid when they arise
from the foundation, and a good way higher up;
but are hollowed out towards the top, and terminate
in a sort of turrets communicating with the interior
of the keep itself. The distant appearance of this
huge building, with these singular accompaniments,
is as interesting to the lovers of the picturesque as
the interior of the castle is to the eager antiquary,
whose imagination it carries back to the days of the
Heptarchy. A barrow, in the vicinity of the castle,
is pointed out as the tomb of the memorable Hengist; and various monuments, of great antiquity
and curiosity, are shown in the neighbouring
churchyard.

When Cœur-de-Lion and his retinue approached
this rude yet stately building, it was not, as at
present, surrounded by external fortifications. The
Saxon architect had exhausted his art in rendering
the main keep defensible, and there was no other
circumvallation than a rude barrier of palisades.

A huge black banner, which floated from the top
of the tower, announced that the obsequies of the

late owner were still in the act of being solemnised. It bore no emblem of the deceased's birth or quality, for armorial bearings were then a novelty among the Norman chivalry themselves, and were totally unknown to the Saxons. But above the gate was another banner, on which the figure of a white horse, rudely painted, indicated the nation and rank of the deceased, by the well-known symbol of Hengist and his Saxon warriors.

All around the castle was a scene of busy commotion ; for such funeral banquets were times of general and profuse hospitality, which not only every one who could claim the most distant connexion with the deceased, but all passengers whatsoever, were invited to partake. The wealth and consequence of the deceased Athelstane occasioned this custom to be observed in the fullest extent.

Numerous parties, therefore, were seen ascending and descending the hill on which the castle was situated ; and when the King and his attendants entered the open and unguarded gates of the external barrier, the space within presented a scene not easily reconciled with the cause of the assemblage. In one place cooks were toiling to roast huge oxen and fat sheep ; in another, hogsheads of ale were set abroach, to be drained at the freedom of all comers. Groups of every description were to be seen devouring the food and swallowing the liquor thus abandoned to their discretion. The naked Saxon serf was drowning the sense of his half-year's hunger and thirst in one day of gluttony and drunkenness ; the more pampered burgess and guild-brother was eating his morsel with gust, or curiously criticising the quantity of the malt and the skill of the brewer. Some few of the poorer Norman gentry might also be seen, distinguished by their shaven chins and short cloaks, and not less so by their keeping together, and looking with great scorn on the whole solemnity, even while

condescending to avail themselves of the good
cheer which was so liberally supplied.

Mendicants were, of course, assembled by the
score, together with strolling soldiers returned from
Palestine (according to their own account at least);
pedlars were displaying their wares; travelling
mechanics were inquiring after employment; and
wandering palmers, hedge-priests, Saxon minstrels,
and Welsh bards, were muttering prayers, and ex-
tracting mistuned dirges from their harps, crowds,
and rotes.[1] One sent forth the praises of Athelstane
in a doleful panegyric; another, in a Saxon genea-
logical poem, rehearsed the uncouth and harsh
names of his noble ancestry. Jesters and jugglers
were not awanting, nor was the occasion of the
assembly supposed to render the exercise of their profession indecorous or improper. Indeed, the ideas
of the Saxons on these occasions were as natural
as they were rude. If sorrow was thirsty, there
was drink; if hungry, there was food; if it sunk
down upon and saddened the heart, here were the
means supplied of mirth, or at least of amusement.
Nor did the assistants scorn to avail themselves of
those means of consolation, although, every now
and then, as if suddenly recollecting the cause
which had brought them together, the men groaned
in unison, while the females, of whom many were
present, raised up their voices and shrieked for
very woe.

Such was the scene in the castle-yard at Coningsburgh when it was entered by Richard and his
followers. The seneschal or steward deigned not
to take notice of the groups of inferior guests who
were perpetually entering and withdrawing, unless
so far as was necessary to preserve order; nevertheless, he was struck by the good mien of the Monarch

---

[1] The *crowth*, or *crowd*, was a species of violin; the *rote*
a sort of guitar, the strings of which were managed by a
kind of wheel, from which the instrument took its name.

and Ivanhoe, more especially as he imagined the
features of the latter were familiar to him. Besides,
the approach of two knights, for such their dress
bespoke them, was a rare event at a Saxon solemnity,
and could not but be regarded as a sort of honour
to the deceased and his family. And in his sable
dress, and holding in his hand his white wand of
office, this important personage made way through
the miscellaneous assemblage of guests, thus conducting Richard and Ivanhoe to the entrance of the
tower. Gurth and Wamba speedily found acquaint-
ances in the courtyard, nor presumed to intrude
themselves any farther until their presence should
be required.

CHAPTER XLII

I found them winding of Marcello's corpse.
And there was such a solemn melody,
'Twixt doleful songs, tears, and sad elegies,—
Such as old grandames, watching by the dead,
Are wont to outwear the night with.

Old Play.

THE mode of entering the great tower of Coningsburgh Castle is very peculiar, and partakes of the
rude simplicity of the early times in which it was
erected. A flight of steps, so deep and narrow as
to be almost precipitous, leads up to a low portal
in the south side of the tower, by which the
adventurous antiquary may still, or at least could a
few years since, gain access to a small stair within
the thickness of the main wall of the tower, which
leads up to the third story of the building—
the two lower being dungeons or vaults, which
neither receive air nor light, save by a square hole
in the third story, with which they seem to have
communicated by a ladder. The access to the
upper apartments in the tower, which consist in all
of four stories, is given by stairs which are carried
up through the external buttresses.

By this difficult and complicated entrance, the
good King Richard, followed by his faithful Ivanhoe, was ushered into the round apartment which
occupies the whole of the third story from the
ground. Wilfred, by the difficulties of the ascent,
gained time to muffle his face in his mantle, as it

had been held expedient that he should not present himself to his father until the King should give him the signal.

There were assembled in this apartment, around a large oaken table, about a dozen of the most distinguished representatives of the Saxon families in the adjacent counties. These were all old, or at least elderly, men; for the younger race, to the great displeasure of the seniors, had, like Ivanhoe, broken down many of the barriers which separated for half a century the Norman victors from the vanquished Saxons. The downcast and sorrowful looks of these venerable men, their silence and their mournful posture, formed a strong contrast to the levity of the revellers on the outside of the castle. Their grey locks and long full beards, together with their antique tunics and loose black mantles, suited well with the singular and rude apartment in which they were seated, and gave the appearance of a band of ancient worshippers of Woden, recalled to life to mourn over the decay of their national glory.

Cedric, seated in equal rank among his countrymen, seemed yet, by common consent, to act as chief of the assembly. Upon the entrance of Richard (only known to him as the valorous Knight of the Fetterlock) he arose gravely, and gave him welcome by the ordinary salutation, *Waes hael*, raising at the same time a goblet to his head. The King, no stranger to the customs of his English subjects, returned the greeting with the appropriate words, *Drinc hael*, and partook of a cup which was handed to him by the sewer. The same courtesy was offered to Ivanhoe, who pledged his father in silence, supplying the usual speech by an inclination of his head, lest his voice should have been recognised.

When this introductory ceremony was performed, Cedric arose, and, extending his hand to Richard, conducted him into a small and very rude chapel,

which was excavated, as it were, out of one of the
external buttresses. As there was no opening,
saving a very narrow loophole, the place would
have been nearly quite dark but for two flambeaux
or torches, which showed, by a red and smoky light,
the arched roof and naked walls, the rude altar of
stone, and the crucifix of the same material.

Before this altar was placed a bier, and on each
side of this bier kneeled three priests, who told their
beads, and muttered their prayers, with the greatest
signs of external devotion. For this service a
splendid 'soul-scat' was paid to the convent of
St. Edmund's by the mother of the deceased; and,
that it might be fully deserved, the whole brethren,
saving the lame sacristan, had transferred themselves
to Coningsburgh, where, while six of their number
were constantly on guard in the performance of
divine rites by the bier of Athelstane, the others
failed not to take their share of the refreshments
and amusements which went on at the castle. In
maintaining this pious watch and ward, the good
monks were particularly careful not to interrupt
their hymns for an instant, lest Zernebock, the
ancient Saxon Apollyon, should lay his clutches on
the departed Athelstane. Nor were they less careful to prevent any unhallowed layman from touching
the pall, which, having been that used at the funeral
of St. Edmund, was liable to be desecrated if handled
by the profane. If, in truth, these attentions could
be of any use to the deceased, he had some right to
expect them at the hands of the brethren of St.
Edmund's, since, besides a hundred mancuses of
gold paid down as the soul-ransom, the mother of
Athelstane had announced her intention of endow-
ing that foundation with the better part of the lands
of the deceased, in order to maintain perpetual
prayers for his soul and that of her departed
husband.

Richard and Wilfred followed the Saxon Cedric

into the apartment of death, where, as their guide pointed with solemn air to the untimely bier of Athelstane, they followed his example in devoutly crossing themselves, and muttering a brief prayer for the weal of the departed soul.

This act of pious charity performed, Cedric again motioned them to follow him, gliding over the stone floor with a noiseless tread; and, after ascending a few steps, opened with great caution the door of a small oratory, which adjoined to the chapel. It was about eight feet square, hollowed, like the chapel itself, out of the thickness of the wall; and the loophole which enlightened it being to the west, and widening considerably as it sloped inward, a beam of the setting sun found its way into its dark recess, and showed a female of a dignified mien, and whose countenance retained the marked remains of majestic beauty. Her long mourning robes, and her flowing wimple of black cypress, enhanced the whiteness of her skin, and the beauty of her light-coloured and flowing tresses, which time had neither thinned nor mingled with silver. Her countenance expressed the deepest sorrow that is consistent with resignation. On the stone table before her stood a crucifix of ivory, beside which was laid a missal, having its pages richly illuminated, and its boards adorned with clasps of gold and bosses of the same precious metal.

'Noble Edith,' said Cedric, after having stood a moment silent, as if to give Richard and Wilfred time to look upon the lady of the mansion, 'these are worthy strangers come to take a part in thy sorrows. And this, in especial, is the valiant knight who fought so bravely for the deliverance of him for whom we this day mourn.'

'His bravery has my thanks,' returned the lady; 'although it be the will of Heaven that it should be displayed in vain. I thank, too, his courtesy, and that of his companion, which hath brought them hither to behold the widow of Adeling, the mother of Athelstane, in her deep hour of sorrow and lamentation. To your care, kind kinsman, I entrust them, satisfied that they will want no hospitality which these sad walls can yet afford.'

The guests bowed deeply to the mourning parent, and withdrew with their hospitable guide.

Another winding stair conducted them to an apartment of the same size with that which they had first entered, occupying indeed the story immediately above. From this room, ere yet the door was opened, proceeded a low and melancholy strain of vocal music. When they entered, they found themselves in the presence of about twenty matrons and maidens of distinguished Saxon lineage. Four maidens, Rowena leading the choir, raised a hymn for the soul of the deceased, of which we have only been able to decipher two or three stanzas :—

> Dust unto dust,
> To this all must.
> The tenant hath resign'd
> The faded form
> To waste and worm :
> Corruption claims her kind.
>
> Through paths unknown
> Thy soul hath flown,
> To seek the realms of woe,
> Where fiery pain
> Shall purge the stain
> Of actions done below.
>
> In that sad place,
> By Mary's grace,
> Brief may thy dwelling be !
> Till prayers and alms,
> And holy psalms,
> Shall set the captive free.

While this dirge was sung, in a low and melancholy tone, by the female choristers, the others were divided into two bands, of which one was

engaged in bedecking, with such embroidery as their
skill and taste could compass, a large silken pall,
destined to cover the bier of Athelstane, while the
others busied themselves in selecting, from baskets
of flowers placed before them, garlands, which they
intended for the same mournful purpose. The
behaviour of the maidens was decorous, if not
marked with deep affliction; but now and then a
whisper or a smile called forth the rebuke of the
severer matrons, and here and there might be seen
a damsel more interested in endeavouring to find
out how her mourning-robe became her than in the
dismal ceremony for which they were preparing.
Neither was this propensity (if we must needs
confess the truth) at all diminished by the appearance of two strange knights, which occasioned some
looking up, peeping, and whispering. Rowena
alone, too proud to be vain, paid her greeting to
her deliverer with a graceful courtesy. Her demeanour was serious, but not dejected; and it may
be doubted whether thoughts of Ivanhoe, and of the
uncertainty of his fate, did not claim as great a
share in her gravity as the death of her kinsman.

To Cedric, however, who, as we have observed,
was not remarkably clear-sighted on such occasions,
the sorrow of his ward seemed so much deeper than
any of the other maidens that he deemed it proper
to whisper the explanation, 'She was the affianced
bride of the noble Athelstane.' It may be doubted
whether this communication went a far way to
increase Wilfred's disposition to sympathise with
the mourners of Coningsburgh.

Having thus formally introduced the guests to
the different chambers in which the obsequies of
Athelstane were celebrated under different forms,
Cedric conducted them into a small room, destined,
as he informed them, for the exclusive accommodation of honourable guests, whose more slight connexion with the deceased might render them

unwilling to join those who were immediately affected by the unhappy event. He assured them of every accommodation, and was about to withdraw when the Black Knight took his hand.

'I crave to remind you, noble thane,' he said, 'that when we last parted you promised, for the service I had the fortune to render you, to grant me a boon.'

'It is granted ere named, noble Knight,' said Cedric; 'yet, at this sad moment——'

'Of that also,' said the King, 'I have bethought me; but my time is brief; neither does it seem to me unfit that, when closing the grave on the noble Athelstane, we should deposit therein certain prejudices and hasty opinions.'

'Sir Knight of the Fetterlock,' said Cedric, colouring, and interrupting the King in his turn, 'I trust your boon regards yourself and no other; for in that which concerns the honour of my house, it is scarce fitting that a stranger should mingle.'

'Nor do I wish to mingle,' said the King, mildly, 'unless in so far as you will admit me to have an interest. As yet you have known me but as the Black Knight of the Fetterlock. Know me now as Richard Plantagenet.'

'Richard of Anjou!' exclaimed Cedric, stepping backward with the utmost astonishment.

'No, noble Cedric—Richard of England! whose deepest interest—whose deepest wish, is to see her sons united with each other. And, how now, worthy thane! hast thou no knee for thy prince?'

'To Norman blood,' said Cedric, 'it hath never bended.'

'Reserve thine homage then,' said the Monarch, 'until I shall prove my right to it by my equal protection of Normans and English.'

'Prince,' answered Cedric, 'I have ever done justice to thy bravery and thy worth. Nor am I ignorant of thy claim to the crown through thy descent from Matilda, niece to Edgar Atheling, and daughter to Malcolm of Scotland. But Matilda, though of the royal Saxon blood, was not the heir to the monarchy.'

'I will not dispute my title with thee, noble thane,' said Richard, calmly; 'but I will bid thee look around thee, and see where thou wilt find another to be put into the scale against it.'

'And hast thou wandered hither, Prince, to tell me so?' said Cedric—'to upbraid me with the ruin of my race, ere the grave has closed o'er the last scion of Saxon royalty?' His countenance darkened as he spoke. 'It was boldly—it was rashly done!'

'Not so, by the holy rood!' replied the King; 'it was done in the frank confidence which one brave man may repose in another, without a shadow of danger.'

'Thou sayest well, Sir King—for King I own thou art, and wilt be, despite of my feeble opposition. I dare not take the only mode to prevent it, though thou hast placed the strong temptation within my reach!'

'And now to my boon,' said the King, 'which I ask not with one jot the less confidence, that thou hast refused to acknowledge my lawful sovereignty. I require of thee, as a man of thy word, on pain of being held faithless, man-sworn, and "nidering," to forgive and receive to thy paternal affection the good knight, Wilfred of Ivanhoe. In this reconciliation thou wilt own I have an interest—the happiness of my friend, and the quelling of dissension among my faithful people.'

'And this is Wilfred!' said Cedric, pointing to his son.

'My father!—my father!' said Ivanhoe, prostrating himself at Cedric's feet, 'grant me thy forgiveness!'

'Thou hast it, my son,' said Cedric, raising him up. 'The son of Hereward knows how to keep his word, even when it has been passed to a Norman.

But let me see thee use the dress and costume of thy English ancestry: no short cloaks, no gay bonnets, no fantastic plumage in my decent household. He that would be the son of Cedric must show himself of English ancestry. Thou art about to speak,' he added, sternly, 'and I guess the topic. The Lady Rowena must complete two years' mourning, as for a betrothed husband: all our Saxon ancestors would disown us were we to treat of a new union for her ere the grave of him she should have wedded—him so much the most worthy of her hand by birth and ancestry—is yet closed. The ghost of Athelstane himself would burst his bloody cerements, and stand before us to forbid such dishonour to his memory.'

It seemed as if Cedric's words had raised a spectre; for scarce had he uttered them ere the door flew open, and Athelstane, arrayed in the garments of the grave, stood before them, pale, haggard, and like something arisen from the dead !

The effect of this apparition on the persons present was utterly appalling. Cedric started back as far as the wall of the apartment would permit, and, leaning against it as one unable to support himself, gazed on the figure of his friend with eyes that seemed fixed, and a mouth which he appeared incapable of shutting. Ivanhoe crossed himself, repeating prayers in Saxon, Latin, or Norman-French, as they occurred to his memory, while Richard alternately said ' *Benedicite,*' and swore, ' *Mort de ma vie !*'

In the meantime, a horrible noise was heard below stairs, some crying, ' Secure the treacherous monks !' —others, ' Down with them into the dungeon !'— others, ' Pitch them from the highest battlements !'

' In the name of God !' said Cedric, addressing what seemed the spectre of his departed friend, ' if thou art mortal, speak !—if a departed spirit, say for what cause thou dost revisit us, or if I can do aught that can set thy spirit at repose. Living or dead, noble Athelstane, speak to Cedric!'

'I will,' said the spectre, very composedly, 'when I have collected breath, and when you give me time. Alive, saidst thou? I am as much alive as he can be who has fed on bread and water for three days, which seem three ages. Yes, bread and water, father Cedric! By Heaven, and all saints in it, better food hath not passed my weasand for three livelong days, and by God's providence it is that I am now here to tell it.'

'Why, noble Athelstane,' said the Black Knight, 'I myself saw you struck down by the fierce Templar towards the end of the storm at Torquilstone, and, as I thought, and Wamba reported, your skull was cloven through the teeth.'

'You thought amiss, Sir Knight,' said Athelstane, 'and Wamba lied. My teeth are in good order, and that my supper shall presently find. No thanks to the Templar though, whose sword turned in his hand, so that the blade struck me flatlings, being averted by the handle of the good mace with which I warded the blow; had my steel-cap been on, I had not valued it a rush, and had dealt him such a counterbuff as would have spoilt his retreat. But as it was, down I went, stunned, indeed, but un-wounded. Others, of both sides, were beaten down and slaughtered above me, so that I never recovered my senses until I found myself in a coffin—an open one, by good luck!—placed before the altar of the church of St. Edmund's. I sneezed repeatedly—groaned—awakened, and would have arisen, when the sacristan and abbot, full of terror, came running at the noise, surprised, doubtless, and no way pleased, to find the man alive whose heirs they had proposed themselves to be. I asked for wine; they gave me some, but it must have been highly medi-cated, for I slept yet more deeply than before, and

wakened not for many hours. I found my arms
swathed down, my feet tied so fast that mine ankles
ache at the very remembrance ; the place was utterly
dark—the oubliette, as I suppose, of their accursed
convent, and from the close, stifled, damp smell I
conceive it is also used for a place of sepulture.
I had strange thoughts of what had befallen me,
when the door of my dungeon creaked, and two
villain monks entered. They would have persuaded
me I was in purgatory, but I knew too well the
pursy, short-breathed voice of the father abbot. St.
Jeremy ! how different from that tone with which
he used to ask me for another slice of the haunch !
the dog has feasted with me from Christmas to
Twelfth Night.'

'Have patience, noble Athelstane,' said the King,
'take breath—tell your story at leisure ; beshrew
me but such a tale is as well worth listening to as
a romance.'

'Ay but, by the rood of Bromholme, there was
no romance in the matter !' said Athelstane. 'A
barley loaf and a pitcher of water—that *they* gave
me, the niggardly traitors, whom my father, and I
myself, had enriched, when their best resources
were the flitches of bacon and measures of corn out
of which they wheedled poor serfs and bondsmen,
in exchange for their prayers. The nest of foul,
ungrateful vipers—barley bread and ditch water to
such a patron as I had been ! I will smoke them
out of their nest, though I be excommunicated !'

'But, in the name of Our Lady, noble Athelstane,' said Cedric, grasping the hand of his friend,
'how didst thou escape this imminent danger ? did
their hearts relent ?'

'Did their hearts relent !' echoed Athelstane. 'Do
rocks melt with the sun ? I should have been there
still, had not some stir in the convent, which I find
was their procession hitherward to eat my funeral
feast, when they well knew how and where I had been

buried alive, summoned the swarm out of their hive.
I heard them droning out their death-psalms, little
judging they were sung in respect for my soul by
those who were thus famishing my body. They
went, however, and I waited long for food ; no
wonder—the gouty sacristan was even too busy with
his own provender to mind mine. At length down
he came, with an unstable step and a strong flavour
of wine and spices about his person. Good cheer
had opened his heart, for he left me a nook of pasty
and a flask of wine instead of my former fare. I
ate, drank, and was invigorated ; when, to add to
my good luck, the sacristan, too totty to discharge
his duty of turnkey fitly, locked the door beside
the staple, so that it fell ajar. The light, the food,
the wine set my invention to work. The staple to
which my chains were fixed was more rusted than
I or the villain abbot had supposed. Even iron
could not remain without consuming in the damps
of that infernal dungeon.'

'Take breath, noble Athelstane,' said Richard,
'and partake of some refreshment, ere you proceed
with a tale so dreadful.'

'Partake !' quoth Athelstane. 'I have been partaking five times to-day ; and yet a morsel of that
savoury ham were not altogether foreign to the
matter : and I pray you, fair sir, to do me reason
in a cup of wine.'

The guests, though still agape with astonishment,
pledged their resuscitated landlord, who thus proceeded in his story :—He had indeed now many
more auditors than those to whom it was commenced,
for Edith, having given certain necessary orders for
arranging matters within the castle, had followed
the dead-alive up to the strangers' apartment, attended by as many of the guests, male and female,
as could squeeze into the small room, while others,
crowding the staircase, caught up an erroneous
edition of the story, and transmitted it still more

inaccurately to those beneath, who again sent it
forth to the vulgar without, in a fashion totally
irreconcilable to the real fact. Athelstane, however, went on as follows with the history of his
escape :—

'Finding myself freed from the staple, I dragged
myself upstairs as well as a man loaded with shackles,
and emaciated with fasting, might ; and after much
groping about, I was at length directed, by the
sound of a jolly roundelay, to the apartment where
the worthy sacristan, an it so please ye, was holding
a devil's mass with a huge beetle-browed, broad-
shouldered brother of the grey-frock and cowl, who
looked much more like a thief than a clergyman.
I burst in upon them, and the fashion of my grave-
clothes, as well as the clanking of my chains, made
me more resemble an inhabitant of the other world
than of this.   Both stood aghast ; but when I
knocked down the sacristan with my fist, the other
fellow, his pot-companion, fetched a blow at me
with a huge quarter-staff.'

'This must be our Friar Tuck, for a count's
ransom,' said Richard, looking at Ivanhoe.

'He may be the devil, an he will,' said Athelstane. 'Fortunately, he missed the aim ; and on
my approaching to grapple with him, took to his
heels and ran for it. I failed not to set my own
heels at liberty by means of the fetter-key, which
hung amongst others at the sexton's belt ; and I
had thoughts of beating out the knave's brains with
the bunch of keys, but gratitude for the nook of
pasty and the flask of wine which the rascal had
imparted to my captivity came over my heart ; so,
with a brace of hearty kicks, I left him on the floor,
pouched some baked meat and a leathern bottle of
wine, with which the two venerable brethren had
been regaling, went to the stable, and found in a
private stall mine own best palfrey, which, doubtless, had been set apart for the holy father abbot's

particular use. Hither I came with all the speed
the beast could compass—man and mother's son
flying before me wherever I came, taking me for a
spectre, the more especially as, to prevent my being
recognised, I drew the corpse-hood over my face.
I had not gained admittance into my own castle,
had I not been supposed to be the attendant of a
juggler who is making the people in the castle-yard
very merry, considering they are assembled to cele-
brate their lord's funeral. I say the sewer thought
I was dressed to bear a part in the tregetour's
mummery, and so I got admission, and did but
disclose myself to my mother, and eat a hasty
morsel, ere I came in quest of you, my noble
friend.'

'And you have found me,' said Cedric, 'ready to
resume our brave projects of honour and liberty.
I tell thee, never will dawn a morrow so auspicious
as the next for the deliverance of the noble Saxon
race.'

'Talk not to me of delivering any one,' said
Athelstane; 'it is well I am delivered myself. I
am more intent on punishing that villain abbot.
He shall hang on the top of this Castle of Coningsburgh, in his cope and stole; and if the stairs be
too strait to admit his fat carcass, I will have him
craned up from without.'

'But, my son,' said Edith, 'consider his sacred
office.'

'Consider my three days' fast,' replied Athelstane; 'I will have their blood every one of them.
Front-de-Bœuf was burnt alive for a less matter,
for he kept a good table for his prisoners, only put
too much garlic in his last dish of pottage. But
these hypocritical, ungrateful slaves, so often the
self-invited flatterers at my board, who gave me
neither pottage nor garlic, more or less—they die,
by the soul of Hengist!'

'But the Pope, my noble friend,' said Cedric——

'But the devil, my noble friend,' answered Athelstane; 'they die, and no more of them. Were they the best monks upon earth, the world would go on without them.'

'For shame, noble Athelstane,' said Cedric; 'forget such wretches in the career of glory which lies open before thee. Tell this Norman prince, Richard of Anjou, that, lion-hearted as he is, he shall not hold undisputed the throne of Alfred, while a male descendant of the Holy Confessor lives to dispute it.'

'How!' said Athelstane, 'is this the noble King Richard?'

'It is Richard Plantagenet himself,' said Cedric; 'yet I need not remind thee that, coming hither a guest of free-will, he may neither be injured nor detained prisoner: thou well knowest thy duty to him as his host.'

'Ay, by my faith!' said Athelstane; 'and my duty as a subject besides, for I here tender him my allegiance, heart and hand.'

'My son,' said Edith, 'think on thy royal rights!'

'Think on the freedom of England, degenerate prince!' said Cedric.

'Mother and friend,' said Athelstane, 'a truce to your upbraidings! Bread and water and a dungeon are marvellous mortifiers of ambition, and I rise from the tomb a wiser man than I descended into it. One half of those vain follies were puffed into mine ear by that perfidious Abbot Wolfram, and you may now judge if he is a counsellor to be trusted. Since these plots were set in agitation, I have had nothing but hurried journeys, indigestions, blows and bruises, imprisonments, and starvation; besides that they can only end in the murder of some thousands of quiet folk. I tell you, I will be king in my own domains, and nowhere else; and my first act of dominion shall be to hang the abbot.'

'And my ward Rowena,' said Cedric—'I trust you intend not to desert her?'

'Father Cedric,' said Athelstane, 'be reasonable. The Lady Rowena cares not for me; she loves the little finger of my kinsman Wilfred's glove better than my whole person. There she stands to avouch it. Nay, blush not, kinswoman; there is no shame in loving a courtly knight better than a country franklin; and do not laugh neither, Rowena, for grave-clothes and a thin visage are, God knows, no matter of merriment. Nay, an thou wilt needs laugh, I will find thee a better jest. Give me thy hand, or rather lend it me, for I but ask it in the way of friendship. Here, cousin Wilfred of Ivanhoe, in thy favour I renounce and abjure—— Hey! by St. Dunstan, our cousin Wilfred hath vanished! Yet, unless my eyes are still dazzled with the fasting I have undergone, I saw him stand there but even now.'

All now looked around and inquired for Ivanhoe; but he had vanished. It was at length discovered that a Jew had been to seek him; and that, after very brief conference, he had called for Gurth and his armour, and had left the castle.

'Fair cousin,' said Athelstane to Rowena, 'could I think that this sudden disappearance of Ivanhoe was occasioned by other than the weightiest reason, I would myself resume——'

But he had no sooner let go her hand, on first observing that Ivanhoe had disappeared, than Rowena, who had found her situation extremely embarrassing, had taken the first opportunity to escape from the apartment.

'Certainly,' quoth Athelstane, 'women are the least to be trusted of all animals, monks and abbots excepted. I am an infidel, if I expected not thanks from her, and perhaps a kiss to boot. These cursed grave-clothes have surely a spell on them, every one flies from me. To you I turn, noble King

Richard, with the vows of allegiance, which, as a
liege subject——'

But King Richard was gone also, and no one
knew whither. At length it was learned that he
had hastened to the court-yard, summoned to his
presence the Jew who had spoken with Ivanhoe,
and, after a moment's speech with him, had called
vehemently to horse, thrown himself upon a steed,
compelled the Jew to mount another, and set off at
a rate which, according to Wamba, rendered the
old Jew's neck not worth a penny's purchase.

'By my halidome!' said Athelstane, 'it is certain
that Zernebock hath possessed himself of my castle
in my absence. I return in my grave-clothes, a
pledge restored from the very sepulchre, and every
one I speak to vanishes as soon as they hear my
voice! But it skills not talking of it. Come, my
friends, such of you as are left, follow me to the
banquet-hall, lest any more of us disappear. It is,
I trust, as yet tolerably furnished, as becomes the
obsequies of an ancient Saxon noble; and should
we tarry any longer, who knows but the devil may
fly off with the supper?'

CHAPTER XLIII

Be Mowbray's sins so heavy in his bosom,
That they may break his foaming courser's back,
And throw the rider headlong in the lists,
A caitiff recreant!

Richard II.

OUR scene now returns to the exterior of the castle,
or preceptory, of Templestowe, about the hour
when the bloody die was to be cast for the life or
death of Rebecca. It was a scene of bustle and life,
as if the whole vicinity had poured forth its inhabitants to a village wake or rural feast. But the
earnest desire to look on blood and death is not
peculiar to those dark ages; though, in the gladia-
torial exercises of single combat and general tourney,
they were habituated to the bloody spectacle of
brave men falling by each other's hands. Even in
our own days, when morals are better understood,
an execution, a bruising-match, a riot, or a meeting
of radical reformers, collects, at considerable hazard
to themselves, immense crowds of spectators, otherwise little interested, except to see how matters are
to be conducted, or whether the heroes of the day
are, in the heroic language of insurgent tailors,
'flints' or 'dunghills.'

The eyes, therefore, of a very considerable multitude were bent on the gate of the preceptory of
Templestowe, with the purpose of witnessing the procession; while still greater numbers had already surrounded the tiltyard belonging to that establishment.

This inclosure was formed on a piece of level ground adjoining to the preceptory, which had been levelled with care, for the exercise of military and chivalrous sports. It occupied the brow of a soft and gentle eminence, was carefully palisaded around, and, as the Templars willingly invited spectators to be witnesses of their skill in feats of chivalry, was amply supplied with galleries and benches for their use.

On the present occasion, a throne was erected for the Grand Master at the east end, surrounded with seats of distinction for the preceptors and knights of the order. Over these floated the sacred standard, called *Le Beau-seant*, which was the ensign, as its name was the battle-cry, of the Templars.

At the opposite end of the lists was a pile of faggots, so arranged around a stake, deeply fixed in the ground, as to leave a space for the victim whom they were destined to consume to enter within the fatal circle, in order to be chained to the stake by the fetters which hung ready for that purpose. Beside this deadly apparatus stood four black slaves, whose colour and African features, then so little known in England, appalled the multitude, who gazed on them as on demons employed about their own diabolical exercises. These men stirred not, excepting now and then, under the direction of one who seemed their chief, to shift and replace the ready fuel. They looked not on the multitude. In fact, they seemed insensible of their presence, and of everything save the discharge of their own horrible duty. And when, in speech with each other, they expanded their blubber lips, and showed their white fangs, as if they grinned at the thoughts of the expected tragedy, the startled commons could scarcely help believing that they were actually the familiar spirits with whom the witch had communed, and who, her time being out, stood ready to assist in her dreadful punishment. They whispered to each other, and communicated all the feats which Satan had performed during that busy and unhappy period, not failing, of course, to give the devil rather more than his due.

'Have you not heard, father Dennet,' quoth one boor to another advanced in years, 'that the devil has carried away bodily the great Saxon thane, Athelstane of Coningsburgh?'

'Ay, but he brought him back though, by the blessing of God and St. Dunstan.'

'How's that?' said a brisk young fellow, dressed in a green cassock embroidered with gold, and having at his heels a stout lad bearing a harp upon his back, which betrayed his vocation. The Minstrel seemed of no vulgar rank; for, besides the splendour of his gaily broidered doublet, he wore around his neck a silver chain, by which hung the 'wrest,' or key, with which he tuned his harp. On his right arm was a silver plate, which, instead of bearing, as usual, the cognizance or badge of the baron to whose family he belonged, had barely the word SHERWOOD engraved upon it. 'How mean you by that?' said the gay Minstrel, mingling in the conversation of the peasants; 'I came to seek one subject for my rhyme, and, by'r Lady, I were glad to find two.'

'It is well avouched,' said the elder peasant, 'that after Athelstane of Coningsburgh had been dead four weeks——'

'That is impossible,' said the Minstrel; 'I saw him in life at the passage of arms at Ashby-de-la-Zouche.'

'Dead, however, he was, or else translated,' said the younger peasant; 'for I heard the monks of St. Edmund's singing the death's hymn for him; and, moreover, there was a rich death-meal and dole at the Castle of Coningsburgh, as right was; and thither had I gone, but for Mabel Parkins, who——'

'Ay, dead was Athelstane,' said the old man, shaking his head, 'and the more pity it was, for the old Saxon blood——'

'But, your story, my masters—your story,' said the Minstrel, somewhat impatiently.

'Ay, ay—construe us the story,' said a burly friar, who stood beside them, leaning on a pole that exhibited an appearance between a pilgrim's staff and a quarter-staff, and probably acted as either when occasion served—'your story,' said the stalwart churchman. 'Burn not daylight about it; we have short time to spare.'

'An please your reverence,' said Dennet, 'a drunken priest came to visit the sacristan at St. Edmund's——'

'It does not please my reverence,' answered the churchman, 'that there should be such an animal as a drunken priest, or, if there were, that a layman should so speak him. Be mannerly, my friend, and conclude the holy man only wrapt in meditation, which makes the head dizzy and foot unsteady, as if the stomach were filled with new wine: I have felt it myself.'

'Well, then,' answered father Dennet, 'a holy brother came to visit the sacristan at St. Edmund's —a sort of hedge-priest is the visitor, and kills half the deer that are stolen in the forest, who loves the tinkling of a pint-pot better than the sacring-bell, and deems a flitch of bacon worth ten of his breviary; for the rest, a good fellow and a merry, who will flourish a quarter-staff, draw a bow, and dance a Cheshire round with e'er a man in Yorkshire.'

'That last part of thy speech, Dennet,' said the Minstrel, 'has saved thee a rib or twain.'

'Tush, man, I fear him not,' said Dennet; 'I am somewhat old and stiff, but when I fought for the bell and ram at Doncaster——'

'But the story—the story, my friend,' again said the Minstrel.

'Why, the tale is but this—Athelstane of Conings-burgh was buried at St. Edmund's.'

'That's a lie, and a loud one,' said the friar, 'for I saw him borne to his own Castle of Coningsburgh.'

'Nay, then, e'en tell the story yourself, my masters,' said Dennet, turning sulky at these repeated contradictions; and it was with some difficulty that the boor could be prevailed on, by the request of his comrade and the Minstrel, to renew his tale. 'These two *sober* friars,' said he at length, 'since this reverend man will needs have them such, had continued drinking good ale, and wine, and what not, for the best part of a summer's day, when they were aroused by a deep groan, and a clanking of chains, and the figure of the deceased Athelstane entered the apartment, saying, "Ye evil shepherds——!"'

'It is false,' said the friar, hastily, 'he never spoke a word.'

'So ho! Friar Tuck,' said the Minstrel, drawing him apart from the rustics; 'we have started a new hare, I find.'

'I tell thee, Allan-a-Dale,' said the hermit, 'I saw Athelstane of Coningsburgh as much as bodily eyes ever saw a living man. He had his shroud on, and all about him smelt of the sepulchre. A butt of sack will not wash it out of my memory.'

'Pshaw!' answered the Minstrel; 'thou dost but jest with me!'

'Never believe me,' said the Friar, 'an I fetched not a knock at him with my quarter-staff that would have felled an ox, and it glided through his body as it might through a pillar of smoke!'

'By St. Hubert,' said the Minstrel, 'but it is a wondrous tale, and fit to be put in metre to the ancient tune, "Sorrow came to the Old Friar."'

'Laugh, if ye list,' said Friar Tuck; 'but an ye catch me singing on such a theme, may the next ghost or devil carry me off with him headlong!

No, no—I instantly formed the purpose of assisting at some good work, such as the burning of a witch, a judicial combat, or the like matter of godly service, and therefore am I here.'

As they thus conversed, the heavy bell of the church of St. Michael of Templestowe, a venerable building, situated in a hamlet at some distance from the preceptory, broke short their argument. One by one the sullen sounds fell successively on the ear, leaving but sufficient space for each to die away in distant echo, ere the air was again filled by repetition of the iron knell. These sounds, the signal of the approaching ceremony, chilled with awe the hearts of the assembled multitude, whose eyes were now turned to the preceptory, expecting the approach of the Grand Master, the champion, and the criminal.

At length the drawbridge fell, the gates opened, and a knight, bearing the great standard of the order, sallied from the castle, preceded by six trumpets, and followed by the knights preceptors, two and two, the Grand Master coming last, mounted on a stately horse, whose furniture was of the simplest kind. Behind him came Brian de Bois-Guilbert, armed cap-à-pie in bright armour, but without his lance, shield, and sword, which were borne by his two esquires behind him. His face, though partly hidden by a long plume which floated down from his barret-cap, bore a strong and mingled expression of passion, in which pride seemed to contend with irresolution. He looked ghastly pale, as if he had not slept for several nights, yet reined his pawing war-horse with the habitual ease and grace proper to the best lance of the order of the Temple. His general appearance was grand and commanding ; but, looking at him with attention, men read that in his dark features from which they willingly withdrew their eyes.

On either side rode Conrade of Mont-Fitchet and

Albert de Malvoisin, who acted as godfathers to the champion. They were in their robes of peace, the white dress of the order. Behind them followed other companions of the Temple, with a long train of esquires and pages clad in black, aspirants to the honour of being one day knights of the order. After these neophytes came a guard of warders on foot, in the same sable livery, amidst whose partizans might be seen the pale form of the accused, moving with a slow but undismayed step towards the scene of her fate. She was stript of all her ornaments, lest perchance there should be among them some of those amulets which Satan was supposed to bestow upon his victims, to deprive them of the power of confession even when under the torture. A coarse white dress, of the simplest form, had been substituted for her Oriental garments; yet there was such an exquisite mixture of courage and resignation in her look that even in this garb, and with no other ornament than her long black tresses, each eye wept that looked upon her, and the most hardened bigot regretted the fate that had converted a creature so goodly into a vessel of wrath, and a waged slave of the devil.

A crowd of inferior personages belonging to the preceptory followed the victim, all moving with the utmost order, with arms folded and looks bent upon the ground.

This slow procession moved up the gentle eminence, on the summit of which was the tiltyard, and, entering the lists, marched once around them from right to left, and when they had completed the circle, made a halt. There was then a momentary bustle, while the Grand Master and all his attendants, excepting the champion and his godfathers, dismounted from their horses, which were immediately removed out of the lists by the esquires, who were in attendance for that purpose.

The unfortunate Rebecca was conducted to the

black chair placed near the pile. On her first glance at the terrible spot where preparations were making for a death alike dismaying to the mind and painful to the body, she was observed to shudder and shut her eyes, praying internally, doubtless, for her lips moved, though no speech was heard. In the space of a minute she opened her eyes, looked fixedly on the pile as if to familiarise her mind with the object, and then slowly and naturally turned away her head.

Meanwhile, the Grand Master had assumed his seat; and when the chivalry of his order was placed around and behind him, each in his due rank, a loud and long flourish of the trumpets announced that the court were seated for judgment. Malvoisin then, acting as godfather of the champion, stepped forward, and laid the glove of the Jewess, which was the pledge of battle, at the feet of the Grand Master.

'Valorous lord and reverend father,' said he, 'here standeth the good knight, Brian de Bois-Guilbert, Knight Preceptor of the Order of the Temple, who, by accepting the pledge of battle which I now lay at your reverence's feet, hath become bound to do his devoir in combat this day, to maintain that this Jewish maiden, by name Rebecca, hath justly deserved the doom passed upon her in a chapter of this most holy order of the Temple of Zion, condemning her to die as a sorceress—here, I say, he standeth, such battle to do, knightly and honourable, if such be your noble and sanctified pleasure.'

'Hath he made oath,' said the Grand Master, 'that his quarrel is just and honourable? Bring forward the crucifix and the *Te igitur.*'

'Sir and most reverend father,' answered Malvoisin, readily, 'our brother here present hath already sworn to the truth of his accusation in the hand of the good knight Conrade de Mont-Fitchet;

and otherwise he ought not to be sworn, seeing
that his adversary is an unbeliever, and may take
no oath.'

This explanation was satisfactory, to Albert's
great joy; for the wily knight had foreseen the
great difficulty, or rather impossibility, of prevailing
upon Brian de Bois-Guilbert to take such an oath
before the assembly, and had invented this excuse
to escape the necessity of his doing so.

The Grand Master, having allowed the apology
of Albert Malvoisin, commanded the herald to
stand forth and do his devoir. The trumpets then
again flourished, and a herald, stepping forward,
proclaimed aloud, 'Oyez, oyez, oyez. Here standeth
the good knight, Sir Brian de Bois-Guilbert, ready
to do battle with any knight of free blood who will
sustain the quarrel allowed and allotted to the
Jewess Rebecca, to try by champion, in respect of
lawful essoine of her own body; and to such
champion the reverend and valorous Grand Master
here present allows a fair field, and equal partition
of sun and wind, and whatever else appertains to a
fair combat.' The trumpets again sounded, and
there was a dead pause of many minutes.

'No champion appears for the appellant,' said
the Grand Master. 'Go, herald, and ask her
whether she expects any one to do battle for her
in this her cause.'

The herald went to the chair in which Rebecca
was seated; and Bois-Guilbert, suddenly turning
his horse's head toward that end of the lists, in
spite of hints on either side from Malvoisin and
Mont-Fitchet, was by the side of Rebecca's chair
as soon as the herald.

'Is this regular, and according to the law of
combat?' said Malvoisin, looking to the Grand
Master.

'Albert de Malvoisin, it is,' answered Beaumanoir; 'for in this appeal to the judgment of God

we may not prohibit parties from having that communication with each other which may best tend to bring forth the truth of the quarrel.'

In the meantime, the herald spoke to Rebecca in these terms: 'Damsel, the honourable and reverend the Grand Master demands of thee, if thou art prepared with a champion to do battle this day in thy behalf, or if thou dost yield thee as one justly condemned to a deserved doom?'

'Say to the Grand Master,' replied Rebecca, 'that I maintain my innocence, and do not yield me as justly condemned, lest I become guilty of mine own blood. Say to him, that I challenge such delay as his forms will permit, to see if God, whose opportunity is in man's extremity, will raise me up a deliverer; and when such uttermost space is passed, may His holy will be done!'

The herald retired to carry this answer to the Grand Master.

'God forbid,' said Lucas Beaumanoir, 'that Jew or Pagan should impeach us of injustice! Until the shadows be cast from the west to the eastward, will we wait to see if a champion shall appear for this unfortunate woman. When the day is so far passed, let her prepare for death.'

The herald communicated the words of the Grand Master to Rebecca, who bowed her head submissively, folded her arms, and, looking up towards heaven, seemed to expect that aid from above which she could scarce promise herself from man. During this awful pause, the voice of Bois-Guilbert broke upon her ear; it was but a whisper, yet it startled her more than the summons of the herald had appeared to do.

'Rebecca,' said the Templar, 'dost thou hear me?'

'I have no portion in thee, cruel, hard-hearted man,' said the unfortunate maiden.

'Ay, but dost thou understand my words?' said

the Templar; 'for the sound of my voice is frightful
in mine own ears. I scarce know on what ground
we stand, or for what purpose they have brought
us hither. This listed space—that chair—these
faggots—I know their purpose, and yet it appears
to me like something unreal—the fearful picture of
a vision, which appals my sense with hideous fan-
tasies, but convinces not my reason.'

'My mind and senses keep touch and time,'
answered Rebecca, 'and tell me alike that these
faggots are destined to consume my earthly body,
and open a painful but a brief passage to a better
world.'

'Dreams, Rebecca—dreams,' answered the Templar—'idle visions, rejected by the wisdom of your
own wiser Sadducees. Hear me, Rebecca,' he said,
proceeding with animation; 'a better chance hast
thou for life and liberty than yonder knaves and
dotard dream of. Mount thee behind me on my
steed—on Zamor, the gallant horse that never failed
his rider. I won him in single fight from the Soldan
of Trebizond. Mount, I say, behind me; in one
short hour is pursuit and inquiry far behind—a new
world of pleasure opens to thee—to me a new career
of fame. Let them speak the doom which I despise,
and erase the name of Bois-Guilbert from their list
of monastic slaves! I will wash out with blood whatever blot they may dare to cast on my scutcheon.'

'Tempter,' said Rebecca, 'begone! Not in this
last extremity canst thou move me one hair's-
breadth from my resting-place. Surrounded as I
am by foes, I hold thee as my worst and most
deadly enemy; avoid thee, in the name of God!'

Albert Malvoisin, alarmed and impatient at the
duration of their conference, now advanced to interrupt it.

'Hath the maiden acknowledged her guilt?' he
demanded of Bois-Guilbert; 'or is she resolute in
her denial?'

'She is indeed *resolute*,' said Bois-Guilbert.

'Then,' said Malvoisin, 'must thou, noble brother, resume thy place to attend the issue. The shades are changing on the circle of the dial. Come, brave Bois-Guilbert—come, thou hope of our holy order, and soon to be its head.'

As he spoke in this soothing tone, he laid his hand on the knight's bridle, as if to lead him back to his station.

'False villain! what meanest thou by thy hand on my rein?' said Sir Brian, angrily. And shaking off his companion's grasp, he rode back to the upper end of the lists.

'There is yet spirit in him,' said Malvoisin apart to Mont-Fitchet, 'were it well directed; but, like the Greek fire, it burns whatever approaches it.'

The judges had now been two hours in the lists, awaiting in vain the appearance of a champion.

'And reason good,' said Friar Tuck, 'seeing she is a Jewess; and yet, by mine order, it is hard that so young and beautiful a creature should perish without one blow being struck in her behalf! Were she ten times a witch, provided she were but the least bit of a Christian, my quarter-staff should ring noon on the steel cap of yonder fierce Templar, ere he carried the matter off thus.'

It was, however, the general belief that no one could or would appear for a Jewess accused of sorcery; and the knights, instigated by Malvoisin, whispered to each other that it was time to declare the pledge of Rebecca forfeited. At this instant a knight, urging his horse to speed, appeared on the plain advancing towards the lists. A hundred voices exclaimed, 'A champion!—a champion!' And, despite the prepossessions and prejudices of the multitude, they shouted unanimously as the knight rode into the tiltyard. The second glance, however, served to destroy the hope that his timely arrival had excited. His horse, urged for many miles to its utmost speed, appeared to reel from fatigue, and the rider, however undauntedly he presented himself in the lists, either from weakness, weariness, or both, seemed scarce able to support himself in the saddle.

To the summons of the herald, who demanded his rank, his name, and purpose, the stranger knight answered readily and boldly, 'I am a good knight and noble, come hither to sustain with lance and sword the just and lawful quarrel of this damsel, Rebecca, daughter of Isaac of York ; to uphold the doom pronounced against her to be false and truthless, and to defy Sir Brian de Bois-Guilbert, as a traitor, murderer, and liar ; as I will prove in this field with my body against his, by the aid of God, of Our Lady, and of Monseigneur St. George, the good knight.'

'The stranger must first show,' said Malvoisin, 'that he is good knight, and of honourable lineage. The Temple sendeth not forth her champions against nameless men.'

'My name,' said the knight, raising his helmet, 'is better known, my lineage more pure, Malvoisin, than thine own.   I am Wilfred of Ivanhoe.'

'I will not fight with thee at present,' said the Templar, in a changed and hollow voice. 'Get thy wounds healed, purvey thee a better horse, and it may be I will hold it worth my while to scourge out of thee this boyish spirit of bravade.'

'Ha ! proud Templar,' said Ivanhoe, 'hast thou forgotten that twice didst thou fall before this lance? Remember the lists at Acre ; remember the passage of arms at Ashby ; remember thy proud vaunt in the halls of Rotherwood, and the gage of your gold chain against my reliquary, that thou wouldst do battle with Wilfred of Ivanhoe, and recover the honour thou hadst lost ! By that reliquary, and the holy relic it contains, I will proclaim thee, Templar, a coward in every court in Europe—in

every preceptory of thine order—unless thou do
battle without farther delay.'

Bois-Guilbert turned his countenance irresolutely
towards Rebecca, and then exclaimed, looking
fiercely at Ivanhoe, 'Dog of a Saxon! take thy
lance, and prepare for the death thou hast drawn
upon thee!'

'Does the Grand Master allow me, the combat?'
said Ivanhoe.

'I may not deny what thou hast challenged,' said
the Grand Master, 'provided the maiden accepts
thee as her champion. Yet I would thou wert in
better plight to do battle. An enemy of our order
hast thou ever been, yet would I have thee honourably met with.'

'Thus—thus as I am, and not otherwise,' said
Ivanhoe; 'it is the judgment of God—to His keeping I commend myself. Rebecca,' said he, riding
up to the fatal chair, 'dost thou accept of me for
thy champion?'

'I do,' she said—'I do,' fluttered by an emotion
which the fear of death had been unable to produce
—'I do accept thee as the champion whom Heaven
hath sent me. Yet, no—no—thy wounds are un-
cured. Meet not that proud man; why shouldst
thou perish also?'

But Ivanhoe was already at his post, and had
closed his visor, and assumed his lance. Bois-
Guilbert did the same; and his esquire remarked,
as he clasped his visor, that his face, which had,
notwithstanding the variety of emotions by which
he had been agitated, continued during the whole
morning of an ashy paleness, was now become
suddenly very much flushed.

The herald then, seeing each champion in his
place, uplifted his voice, repeating thrice—*Faites
vos devoirs, preux chevaliers!* After the third cry,
he withdrew to one side of the lists, and again proclaimed that none, on peril of instant death, should

dare by word, cry, or action to interfere with or
disturb this fair field of combat. The Grand Master,
who held in his hand the gage of battle, Rebecca's
glove, now threw it into the lists, and pronounced
the fatal signal words, *Laissez aller*.

The trumpets sounded, and the knights charged
each other in full career. The wearied horse of
Ivanhoe, and its no less exhausted rider, went down,
as all had expected, before the well-aimed lance and
vigorous steed of the Templar. This issue of the
combat all had foreseen ; but although the spear of
Ivanhoe did but, in comparison, touch the shield of
Bois-Guilbert, that champion, to the astonishment
of all who beheld it, reeled in his saddle, lost his
stirrups, and fell in the lists.

Ivanhoe, extricating himself from his fallen horse,
was soon on foot, hastening to mend his fortune with
his sword ; but his antagonist arose not. Wilfred,
placing his foot on his breast, and the sword's point
to his throat, commanded him to yield him, or die
on the spot. Bois-Guilbert returned no answer.

'Slay him not, Sir Knight,' cried the Grand
Master, 'unshriven and unabsolved ; kill not body
and soul ! We allow him vanquished.'

He descended into the lists, and commanded them
to unhelm the conquered champion. His eyes were
closed ; the dark red flush was still on his brow.
As they looked on him in astonishment, the eyes
opened ; but they were fixed and glazed. The flush
passed from his brow, and gave way to the pallid
hue of death. Unscathed by the lance of his enemy,
he had died a victim to the violence of his own
contending passions.

'This is indeed the judgment of God,' said the
Grand Master, looking upwards—'*Fiat voluntas
tua !*'

CHAPTER XLIV

So! now 'tis ended, like an old wife's story.

WEBSTER.

WHEN the first moments of surprise were over, Wilfred of Ivanhoe demanded of the Grand Master, as judge of the field, if he had manfully and rightfully done his duty in the combat.

'Manfully and rightfully hath it been done,' said the Grand Master; 'I pronounce the maiden free and guiltless. The arms and the body of the deceased knight are at the will of the victor.'

'I will not despoil him of his weapons,' said the Knight of Ivanhoe, 'nor condemn his corpse to shame: he hath fought for Christendom. God's arm, no human hand, hath this day struck him down. But let his obsequies be private, as becomes those of a man who died in an unjust quarrel. And for the maiden——'

He was interrupted by a clattering of horses' feet, advancing in such numbers, and so rapidly, as to shake the ground before them; and the Black Knight galloped into the lists. He was followed by a numerous band of men-at-arms, and several knights in complete armour.

'I am too late,' he said, looking around him. 'I had doomed Bois-Guilbert for mine own property. Ivanhoe, was this well, to take on thee such a venture, and thou scarce able to keep thy saddle?'

'Heaven, my Liege,' answered Ivanhoe, 'hath

taken this proud man for its victim. He was not
to be honoured in dying as your will had designed.'

'Peace be with him,' said Richard, looking stead-
fastly on the corpse, 'if it may be so; he was a
gallant knight, and has died in his steel harness full
knightly. But we must waste no time. Bohun, do
thine office !'

A knight stepped forward from the King's attendants, and, laying his hand on the shoulder of
Albert de Malvoisin, said, 'I arrest thee of high
treason.'

The Grand Master had hitherto stood astonished at
the appearance of so many warriors. He now spoke.

'Who dares to arrest a knight of the Temple of
Zion, within the girth of his own preceptory, and in
the presence of the Grand Master? and by whose
authority is this bold outrage offered?'

'I make the arrest,' replied the knight—'I,
Henry Bohun, Earl of Essex, Lord High Constable
of England.'

'And he arrests Malvoisin,' said the King, raising
his visor, 'by the order of Richard Plantagenet,
here present. Conrade Mont-Fitchet, it is well for
thee thou art born no subject of mine. But for thee,
Malvoisin, thou diest with thy brother Philip ere
the world be a week older.'

'I will resist thy doom,' said the Grand Master.

'Proud Templar,' said the King, 'thou canst not :
look up, and behold the royal standard of England
floats over thy towers instead of thy Temple banner !
Be wise, Beaumanoir, and make no bootless opposition. Thy hand is in the lion's mouth.'

'I will appeal to Rome against thee,' said the
Grand Master, 'for usurpation on the immunities
and privileges of our order.'

'Be it so,' said the King; 'but for thine own
sake tax me not with usurpation now. Dissolve thy
chapter, and depart with thy followers to thy next
preceptory, if thou canst find one which has not been

made the scene of treasonable conspiracy against
the King of England. Or, if thou wilt, remain, to
share our hospitality, and behold our justice.'

'To be a guest in the house where I should
command?' said the Templar; 'never! Chaplains,
raise the Psalm, *Quare fremuerunt gentes?* Knights,
squires, and followers of the Holy Temple, prepare
to follow the banner of *Beau-seant!*'

The Grand Master spoke with a dignity which
confronted even that of England's king himself, and
inspired courage into his surprised and dismayed
followers. They gathered around him like the sheep
around the watch-dog, when they hear the baying
of the wolf. But they evinced not the timidity of
the scared flock: there were dark brows of defiance,
and looks which menaced the hostility they dared
not to proffer in words. They drew together in a
dark line of spears, from which the white cloaks of
the knights were visible among the dusky garments
of their retainers, like the lighter-coloured edges of
a sable cloud. The multitude, who had raised a
clamorous shout of reprobation, paused and gazed in
silence on the formidable and experienced body to
which they had unwarily bade defiance, and shrunk
back from their front.

The Earl of Essex, when he beheld them pause
in their assembled force, dashed the rowels into his
charger's sides, and galloped backwards and forwards
to array his followers, in opposition to a band so
formidable. Richard alone, as if he loved the
danger his presence had provoked, rode slowly
along the front of the Templars, calling aloud,
'What, sirs! Among so many gallant knights,
will none dare splinter a spear with Richard? Sirs
of the Temple! your ladies are but sun-burned, if
they are not worth the shiver of a broken lance!'

'The brethren of the Temple,' said the Grand
Master, riding forward in advance of their body,
'fight not on such idle and profane quarrel; and

not with thee, Richard of England, shall a Templar cross lance in my presence. The Pope and princes of Europe shall judge our quarrel, and whether a Christian prince has done well in bucklering the cause which thou hast to-day adopted. If unassailed, we depart assailing no one. To thine honour we refer the armour and household goods of the order which we leave behind us, and on thy conscience we lay the scandal and offence thou hast this day given to Christendom.'

With these words, and without waiting a reply, the Grand Master gave the signal of departure. Their trumpets sounded a wild march, of an Oriental character, which formed the usual signal for the Templars to advance. They changed their array from a line to a column of march, and moved off as slowly as their horses could step, as if to show it was only the will of their Grand Master, and no fear of the opposing and superior force, which compelled them to withdraw.

'By the splendour of Our Lady's brow!' said King Richard, 'it is pity of their lives that these Templars are not so trusty as they are disciplined and valiant.'

The multitude, like a timid cur which waits to bark till the object of its challenge has turned his back, raised a feeble shout as the rear of the squadron left the ground.

During the tumult which attended the retreat of the Templars, Rebecca saw and heard nothing : she was locked in the arms of her aged father, giddy, and almost senseless, with the rapid change of circumstances around her. But one word from Isaac at length recalled her scattered feelings.

'Let us go,' he said, 'my dear daughter, my recovered treasure—let us go to throw ourselves at the feet of the good youth.'

'Not so,' said Rebecca. 'O no—no—no ; I must not at this moment dare to speak to him. Alas !

I should say more than—— No, my father, let us
instantly leave this evil place.'

'But, my daughter,' said Isaac, 'to leave him
who hath come forth like a strong man with his
spear and shield, holding his life as nothing, so he
might redeem thy captivity; and thou, too, the
daughter of a people strange unto him and his—
this is service to be thankfully acknowledged.'

'It is—it is—most thankfully—most devoutly
acknowledged,' said Rebecca; 'it shall be still more
so—but not now—for the sake of thy beloved
Rachael, father, grant my request—not now!'

'Nay, but,' said Isaac, insisting, 'they will deem
us more thankless than mere dogs!'

'But thou seest, my dear father, that King
Richard is in presence, and that——'

'True, my best—my wisest Rebecca. Let us
hence—let us hence! Money he will lack, for he
has just returned from Palestine, and, as they say,
from prison; and pretext for exacting it, should he
need any, may arise out of my simple traffic with
his brother John. Away—away, let us hence!'

And hurrying his daughter in his turn, he
conducted her from the lists, and by means of
conveyance which he had provided, transported her
safely to the house of the Rabbi Nathan.

The Jewess, whose fortunes had formed the
principal interest of the day, having now retired
unobserved, the attention of the populace was
transferred to the Black Knight. They now filled
the air with 'Long life to Richard with the Lion's
Heart, and down with the usurping Templars!'

'Notwithstanding all this lip-loyalty,' said Ivanhoe to the Earl of Essex, 'it was well the King
took the precaution to bring thee with him, noble
Earl, and so many of thy trusty followers.'

The Earl smiled and shook his head.

'Gallant Ivanhoe,' said Essex, 'dost thou know
our master so well, and yet suspect him of taking

so wise a precaution! I was drawing towards York, having heard that Prince John was making head there, when I met King Richard, like a true knight-errant, galloping hither to achieve in his own person this adventure of the Templar and the Jewess, with his own single arm. I accompanied him with my band, almost maugre his consent.'

'And what news from York, brave Earl?' said Ivanhoe; 'will the rebels bide us there?'

'No more than December's snow will bide July's sun,' said the Earl; 'they are dispersing; and who should come posting to bring us the news, but John himself!'

'The traitor!—the ungrateful, insolent traitor!' said Ivanhoe; 'did not Richard order him into confinement?'

'O! he received him,' answered the Earl, 'as if they had met after a hunting party; and, pointing to me and our men-at-arms, said, "Thou seest, brother, I have some angry men with me; thou wert best go to our mother, carry her my duteous affection, and abide with her until men's minds are pacified."'

'And this was all he said?' inquired Ivanhoe; 'would not any one say that this prince invites men to treason by his clemency?'

'Just,' replied the Earl, 'as the man may be said to invite death who undertakes to fight a combat, having a dangerous wound unhealed.'

'I forgive thee the jest, Lord Earl,' said Ivanhoe; 'but, remember, I hazarded but my own life— Richard, the welfare of his kingdom.'

'Those,' replied Essex, 'who are specially careless of their own welfare are seldom remarkably attentive to that of others. But let us haste to the castle, for Richard meditates punishing some of the subordinate members of the conspiracy, though he has pardoned their principal.'

From the judicial investigations which followed

on this occasion, and which are given at length in the Wardour Manuscript, it appears that Maurice de Bracy escaped beyond seas, and went into the service of Philip of France, while Philip de Malvoisin and his brother Albert, the preceptor of Templestowe, were executed, although Waldemar Fitzurse, the soul of the conspiracy, escaped with banishment, and Prince John, for whose behoof it was undertaken, was not even censured by his good-natured brother. No one, however, pitied the fate of the two Malvoisins, who only suffered the death which they had both well deserved, by many acts of falsehood, cruelty, and oppression.

Briefly after the judicial combat, Cedric the Saxon was summoned to the court of Richard, which, for the purpose of quieting the counties that had been disturbed by the ambition of his brother, was then held at York. Cedric tushed and pshawed more than once at the message; but he refused not obedience. In fact, the return of Richard had quenched every hope that he had entertained of restoring a Saxon dynasty in England; for, whatever head the Saxons might have made in the event of a civil war, it was plain that nothing could be done under the undisputed dominion of Richard, popular as he was by his personal good qualities and military fame, although his administration was wilfully careless—now too indulgent and now allied to despotism.

But, moreover, it could not escape even Cedric's reluctant observation that his project for an absolute union among the Saxons, by the marriage of Rowena and Athelstane, was now completely at an end, by the mutual dissent of both parties concerned. This was, indeed, an event which, in his ardour for the Saxon cause, he could not have anticipated; and even when the disinclination of both was broadly and plainly manifested, he could scarce bring himself to believe that two Saxons of royal descent should scruple, on personal grounds, at an alliance so necessary for the public weal of the nation. But it was not the less certain. Rowena had always expressed her repugnance to Athelstane, and now Athelstane was no less plain and positive in proclaiming his resolution never to pursue his addresses to the Lady Rowena. Even the natural obstinacy of Cedric sunk beneath these obstacles, where he, remaining on the point of junction, had the task of dragging a reluctant pair up to it, one with each hand. He made, however, a last vigorous attack on Athelstane, and he found that resuscitated sprout of Saxon royalty engaged, like country squires of our own day, in a furious war with the clergy.

It seems that, after all his deadly menaces against the abbot of St. Edmund's, Athelstane's spirit of revenge, what between the natural indolent kindness of his own disposition, what through the prayers of his mother Edith, attached, like most ladies (of the period), to the clerical order, had terminated in his keeping the abbot and his monks in the dungeons of Coningsburgh for three days on a meagre diet. For this atrocity the abbot menaced him with excommunication, and made out a dreadful list of complaints in the bowels and stomach, suffered by himself and his monks, in consequence of the tyrannical and unjust imprisonment they had sustained. With this controversy, and with the means he had adopted to counteract this clerical persecution, Cedric found the mind of his friend Athelstane so fully occupied, that it had no room for another idea. And when Rowena's name was mentioned, the noble Athelstane prayed leave to quaff a full goblet to her health, and that she might soon be the bride of his kinsman Wilfred. It was a desperate case, therefore. There was obviously no more to be made of Athelstane; or, as Wamba expressed it, in a phrase which has descended from Saxon times to ours, he was a cock that would not fight.

There remained betwixt Cedric and the determination which the lovers desired to come to only two obstacles—his own obstinacy, and his dislike of the Norman dynasty. The former feeling gradually gave way before the endearments of his ward and the pride which he could not help nourishing in the fame of his son. Besides, he was not insensible to the honour of allying his own line to that of Alfred, when the superior claims of the descendant of Edward the Confessor were abandoned for ever. Cedric's aversion to the Norman race of kings was also much undermined—first, by consideration of the impossibility of ridding England of the new dynasty, a feeling which goes far to create loyalty in the subject to the king *de facto*; and, secondly, by the personal attention of King Richard, who delighted in the blunt humour of Cedric, and, to use the language of the Wardour Manuscript, so dealt with the noble Saxon that, ere he had been a guest at court for seven days, he had given his consent to the marriage of his ward Rowena and his son Wilfred of Ivanhoe.

The nuptials of our hero, thus formally approved by his father, were celebrated in the most august of temples, the noble minster of York. The King himself attended, and, from the countenance which he afforded on this and other occasions to the distressed and hitherto degraded Saxons, gave them a safer and more certain prospect of attaining their just rights than they could reasonably hope from the precarious chance of a civil war. The church gave her full solemnities, graced with all the splendour which she of Rome knows how to apply with such brilliant effect.

Gurth, gallantly apparelled, attended as esquire upon his young master, whom he had served so faithfully, and the magnanimous Wamba, decorated with a new cap and a most gorgeous set of silver bells. Sharers of Wilfred's dangers and adversity,

they remained, as they had a right to expect, the
partakers of his more prosperous career.

But, besides this domestic retinue, these distinguished nuptials were celebrated by the attendance of the high-born Normans, as well as Saxons,
joined with the universal jubilee of the lower orders,
that marked the marriage of two individuals as a
pledge of the future peace and harmony betwixt
two races, which, since that period, have been so
completely mingled that the distinction has become
wholly invisible. Cedric lived to see this union
approximate towards its completion; for, as the two
nations mixed in society and formed intermarriages
with each other, the Normans abated their scorn,
and the Saxons were refined from their rusticity.
But it was not until the reign of Edward the Third
that the mixed language, now termed English, was
spoken at the court of London, and that the hostile
distinction of Norman and Saxon seems entirely to
have disappeared.

It was upon the second morning after this happy
bridal that the Lady Rowena was made acquainted
by her handmaid Elgitha, that a damsel desired
admission to her presence, and solicited that their
parley might be without witness. Rowena wondered,
hesitated, became curious, and ended by commanding the damsel to be admitted, and her attendants
to withdraw.

She entered—a noble and commanding figure,
the long white veil, in which she was shrouded,
overshadowing rather than concealing the elegance
and majesty of her shape. Her demeanour was
that of respect, unmingled by the least shade either
of fear or of a wish to propitiate favour. Rowena
was ever ready to acknowledge the claims, and
attend to the feelings, of others. She arose, and
would have conducted her lovely visitor to a seat;
but the stranger looked at Elgitha, and again intimated a wish to discourse with the Lady Rowena

alone. Elgitha had no sooner retired with unwilling steps than, to the surprise of the Lady of Ivanhoe, her fair visitant kneeled on one knee, pressed her hands to her forehead, and bending her head to the ground, in spite of Rowena's resistance, kissed the embroidered hem of her tunic.

'What means this, lady?' said the surprised bride; 'or why do you offer to me a deference so unusual?'

'Because to you, Lady of Ivanhoe,' said Rebecca, rising up and resuming the usual quiet dignity of her manner, 'I may lawfully, and without rebuke, pay the debt of gratitude which I owe to Wilfred of Ivanhoe. I am—forgive the boldness which has offered to you the homage of my country—I am the unhappy Jewess for whom your husband hazarded his life against such fearful odds in the tiltyard of Templestowe.'

'Damsel,' said Rowena, 'Wilfred of Ivanhoe on that day rendered back but in slight measure your unceasing charity towards him in his wounds and misfortunes. Speak, is there aught remains in which he or I can serve thee?'

'Nothing,' said Rebecca, calmly, 'unless you will transmit to him my grateful farewell.'

'You leave England, then?' said Rowena, scarce recovering the surprise of this extraordinary visit.

'I leave it, lady, ere this moon again changes. My father hath a brother high in favour with Mohammed Boabdil, King of Grenada; thither we go, secure of peace and protection, for the payment of such ransom as the Moslem exact from our people.'

'And are you not then as well protected in England?' said Rowena. 'My husband has favour with the King; the King himself is just and generous.'

'Lady,' said Rebecca, 'I doubt it not; but the people of England are a fierce race, quarrelling ever with their neighbours or among themselves, and

ready to plunge the sword into the bowels of each
other. Such is no safe abode for the children of
my people. Ephraim is an heartless dove; Issachar
an over-laboured drudge, which stoops between two
burdens. Not in a land of war and blood, surrounded by hostile neighbours, and distracted by
internal factions, can Israel hope to rest during her
wanderings.'

'But you, maiden,' said Rowena—'you surely
can have nothing to fear. She who nursed the
sick-bed of Ivanhoe,' she continued, rising with
enthusiasm—'she can have nothing to fear in
England, where Saxon and Norman will contend
who shall most do her honour.'

'Thy speech is fair, lady,' said Rebecca, 'and thy
purpose fairer; but it may not be—there is a gulf
betwixt us. Our breeding, our faith, alike forbid
either to pass over it. Farewell; yet, ere I go,
indulge me one request. The bridal veil hangs
over thy face; deign to raise it, and let me see the
features of which fame speaks so highly.'

'They are scarce worthy of being looked upon,'
said Rowena; 'but, expecting the same from my
visitant, I remove the veil.'

She took it off accordingly; and, partly from
the consciousness of beauty, partly from bashfulness, she blushed so intensely that cheek, brow,
neck, and bosom were suffused with crimson.
Rebecca blushed also; but it was a momentary
feeling, and, mastered by higher emotions, past
slowly from her features like the crimson cloud
which changes colour when the sun sinks beneath
the horizon.

'Lady,' she said, 'the countenance you have
deigned to show me will long dwell in my remembrance. There reigns in it gentleness and goodness;
and if a tinge of the world's pride or vanities may
mix with an expression so lovely, how should we
chide that which is of earth for bearing some colour

of its original? Long, long will I remember your
features, and bless God that I leave my noble
deliverer united with——'

She stopped short—her eyes filled with tears.
She hastily wiped them, and answered to the
anxious inquiries of Rowena—'I am well, lady—
well. But my heart swells when I think of Torquilstone and the lists of Templestowe. Farewell. One,
the most trifling, part of my duty remains undis-
charged. Accept this casket; startle not at its
contents.'

Rowena opened the small silver-chased casket,
and perceived a carcanet, or necklace, with ear-
jewels, of diamonds, which were obviously of immense
value.

'It is impossible,' she said, tendering back the
casket. 'I dare not accept a gift of such consequence.'

'Yet keep it, lady,' returned Rebecca. 'You
have power, rank, command, influence; we have
wealth, the source both of our strength and weakness; the value of these toys, ten times multiplied,
would not influence half so much as your slightest
wish. To you, therefore, the gift is of little value;
and to me, what I part with is of much less. Let
me not think you deem so wretchedly ill of my
nation as your commons believe. Think ye that
I prize these sparkling fragments of stone above
my liberty? or that my father values them in comparison to the honour of his only child? Accept
them, lady—to me they are valueless. I will never
wear jewels more.'

'You are then unhappy!' said Rowena, struck
with the manner in which Rebecca uttered the last
words. 'O, remain with us; the counsel of holy
men will wean you from your erring law, and I will
be a sister to you.'

'No, lady,' answered Rebecca, the same calm
melancholy reigning in her soft voice and beautiful

features; 'that may not be. I may not change the faith of my fathers like a garment unsuited to the climate in which I seek to dwell; and unhappy, lady, I will not be. He to whom I dedicate my future life will be my comforter, if I do His will.'

'Have you then convents, to one of which you mean to retire?' asked Rowena.

'No, lady,' said the Jewess; 'but among our people, since the time of Abraham downwards, have been women who have devoted their thoughts to Heaven, and their actions to works of kindness to men—tending the sick, feeding the hungry, and relieving the distressed. Among these will Rebecca be numbered. Say this to thy lord, should he chance to inquire after the fate of her whose life he saved.'

There was an involuntary tremour on Rebecca's voice, and a tenderness of accent, which perhaps betrayed more than she would willingly have expressed. She hastened to bid Rowena adieu.

'Farewell,' she said. 'May He who made both Jew and Christian shower down on you His choicest blessings! The bark that wafts us hence will be under weigh ere we can reach the port.'

She glided from the apartment, leaving Rowena surprised as if a vision had passed before her. The fair Saxon related the singular conference to her husband, on whose mind it made a deep impression. He lived long and happily with Rowena, for they were attached to each other by the bonds of early affection, and they loved each other the more from the recollection of the obstacles which had impeded their union. Yet it would be inquiring too curiously to ask whether the recollection of Rebecca's beauty and magnanimity did not recur to his mind more frequently than the fair descendant of Alfred might altogether have approved.

Ivanhoe distinguished himself in the service of Richard, and was graced with farther marks of the

royal favour. He might have risen still higher but
for the premature death of the heroic Cœur-de-Lion,
before the Castle of Chaluz, near Limoges. With
the life of a generous, but rash and romantic,
monarch perished all the projects which his ambition
and his generosity had formed; to whom may be
applied, with a slight alteration, the lines composed
by Johnson for Charles of Sweden—

> His fate was destined to a foreign strand,
> A petty fortress and an 'humble' hand;
> He left the name at which the world grew pale,
> To point a moral, or adorn a TALE.